Dictionary of Library and Information Science

ग्रंथालय व माहितीशास्त्र परिभाषा कोश

मराठी – इंग्रजी
इंग्रजी – मराठी

डॉ. सु. प्र. सातारकर
डॉ. उद्धव रा. अघाव

डायमंड पब्लिकेशन्स

ग्रंथालय व माहितीशास्त्र परिभाषा कोश

(मराठी–इंग्रजी) (इंग्रजी–मराठी)

डॉ. सु. प्र. सातारकर, डॉ. उद्धव रा. अघाव

Dictionary of Library and Information Science
Dr. S. P. Satarkar, Dr. Uddhav R. Aghav

प्रथम आवृत्ती : २०१२

ISBN 978-81-8483-442-0

© डायमंड पब्लिकेशन्स

मुखपृष्ठ
शाम भालेकर

प्रकाशक
डायमंड पब्लिकेशन्स
१२५५ सदाशिव पेठ, लेले संकुल, पहिला मजला
निंबाळकर तालमीसमोर, पुणे–४११ ०३०
☎ ०२० – २४४५२३८७, २४४६६६४२
diamondpublications@vsnl.net
www.diamondbookspune.com

प्रमुख वितरक
डायमंड बुक डेपो
६६१ नारायण पेठ, अप्पा बळवंत चौक
पुणे–४११ ०३० ☎ ०२०–२४४८०६७७

ग्रंथालय व माहितीशास्त्राचे

अध्ययन, अध्यापन आणि संशोधन यामध्ये
अभ्यासपूर्ण कार्य करणाऱ्या
सर्व ग्रंथालय व्यावसायिकांना समर्पित...

लेखकांचा परिचय

डॉ. सु. प्र. सातारकर

स्वामी रामानंद तीर्थ मराठवाडा विद्यापीठ, नांदेड येथे १९९६ पासून विद्यापीठ ग्रंथपाल पदावर कार्यरत होते. चार दशके ग्रंथपालन व्यवसायात ग्रंथपाल म्हणून काम. चार विद्यार्थ्यांनी त्यांच्या मार्गदर्शनाखाली पीएच.डी. पदवी संपादन केली आहे. ग्रंथालयशास्त्र विषयातील प्रमाणपत्र, पदवी, पदव्युत्तर व एम.फिल. वर्गांना अनेक वर्षांपासून अध्यापन. विविध चर्चासत्रे, संमेलने, परिषदा, कार्यशाळांमध्ये तज्ज्ञ, साधनव्यक्ती म्हणून मार्गदर्शन व आयोजन. ग्रंथपरिवार, ज्ञानतीर्थ, ज्ञानगंगोत्री नियतकालिकांच्या संपादनाच्या कामी सहभाग. विविध विद्यापीठात ग्रंथालयशास्त्राच्या निरनिराळ्या समित्यांवरील कार्यांचा अनुभव. दक्षिण रत्नागिरी शिक्षण संस्था, सावंतवाडी यांच्यातर्फे राणी पार्वतीदेवी भोसले 'ग्रंथमित्र' पुरस्काराने सन्मानित. तसेच भारतीय ग्रंथालय संघ, नवी दिल्ली यांचा २००९ या वर्षीचा उत्कृष्ट शैक्षणिक ग्रंथपाल पुरस्कार प्राप्त.

लेखकाची इतर ग्रंथसंपदा

प्रकाशित ग्रंथ

(अ) मराठी

१. 'ग्रंथ वर्गीकरण तात्त्विक', आ.३री, संगत प्रकाशन, नांदेड, २००२.

२. 'ग्रंथालय व्यवस्थापन : तंत्र व मंत्र', आ. ३री, अभय प्रकाशन, नांदेड, २००६.

३. 'जनशिक्षण नियम ग्रंथालयाचे व्यवस्थापन', म. रा. प्रौढ शिक्षण संस्था, औरंगाबाद, १९९५.

४. 'संशोधन ग्रंथालये', य.च.म.मु. विद्यापीठ, नाशिक, २०००.

५. 'तालिकीकरण तत्त्व आणि व्यवहार', आ. २री, अभय प्रकाशन, नांदेड २००६.

६. 'सार्वजनिक ग्रंथालय, सद्य:स्थिती आणि बदलते स्वरूप' शांभवी प्रिंटर्स ॲण्ड पब्लिशर्स, औरंगाबाद, २००७. (भास्कर आर्वीकर यांच्यासोबत सहसंपादन)

(ब) इंग्रजी

१. 'Personnel Management in College Libraries', Rawat Publications, Jaipur, 2000.

२. 'Intellectual Property Rights and Copyrights', Ess Ess Publications, New Delhi, 2003.

३. Modern Teaching Techniques for Library and Information Science, Current Publications, Agra, 2008 (with Mrs. Eraj Siddiqui)

(क) लेख

(२४ लेख इंग्रजीत आणि २२ लेख मराठीत प्रकाशित.)

डॉ. उद्धव रा. अघाव

श्री संत जनाबाई शिक्षण संस्थेचे कला, वाणिज्य व विज्ञान महाविद्यालय, गंगाखेड, जि. परभणी येथे १९९९ पासून ग्रंथपाल (सहयोगी प्राध्यापक श्रेणी) पदावर कार्यरत. गेल्या दोन दशकांहून अधिक काळ औद्योगिक ग्रंथालय, शिक्षणशास्त्र ग्रंथालय, महाविद्यालय ग्रंथालय व विद्यापीठात ग्रंथालयशास्त्राचे अधिव्याख्याता म्हणून अनुभव. स्वा. रा. ती. म. विद्यापीठाकडून पीएच.डी. पदवी २००९ मध्ये प्राप्त. ग्रंथालय व माहितीशास्त्र या विषयातील प्रमाणपत्र, पदवी, पी.जी.डी.लॅन. आणि पदव्युत्तर वर्गांना गेल्या दशकापासून अध्यापन. विविध चर्चासत्रे, संमेलने, परिषदा, कार्यशाळा इ.मध्ये पेपर वाचन व सक्रिय सहभाग. ग्रंथालयशास्त्रावर पाच पुस्तके व ५० लेख (मराठी २१ आणि इंग्रजीत २९) नामांकित नियतकालिकांत प्रकाशित. यु.जी.सी. तर्फे एम.आर.पी. अंतर्गत दोन प्रकल्प पूर्ण. वाचन, लेखन, अध्यापन, संपादन व संशोधनात विशेष रुची.

लेखकाची इतर ग्रंथसंपदा

प्रकाशित ग्रंथ

(अ) मराठी

१. पद्मश्री डॉ. एस. आर. रंगनाथन् : 'जीवन व कार्य', आ. २ री, क्रिएटिव्ह पब्लिकेशन्स, नांदेड, २०१२, पृ.१२८

२. ग्रंथायन, न्यू मॅन पब्लिकेशन, परभणी, २०१२, पृ.१२८

(ब) इंग्रजी

१. 'Comprehensive Objective Questions in Library and Information Science' (As per revised NET/SET (2001) syllabus for Paper -II, Pawan Prakashan, Parbhani, 2001. P. 310

२. 'Dictionary of Acronyms in Library Science and Information Technology, Mrs. Vidya Uddhav Aghav, Parli Vaijanath, 2006, P. 98.

३. 'Industrial Information System', Creative Publications, Nanded, 2010, P.272

(क) लेख

(२१ लेख मराठी आणि २९ लेख इंग्रजीत प्रकाशित.)

लेखकांचे मनोगत

ग्रंथालय आणि माहितीशास्त्र हा विषय आता विविध महाविद्यालये आणि विद्यापीठांतून एक महत्त्वपूर्ण विषय मानला जात आहे. गतिशीलता व परिवर्तनीयता हा शास्त्रांचा नियम असतो. हा विषय या नियमास अपवाद नाही. या विकासक्रमात संगणक, इंटरनेट, ई-लायब्ररी, अंकीय तसेच अदृश्य ग्रंथालये इत्यादींसारख्या माहितीच्या भांडाराशी जुळते घेऊन ग्रंथालय व माहितीशास्त्राला विविध आयाम प्राप्त होत असल्याचे आपण पहात आहोत.

प्रत्येक शास्त्राची स्वतंत्र अशी परिभाषा असते व शास्त्रांच्या विकास प्रक्रियेत नवनवीन संकल्पनांचे निर्माण होणे व स्थिरावणे ही एक अखंड प्रक्रिया असते. ग्रंथालये अद्ययावत माहितीची दालने म्हणून पुढे येत असताना व ग्रंथालयांशी निगडित अभ्यासक्रमांची लोकाभिमुखता वाढत असताना त्याच्याशी संबंधित अध्ययन व अध्यापन सामग्रीची जशी गरज असते तद्वतच त्या शास्त्रातील संकल्पनांचे अर्थनिर्वचन करण्यासाठी परिभाषा कोशाची गरज असते.

शास्त्रनिहाय परिभाषा वेगळी असते म्हणून शास्त्रनिहाय परिभाषा कोश असतात. वा. गो. आपटेकृत 'विस्तारित शब्दरत्नाकरात', 'शास्त्रीय ग्रंथालया विशेष अर्थांच्या शब्दांची सूची म्हणजे परिभाषा कोश' अशी व्याख्या करण्यात आली आहे. प्रस्तुत कोश हा शब्दकोशही नाही आणि ज्ञानकोशही नाही. हा ग्रंथ केवळ परिभाषा शब्दसंग्रह नव्हे तर प्रत्येक परिभाषेचा यथोचित अर्थ विश्लेषणासह सदरह्न ग्रंथात दिला आहे. तेव्हा रूढार्थाने हा शब्दकोशही नाही किंवा विस्तृत ज्ञानकोशही नाही, तर संक्षिप्त ज्ञानकोश आणि शब्दकोश यामधील एक संपन्नावस्था असे याचे विश्लेषण करता येईल. इंग्रजीत यास Glossary असे म्हणतात. Harrod, L.M. यांनी 'The Librarian's Glossary' यामध्ये Glossary म्हणजे 'An alphabetical list of abstruse, obsolete, unusual, technical, dialectical or other, terms concerned with a subject field, together with definitions.' अशी व्याख्या दिली आहे.

हा परिभाषा कोश आहे किंवा यालाच लॅरूस धर्तीचा संज्ञा ज्ञानकोश असेही म्हणता येईल. ग्रंथालय व माहितीशास्त्रामध्ये अशा प्रकारच्या संज्ञा अथवा कोशांचे लेखन यापूर्वी झाले होते की नाही? परिभाषा कोशाचे काम करणे आम्ही का स्वीकारले? या प्रश्नाचे उत्तर असे की, (१) भाषा संचालनालयकृत 'ग्रंथालयशास्त्र परिभाषा कोश' सुधारित आवृत्ती, १९९४ (भाषा संचालनालय, महाराष्ट्र राज्य, मुंबई), (२) भाग्यश्री जयंत साने संकलित 'ग्रंथालय, माहिती, संगणकविषयक परिभाषा कोश' (इंग्लिश, मराठी), युनिव्हर्सल प्रकाशन, पुणे २000, (३) सुजाता कोण्णूर संकलित 'ग्रंथालयशास्त्र शब्दकोश' (इंग्रजी-इंग्रजी-मराठी), डायमंड पब्लिकेशन्स, पुणे २००७ इ. कोश उपलब्ध आहेत.

हिंदीमध्ये पुष्पा ध्यानी यांचा 'Dhyani's Glossary of LIS Terms (English-Hindi)' तसेच इंग्रजीत L. M. Harrod's 'The Librarian's Glossary' 4th Rev.Ed. आणि इतर अनेक लेखकांच्या अंदाजे वीस Dictionary and Encyclopaedic Dictionary for LIS उपलब्ध आहेत. यापैकी सुजाता कोण्णूर यांनी तयार केलेल्या ग्रंथाचे शीर्षकच 'शब्दकोश' असे आहे. भाग्यश्री जयंत साने आणि भाषा संचालनालय यांनी संकलित केलेले परिभाषा कोश ज्ञान वाढीचा वेग लक्षात घेता जुने झाले आहेत. त्यामुळे ग्रंथालय व

माहितीशास्त्रातील नव्या शब्दांचा त्यात समावेश नाही. याशिवाय महत्त्वाचे म्हणजे हे तिन्हीही कोश इंग्रजी शब्दांचा, मराठी भाषेमध्ये अर्थ स्पष्ट करतात मात्र मराठी शब्दांचा अथवा परिभाषेचा इंग्रजीत अर्थ देणारा अथवा स्पष्टीकरण देणारा ग्रंथ उपलब्ध नव्हता. प्रस्तुत कृतीमुळे वाचकांची ही अडचण दूर होईल असे लेखकद्वयांना वाटते, कारण यामध्ये वरील दोन्ही भाषांतील शब्द समाविष्ट केले आहेत.

प्रस्तुत ग्रंथामध्ये ग्रंथालय व माहितीशास्त्रातील संशोधक, अध्यापक, विद्यार्थी, ग्रंथपाल, कार्यकर्ते व जिज्ञासू वाचक यांना उपयुक्त अशा मराठी (२,७००) व इंग्रजी (४,३००) परिभाषांची माहिती देण्यात आली आहे. या विषयात होत गेलेल्या आजपर्यंतच्या अद्ययावत पारिभाषिक परिवर्तनाचे अंतरंग उलगडून दाखविण्याचा प्रयत्न केलेला आहे. ग्रंथालय व माहितीशास्त्र शिक्षणाचे माध्यम मराठी करण्याचा प्रयत्न विविध विद्यापीठांतून सुरू आहे. त्यामुळे मराठी माध्यमांतून या विषयाचे ज्ञान मिळविणाऱ्या विद्यार्थ्यांची सोय होणार आहे.

समाज बदलतो तसतशी ज्ञानक्षेत्रेही बदलत असतात. परिवर्तनशीलता हा दोहोंचाही गुणधर्म असतो. ज्ञानप्राप्तीचे साधन मानवी भाषा असते. 'कोश' हा भाषिक प्रगती जोखण्याचा मापदंड असतो. आपण आपली मातृभाषा सहज आत्मसात करतो हे खरे असले तरी आपल्याला आपली मातृभाषा चांगली येते असे नव्हे. भाषा अर्जनाच्या प्रक्रियेत कोशाचे महत्त्व विशद करताना प्रमोद तलगेरी यांनी म्हटले आहे की, ''कोशामुळे प्रमाणभाषेतील शब्द समाजाच्या सर्व स्तरांपर्यंत जाऊन झिरपतात, शिवाय प्रमाण भाषेतील शब्दाला किती प्रादेशिक शब्दांचा पर्याय आहे हेही कळते. कोशामुळे भाषेचे प्रमाणीकरण होते आणि त्याचे संवर्धनही.'' हाच नियम परिभाषा कोशालाही लावता येईल. शास्त्रीय परिभाषा प्रमाणीकरण, संवर्धन व विकास परिभाषा कोशांतून होतो हे म्हणण्यास पुरेसा वाव आहे.

शास्त्रीय परिभाषा शब्दकोश वा कोशांनाही फारसा वाचक वर्ग मिळत नाही; पण म्हणून शास्त्रांचा विकास थांबत नाही. प्रमोद तलगेरी (दैनिक सकाळ, २ जुलै, २००८, पृष्ठ ४)च्या अंकात म्हटले आहे की, ''शब्दकोश भाषेचा आरसा असतो. समाजातील छोट्या छोट्या बदलांचे, नव्या गोष्टींचे प्रतिबिंब शब्दकोशात पडायलाच हवे तसे झाले तर त्या भाषेचा विकास होतो.'' कोणत्याही भाषेतील प्रादेशिक शब्द, साहित्य अथवा वाङ्मयनिर्मिती व उपेक्षित ज्ञानक्षेत्रांचा विकास भाषा विकासाला कारण ठरतो. त्याचप्रमाणे शास्त्रांतील ज्ञानशाखांचा विस्तार परिभाषा कोशाच्या विस्ताराचे कारण ठरतो.

ग्रंथालय व माहितीशास्त्र विषयातील तालिकीकरणाच्या पारंपरिक पद्धतीमध्ये संगणकाच्या उपयोजनाने आमूलाग्र बदल झाले आहेत. ग्रंथालयशास्त्र हे ग्रंथालय व माहितीशास्त्र या नावाने लोकप्रिय झाले. नेटवर्किंग, ग्रंथालय व्यवस्थापन यासारख्या ज्ञानशाखांच्या उदयाने ग्रंथालय व माहितीशास्त्राचा आवाका वाढत गेला. त्यातूनच ग्रंथालयीन शास्त्रीय परिभाषाही वाढल्या. त्या समजून घेऊन त्यांचे उपयोजन करण्यासाठी हा परिभाषा कोश महत्त्वपूर्ण भूमिका बजावेल असे म्हटल्यास वावगे ठरणार नाही असे वाटते.

जुन्या ग्रंथालयशास्त्र या विषयाला विसाव्या शतकाच्या अखेरीस माहितीशास्त्र हा शब्द जोडला गेला. ग्रंथालयक्षेत्रात संगणकाचा व माहिती तंत्रज्ञानाचा वापर एकविसाव्या शतकाच्या प्रारंभापासून मोठ्या प्रमाणावर सुरू झाला व त्यामुळे माहितीशास्त्र आणि संगणकशास्त्र या विषयावरील परिभाषा ग्रंथालयशास्त्रात वापरल्या जाऊ लागल्या. साहजिकच त्यासाठी मराठी पर्यायी शब्द निर्माण होणे ही काळाची गरज होती. ही उणीव लक्षात घेऊन प्रस्तुत परिभाषा कोशाची निर्मिती करण्यात आली आहे.

सदरहू ग्रंथ तयार करताना महाविद्यालय ग्रंथपाल ज्योती शामराव मगर-ताटे आणि विवेक मिलिंद मोरे यांनी रचनेच्या कामी मदत केली त्याबद्दल त्यांचे आभार.

या परिभाषा कोशाच्या निर्मितीमागे 'डायमंड पब्लिकेशन्स' या अल्पावधीतच कोशनिर्मितीच्या कार्यात गरुडझेप घेणाऱ्या प्रकाशन संस्थेचे श्री. दत्तात्रेय गं. पाष्टे यांच्यामुळेच हा परिभाषा कोश तयार झाला व आपणासमोर ठेवता आला. त्यामुळे त्यांचे आम्ही अत्यंत आभारी आहोत.

कोश निर्मितीची प्रक्रिया सातत्याने चालणारी प्रक्रिया आहे. ग्रंथालय व माहितीशास्त्र या विषयात असणारे ज्ञानसाहित्य बव्हंशी आजही इंग्रजी भाषेत आहे. जोपर्यंत या इंग्रजी भाषेतील परिभाषेला सुयोग्य मराठी पर्यायी शब्द उपलब्ध करून दिला जात नाही, त्यास समाजमान्यता मिळत नाही, तोपर्यंत त्याचा वापर करून या विषयात मराठीतून ग्रंथनिर्मिती होणार नाही असे लेखकांना वाटते. हे काम केवळ एकदाच करून चालत नाही तर कालांतराने त्याच्या सुधारित आवृत्त्या प्रकाशित कराव्या लागतात. त्या दृष्टीने या परिभाषा कोशात काही उणिवा, चुका आढळल्यास सुजाण वाचकांनी जरूर कळवाव्यात. त्याचा अंतर्भाव पुढील आवृत्तीत करणे शक्य होईल. त्यादृष्टीने ग्रंथालयशास्त्रातील अभ्यासकांकडून सहकार्याची अपेक्षा आहे.

डॉ. सु. प्र. सातारकर

डॉ. उद्धव रा. अघाव

अनुक्रम

मराठी – इंग्रजी

अ

अँग्लो अमेरिकन तालिका संहिता - **Anglo - American Cataloguing Rules -** the cataloguing code devised by the LA and ALA and published in 1908. Revised edition of AACR was published in 1978 & is known as AACR II.

अँटिक (अलंकरण) - **antique tooling -** a form of blind tooling.

अँटिक - **antique -** the name given to printing papers made from esparato grass. They usually have a rough surface and the poorer qualities are called featherweight, so loosely woven that 75 percent of the bulk is air space.

अँटिक कागद - **antique paper -** originally paper made on moulds of which the chain wires were laced or sewn direct to the wooden ribs or supports of the moulds.

अंक - **digit = numerals -** 1) number, (arabic, roman etc.) any one of the figures e.g. 0,1,2,..........8,9
2) figure, word or group of figures denoting a number.

अंक / अंकीय संगणक - **digital computer -** a computer that uses digital techniques, most computers use this approach.

अंक - **numbering -** an act of allotting numbers in a sequence.

अंकांची अखंडता - **integrity of numbers -** the numbers or other symbols used to denote items in a scheme of classification, should not get drastically altered in later revisions of the scheme.

अंकीय - **digital** - consists of numbers and numeric representations, typically binary numbers. computers use digital technique for storing & manipulating data.

अंगभूत पैलू - **basic facet** - characteristic denoting inherent quality.

अंगरेषा - **leading line** - 1) first horizontal line.
2) the top horizontal line on a standard ruled catalogue card; the one on which the author heading is entered.

अंगुलास्थि - **phalanx** - it was a close formation especially of infantry ready for battle in ancient Greece.

अंगुष्ठ निर्देश - **thumbs index** - a series of rounded notches cut into the fore edges of a book, from top to bottom. Usually provided for Bibles and dictionaries.

अंतप्रज्ञ - **intuitive** - feelings that something is true or exists, although one may have no evidence or proof of it.

अंतर संघटन किंमती - **intra organization pricing** - where investment centre or profit centres exist and one centre provides products or services for another centre, an intra-organization pricing system is established. Methods used to determine transfer price of products.

अंतर संयोजन/योजन - **spacing** - the distribution of printed matter on a printed page or pair of pages so that it is aesthetically satisfactory. It relates to the space between letters, words, lines, paragraph and any decorative or illustrative matter.

अंतर–स्तरीय स्थानांतरण/अंतरण - **inter layer transfer** - a phenomenon in which the magnetic field of a medium affects its own part during storage. It usually occurs in magnetic tapes, catridges etc.

अंतरदांडा - **space bar, bands** - automatic justifying devices in a line, a rectangular bar used to add space in between words.

अंतराल मापक्रम - **interval scale** - a scale based upon the metric system.

अंतर्गत संशोधन अहवाल - **internal research report** - research report prepared by internal staff members of an institution.

अंतर्गत संस्थापत्रिका - **internal house journal** - a journal meant for internal public namely the employees, management people etc.

अंतर्गत स्वरूप - **inner form** - a) in classification scheme, adjunct to a classification which enables books to be arranged (within their subject) acording to the form in which they are written. They usually have a mnemonic notation which can be applied to any part of a scheme. There are two kinds of form divisions ; outer &inner form. Inner form indicates modes of approach such as the theory, history or philosophy of a subject.

Outer form indicates books of which the content is arranged in a particular way, such as in classified or alphabetical order as in dictionaries, or according to the form of writing or presentation, as essay, bibliography, periodical.

b) In cataloguing - The following are the chief types of catalogues based on the internal form of the catalogue :

1) The alphabetic catalogue: a) Author catalogue, b) Name catalogue, c) Subject catalogue, d) Title catalogue, e) Dictionary catalogue.

2) Classed catalogue or classified catalogue.

3) Alphabetico - classed catalogue.

अंतर्लेखन - **inscribing** - to write or carve (words or symbols) on a surface especially as a formed or permanent record.

अंतर्वासित - **intern** - 1) in America, a graduate who works full time in a library while attending part time education in a school of librarianship.

2) a person undergoing training. Working for experience with less or no remuneration.

अंतर्वासिता - **internship** - a student or trainee who does a job to get work experience while obtaining a qualification.

अंतर्वेशन क्लृप्ती - **interpolation device** - insertion of a new topic at any point in a scheme of classification.

अंतर्वेशन टीप - **interpolated note** - insertion of a new topic/ note at any point in scheme of classification by a compiler.

अंतिम दुवा - **last link** - the term used in chain indexing explaining meaning carried by the last digit of a notation.

अंतिम भाग - **back matter, end matter** - the items which follow the text of a printed book.

अंतिम मुद्रिते - **author's correction** - final copy of a document prepared after typesetting is completed.

अंतिम वर्ग - **ultimate class** - the class of the smallest extension admitted by the scheme of classification, into which a document can be placed.

अंतिम सत्य - **ultimate truth** - last truth, proved fact.

अंत्यस्वरलोप - **elision** - the contraction of pair of numbers, e.g. 93-98 becomes 93-8, 1974-75 becomes 1974-5.

अंदाजपत्रक - **budget** - 1) a plan of expected income and expenditure ; generally for a financial year.
2) an itemized list of expected income & expenditure for a specific future period.

अंदाजपत्रक केंद्र - **budget centre** - a section of the organization of the undertaking defined for the purpose of budgetary control.

अंदाजपत्रकाचे समर्थन - **budget justification** - estimation facilitating the qualification of activities & suggestions, inadequacy in activities, for improvement and / or start of new activities.

अंमलबजावणी करणे - **execute** - 1) carry out a plan. 2) perform an activity or manoeuver.

अकादमी प्रकाशन - **publication published by academy.**

अक्षर आकलन/लावणे - **decipher** - convert from code into normal language, succeed in understanding or interpreting (something).

अक्षरचिन्ह संकेत - **character code** - refers to code, such as ASCII (American Standard Code for Information Interchange) or ISO (International Standards Organization), that assigns a special standardized group of binary digit to each printed character.

अक्षरचिन्हांचा संच - **set of characters** - a group of characters; specifically the one with common characters.

अक्षरप्रतिरूप - **offset** - 1) printing process in which the impression is transferred from a litho stone or plate to rubber covered cylinder, and then offset by pressure onto the paper.
2) sometimes erroneously used to describe the unintentional transfer of ink from one sheet to another, this is correctly called 'set off.'

अक्षरप्रतिरूप मुद्रण - **offset printing** - an adoption of the principles of stone lithography, in which the design is drawn or reproduced upon a thin, flexible metal plate which is curved to fit one of the revolving cylinders of the printing press, the design from this plate is transferred or 'offset' to the paper by means of rubber blanket which runs over another cylinder and which has received its impression from the plate.

अक्षरमुद्रण - **letter press** - 1) the text of a book as distinguished from its illustrations.
2) matter printed from type as distinct from plates.
3) a method of relief printing as opposed to intaglio or planographic.

अक्षरेखन - **lettering** - the emplacement of the library call number on the spine of a book.

अक्षरेखनकला - **calligraphy** - the art of fine handwriting penmanship. A calligrapher is a trained pressman. Calligraphic types are designed in close sympathy with the spirit of good handwriting.

अक्षरवळण - **typeface** - 1) printing surface of the upper end of a piece of type which bears the characters to be printed.
2) the style, or design of characters on a set of pieces of type, comprising all the sizes in which the particular design is made.

अक्षरसंच (शब्द) - **word** - in information retrieval, a spoken or written symbol or an idea. In computer terminology, the contents of a storage location.

अक्षरसंच - **font/fount** - 1) a full set of type of one style and size containing of the correct number of the various characters i.e. upper and lower case, numerals, punctuation marks, accents, ligatures. etc. A type family includes fonts like roman, italic, semi bold, condensed and sanserif.

अक्षरानुसारी क्रम रचना - **letter by letter arrangement** - arranging text alphabetically according to letters considering each alphabet is one entity.

अक्षरानुसारी तालिका - **alphabetical device** - one of the principles used in the colon classification for determining the sequence of subjects. It is used when no better systematic order is apparent e.g. for proper names, trade names etc.

अक्षरे व अंक यांची एकत्रित रचना - **alphanumeric** - an arrangement of matter which consists of alphabets and numericals together.

अखंडता - **integrity** - a state of being whole or unified.

अग्रंथित पाने - **advance sheet** (copy) - a copy of a book, usually bound, but sometimes in sheets to serve as a proof of the binder's work, for review notice, advertising or other purposes

अग्रदूत - **harbinger** - person or thing that announces about something is coming.

अग्रलेख - **editorial-leading article** - a newspaper article giving the editorial opinion describing a current issue in detail.

अग्रलेखकार - **leader writer** - the writer of newspaper editorials.

अग्रवर्ती सामान्य उपविभाग - **anteriorising sub division** - sub-division of a subject to be placed before or preliminary to a general treatment of subject.

अग्रीय/अंतिम - **terminal** - a work station, typically consisting of a keyboard & display screen, which performs input and output when connected to a computer.

अग्रेसर विभाग/अग्रविभाग - **leading section** - first section in a catalogue entry which decides place to file the card in the catalogue, it appears at the top line of the card.

अचूक वर्गांक तयार करणे - **number building** - to prepare or assign correct class number.

अचूक स्थान - **subordination** - arranging subjects in the order of decreasing extension in a scheme of classification.

अजूर बांधणी - **ajour binding** - a style of binding practised in the last third of the 15th century at Venice. It was in the traditional eastern manner with arabesques, gilding, and cut-out leather, over a coloured background.

अइयुअर बांधणी - **azure tooling (book-binding)** tooling in which horizontal lines are shown close together.

अतिमहत्त्वाचे नियतकालिक - **core journal** - most important periodical for a subject.

अतिरिक्तता - **redundancy** - use of more words than is necessary to convey an idea or thought.

अतिसंक्षिप्त सूची - **finding list** - a very brief list of books and documents in a library system usually limited to author, title and class mark or location symbol.

अत्यंत छोटया आकाराचा ग्रंथ - **bibelot** - a very small book, valuable as a curiosity because of its format or rarity also called as 'Dwarf book' or 'Thumb Book'.

अत्यल्प अंतर - **hair space (printing)** - the thinnest spacing. It is used between letters or words. Hair spaces vary in thickness from eight to twelve em, according to body size, thus in 6pt. the hairspace is 1/2 pt. ; in 18pt. it is $1\frac{1}{2}$ pts.; e.g. Thissentenceishairspaced.

अदलाबदल ग्रंथनाम निर्देश - **permuted title index** - a method of indexing which can be carried out, whereby entries are made for every important word in a title.

अदलाबदल निर्देशन - **permutation indexing** - change the order in the title of book for indexing.

अदलाबदल विषयनाम निर्देश - **permuted subject index** - a method of indexing which can be carried out whereby entries are made for every important subject in a title.

अदलाबदल/विनिमय - **exchange** - to give something and receive something else in return.

अदृश्य महाविद्यालय - **invisible college** - an elite or high performing personality who has an informal network of scientific communication and the published literature.

अद्ययावत - **up-to-date** - incorporating all available knowledge of the latest development and trends.

अद्ययावत आवृत्ती - **recent or latest edition** - updated new edition.

अध:संरचना - **infrastructure** - 1) institutional physical holdings including information resources and facilities.

2) a set of institution / organizations, resources which support flow, handling and delivery of information from the generator to the user including its acquisition, processing, replacing & transfer.

अधिक नोंद/पूरक नोंद - **added entry** - a secondary catalogue entry i.e. other than the main entry. Where printed cards are used, it is a duplicate of the main entry with the addition of a heading for subject, title, editor, series or translator. When printed cards are not used, the added entry is prepared by the omission of all or part of the imprint collation, sometimes of subtitles and the addition of an appropriate heading. It should not be confused with a cross reference. Added entries may be made for editor, translator title, subjects, series, illustrator, etc. In the case of music additional entries for arranger, libretti, title, medium, form etc. are to be made.

अधिकार पंजी - **authority file**- 1) this term is synonymous with 'Authority list'. It enlists of all personal corporate names of anonymous classic, sacred books, titles of anonymous books and headings for series cards, which are used as headings in the catalogue; sometimes references are given to books in which each name along with its variants was found. In case of corporate entries it enlists sources, a brief history, particulars as to changes of name. The entries, are made when a heading is first decided upon.
2) a file consisting of major decisions or orders so as to maintain consistency in office work.

अधिकाराचे प्रत्यायोजन - **delegation of authority** - the process of assiging responsibility along with the needed authority by a supervisor to a subordinate. The authority includes responsibility for the job.

अधिकारिता - **jurisdiction** - 1) the official power to make legal decisions and judgements.
2) the territory or sphere over which the legal authority of account or other institution extends. 3) a system of law courts.

अधिकृत आवृत्ती - **authorized edition** - an edition issued with the consent of the author, or his representative to whom he may have delegated his rights and privileges.

अधिकृत ग्रंथांक - standard book number - 1) a book number having recognized as a permanent value.

2) the use of a sequence of nine digits to individualize title, editor or volume.

अधिकृत परवानगी - authorised permission - approval to allow, give opportunity officially.

अधिकृत संकेत - authorization code - the code which is used for authorization; generally used to get information from computer.

अधिक्षमता सूत्र - canon of prepotence - a principle stated by Dr. S. R. Ranganathan stating that within a set of words, while cataloguing a document, importance should be given to the word having more value or potentiality.

अधिनिक्षेप/स्वामित्व ग्रंथालय - copyright library - it is a library entitled under copyright laws to receive a free copy of any and every book published in the country.

अधिनियम - Act - a set of rules formed by a government.

अधिसमावेशन क्लृप्ती - super imposition device - device for sharpening a focus in the form of an isolate by restricting its extension to the portion of its falling within.

अधिसूचना - notification - letter providing information of some events in a formal or official manner.

अधिस्वीकृत ग्रंथालयशास्त्र शिक्षणसंस्था - accredited library school - library school having accreditation of official body.

अधोरेखन - underline - line drawn under a word to highlight it.

अध्यापनशास्त्र दृष्टया - pedagogic - concerning to teaching methods

अध्याय - chapter - lesson, a division of book usually being complete in itself in subject matter but related to the preceding and following ones.

अनधिकृत आवृत्ती - unauthorized edition - an edition which is published without permission of author or publisher. A pirated work, reprint of a work that has violated copyright provisions.

अनधिकृत ग्रंथ प्रकाशन - piracy, pirated book - a publication which is published without the permission of copyright holder of the document.

अनाम - anonym - an anonymous person or publication. a pseudonym.

अनामत घर - cloak room - a room usually in a public building where coats, hats or baggages etc. can be kept for a time.

अनामत संग्रह - **deposit collection** - 1) a collection of particular author or publisher kept separately for readers use.

2) a collection of materials from a single publisher or owner placed in a library organization so as to make it available to the public.The depositor often prescribe regulations for access. Generally such collection is received as gratis.

अनामत रक्कम/ठेव - **deposit, caution money** - money deposited by a borrower, which is returned after cancellation of membership.

अनामतदार - **depositors** - readers who pay a deposit, in lieu of obtaining a guarantee, to enable them to borrow books from a library.

अनामिक ग्रंथकाराचा अभिजात ग्रंथ - **anonymous classic** - a work of unknown or doubtful authorship commonly designated by title which may have appeared in the course of time in many editions, versions and / or translation. Such work is considered to be anonymous.

अनामिक कृती - **anonymous work** - a publication is said to be anonymous when the author's name does not appear anywhere on it, either on the title page or cover or the preface or introduction or foreword.

अनामिक लेखक - **anonymous author** - author of a document whose name does not appear on it.

अनामिक - **anonymous** - without a name / unknown.

अनावर्ती खर्च - **non-recurring expenditure** - expenditure that is not repeated every year e.g. building, equipment, machinery etc.

अनावर्ती साहाय्यक अनुदान - **non-recurring grant** - financial aid given only once.

अनियतकालिक - **irregular periodical** - a periodical which is issued in series but with no specific periodicity.

अनिर्बंध नेतृत्व - **laissez - faire leadership** - a leadership style in which the leader exercises very little control or influence over group members.

अनिर्बंध प्रकाशन/अग्रंथित प्रकाशन - **advance copy (sheets)** -
1) pre publication copy.
2) copy of a book usually bound, but sometimes in sheets to serve as a proof of the binder's work, for review notice, advertising or other purposes.

अनिर्बंधित निधी - **unrestricted funds** - unrestricted funds allow flexibility in use of funds and reallocation of funds from one head to another.

अनुकरण कला कागद - **imitation art paper** - unlike art paper, which is coated. Imitation art paper is loaded by adding clay and glue to the pulp.

अनुकूलन/अनुयोजन/समायोजन - **adaptation** - a character by which anything is adopted to conditions, including adjustments.

अनुक्रम - **sequence** - a particular order in which related things follow each other.

अनुक्रम निर्देशक शब्द - **entry word** - 1) the first word other than an article of a heading in a catalogue by which the entry is arranged.
2) the word determining the place of an entry or group of related entries in the catalogue.

अनुक्रमणिका यादी पत्रिका - **contents list bulletin** - a periodical bulletin consisting of reproduction of the contents of selected periodicals, assembled into some form of cover. Also called 'Current Awareness Journal'.

अनुक्रमणिका - **list or table of contents** -
1) a list of contents in various periodicals, books, documents etc.
2) index giving the details of chapters viz. chapter no., title.
3) a list of articles in a book according to sequence.
4) the table depicting the subjects topics, chapters etc. covered in a book or documents usually with corresponding page numbers. Also known as contents.

अनुक्रमांक - **serial number** - a number identifying the place in sequence of a publication issued as a part of a series.

अनुगामी क्रमांक - **successive numbers** - numbers following in order or uninterrupted course, as a series of numbers or things; either in time or place; coming in succession; consecutive.

अनुचित्र प्रेषण - **fascimile transmission** - transmission of an image, or communication line in the form of electric signals in such a way that the image is reproduced at the destination using special equipment and paper.
2) the rapid transmission of printed pages from one point to another using electronic devices.

अनुदान - **grants** - sum or money given by a govt. or public body for a particular purpose so as to extend support for useful activity.

अनुदान नियतवाटप/वाटप - **allotment of grants** - grants which are alloted; a share, part or portion granted or distributed.

अनुपयोगी - **unserviceable** - not in working order, unfit for use.

अनुबद्ध पुस्तक - **linked books** - separately bound book where the relationship between each other is indicated in various ways, such as collective or series title pages, continuous paging, series or signatures; mention in contents or other preliminary leaves.

अनुभवजन्य/अनुभविक/अनुभवसिद्ध संशोधन - **empirical research** - a research based on factual information, observation, as opposed to theoretical knowledge.

अनुमान पद्धती - **inferential** - a system which works out through evidence rather than from direct statement.

अनुरूप संगणक - **analogue computer** - a computer designed to respond to an infinite number of variations in signal, compared to a digital computer which responds to discrete off and on (binary 0 and 1) signals.

अनुरूपता - **compatibility** - the characteristic or ability of systems to co-exist and function in the same environment without mutual interference.

अनुरूपता - **compatibility** - the quality of two or more thesauri which are compiled by the same method and in which the descriptors can be interchanged and which may be used to index, or for searching, in equivalent subject fields.

अनुवर्ती संचिका/पंजी – **subsequent file** - a file following in time, place, or order; coming after; as subsequent files.

अनुवर्ती स्मरणपत्र - **follow-up notices** - the American term for second & subsequent overdue notices.

अनुवाद कुंड - **translation pool** - 1) a centre where names and addresses of persons or agencies who can translate, sources of announcement and location or indexes are readily available for users.
2) a centrally held collection of translations acquired from a variety of sources and available for use on a co-operative basis.

अनुवाद(कला)अभिसाधन - **rendering** - a performance of a piece of music or drama translation or an artistic depiction.

अनुवाद - **translation** - 1) the act of turning a literary composition from one language into another. The work so produced.
2) put into another language. express the sense of words or texts in another language.
3) a process of transferring precisely the information content of the text from one language into another language.

अनुवादक नामिका - **panel of translators** - a list of translators who can undertake work in their spare time and are not employed as staff translators.

अनुवादक नोंद - **translator entry** - a catalogue card bearing an entry under the name of translator; entry made in a catalogue under the name of the person who translated the work.

अनुवादक/भाषांतरकार - **translator** - one who translates text from one language to another.

अनुवादनिर्देश/निर्देशसूची - **index translationum - translation index** -
1) an alphabetical list of translation.
2) a UNESCO publication which lists translation of literary, scientific, educational and cultural works published in pamphlet or book form. Resumed as annual in 1949, it continues a similar publication issued regularly from July 1932 to October 1940, as a quarterly publication (thirty one issues being published) by the former International Institute of Intellectual Co-operation. The present ('New' UNESCO) series began with a volume number No. 1, 1948, dated 1949 © 1950.

अनुसूची - **annexure** - detailed information which could not be accommodated in the text report of research and is incorporated at the end of the report.

अनुसूची - **schedule** - the long series of numbers arranging all the subjects and their branches in numerical order from 000 to 900. In DDC Volume - 2 contains the schedules.

अनुसूचीबद्ध स्मृतिसुलभता - **scheduled mnemonics** - Canon of Scheduled Mnemonics : A scheme of classification should include a preliminary set of schedules of divisions based on characteristics likely to recur in an array of some order or other of all or many classess, or refer to any recurrent array of divisions to the one schedule of them giving in connection with an appropriate class.

अनेक प्रती - **multiple copies** - copies of a single title.

अनेक वस्तू वर्ग - **multiple class** - a group of many subjects / items.

अनेक शीर्षकांखाली निर्देशनोंद केलेला निर्देश - **cross reference entry**-catalogue card prepared as per cross reference index entries.

अनौपचारिक संप्रेषण - **informal communication** - knowledge imparted without formal learning processes.

अन्वेषणोपयोगी तंत्र - **heuristic techniques** - in machine indexing, simulations of human methods of learning and problem solving. Functionally heuristic programmes are designed to discover solutions to problems which occur by setting up goals and sub-goals, which are then put in order and tested to determine whether in fact any of the solution sequences fully satisfy requirements of the problem.

अन्वेषणोपयोगी शोधन - **heuristic searching** - the searching for information or a document by the user of a library, the search being modified as it progresses, each piece of information or document found tending to influence the use for continuous search.

अपकृंतन - **bleeding** - the diffusion of printing inks or colours into surrounding areas.

अपकृंतित पृष्ठ - **bleeding page** - the page of document having the diffusion of printing inks or colours into surrounding areas.

अपर ग्रंथायान - **later title** - changed title; parallel title.

अपरिवर्तन सूत्र - **canon of modulation** - a chain of classes it should comprise of one class of each and every order that lies between the orders of the first and the last link of the chain.

अपलक - **Sans Serif** - a type face without series. The best known is 'Gill Sans' designed by Eric Gill ; other well-known sans serif types are Futura & Vogue. The first sans serif type, designed by William Caslon, was named Egyptian ; it was afterwards re-named Sanserif.

अपवर्जकता सूत्र - **canon of mutual exclusiveness** - Canon of Exclusiveness : The classes in an array of classes should be mutually exclusive.

अपसरण/विसरण - **dispersion** - scattered in different directions.

अपहृत आवृत्ती - **unauthorized edition /pirated edition** - publication which violates the copyright law and produces a book.

अपारंपरिक प्रलेख - **non-conventional document** - document having non-conventional nature.

अपारदर्शक सूक्ष्मप्रत - **opaque microcopy** - a microcopy made on opaque or non-transparent material, usually paper or card also called micro-opaque.

अपारदर्शी पडदा - **opaque screen** - a screen which is not transparent.

अपुरा संदर्भ - **blind reference** - a reference in an index to a catchword which occurs in the index or a reference in a catalogue or bibliography used as heading under which no entry will be found.

अपूर्ण प्रत - **incomplete copy** - damaged copy, a book wherein pages or sections are omitted.

अपूर्ण संच - **incomplete set** - periodical issues or books in series wherein some parts are missing.

अपूर्णता - **imperfections** - printed sheets rejected by the binder on account of being in some respect imperfect, others are required to complete the work.

अपेक्षित प्रलेखन यादी - **anticipatory documentation list** - documentation list prepared before the time; occuring in advance.

अपेक्षित मूल्य - **expected value** - the value of dependent variable calulated after the estimation from the quotation.

अप्रकाशित साहित्य - **grey literature** - literature that appears in documents which are not published formally and usually are not available commercially e.g. internal reports, office records inflows etc.

अप्रकाशित साहित्य - **in edital** - unpublished works.

अप्रकाशित - **ineditus (unpublished)** - an unpublished.

अप्रचलित नोंदी - **non-current records** - records which are not currently used .

अप्रत्यक्ष कर **indirect taxes** - taxes on goods or services, sometimes known as outlay taxes, as distinct from taxes on income.

अप्रत्यक्ष किमती - **indirect costs** - the overhead costs which cannot be exclusively assigned to a particular activity, services or product.

अप्रत्यक्ष संचिका / पंजिका - **hidden file** - 1) file in a computer that is not normally displayed by a file listing. For example the MSDOS and VAX DIR command. Under MS - DOS the files IO SYS and DAS. SYS are hidden files.
2) files in a computer which are kept in such a folder which cannot be changed.

अप्राप्य साहित्य - **fugitive literature** - such publications as pamphlets, programmes and duplicated material produced in small quantities and of immediate, transitory or local interest.

अभावदर्शक नोंदपत्र - **gap card** - an entry in a catalogue showing absence of specific issues/ volumes of periodicals or serials.

अभिगम्य - **access** - the means to enter a place.

अभिगम्यता - **accessible** - 1) ability to be accessed.
2) friendly and easy to talk to, approachable.
3) easily understood or appreciated.

अभिजात (ग्रंथ) लिहिणारा लेखक - **classical author** - for the purposes of the Colon Classification, an author, whose at least one work is a classic.

अभिजात (ग्रंथ) - **classics** - an outstanding work usually appearing in several versions and translations and sometimes adapted being the subject of commentaries and writings. It continues to be in print for longer period after first publication. In classification it is often treated as if it is a class or a subject.

अभिजात क्लृप्ती/युक्ती - **classic device** - in Colon Classification the digit 'x' is put after the class number and precedes a work facet or author facet. This is done to bring the different editions of classics and commentaries together.

अभिजात - **classical** - 1) relating to ancient Greek or Latin literature, art or culture (of act or architecture) influenced by ancient Greek or Roman forms or principles.
2) literature in use since generations.

अभिनत प्रावस्था - **biasing phase** - approach to classification according to subject approach classification.

अभिपत्रक - **communique** - an official announcement or statement especially one made to the media.

अभिप्राय/ग्रंथ समीक्षा - **book review** - view again, examine again, opinion regarding the book.

अभिरुची नोंद/अभिलेख - **interest's record** - a record of the interests of individuals habitually using a library. It is complied from statements made on their membership application forms, from requests for books or information, deliberate interviews, or contacts and in an organization of fixed and limited numbers such as a firm or research laboratory, by reading correspondence. It is maintained, usually in subject order to determine what current matter shall be routed or abstracted and to whom lists of additions and other information shall be disseminated.

अभिलिखित ज्ञान – **recorded knowledge :** knowledge that is recorded in any format of communication.

अभिलिखित माहिती - **record information** - information that is recorded in any format of communication.

अभिलेख - **record** - 1) a document preserving an account of fact in permanent form, irrespective of media or characteristics.
2) the data relating to a document on which a catalogue or other entry is based.

अभिलेखापाल - **archivist** - a custodian of documents or records relating to the activities constitutions, claims, rights, treatise of a historical figure, family, community, corporation or a nation.

अभिवृत्ती - **attitude** - opinion, feelings or emotion concerning an event, fact or state.

अभिसरण/प्रसरण - **diffusion** - it is a transfer process in which there is movement of technical know-how within a group of users.

अभिसारी ग्रंथकेंद्र - **circulating library** - a library which lends books for use with door delivery. In England, the term usually indicates a commercial library where fees are to be paid for the use of books.

अभ्यागत वही - **visitors notebook** - a note book in which visitors can write their remarks.

अभ्यासक्रम/शिक्षणक्रम - **curriculum** - all the courses related to study in school, college, university etc.

अभ्यासक्रम/माहिती पुस्तिका - **prospectus, brochure, syllabus** -
1) a leaflet or pamphlet issued by a publisher describing a new publication.
2) a publication written to inform, arowse interest in and to encourage the reader to take some action regarding a school or other education institution or the issue of stock or shares of a company etc.

अभ्यासिका - **alcove / research carrel / cubicle / reading room / studyroom-** a small compartment connected to a reference library, which is set aside for continuous research work by a reader and in which books, notebooks etc. may be securely locked during the temporary absence of the reader.

अमुद्रित - **non print** - the documents wherein printing technology is not used.

अमूर्त - **intangible** - costs or benefits that cannot be quantified, or at least cannot be priced.

अमूर्त वर्गीकरण - **abstraction** - quality or process of treating something in a theoretical way. The process of abstracting knowledge.

अमेरिकन लायब्ररी असोसिएशन (ए. एल. ए.) - **American Library Association** - founded in 1876, to promote library service of excellent quality. Freely available to all the association, caters for special needs through thirteen divisions, each division acting for the association within its field of responsibility.

अरेबिक अंक/आकडे - **arabic numbers / figures** - the numerical characters 1,2,3 etc. as distinct from roman numerals I, II, III, etc.named from having been introduced from Arab use to Europe.

अर्जन/उपार्जन/ग्रंथोपार्जन - **acquisition** - the process of obtaining books and other documents for a library, documentation centre or archive.

अर्थपूर्ण ग्रंथनाम - **significant title** - meaningful title, important title.

अर्थपूर्ण दुवा - **significant line** - the term is used in chain procedure to denote a part of notation carrying a specific meaning.

अर्थमिती - **econometric** - application of statistical techniques to economic theories.

अर्थवाहक चिन्हांकन - **expressive notation** - one of the Ranganathan's canon of notation, that the notation should be designed to show that two terms are in the same array or the same chain.

अर्थवाहकता - **expressiveness** - effectively conveying thought or feeling through notation.

अर्थविचार - **semantics** - the study of relations between linguistic symbols (words, expression, phrases) and the objects or concepts to which they refer.

अर्थव्याप्ती - **denotation connotation** - a term in classification indicative of all the qualities conveyed by or comprised in a class name e.g. 'man' in connotation means the qualities (mammalian structure, upright gait, reason etc.) that go to make up man, as opposed to denotation, where the term merely marks down or indicates. The phrase : 'That man is really a man', shows the denotative followed by the connotative use of the word. Connotation and denotation may be considered synonymous to intension and extension respectively.

अर्थसंकल्प/अंदाजपत्रक - **budget** - estimate of probable future income and expenditure.

अर्थसंकल्पीय अंदाज - **budget estimates** - a tentative allocation of funds for different activities of an institution.

अर्थसंकल्पीय नियतवाटप - **budget allotment** - specific amount made available for an activity of an institution.

अर्थसंकल्पीय समिती - **budget committee** - a committee responsible for preparation of budget estimates of an institution.

अर्थहीन दुवा - **false link** - in chain indexing it refers to the step in the notational hierarchy where the notational chain gets lengthened by a symbol without an appropriate term being supplied, hence such link does not carry any verbal meaning.

अर्ध कातडी बांधणी - **half - leather binding** - binding of a book, periodical volume using leather for half part (spine and corners) of the cover.

अर्ध कापडी बांधणी - **half - cloth binding** - binding of a book, periodical volume using cloth for half part (spine and corners) of the cover.

अर्ध बांधणी - **half-binding /quarter binding** - a binding in which the spine and a very small part of the sides is covered with a strong material than the rest of the sides. 'Half binding' has the corners covered with the same material as the spine. In three quarter binding the material used on the spine extends up to three quarters of the width of the sides.

अर्ध लिनन - **half - linen / half - cloth** - a book with a cloth spine, usually with the title printed on a paper label and having proper covered 'board' (i.e. strawboard) sides.

अर्ध–पत्र संयोजन - **half - sheet imposition** - half sheet work; printing (with two machines) sheets of paper on both sides with the same form. The paper is then cut in half to give two copies.

अर्ध–प्रकाशित साहित्य - **grey literature** - literature that is not accounted for an official statistics.

अर्धउकल - **version** - a rendering in graphic art form or sequence of words, of a record, publication or document, especially translation of the bible.

अर्धपृष्ठ मुद्रित ग्रंथ - **double book / double documents** - a defect in microfilming whereby a rotary camera photographs two documents simultaneously in such a way that one covers or overlaps the other. Adjustment of the document will usually prevent this.

अर्धवार्षिक- **biannual, half-yearly, semi annual** - a publication which is issued twice a year. This word is sometimes used synonymously with biennial which strictly means 'published every two years' to avoid misunderstanding. The terms 'half-yearly' or 'twice a year' are tending to be used instead of bi-annual.

अर्धशीर्षक/लघुशीर्षक - **half title** - the brief title of a book appearing on the recto of the leaf preceding the title page. It serves to protect the title page and help the printer to identify the book to which the first sheet belongs. The wording of long title is often abbreviated. The use of such a page dates from the later half of the 17th century although a blank sheet had been used to protect title pages for a very long time. Also called 'Basterd title', 'fly - title'.

अर्धसाप्ताहिक - **semi weekly** - a serial publication issued twice a week.

अर्पणपत्रिका पृष्ठ - **dedication page** - page of the book where the author mentions the name of the person to whom the work is dedicated.

अर्पणपत्रिका - **dedication** - the author's inscription to a person or persons denoting respect and often referring to the special help and favour, it usually appears on the recto of the leaf following the title page. In 16th and 17th century this dedication often took the form of a dedicatory letter written by the author to his patron.

अलंकरण - **land tooling.**

अलंकारी मुद्रण - **decorative type** - a class typeface having exaggerated charcteristics of the other three classes, Abstract, Cursive and Roman.

अलंकृत आद्याक्षरे - **guide / initial / illuminated letters** -
1) a letter printed in the space to be filled by the rubrisher or illuminator of an early printed book as a guide to prevent him inserting a wrong letter.
2) a capital letter, being the first letter of a word, sentence or paragraph, larger in size than the subsequent letters and so set to give emphasis or for decoration. In typography, its size is indicated by the number of lines of body type it occupies, as '3 line initial' sometimes called 'ornamental initial'.

अलंकृत ग्रंथ - **illuminated book** - a book or manuscript, usually on vellum decorated by hand with designs and pictures in gold, silver and bright colours not primarily to illustrate the text, but to make it unified whole.

अलंकृत बांधणी - **illuminated binding** - a term used for all bindings which includes extra colours but particularly to those where a design was blocked in blind and the outline afterwards filled in with colour. Originally a French innovation, this style was practised in Britain from about 1830 to 1860.

अलंकृत वेष्टन - **decorated cover** - the front cover of a book which bears distinct lettering or an illustration or design.

अलिकडची आवृत्ती - **recent edition** - new edition, latest edition.

अल्क प्रक्रिया - **alkali process** - process used in manufacturing of paper of any soluble mineral salt or mixture of salts found in certain deserts and capable of neutralizing acids.

अल्डाईन शैली - **aldine style** - ornaments of solid face without any shading whatever, used by Aldus and other early Italian printers. The ornaments are Arabic in character, and are suitable for early printed books (binding). Late 15th & 16th century Venetian bindings in brown or red Morocco were carried out for Aldus Manutius.

अल्पकाळ महत्त्वाचे असणारे साहित्य - **ephemera** - 1) pamphlets, cutting and other material of ephemeral interest and value.

2) material of earlier periods which has acquired literary or historical importance.

अवतरण चिन्ह - **quotation mark** - 1) a set of single or double punctuation marks used to mark the beginning and end of a word/group of words to highlight their meaning.

अवतरण चिन्हे - **inverted commas** - another term for quotation mark. One inverted comma is sometimes used in the abbreviation for Mac, Thus; M'c

अवतरण - **quotation** - group of words taken from a book, play, speech etc. and used again by persons other than the original author.

अवतरण/दरपत्रक - **quotation** - 1) a formal statement of the estimated cost of a job stating rates of supply and term and conditions.

अवयव लक्षण - **organ characteristic** - characteristic related to the part of the book (subject).

अवयव - **1) organ** - a newspaper or periodical which puts forward the views of a political party or movement.
2) syllable - part of a word that contains a single vowel sound and that is pronounced as a unit. The word 'book' consists of one syllable and reading of two syllables.

अवरकत प्रकाश - **infra red light** -light designating of those invisible rays just beyond the red visible spectrum : their waves are longer than those of the spectrum colours but shorter than radio waves, and have a penetrating heating effect.

अवरोही अक्षरमुद्रा - **descender** - the vertical descending stem of lower case letters such as j, p, q, etc.; that part which extends below the x height.

अवलंबी चल - **dependent variable** - also called as explained variable ; these variables respond to changes in the independent variables.

अवलोकन - **perusal** - read or examine thoroughly or carefully.

अवशेष/शिलकी ग्रंथ - **remainders** - when books have ceased to sell, the remaining stock is sold off by auction or at a low price to a wholesaler or bookseller termed as remainders.

अवांछित दुवा - **unsought link** - a link describing a subject which do not have any demand by user under its verbal meaning, the term is used in chain indexing.

अवाप्ती विभाग - **accession section** - a section of a cataloguing or processing department which is carrying out the work of entering of library materials.

अविभाज्य चिन्हांकन – **integral notation** - the notation of a scheme of classification, which uses numbers arithmetically (as done in the Library of Congress Scheme) and not decimally, also called an 'arithmetical' notation.

अविभाज्य - **integral** - a leaf which is part of a section and distinct from one which is printed, independent from a section but inserted in it.

अविरत आधारसामग्री - **continuous data** - data which can take any value within a range and are measured to any degree of fineness. For example, height, weight & temperature.

अश्लील वाङ्मय साहित्य - **pornography / facetial / curiosa / erotica** -
1) writings of an absence or licentious character originally applied only to treatises on prostitutes and prostitution. It comes from the Greek word meaning 'writing about harlots'. Many catalogues of old and rare books include such items under the term Erotica.
2) coarsely written books; objectionable or indecent works collectively.

अष्टक - **octave** - 1) a series of eight notes occupying the interval between (and including) two notes, one having twice or half the frequency of vibration of other.
2) a group or stanza of eight lines.

अष्टक क्लृप्ती - **octave device** - in classification Dr. S.R.Ranganathan has used a method to extend the equal base of Arabic numerals to infinity, by setting aside the figure nine as an extender of the eight groups that are formed is each round. This is known as the octave device. A number system based on the base of each octal digit can be directly mapped on to three binary digits.

अष्टक तत्त्व - **octave principle** - a principle which operates with a base (compare binary)

अष्टपत्री आवृत्ती - **octavo edition** - one issued in octavo form.

अष्टपत्री - **octavo** - a sheet of paper folded three times to form a section of eight leaves, or sixteen pages.
2) a book having sections of eight leaves or sixteen pages.
3) any book whose height is between 6.25 to 10 inches.

अष्टपृष्ठी आवृत्ती - **quarto edition** - one issued in quarto form.

अष्टपृष्ठी कपाटरचना - **quarto shelving** - shelves to accommodate quarto books.

अष्टपृष्ठी - **quarto** - 1) a sheet of paper folded twice to form a section of four leaves. The sheets given under the definition octavo are folded twice to give the following quarto book sizes in inches, double size sheets folded three time would give the same size but would be described bibliographically as octavos not quartos.

2) a book having sections of four leaves or eight pages.

3) a book cover with height between10 to 13 inches. This is the popular or book trade definition.

असमानता - **asymmetry** - imbalance of information between a buyer and a seller.

असाधारण ग्रंथ - **abnormal book** - document having small or large size than normal one.

असोसिएशन ऑफ कॉलेज ॲन्ड रिसर्च लायब्ररीज - **Association of College and Research Libaries (ACRL)** - a division of the American Library Association since 1938; found in 1889 to represent and promote 'libraries of higher education', (institutions supporting formal education above the secondary school level) independent research libraries and specialized libraries; has eleven sections. It is the largest division of the ALA.

अस्तर कागद - **lining paper** - 1) that portion of an end paper which is pasted on the inner cover of a book. The other portion of the endpaper is known as the 'free end paper'.

2) coloured or marble paper used as an endpaper.

अस्तर पृष्ठ - **lining page** - **end papers** - pages attached to a book in the beginning and at the end so as to protect the text.

अस्तित्व पत्र/शोधयादी/वस्तूसूची - **inventory** - checking the book collection in a library with the shelf record to discover missing books.

अस्थायी ग्रंथालय सेवा - **floating library service** - a mobile library accommodated on a boat, ship.

अस्थायी किंवा तात्पुरता - **tentative / temporary** - the nature of an experiment, trail or attempt made or done provisionally.

अस्थिर/बदलणारा/चल - **variable** - a quantity which changes characteristics used for differentiation.

अहवाल - **report** - 1) gives a spoken or written account about work of the organization.

2) a special type of publication with a given format and structure used to communicate facts, ideas, results of research etc. to the person who needs it. Also used for inter office correspondence, which can be formal or informal.

अहस्तांतरणीय - **not transferable** - one which is used by a person to whom it is issued.

अॅटलास (नकाशासंग्रह) - **atlas** - collection of maps in book form with or without descriptive letterpress. It may be issued to supplement or accompany a text, or be published independently.

अॅथेनिअम - **athenaeum** - used in the names of libraries or institutions for literary or scientific study.

अॅम्पिअर वर्गीकरण (पद्धती) - **ampere classification** - Andre Marie Ampere (1775-1836) gave his scheme of knowledge classification, in which subjects were arranged in a very clear way. It may be noted that arrangement of subejcts in Colon Classification resembles. Ampere's Classification to a great extent. e.g. Physics. Engineering, Geology, Mining, Botany, Agriculture, Zoology, Anima Husbandary, Medicine.

अॅसिटेट फिल्म - **acetate film** - a film produced by using a salt of acetic acid.

अॅस्लिब - **ASLIB - Association of Special Libraries and Information Bureaux)** - an international association established in 1926 (UK), works for special libraries.

आ

आंतरराष्ट्रीय ग्रंथसूची - **universal / international bibliography** - a bibliography of the books which covers publications throughout the world. None exists at present, but an attempt has been made by the FID.

आंतरराष्ट्रीय ग्रंथालय - **international library** - universal library.

आंतरराष्ट्रीय प्रमाण कालिक क्रमांक - **International Standard Serial Number (ISSN)** - a unique eight digit standard number assigned to periodicals by the ISDS to identify a specific serial publication.

आंतरराष्ट्रीय प्रमाण ग्रंथ क्रमांक - **International Standard Book Number (ISBN)** - a number given to every book or edition of a book before publication to identify the publisher, the title, the edition and volume number. The ISBN consists of ten digit (Arabic 0 to 9)

आंतरराष्ट्रीय मानक संघटना - **International Organization for Standardization (ISO)** - an orgnization formed to achieve worldwide agreement on international standards with a view of expansion of trade, improvement of quality, increase of productivity and lowering of prices.

आंतरराष्ट्रीय ग्रंथालय महासंघ - **International Federation of Library Associations (IFLA)**- founded June, 1929 at Edinburgh to promote and facilitate international cooperation in librarianship and bibliography.

आंतरराष्ट्रीय प्रमाण ग्रंथसूची वर्णन - **International Standard for Bibliographic Description (ISBD)** - a group of standards, the first of which was officially adopted by the IFLA's committee on cataloguing at its meeting in Liverpool in 1971 and published by this committee the same year. Its primary objective is to provide a standard for preparing the descriptive portion of bibliographic entries (including catalogue entries) prepared by the national bibliographic and cataloguing agencies of all countries.

आंतरराष्ट्रीय संगणकजाळे - **internet** - 1) a global collection of interconnected local, midlevel and wide area networks. 2) network of networks.

आंतरग्रंथालयीन देवघेव - **Inter Library Loan (ILL)** - 1) a loan of library material by one library to another library. Also termed as resource sharing.
2) library activity which provides documents for circulation to the outside libraries as clientele.

आंतरग्रंथालयीन सहकार्य - **inter library cooperation** - a cooperative arrangement among libraries by which one library may borrow material from another library.

आंतरशासकीय - **inter -governmental** - international organization in which the members are national governments.

आंतरपृष्ठे - **end paper** - a folded sheet of paper whose one half is attached to a board of the book and forms a fly leaf.

आंतरिक माहिती प्रतिप्राप्ती - **interactive information retrieval** - online continuous conversation with the database placed at a central store of information in the form of a CD stored memory with telecommunication link to remote areas and within the campus.

आंशिक ग्रंथनाम - **partial title** - 1) it is part of a title. 2) one which consists of only a secondary part of the title as given in the title page. It may be a catchword title, subtitle or alternative title.

आंशिक ग्रंथसूची - **partial bibliography** - one in which a mechanical limit has been put on the material included ; e.g. only periodicals, books or articles from a certain period or in a certain country or library.

आशय - **contents** - thoughts & ideas expressed in a document irrespective of its physical form, includes other means of communication also.

आशय विश्लेषण - **contents analysis** - studying all types of communications covered in a periodical. Its nature, its underlying meanings, its dynamic processes and the people engaged in the act of communication etc.

आकृती/प्रतिमा - **image** - picture, a likeness of something in a form of a picture.

आकृती/संख्या - **figure** - a traditional term for line or number illustration incorporated within the text.

आकडेवारी - **statistics** - science of numerical description or analysis. A collection of numerical facts or data, body of methods and techniques for analyzing numerical data.

आकड्यात - **in figures** - by using numbers.

आघात/न्यास - **accent** - features of a person's pronunciation which help us identify where he is from i.e. from which region or social strata.

आगामी प्रकाशन - **in print** - future publication. Manuscript of a book available with the publisher but not yet published.

आजुर बांधणी - **adjure binding** - a style of binding practised in the last third of the 15th century at Venice.

आचार संहिता - **code of conduct** - set of manners or rules for an institution.

आर्ट पेपर - **art paper** - the name given to papers coated on one or both sides by brushing of china clay, sulphate of barium or sulphate of lime and alumina (the last for the 'satin - like finish) and afterwards published.

आर्ट वेलम - **art vellum** - 1) a brand name for lightweight book cloth. 2) a fabric used for classes of works which do not require a very strong cloth.

आटोपशीर संग्रह - **compact storage** - closely packed stock room.

आडनांव - **surname** - family name, an inherited name common to all members of a family.

आडपडदा/विभाजन - **partition** - division into parts.

आडनांवानुसार निर्देशन - **surname indexing** - an index where symbols are allocated to surnames so that they may be arranged in order other than by alphabetization.

आडवी रेघ - **horizontal line** - a line parallel to the horizon or not inclined to it; in perspective, a line paralled to the horizon, passing through the centre of vision and cutting the prespective line at right angle. This line is used in catalogue to show that succesive part is sub unit of preceding one.

आडवे पुस्तक - **landscape/oblong** - 1) a document having width more than length. 2) a book or documents that is wider than its height; one that is designed to be read with its longer edges towards the reader. More often called 'oblong'.

आढावा घेणे - **review** - view again, examine again.

आद्यपद नोंद - **first word entry** - an entry in a catalogue according the first word from the title.

आतिथ्यशीलता चिन्हांकनाची - **hospitality of notation** - an essential quality of any notational system enabling it to accommodate new subjects at their logical places without disturbing the already existing subjects and their positions.

आद्याक्षर वर्ग तालिका - **alphabetico classed catalogue** - 1) classed catalogue is arranged according to alphabets.

2) an alphabetical subject catalogue, in which entries are not made under specific subjects, as in the dictionary form, but under broad subjects arranged alphabetically, and each sub-divided alphabetically by subjects to cite more specific sub-divisions. Author and title entries may be included in the same alphabet under the appropriated subject headings.

आद्याक्षर विशेष विषय तालिका - **alphabetico specific subject catalogue** - one in which alphabetically arranged headings state precisely the subject of the literary unit indexed, whether it is a whole document or only a portion such as a chapter section or paragraph of it.

आवेदन पत्र/आकृतिबंध - **form** - a document in an office system in which certain items have been provided and against which variable information is entered.

आत्मचरित्र - **autobiography** -1) the life of a person written by himself. 2) a work dealing with the life of the author himself.

आतिथ्यशीलता/स्वागतशीलता - **hospitality** - the friendly and generous treatment of subjects in classification; capacity of a classification scheme to accomodate new subjects at appropriate place.

आर्थिक तरतूद/अर्थसंकल्प/अंदाजपत्रक - **budget** - an estimate of probable future income and expenditure.

आद्याक्षर क्लृप्ती - **alphabetical device** - one of the principles used in the colon classification for determining the sequence of subjects. It is used only when no better systematic order is apparent, e.g. to proper names, trade names etc.

आदर्श विविधता - **standard variety** - a prestige variety of language used within a community, standard languages dialects varieties cut across regional differences, providing a unified means of communication and thus creating an institutionalized norm, which can be used in mass media in education and so on.

आधारतत्त्वे/गृहीतक - **postulates** - to suggest or accept that formulation is true as a basis for a theory.

आर्द्रता - **humidity** - 1) pounds of water vapour carried by one pound of dry air.
2) a quantity representing the amount of water vapour in the atomosphere or a gas.

आधारभूत - **basic/fundamental** - 1) forming an essential foundation .2) The essential facts or principles of a subject or skill.

आदर्श किंमत - **standard cost** - a predetermined cost of using some resource (such as labour or materials) in a production by a manufacturer.

आदेश/मागणी - **order** - letter sent to book seller/publisher for supply of books.

आधारभूत ग्रंथ - **basic book** - first book giving comprehensive account on a subject.

आधारभूत मूल्य - **cardinal value** - any of the numbers that express amount as one, two, three etc.

आधारभूत वर्ग/मूळ वर्ग - **summun genus / basic class** - the first comprehensive class from which the division of a classification commences. Basic class; main class in scheme of classification enumerated as such.

आधारभूत संग्रह - **basic stock** - standard books which may be considered to form the basis of a well balanced and authoritative book stock.

आधारसामग्री - **data** - fundamental information.

आधारसामग्री/डेटाबेस - **database** - a collection of data, usually related in some manner e.g. Telephone directory.

आधारसामग्रीची हाताळणी - **manipulation of data** - processes on data so as to bring out various print output and search output.

आधारसामग्री संकलन - **data storage** - one which stores items for later reuse and modification.

आधारसामग्री जोडणी - **datalink** - in data communications. 1) physical means of connecting two locations. e.g. a telephone wire,
2) the physical medium of transmission the protocol, associated devices and programmes that together data source to a datasink.

आधारसामग्री संस्करण - **data processing** - recording information by some means where it could be obtained immediately by some mechanical or semi-mechanical process.

आधारसामग्री कुंडी - **datasink** - in data communications, that part of a data terminal device that receives data.

आधार रेषा - **base line (printing)** - the lowest limit of the body of a piece of type, the imaginary line on which the bases of capitals rest.

आधारपृष्ठ - **end paper** - a sheet of paper of each end of a book which is inserted by the binder to help fasten the sewn sections to the cover. One half, the paste down endpaper' is pasted on to the cover of the book (with the tapes between); the 'free endpaper' or 'fly-leaf' is pasted with a narrow strip of paste at the fold to the end leaf of a section. Endpaper are best left plain but are frequently used for maps and tables.

आधिक्य - **redundancy** - use of a several devices that all perform the same function in order to increase the reliability or accuracy.

आधुनिक संगणक विकसित करण्याचे शास्त्र - **artificial intelligence** - a field of computer science research aimed at understanding how the human mind thinks and creating intelligent machines that can learn from their experiences.

आधुनिक वर्तनवाद - **modern behaviourism** - the current stage of evolution of the behavioural school management, which gives primacy to psychological considerations but treats fulfillment of emotional need mainly as a means of achieving other primarily economic goals.

आध्यात्मिक विभाजन - **metaphysical division** - division of having the nature of metaphysics, the nature of being or essential reality.

आणि इतर - **and others** - when there are more than three joint authors, collaborators, etc. a catalogue entry is to be made only under the first, followed by "and others."

आणि इतर - **et. al** - abbreviation of et al is used for second or subsequent authors in foot notes.

आणि इतरत्र - **et. alibi** -

आणि इतर गोष्ट – **et alia** -

आणखी पाहा - **see also** - a direction in a catalogue for a heading under which entries have been listed to another term or name under which additional information may be found.

'आणखी पाहा' नोंद - **see also entry** - an entry, that directs the user from one term or name to other related terms or names.

'आणखी पाहा' संदर्भ - **see also reference** - a direction in a catalogue for a heading under which entries have been listed to another terms or name under which additional information may be found.

आणखी प्रकाशन नाही - **no more published** - notice issued by publisher for discontinuing future publications.

आनुवंशिकी - **genetics** - the branch of biology dealing with heredity.

आभासी अभिजात ग्रंथ - **pseudo - classics** - a classic which is not genuine, a fake, make that seems genuine.

आभासी वर्ग - **pseudo - class** - a class which is is false : spurious : pretended counterfeit.

आयताकृती ग्रंथ - **square book** - document with equal sides and equal angles.

आयकर - **income tax** - a tax charged by govertment on all types of income, rent, wages, interest and profit.

आयोग - **commission** - a group of persons having given official authority to suggest or investigate some specific issue.

आयात - **import** - bring (goods, services, books etc.) in the country from abroad; computing transfer (data) into a file or documents.

आयुधांकित ग्रंथालयमुद्रा - **armorial book plate** - a book plate which is bearing a coat of arms.

आरक्षण - **reservation** - kept for special use.

आरक्षित ग्रंथ - **reserved book** - book that is kept separate for the use of some reader.

आरंभिक सामग्री - **front matter - preliminaries** - parts of the book which precede the first page of the text.

आरोही / आरोदक - **ascender** - the vertical ascending stem of lower-case letters such as b,d,k etc. that part which extends above the x-height.

आरक्षित संग्रह - **reserved collection** - library materials having frequent demand and which consequently is not kept on open shelves, but individual items of which can be obtained on request.

आरक्षण पत्र - **reservation card** - a card on which borrowers enter particulars of books required but are not available, at a particualr time as borrowed by other users,

आरंभीचा भाग - **preliminaries** - 1) those parts of the book which precede the first page of the text. 2) printed portion which precedes the text of a work, it includes half title, front piece general & special title pages, dedication, preface, introduction etc.

आरंभिक पृष्ठे - **preliminary pages** - unnumbered pages, printed on one or both sides, which are at the begining of a book before the numbered pages.

आराखडा - **design** - to plan the entire format of a book.

आराखडा/आकार/रुपरेषा - **format** - it is used to describe the appearance and make up of a book, size, shape etc. The physical form in which information appears.

आरेखी अभिलेखन - **graphic record** - records by using styles of type faces which suggest that the characters have not been written but drawn. Of e.g. Cartoon and Old English (monotypes).

आवरण **wrapper/book jacket** - The paper wrapping or covering of a book as issued by the publisher. It serves the purpose of protecting the book, and if illustrated (as it usually is) of attracting attention.

आलंबित समासांतर - **hanging indentation** - 1) a paragraph of which the first line is set to the full width of the measure, the second and all subsquent lines of the paragraph being indented one or more cms from the left hand margin as for this definition.

आलेख - **graph** - 1) diagram showing the relation between variable quantities.
2) a pictorial representation of numerical data. Graphs may take various forms and are described as pictograms or as bar, line, broken-line or circular graphs.

आयताकृती - **square** - portion of binding cover that projects beyond leaves.

आशय टीप - **contents note** - refers to the part of the entry for a work in a catalogue which lists contents of the work. It bears the name of the author, the title and usually has a blurb on the first flap, particulars of other books by the same author or issued by the same publisher are mentioned elsewhere.

आवर्तन/पुनरावर्ती खर्च - **recurring expenditure** - 1) expenditure related to ongoing items.
2) repeated expenditure on same issue, e.g. expenditure on books, journals, staff salaries etc.

आवर्ती ग्रंथशीर्षक - **running title** - the title appearing through a book or section of a book, repeated at the top of each page or at the top of the left hand pages with the chapter heading or the subject contents of both open pages on the right hand page.

आवर्ती देवघेव - **routing** - a particular way or system direction of movement of books or documents among staff or users in an organisation.

आवर्ती/चक्रीय फेरबदल/विभिन्नता - **cyclic variation** - periodical fluctuation in the data usually longer than a year, caused by extraneous factors like business cycles, general recession or boon etc.

आवृत्ती - **edition** - reprinting of a document by making changes in the orinigal text.

आवेष्टन - **packaging** - the act or process of packing a book or item.

आवेदन पत्राचा नमुना - **application form** - a term used for a printed form which a person fills out to become a member.

आवृत्ती नोंद -**edition statement** - that part of a catalogue entry which relates to the edition of the book catalogued, as : 2nd rev. ed.

आसमंत/परिस्थिती(समाज) - **milieu social** - refers to man's social environment or surroundings.

आसनव्यवस्था - **seating arrangement** - the arrangement of seats in a library.

आसनक्षमता - **seating capacity** - the capacity of seats for users in a section of library.

आसंवेदन/अनुव्यवसाय/अध्यवसाय - **apperception** - the assimilation of a new sense or experience of an idea already in mind.

आक्षेपार्ह मजकूर - **expurgated edition** - an edition from which objectionable text is amended or removed.

आज्ञावलीकार - **programmer** - person responsible for producing a working programme from a programme specification.

आज्ञावली प्रलेखन - **software documentation** - documenting computer programs, procedures, rules for use in a library / any organization using such equipment. (see documentation)

आज्ञावलीकाराने लिहिलेली सांकेतिक भाषेतील आज्ञावली - **assembler** - the program which converts the symbolic language program written by the programmer to a machine language program.

आज्ञावलीची भाषा - **programming languages** - in computer programming, a set of rules to define the manner in which data structures are formulated and the processing instructions are written & organized.

आज्ञेवर चालणारी (आज्ञावली) - **command driver** - an operating system or software application that responds to direct typed commands from the computer user. The alternative is a menu driven system in which the computer operator passively selects an item from a menu.

अचूक वर्गीक तयार करणे - **classification number building** - the process of further synthesising a number by an add-to-note.

अंकांचे संश्लेषण - **synthesis of numbers** - another term for number building.

अन्यत्र वर्ग/वर्गीक टीप - **class elsewhere note** - an instruction given under a heading, directing to a distinct number for a related subject, or for a part of that subject.

अभिजात युक्ती - **classic device** - a notational device in library classification for bringing together, along with a classic, its editions and commentaries on it.

आभासी –अभिजात - **pseudo - classic** - a work not fit to be treated as a classic and provoking evaluations and parodies on itself.

अल्पायुषी साहित्य - **ephemeral material** - documents which become valueless within a short period of time e.g. old catalogues, old text books, news bulletin etc.

अर्ध–व्यावसायिक - **semi-professionals** - persons with basic qualification and a short training in the professional field.

अवकाश/विश्व - **universe** - it is a traditional concept, the material world, the sum total of material objects is qualitatively different forms of matter. The concept has now been given greater precision : the universe is the object of cosmology, the part of the material world which at the present level of science, is accessible to astronomical investigations. In library science, it cannotes total available knowledge.

अनंत/अपरिमित - **infinite** - unlimited or which cannot be measured.

अग्रषित - **forwarding** - onward transmission of letter.

अध्यारोपण - **superimposition** - it is connecting two or more isolate ideas belonging to the same universe of isolate idea.The isolate ideas resulting from superimposition is called a superimposed idea. It is characterized by influence of one idea on other.

असमजात - **antithetic** - a contrast or opposition of thoughts, usually in two phrases or sentences.

आधार द्रव्य - **matrix** - a rectangular arrangement of ideas into rows and columns. In table, the facets are numbered in a row and the corresponding facets of subjects are in column.

अधिकार पंजी - **authority file** - an authentic list of names of authors, subjects, keywords etc. consulted and used while making entries.

अंत–सहसंबंध निर्देशन पद्धत - **post -coordinate indexing system** - an indexing system, in which the grouping of large number of entries under simple concepts is in such a way that the user can combine them to locate material on compound subjects in which user is interested.

अर्क/निकर्ष/सार - extract - a document which embodies a summary of another document.

अनाकर्षक/भिकार कार्य - pedestrian work - work having low quality & hence is not durable and important too.

आडनांव - surname - a family name which a person uses in conjuction with his personal name. He bears it in common with other members of a group who are related to him. It is used often without his personal name and sometimes in conjunction with a title or address, when referring to him outside the circle of his personal acquaintance. It is the name used as the heading for entries in a catalogue or bibliography.

अर्क/निष्कर्ष टीप - extract note - a note in the catalogue entry indicating that the document catalogued is an extract from another document.

अग्र विभाग - leading section - first part of a catalogue entry which determines its filing position in catalogue.

अंशात्मक नोंदी - analytical entries - entries that go into a catalogue for parts or chapters of a document.

अर्थ हरवलेले वचन किंवा कल्पना - cliche - phrase or idea which is used so often that it has become stale or meaningless.

अक्षरे जुळवून शब्द तयार करण्याचा एक खेळ - scrabble - game in which words are built up on a board marked with squares using letters printed on blocks of wood etc.

अक्षरेविपर्यास सिद्ध शब्द - anagram - words or phrases made by rearranging the letters of another word or phrase eg: cart house in an anagram or orchestra.

आर्षप्रयोग/पुराणोपयोग - archaisms - archaic word or expression, Archaic -primitive ; especially of words , etc. in a language no longer in current use.

आधारसामग्री - databases - a collection of related items of information which together make up the record for a single topic/aspect, usually computer generated. Also called as 'Data Bank'.

अन्वर्थकता/सुसंबंध/संगति - relevance - to retrieve items from a store of information which are precise and relevant to a query.

ॲग्रिस - AGRIS - International System for Agricultural Sciences and Technology, a cooperative worldwide information system on current agricultural literature.

अनामिक – **anonymous** - a work by an author whose name is not mentioned in a document.

आशय विश्लेषण - **content analysis** - a methodology used to analyse the subject content of documents. It is an intellectual operation. By and large, computers are being used for this purpose by using statistical methods regarding term occurrences etc.

ओ. सी. एल. सी. - **OCLC** - it was formerly an abbreviation for Ohio College Library Center but now it stands for Online Computer Library Center.

ओपॅक - **OPAC** - it is an acronym for Online Public Access Catalogue; computerised catalogue of a library.

ऑनलाईन - **online** - direct access from a computer i.e. CPU enabling immediate processing of input.

ऑनलाईन शोध सेवा - **online search service** - an organization which provides facilities for online searching of bibliographic or non-bibliographic databases using remote terminals. eg: SDC , DIALOG , BRS, etc.

आज्ञावली/संयोजन संच - **software** - 1) it is a collection of programs. it is the means by which a computer system is made to perform specific tasks. It contains the complete and unambiguous description of each task in terms of the available operations of the computer.

2) the instructions or programs which are used to direct the operation of a computer.

इंटरनेट (आंतरराष्ट्रीय) - **internet** - world wide network of computers providing information on various aspects.

इंटरनेट सुविधा वापरताना पाळण्याचे शिष्टाचार - **netiquette etiquettes** - protocols while using internet.

इंट्रानेट - **intranet** - network of computer within an institution or organisation.

इंडो अरेबिक अंकसंग्रह - **indo arabic numerals** - e.g.1,2,3,4...............9 and 0

इंद्रिय विभाजन गुण - **organ characteristics** - characteristics used in classification scheme related to part of the body of a living thing.

इंद्रियानुबोध - **sense impression** - beware of, pursive.

इटालिक - **Italic** - type face used especially for emphasis and foreign words.

इतिवृत्त - **proceedings** - record of meeting of an institution, association or society wherein administrative decisions are taken.

इतिहास - **history** - authentic record of person, place or geographical area.

इत्यादी - **etc** - abbreviation for et-cetera.

इन्ग्रेन कागद - **ingrain** - rough and shaggy quality of tinted paper used for pamphlet covers & wall hangings.

इन्स्पेक - **INSPEC** - acronym for information services for physics, electro-technology, computers and control, brought out by the Information Services Division of the Institution of Electric Engineers.

इष्टिका - **brick book / clay tablets** - 1) an ancient Mesopotamian form of record which got inscribed in cuniform writing on a piece of clay.
2) records were made by making marks on wet clay which was baked in the sunlight or kilns to give the writing permanence.

इष्ट दुवा/वांछित दुवा - **sough link** - correct link. The term used by Ranganathan in preparation of class number of a subject through chain prodecure.

इष्ट शीर्षक - **sought heading** - correct, appropriate heading / title.

इष्ट स्थान चिठ्ठी - **destination slip** - pieces of paper which project books in the order cataloguing department to indicate by their colour or marking showing libraries to which they are allocated.

ई मेल - **electronic mail** - i) transfer of message, memoranda, letters, reports etc. between individuals or organisation using videotex, online systems and online networks.
ii) transmission of messages at high speeds over telecommunication facilities.

उ

उघड/स्पष्ट करणे - **expound** - present and explain systematically.

उच्चतंत्र अवगत असलेला वाचक - **high -tech reader** - reader who is well versed in any discipline or profession.

उच्चप्रतीची बांधणी - **deluxe binding** - binding of very high quality.

उच्चप्रतीची/उत्तम आवृत्ती - **deluxe edition** - it is characterized by superior materials and fine workmanship, generally published with limited copies.

उच्चार चिन्ह/उच्चार भेददर्शक चिन्ह - **diacritical mark** - a mark placed over, under or attached to a letter to indicate pronunciation, stress, accent or other value of words.

उच्चारण्यास सहज/सोपे चिन्हांकन - **pronounceable notation** - syllabic notation.

उठावरेखन/उमटरेखन - **embossing** - decorate with raised design.

उठावाचा/उठावदर्शी नकाशा – **relief map** -1) a map indicating hills and valleys with ups and downs rather than by contour lines alone. 2) a map model with elevation and depressions representing hills and valleys.

उणीव - **lacuna/gap** - missing portion in the stock of a library.

उणीव ग्रंथ - **misses** - (information retrieval) relevant documents which were not retrieved in a search.

उतरंड/श्रेणीय पद्धती - **hierarchy** - it is used in classification, a series of classes in successive subordination such as science- physics - light.

उतरंडीय पद्धतीतील स्तर/श्रेणी रचना - **hierarchical tiers** - tiers of subjects according to their relative levels.

उतरंडीय/श्रेणीनुसार वर्गीकरण - **hierarchical classification** - a classification of things according to their relative levels.

उतरंडीय/श्रेणीय संरचना - **hierarchical structure** - structure of subjects according to their relative level.

उतरंडीय/श्रेणीवार संबंध - **hierarchical relation** - relation among the subjects according to their relative levels.

उतरंडीय/श्रेणीनुसार रचना असलेला माहिती संच - **hierarchical database** - database prepared according to the relative importance of data.

उतरंडीय/श्रेणीनुसार वैशिष्ट्यगुण - **hierarchical force** - the property by which headings and certain notes apply to all subdivisions of the topic described and defined.

उतरंडीय/श्रेणीयुक्त चिन्हांकन - **hierachical notation** - notation assigned to subjects according to their relative levels.

उतारा (सारांशरुपी) - **extract** - to remove a selected part from an item of set or items of information.

उतारा टीप - **extraction note** - note giving details of action of extracting.

उतारा - **excerpt** - a verbatim extract from a book or piece of music whether printed or manuscript. An extract or selection.

उत्कर्ष/प्रगती/वाढ/पदोन्नती– **promotions** - development ; progress ; movements to higher position.

उत्क्रांती - **evolution** - gradual development.

उत्क्रांतीक्रम युक्ती - **evolutionary device** - in a classification system, it refers to the method by which subjects are arranged in the order of their history or development.

उत्कीर्ण मुद्रण - **gravure printing** - a french word, meaning cutting or engraving, used as a continuing word, like photogravure, rotogravure.

उत्कीर्ण मुद्रणचिती - **gravure cylinder** - cylinder of metal on which engraving is made by means of plates made by a photographic process ; photogravure.

उत्कीर्ण लेखन - **glyphography** - a process of making printing plates by engraving on a copper plate covered with a wax film, then dusting with powdered graphite, producing a surface that is used to make an electrotype.

उत्कीर्ण - **etching / deep etching** -1) the art or process of producing impression.

2) a print produced by etching (mark with carved text or design).

3) the art of producing impressions on paper or other material from an etched plate.

उत्तम खप असलेला ग्रंथ(पुस्तक) - **best seller (book)** - books having a large sale.

उत्तम खप असलेले ग्रंथ(पुस्तके) - **best books** - a group of books considered to be the most authoritative on a subject or a group of subjects.

उत्तर समावेशनासाठी - **insert key** - a key on the keyboard of the computer which allows insertion of characters.

उत्तरदाता - **respondent** - a person who responds to a questionnaire by returning the same to a researcher.

उत्तरदायित्व/जबाबदारी - **accountability** - employee is answerable to superior for the results of his or her work.

उत्तरभाग - **sequel** - publication that follows a previous literary work e.g. Kosala - Bidhar Jarila Zool - Hindu (Bhalchandra Nemade).

उत्तरवर्ती/परवर्ती - **posterioring** - opposite of anterior ; coming later in an arrangement.

उत्तरावर्ती (परवर्ती) विभाग - **posterior division** - sub divisions in a classification which can be affixed after main class.

उत्तरावर्ती सामान्य उपविभाग - **posteriorising common isolate** - when these are added to the host class, they decrease the extension of the same. The purpose of PCI is to sharpen the host class. The addition of a PCI leads to posterior value.

उत्तरासमावेश/समावेश - **insertion** - 1) an addition in manuscript between two lines or two words made by author or editor. 2) an additional sentence or a paragraph added to a proof to be inserted in a revised or final proof.

उत्तेजक कारक - **contingent condition** - varible which increases effect of original event.

उत्तेजक/प्रेरक/चेतक - **stimulus** - something that causes a reaction or that promotes activity.

उत्पाद प्रारुप - **output format** - data structure at the output stage using formatting instructions.

उत्पादकता - **productivity** - relationship between input and output of an organisation. Input being measured in man, machines, materials and money and output in products and services.

उत्पादन उद्बोधन - **production orientation** - stresses the production and the technical aspects of the job. Employees are seen as tools to accomplish the goals of the organisation.

उत्पादन किंमत - **production cost** - face value including costs of indirect material, indirect labour and indirect expenses.

उत्पादने (प्रकाशने) - **products (information)** - an article or substance or publication manufactured for sale.

उत्पादने व सेवा - **products & services** - information packed as products & services offering access to information from any source.

उत्पादने - **products** - indexes, abstracts, digests and others which are offered as finished products.

उत्स्फूर्तता - **spontaneity** - acting with a natural impulse.

उद्दिष्टे/लक्ष्य/ध्येय - **objectives** - 1) aim.   2) Goal or aim.
3) expected achievements of a research. 4) specific aims, goals to be achieved.

उद्बोधन - **orientation** - to provide formal information of the library to the user through direct and indirect method.

उद्भासन - **exposure** - to reveal or explain something unknwon. The publishing of information or an event.

उद्भासन कालावधी - **exposure time** - the time required for the publishing of information or an event.

उधार शोधन - **book on loan** - a book, or a number of books given, on loan to an individual, a group of persons, an institution or a library.

उद्धरण टीप/उतारा टीप - **extraction note** -note giving details of action of extracting.

उद्धरण विश्लेषक **citation analyst** - a person skilled in citation analysis.

उद्धरण शोधन - **citation searching** - using citation indexes or their online equivalent to search for references to documents which cite a known document or author's work.

उद्धरण/उल्लेख - **citation** -1) sources mentioned as authority for a statement.
2) a quotation from or reference to a book or author
3) when a reference 'A' is cited in the citing article 'B' then the article 'B' is referred as 'citation' of reference 'A'.

उद्धरित प्रलेख - **cited documents** - a document that has been quoted in another documents.

उप समिती - **sub - committee** - a committee formed from members of a larger committee to consider one or more matters on behalf of the larger committee. Report and deliberations of subcommittee are finalized by large committee.

उपकर/कर - **cess/tax** - an amount levied by government or local body for a particular purpose.

उपकरण - **gadget** - a mechanical device or tool.

उपग्रंथनाम/उपशीर्षक - **sub - title heading** - a secondary or subordinate title usually explanatory and often following a semicolon, 'or','an', or 'a'

उपग्रंथपाल - **deputy librarian** - the immediate subordinate of librarian. One who becomes acting chief librarian in the absence of the Principal Librarian, formerly called "Sub-librarian', in America called as "Associate librarian".

उपग्रहाद्वारा प्रसारण - **satellite broadcasting** - message sent through satellite, the artificial object put into orbit around the earth.

उपग्रहाद्वारा संगणकजाळे - **satellite network** - information sent out by satellite networking.

उपनिर्देश - **sub-index** - secondary index.

उपनोंद - **sub-entry** - a secondary entry.

उपमाला/उपमालिका - **sub-series / minor series** - a series published in conjuction with another.

उपयुक्त अनुक्रम - **helpful order/sequence** - items in a classification schedule which displays the subjects in such a way that the order itself leads the user to the specific subject needed.

उपयुक्त अनुक्रमाची तत्त्वे - **principle of helpful sequence** - sequence of the classes in an array of a class and of the ranked isolates should be helpful to the purpose served. This should be according to some accepted principles and not arbitrary. It is a part of guiding principles.

उपयुक्तता - **utility** - 1) usefulness 2) The state of being useful, profitable or beneficial. The value of which is sought to be maximum in any situation involving a choice. 3) functional rather than attractive.

उपयुक्ततेनुसार वर्गीकरण - **utilitarian classification** - a classification based on utility.

उपयुक्तवादी - **utilitarian** - useful or practical rather than attractive.

उपयोक्ता नमुना - **user modelling** - User modeling is a subdivision of human-computer interaction and describes the process of building up and modifying a user model. The main goal of user modeling is customization and adaptation of systems to the user's specific needs.

उपयोक्ता/वाचक/उपयोजन - user/reader/clientele/patron - borrower who uses a library.

उपयोक्ताचे समाधान - user satisfaction - reader satisfaction by offering infra-structure, sources and services provided by the library.

उपयोक्ताशी मैत्रीपूर्ण व्यवस्था पद्धत - user friendly system - a system which can be directly operated by the user without the assistance of other professionals.

उपयोक्ताशी मैत्रीपूर्ण - user friendly - a service or institution that user, reader can understand easily.

उपयोगिता लक्षण/वैशिष्ट्ये- utility characteristic - a characteristic which is useful for classification.

उपयोगिता - utility - the quality or state of being useful.

उपयोजक गट - user group - a group of users.

उपयोजकांसाठी शिक्षण - user education - training of users.

उपयोजकाचा अभ्यास - user study - study of user's reading habits and other particulars.

उपयोजन - application - 1) The action of putting something into operation.
2) the action of applying something to an operation.

उपयोजित ग्रंथसूची - applied bibliography - synonymous term for historical bibliography.

उपरि प्रक्षेपक - overhead projector - a device for projecting images printed on transparent sheet of about nine inches square. The large image appears on to a screen in front of, or to one side of the audience while the operator faces them. The transparency is known as 'overhead transparency.

उपलब्ध नाही - not available - material not available or not in stock in a library.

उपलब्धतेच्या अटी - terms of availability - conditions or terms laid down by supplier to supply docuements to a library.

उपलब्धी पत्र - holding card - a catalogue card which shows the volumes or parts of a work which the library possesses. It is usually the main entry card.

उपवर्ग - sub-class / species- 1) in classification, the groups into which a genus is divided.
2) in computer coding each conventional set of 'sorts' comprising a symbol.

उपवर्गांचे सहव्यवस्थापन करण्याची पद्धत - collocation - an arrangement of sub classes of classification by degree of likeness.

उपविभाग - sub- division/sub-section/ isolates - action of dividing into smaller parts. A secondary division of a main class.

उपविभागीय ग्रंथालय - sub-divisional library - library which works under the divisional library.

उपविषय साहित्याची सूची - topical bibliography - a subject bibliogarphy which consists of short list of books or references placed at the ends of the chapters.

उपविषय - topic - a group of words which describes a given subject, text, speech, conversation etc.

उपविषयक मार्गदर्शक - topic guide - a guide to specific subject, it is usually a narrow block of wood or piece of cardboard bearing a subject and class number, placed on the shelf at the beginning of the books related to that subject, also called 'Subject Guide'.

उपविषयानुसार निर्देश सूची - sectionized index - an index to a periodical literature split into sections such as (a) long articles of importance (b) short paragraphs and brief news items (c) literature abstract, and similar well defined groups.

उपशीर्षक - sub-title/heading-
1) a heading given as a subsection of a piece of writing.
2) a secondary heading used in the subdivision of a subject. In a verbal headling it is the second or subsequent word, separated from the preceeding by punctuation.

उपशीर्षकापूर्वीचे शीर्षक - main title - 1) the part of title which precedes in the sub title.
2) to select a heading in a process of cataloguing and indexing.

उपसंपादक - sub - editor - assistant editor who checks and corrects the text before printing

उपसंस्कृती - sub-culture - cultural group within a larger culture having beliefs or interest that are different from those of the general one.

उपसंहार - epilogue - a closing section added to a novel, play etc. providing further comment, interpretation or information.

उपसमष्टी - dependent body - body which relies on another for support, existence, aid etc.

उपांग - isolate - a generic term denoting an isolate concept having subordinate level of subject.

उपांत्य अष्टक - penultimate octave - last but one octave.

उपांत्य टिपण - cutting note / in cut note - a side note which is laid at the outer edge of a paragraph of text instead of appearing in the margin usually set in smaller and heavier type than the text, also called 'cut in note' 'cut in side note', ' a late in note'.

उपांत्य वर्ग - penultimate class - subject before the next desired order.

उपांत्य शीर्षक - cut in heading - a paragraph or section heading set in a bold or otherwise distinguishing type in a space made available against the outer margin but within the normal type area. Also called 'in cut heading'.

उपांत्य - penultimate - last but one, second last.

उपार्जन (ग्रंथोपार्जन) अधिकारी - acquisition officer - an assistant who undertakes the duties necessary for acquiring new books for a library.

उपार्जन (ग्रंथोपार्जन) कार्य - acquisition work - the work of book selection, ordering obtaining by gift or exchange, serials control and rebinding.

उपार्जन (ग्रंथोपार्जन) विभाग - acquisition department - the department of a library concerned with ordering of books and possibly their cataloguing and processing also, often other functions such as obtaining books by exchange or gift, administration of serials and binding are also undertaken.

उपार्जन/ग्रंथोपार्जन - acquisition - 1) process of obtaining books and other documents for a library, documentation centre or archive.
2) commonly refers to 'hunting and gathering' of information/documents, the foundation of efficient reference service.

उपार्जित साहित्याची(ग्रंथाची) नोंद - acquisition record -
1) record of books (articles) acquired for the library.
2) a record of all books and other material added or in process of being added, it is usually kept in alphabetical order.

उभय प्रतिरोधी विद्राव - buffer solution - substances used for controlling the active & potentially harmful effects of chemical changes in materials.

उमटरेखन - embossing - relief printing by the use of a sunken die and raised counterpart. called female and male, the surface of the paper being raised in relief. It may also be done by use of certain substances dusted on the printed surface and caused to be raised by heating. Also called 'Process embossing', 'Relief printing', 'Bas relief printing'

उमटरेखित/कोरीव ग्रंथ - embossed book - a book in which the text is printed in embossed characters, e.g. Braille for the use of the blind.

उमेदवार (शिकाऊ) - apprentice - a person who is newly included in staff to learn the routine of actual work.

उलट पाहा/आणखी पाहा संदर्भ - cross reference entries - general added entries referring from one word or set of words to another synonymous word or to a set of words.

उलट संदर्भ नोंद पाहा/आणखी नोंद पाहा - **cross reference index entry** - general added entry referring from one word or set of words to another synonymous word or set of words.

उलट संदर्भ नोंद पाहा/आणखी पाहा - **cross reference entry** - a title which refers to other title in a classification system or in indexing.

उलटे न करता येणारे संबंध - **irreversible relations** - the relation where reversible relations are not possible e.g. mathematics for engineers.

उल्लेख निर्देश/सूची - **citation index** - a list of articles subsequent to the appearance of the original article.

उल्लेख सूची संकलित करण्याची प्रक्रिया (निर्देशन) - **indexing** - the art of compiling an index.

उल्लेख सूचीमधील विषय निर्देशनाची संकेत भाषा (निर्देशी भाषा) - **indexing language-**
1) an artificial language which is used for indexing.
2) a set of indexing terms as used in particular retrieval system. The 'language' can be 'natural' or 'structured' or 'controlled'. Text carried out on a number of vocabularies have shown that, those based on natural language might give better results than those based on that structured language. (see also 'Artifiticial indexing language' and 'natural language'.)

उल्लेख सूचीमध्ये समाविष्ट केलेली नोंद (निर्देशी नोंद) - **index entry** - an individual line or item of data present in an index such as an entry in a dictionary.

उल्लेख - **citation** - source item mentioned as an authority for a statement.

उसनवार ग्रंथ - **book on loan** - to lent books from library.

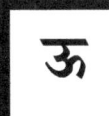

ऊर्जा/क्रिया - **energy** - the strength and vitality required to keep active. In colon classification this term is used as one of the prime characteristic.

ऊर्जा उपांग - **energy isolate** - one of the isolates in colon classification related to energy, process or action.

ऊर्जा मुख/पैलू - **energy facet** - one of the facet of colon classification enunciating the process or action for a subject.

ऊर्जापरिवर्तक/परांतरित्र - **transducer** - a device that converts a physical input into an electrical signal.

ऊर्जा पैलूच्या फेऱ्या - **rounds of energy** - the facet energy coming again and again in a sequence in classifying documents.

ऊर्जा सामान्य उपविभाग - **energy common isolate** - common isolates related to energy facet in colon classification.

ऊतक कागद - **tissue paper** - fine quality paper, ideal for repair and restoration work.

उद्धरण अभ्यास - **citation study** - A study of the references made to previously published documents by author in his work. These references may be in the form of footnotes or bibliography. The word citation is also used to mean the information given in the entries of a catalogue or bibliography to describe a document.

उद्धरण क्रम - **citation order** - The order of sequencing facets of a subject.(Synonymous with facet sequence and facet synthesis.)

उपविभाग - **sub-section** - a first division of section e. g. 531.1.It is a four digit number representing first subdivision of main class 531.

उप –उपविभाग - **sub-subsection** - a further division of subsection e.g. 531.1.1. It is a five digit number, and subsection of 531.1.

उप –शीर्षक - **sub- title** - 1) an explanatory title which follows the title proper. It elucidates the theme of book.
2) a secondary or subordinate title.This is usually an explanatory part of the title which either expands or limits the title proper.

उप –माला - **sub-series** - a series within a series or a series appearing along with a comprehensive series which in turn forms a section.

उपशाखन/शाखायन - **ramification** - divisions and sub- divisions of a subject.

उद्दिष्ट/हेतू/अभिप्राय - **intention** - depth of coverage of a subject.

उद्दिष्टेपेक्षी/अपेक्षामूलक/प्रत्याशी सेवा - **anticipatory service** -information service given in anticipation of demand after a general assessment of need; given to groups, not to individuals.

उद्धरण निर्देश - **citation index** - an ordered list of articles that, subsequent to the appearance of the original article refers to or cite that article.This method has been used extensively in the legal profession and is particularly applicable to scientific literature.

उद्राती/नष्ट होणारी स्मृती - **volatile memory** - memory that is erased when the electric current to the computer is turned off.

उपयोजित आज्ञावली - **application software** - it is a set of programmes which is written to deal with a particular task.

उपयोजित कार्यक्रम - **application programme** - a precoded set of generalized instructions for the computer written to accomplish a certain goal. Examples of such programmes include a book acquisition package etc.

उपार्जन पद्धत - **acquisition system** - the method of procurement of all types of library materials, whether by purchase, gift or exchange.All the physical processes from the request stage till the book is made available for cataloguing are included within acquisitions function.

ए.ए.सी.आर.- I- AACR -I (Anglo American Cataloguing Rules-I) - cataloguing rules prepared by American Library Association, published in 1967.

ए.ए.सी.आर. - II- AACR - II (Anglo American Cataloguing Rules-II) - cataloguing rules published in 1979 by incorporating rules to catalogue non-book materials.

ए.सी.आर.एल. - ACRL (Association of College and Research Libraries) - a division of the American Library Association since 1938, founded in 1889 to represent and promote 'libraries of higher education (institutions supporting formal education above the secondary school level), independent research libraries and specialized libraries'. Has eleven sections. It is the largest of the divisions of ALA.

एक संधी एकात्मता - seamless integration - integration of text, image and sound in a digital information environment without any binding chord fastening each form.

एकक (गुणविशेष)- character - the particular quality.

एकक (घटक) - unit - smallest part of a whole number used in various measurements.

एकक ग्रंथसूची - unit bibliography - a bibliography of different editions of a book with the small title.

एकक पत्र पद्धती - unit card system - system which uses machine sorted punched cards each of which bears a single term and a single document number. It was developed by G. L. Peakes.

एकक पत्र - **unit card** - a basic catalogue card, in the form of a main entry a duplicate of which may be used as a unit weather an entry for that particualr book is required in any catalogue, after the addition of any heading which may be necessary.

एकक संज्ञा निर्देश - **uniterm index** - a method of indexing which involves the selection of 'key words' from graphic record.

एकक/घटक नोंद - **unit record** - records which comprise of a descriptor file such as specification of documents, addresses etc.

एकक/घटक मूल्य - **unit cost** - cost of one operation or transaction or production.

एकघाती कार्यक्रमण - **linear programming** - a mathematical simulating method and process of calculating, evaluating and programming optimum path of action, process or operation for management consideration.

एकघाती समीकरण - **linear equation** - an equation in which the highest power of an unknown variable is one. The general form of a linear equation is $mx + c = 0$

एकत्र बांधणे - **bind** - hold together.

एकत्रित करण्याचा क्रम - **collating sequence** - an order in which various sets of data are merged into one.

एकत्रित तालिका - **consolidated catalogue** - combined catalogues of various libraries.

एकत्रित निर्देश - **consolidated index** - a combined index to several volumes of one subject or to several independent works.

एकत्रित नोंद - **consolidated entry** - entries combined into a single unit.

एकत्रित व्यक्तींचा समूह/समष्टी समिती - **corporate body** - a committee responsible for document production which is considered as author for the purpose of cataloguing.

एकत्रीकरण - **amalgamation** - 1) the union or combination of two or more concepts, organizations into one. 2) collating : the process of gathering and merging separate groups of sequenced documents such as signatures in a book, pages of report etc. 3) consolidation : comprehensive account, descriptive or critical, reported separately or journal articles and technical reports, conference papers etc.

एकधागा बांधणी - **all along binding** - the method of sewing by hand the sections (usually on cords or tapes) of a book, when the thread goes 'all along' or from kettle stitch to kettle stitch of each section. Also used to describe machine book sewing when each section is sewn with the full number of stitches.

एकपांक निर्देश - entry-a-line index - an entry in an index, with its page or other reference, which is printed on a single line. Where the entries consist of titles which are similarly confined to one line, it is known as a 'Title-a-line Index'.

एकभाषिक एकभाषीय शब्दकोश - monolingual dictionary - dictionary having words and their meaning in single (same) language.

एकमितीयता - unidimensionality - Item having only one dimension.

एकमुद्राक्षर - monotype - paper perforating and type founding machines invented by Tolbert Lanston for composing and casting single types. Individual types are cased on the casting machine from paper rolls perforated on the perforating machine in which a keyboard is incorporated.

एकरूप आवृत्ती - uniform edition - the individual work of an author published in an identical format and binding.

एकरूप ग्रंथनाम - uniform title - the distinctive title by which a work is indentified although it has appeared under varying titles and catalogue entries are made under such common title in different versions. Also called 'Conventional title', 'Filing title', 'Standard title'.

एकरूप शीर्षक - uniform heading -a heading adopted for use in the catalogue for an author (personal or corporate), title or for any other component to keep consistency.

एकरूप - uniform - 1) always the same. 2) not varying or changing in form, rate, degree, manner etc. 3) having a consistent action, effect etc. being identical throughout a state, country etc.

एकरूपता आत्मसात करणे - assimilation - absorb; the act of bringing together or coming to resemblance.

एकरूपता - uniformity - 1) empirical which relies solely on experience rather than theory, exact resemblance.

एकवर्णक - monochrome - illustration in one colour.

एकवस्तू गट - unitary group - a group of ideas or items where each item resembles other.

एकविषयी ग्रंथ - monograph - a separate treatise on a single subject.

एकसंज्ञा निर्देश - uniterm index - a method of indexing which involves the selection of 'key words' from graphic records. Keywords represent the content of the record or document that is being indexed. It is not necessary to create or maintain a list of approved headings since a list is compiled as the work proceeds. The keywords must be predicted when analysing a question in order to provide searching clues.

एकसूत्रता/समन्वय - **coordination** - interaction among constituents of a system towards maximum utilization of resources.

एकस्व साहित्य - **patents literature** - a government licence for writings & other form giving sole right to make use or sell invention for a set period.

एकस्व - **patent** - a specification dealing with the design or manufacture of item or product which is protected by letter of patent and secured for the exclusive profit of the designer or inventor for a limited number of years, period of which varies in different countries.

एका ओळीत एकच नोंद केलेला निर्देश - **line - by - line index** - Index having only one entry in a line.

एका ओळीतील रचना - **liner arrangement** - an arrangement made or extended along a straight line.

एका पंक्तीमध्ये असणारे वर्ग/सहसंबंधी वर्ग - **co-ordinate classes** -classes formed by same order of division.

एका मागोमाग येणारे विषय - **modulated subjects** - controlled or regulated subjects.

एका मागोमाग येणाऱ्या गौण विषयांची साखळी - **chain of modulated subjects** - a chain of classes of each and every order that lies between the order of the first link and the last link of the chain.

एकाकी नोंद - **single entry** - entry showing only expenditure or receipt.

एकूण उपयोगिता - **total utility** - the total amount of satisfaction derived by the consumer after consuming a product at different prices.

एकूण किंमत - **total cost** - the sum total of the fixed and variable costs.

एफ.आय.डी. – **FID (Federation International Documentation)**- 1) The organization (Formerly The International Institute for Documentation (Institut International de Documentation, IID) Which publishes the UDC and many other publications in the field of information and documentation in which it is the major international non-governmental scientific organisation.
2) the English name of the Federation Internationale de Documentation (FID) by which the International Institute of Bibliography was known in 1938.

एम.एस.डॉस - **MS-DOS - (microsoft disk operating system)**- an operating system in computing having package that controls the operation of user programmes.

ऐच्छिक - voluntary -

1) doing things without compulsion. 2) of once own free will. 3) done on one's own accord by free choice with all good intentions.

ऐतिहासिक हेतूसाठी केलेला साठा/पुराभिलेखागार - archive -

1) storage of items of interest for historical purposes.

2) a place where old public records, documents etc. are kept.

ओ

ओतशाळा साधक/सिद्धता - **foundry proof -** a proof pulled before the form is sent to the foundry.

ओतशाळा - **foundry -** department of a printing works where matrices are made from the type forms and blocks, and where stereo plates are cast. Other operations concerned with the casting or fabricating of type and other printing surfaces are also carried out here; the casting and routing of machines, type-metal, stereo-metal & similar materials and the necessary tools are available here.

ओपवणे - **bleach -** Removing or reducing colouration from paper or cotton fabric by use of acid or alkaline solution (Unbleached).

ओपॅक - **OPAC (online public access catalogue) -** an automated catalogue system stored in machine readable form and accessed online by the library clientele via Video Display Unit and employing user friendly software.

ओलावा/सांद्रता - **moisture -** percentage of water in air which makes it slightly wet, at a given relative humidity and temperature.

ओळखचिन्हं पत्र - **identification card -** generally used in place of borrower's ticket in the network charging system and transaction card system. This card is bearing borrower's name, address and registration number.

ओळखपत्र - **identity card -** 1) a card which proves as being specified person.
2) the condition or fact of being the same in all qualities under consideration sameness.

औद्योगिक ग्रंथालय - industrial library - 1) libraries provided by and in, industrial firms. 2) a library established, maintained by and in industrial firm.

औपचारिक नेतृत्व - formal leadership - a manager is a formal leader by virtue of authority coming from the organization. A formal leader is usually selected by the organization.

औपचारिक - formal - customary, traditional.

औपचारिक संघटन/संस्था - formal organization - an organization with a well defined structure, clearly specified jobs for members and a hierarchy of objectives.

औपचारिक हस्तलिखित प्रलेख - chirograph - formerly, writing which required a duplicate, was engrossed twice on the same piece of parchment with a space between in which was written the word chirographum or other word or words, through which the parchment was cut, and one part was given to each party.

औपचारिक/शाब्दिक व्याख्या – formal definition - definition prepared according to the forms that make explicit, definite, valid, etc. as a formed explanation of the term.

कटर अंक/चिन्ह - **cutter number or cutter mark** - cutter number is also known as "Author number" or "Book number".It is a combination of letters and numbers used to individualize and distinguish books having the same class number.

कट्टा - **counter** - long, narrow, flat, high surface over which books are kept in shop or circulated for reading in library.

कठीण तबकडी - **hard disk** - a high performance magnetic storage media usually fixed inside the computer.

कडांना खाचा असलेली पत्र - **edge - notched card** - a card having holes at one or more edges, used in a simple mechanical search technique; each hole position is assigned a coded significance and for particualar cards the holes are turned into notches by removing the part of the card between hole and edge.

कणा/पाठ - **back** - binding edge of the book, in some cases author's name and title of the document is mentioned on this area.

कनिष्ठ साहाय्यक - **junior assistant** - a professional who works under the supervision of senior professional.

कनिष्ठ - **junior** - a person of lower level in a cadre.

कपाट क्रमांक - **shelf number** - a number assigned to a shelf to describe its location.

कपाट फलक/मार्गदर्शक - **shelf guide** - an indicator showing details of documents available in a particular shelf.

कपाट यादी - **shelf list** - a catalogue of library holdings arranged in same order as they are available on shelves. For each document one entry with full details is prepared and such list is referred only by library staff.

कपाट शोधन - **shelf rectification** - the process of reforming order of the scheduled documents.

कपाट - **shelf** - compartment of library cupboard or stack.

कपाटवार रचना/मांडणी - **block arrangement** - arrangement of sections of library collection based on subject/type of documents.

कपाटाची क्षमता - **shelf capacity** - capacity of holding number of volumes on a shelf.

कपाटातील खूण/चिन्ह -**shelf mark** - a symbol showing the contents of a shelf.

कपाटावरील रचना - **shelf arrangement** - arrangement of documents on shelves.

कप्पेनिहाय रचना/मांडणी - **ribbon arrangement** - a method of arranging documents in a library with non-fiction on upper shelves and novels on lower shelves or vice- versa, or novels on middle shelves and non-fiction above and below, the object being to dispense the readers around the library and avoid congestion at the fiction shelves.

कर - **cess / tax** - amount to be paid by people or business to a government for public utility purposes.

कर्तव्य चुकार/कामचुकार - **defaulter** - 1) a person who fails in returning library documents on due date. 2) a person having library dues.

कर्मचारी उद्बोधन - **employee orientation** - making staff abrest for the new service, operation, equipment etc.

कर्मचारी नियमपुस्तिका - **staff manual** - a handbook or a guide explaining procedures, activities for regular work of the staff.

कर्मचारी वर्ग - **personnel / staff** - people employed in firm or public office.

कर्मचारी वर्ग - **staff** - human resources available in an institution or deportment.

कर्मचारी व्यवस्थापन - **personnel management**- the total administration of human resources of an organisation.

कलनशास्त्र - **calculus** - a branch of mathematics that deals with rates of change in variable quantities, used to solve many mathematical problems. It is divided into two main parts i.e. differential calculus and integral calculus.

कला दालन - art gallery - the gallery or that area used for display or exhibit photographs, pictures and other forms of art.

कलित सार - slanted abstract / biased abstract - an abstract giving emphasis to a particular aspect of the contents of a documents so as to safeguard the interests of a particular group of readers.

कल्पना क्षेत्र - idea plane - to differentiate ideas / concepts imaginatively but in logical order specially for the purpose of classification.

कल्पनाचित्र - ideogram - a form of primitive writing expressing a way of expressing ideas, not necessarily in words, is called ideography. Pictures drawn for purpose of communication differ slightly from pictures drawn for artistic purposes. Communication pictures are however, simplified and stereotyped with no details that are needed as part of the communication.

कल्पनारम्य ग्रंथनाम - fanciful title - the title of document with unreal, imaginative, attractive words.

कल्पनारम्य ग्रंथशीर्षक - fanciful title - the title of document with unreal, imaginative, attractive words.

कल्पित नाव - fictious name - an assumed name of document imaginatively created for the purpose of writing.

कळफलक - key board - a board used for typing using typewriter or computer having number of keys associated with the code linked with electric switches. The system hardware used to input characters, commands and functioning to the computer.The keyboard normally consist of 83& 108 keys and is organized into three sections : the function keys, the typewriter keyboard and numeric key pad.

कवक - fungus - a type of plant without leaves and flowers, growing on paper, other plants, decaying matter, or wet surface.

कवककण - fungus spores - destructive mildews in dormant forms flourishing in damp conditions. They appear in dull shades of green, grey, brown, blue & purple.

कशिदा/वेलबुट्टी काढलेली आच्छादने/बांधणी- embroidered covers / binding - binding in which the covering material is with embroidered cloth, also called as needle work binding.

कशिदा/वेलबुट्टी - embroidery - preparation of designs on cloth by using thread.

कसर/बट्टा - discount - the rebate on printed price.

कांटचे वर्गीकरण - Kant's classification - scheme of classes implied in the critique of pure reason. (1781) by Immanuel Kant.

कागद रंगीबेरंगी/गुलगुलीत - immitation paper - paper having soft surface.

कागद (पातळ/पारदर्शक) - tissue paper - very thin, unsized, nearly transparent paper.

कागद - paper - sheet of fibrous material on which one can write.

कागदाची एक घडी - folio - large sheet of paper folded once, making two leaves or four pages of a book.

कागदी आवरण - cover, book jacket - made of paper, cloth, leather etc. to which the body part of a book gets attached by gluck thread.

कागदी बांधणी - paperback binding - binding backed with paper for student edition.

कागदी रोगण - paper varnish -

काटकसर सिद्धान्त - law of parsimony - enunciated by Dr. S. R. Ranganathan stating that while cataloguing a document, one should write only essential information.

काटेकोर - tailored exact - punctual particular.

काठावरचा - peripherals - a general term for the various devices used with computers, operating under computer control. It includes input and storage devices.

काढून टाकणे discard - a book that is withdrawn from circulation in a library because it is outdated or is torned or unusable.

काढून टाकणे/निष्कासन/निर्लेखन - terminate (from service) ; weeding out-the process of removing mutilated collections from the library.

कातडी कमावणे - tanning - the treatment of animal pelts using vegetables, minerals and animal fats to make leather soft.

कात्रण सेवा - clipping services - service generated on the basis of the newpaper clippings. Generally the clippings are provided in subject order so as to make the specialist users aware of the current trends of the subject.

कात्रण - clipping - a printed paper piece clipped from a newspaper or magazine which contains information on a given subject.

कात्रणे - news / press clippings / newspaper clippings.

कादंबरी - novel / fiction - narrative prose writing. A form of literary writing.

कापडी बांधणी - cloth binding - a binding in which cloth is used with hardboard to protect a document.

काम (नेमून दिलेले) - task - a coordinated and aggregated series of work elements used to produce a desired output.

काम/कार्य विश्लेषण - task /job analysis - the process of identifying the tasks of a particular job in a particular organizational context by analyzing activities, establishing performance criteria, determining required competencies and analyzing any discrepancies uncovered by this process.

कायदा ग्रंथालय - law library - specialized library for practising lawyers, teachers and research scholars working in the field of law. The collection of such library includes judicial decisions, administrative orders, notifications, amendments of rules etc.

कायदा/विधी/नियम - law - a rule of action established by authority.

कायमचा (स्थायी) - standing - permanent, continuing without occasion or charge.

कायमची (स्थायी) समिती - standing committee - a committee having powers of administrative decisions.

कार्य अभ्यास - work study - it is the collective term used to describe the combination of techniques involved in method study and work measurement.

कार्य घटकाचे मूल्य/एकक मूल्य - unit cost - normal and average cost to carry out an unit amount of work.

कार्य पृथक्करण - job analysis - analysis of different kinds of jobs, works, activities.

कार्य मूल्यमापन - job evaluation/performance evaluation -
1) assessment of the quality and quantity of job performed.
2) specifying the value of a job in relation to other jobs.

कार्य विश्लेषण विवेचन - job description - details of jobs assigned to a post or cadre.

कार्य स्थानक - work station - a system comprising of a single word processing station that does not share the power of a control computer.

कार्य/अर्थक्रिया - function - a type of work activity that can be identified and distinguished from other work.

कार्य - job - a set of task prescribed for execution.

कार्यकारी आदेश/सूचना - executive order - order issued by an executive authority.

कार्यकारी - executive - the person who administers an organisation : a person who performs duties to satisfy the policies to run the organisation.

कार्यकुशल कर्मचारी - professional staff - a person with minimum basic qualifications in a subject and having preliminary profession skill of an occupation.

कार्यक्रम मूल्यमापन व परीक्षण तंत्र - PERT (Programme Evaluation Review Technique) - a planning & control technique that involves the display of a complex project as a network of events & activities with three time estimates used to calculate & expected time for each activity.

कार्यक्रम - programme - sequence of instructions given to a computer or an arrangement of jobs to take up. Also known as software/computer programmes recreational activity.

कार्यक्रमकार - programmer - a specialist who designs, writes and maintains the computer programme.

कार्यक्रमण/आज्ञावली/कार्यक्रम - program - a program is a complete specifications of the processing to be performed on data supplied in terms of available operations of a computer.

कार्यक्रमाची भाषा/आज्ञावलीची भाषा - programming language - language used to express programme.

कार्यक्षमता - efficiency - capacity of a person or machine for doing things accurately with the minimum use of time and other necessary resources. It is also expressed as the proportional relationship between the quality & quantity of inputs and outputs.

कार्यदल - task force - a group of committee formed for analysing, investigating or solving a specific problem.

कार्यवाह (सचिव) - secretary - trustee of an institution having administrative power.

कार्यवाहक - operator - a person who operates / performs various jobs with machines.

कार्यवाही पुस्तिका - operational manual - manual which contains instructions and specifications for a given assignment, appliance or application.

कार्यवाही - operation - 1) generally refers to the action / job performed by a computer. 2) process of operation or action / job performed by a computer.

कार्यवृत्त/सभावृत्त - minutes -1) note of decisions in an official memorandum; record of decisions taken in a meeting. 2) an official record of the meeting of an organisation or institution or committee.

कार्यवृत्ताची नोंदवही - **minute book** - book in which minutes are recorded.

कार्यशाळा - **workshop** - meeting for a continuous period of time combining instructions as well as laboratory work to upgrade skill.

कार्यसुलभ भाषा - **assembly language** - a language based on machine code using memory or a language between high level language and machine language.

कार्यसूची - **agenda** - a list, planned outline of the things to be considered for decision, matters to be acted upon.

कार्यालयीन मुखपत्र - **official organ** - a journal, newspaper or other publication representing a special group.

कालक्रम युक्ती (विचार स्तर) - **chronological device (idea plane)** - device for forming an isolate or sharpening a host focus in the form of an isolate or an array isolate with the help of characteristic of being occurred first.

कालक्रमानुसारी क्रम - **chronological order** - Arrangement in order of date of appearance. Applies to order in a catalogue (date of publication - imprint or copyright or of the material itself (books, pamphlets or cuttings).

कालगणना/कालक्रम - **chronology** - science of arranging historical events based on their time of occurrence/arrangement of list events in the order in which they occured.

कालबाह्य/अनुपलब्ध ग्रंथ - **out - of - print - books** - completely sold out document of which not a single copy is available in the market.

कालातीत प्रकाशन - **out of print** - a document of which all the copies are sold & not a single is available in the market for sale.

कालातीत संग्रह - **out of stock** - document which is not available with stockist and distributors.

कालानुक्रम युक्ती - **chronological device - (notational plane)** - Chronological Device : it consists of use of and appropriate chronological number for the further sub-division of a class which is capable of chronological division.

कालानुक्रम - **chronological order** - an arrangement of classes achieved by applying time and date as differentiating characteristics.

कालानुक्रम - **chrononomics** - organization of events according to their year of appearance.

कालिक नियंत्रण - **serial control** - acquisition of the serial publications.

कालिक तालिका - **serial catalogue** - a catalogue of serial publications.

कालिक संख्या/अंक - **serial number** - the successive number which fixes the position of the serial volume amongst other volumes of the publication.

कालिक - **serial** - a periodic publication with a specific name and articles on varying topics. These articles supplement previous knowledge published in its earlier volumes.

काल्पनिक नांव - **fictious name** - an imaginary or fanciful name.

काल/कालावधी - **period** - in the scheme of classification the term is used for literary piece that is composed. For every language or literature, there is a separate and unique period table. Every literature has its own historical approach.In case of critical appraisal or literary anthologies regardless of a language, the period is to be taken from ss09 in table 1of DDC.

काळ/वेळ पैलू - **time facet** - the characteristic used in classification schemes denoting period of occurance of an event on which the document is based upon.

काळसारणी – (वेळापत्रक) - **time table** - a schedule of time to operate a service.

किंमत केंद्र - **cost centre** - it is a location, person, item or equipment (or group of these) for which costs may be determined for the purpose of cost control.

किंमत घटक - **cost unit** - it is a unit into which a product or service or item is divided for costing purpose. It is a unit of measurement of an item for costing purpose.

किंमत फायदा विश्लेषण - **cost benefit analysis** - analysis relating to the cost of providing a particular service to the beneficiaries of this service.

किंमत - **cost** - it is the measure of what has to be given up to achieve something.

किंमतीची परिणामकारकता - **cost effectiveness** -measurement of cost to its effectiveness.

कीलकार - **cuneiform** - a term derived from a Latin word, meaning 'wedge-shaped'. It is one of the most widespread & historically significant writing system in the ancient North East. The origin of the cuneiform may be traced back approximately to the end of the 4th millennium B C and is attributed to the submarine. Due to the prevalent use of clay tablets as writing material the linear strokes acquired a wedgeshaped appearance by being pressed into the soft clay with the slanted edge of stylus.

कुटुंब/परिवार नांव/कुलनाम - **family name-surname** - a name which is in use in a family representing heredity. a name that preceds the family name or class or surname; a christian or personal name.

कुलनाम/वर्गनाव/आडनावापूर्वी येणारे नांव - **forename** - part of the name which individualises a person. It is a name or a part of a name which designates a person or individual and distinguishes him from others bearing the same family name surname or class name. Also called given name or family name.

कृती कार्यमापन - performance appraisal - an assessment of the performance of work accomplished by employees to determine their contributions, strengths and weaknesses.

कृती मूल्यमापन - performance evaluation - it helps to assess how well a system or person or section is working with respect to the targets set out.

कृती योजना - strategy - a predetermined course of action, usually selected from a number of alternatives.

कृती/रचना/काम - work - expressed thoughts in language, symbols or any other mode.

कृती मोजमाप - performance measurement - it means how well an operational system meets the needs of its users.

कृत्रिम निर्देश भाषा - artificial indexing language - an indexing language; a group of signs, symbols or digits or of phrases or words arranged in an invested order according to rules and so becoming controlled language to represent facts and ideas.

कृत्रिम बुद्धिमत्ता - artifical intelligence - 1) an intelligent work undertaken and completed by using machines, computers etc.
2) the branch of computer science that is attempting to replicate some aspects of human intelligence, for example solving problems and drawing conclusions.

कृत्रिम भाषा - artificial language - 1) a group of signs, symbols or digits (or of phrases, words arranged in an inverted order according to rules and so becoming 'controlled' language to present facts & ideas.
2) a symbolic language used in library classification. The language used arbitrary and rules for its use are provided with it.

कृत्रिम लक्षण - artificial characteristic - 1) a quality which is possessed in common by a group e.g. colour or height of men.
2) a quality which is possessed by a group of things in common, but is not a necessity for their being.

कृत्रिम समासित ग्रंथ - artificial composite book - a composite book without a generic title, generally created by the binder. The books put together in one binding for the sake of convenience.

कृत्रिम - artificial - one which is not natural.

कृषिविषयक संशोधन माहिती प्रणाली/व्यवस्था - **Agricultural Research Information System (AGRIS)** - an acronym for worldwide cooperative agricultural research information system set up in 1970-71 for current information in the field of agriculture, science and technology.

कृषी अभियांत्रिकी - **agricultural engineering** - engineering education related to agriculture.

कृषी महाविद्यालय - **agricultural college** - the college offerring agriculture education.

कृषी विद्यापीठ - **agricultural university** - university imparting agriculture & allied education.

कृषी शाळा - **agricultural school** - school imparting agriculture education.

कृषी - **agriculture** - the science and art of farming ; tillage; the cultivation of the crops for the purpose of producing vegetables & fruits.

कृषीप्रधान समाज - **agrarian society** - a society in which the work force is predominantly from the agricultural class.

कृषीविषयक ग्रंथालय - **agricultural library** - a library maintained to disseminate information to agriculture sector and R & D units.

कृषीविषयक संशोधन माहिती केंद्र - **Agricultural Research Information Centre (ARIC)** - the centre established to collect information of agricultural research of the country for creating database for onward transmission to database known as AGRIS.

केंद्र - **nodes / nucleus / centre** - a point of function of the link or a control point in a network.

केंद्रबिंदू - **focal point / focus** - 1) generic term to denote an isolate ideal basic class/ compound class/ complex class.
2) the central or principal body of activity or attention.

केंद्रस्थान शीर्षक - **central heading/entry** - a typographical device used in the decimal classification scheme.

केंद्रीभूत तालिकीकरण - **centralized cataloguing** - cataloguing of information sources acquired for branch or member libraries or group of libraries by a central agent to achieve uniformity.

केंद्रीभूत पंजीकरण - **centralized registration** - registration made at central place of the branches, gathered together to draw a central point, to bring to a centre.

केंद्रीभूत सोपस्कार - **centralized processing** - processing of documents at one place so as to organize or systematize under one authority or control.

केंद्रीय नोंद/शीर्षक - centred entry / centred heading - a heading denoted by a span of numbers, as there is no specific number for that heading.

केंद्रीय प्रक्रियक घटक - CPU (central processing unit) - it is a primary data storage unit of a computer. A control unit directs the sequence of operations. It accepts and transfers the data. It is a principle operating part of a computer.

केंद्रीय प्रवृत्ती - central tendency - a series of data can often be expressed in terms of summary figure for better comprehension and analysis. This summary figure, expressed as some middle or central value of the data, calculated by a properly defined method, is called a measure of central tendency. There are five important measures of central tendency mean, median, mode, geometric mean, and harmonic mean.

कॅम - CAM - computer aided microform - computer aided microforms are any forms, either films or paper, containing micro reproductions of documents for transmission, storage, reading, and printing. Microform images are commonly reduced to about one twenty-fifth of the original document size.

कोण आहे/होता/चरित्रकोश - who's who / who was who - collection of biographies either of alive or dead persons.

कोन - angle - space between two lines or surfaces meeting at one point.

कोबाल - COBOL (common business oriented language) - language used for data processing of business purpose. A high level language oriented toward organizational data processing procedures.

कोरडी छपाई - zerography - method of making copies of printed page by the use of light and an electrostatically charged plate. The method was invented by Chester F. Carlson patented by him in 1937.

कोरणी - engraving - an art of cutting or carving designs on metal, stone, wood, book, cover etc.

कोरीवकाम/उत्कीर्णन - engraving - the art or process of carving letters or designs on wood, metal or other substances, by cutting or etching for the purpose of printing or stamping by intaglio or recess process on paper or other material.

कोश विभाग/अनुवर्ग विभाग - dictionary, part of the catalogue - where entries are arranged alphabetically.

कोशकला - lexicology - the branch of knowledge which is concerned with words, their history, form and meaning.

कोशस्वरुपाची प्रलेखन यादी - **dictionary documents list** - a series or entries having verbal headings which are arranged in alphabetical order. Also termed as alphabetico - subject catalogue.

कोष्टक पत्र - **tabular work** - numerical figures arranged vertically in columns.

कौशल्य क्षमता - **aptitude** - a combination of native & acquired abilities & characteristics which can be regarded as predictive of a person's ability to become proficient in a line of activity with a given amount of training.

कॉम्पेन्डेक्स - **COMPENDEX** - abbreviation for Computerized Engineering Index, the machine readable version of Engineering Index, the principal agency for abstracting and indexing periodical covering the broad field of engineering.

क्रम (पंक्तिचा) - **order of an array** - the number of successive characteristics on the basis of which the classes in the array are derived from universe.

क्रम (मिश्र पंक्ती/पृथक घटकांचा) - **order of complex array isolate**-arrangement of isolates in a complex array.

क्रम (मिश्र वर्गाचा)– **order of the complex class** - arrangement of number of basic or compound classes combined to form one class.

क्रम (वर्गाचा) - **order of class** - the number of successive characteristics on the basis of which class of a subject is derived from universe.

क्रम (श्रृंखलेचा) - **order of chain** - the order of link in a chain.

क्रम (संयुक्त वर्गाचा) - **order of compound class** - number of isolates in a class.

क्रम (साखळीचा) - **order of a link** - order of classes representing the sequence.

क्रम प्रपत्र - **order form / format** - form or format used to place order of supply of items.

क्रम सूची - **order list** - list of orders placed with the suppliers, a list of documents of which letters for supply are sent.

क्रम - **order/sequence** - arrangement of ideas / concepts / things using logical arrangement.

क्रमपत्र - **order card** - card containing the information about documents asked to supply.

क्रमबद्ध ग्रंथसूची - **systematic biography** - an enumeration and classification of books. Assembling of bibliographical details of documents into logical and useful arrangements so as to locate them perfectly.

क्रमरचना - **interfile** - to arrange in a file or rank.

क्रमवाचक अंक - ordinal number - 1) a number having ordinal value which shows its relationship with other number.

2) a number given to a document that fixes its position relative to other documents in a collection.

क्रमवाचक चिन्हं - ordinal symbol - a symbol showing relative position of each other . Symbols merely indicate order sequence and are devoid of any cardinal value.

क्रमवाचक चिन्हांकन - ordinal notation - symbols for notation used in a classification scheme, showing relationship with each other.

क्रमवाचक नांव - ordinal name - number of a class in a scheme of classification, denoting its reference and place with other classes.

क्रमवाचक मूल्य - ordinal value - value denoting order or sequence as the ordinal numbers like first, second, third etc.

क्रमविक्षण - scanning -the examination of tallies records / sequentially, simultaneously and fractionally in information retrieval.

क्रमसंचय - cumulation - to accumulate.

क्रमसंचयी सूचीकरण/निर्देशन - cumulative indexing - progressive indexing of entries in a predetermined order which is circulated for use after specific period.

क्रमिक पुस्तके - text books - books written specifically for use by those studying for an examination in any particular subject. and class

क्राफ्ट कागद - craft paper - paper made especially by manual efforts. A type of handmade paper.

क्रिया/कार्य - action / process - an activity performed.

क्लिष्टता/गुंतागुंत/जटिलता - complexity - the state or quality of being complex ; complexness.

क्वीक – KWIC (keyword in context indexing) - a method of achieving index with the help of keywords.

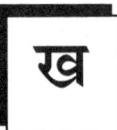

खंड/वर्ग - quasi - class - work which is treated as a class in a classification scheme although it is not a separate brand of subject or whose title is used as a subject heading in a cataloguing practice. A quasi class is usually a sacred work or a work of literature or a classic.

खंडित प्रक्रिया - batch processing - a method of processing in which the programs or data is accumulated and fed into (input) to the computer in a single block. Batch processing always involves delay between the occurrence of the event and processing of the resultant transactions.

खण - tray / drawer - flat piece of wood, metal, plastic etc. with raised edges, used for carrying or holding things, especially cards.

खराब ग्रंथ - damaged book - a book which has become unserviceable due to continuous use and could not be repaired.

खळ देणे – sizing : 1) gelatious solution used in coating and glazing paper surface. 2) the act of applying size.

खाजगी/व्यक्तिगत ज्ञान - private knowledge - the knowledge of the mind of an individual and as such is available to him / her or through him/her, to others if communicated.

खातेवही - ledger/register -book showing receipts and expenditure of each head of a budget.

खात्रीशीर - **authentic** - genuine, known to be true.

खिळा - **bolt** - metal bar that slides into a socket to lock a door, window etc.

खूणचिठ्ठी - **separator / marker / book-marker** - book mark, piece of thick paper to be used as an identifier or separator while reading a book.

खूणचिठ्ठी लावण्याचे काम - **labelling** - work of pasting and writing information on the label.

खोळ/कोश - **case** - a book cover that covers completely before it is affixed to a book. Pasting a book into its cover is expressed as 'casting in'.

ग

गट (सम्मुचय) - **group** - any sub aggregate of the entities formed with the entities obtained by the division of the entities of a universe; unit composed of similar characters.

गट क्रमांक - **batch number** - identification number to the information having uniform characteristics.

गट चिन्हांकन युक्ती - **group notation device** - device of using ordinal decimal fraction numbers of two or more digits to represent the number of co-ordinate isolate or array isolates, when they are too many to be represented economically by sector device alone.

गट - **batch** - a group of transactions carried out in a single unit.

गणकयंत्र - **calculator** -machine especially designed for performing arithmetic operations.

गणितीय प्रारूपे - **mathematical models** - a mathematical equations that defines & represents the relationship among elements of a system.

गतिशास्त्र/यंत्रशास्त्र - **mechanics** - mechanical or functional details that have to be attended to in the production.

गुंडाळलेला नकाशा - **rolled map** - map which can be rolled, stored and preserved.

गुंतागुंतीचा वर्ग/संमिश्र वर्ग - **complex class** - class framed by the combination of two or more basic or compound classes expressing relationship between them, but excluding the case when one of the classes forms an isolate of the other, formed by subject device.

गुंतागुंतीचा विषय - complex subject - a subject with one basic class alongwith one or more isolate ideas, subject which has more than one notable characteristics of subject.

गुटेनबर्ग - Guttenberg - Johannes Guttenberg (1398-1468) who invented printing press (letter) machine.

गुणकांक/गुणक - multiplier - the number by which another number is or to be multiplied.

गुणधर्म वस्तुमुख - property phase relation - device used in colon classification to represent characteristics of matter.

गुणवत्ता नियंत्रण - quality control - QC is a process to determine how the technological, human information and financial resources are being used effectively to get the best results.

गुणवत्ता वर्तुळ - quality circle - it is a small group between three to twelve people who do the same or similar work voluntarily, meeting regularly for about one hour per week, in paid time usually under the leadership of their own supervisor to identify, analyse, and solve some of the problems in their work. Presenting recommendations to management and where possible, implementing the solutions themselves.

गुणवत्ता सुधारणा - quality improvement - adding value to information products and services using appropriate performance standards.

गुणवत्ता/खात्री/विश्वास/वचन - quality assurance - QA is the method of and a philosophy for achieving better quality. It incorporates such areas as customer care, standards and performance setting. It encompasses all activities and operations.

गुणवत्ता - quality - the dictionary definition of 'Quality' of a person or thing is a characteristic innate which in particular, determines the nature & behaviour of the person or thing.

गुणविशेषणे – characteristics - quality of an attribute with reference to which two things can be distinguished.

गुणविशेष लक्षणे - characteristic features - set of elements or components that gives a structural outline of a technical communication.

गुणांक वाचक - multiplier reader - more or less similar to mixed readers.

गुणित वृद्धी – exponential growth - growth in Algebra, relating to exponents, especially involving the variable or unknown quantity as an exponent.

गुणोत्तर मापक्रम - ratio scale - it is an interval scale in which an absolute zero point exists, a point at which zero indicates a total absence of that which is being measured.

गुणोत्तरमध्य – **geometric mean** - refers to mean defined as

G. M. = where, $f_1 + f_2 + \text{-----}+ f_n = N$

गुप्त निरीक्षण - **clandestine observation** - secret observation.

गूढ - **occult** - involving supernatural or magical power.

गृह ग्रंथालय/व्यक्तिगत ग्रंथालय - **home library / personal library** - individual collection of documents for home / personal use.

गृह शैली - **house style** - conventions used by a publisher while preparing material for printing, which may be different for different publishing houses depending on their needs, requirements and preferences.

गृह/संस्था पत्रिका - **house journal** - a publication issued by the organisation to inform public of its performance and style of functioning and also to know the reactions, opinions and methods of public.

गृहीतक/आधारतत्त्व - **postulate** - a concept in colon classification scheme ; postulate is an assumption which is never put to test.

गॅन्ट तक्ता - **Gantt chart** - a two dimensional graph with lines on the horizontal axis and listing of the parts of a program on the vertical axis.

गोपनीय पंजी - **confidential file** - file containing very important papers available for use to restricted persons.

गोल कंस - **parentheses** - two curved lines ( ) used to include words to be inserted; used in cataloguing to enclose explanatory or qualifying words or phrases to set of some items in the entry, such as a series note.

गोलाई काढणे/ठोकणे - **backing** - preparation of semicircular spine of a book while binding by using cloth, rubber, rexin, leather etc.

गौण उपवर्गांचे सूत्र - **canon of sub-ordinate classes** - canon in classification stating that all sub-ordinate classes in whatever chain they may occur, should immediately follow it without being separated or among themselves by any other class.

गौण - **grid** - network of squares on a map, numbered for reference.

गौण - **subsidiary** - of having sub-ordinate importance or of secondary importance.

गौरवग्रंथ - **Festschrift** - a memorial volume issued in honour of a person. Contains contributions of different people, one theme, sometimes contains biography of the person who is honoured.

ग्रंथसूचीकार - **bibliographer** - a person who prepares bibliographies.

ग्रंथ अनुदान - **book grant** - the amount made available to increase library collections mostly by the government or non-governmental organizations.

ग्रंथ आधार - **book support** - rectangular piece of word or steel placed at the end of a row of books to keep them upright also called 'Book end'.

ग्रंथ आवरण/वेष्टन - **book jacket** - 1) the outer paper cover of the book which usually contains title of the document, information about book and its author. 2) a detachable protective wrapper of a book, also called book wrapper, dust jacket, or dust wrapper.

ग्रंथ उपयोगासाठी आहेत - **books are for use** - the first law of library science enunciated by Dr. S.R.Ranganathan. This law advocates for use of documents instead of preservation. The law demands that all situations like collection, hours, staff, building etc. should satisfy the requirements of the law.

ग्रंथ कणा - **spine** - the edge of a book where sections are sewed together in binding, also called 'back'.

ग्रंथ खरेदी - **purchase of book** - acquiring documents by payment of its cost.

ग्रंथ चिठ्ठी - **book label** - a label either circular or square in shape pasted on the spine of the book or at the bottom of cover of a document denoting the call number.

ग्रंथ निधी - **book fund** - an amount generated for purchase of information sources in a library.

ग्रंथ पत्र - **book card** - a card prepared for a book showing selected information about the book and kept either in book or in book pocket to use it at the time of charging. At the time of laying the document the date of issue or due date and name of the borrower is indicated on it.

ग्रंथ पेटी - **book case** - a cupboard used to hold books for storage.

ग्रंथ प्रदर्शन - **book exhibition** - display of books so as to give more publicity amongst users, book fair.

ग्रंथ प्रदान अधिनियम - **delivery of books Act** - Act inacted by the Central Government of India making it compulsory to deposit four copies of the published works at respository libraries.

ग्रंथ बांधणीचे दुकान - **bindery** - a place where books are bound.

ग्रंथ भांडार - **stack room** - an area in a library where collection is kept.

ग्रंथ मंडळ - **book club** - group of users who are producing / distributing /using books.

ग्रंथ वर्गीकरण – **book classification** : arrangement of documents in a systematic way by applying common characteristics to the subject.

ग्रंथ वर्गीकरणाची अनुसूची/तक्ता - **schedule of classification** - subjective directory helpful in finding the class number of each subject as expressed in a natural language, a jargon of library profession or a trade series of terms used to represent subject and their sub-branches in a scheme of classification.

ग्रंथ संग्रह/वाचनसाहित्य –**book collection** - collections of a library including all types of print and non-print documents.

ग्रंथ साठा/संग्रह - **book reservoir** - a place either within the library or at a predominated place within a region or country where weeded docuements can be stored or preserved.

ग्रंथ सूची/तालिका - **book catalogue** - a list of documents available A list or itemized display, as of titles or articles usually including descriptive information or illustrations; a publication, such as a book or pamphlet, containing such a list or display. & produced in book form, also known as "printed catalogue".

ग्रंथ/पुस्तक/प्रलेख - **book, document** - physically independent work other than a periodical publication, completed or intended to be completed in a finite number of pages or of volumes. It can have many volumes. It may be in printed form, manuscript, photocopy, microfilmed, audio-video cassettes, photographs, maps, newspapers, periodicals and tapes etc. A book is collection of information on a given subject or for recreation having a distinct title and at least 48 (forty-eight) pages. Thus, it is a macro document which deals with a subject in a great extension and less intension.

ग्रंथकार विश्लेषक नोंद - **author analytical entry** - an added entry referring the name of the author and the title of the contributor forming a part of a document, to the host document and giving place of occurrence of contribution in the host document.

ग्रंथकार/ग्रंथकर्ता/लेखक - **author** - the person, persons or corporate body responsible for the published or unpublished work.

ग्रंथदालन मार्गदर्शक – **gangway guide** - guide boards used in a big library to denote the location of the stock of particular subject.

ग्रंथनाम विश्लेषक नोंद – **title analytical entry** - an added entry referring the a title of a contribution forming a part of document and giving the place of occurrences of the contribution in the host document.

ग्रंथपाल - **librarian** - a person responsible for arranging library services; manager of a library.

ग्रंथपालन - **librarianship** : the profession of a librarian.

ग्रंथबद्ध असे ज्ञानविश्व - **universe of knowledge** - known knowledge represented in the documents.

ग्रंथमांडणी - **shelving of books** - an activity of keeping documents at its assigned place in a stack room, after receipt from users.

ग्रंथमापनशास्त्र - **bibliometrics** - पहा ग्रंथात्मक सांख्यिकी.

ग्रंथवर्गीकरण पद्धतीचा संकल्पक/रचनाकार/वर्गीकरणकार - **classificationist** - one who prepared a classification system for library classification.

ग्रंथवर्णनाचा माहितीसंग्रह - **bibliographical database** - a collection of computer generated, related items of information which together make the record of a single topic aspect.

ग्रंथवर्णनाच्या बाबी/विवरण - **bibliographic data / description** - information record of document consisting name of author, co-author, editor, translator, title, edition, publisher, series and publication date, etc. as to locate the document.

ग्रंथविषयक अभिलेख - **bibliographic record** - information giving bibliographic data.

ग्रंथविषयक नोंदीचे प्रारुप - **bibliographic record format** - layout of bibliographic data on a mechanical device or computer.

ग्रंथशीर्षक/ग्रंथनाम - **title** - the word / group of words used to denote name of the work.

ग्रंथसूची - **bibliography** - systematic list of documents to keep user abreast with the development of the discipline for which it is prepared. It constitutes the basic material of the reference section of every library. It includes both macro and micro documents.

ग्रंथसूचीत्मक केंद्र - **bibliographic centre** - place where bibliographic information is generated for disseminating among its users.

ग्रंथसूचीय अभिलेख प्रारुप - **bibliographic record format** - the layout or presentation of bibliographical data of a document in a machine readable form or machine printout.

ग्रंथांक - **book number** - 1) ordinal number which decides the position of a document in a library in relation to the other documents having the same ultimate class or a set of numbers, digits, symbols or combination of all, used to distinguish an individual development from every other documents of the same class to arrange it on the shelves in a desired manner.

2) the ordinal number which fixes the place of a document in a library relative to other document having same class number.

ग्रंथांक - **book number** - 1) the ordinal number which fixes the place of a document in a library relative to other documents having the same class number.

2) The layout or presentation of bibliographical data of a document in a machine readable form or machine printout.

ग्रंथाचा कणा - **spine of a book/back** - binding edge of the book; in some cases information like name of the author, title and call number of the document is mentioned on it.

ग्रंथाची फार जुनी हस्तलिखित प्रत - **codex** - the name given to the earliest forms of manuscripts in book form, i. e. the collection of written pages stitched together. This form replace the earlier roll form of papyrus or leather manuscripts.

ग्रंथाच्या आरंभीचे वा शेवटचे पान - **fly-leaf** - a blank leaf at the beginning or end of a book, specially the free half of end paper.

ग्रंथात्मक नियंत्रण - **bibliographic control** - management of publications.

ग्रंथात्मक नियतकालिक - **bibliographic periodical** - periodical giving a catalogue of books and aritcles currently published.

ग्रंथात्मक माहितीसंग्रह - **bibliographic database** -
1) computerised storage collection of information / data in machine readable form.
2) typical databases include segregates (i.e. name, title abstract) of library holdings or of published journal articles.

ग्रंथात्मक वर्गीकरण - **bibliographic classification** - scheme of classification of documents designed by Henry Evelyn Bliss, first published in 1935.

ग्रंथात्मक वर्णन - **bibliographic description** -
1) Information about a document regarding its author, title, edition, publishing and other details in a catalogue entry. 2) the description of published work of literary or musical composition, giving particulars of authorship, of others who have contributed to the presentation of the text (editor, translator, illustrator, arranger etc.), title, edition, data, particulars of publication (place and name of publisher and possibly of printer) etc. 3) of bibliographic description is used to locate the original source in order to refer the required information in the original form.

ग्रंथात्मक विवरण - bibliographic description - information of author, co-author, editor, translator, title, edition, publisher, series, publication date etc., information about document useful to locate.

ग्रंथात्मक सांख्यिकी/ग्रंथमापनशास्त्र - bibliometrics - 1) statistical analysis of the literature, information on any published work. 2) application of various statistical techniques to study patterns of authorship, publication and use of literature etc.

ग्रंथात्मक सूचना - bibliographic instruction - course related, classroom based library instruction.

ग्रंथात्मक सेवा - bibliographical services - the act of producing bibliographies.

ग्रंथायतन - pool of libraries - group of libraries.

ग्रंथालय अंदाजपत्रक - library budget - allocation of funds made available to a library for offering library services.

ग्रंथालय अधिनियम - library Act - Act legistation prepared and approved by government to create library services in a systematic order.

ग्रंथालय अभिलेख - library records - information maintained by a library such as accession register, issue record etc.

ग्रंथालय अभ्यागत - library visitor - a person visiting a library who is not a regular member.

ग्रंथालय अर्थव्यवस्था - library economy - aspects concerning with library finance.

ग्रंथालय आज्ञावली - library software - a computer program designed for handling library operations.

ग्रंथालय आय - library income - funds in the form of grants, membership fee, endowments, fines, service charges, sale of publications etc.

ग्रंथालय आवृत्ती - library edition - an edition especially brought out for use in libraries having good paper and hard binding.

ग्रंथालय इमारत व साधनसामुग्री - library building and furniture - the building and furniture meant for a library.

ग्रंथालय उपकरण - library equipment - the equipments used in library.

ग्रंथालय उपक्रम - library activities - various operations carried out to offer library service.

ग्रंथालय कपाट - library stack - special racks used for storage or collection in which height of the shelves is adjustable, further, in some model, book supporters are available in each shelf.

ग्रंथालय कर - **library cess** - provision made under the Act for generation of funds to provide essential library services.

ग्रंथालय कर्मचारी - **library staff** - staff engaged to perform various activities carried out by a library.

ग्रंथालय कामगार - **library worker** - non professional working a library supportive staff.

ग्रंथालय कायदा - **library legislation** - Act passed by a legislature for promotion of library services in a province.

ग्रंथालय कार्य - **functions of library** - work carried out by a library.

ग्रंथालय खर्च - **library expenditure** - 1) expenditure incurred by a library. 2) money spent by a library on different heads such as purchase of reading materials salaries & allowances, stationery, postage, furniture, equipment etc.

ग्रंथालय गणनशास्त्र - **librametry** - quantitative analysis of various facets of library activities and library documents by application of mathematical and statistical calculus to seek solution to library problems.

ग्रंथालय चळवळ - **library movement** - activity undertaken by group of people or libraries to improve library services.

ग्रंथालय जाळे - **library network** - 1) group of libraries connected with a communication link.
2) interlinking library document resources and services by means of computer & communication technologies.

ग्रंथालय तालिका - **library catalogue** - record of document holdings of a library arranged in a definite order.

ग्रंथालय धोरण/नीती - **library policy** - a policy formulated to develop library services in various sectors.

ग्रंथालय नियम व नियमावली - **library rules and regulations** - guiding principles for the library professionals and users.

ग्रंथालय नियोजन - **library planning** - a plan through which library services are arranged.

ग्रंथालय पत्र - **library card / borrowers card** - a membership card or cards isssued to holder to borrow books from the library.

ग्रंथालय पत्र - **library ticket** - membership card used to borrow library books for using them outside the library premises.

ग्रंथालय परिचर - library attendant - semi-professional person working in a library. A person who serves in a library having lowest professional qualification.

ग्रंथालय प्रलेख - library documents, library holdings - sources of information available in a library.

ग्रंथालय प्रशासन - library administration - a method of supervision of a library by which aims and objectives of a library are fulfilled and routine works are carried out.

ग्रंथालय प्रसार/विकास - library development - increase in the number of libraries.

ग्रंथालय प्रसिद्धी - library publicity - activity undertaken to make a library popular.

ग्रंथालय प्राधिकरण - library authority - 1) an authority which is responsible for implementing library policies.
2) person or a collective body of persons empowered by law to act on behalf of the library concerned.

ग्रंथालय बांधणी - library binding - binding of a document especially prepared with a view to make the document more durable.

ग्रंथालय मंडळ - library board - the committee responsible for the control of an American library system. It is also known as "Library trustees" "Board of directors", " Board of library trustees" & sometimes as "Library commission".

ग्रंथालय लिपिक - library clerk - person performing clerical operations in a library.

ग्रंथालय लेखा - library accounts - accounts maintained for a library.

ग्रंथालय वर्गीकरण - library classification - translation of the subject into a preferred artificial language of symbols. An arrangement of collection on shelves for effective use.

ग्रंथालय वित्त/निधी - library finance - 1) funds of a library.
2) sources of financial flows and expenditure.

ग्रंथालय विस्तार कार्यक्रम - library extension programme - activities undertaken by a library for increasing its popularity.

ग्रंथालय वेळा - library hours - the period during which library remains open.

ग्रंथालय शिक्का - library stamp - a stamp bearing the name of the library, which is put on a document to indicate ownership.

ग्रंथालय शुल्क - library fee - subscription amount to be paid by an user to avail facility of library services on a monthly basis.

ग्रंथालय संग्रह - **library collection** - number of documents acquired by a library.

ग्रंथालय संघ/संघटना - **library association** - a forum of library professionals to exchange their views/experiences, to solve professional problem. It can be of regional, national and international level.

ग्रंथालय संघटन - **library organisation** - principles of structure / layout of library resources.

ग्रंथालय संचय - **library holdings** - पहा ग्रंथालय प्रलेख.

ग्रंथालय संचालक - **director of libraries** - head / officer of the library services appointed by the state government.

ग्रंथालय संचालनालय - **directorate for libraries** - section / department of government related to library services.

ग्रंथालय समिती - **library committee** - the committee set up for the governance of the library.

ग्रंथालय सल्लागार समिती - **library adivisory committee** - committee constituted to advise in matters related to library. It may consist of members from professionals, users, scholars and policy makers.

ग्रंथालय सल्लागार - **library consultant** - an advisor who proposes solutions for library related matters.

ग्रंथालय सहकार - **library co-operation** - sharing of resources.

ग्रंथालय साधने - **library resources** - resources such as finance, collection and man power etc. required to maintain library services.

ग्रंथालय साहित्य - **library materials** - different types of information sources.

ग्रंथालय सूट - **library discount** - discount allowed by a vendor on the printed price of the document during purchase.

ग्रंथालय सेवा - **library service** - the efforts / facilities extended for using library collection.

ग्रंथालय स्थळ - **library location** - the place where library is situated.

ग्रंथालय स्वयंचलन/संगणकीकरण - **library automation** - library automation is the use of automatic and semi-automatic data processing machines to perform library activities like acquisition, cataloguing, circulation, serials control etc. Library automation is the most commonly used term for mechanization of library activities using modern electronic computers.

ग्रंथालय स्वयंचालन - library automation - application of computers in library and utilisation of computer products and services for various library service operations.

ग्रंथालय हस्त/हस्ताक्षर - library hand - a special writing style recommended by Ranganathan for handwritten catalogue where the letters are written in a bold and detached manner so as to avoid the personal handwriting styles.

ग्रंथालय - library - library is the store house of our history & culture. In modern sense it is an information dissemination centre, especially a service institution.

ग्रंथालयशास्त्र संकुल/प्रणाली - library science school - a school where education of library science is imparted.

ग्रंथालयशास्त्र - library science - science in which systematic study of library services and education is covered.

ग्रंथेतर साहित्य - non-documentary resources - non-book material, the information sources which are not in printed form.

ग्रंथो सोपस्कार - processing of book - technical operations carried out by a library for each document received e.g. classification, cataloguing, accession etc.

ग्रंथोपार्जन - acquisition of books - acquiring of sources of information through purchase, gift or exchange etc.

ग्रंथोपार्जन अभिलेख - acquisition record - records generally maintained in acquisition section in the form of register or files. These may have variety such as selection files, files for complete orders, and so on. A library may have separate accession register for purchased documents and documents received through various other resources such as gift, exchange etc.

ग्रंथोपार्जन कार्य - acquisition work - the work related to selection, approval, while ordering and collection of a document.

ग्रंथोपार्जन विभाग - acquisition department / section - the section of the library which has concern with identification, selection and collection of records/books.

ग्रंथोपार्जन संख्या - acquisition number - latest serial number under which entry is made of the acquired documents in the accession register of library.

ग्राहक वर्ग - clientele - users of the library and its services.

ग्राहक - recipient - the ultimate receiver of information who may also generate or create information.

घटक पैलू - **facet / fundamental category** - concept used in colon classification, the totality of the isolates, each one of which can itself be attached to a specified basic class or a class derived from it. These are enumerated in the schedule as possible manifestation of a particular fundamental category in a specified level of a specific round, a generic name for a basic class or an isolate of a subject or group of divisions. This is obtained from a subject dividing on the basis of using single characteristic at a time.

घटक मूल्य - **unit cost** - cost of a single unit of operation e.g. cost of cataloguing a single book.

घटक/पदार्थ–प्रकार/वर्ग - **category** - a fundamental concept used in colon classification to group knowledge into desired manner, see also facet.

घटना/दृश्यघटना/निसर्गघटना/आविष्कार - **phenomenon** - fact or occurrence (phenomena is the plural form).

घातांकीय वाढ - **exponential growth** - quantitative growth of a thing, at a particular rate of growth; e.g. chemical literature doubles every seven years.

घृणा/प्रतिकर्षण - **repulsion** - feeling of disgust or unfriendly treatment.

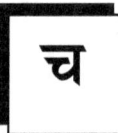

च

चकाकी/तकाकी/झळाळी - **brightness / shine** - fluorescence : the property of some substances of emitting when exposed to radiation those receive rays of greater wavelength.

चटकन उपलब्ध - **readily available** - available without delay.

चढता क्रम - **ascending order** - arrangements in which the ordinal values increase.

चमत्कारिक शीर्षक - **fanciful title** - a title from which it is difficult to find out the subject of the work. ("Title that does not disclose the subject of the work." - Ranganathan.)

चरित्र – ग्रंथसूची - **bio-bibliography** - list of books describing biographies of various persons.

चरित्र पंजी - **biography file** - a file of records on standard size cards or of cuttings, giving information about individuals. Also called as whose who file.

चरित्र - **biography** - a written account of important events of a person's life. Branch of literature concerned with the lives of people.

चरित्रकार - **biographer** - a person who writes biography.

चरित्रनायक/चरित्र व्यक्ती - **biographee** - a person who is the subject of biography.

चरित्रनायक/चरित्र व्यक्ती नोंद - **biographee entry** - the entry in a catalogue (dictionary name or subject) under the name of a person on whom the biography is written.

चरित्रात्मक शब्दकोश - **biographical dictionary** - a collection of lives of people arranged in alphabetical order.

चरित्रीय कोश/चरित्रकोश - **biographical dictionary** - a collection of information about eminent persons, arranged in alphabetical order also known as whos who.

चर्चापीठ - **forum** - public place for discussion of matters of common interest to a given group.

चर्मग्रंथ/चर्मपत्र - **parchment** - skin of sheep or goat which undergoes a process and treatment for writing purpose.

चल ग्रंथालय - **travelling library / mobile library** - library on wheels which reaches door and gives services.

चल/बदलत्या किंमती - **variable costs** - costs directly related to the volume or quantity of an activity, service or product.

चलचित्रवत योजना - **scenario** - the outline of a film plot.

चाचणीचा अभ्यास - **pilot study** - a study preceding the main study usually to check the viability of the study design.

चातुर्य/बुद्धी/विवेक/प्रज्ञा - **wisdom** - the quality of being wise, the activity of making the best use of knowledge, experience, understanding etc. with good judgement.

चामडे - **leather** - calf leather used for book binding.

चिंतन/विचारप्रणाली/विचार/विमर्श/प्रज्ञा/शाखा - **thought** - series of ideas having logical base.

चिकित्सात्मक ग्रंथसूची/फलित ग्रंथपाठ - **textual bibliography** - the study and comparison of texts and their transmission through different information sources and their editions.

चिठ्ठी/तालिका - **sheet/sheaf form catalogue** - catalogue entries are prepared on loose slips of paper and are arranged in a helpful sequence.

चिठ्ठी/लेबल - **tag** - field identifier or label. Each tag consists of numerical digits.

चिठ्ठी - **slip / sheaf** - a piece of paper.

चित्र/आकृती - **illustration** - graphics & images in the text.

चित्रकार - **illustrator** - a person who draws the charts and pictures for content of document.

चित्रयुक्त - **illustrations** - the photographs, charts, maps, figures etc. appeared in a book documents.

चित्रलिपी/चित्राक्षर - **hieroglyphics** - the Egyptians developed a word-syllabic writing, know as hieroglyphic, about 3000 B.C. It is a kind of picture writing. The Greek word hieroglyphic means sacred carving the Greeks believed that only Egyptian priests understood and used this system of writing. This belief persisted until the 1800's when scholars deciphered it.

चिन्ह - **symbol** - a figure that represents something other than itself. The value or meaning of which is generally defined.

चिन्हांकन क्षेत्र - **notational plane** - a group of symbols / class numbers used in a scheme of classification.

चिन्हांकन - **notation** - 1) the system of ordinal numbers representing the classes in a scheme of classification, it is a set of symbols used to represent subject in a classification scheme.
2) a system of ordinal numbers representing the classes in a scheme of classification.
3) a type of signs or symbols used in a scheme of classification to denote subjects.

चिन्हांक - **number** - any numerical digit used as notation.

चिन्हांकन पद्धत – **notational system** - a system of ordinal numbers used to represent the classes in a scheme of classification. A system of symbols comprising a notation.

चिप (पटलिका) - **chip** - 1) an electronic entity containing one or more semiconductors on a wafer of silicon, within which an integrated circuit is formed. 2) Short form for microchip. It is a tiny but complex module that stores the computer's memory or logic circuit. Basically an IC, it is manufactured as a silicon wafer, which is first cut to size and then etched with the necessary circuit.

चुंबकीय चकती - **magnetic disc** - computer device used to store data, combination of a number of flat circular plates of magnetic electronic readable substance put together to enhance storing capacity.

चुंबकीय पट्टी - **magnetic tape** - 1) plastic tape coated with magnetic material on which information can be recorded / located by mechanical device.
2) a magnetic storage medium in tape form usually wound in spools and catridges.

चुंबकीय संग्रह - **magnetic storage** - any form of storage device whose operating depends on the properties of a magnetic material.

चुंबकीय - **magnetic** - having the properties of a magnet.

चुटका/कथाप्रसंग - **anecdotal** - a published short narrative of an incident.

चूक मूल्य - **error value** - the difference between observed and the expected value.

चूक - **error / mistake** - a wandering or straying about, fault, error.

चौकट - **frame** - boundary, outline having shape of square.

चौकोनात्मक बांधकाम - **modular construction** - construction of building having module or modulus. Internal arrangements in such constrution can be altered easily.

चौकोनी पुस्तक - **quarto** - a full sheet of paper folded twice to give eight pages.

छ

छाननी/समीक्षण/परिनिरीक्षण - scrutiny - a careful enquiry; an inspection.

छापखाने आणि ग्रंथनोंदणी अधिनियम - Press & Registration of Books Act, 1867- an Act for the regulation of printing presses and newspapers, for the preservation of copies of books (and newspapers) printed in India, and for the registration of such books (and newspapers), inacted in 1867.

छायाचित्र यंत्र - photo-copier - a photocopying machine.

छायापत्र - photocopy / zerox - photostat copy of a document.

छिद्रित पत्र - aperture card - a micro transparent document mounted on opaque card of 7^{inch} x 3^{inch} size.

छेद/संकर वर्गीकरण - cross classification - situations in classification of complex subjects having inconsistency in the use of characteristics.

छेदक - divider - one that divides, characteristic reponsible to form classes /groups.

छेदन - truncation - when a search term in a profile is not truncated, it will retrieve only if it matches exactly with the same term in the database. Terms may be truncated to facilitate retrieval of terms with a common root or containing common fragments. Incorporating truncation device makes it is possible to search for a portion of a term only.

छोटा संगणक - mini computer - 1) type of computer having comparatively less memory. 2) medium sized processing unit. It comprises of 128-512 k bytes, terminals, disc units, tape drives and printers.

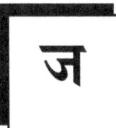

ज

जकात - **octroi** - tax on goods brought within the limit of municipality imposed by municipal authorities.

जटिलता वृद्धी - **increasing complexity** - the order used in arranging subjects in the scheme of classification wherein arrangement is from simple to complex.

जडवस्तुसामग्री/जडसंग्रह नोंदवही - **dead stock register** - register used to enter the furniture and other such items available in an institution.

जनसंपर्क माध्यम - **mass media / multimedia** - integrated or independent form through which information is communicated to mass audience.

जनसंवाद - **mass communication** - information communicated to a large mass audience.

जन्म वर्ष - **year of birth** - the year of birth of author as per christian era which is generally traced in catalogue entry or in book number to identify the author.

जबाबदारी केंद्र - **responsibility centre** - a personalized group of cost centres under the control of a 'responsible' individual.

जबाबदारी - **responsibility** - an obligation to perform work activities. It is described for someone when he or she accepts an assignment.

जमाखर्च - **accounting** - a systematic record of income & expenditure.

जमीन महसूल - **land revenue** - tax imposed on the owner of a land towards the property.

जळणे/ज्वलन - **combustion** - act or process of burning chemically.

जागतिक ग्रंथसूची/आंतरराष्ट्रीय ग्रंथसूची - **universal bibliography** -a bibliography of the books published throughtout the world during a given period.

जागतिक माहिती पद्धती - **global information system** - an international venture in terms of coverage of documents, variety of services and products specially for the users for achieving economy in money time and effort.

जाणकार तज्ज्ञ - **stalwart/an expert** - a person having thorough knowledge of a particular subject.

जातिपट - **generically** - characteristics of a large group or class, general, non-specific.

जाती - **genus** - a class, a kind, sort.

जालक/वृत्तजाळी - **grid** - a referencing system using distances measured on a chosen project.

जाळयांचे विश्लेषण - **network analysis** - analysis of computer network showing its components.

जाळे पसरविणे - **networking** - method of interlinking number of computer centres.

जाळे (माहितीचे) - **network (information)** - a set of inter related information centers and systems associated with communication facilities which are cooperating through more or less formal and institutional agreements, in order to jointly implement information handling operations with a view to pooling their resources and better services for the users.

जाळे विश्लेषण - **network analysis** - it helps in designing, planning, coordinating, controlling information in minimum available time with the limited available resources.

जाळे - **network** - a set of inter connected communication channels for transferring information to all connected centres through computers.

जाहिरनामा - **manifesto** - a public declaration of plans and intentions by a govt. or by a person or groups having some public importance.

जाहीरात पंजी - **advertisement file** - advertisement issued by various agencies are arranged in alphabetical/jobwise order and are made available to users of the library.

जिलेटिन कागद - **giletin paper** - paper prepared with a coating of gelatin.

जिल्हा ग्रंथालय - **district library** - a public library recognized by public library act and functioning as main library of a district.

जिल्हा मध्यवर्ती ग्रंथालय - **district central library** - district public library established by government having geographical limitation of a district.

जुळवणीकार/जोडणीकार - **assembler** - a program that converts the mnemonics and symbols of assembly language into the opcodes and operands of machine language.

जोडणी/जुळवणी भाषा - **assembly language** - a language similar in structure to machine language, mnemonics and symbols. Programs written in assembly language are less difficult to write and understand than programs in machine language.

जोडरेषा - **dash (-)** - a horizontal line used to connect two words.

झुबका - **cluster** - a group of similar things or people positioned or occurring close together.

झरणी - **pen** - an instrument for writing or drawing with ink, typically consisting of a metal nib or ball, or a nylon tip, fitted into a metal or plastic holder.

झरोका - **small window** - window of a small size kept in the structure of building to get sunlight.

झिरपणे - **leakage** - a hole through which contents lose.

झिलई - **glazing** - a vitreous substance fused on to the surface or cover to form a hard impervious coating.

झीज - **erosion/corrosion/denudation** - the process or result of eroding or being eroded.

झुरळ - **cockroach** - a bettle like scavenging insect with long antennae & legs, some kinds of which are household pests.

ट

टंकलिखित संदेश - **telex -** a telegraph service enabling its subscribers to communicate directly with one another over the public telegraph network using start stop apparatus, usually teleprinters using public telecommunication network.

टिप्पणासह प्रलेखन यादी - **annoted documentation list -** list of documents alongwith comments on its special features.

टिप्पणी/विवरण टीप - **notes / annotation -** a brief statement added at the end of an entry of a document, explaining or evaluating the contents.

टीकात्मक/चिकित्सक - **critical -** document with critics or criticism, based on or in accordance with the principles of criticism.

टीप (विवरण) - **annotation -** a note added to an entry in a catalogue, reading list or bibliography, to elucidate, evaluate or describe the subject and contents of a book.

टीप अनुच्छेद - **note section / area -** an area which consists of notes in the catalogue entry such as series etc.

टोपणनाव - **pseudonym -** 1) an adopted name of an author used to hide real name. 2) a fictitous name adopted by an author.

ठ

ठराव - **resolution** - a firm decision, a formal expression of opinion or intention agreed on by a legislative body.

ठराविक निश्चित क्षेत्र – **fixed field** - the field with has predetermined length, it cannot accommodate more characters than those a specified earlier.

ठळक मथळा - **headline** - a heading at the top of article or page in a newspaper or magazine.

ठशाची/ठोकळ्याची छपाई - **block printing** - making an illustration, or printing a design on paper or material using wood or metal blocks with the design in relief.

ठसा/ठोकळा - **block stamp** - a piece of hard wood used after engraving by printers for printing purpose.

ठिकाण/स्थळांची नावे – **place names** - the name of a place, as of a city, province etc. used in bibliographic description.

ठिपका रेखन – **blot drawing** - a drawing in which a spot or stain; especially one made by ink.

ठिसूळ - **brittle** - hard but liable to break easily.

ठेव - **deposit** - a returnable sum paid to cover possible loss or damage.

ठोकळा आलेख - **block diagram** - to roughly sketch a diagram, omitting details.

ड

ड्यूईचे दशांश वर्गीकरण – **Dewey's decimal classification** - a library classification scheme first published in 1876 in USA by Dr. Melvil Dewey. It divides knowledge into ten groups. Indo-Arabic numerals with decimal point are used as notation having atleast three digits to denote subjects. 22nd edition of the scheme in four volumes is available for use.

डांबर गोळी - **napthalene ball** - chemical product used as antipest.

डंबर - **coal tar** - a thick, black, viscid, opaque liquid obtained by the destractive distillation of bituminous coal.

डाऊन वेळ - **down time** - time taken by the computer for transfer of data.

डाऊनलोडिंग - **downloading** - 1) transferring data via telecommunication or direct line from a remote database usually on a main frame or large mini computer, to a local computer.
2) transfer of data from one computer unit to another storage media.

डाक नोंदणी - **registered post** - a letter where address of receiver is registered at a post office, for which special charges are paid.

डाक परिचलन - **postal circulation** - communication through postal services.

डाक मुद्रविद्या – **philately** - The collection & study of postage stamps, postmarks, stamped envelops, etc. usually as a hobby.

डाग – **stain -** imprint or impressions left.

डी.बी.एम.एस. - **DBMS (database management system) -** a set of programmes which facilitates the creation and maintenance of a database and the execution of programmes using the database information.

डी.बी.एस. श्री. - **DBS-III -** data base management system for micro computers, popular in use on IBM PCs.

डेल्फी तंत्र – **delphi technique -** an intuitive technique for obtaining and sharing experts judgements, speculation and forecasts about some future events for purpose of more successful planning, organizing and decision making.

डोल - **rolling -** folded over or back. Moving by turning over and over.

ड्राय रन - **dry-run -** practice in firing small arms or guns without using live ammunition, A rehearsal for any events.

त

तंतुमय काच – **cellular glass -** glass consisting of or containing cells.

तंतुमय – **fibrous -** composed or consisting of fibers; as a fibrous body or substance.

तंतुरुप काच - **fibre glass -** finespun filaments of glass made into yarn that is woven into textiles or used in wolly masses as insulation matertial.

तंतू प्रकाशकी – **fibre optics -** a communication tool where information is transmitted in the form of light over a transparent fibre material such as strand of glass. Advantages are noise free communication, not susceptible to electromagnetic interference.

तंत्र निकेतन – **polytechnic -** institution, usually one offering diploma courses in enginering.

तंत्र/पद्धत – **technique -** the method of procedure (with reference to practical or formal details).

तंत्रजड भाषा – **jargon -** every profession has a specialised language which conveys facts and concepts quickly and efficiently among the group. Jargon also refers to terms and expressions that are unclear because the reader is not familiar with them.

तंत्रज्ञ – **technologist-** person well versed in technology.

तंत्रविज्ञान/तंत्रविज्ञा – **technology -** the science or study of the practical or industrial arts, applied science.

तंत्रशिक्षण – **technical education-** eduction having to do with practical industries or mechanical arts or the applied sciences.

तकाकी/चकाकी - **gloss / glaze** - brightness or luster of a smooth surface polish. The vitreous coating.

तक्ता/रेषा तक्ता – **chart** - display of information on paper using proportionate designed layout.

तक्ता/सारणी – **schedule** - a written statement of classes alongwith their notation in a scheme of classification.

तक्षण – **carving** - the act or art of cutting figures in wood or stone.

तज्ज्ञ प्रणाली – **expert system** - a specialist problem solving system programmed with knowledge from human expert.

तज्ज्ञमत धारणेवर आधारित तंत्रे – **delphi technique** - techniques in contemporary operations or research, a prophetic method of forecasting technique whereby experts solicit the opinions of a group of advisors through a series of carefully designed questionnaires.

तटस्थ – **neutral** - neither one nor the other. Belonging to neither of two classes; in a middle position between extremes; not one thing or the other, indifferent.

तत्त्व - **principle** - a fundamental truth, law, doctrine or motivating force, upon which others are based.

तत्त्व मीमांसा – **metaphysics** - 1) the branch of philosophy concerned with first principles of things, including abstract concepts such as being or knowing reality (ontology) and of the origin & reality (ontology) structure of the world (cosmology) ; it is closely associated with a theory of knowledge (epistemology). 2) branch of philosophy dealing with the nature of existence, truth and knowledge for e.g. it discuses whether existence is only in the mind or if there is an independent external physical reality.

तत्त्वज्ञान - **philosophy** - a study of the processes governing thought and conduct; theory or investigation of the principles or laws that regulate the universe and underlie all knowledge & reality; included in the study are aesthetics, ethics logic, metaphysics etc.

तथ्य/तथ्यता - **fact** - a thing that has actually happened or is true .

तदर्थ - **ad hoc / temporary** - for specific purpose, for this case only.

तपास - **inquest / investigation** - an investigating; careful search; detailed examination; systematic inquiry; as the investigations of the scientist.

तपासणी यादी – **check list** - a list used for verification.

तबकडी – **disc** - popular name for a gramophone, a circular disc containing record i.e. CD

तर्कशास्त्र – **logic** - the science of correct reasoning; the science which deals with the criteria of valid thought.

तर्क - **reason** - the ability to think, form judgements, draw conclusions etc.

तर्कदोष – **fallancies** - false or mistaken beliefs.

तर्षण/परासरणाचे तत्त्व – **principle of osmosis** - when a library switches over to a new scheme of classification or to a new catalogue code the principle of osmosis suggests a smooth change over. According to this principle new accessions and frequently used present collection should first of all be classified or catalogued according to the new scheme or new code or both as the case may be. Users should be informed through reference department and the library staff about the existence of two collections in the library. For the books borrowed, on its return it should be recatalogued and reclassified and absorbed in the new collection. The principle was suggested by Ranganathan.

तळ - **base / camp / floor** - the bottom of a thing considered as its support, or the part of a thing on which it rests; foundation; as, the base of a column.

तळघर – **basement / cellar** - the lowest story of a building or the one just below the ground floor, usually wholly or partically lower than the surface of the ground floor of a building below the ground level.

तळटीप - **foot note** - a note supplementary to the main text, specifying the bibliographic details of the document cited.

तसबीर - **portrait** - a photograph or information mount with glass / plastic lamination.

तहनाम्याचा मसुदा - **protocol** - an original draft or record of a document, negotiation, etc.

तांत्रिक अहवाल – **technical report** - 1) a report presenting scientific result.
2) a report concerning the result of scientific investigations or a technical development test or evaluation.

तांत्रिक ग्रंथालय - **technical library** - a library which has most of the collections on technical subjects.

तांत्रिक द्वाररक्षक – **technological gatekeeper** - the experts in an organization who keep track on the information on a subject & guide or provide the users with the required information. These persons are available mostly in science & techonology organizations & function informally.

तांत्रिक पत्रिका – **technical journal -** a journal devoted to a branch of technology. Also known as technical periodical.

तांत्रिक बदल/नावीन्य – **technological innovations -** recent and highly acclaimed developments in technology.

तांत्रिक योग्यता – **technical qualification -** qualification of specialised nature helpful to carryout technical work of libraries and information service centres.

तांत्रिक व व्यवस्थापन शिक्षण - **technical and management education -** education imparted to develop technical know how and knowledge of management techniques.

तांत्रिक संज्ञा – **technical term -** the terms used in technical disciplines.

तांत्रिक संप्रेषण – **technical communication -** transmission of commercial, industrial or scientific facts or news to the intended user to achieve a predetermined aim.

तांत्रिक सारसंग्रह – **technical digest -** a digest service directed to executives, engineers, technical workers etc. working in industries. It provides up-to-date technical information on a given subject.

तांत्रिक सेवा – **technical service -** service like cataloguing and classification through which information is processed for use.

ताड/कडकडीत – **buckram -** coarse linen or cloth stiffened with paste etc.

तात्काळ/तयार संदर्भ सेवा - **ready reference service -** a quick library search service based generally on reference documents.

तात्त्विक/सोपत्तीक – **theoretical -** limited to or based on theory hypothetical, ideal opposed to practical or applied.

तादात्म्य – **coincidence -** coincident, identity.

ताम्रपट/ताम्रपत्र – **copper -plate -** a flat piece of copper on which lettering or a design is engreaved, the sunken lines being filled with ink.

ताम्रयुग - **copper age -** age in which copper has been widely used as a metal for writing, vessels, pots etc.

तारांकित – **asterisk -** to mark with an asterisk sign.

तारायंत्र – **telegraphy -** the operation of telegraph apparatus or study of subject talegraph.

तारीय जाळे – **star network -** a network where one participant holds substantially all the resources, to be utilised by other participants.

तार्किक रचना - **logical arrangement** - arrangement of entries by principles associated with the subject matter i.e. chronological, hierarchical, numerical etc. other than alphabetical one.

तार्किक व्यवस्था - **logical arrangement** - a departure from the normal alphabetical order so as to arrange entries by principles associated with the subject matter or type of the entries e.g. chronological, hierarchical, numerical.

तालिका नोंद - **catalogue entry** - an entry which is prepared for a document to include in a catalogue.

तालिका पत्र - **catalogue card** - a standard size 12.5 cm x 7.5 cm white ruled or blank paper card used for preparing entries of library records for vertical filing.

तालिका पेटी - **catalogue cabinet** - cupboard made of wood or steel in standard size to hold catalogue cards.

तालिका संहिता - **catalogue code** - a set of rules for guidance of cataloguers to achieve uniformity, popularly used codes are AACR -II and CCC.

तालिका/सूची - **catalogue** - catalogue is a list of holding of a library which is developed with definite purpose. It is a key to collections arranged on a set plan showing the place of documents on shelves. One can know by it which publication is available in a library. It may include collection of one library or a group of libraries.

तालिकाकार - **cataloguer** - a person who prepares catalogue entries and knows cataloguing rules.

तालिकीकरण - **cataloguing** - an art of making entries for a catalogue.

तालिकीकरण तंत्र - **calaloguing technique** - the method adopted under the rules to develop catalogue entries.

तालिकीकरण नियम - **cataloguing rules** - पहा : तालिका संहिता.

तालिकीकरण विभाग - **cataloguing department** - the department that processes documents for cataloguing.

ताळा/तपासणी - **verification** - the establishement or confirmation of the truth of a fact, theory etc.

ताव - **sheet** - a rectangular piece of paper, especially one ut to a definite, uniform size, for writing, printing etc.

तुकडी - **section / division** - a part separated or removed by cutting; a slice, a division.

तुरुंग ग्रंथालय/कारागृह ग्रंथालय - **prison library** - a library maintained in a prison for the use of prisoners.

तुलना विषयांग संबंध – **comparison phase relation** - phase relation in which Phase-I is compared with phase II (Dr. Ranganathan).

तूट – **deficit** - the amount by which a sum of money is less than what is expected, due needed etc; shortage.

तूलीर/सेल्यूलोज – **cellulose** - highly purified and bleached wood pulp.

तृतीयक साधने – **tertiary sources** - sources of third rank in order of formation etc.;

त्रितयी – **trivialization** - the three subjects of study (grammar, rhetoric and logic) consisting a common interest.

त्रुटी – **error** - the state of believing what is untrue, incorrect or wrong.

त्रैमासिक – **quarterly journal** - a publication brought out after every three months or four issues in year.

थकबाकी – **arrears -** unpaid and overdue amounts. Behind in paying a debt.

थर – **layer / bed -** thin coating laid on any surface; a stratum; a thickness or fold spread over another; as a layer of clay or sand.

थाटणी – **get-up -** general arrangement or composition of a thing.

थोडक्यात - **in short / briefly -** in a few words.

द

दंड/द्रव्यदंड – **fine -** penalty for overdue documents which is calculated on the basis of number of days it is retained.

दंडचित्र – **bar diagram -** diagram in which various line bars are used to show level of information.

दप्तरनोंद प्रारुप – **record format -** the field structure and its identifications.

दप्तरनोंद – **record -** collection of related items of data, which is treated as a unit of information for computerised information processing.

दमनकारी सत्ता – **coercive power -** the power of a leader that is derived from fear. The follower perceives the leader as a person who can punish deviant behaviour and action.

दर - **charge / rate -** price or amount stated or fixed on product or service

दरपत्रक – **quotation -** a bid or terms & conditions offered by a merchant for completion of job or supply of material.

दर्जा - **rank -** standard, status, level or position in a job. High in social position; eminence; excellence; distinction; high degree; as, a man of rank.

दर्जात्मक उपांग - **ranked isolate -** an isolate whose place is assigned in the scheme of classification.

दर्शक अंक – **indicator digit** - a digit prefixed to an isolate number to indicate the fundamental category of which the isolate is a manifestation. Till recently, it was called connecting digit.

दर्शक अनुच्छेद – **direction section** - entry in a catalogue which guides user to search correct entry.

दर्शक काटा – **pointer** -term in data structures, a variable that holds the address of an item of data.

दर्शकांक निर्देश – **index** – systematically arranged bibliographical details. A table of reference which is held in memory in some key sequence. A systematically arranged list giving enough information for each item to be traced by means of page number or other symbol indicating its position in sequence.

दर्शनिका - **gazetteer** - 1) a book containing geographical names and descriptions, alphabetically arranged; a geographical dictionary or index. 2) consolidated recrod of information as social, religious features of a district or state.

दर्शनी धनाकर्ष – **demand draft** - draft issued by a bank for amount paid by customer.

दर्शनी मूल्य – **face value** - the value printed or written on an item, bond, etc. without allowing any discount.

दल - **sector** - a range of numbers begining with a semantically rich digit, or with one empty digit and so on.
example - (s-1) stands for sector 1,2............8
(S-91) stands for sector 91,92..................98
(S-A) stands for sector A,B..................Y
(S-Z1) stands for sector Z_1, Z_2 ....Z8
(S-ZA) stands for sector ZA, ZB..................ZY

दळणवळण – **communication** - the act of imparting, confering, or delivering, from one to another communication of knowledge, opinion or facts.

दशमान चिन्हांकन – **decimal notation** - a notation consisting of a numeral used decimally so as to permit the logical subdivision of a subject.

दशांश चिन्हांकन - **decimal notation** - decimal notation is widely used in Dewey decimal classification scheme, minimum digits for a call number are three but it is presumed that these are decimal numbers having ordinal value.

दशांश युक्ती – decimal fraction device - device for taking the place value of each digit in a number as in a pure decimal fraction, though the decimal point to its equivalent mark is not actually put in front of the number (Dr. S.R.Ranganathan).

दशांश वर्गीकरण - decimal classification : it is a widely used library classification scheme devised by Melvil Dewey and firstly published in 1876 in USA. 22nd edition has been brought out in four volumes to make scheme more effective and workable. It has used Indo-Arabic numeral notation in decimal fraction, the universe of knowledge is classified in ten main classes.

दहा मुख्य वर्ग - ten main classes - first division mentioned in Dewey decimal classification scheme for universe of knowledge. Also called "first summary."

दहिया भुरी – mildew - destructive growth of minute fungi on paper, leather etc. when come in contact with warm, damp, climate.

दाखल अंक – accession number - 1) the serial number given to the document of a library as per the record / accession register.
2) the number given to a book from the accession register serially in the order of its receipt.

दाखल अभिलेख – accession record - the progressive collection record of a library in which documents are entered as they are received. The information details are worked out by the monitoring authority of the library.

दाखल क्रम – accession order - the arrangement of documents on shelves in their acquisition order.

दाखल दिनांक – accession date - the date on which a publication is listed in library accession register.

दाखल नोंदणी – accessioning - an act of doing accession which includes the verification of document, posting of information in record register and accession number on the document.

दाखल मुद्रा/ठसा – accession stamp - a stamp used to fix up accession number on a library document.

दाखल यादी – accession list - a list of accession numbers generally prepared to perform internal jobs like verification.

दाखल विभाग – accession department / section - a department/section where acquisitions of library are entered in accession register.

दाखल व्यवस्था रचना – **accession arrangement** - an arrangement of books in a library in order of their receipt or in their collection order number.

दाखलनोंद अंक अनुच्छेद - **accession number section** - the section of an entry giving the accession number of its document, the place of which is decided on the basis of cataloguing code followed.

दाखलनोंदवही/ग्रंथपट **accession register** - register in which entry document received in a library is entered by allotting serial number in a sequence. This register is a basic and main record of any library documents.

दालन दर्शक – **bay guide** - a guide to the subjects of the books shelved in a row of book shelves.

दावा - **legal statement** - a statement based upon or authorized by law. Statement in conformity with the positive rules of law permitted by law as a legal statement.

दिग्दर्शनस्वरुप/दर्शिका – **directory** - a book containing list of names of residents, organizations or business houses in a town, a group of towns or a country, in alphabetical order, and or in order of situation in road or of firms in trade classifications arranged in alphabetical order; or of professional people, manufactures or business houses in a particular trade or profession.

दिनदर्शिका - **calender** - chronological schedule of events or an almanac giving list of days & months, yearly publication giving details of festivals, special feature of a day/ month.

दिनांक मुद्रा – **date stamp / dater** - a stamp used by the library circulation counter to fix up either date of issue or date of return on the loaned document.

दिनांक चिठ्ठी – **date slip / label** - a paper slip generally pasted inside the cover of the document to indicate date of issue or date of returning the documents to a library.

दिनांक दर्शक - **date guide** - a guide card used to indicate the date of loan of documents.

दिनांक पत्र – **date card** - see book card.

दिनांक प्रकाशनाचा – **date of publication** - year in which a document is published.

दिनांक – **date** - a statement of time/period on a letter book, document etc.

दीर्घकालीन प्रवृत्ती – **secular trend** - the long run behaviour of the data; it may be increasing, decreasing or constant.

दुडा/पोथीप्रमाणे असलेले पुस्तक - **folio** - a full sheet of paper folded twice to give four pages.

दुय्यम घटक – **secondary elements** - word added after entry element.

दुय्यम पत्रिका/नियतकालिक – **secondary journal / periodical -**
1) a journal based on published information like published articles, abstracts and reviews etc.
2) an abstracting, indexing or review periodical.

दुय्यम प्रकाशने – **secondary publications** - documents such as an abstract, digest, index to periodicals, current awareness journals, or popularization, which are prepared in order to dissminate more widely information which has already appeared in another form, particularly in primary publication.

दुय्यम प्रलेख – **secondary document** - 1) publication publishing the contents of primary document in a condensed form or listing them in a helpful way so that existence of primary documents is known and access to them is made easy.
2) the publication generated to know the flow of primary documents. Source material giving information already published in primary documents.

दुय्यम विश्लेषण – **secondary analysis :** analysis of the already existing data collected initially for some other purpose.

दुय्यम साधने – **secondary sources** - compilation consisting of references of primary sources.

दुय्यम स्रोत – **secondary sources** - books or unpublished literary material in the compilation of which primary sources have been used.

दुय्यम हाताळणी ग्रंथ – **secondhand book** - a book sold after use.

दुय्यम – **secondary** - a thing of secondary or subordinate importance.

दुरुस्त केलेले – **reconditioned** - the one which is repaired or changed.

दुरुस्ती – **correction** - amendment.

दुरुस्ती/विशोधन/सुधारणा – **amendment** - an alteration or change for better improvement.

दुर्मिळ ग्रंथ – **rare book** - a book of importance which is scarce & not easily available.

दुर्लभ मुद्रा/दुर्मिळ चलन – **hard currency** - scarce currency.

दुवा - **interface** - point at which one computer system ends & another begins, boundary between computer or telecom hardware devices or functions.

दुवा – **interface** - the connection or junction between two systems or compenents of the same system.

दुव्याचा/परिभाषिक शब्द - **keyword** - significant words or the words representing certain important concepts in any article or writing.

दुसरा समास – **second indention** - second allotted space, line from the left edge of catalogue card which is used to design information, in a paragraph.

दुसरी नक्कल प्रत/प्रतिलिपी - **duplicate copy** - exact copy of the original.

दुसरी प्रतिलिपी नोंद - **duplicate entry** - an additional entry.

दूर/निराळा/ठेवणे/काढणे - **segregate** - to separate from the main class or to separate from others.

दूरचित्रवाणी – **television** - 1) the process transmitting senses or views by radio or rarely, by direct wire : the transmitting televisor, by means of an electronic tube, converts light rays into radio waves. 2) the science of making or operating television apparatus.

दूरध्वनी - **telephone** - transmission of voice from one place to another by using cable.

दूरपरिषद - **teleconference** - a conference where participants having different locations are linked by telecommunication devices; personal presence at one site is not essential.

दूरमुद्रक - **teleprinter** - teletypewriter. printing of messages mechanically with transmission through cables.

दूरलेखन - **fascimile** - an electronic system for transmitting pictures & graphic materials over very high frequency airwaves.

दूरलेखन – **telefacsimile** - an exact copy, especially written or printed material with the help of telecommunication e.g. Fax.

दूरलेखा – **telegraph** - an apparatus or system for transmitting messages by electronic impulses sent through a wire or converted into radio waves.

दूरसंचरण/दूरसंदेशवहन - **telecommunication** - essentially the transmission of information from one point to another by wire, radio, optical or other electromagnetic system.

दूरस्थ स्थानांतरण – **facsimile transmission** - the rapid transmission of printed pages from one point to another, using electronic devices. The process involves converting the original picture into electrical impulses which is then transmitted over telephone lines, private lines, microwave, or a combination of these communication media.

दृक श्राव्य साधन – **audio-visual equipment** - technical devices used to make use of electronic recording.

दृक श्राव्य - **audio-visual** - the document which is used on electronic device for getting the original voice or picture or both to hear or see as the case may be.

दृक श्राव्य केंद्र - **audio-visual centre** - a place where audio - visual aids are used.

दृक श्राव्य संप्रेषण - **audio-visual communication** - communication through audio - visual media.

दृक श्राव्य साहाय्यक साधने - **audio -visual aids** - non-book materials such as records slides, gramophone records cassetters, tapes, CDs, DVDs produced by educational technology.

दृकश्राव्य शिक्षण - **audio-visual education** - an education imparted to make use of audio-visual aids.

दृश्यपट्टिका - **slides** - a transparent plate bearing information for projection on a screen, with enlargement.

दृष्टिकोन - **point of view / aspects** - characteristic showing intention.

दृष्टिकोन वर्गीकरण - **aspect classification** - see "facet classification."

दृष्टिकोन/छाया/कल युक्ती - **bias device** - influence device used in the classification to specify the influence or impact of one subject on other.

दृष्टिमूलक उपकरण - **visual aids** - aids to project information on monitor.

दृष्टिमूलक प्रदर्शनी पथ - **visual display terminal** - a device capable of displaying input and output on screen.

दृष्टिविषयक युक्ती - **optical device** - making a copy of a document on photographic material in the same scale or one different from the original.

दृष्टिकोन - **spectrum** - a broad range of varied but related ideas, the individual features of which tend to develop so as to form a continuous series or sequence.

देणगी अभिलेख नोंद - **donating record** - record for gifts received. It may contain record for cash or items or for both.

देणगी - **endowments** - giving a large amount of money or property for the use & benefit of an organisation.

देणगी/धर्मार्थ निधी - **endowment fund** - a fund which is created for the purpose of endowment.

देणगीदार दाता - **donor** - one who gives or bestows : one who makes a donation.

देयक – **bill / invoice** - demand slip claiming the amount of cost for the items supplied.

देयक पुस्तक – **bill book** - a register in which bill record is kept or a book of blank proformas of bill copies.

देवाण कट्टा – **issue counter** - a counter in a library from whose books are issued..

देवाण – **issue** - loaning of library documents or a part of the periodical publication.

दैनंदिन कामकाज – **day to day work** - everyday, daily; routine work day by day : day labour.

दैनंदिन दृष्टिकोन – **everyday approach** - a common idea or solution.

दैनंदिनी - **diary** - a daily written records, especially of the writer's own experiences, thoughts etc.

दैनिक - **daily** - a publication brought out every day to disseminate current news.

दैववाद – **fatalism** - belief that all events are predetermined by orbitary decree, submission to all that happens is inevitable.

दोलामुद्रिते - **incunabula** - 1) books printed before 1500 A.D., this date limitation probably derived from the earliest known catalogue of incunabula. These are the specimens is derived of the cradle-period of printing and typographic art.
2) incunabula derived from the Latin 'canae' (cradle) and indicates books produced in the infancy of printing i.e. before 1500.

दोषयुक्त प्रत – **defective copy** - a copy which has some printing / binding defects.

द्वार – **gateway** - a system permitting the users of one computer system to access another, particularly connections between local area networks also termed as bridge.

द्वारमार्ग – **gateways** - any system permitting users of one computer system to access another.

द्वि –वार्षिक – **bi-ennial** - a publication which is issued twice a year.

द्विअंगी अंक – **binary digit** - numbers used in computer language.

द्विअंगी शोध - **binary search** - a search method in which only binary digits 0 and 1 are used.

द्विअंगी संख्या पद्धत – **binary number system** - method of using binary numbers.

द्विअंगी संख्या - **binary number** - see 'binary' and see also 'bit'.

द्विअंगी संहिता – **binary code** – a code that makes use of only two numbers, i.e. 0 (zero) and 1(one).

द्विअंगी – **binary** - computer used number system when zero (0) and one (1) are only used to represent entire base.

द्विबिंदुग्रंथ क्रमांक – **colon book number** - the number may consist of one or more from the successive facet like language form, year, acquisition, volume, supplement, copy, evaluation and acquisition number (Dr. S. R. Ranganathan)

द्विबिंदू वर्गीकरण – **colon classification** - it is freely faceted and analytico synthetic scheme of classification, first published in 1933. It has a very sound theory to understand. The scheme has number of principles and postulates to analyse and synthesise the subject into five fundamental categories (Dr. S. R. Ranganathan).

द्विबिंदू - **colon** - a symbol used by Universal Decimal Classification and very intensively used by Colon Classification, to express facet of a document.

द्विभंजन – **fission** - breaking up into parts; splitting apart; cleavage.

द्विभाजन – **binary fission** -

द्विमान – **binary** - compounded or consistinting of two things or parts : double; two fold.

द्वै मासिक – **bi-monthly** - a serial publication brought out / published everu alternate month or after every two months.

द्वै –वार्षिक – **bi- annual** - a publication once in two years.

धंदा - **profession** - a vocation or occupation requiring advanced training in some liberal art or science, and usually involving mental rather than natural work, as teaching, engineering, librarianship, writing. etc. The collective body of persons engaged in or practicing a particular calling or vocation.

धंदेशिक्षण/व्यावसायिक शिक्षण – **vocational education** - education of any trade, profession or occupation.

धनादेश - **cheque** - a bank cheque; authority to pay an amount with the help of paper transaction.

धर्म – **religion** - any specific system of belief, worship, conduct etc., often involving a code of ethics and a philosophy. Belief in the divine, the creators(s) and ruler(s) of universe.

धर्मसूत्र – **canon** - a law or rule in general stated in religious document.

धर्म संस्था – **parochial** - term related to a Church.

धर्मसुधारणा – **reformation** - 16th century European movement for reforms in the Roman Catholic Church which resulted in the establishment of reformed or protestant .

धर्ती/नमुना/साचा – **pattern** - a specimen volume or rubbing, sent to a binder to indicate the style of lettering to be used.

धारक - **receiver** - the person or equipment that receives the message.

धारणा/गृहीतक – **presumption -** an act of supposing something as true or as a fact without direct proof but with some feeling of being certain.

धारणाधिकार – **lien -** a claim on the service or property.

धार्मिक कार्य/पवित्र कार्य – **sacred work -** religious work.

धार्मिक ग्रंथ/पवित्र ग्रंथ – **sacred book -** basic work of a religion, generally accepted as such among its followers.

धुमारा/धुरी/धूसन – **fumigation -** 1) vapours raised by fumigating. The method is used to preserve books from pests.
2) exposure to vapours or fumes for disinfection or destruction of pests etc.

धूप्रदान – **fumigate -** activity to destroy infections, germs, insects etc. with the fumes of certain chemicals.

धूळपाटी – **abacus -** anything flat, as a side board, a bench, a slate, a table or board for games; a counting board. An instrument for doing or teaching arithmetic.

धोके – **hazards :** anything which might cause harm or create danger.

धोरण – **policy -** a statement of a commitment to a generic course of action, necessary for or conducive to the attainment of a goal.

ध्वनिक्षेपण – **broadcasting -** equipment for radio broadcasting; transmitter. Of or for radio broadcasting.

ध्वनिमुद्रिका – **gramophone record -** a device prepared to transfer sound by electrical or mechanical means and register it in some permanent form, as the grooved track of a phonograph record, the magnetization of fine wire etc. so that it can be reproduced.

ध्वनिमुद्रिका ग्रंथालय – **gramophone library -** a library having gramophone records as a prime document in its collection.

ध्वनिविचार लेखन - **phonetic writing -** it is a word syllabic system of writing. The Sumerians devised a fully developed form of it around 3000 BC. Later on, this system was developed as alphabetic system, first by the Greeks in the second millennium BC in which a symbol represents a single sound of a language.

ध्वनीवर्धक - **loud - speaker -** a device for converting audio-frequency electric currents into sound waves and for amplifying this sound to the desired volume, used in radio and other oral communications.

न

नकली वर्ख – **imitation foil** - made to resemble a thin metal sheet; not real; sham; bogus; as, imitation foil (gold, silver, aluminium) etc.

नकाशा संग्रह – **atlas** - collection of maps and photographs of land. It may be an independent volume of maps, followed with description.

नकाशा – **map** - maps are the projection of a part or whole of the surface of the earth, traced on a plane surface at proportionately reduced scale showing physical structure or political boundries of nations or regions.

नगरपालिका ग्रंथालय – **municipal library** - public library functioning through urban municipal council.

नफा केंद्र – **profit centre** - a form of responsibility centre in which a manager is held responsible for both revenues and costs and hence for the resultant level of profit.

नमुना नियंत्रण – **format control** - in computer, format control protects date block.

नमुना पृष्ठ – **sample page** - a selected page to project the document.

नमुना संग्रह – **format storage** - a system in which storage is done on a fixed available format.

नमुना/प्रारूप –**format** - 1) the term used to denote physical space and size of document or structuring of information record in predetermined arrangement.
2) A statement of height & width of a typical leaf of a document.

नवनिर्मित शब्द – **neologisms** - a new word or expression in a language or a familiar word or expression that is now being used with a new meaning a formal word.

नवप्रवर्तक – **innovative** - to bring in novelties, make changes in.

नष्ट न होणारी स्मृती - **non-volatile memory** - a form of storage device that does not loose its contents when the system's power is turned off. It may take the form of bubble memory or it may be powered by batteries.

नविनीकरण (ग्रंथाचे) – **renewal of books** - reissueing of library book to the same borrower.

नविनीकरण/नूतनीकरण – **renewal** - extension or revision of the existing arrangement.

नवीन आवृत्ती – **new edition** - a reprint with additions and corrections or same publication which is different in same aspect from the existing one.

नवीन भरती – **new additions** - acquisition of new books of a particular library, : the books published and / or added to a library recently.

नवीनतम प्रलेख – **nascent document** - article or other material offering latest information.

नवीनतम – **nascent** - newly developed, recent.
1) latest coming into being : being born or beginning to form, start, grow or develop, cluster of ideas, cultures etc.
2) newly born, starting to grow or develop.

नात्यानुसारी क्रम – **filiatory sequence** - sequence of subjects on the basis of their relative relationships.

नाव तालिका – **name catalogue** - a catalogue in which entries are arranged in alphabetical order, according to the name of authors.

नाव शीर्षक – **name heading** - a heading which refers to a of person, place, corporate body etc.

नाव संज्ञा ; नामपद्धती – **nomenclature** - a system of names for a classes, or classification.

नाव संदर्भ– **name reference** - a reference used in catalogue to indicate more than one name used by the author.

नाव – **name** - identification of an entity.

निःसंदिग्ध – **unambiguous** - clear, perfect.

निकटता/सानिध्य/निकटस्थिती - **juxtapose** - to place side by side for comparison.

निकनेट - NICNET (National Information Centre Network) - a computer network developed by the National Information Centre, New Delhi.

निकष/कसोटी/निर्णायक लक्षण – criterion - a standard of judging; any established law, rule, principle or fact by which a correct judgement may be formed.

निकेम – NICHEM (National Information Centre for Chemistry and Chemical Technology) -is an information centre developed under NISSAT, functioning from 1986. The centre is operational with library and documentation services of National Chemical Laboratory, Pune. The centre has comprehensive collection in chemistry & chemical technology on mechanical retrieval system.

निगमन – deduction - a style of reasoning which seeks to explain any phenomena by arguing from the general to particular.

नीती/धोरण – policy - guideline to achieve the set goals.

नीतीशास्त्र/नीतीमूल्ये – ethics - 1) science of morals. 2) rules of conduct recognised with respect to a particular group.

नित्यक्रम – routine - general procedure or activity carried out regularly.

निदेश/ग्रंथ हस्त पोथी/ हस्ताध्यायी – handbook - a small size book which contains concise information. see also "manual."

निधी – fund - see 'book fund.'

नियंत्रण भाषा – command language - set of commands or instructions used for storage & retrieving information from a database.

नियंत्रण व संदेशवहनशास्त्र – cybernetics - study of mechanical-electrical communication systems such as computing systems.

नियंत्रण – controlling - it is checking, verifying, testing, regulating & exercising restrain in order to carry out a management process successfully.

नियंत्रित अलमारी/कपाट – closed shelves - see 'closed access'.

नियंत्रित क्रम - closed sequence - see 'closed array'.

नियंत्रित चिन्हांकन – closed notation - a notation which does not accept new digits to represent new classes.

नियंत्रित नोंद – closed entry - an entry which consists complete information about a document and no addition is required.

नियंत्रित पंक्ती – closed array - an array of classes which could not accept new classes and which cannot be extended further more.

नियंत्रित प्रवेश – closed access - library where the user is not allowed to enter in the stackroom for selection of documents required.

नियत निधी - allotted fund - fund distributed, granted, assigned.

नियत/देय दिनांक – due date - date on which a document is due for return to the library from which it was borrowed.

नियतकाल - periodicity - interval after which issue of a periodical is brought out.

नियतकालिक पेटी – periodical box - a box used to collect loose issues of the current periodicals. see also pamphlet box.

नियतकालिक प्रदर्शनी रॅक – periodical display rack : especially designed rack used to display current issues of the periodicals received in a library.

नियतकालिक – periodical - a publication which appears in parts with regular intervals, having distinctive features like common names, periodicity and issue number to volume etc. Each issue contains different information.

नियतकालिकाचा पूर्वी प्रकाशित झालेला खंड – 1) back issue : synonymous with back number.
2) back number : any issue of periodical which precedes the current issue.

नियतरिती/गणनविधी – algorithm - instructions of carrying out a series of logical procedural steps in a specific order.

नियम (वर्गीकरणाचे) – rules of classification - set of rules framed to guide classifier.

नियम – rules - set of guidelines put to practice, principles.

नियमपुस्तिका – manual - a handbook published by an organisation giving practical step by step instructions on how to do a particular job; can be used to impart training for the job.

नियमावली – regulation - a principle or guideline governing conduct, procedure etc.

नियामक मंडळ संस्था – governing body - body having the power to govern.

नियुक्त/नामनिर्देशित - nominated - appointment of a person to an office, nominated by a committee, constituted for the selection.

नियोजन – planning - process of preparation of plans that state the ways and means by which the organization can achieve the set goals and objectives through the proper utilization of financial, material & manpower resources.

नियोजनानुसार अनुदान - **non-plan grants** - regular budgeted grants given every year.

निरंकुश सत्ता असलेला नेता - **autocratic leader** - a person who tells subordinates what to do and expects to be obeyed without question. A leadership style in which practically all authority centres in the leader.

निरंतर (प्रलेख) - **routing of documents** - circulation of documents to users to inform about their presence and use.

निरंतर शिक्षण - **continuing education** - non-formal education for the benefit of working professionals / working class to improve their skill or to update them in the area of their work.

निरर्थक अंक/रिकामा अंक – **empty digit** - a digit which has no semantic value, but retains the ordinal value and generally used to expand notational capacity.

निरर्थक आणि निरर्थकारक अंक – **empty and emptying digit** - a digit with ordinal value, without representing any specific local idea and depriving the preceding digit of local idea. This concept is used in colon classification.

निरर्थकारक अंक - **emptying digit** - a digit with ordinal value and also depriving the preceding digit of its local idea.

निरर्थकारक स्थायी अंक - **emptying substantive digit** - a digit with ordinal value representing a local idea and depriving the preceding digit or its local idea.

निरीक्षक/पर्यवेक्षक – **supervisor** - person who supervises.

निरीक्षण - **observation** - 1) action of observing, state of being observed.
2) a recording of a single datum.

निरीक्षणात्मक मूल्य – **observed value** - the values recorded in an empirical survey.

निर्जलीकरण/निर्जलीभवन – **dehydration (chemical)** - removal of free or combined water from a compound.

निर्णय प्रक्रिया – **decision making** - the process of generating and evaluating alternatives and making choices among them.

निर्णय प्रवाह तक्ता – **decision flow chart** - graphic means of representing work flows which include the Yes -No decision and actions required to perform a designated task or series of tasks.

निर्णय – **decision** - decision stating what actions are to be taken.

निर्णायक/खडतर/कठीण – **crucial** - of supreme importance, decisive, critical or extremely trying, severe, difficult.

निर्देश/निर्देशांक/दर्शक /सूची - **index** - an alphabetical list of terms, topics, names, places etc. which is used to operate the text or relative position of entries in a file / record.

निर्देश अंक विभाग – **index number section** - the section of an entry giving an index number if any.

निर्देश अंक – **index number** - the number in a specific entry representing its documents or the number in a class index entry representing its heading.

निर्देश नोंद – **index entry** - an entry which is formulated to develop an index.

निर्देश – **index** - the alphabetical list of names, subjects, topics etc. with the note of exact location.

निर्देशक – **director** - the chief executive / head of the institution.

निर्देशांक – **index number** - a class number or a call number of a document, or class number relevant to the class mentioned in a class index entry.

निर्देशात्मक नियतकालिक – **indexing periodical** - a periodical similar to an abstract but without giving abstract / annotations for the entries listed in it, or a periodical listing only the bibliographical details of articles, books and other collections on a subject in systematic order.

निर्देशिकरण भाषा – **indexing language** - specially designed language, suitable for indexin with reference to information storage and retrieval system.

निर्देशिका (ग्रंथालयाची) – **directory of libraries** - an alphabetical list of the libraries with brief information about each library included in it, such directories are brought out by ILA and Raja Ram Mohan Roy Library Foundation (RRMRLF)

निर्देशिका - **directory** - an alphabetical list of names, places, countries, institutions, etc. with brief or specific information. Telephone Directory, Publisher Directory etc.

निर्देशीकरण सेवा – **indexing service** - a periodical publication which regularly & systematically indexes the content of periodicals & sometimes other forms of publication, either of a general nature or within specified subject fields. They are usually cumulated at regular intervals.

निर्देशीकरण – **indexing** - an art / technique of preparing an index.

निर्धारित पाठ्यक्रम – **prescribed curriculum** - recommended subject contents.

निर्धारित – **allocate** - scheduled , errmarked, fixed.

निर्धारित – **prescribed** - recommended for particular courses.

निर्बंधित निधी – **restricted funds** - restricted funds do not allow flexibility in use of funds, like grants for specific purposes, restricted funds cannot be used for purpose other than for which it is sanctioned.

निर्मिती लाभ – **cost benefit** - relationship between cost involved and service generated by the programme.

निलेखित करणे – **write off** - to cancel or remove document from accounts of the library accession register.

निर्विष्टी युक्ती – **input devices** - in computer keyboard is next visible device used for input. Thus, it is a mechanical unit which brings data into a computer for processing. See also 'input equipment'.

निर्विष्टी संग्रह – **input** - information stored into the internal memory of the computer or the information, data signal, or the like supplied to a system of device.

निर्विष्टी साधन/उपकरण – **input equipment** - the equipment used for transferring data into a data processing system.

निर्विष्टीक्षेत्र – **input area** - area of storage, a section that has been reserved for input data.

निवड ग्रंथसूची – **select bibliography** - list which gives only a selection of the literature of a subject, the selection having been made with a view to exclude non-essential material or to meet the needs of a special class of people.

निवड – **selection** - process of assessment of those who apply for employment, by one or more methods, as to their suitability for particular position and the choice of the most suitable candidate.

निवडक माहितीचे प्रसारण – **SDI (selective dissemination of information)** - an automated system of information retrieval utilizing a computer for disseminating relevant information to users. An interest profile depicting & defining each area of interest as complied for each user, it consists of terms which are likely to appear in relevant documents.

निवडक ग्रंथसूची – **selected bibliography** - list which gives only a selection of the literature of subject, the selection having been made with a view to exclude worthless material or to meet the needs of a special class of people. Also called 'selective bibliography'.

निवडक माहितीची वितरण सेवा – SDI - (selective dissemination of information) - a computer aided service providing relevant information to specific users on the basis of their interest profile.

निविदा – tender - formal offer to supply goods or carryout work at a stated price, which is open to all vendors.

निवेश प्रारुप – input format - data structure at the time of inputting, specifying various fields and their rendering.

निश्चल – invariant - a function of the coefficient which remains unchanged by a specified transformation or operation.

निश्चित किमती – fixed costs - the costs that do not change with the volume or size of an activity, services or product.

निश्चित स्थान – fixed location - a method of arrangement by making a book with shelf and other location marks so that its position on a particular shelf remains the same.

निश्चितपणा/मानक – specification - Nationality or internationally approved quantum of space, item, size of furniture, equipment or for setting out the details of work to be carried out.

निष्कर्ष/अनुमान - conclusion - belief or opinion that is the result of reasoning.

निष्कर्षण/अमूर्तीकरण – abstraction - an idea of quality as separate from any object.

निष्कर्षण/नि:सारण टीप – extraction note - a note in the catalogue entry indicating the presence of extracts for a documents.

निष्कासन घटक – omission factor - ratio of the number of relevant documents not selected to the total number of relevant document for the machine had been fed with entries.

निसर्गघटना – phenomenon - 1) occurrence (phenomena - plural). 2) any fact, circumstance, or experience that is apparent to the senses and that can be scientifically described or appraised; as, an eclipse is a phenomenon of astronomy.

निसाट – NISSAT (National Information System for Science & Technology) - was set up to co-ordinate the resource of science and technology library. so the wasteful expenditure is avoided.

नूतनीकरण (ग्रंथाचे) - renewal of book/document - reissue of library book to the same borrower for extemded period.

नूतनीकरण (वर्गणीचे) – renewal of subscription - 1) the subscription of the same periodical is paid in advance to keep the supply continued.

2) Subscription of the periodical which is paid in advance.

नेतृत्व शैली – **leadership style** - a leader's typical way of behaving towards group members.

नेतृत्व – **leadership** - for further period of time. To guide, lead the subordinates for getting the work done.

नैमित्तिक/प्रासंगिक/तदर्थ समिती – **advoc committee** - committee constituted to suggest measures to deal with a certain situation or to deal in detail with some specific assignment; such committee works under fix terms of reference provided to it. Sometimes it is constituted from the member of the main committee.

नैसर्गिक लक्षण – **natural characteristics** - 1) a quality or complex of qualities in the things classified, inherent and inseparable from the things and without which they could not be the things they are.

2) an inherent and inseparable characteristics by use of which the things are classified.

नैसर्गिक/प्राकृतिक भाषा – **natural language** - 1) human spoken language such as Hindi, Gujarathi, Marathi etc.

2) a language which reflects current usage without being specifically prescribed.

नैसर्गिक/प्राकृतिक संपदा – **natural material** - concrete entity found in and extracted from nature.

नॅसडॉक – **NASSDOC (National Social Science Documentation Centre)** - the center is working in New Delhi under Indian Council of Social Science Research (ICSSR), It is generating publication based on current information acquired in the field of social sciences.

नोंद घटक – **entry element** - word or group of words under which an entry is made.

नोंद घटक/तत्व – **entry element** - the block of information such as author, title, publisher, year, series, note etc.

नोंद चिट्ठी – **coupon** - usually a small detachable piece of paper that gives the holder the right to do or receive something.

नोंद शब्द – **entry word** - a word used to arrange the entry.

नोंद – **entry** - unit record of information in a catalogue or documentation list.

नोंदवही - **register** - a record or list of events, items, etc., often kept by an official appointed to do so; a book in which this is kept.

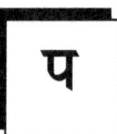

प

पंक्ति दूरस्थ बिंदू – **array telescoping point** - isolate in a telescoped array, a sub-isolate.

पंक्ती/उपांग/विचार – **array** - isolate idea : thought unit enumerated in single array taken by itself.

पंक्ती – **array** - 1) set of classes arranged in the proper sequence and derived from a universe on the basis of a single characteristic at any step in the progress towards a complete assortment of the entities of their universe. A set of coordinate classes of its immediate universe or set of related variables.
2) a set of classes derived from a universe by applying a single characteristic. A group of coordinate classes.

पंचांग – **almanac** - annual publication containing information about calender /astronomy, low and high tides, sunrise and sunset timings etc.

पंजीकरण अभिलेख – **registration record** - record of membership in library which is used to give clearance / attendance certificates as and when required.

पंजीकरण पत्र – **registration card** - a card which keeps identification of the user.

पंजीकरण प्रपत्र – **registration form** - a form used to register the user in a library.

पंजिका (संचिका)/गाठवण व्यवस्थापन पद्धती – **file management system** : a system used to control the files available in any database, or computer software to define data in specified records and files to make use on demand.

पंजिका/गाठवण निर्देश - **file index** - a table or list of files.

पंजिका/गाठवण सोपस्कार – **file processing** - updating of the file .

पंजिका/संचिका/गाठवण – **file** - 1) organised collection of information for some particular purpose, or a collection of related records as one unit. 2) Maintaining the record of all correspondence on one subject.

पंजी देवघेव पद्धती – **register issue system** - it is the earliest system in which page / pages in a register are allotted to a user and issued details of document are traced on the page marked to him.

पंजी प्रपत्र तालिका – **register form catalogue** - a catalogue where entries are written by hand in a bound register. The entries are made in the sequence of their receipt.

पंजी – **register** - a bound folder of papers used to record specific information.

पंजीकरण - **copy filing** - when the copies are arranged in a file.

पंजीकरण/पंजीयन - **registration** - an act of allowing library membership.

पंजीकृत नसलेला ग्रंथ - **unaccessioned book** - a book which is not entered in the library accession register.

पट/नोंदवही देवघेव पद्धती – **register issue system** - it is the earliest system in which page/pages in a register are allotted to a user and at the time of issue, details of document lent are mentioned on it.

पट/नोंदवही रुप तालिका – **register form catalogue** - a catalogue in which entries are written by hand. The entries are made in the order of their receipt. It is a bound register.

पट/नोंदवही – **register** - a bound folder of papers used to record specific information.

पटल/पापुद्रा – **film** - a sensitive -surfaced flexible transparent material in the form of sheets, strips or rolls.

पडताळणी(ग्रंथ) – **collation** - the process of examining and checking new books for completeness, presence of all the illustrations, variation of the number and order of the pages and sections of a volume.

पणन तंत्रविज्ञ - **marketing technology** - technology of the act or business of buying or selling in the market.

पत्ता - **address** - group of characters which identifies the data to communicate in a computer. It is a memory location, delivery direction on a letter, parcel etc. including the name, title and place of residence of the person for whom it is intended.

पत्ता अंक/संख्या – **address number** - location number assigned in computer programme to aid its memory.

पत्ता नोंदवही – **address register** - it is a CPU register in computer.

पत्ता रस्ता – **address path** - the selection path for memory and input / output data.

पत्र खण - **card drawer** - steel or wooden drawers meant for holding catalogue cards kept in a card cabinet.

पत्र खण/कपाट –**card cabinet** : a set of drawers in which cards are filed in vertical order, but in desired sequence.

पत्र तबक – **card tray** - a drawer which holds cards to keep these in a card cabinet.

पत्र तालिका खण/कपाट – **card catalogue cabinet** - see 'card cabinet.'

पत्र तालिका – **card catalogue** - a catalogue prepared on standard uniform 5" x 3" size cards. Each entry has information according to approach and these are kept in dictionary order or in classified order as the case may be. It is a unit of card filing drawers made of either wood or steel.

पत्र देवघेव पद्धत – **card charging system** - an issue system wherein circulation control is affected through the use of a book card containing information about a document and a borrower's ticket containing information about a borrower.

पत्र देवघेव पद्धती – **card issue system** - to arrange circulation of library documents, cards are introduced for identification of the borrower and also for document loan, number of cards are issued on the basis of the policy followed.

पत्र निर्देश/अनुक्रमणिका – **card index** - an index or entires in card form arranged in alphabetical order.

पत्र – **card** - a small sheet of thick paper.

पत्रक पेटी – **pamphlet box** : a box used for holding pamphlet.

पत्रक/पत्रके – **pamphlet** - 1) single page or few printed pages of information of immediate use. Generally developed to disseminate information of current interest. 2) a non-periodical publication of at least five but not more than 48 pages.

पत्रकार – **journalist** - one who contributes for publication of periodicals and newspapers.

पत्रकारिता – **journalism** - the profession of compiling, writing and editing of information for the use of publication in periodicals.

पत्रव्यवहार – **correspondence** - official writing of letters connected with specific functions of professional management.

पत्रिका खोली/कक्ष – **periodical room** - a room which is used exclusively for keeping and reading the periodicals.

पत्रिका दर्शक घोडा – **periodical stand** - a stand used to display periodicals.

पत्रिका पेटी – **periodicals box** - a box used to collect loose issues of the current periodicals. see also pamphlet box.

पत्रिका प्रदर्शनी रॅक – **periodical display rack** - a specially designed rack used to display recent issues of the periodicals received in a library.

पत्रिका लेख – **periodical article** - an article which appears in any periodical.

पत्रिका साठा – **periodical stock** - a place where back issues of the periodicals are arranged.

पत्रिका/नियतकालिका/ज्ञानपत्रिका – **journal** - a serial publication and an important source for dissemination of primary information on any subject. It may comprise of one or more subjects.

पत्रिका/नियतकालिक – **periodical** - a publication which appears in parts with regular intervals, having distinctive features like name, periodicity and issue number to a volume etc.

पद्धती (निवडीची) – **scheme of assortment** - method of sorting entities of a universe.

पद्धती (वर्गांची) – **scheme of classes** - statement showing the filiatory sequence of the classes.

पद्धती विश्लेषण – **system analysis** - systematic study of activities, methods, procedures and techniques to make best use of the system.

पद्धती/पद्धती शास्त्र – **methodology** - 1) the science of applying method. 2) Scientific way of solving a problem of research.

पद्धत (ग्रंथालय) - **system library / library system** - a library which has number of extensions.

पद्धती/प्रणाली – **system** - it can be a machine system for collection of instructions which forms operating system or organised grouping of people, methods, machines and materials collected together to perform specific objectives.

पद्धती/योजना – **scheme** - complete description of a plan.

पपायरस – **papyrus** - an ancient paper like material made from the long stem of a water plant.

परकीय विषय – **alien subject** - subject of distant or no relationship.

परकीय प्रदेश – **alien region** - regions in an arrangement consisting on either side of the umbral region, beyond the penumbral region concerned, consisting of classes of isolates or array, isolates not of interest to the reader at the moment or a subject totally irrelevant to the subject sought.

परत कट्टा – **return counter** - also called 'charging desk', 'delivery desk' 'discharging desk' 'issue desk' 'lending desk' 'fan desk' 'receiving desk' 'return desk' 'slipping desk' etc. It is a place in the library where books are returned.

परस्पर वर्जक – **mutually exclusive** - two or more subjects excluding or not admitting things, restricted to group or area concerned.

परस्परव्यापक – **overlapping** - fact or process of overlapping, subjects which cover subsubjects of each other.

परस्परांवर परिणामकारी माहिती पद्धत – **interactive information system** - an adjective applied to a computer-based information system, which allows a user to communicate with a programme and provides the user with immediate responses, rather than delayed ones.

परस्परावलंबी – **interdependent** - factors depending on each other.

परा प्रलेख – **meta document** - an instrument record of natural and social phenomena made directly unmediated by the human mind even before it got transformed into thought and human mind.

परागती – **regress** - opposite of progress, decrease in existing one.

परिक्षण आढावा नियतकालिक – **review periodical** - periodical publishing reviews of progress, usually in the field of science and technology.

परिगणनात्मक पंक्ती उपांग – **enumerated array isolate** : array isolate of an array attained by enumeration device.

परिगणनात्मक – **enumeration** - 1) listing of subjects for past, present and anticipated future.

परिगणात्मक युक्ती – **enumeration device** - 1) device using successive digits for forming the classes or the isolates in facet or the array isolate in an array be directly enumerating them.
2) device which is helpful in counting.

परिगणात्मक वर्गीकरण – **enumerative classification -** 1) a classification which identifies all possible classes and lists them after assigning notation.
2) a classification scheme which consists essentially of a single schedule enumerating all the subjects of the past, present and anticipatable future.

परिगणात्मक विशिष्ट उपांग – **enumerated special isolate -** special isolate got by enumeration device.

परिघीय कंस – **circular brackets -** curves or half round brackets in which first is called starter and last is called arrester. These are used with notation to identify subject device used.

परिघीय – **circular** : shaped like a circle, round.

परिचर – **attendant -** see 'library attendant.'

परिचलन नियंत्रण – **circulation control -** it covers all the aspects associated with the borrowing of library materials by the users of the library.

परिचालन पद्धत – **operating system -** in computing a software programming package, this program controls the operation of user programmes.

परिचालन विवरणपत्र – **operating statement -** a summary of operating cost card, where appropriate the revenues and profit margins of the whole or part of the activities of an enterprise for a given period are given.

परिच्छेद खूण – **paragraph mark -** proof to indicate the commencement of a new paragraph.

परिच्छेद दंड – **paragraph indention -** setting the first line of a paragraph 1 cm or so from the margin.

परिच्छेद – **paragraph -** distinct section of a written or printed text, usually consisting of several sentences dealing with a single theme and starting on a new line.

परिणामकारक घटक – **anticedent variable -** a thing that occurs before another which is responsible for occurrence of the latter.

परिणामकारकता – **effectiveness -** the degree to which the process produces the intended outputs. Effectiveness involved doing those things necessary to accomplish organizational objectives.

परिणामशून्य गृहीतक – **null hypothesis -** a hypothesis which states that there is no difference between two entities.

परिनिरीक्षण – **censorship** - assessment and prohibition of production, distribution and circulation or sale of material considered to be objectionable on grounds of politics, religion, obscenity or blasphemy.

परिपत्रक – **circular / letter** - an official letter which is used to convey a policy or revision of previous decision to the concerned people.

परिभाषा/व्याख्या/संज्ञा – **terminology** - set of terms used in science, arts, system of terms used.

परिमाण/एकक/घटक – **unit** - unit of measurement, smallest of a whole number.

परिमित/सांत – **finite** - limited or measurable.

परिरक्षण/जतन/निगा – **maintenance** - the action of maintaining, up keep, preservation, repair etc.

परिवर्तन/बदल अभिलेख – **change record** - master record in which amendments are incorporated as and when made.

परिवर्तनशील क्षेत्र – **variable field** - a field which can be extended to accommodate longer data as per requirement.

परिवर्तित नाव – **changed name** - a note made in cataloguing of documents when an author contributes under various pseudonyms then for all such names except original.

परिवर्तित शीर्षक – **changed title** - a different title for a document other than the title appeared in the earlier edition.

परिवर्तिक सामान्य उपविभाग – **posteriorising common isolate** - common isolate idea whose attachment to a host class makes the resulting class succeed the host class.

परिवर्तीत शीर्षक – टीप - **changes of title note** - a note stating the term under which the work has appeared earlier with different title.

परिवहन/वितरण - **circulation** - the total number of books issued from a library in a given period.

परिवहन/देवघेव अभिलेख – **circulation record** - record of the lent documents of a library.

परिवहन/देवघेव कार्य – **circulation** - process of lending library documents.

परिवहन/देवघेव डेस्क – **circulation desk / counter** - place where record of home lent of documents is made.

परिवहन/देवघेव नियंत्रण – **circulation control** - supervision of all activities relating to issue and return of library documents.

परिवहन/देवघेव विभाग – **circulation department / section** : the section of a library in which documents are lend on demand for use and received back.

परिवहन/देवघेव सांख्यिकी – **circulation statistics** - statistical profile for the documents circulated by a library.

परिवाह/दूरदर्शनचे केंद्र – **channel** - established relay centre that disseminate information or knowledge or any type of their surrogates.

परिशिष्ट – **appendix / addenda** - subject matter which supplements the text of the document specifying detail information. It is usually placed at the end of the text.

परिशुद्धता – **precision** - tells how efficiency of the system provides only relevant items.

परिषद खोली (कक्ष) – **conference room** - a room, hall, used for a conference.

परिषद/प्रशासकीय मंडळ – **council** - group of people elected to manage the affairs of an association, to give advice, make rules, manage work etc.

परिषद/संमेलन – **conference** - a meeting of the members of association, generally arranged to discuss issues of the profession.

परिसंवाद कक्ष/खोली – **seminar room** - a room meant for debate or discussions.

परिसंवाद – **seminar** - discussion having a theme of nascent thought.

परिसर – **campus** - area including grounds and buildings of an institution.

परिसूत्र/सूत्र – **formula** - guidelines, rule expressed in symbols.

पर्टं/सी.पी.एम. (कार्य मूल्यमापन आणि अवलोकन तंत्र) – **PERT/ CPM (programme evaluation review technique / critical path method)** - a time event network analysis system in which the various events in a programme or project are identified, with the planned time for each, and are placed in a network showing the relationship of each event to other events, from the sequence of interrelated events, the path of those events in which there is the least "slack" time in terms of planned completion is the "critical path" PERT/TIME : PERT / COST systems introduce costs of each event and are usually combined with elapsed time of each event or series of events.

पर्याय – **surrogate** - person or thing that acts or is used instead of another as substitute.

पर्यायी ग्रंथ नाव/शीर्षक – **alternative title** - a sub-title introduced by or its equivalent, sometimes more than the language or various types of type face are needed to individualise.

पर्यायी शीर्षक – **alternative title** - second part of a title proper, which consists of two parts, each of which is a title by itself and both of them joined by the word or its equivalent in another language.

पर्यायीस्थान – **alternative location** - provision in a scheme of classification for adaptation of logical order or practical convenience. Two alternative places for a subject in a scheme.

पर्यावरण – **environment** - conditions, circumstances etc. affecting people's lives.

पर्सियन सूचना (नियम) - **Pursian instructions (rules)** - the German cataloguing rules of an English translation published by University of Michigan in 1938.

पश्च भरण – **feedback** - response or opinion obtained from a person stating the effectiveness of the programme conducted.

पसंतीसाठी ग्रंथ – **books on approval** - the books sent by bookseller for selection, purchase, consideration or peursal.

पहिली आडवी ओळ – **leading line** - the first horizontal line on a catalogue card which is used for recording heading of an entry.

पहिली उभी रेषा – **first vertical line** - the first left of the two vertical lines printed on a catalogue card from which the new section of an entry begins.

पहिली छपाई – **first printing** - the first quality of a book to be printed, equivalent to first impression.

पहिली मुद्रित – **first proof** - a proof of type set matter which is read by the printer's reader & corrected before the final galley proof is made. See also proof.

पहिली शब्द नोंद – **first word entry** - entry under the first word of a title of the document.

पहिले नाव – **first name** - the first name of a person excluding family name and parent's name.

पाच मूलभूत घटक/वर्ग – **five fundamental categories** - a concept under colon classification scheme. It states that there are only five fundamental categories, personality, matter, energy, space & time. Each facet of a subject is regarded as manifestation of one or other of these categories. These are arranged in order of PMEST in their decreasing concreteness.

पाच सूत्रे (नियम ग्रंथालयशास्त्राचे) - **five laws of library science** - the five laws enunciated by Dr. S.R. Ranganathan are :

1. books are for use.
2. every reader his / her book.
3. every book its reader.
4. save the time of the reader.
5. library is a growing organism.

पाठचिकित्सा – **textual criticism** - linguistic analysis of a text.

पाठपुरावा – **follow-up** - 1) action taken to continue or exploit what has already been started or done.

2) an act following up a decision to implement it.

पाठपुरावा/बाजू मांडणे/मार्गदर्शन करणे – **advocate** - speak publically in favour of something, recommend, support.

पाठ्य/क्रमिक पुस्तक – **text book** - the book developed as per curricula to support teaching programme or a standard contribution which helps in understanding a specific branch of knowledge.

पाठ्य/क्रमिक पुस्तके ग्रंथालय - **text books library** - a library having only text books collection.

पाठ्य/विषय – **text** - the main part of the document.

पातबिंदू - **nodes** - a centering point of component parts.

पात्रता/योग्यता – **qualification** - training, educational conditions, or experience that is prescribed to select an employee.

पायस – **emulsions** - a coating consisting of light - sensitive materials contained in a medium, used on a film base.

पायाभूत सुविधा - **infrastructure** - subordinate parts, installations, physical facilities etc. that form the basis of system, an organisation or an enterprise.

पारंपरिक/सूत्रबद्ध वर्ग – **canonical class** - traditional sub-class of main class enumerated in a scheme of classification for the universe of knowledge, and not derived on the basis of definite characteristics.

पारंपरिक प्रलेख – **conventional document** - a document where the thought content is recorded in a natural language by means of writing, typing, printing or by some near-printing process.

पारंपरिक/सूत्रबद्ध क्रम (आदेश) – **canonical order** - the order in which sub-classes of main class are arranged.

पारंपरिक/सूत्रबद्ध क्रम – **canonical sequence -** traditional arrangement of subjects which is not derived on the basis of any definite characteristic.

पारदर्शक – **transparent -** clear, certain easily understandable, about which there is no doubt.

पारदर्शक सूक्ष्मपत्र – **microfiche -** a flat sheet of standard pictographic film used to record information. The record may be in rows and colums.

पारदर्शिका – **transparency -** an image, in black & white or colour, on transparent base stock, usually film, contents of which may be viewed by transmitted light, with the aid of a projector.

पारभासी पडदा – **translucent screen -** a sheet of glass treated in some way (ground, opal, coated etc.) or plastic on to which an image is projected in a microfilm reader.

पारिभाषिक कोश – **glossary -** an alphabetical list of terms with its description. It may be only for selected terms.

पारिश्रमिक पत्रक – **payment sheet -** sheet shorting the details of payment made.

पाश्र्व सोपस्कार – **background processing -** programme which works to prepare for goals.

पाश्र्वचित्र – **profile -** an organised list of specific topics or information heads compiled out of a set of information users. The profile explains who is interested in which information and vice versa.

पाहा आणखी – **see also -** a direction note to refer the same subject available under another parallel term.

पाहा – **see -** a direction note to shift subject search under another synonymous term.

पिरॅमिड (घनाकृती) - **pyramid -** things or pile of things with shape of a pyramid.

पुढील बाजू/टोक शीर्षक – **fore-edge title -** a hand written title on the fore - edge of a book so that it could be identified when standing on a shelf with its fore-edge outwards.

पुढील बाजू/टोक समास – **fore-edge margin -** the space between the typed matter and the fore-edge of a book or periodical. Also called 'outside margin'.

पुढील बाजू/टोक – **fore-edge -** the front edge of a sheet of a paper or of the sections of a book opposite the folded edge through which the sewing passes. Also called 'front edge'.

पुनर्गठन - **repackaging** - rearrangement of the imformation already available.

पुनर्प्राप्ती घटक - **recall factor** - ratio of number of relevant documents selected to the total number of relevant documents for which the machine had been fed with entries.

पुनर्प्राप्ती सूचना - **recall notice** - a notice sent to a reader requesting the return of a book or other item which is overdue or required for use by someone else.

पुनर्प्राप्ती - **recall** - recollect, it is an effort of getting books or ideas back for further use.

पुनर्मांगणी - **recall** - a measure to check how well a system performs at yielding up all relevant items within it.

पुनर्मुद्रण - **reprint** - reproduction of the documents without any change.

पुनर्रचना - **relocation** - keeping at a new place.

पुनर्विलोकन/परीक्षण - **review** - i) primary literature : analysed, synthesized and integrated.
ii) primary literature further impacted and repackaged for specific category of users.
iii) serves as records of evaluated and integrated knowledge for assimilation and use by students, scientists and other scholars.
iv) encourage cross - fertilization of ideas.
v) promote linking of relevant fields of research.

पुनर्शोधन - **rectification** - arrangement of things or items at proper place.

पुरवठा - **supply** - the quantities of goods or services offered for sale.

पुरवठाकार - **feeder** - the various pieces of automatic apparatus by means of which sheets of paper are fed to and positioned on, printing press and paper processing machines of various kinds.

पुरवणी पूरक नियतकालिकाची - **supplement to a periodical** - an issue brought out as additional material on special occasion.

पुरवणी/पूरक पैलू - **supplement facet** - part of the book, number of documents, which is its supplement number.

पुरवणी/पूरक लेखक विवरणाचे - **supplement to author statement** - statement of the year of birth and of the alternative name if any of each person mentioned in author statement.

पुरवणी/पूरक - **supplement** - volume forming a part of the work; an addition.

पुरवणी/पूरकसंख्या - **supplement number** - number assigned to a supplement to individualise it from the original document.

पुरातन ग्रंथ – **antiquarian book** - these are old books and are enough to recon higher prices than ordinary recorded in hand books.

पुराभिलेखागार – पहा– 'ऐतिहासिक हेतूसाठी केलेला साठा.''

पुराभिलेखीय सूक्ष्मपट – **archival microfilm** - a film having the information on ancient topic bearing characteristics retainable for indefinite period.

पुरालेखविद्या – **paleography** - study or ancient modes of writing / hand writing.

पुस्तकी किडा – **annobium domestieum** - a person having bookish knowledge.

पुस्तपत्र/पत्रिका – **pamphlet** - a non - periodical publication of atleast five but not more than 48 pages, exclusive of the cover pages. (General Conference of UNESCO, 1964.)

पूरक टीप – **add note** - an instruction appended to an entry to extend the class number by a part of the number taken either from the schedules (volume 2) or from any of the tables 2 to 6 (volume), in DDC.

पूरक पंजी – **continuation file** - file used for continuation of the original one. This is also called part II and III as the case may be.

पूरक पत्र – **continuation card** - second and subsequent catalogue card which carries to its top the reference, that is classification number and entry word as in main card to follow remaining part of the main entry which was not covered in first card due to pository of space. A card used for ordering a continuation.

पूरक/अतिरिक्त आवृत्ती – **added edition** - a different edition from the one already available

पूरक/अतिरिक्त नोंद - **added entry** - an entry derived from the main entry to widen search approach through author, title, series etc. or duplicate entry with additional heading information. It is a supplementary entry which is generated from the main entry to help user in search.

पूरक/अतिरिक्त शीर्षक नोंद – **added title entry** - an added title entry is made under the title only when the title is very prominent. In this type of entry title is used at top line as search point.

पूर्ण कापडी बांधणी – **full cloth binding** - type of binding wherein hard board cover of book is protected fully by cloth.

पूर्ण चामडी बांधणी – **full leather binding** - type of book binding wherein the whole of the hard cover is covered with leather to ensure safety for longer period.

पूर्ण नांव – **full name -** a name consisting all parts like forename and surname.

पूर्ण बिंदू/थांबा/पूर्णविराम – **full point / stop / fullstop -** the punctuation mark used to end the sentence.

पूर्ण भाग तत्त्व – **whole - organ principle -** if a subject facet 'B' is an organ, and 'A' is body, then 'A' should precede 'B'. This principle is used in preparation of classification schedules.

पूर्ण शीर्षक – **full title -** a part of the title which precedes the subtitle, see also 'main title'.

पूर्व–सहसंबंध निर्देशन पद्धत – **pre-coordinate indexing system -** an indexing system in which a combination of subject terms is accomplished at the time of preparing the index itself for use in the retrieval of information pertaining to complex concepts.

पूर्वग्रह उपांग – **bias phase -** the treatment of a subject generally and fairly completely, if concisely, from the point of view of a class of users whose primary interest is in another subject.

पूर्वपरंपरागत **- patronymic -** derived from the name of one's father or some other male ancestor.

पूर्वलक्षी ग्रंथसूची – **retrospective bibliography -** a bibliography which lists books published in previous years as distinct from a 'current' bibliography which records books recently published. Also called a closed bibliography.

पूर्वलक्षी परिवर्तन – **retro conversion -** to convert a system or procedures for an activity and apply it to complete old stock also.

पूर्वलक्षी प्रभावाने – **with retrospective effect -** application of decision with back effect.

पूर्ववर्तक अंक – **anteriorising digit -** digit, addition of which at the end of any class number makes the resulting to precede the host class number.

पूर्ववर्तक मूल्य – **anteriorising value** (classification) **-** said to be possessed by a digit which, when added to a class number and which is then said to be the 'host class number' causes the resulting class number to have precedence over the host number.

पूर्वान्वयी सूचीकरण पद्धती – **pre- coordinate indexing system -** a system by which terms are combined at the time of indexing a document, the combination of terms being shown in the entries. This system is known as PRECIS.

पूल – **bridge -** in communication, equipment and techniques used to match circuits to each other ensuring minimum transmission impairment.

पृथक्करण घटक – **individualizing element** - part in a class number responsible in making it unique and is identified from the identical class number.

पृथक्करण – **1) abstraction** - the process of separation to achieve grouping in classification. **2) individualization** - separation of an entity in a universe into a unitary class by the process of assortment.

पृथक/विभक्त आधारसामग्री – **discrete data** - data having certain discrete values with gaps in between. For example, the number of persons can be 5 or 6, not something in between 5 and 6.

पृष्ठसंख्यारहित ग्रंथ - **unpaged books** - a book which has leaves without page number.

पृष्ठादिवृत्त – **collation** - the description of document to present physical form such as volume, page, illustration, size etc.

पेपीरस/पपायरस – **papyrus** - an ancient paper like material made from the stem of specific tree.

पैलू दूरस्थ बिंदू – **facet telescoping point** - stage in the enumeration of the isolates in a telescoped facet where change of level of facet occurs.

पैलू युक्ती (चिन्हांकन तल) – **facet device (notational plane)** - device of prefixing a connecting symbol to an isolate number within a class number in order to implement the facet device of the idea plane.

पैलू युक्ती (विचार तळ) – **facet device (idea plane)** - device for sharpening a host focus in the form of a class by the addition of new facet.

पैलू विश्लेषण – **facet analysis** - analysis of a subject into its facets according to the postulates and principles stated for the the purpose.

पैलू संबंध – **facet relation** - relation between different aspects of a subject e.g. substances, properties, reactions etc. in the subject chemistry.

पैलू संश्लेषण – **facet synthesis** - synthesis of the focal number of a subject according to postulates and principles stated for the purpose.

पैलू सूत्र – **facet formula** - a formula used to group characteristics on a desired plan to achieve the sequence of various facets.

पैलू - **facet** - the totality of the isolate, each one of which can itself be attached to a specified basic class or a class derived from it. It is enumerated together in a schedule as possible manifestation of a particular fundamental category in a specified level of a specific round or generic name for a basic class. An isolate of a subject, or group of divisions when a subject is divided on the basis of single characteristic.

पैलूदर्शक चिन्ह – **facet indicator** - a symbol connecting notation of two facets. Also known as 'connecting symbol.'

पैलूबद्ध वर्गीकरण – **faceted classification** - 1) scheme of classification which reflects in its structure, the analysis of subject according to a number of fundamental concepts (PMEST)
2) a classification scheme based on fundamental concept of facet formula provided by Dr. S.R. Ranganathan.

पॅरीस तत्त्व – **Paris principles** - (cataloguing) the twelve principles on which an author/title entry should be based. Named in the International Conference on Cataloguing Principles (ICCP) at which they were drawn up, was held in Paris in October, 1961.

पोच स्थळ/गंतव्य – **destination** - it is the final point in the information chain. It is the intended target of the message.

पॉप्सी – **POPSI** - the abbreviation for postulate based permuted subject indexing. It was developed by the Documentation Research & Training Centre, Bangalore.

प्रकाशक – **publisher** - a person / firm / corporate body responsible for the publication of a document.

प्रकाशकीय चकती – **optical disc** - a type of video disk storage device consisting of a pressed disk with spiral groove at the bottom of which are sub-micro meter sized depression that are sensed by laser beam.

प्रकाशन तंतू – **optical fibres** - a thin glass or plastic fibre used to carry data in the form of lightwaves.

प्रकाशन तालिका – **publisher's catalogue** - list of books prepared by a publisher for the publications available with him. It may be for own publications or for his collections.

प्रकाशन दिनांक – **publication date** - see 'date of publication.'

प्रकाशन दिवस – **publication day** - the day of the week or month on which a periodical is issued. The first day on which a book may be sold to the public.

प्रकाशन पूर्व तालिकाकरण – **pre-natal cataloguing** - see 'cataloguing in source'.

प्रकाशन पूर्व – **pre-natal** - the technical processing of a document done before its publication. The idea was first coined by Dr. S.R. Ranganathan.

प्रकाशन वर्ष – **year of publication** - 1) the year in which a book was published. 2) year in which a book is published.

प्रकाशन विभाग – **publication division** - separate department of an enterprize, government etc. responsible for publishing.

प्रकाशन – **publication** - action of making a book or periodical available to the public action of making something known to the public.

प्रकाशनवृत्त - **imprint** - the statement in a book concerning the publication or printing of a book. Also called 'Biblio'. The publisher's imprint means the name of the publisher, date and place of publications. It usually appears at the bottom of the title page, and sometimes more completely on its back.

प्रकाशित मूल्य – **published price** - the retail sale price indicated on a book.

प्रक्रिया/उपस्कार – **process** - activities carried out an each document possessed by the library which include actions such as labelling and giving marks of ownership.

प्रक्रियारहित ग्रंथ – **unprocessed books** - पहा– 'पंजीकृत नसलेला ग्रंथ.'

प्रक्षेपक - **overhead projector** - equipment used to project the things in focused manner.

प्रक्षेपण करणे – **projection** - process of projecting / broadcasting.

प्रक्षेपण/प्रवर्धक/प्रक्षेप – **projection** - the method used by cartographer for representing on a plane the whole, or vertical part of the earth's surface which is not flat.

प्रगणन/मोजणी/गणती युक्ती - **enumeration device** - device of using successive digits for forming the classes or the isolates in facet or the array, isolate in an array by directly enumerating them.

प्रगणन/मोजणी/गणती - **enumeration** - list of subject of past, present and anticipated future.

प्रगणनात्मक वर्गीकरण – **enumerative classification** - a classification which identifies all possible classes and lists them after assigning notation.

प्रगतीचे आढावे – **review of progress** - an account of researches & their results carried out in recent past.

प्रचलित अंक (संख्या) – **current number** - the last published number /issue of a publication.

प्रचलित अनुक्रमणिका – **current content** - it is a kind of reference service in which current contents of the works are provided to the specialist users.

प्रचलित ग्रंथसूची – **current bibliography** - a bibliography compiled for the recently published books.

प्रचलित जागरूकता सेवा – **CAS (current awareness service)** - service to keep specialist users abreast about additions in areas of their interest.

प्रचलित जागरूकता सेवा – **current awareness service** - service rendered by a library to keep abreast with current developments/advances through recent literature.

प्रचलित जागरूकता – **current awareness** -
1) selectively cites relevant literature of high quality.
ii) alerts users on new developments and trends.
iii) avoids repetition & duplication of research report.

प्रचलित निर्देशिका (मार्गदर्शिका) – **current directory** - directory which contains the information of current nature.

प्रचलित परीक्षण(समीक्षा) – **current review** - the latest reviews which are used to evaluate the contribution.

प्रचलित माहिती – **current information** - an information of immediate value.

प्रचलित यादी – **current list** - a list providing information about acquistions of a library.

प्रचलित विषय संग्रह – **topical collection** - collection dealing with topics of the day of current or local interest.

प्रचालन पद्धती – **operating system** - while computing a software programming package this controls the operation of user programmes.

प्रचालन संशोधन – **operations research** - it is the application of mathematical models that permits comparisons of alternative courses of actions and the determination of the course that will bring maximum results.

प्रच्छाया/भूच्छाया – **umbra** - dark central part of the shadow cast by the earth or the moon during an eclipse. The concept is used in classification scheme to arrange the subject in proper sequence.

प्रणाली आज्ञावली – **system software** - a set of programmes usually supplied readymade, by the computer manufacturer with the intention of making the computer easier to use.

प्रणाली/संप्रदाय/शाळा – **school** - an institution for teaching a particular discipline where group of subjects is taught under one umbrella.

प्रत संख्या – **copy number** - number of a copy of a document of which there are two or more copies, individualizing the said copy.

प्रत संपादन – **copy editing** - placing instructions in code language or signs on the manuscript for the printer, indication of typeface, italics, capitalization, order and relative importance of headings, etc.

प्रत/प्रतिकृती/प्रतिलिपी/नक्कल - **copy** - a single document or a duplicate copy of a document or unchanged transfer of data from original sources to another place for use.

प्रतवारी – **gradation** - any of the stages or steps into which something is divided.

प्रतिआभास तंत्र – **simulation techniques** - techniques which have false resemblance, as through imitation.

प्रतिक्षा यादी – **waiting list** - a list prepared to fix up priority of users for a document in circulation.

प्रतिनिधी मंडळ – **delegation** - group of people deputed by an institution or government which represents it and participate as its official representation.

प्रतिनिधी संस्था – **agency** - it may be an individual or a firm.

प्रतिनिधी - **agent** - an individual or a firm which is used to arrange library collections and other equipments.

प्रतिप्रासी पद्धत/व्यवस्था – **retrieval system** - a sequence of actions which results in obtaining (retrieving) required information. The system requires such components as a selector which enables the information to be identified in the store.

प्रतिप्रासी बिंदू/केंद्र – **access point** - unique heading or a term, name, phase, word or group of words under which a user is expected to search library collections to locate required information.

प्रतिप्रासी वेळ – **access time** - time taken by user from selection of data / information till obtaining the document required.

प्रतिप्रासी – **access** : process used for approaching the information method by which a document is searched, either manually or through computer, process of retrieving or locating information.

प्रतिप्राप्ती/पुन –प्राप्ती - **retrieval** - an act for locating information.

प्रतिभास पद्धती (गणितशास्त्रावर आधारित) – **linear programming** - in mathematics, a procedure for minimizing or maximizing a linear function of many variables, subject to a finite number of linear restrictions on these variables.

प्रतिरुप मुद्रण – **offset printing** - processing where impression from the plate is taken indirectly through rubber blanket.

प्रतिरुप लेखन – **reprography** - the reproduction in facsimile of documents of all kinds by any process using light, heat or electric variation photo-copier, micro copies, blue printer, electro-copies, thermo-copies etc.

प्रतिरुप – **copy** - an identical production.

प्रतिरुप – **facsimile / fax** - a system of communication in which a transmitter scans a photograph, map or other fixed graphic material and converts the information into signal waves for transmission by wire or radio to a facsimile receiver at remote point.

प्रतिरुपलेखन सेवा - **reprography service** - service which provides photocopy of the document.

प्रतिरुपलेखन – **reprography** - an art of reproduction of the documents.

प्रतिलिपी तंत्र – **duplicating technique** - technique for making exact copies of a letter, photograph, drawing etc.

प्रतिलिपीकरण - **duplication** - a process of obtaining number of copies from the original.

प्रतिलिपीकारक – **duplicator** - a machine used to obtain multiple copies of the original.

प्रतिलिपीकृत ग्रंथ – **photocopied book** - a copy of the book obtained by using photocopier.

प्रतिवर्तित प्रत पद्धत – **reflex copying method** - a process for reproducing photographic copies of document which are opaque or printed on both sides.

प्रतिवस्तू – **dummy** - a substitute to the original. It is generally prepared to publish a work.

प्रतिशब्द – **synonyms** - the words/names having similar meaning.

प्रतिष्ठान – **corporate body** - a group of individuals associated together as an organised unit with common objectives.

प्रतिष्ठान/संयुक्त सामुदायिक नोंद - **corporate entry** - an entry which is rendered under a corporate body.

प्रतिष्ठान/संयुक्त सामुदायिक लेखक - corporate author - corporate authorship is an effort where group of persons is identified by a particular common name and considered as author in a catalogue entry. The authorship lies with institution or other such body.

प्रतिसाद/पुनर्निवेश - feed back - it is a process of arranging relevant information. response : the behaviour and reactions of users to a piece of technical writing.

प्रतिसादात्मक सेवा – responsive service - 1) service rendered by the computer to answer a search question. This may vary according to the complexity of the search & the total no. of users accessing the system at any one time.
2) service which offers answering, replying, responding.

प्रतिसादात्मक/प्रतियोगी सेवा – responsive services - reference and information services given on request to individuals.

प्रत्यक्ष कर – direct tax - tax collected by government on salary, goods etc. The direct tax is on income as distinct from tax levied on goods and services.

प्रत्यक्ष किंमती – direct costs - the costs which can be directly assigned to a particular activity, service or product.

प्रत्याभरण – feedback - 1) the act of using the output from a system as part of input to the system to achieve a greater operational efficiency in the performance of the system.
2) opinion received from the participants regarding effectiveness of system.

प्रत्यावाहन – recall - to retrieve from a store of information all that is pertinent to a query.

प्रत्येक ग्रंथास वाचक - every book its reader - it is third law of library science which demands that every collection should be effective and in helpful sequence to put in intensive use.

प्रत्येक वाचकास ग्रंथ - every reader his / her book - it is the second law of library science cited by Dr. S.R.Ranganathan. The law demands that variety of books should be acquired to satisfy the various demonds of the users.

प्रदर्शन ग्रंथांचे – exhibition - public display of items in an art gallery or museum. see also 'book exhibition.'

प्रदर्शन पेट्या – show cases - cases with a glass top or sides for displaying books, periodicals etc. in a library.

प्रबंध – thesis - dissertation; a long piece of written work involving personal research on a particular topic.

प्रबंधिका/व्याप्तीलेख – monograph - a scholarly publication dealing with a single subject.

प्रबोधक – **monitor** - display electronic device which may be in black and white or in colour.

प्रभावी विषयांग - **influencing phase** - phase II of a complex array isolate as the case may be in which the phase relation is influencing relation.

प्रमाण आकार – **standard size card** - a card of commonly accepted size like catalogue card usually of 5" x 3" used in all libraries.

प्रमाण उपविभाग – **standard subdivision** - subdivisions which are used to form characteristic of the document, and are joined to the main class numbers.

प्रमाण ग्रंथ – **standard book** - the publication having permanent value.

प्रमाण प्रारूप (आराखडा) - **standard format** - organised information on accepted guidelines.

प्रमाण प्रारूप – **standard format** - recognized and accepted organisation of bibliographic data of a document.

प्रमाण रचना – **standard work** - see 'standard book.'

प्रमाण विचलन – **standard deviation** - the positive square root of the variance.

प्रमाण/साक्ष – **testimony** - a written or spoken statement.

प्रमाण/मानक – **standard** - 1) publications which provide specifications / standards to achieve uniformity.
2) model, guide or pattern for guidance.

प्रमाणक नियम – **normative rule** - explaining, stating or using obedience to a rule.

प्रमाणक – **norm** - standard or pattern that is typical (of a group etc.)

प्रमाणके - **matrix** - the mould from which a stereotype (stereo) or electrotype (electro) is made.

प्रमाणित प्रत – **standard copy** - a copy evolved after observing guidelines available on the subject.

प्रमाणीकरण/मानकीकरण – **standardisation** - standards for exchange of bibliographical and other types of information.

प्रमाणीकरण - **standardization** - action or process of standardizing making regular.

प्रमुख वैशिष्ट्ये – **salient features** - most noticeable or important main points.

प्रयोगशाळा टिपणे – **laboratory notes** - notes of / or performed in, or as in, a laboratory.

प्रयोजक गृहीतक – **causal hypothesis** - assumption about cause effect relationship between two variables.

प्रलेख पुरवठा – **document supply** - see 'document delivery service.'

प्रलेख प्राप्ती सेवा – **document procurement service** - service in which photo copies of the documents are obtained and made available to the user.

प्रलेख रूपरेखा – **document profile** - 1) a file of machine readable bibliographic records which could be searched with reference to specific criteria laid down by the users of the system.
2) machine readable bibliographic record.

प्रलेख वितरण/सेवा प्रदान – **document delivery service** - 1) a service which arranges document / information at the user's place.
2) the process of providing relevant documents on a specified subject.

प्रलेख वितरण – **document delivery** - the process of providing relevant documents on a specified subject.

प्रलेख प्रदान/वितरण – **document delivery** - this system enables users to order copies of materials retrieved by online searches either by direct dospatch of item by the host or via an agent.

प्रलेख – **document** - the document is the record of knowledge / information which may be in print or non-print form. In computer, a non-book medium that contains stored information for further use.

प्रलेखक – **documentalist** - an officer responsible for the documentation work so as to facilitate dissemination of information to specialist reader.

प्रलेखन कार्य – **documentation work** - method of preparing lists, abstracts etc.

प्रलेखन केंद्र – **documentation centre** - it is an organisation engaged in collecting, evaluating, organisating and repackaging of information for quick retrieval on demand. It generates publications such as abstracts, indexes, annotations lists etc.

प्रलेखन यादी – **documentation list** - list of documents prepared for a specific purpose. The purpose is usually to bring the reader close to exhaustive / select list of document relevant to his enquiry / study. This term is used to emphasis the inclusion of micro document in listing.

प्रलेखन विज्ञान - **documentation science** - it is a science of controlling the enormous growth of information and generating secondary sources.

प्रलेखन संशोधन आणि प्रशिक्षण केंद्र – **DRTC (documentation research & training centre)** - the centre is situated at Bangalore and engaged in the advanced research and training in the field of library & information science. (Est. 1962).

प्रलेखन सेवा – **documentation service** - service through which abstracting, indexing etc. is provided to the users.

प्रलेखन – **documentation** - collection, organisation of recorded information exhaustively, expeditiously and pin-pointed for use of the researchers.

प्रलेखविरहित माहितीस्रोत/साधने – **non-documentary sources of information** - information sources such as oral, technology based database etc.

प्रवर्ग – **category** - a fundamental concept to group knowledge in desired manner. See also 'facet'.

प्रवर्तन/विगमन – **induction** - introduction to the job or an organisation.

प्रवर्तना/अभिप्रेरणा/प्रबलन – **motivations** - the willingness to put forth efforts in the pursuit of goals.

प्रवासी मार्गदर्शक ग्रंथ – **travel guide book** - a booklet consisting information on places, accommodation and transport facilities of tourist interest.

प्रवाह आकृती – **flow diagram** - a flow diagram is a graphic view of a work area upon which the path or movement of worker or the flow of materials is superimposed.

प्रवाह प्रक्रिया तक्ता – **flow / process chart** - it is a graphic means of representing diagra maticaly the work involved in a job where the person or process charted moves from place to place.

प्रवृत्ती अहवाल – **trend report** - gives an account of the general direction of research. It is based on a review of the documents on current developments.

प्रवेश अभिलेख (नोंद) – **admission record** - पहा– 'प्रवेश पत्र.'

प्रवेश केंद्र – **access point / centre** - identified unique heading or a term, name, phrase, word or group of words under which user of the library searches library collection to find out required information.

प्रवेश चिठ्ठी – **admission slip** - पहा– 'प्रवेश पत्र.'

प्रवेश पत्र – **admission card** - it is a card or letter to use library or to get library membership. It is an introductory card / letter issued by competent authority after observing security. The card can be used to borrow library documents for a given period.

प्रवेश बिंदू – **access** - points of approach to information.

प्रवेश बिंदू – **access point** - a term, name or phrase etc. used at the head of a catalogue entry by means of which a document is searched or identified.

प्रवेश वेळ – **access time** - time taken between transfer and selection of data /information from computer programmed data block.

प्रवेश – **entry/access** - process of approaching information or method by which a library document is searched. In computer, it is a process of retrieving or locating information.

प्रवेशद्वार नोंदवही – **gate register/entrance register/visitor register** - entrance register in which persons coming to a library, institution have to give their details.

प्रवेशद्वाराचा मार्ग – **gateway** - 1) a facility which allows the searcher online to online service or to connect it to another online service.
2) interface which automatically dials the telephone and connects the user to the online service.

प्रवेशिका/उपकक्ष – **lobby** - porch, entrance hall or ante-room.

प्रशंसाप्रत/पूरक प्रत – **complimentary copy** - a copy received without payment which may be for publicity or to get the work evaluated.

प्रशासकीय इमारत/वास्तू – **administrative building** - a building of an institution where administrative works are carried out.

प्रशासकीय कार्यालय – **administrative office** - the office which works to implement the policies to achieve the set goals of service.

प्रशासकीय व्यवस्थापन – **administrative management** - this approach seeks to systematically study the management process. Functions that managers perform and effective principles of management have been developed, through such process.

प्रशासन/व्यवस्थापन/कारभार - **administration** - management of public or business affairs.

प्रशिक्षण आणि विकास – **training and development** - a process in which personnel in an organization is deliberately offered, to enable him to absorb some perspectives, understanding, value, attitude, technique or skill with reference to an organization. Development is a method of preparing person to perform work, to accept responsibilities far greater than he presently has.

प्रशिक्षणार्थी - **trainee** - an individual who undergoes training.

प्रशिक्षण – **training** - programme of teaching for practical services.

प्रशिक्षित – **trained** - an individual who has received training.

प्रश्नावली – **questionnaire** - written or printed list of questions to be answered by a number of people, especially to collect information as part of a survey.

प्रश्नावली खुली – **open questionnaire** - series/ list of questions which requires respondents to ensure in their own words.

प्रश्नावली चित्रमय – **pictorial questionnaire** - series of questions using pictures.

प्रश्नावली टपाली – **mailed questionnaire** - quesionnaire which has been mailed by post / courier to obtain response.

प्रश्नावली बंदिस्त – **closed questionnaire** - these are the fixed - choice questions. They require the respondent to choose a response from probable answers provided by the searcher.

प्रसंभाव्य प्रक्रिया – **stonchastic process** - a system which produces a seqeunce of discrete symbols according to certain probabilities e.g. the sequence of letters which makes up a passage of printed English.

प्रसारमाध्यम संप्रेषण – **mass communication** - communication that is produced for the masses. Such as newspapers, radio/ television broadcasting etc.

प्रसारमाध्यम – **media** - 1) channels used for transmission of message e.g. print, sound or vision.
2) the physical media that carries messages or contents of information.

प्रसारमाध्यमातील व्यक्ती – **media person** - specialists & experts of different categories functioning & operating in mass communication.

प्रसिद्धी–पूर्व – **pre-natal** - before publication; the context of cataloguing before the distribution of a publication; the term is used for processing of documents (classification & cataloguing) before actual publication.

प्रस्ताव/योजना – **proposal** - technical writing that deals with a formal offer of undertaking any activity.

प्रस्तावना दिनांक – **preface date** - the date given at the end of the preface.

प्रस्तावना – **preface** - author's statement in a document about purpose/method used for its development.

प्रस्तावना/विषयप्रवेश/भूमिका – **introduction** - preliminary writing in work to introduce the subject, method and sources used.

प्रस्तावित देयक – **invoice** - list of proposed items together with price to be charged.

प्रात्यक्षिक – **practical** - concerned with practice/action rather than theory.

प्राथमिक शाळा ग्रंथालय – **primary school library** - the library which is maintained by the primary school to support studies of the students and also to develop interest in books during their future studies.

प्राथमिक संज्ञा – **primary term** - a term figuring in the source article title appearing as the main entry in the premature subject index.

प्राथमिक नियतकालिक/मासिक – **primary periodical** - a periodical which publishes papers or reports containing original research information so far not published elsewhere.

प्राथमिक प्रलेख – **primary document** - that which contains original information or the first formulation of any new observation, experiment, idea etc.

प्राथमिक माहिती साधने – **primary document sources** - a basic document source containing first hand original information / basic information on a topic.

प्राथमिक स्रोत – **primary sources** - original manuscripts, contemporary records; or documents which are used by an author while writing a book or other literary compilation.

प्राथमिक/मूलगामी नियतकालिक पत्रिका - **primary periodical/ journal** - a periodical journal, that covers unpublished research report / papers on recent thoughts.

प्रादेशिक ग्रंथालय – **regional library** - a library providing service to specific region. It has larger size and greater resources, hence supplies information to smaller libraries in a large country or urban system, as well as serving the individuals.

प्रादेशिक आणि आंतरराष्ट्रीय – **regional and international cooperation** - co-operation among countries in specific geographical areas.

प्राधिकरण/अधिकार फलक - **authority hoarding** - board displaying the powers of a person or of an authority.

प्राधिकरण/प्राधिकारी निर्णयाची संचिका – **authority file** - authentic record . A file wherein the decisions about minor changes or office procedure is recorded.

प्राधिकरण/प्राधिकारी – **authority** - person or group having the power to give orders or take action.

प्राप्ती प्रेरणा/प्रवर्तना/विक्रम – **achievement motivation** - linked by MC cell and with the entrepreneurial spirit needed to take risks and develop a country's economic resources. People with a high need for achievement like to take responsibility for their own actions, engage in moderate risk taking, and receive feedback concerning their performance.

प्रारूप/रूप नोंद - **form entry** - an entry in a catalogue under; (1) the name of the form in which a book is written e.g. poetry, drama, fiction or (2) the form in which the subject material is presented, e.g. periodicals.

प्रारूप - **format** - a specific designator for a form of material, for example sound cassette, microfiche, video disc.

प्रावकल्पना/प्राकथन - **hypothesis** - idea or suggestion that is based on known facts. It is used as a basis for reasoning of further investigation.

प्रावस्था संबंध - **phase relation** - relation between the phases of a complex array isolate.

प्रेसिस - **PRECIS** - the abbreviation for preserved context index system. It was developed by Derek Austin for use in the British National Bibliography.

फ

फलक – **board** - face, plate.

फलज्योतिष – **astrology** - the science or doctrine of the stars, formerly often used as equivalent to astronomy, but now restricted in meaning to the pseudo science which claims to foretell the future by studying the supposed influence of the relative positions of the moon, sun and stars on human affairs.

फलप्रामाण्य – **pragmatic** - dealing with matters in the way that seems best under the actual conditions, rather than following a general principle, practical.

फसवणूक/लबाडी – **deception** - the act or state of being deceived or mislead.

फाईल – **file** - it is an organized named collection of information for some particular purpose, or a collection of related records as one unit.

फिनिक्स अनुसूची – **phoenix schedules** - a completely new development of the schedule for a specific discipline. Unless by chance only the basic number for the discipline remains the same as in earlier editions, all other numbers being freely reused.

फिरते ग्रंथालय – **mobile library** - library on wheels which gives door to door services.

फिल्ड (क्षेत्र)/स्थान – **field** - 1) in a computer programme, format the space provided to keep a block of information data/information group in a record. In cataloguing, a set of columns in a card fixed as to enter. The total area of the card available for information storage.
2) **field** - a subdivision of a record that holds on a piece of data about a transaction.

फिल्ड (क्षेत्र) स्थान चित्र – **field chart** - layout of the data showing the field programme.

फिल्ड (क्षेत्र) स्थान डेटा – **field data** - data generated from the field to plot.

फीत – **tape** - a transparent chemical coated thin ribbon used to keep document intact; or magnetic coated electronic media strip on which information is stored.

फुगवटा – **inflation** - an increase in the amount of currency in circulation, resulting in a relatively sharp and sudden fall in its value and rise in prices; it may be caused by an increase in the volume of paper money issued or of gold mined, or a relative increase in expenditures, as when the supply of goods fails to meet the demand.

फेर तपासणी – **revision** - the act, process or work of revising; review; reexamination for correction ; as, the revision of a book or of a proof sheet; a revision of statutes. The result of revising; a revised form or version, as of a book, manuscript, etc.

फोरट्रन – **FORTRAN (formula translator)** - 1) computer used programming language developed by IBM Corporation widely accepted for commercial mathematical computations. 2) a acronym for FORmula TRANslator, a programming language designed for writing problems, solving programmes that can be stated as arithmetic procedures.

फ्लो चार्ट – **flow-chart** - a graphical or textual representation of the programme showing step by step activities.

फ्लॉपी डिस्क – **floppy disc** - magnetic flexible disc used for digital memory in a computer.

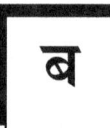

ब

बंदिस्त पद्धती – **closed system -** library, where users are not allowed to enter in the stock room.

बंदिस्त प्रवेश – **closed access -** access to the book shelves is not permitted for users. Required books are brought at counter from the shelves by the library staff.

बंदिस्त वर्गीकरण – **closed classification -** arrangement of subject in a classification scheme in minute sub-divisions under inclusive divisions.

बंधन – **binding / obligation -** compulsory fact - action.

बक्रम – **buckram -** stiff cloth used especially for binding of books.

बग – **bug -** 1) a flow in a program (from the expression "working the bugs out") Also, defined as an undocumented feature in fun. 2) an error. A hardware bug is physical or electrical malfunc or design error; a software bug is an error in programming either in the logic of the program or in typing.

बग्ग – **bugg -** said of software, unstable, unreliable, full of bugs.

बदललेले नांव – **changed name -** when an author contributes under various adopted names then for all such names, a note is made in cataloguing.

बदललेले शीर्षक टिप्पण – **change of title note -** a note mentioning the alternative title, if any, under which the work may have appeared earlier.

बदलेले अभिलेख/नोंद – **changed record** - it is master record in which amendments are incorporated as and when released.

बदलेले शीर्षक - **changed title** - a different title than the title appered in the previous edition.

बनावट कागदपत्र/दस्तऐवज – **forged document** - false, untrue, illegal documents.

बहिस्थ संस्थापत्रिका – **external house journal** - periodical published by institution meant for the external public like the share holders, customer, etc.

बहुकेंद्रीय कार्य – **multi / focal work** - document treating several collateral subjects not having a common universe of the first one according to the preferred scheme of classes.

बहुखंडात्मक ग्रंथ – **multivolumed / voluminous book** - a book which contains many volumes, giving a continuous exposition of the subject, treating all the volumes in separable set. The total set may have a general title and continued pagination even.

बहुजन माध्यम – **mass medium** - medium applicable in large quantities.

बहुजन शिक्षण – **mass education** - edcuation applicable to masses at large quantity.

बहुपैलूक – **multi-faceted** - document having many angles of study.

बहुप्रसार माध्यम – **multimedia** - seamless integration of text, image & sound in a digital information environment. The word is used for the different media operating independently.

बहुभाषिक – **multi-lingual** - speaking or using many languages/written or printed in many languages.

बहुभाषिक – **polygot** - person having multilingual knowledge, using and writing in many languages.

बहुरुपदर्शक/बहुमूर्तीदर्शक – **kaleidoscopic** - a thing which constanlty shifts or changes.

बहुरूपदर्शी/बहुमूर्तीदर्शी – **kaleidoscopic** - chain patterns as a kaleidoscope which is an optical instrument in which bits of glasses, beads, etc. are held loosely at the end of a rotating tube show continuously changing symmetrical forms by reflection in two or more mirrors set at angles to each other. When a person passesses a quality of using different languages easily, this term is used.

बहुसमावेशक ग्रंथसूची – **comprehensive bibliography** - list of as far as possible everything published on the subject.

बहुसमावेशक/सर्वमावेशक निर्देशन पद्धत – **comprehensive indexing system** - indexing system including all index terms, related terms etc.

बहुसमावेशक/सर्वमावेशक बाजार खंडीकरण/खंडीभवन – **market segmentation** - is the act of dividing a market into meaningful parts or segments. Members of a particular segment are alike and different from members of other segments.

बहुसमावेशक/सर्वमावेशक संग्रह – **comprehensive collection** - to have almost all documents on a given subject.

बहुसमावेशक/सर्वसमावेशक – **comprehensive** - one that includes almost everything about the topic covered.

बाँझशिल्प – **bronze statue** - anything, as a work of art, made of bronze.

बांधणी अभिलेख/नोंद – **binding record** - record maintained to take up binding work which may be in the form of cards or register.

बांधणी किनारा – **binding edge** - the edge of the document used to attach in binding.

बांधणी चिठ्ठी – **binding slip** - slip used for keeping records / information of individual volume to be bound.

बांधणी विभाग – **binding department / section** - a place where books are bound.

बांधणी – **binding** - the protection cover of the volume. The process of reinforcement of a document to increase its use.

बांधणीकार – **binder** - a person who carries binding work of documents.

बांधणीकाराचा फलक – **binder's board** - a general term for pulped materials pressed into stiff, flat, smooth sheets of various thicknesses, used over the cover of a book, under the cover of a book, under the cloth, leather or any other material. Also called Book Board, or simply Board.

बांधिलकी/कार्यनिष्ठा – **commitment** - to something / to do something for which one has promised to pledge undertaking.

बांधीव आवृत्ती – **bound edition** - the binding of an edition or a number of copies of the same book in identical style, usually by mass production methods and in relatively large quantities as opposed to hand binding or utility binding.

बाइट – **byte** - 1) a byte is one character of data which is operated as a unit, generally it consists 8 bits to represent one unit. 2) a basic unit of measure of a computer's memory. A byte usually comprises of eight bits, and therefore its value can be from 0 to 256. Each character can be represented by one byte in ASCII.

बाजारभाव – **market price** - the price for which the item is sold in market; the prevailing price.

बाजारमिश्र – **market mix** - it is the combination of produce design, pricing, communication and distribution.

बातमी पत्रक – **news letter** - a report of current happenings issued regularly at some fixed interval. The news covered in such publication remains very brief and generally first hand.

बातमी /वर्तमानपत्र प्रदर्शक – **newspaper stand** - a stand used to display newspaper.

बातमीपत्र – **news bulletin** - a digest of current news which is to be generalized.

बातमीपत्र /वर्तमानपत्र - **newspaper** - a carrier of news of current events. It generally covers almost all areas of the society.

बातम्या – **news** - piece of current information / new information / fresh event.

बातम्याचे कात्रण – **news clipping** - news taken from newspaper for sorting current reported event.

बालवाङ्मय – **children's literature** - literature designed for an audience generally of elementary school age.

बाह्य वाचक – **external reader** - a person who is not a regular member of the library but makes use of library collections as a casual user.

बाह्य /बाहेरचा – **extrinsic** (of qualities, values etc.) not belonging to or part of the real nature of a person or thing coming from outside.

बाह्यपरिघीय – **peripheral** - adjustment to the purview of a subject or any hardware device connected to a computer system.

बिंदुपथ विभाग – **locus section** - section giving information on the location of a microdocuments which is called the host documents.

बिजागर – **hinge** - the flexible part of the binding material (leather, cloth, rexine or paper) on which the book opens, also called 'joints'.

बिट – **bit** - 1) a single unit of word in machine language or the basic element for representing data in computer or a single binary digit. 2) a binary digit-the smallest amount of information a computer can hold. A single bit specifies a single value of 0 or 1, bits can be grouped to form larger values (see byte).

बिनधुवट – **bleach** - (cause something to) become white or pale (by chemical action or sunlight)

बी.एल.आय.एस्सी. – **B.L.I.Sc. (Bachelor in Library & Information Science)** - graduate level degree in library and information science education.

बीजगणिती उपगट - **algebraic sub-grouping.**

बुद्धिजीवी मानव – **human intellectual** - skills of variety necessary for all-round development of human being.

बुद्धिमत्ता – **intelligence** - the ability to learn or understand from experience; ability to acquire and retain knowledge; mental ability.

बुरशी आलेला – **mould** - fine furry growth of fungi that forms on old food or on object left in moist air.

बुरशी/कवक – **fungus** - plant of simple structure, lacking chlorophyll, has no root, stem or leaf and reproduces by spores, e.g. moulds toad-stools, bacteria and yeast.

बुरशीनाशक – **fungicides** - chemical substance that kills fungus.

बुलियन प्रचारक – **Boolean operators :** the operators AND, OR, NOT which are used to link two or more concepts in a retrieval system.

बुलीयन शोध – **Boolean searches** - a device for searching relevant information / items in a database combining any searchable field using the Boolean operators AND, OR, NOT. This device is used either to contract or expand a search.

बेकन वर्गीकरण – **Bacon classification** - scheme of classes implied in advancement learning (1605 B.C.) of Francis Bacon.

बेटल – **bettle** - a kind of book worm.

बेबाकी/नादेय प्रमाणपत्र - **no dues certificate** - certificate issued to a reader stating therein that he does not owe any dues to a library.

बेसिक – **BASIC (beginners all purpose symbolic instruction code)** - 1) widely used computer programming language developed by an American, John G. Kemeny in 1964 and popular for its simplicity.
2) an acronym for beginner's all purpose symbolic instruction code. It is a common-easy-to learn computer programming language. The advanced version of BASIC is called BASIC-A.

बोध/बोधन/ज्ञान – **cognition** - the mental process by which knowledge is acquired by the mind.

बोधक संघ – **monitoring team** - it refers to experts from outside the organization specially selected for guiding, monitoring and controlling certain activities or process.

बोधकथा - fable, parable - a fictitious narrative intended to teach some moral truth or perception in which animals and sometimes inanimate objects are represented as spackers and actors.

बोधचिन्ह – emblem - formerly, a picture with a motto or verses, allegorically suggesting some moral truth.

बोधनिक/बोधीय आवड – cognitive interest - interest knowing empirical factual knowledge.

बोधांक/मागणी अंक उपविभाग – call number section - the section of an entry stating the call number of its document.

बोधांक/मागणी अंक नोंद – call number entry - catalogue entry starting with call number as leading section. In classified catalogue code it is regarded as main entry.

बोधांक/मागणी अंक – call number - the ordinal number which fixes the relative position of a document in a library. It comprises of class number, book number and collection number.

बोली/पोटभाषा – dialect - a variety of a language spoken in one part of a country, which is different in some words, grammar or pronunciation from other forms of the same language.

बोलीभाषा – dialect - 1) any language as part of a larger group or family of languages. In linguistics the form or variety of a spoken language peculiar to a region, community, social group or occupational group : in this sense, dialects are regarded as being to some degree, mutually intelligible while languages are mutually unintelligible.

बौद्धिकक्षमता – academic aptitude - aptitude of or belonging to a learned society.

बौद्धिक स्वातंत्र्य – academic freedom - freedom of or belonging to a learned society.

बॉन्ड कागद – bond paper - a strong, superior quality of paper with smooth surface but tough in nature, used for letterheads, legal documents etc.

ब्रिटिश ग्रंथालय – British Library - British Library is the national library of the United Kingdom. It is serving as the centre for scholarship, research and industry of the country.

ब्रिटिश राष्ट्रीय ग्रंथसूची – British National Bibliography (BNB) - it is a list of books published in Great Britain. The entries are available on international size cards. The list is compiled on the basis of publication received under copyright Act.

ब्रीद – motto - a word, phrase, or sentence inscribed on something, prefixed to a literary work, etc. as expressive of or appropriate to its character.

भग्नक्रम – **broken order** - when the order of chosen classification scheme is broken for arranging documents on shelves, to achieve more helpful sequence it is called 'broken order'.

भर घाला टीप – **add to note** - such notes are provided in classification scheme to direct, to divide a given class further on the pattern of another class available in classification schedule. As DDC has used term 'all divide like' at many places.

भरती – **recruitment** - the process by which an organization obtains the required manpower by carrying out stepwise process.

भवितव्य शास्त्रज्ञ – **futurologists** - a person who systematically forecasts further growth of institute based on present trends.

भविष्यवेत्ता – **futurologists** - specialists in forecasting. पहा : भवितव्य शास्त्रज्ञ

भांडवली अंदाजपत्रक – **capital budget** - budget indicating expenditure of non-recurring items.

भांडवली किंमत – **capital costs** - costs of items used over a long period.

भाग – **part** - portion or division of a whole.

भागधारक – **shareholders** - owner of shares in a business company.

भाडोत्री ग्रंथालय – **rental library** - where the services of library are charged with fee.

भारतीय ग्रंथालय संघ – ILA (Indian Library Association) - it was founded in 1933 as a national body. It is a registered society of library professionals and scholars. Its office is elected from the members by postal ballet system for two 'years' terms. It organizes seminars, conferences & workshops to debate on the issues of library science and service. It has publications like ILA newsletter and ILA bulletin to exchange the views of contributors.

भारतीय नाव – Indic / Indian name - the name that indicates person having Indian origin.

भारतीय प्रकाशन – Indian publication - publications brought out by Indian publishers.

भारतीय राष्ट्रीय ग्रंथसूची – INB (Indian National Bibliography) - a bibliography which lists all the books & other publications published in India.

भारतीय राष्ट्रीय वैज्ञानिक प्रलेखन केंद्र – (INSDOC) Indian National Scientific Documentation Centre - founded by the Govt. of India in 1952 to serve scientific community with bibliographical information support.

भावविस्थापन – displacement - a defining property of human language whereby language can be used to communicate about events removed in time of generation by a process of learning and not genetically.

भावी किमती – perspective pricing - setting price prior to the performance of the service.

भाषा अंक – language number - an ordinal number representing the notation of language of translation.

भाषा अभियांत्रिकी – language engineering - rearragment of concepts concerned with a language.

भाषा उपविभाग – language sub-division - sub division of a subject according to the language of the document as recorded in schedule of scheme.

भाषा तक्ता – languages table - an auxiliary table enlisting all the languages of the world grouped according to their families.

भाषा पैलू – language facet - part of the book number of a document which is its language number.

भाषा प्रक्रम – language processor - a programme or software that translates, interprets & performs other functions required for processing a particular programming language, requirements, specification language, design language etc.

भाषा भिन्नता – language variation - difference in linguistic behaviour due to change in region, social class, occupation, gender, etc.

भाषा वर्गीकरण – **language classification** - when the documents are scheduled according to the language of the document as characteristic.

भाषा – **language** - in computer, any set of symbols and rules governing interrelations between the symbols, which can be used to convey or represent information (DDPT) or a set of characters /rules used for meaningful communication.

भाषेचे भाषाशास्त्रीय घटकगुण – **linguistic features of language** - characteristics of words such as; phonetics (sounds), syntax (grammar) and lexis (vocabulary) of a language.

भाष्य/टीका – **commentary** - explanatory or critical note on a work.

भाष्यकार – **commentator** - a person who prepares commentary.

भित्ती चित्र सिद्धान्त – **wall picture principle** - if two facets A and B of a subject are such that the concept behind B will not be operative unless the concept behind 'A' is conceded. Even a mural picture is not possible unless the wall exists to draw upon then the facet 'A' should precede facet 'B.' This concept is used in preparation of schedules of classfication, in arrangement of subjects therein.

भित्ती चित्र/पत्रक – **poster** - a paper containing information that can be displayed on wall.

भिरकावणे तक्ते – **flip charts** - flip charts are widely used in industry. They are portable, require no special equipment, and do not require darkening the room. They allow spontaneity and one can easily use them for notes. They are not useful for large audience.

भूतलक्षी/पूर्वलक्षी ग्रंथसूची – **retrospective bibliography** - a bibliography which has current documents alongwith documents published during previous years as well.

भूतलक्षी/पूर्वलक्षी शोध – **retrospective search** - search that is carried out over the past period of time.

भूमीस्वरूपीय – **topographical** - a detailed mapping of the features of a relatively small area.

भेट प्रत – **complimentary copy** - a copy received without payment which may be for publicity or for its evaluation.

भेद विषयांग संबंध – **difference phase relation** - relation of phase indicating the condition of being different.

भेद विषयांग/प्रावस्था – **difference phase** - phase indicating the condition of being different.

भेददर्शक पैलू – **differential facet** - characteristics used for distinguishing purpose.

भौगोलिक स्थळ अंक – **geographical notation code** - geographical number, specified for a particular space in a scheme of classification.

भौगोलिक अंक – **geographical numbers** - numbers added to a classification symbol to arrange the books geographically, they are usually applicable throughout a classification scheme.

भौगोलिक क्षेत्र – **geographical area** - an area showing country, region in the class number.

भौगोलिक नोंद – **geographical entry** - the name given to catalogue entries for topographical books and geographical guides, which go under the name of the district to which they refer.

भौगोलिक पैलू – **geographical facet** - facet related to geographical aspect.

भौगोलिक भूखंड/संलग्नता – **geographical continuity** - the arrangement of places and physical features considering the location and its adjuscent area.

भौगोलिक युक्ती – **geographical device** - 1) A method of adding a notation to a class number to represent geographical area covered in a document.
2) device based on geographical (places and physical) features.

भौगोलिक लक्षण/साम्यगुण/वैशिष्टयगुण – **geographical characteristic** - characteristics used in classificiation scheme related to geography (places etc.)

भौगोलिक विभाग – **geographical division** - subdivision in a classification scheme as per country, region or locality.

भौगोलिक स्थानानुसार क्रमरचना – **geographical order** - arrangement of subjects based on geographical aspects.

भौतिकवादी/जडवादी संज्ञा – **mechanistic term** - mechanically determined routine procedure and technical details.

भ्रामक शीर्षक – **misleading / fanciful title** - the title which does not represent the subject covered in a document.

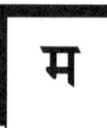

म

मजकूर संयोजन – **text composition** - a process of assembling the print matrices through movable types or key board operation.

मजकूर – **text** - any piece of writing which forms a whole.

मजबूत बांधणी/पुठ्ठा बांधणी – **hard bound** - a book which is published with stiff cover so as to increase its life. It is also called as 'library edition.'

मतैक्य – **consensus** - a general agreement; agreement in all aspect.

मधुरसा/सिंद्रक – **dextrine glue** - water soluble gum prepared with dextrine mixed with water and other materials.

मध्य/सरासरी – **mean** - also called arithmetic mean or average, it is expressed in terms of the following formula x = 1 fixi

मध्यक – **median** - the middle most observation in the series.

मध्यवर्ती ग्रंथालय – **central library** - the main monitoring library of the system or a library which has number of branch or departmental libraries.

मध्यवर्ती तालिका – **central catalogue** - a catalogue of the library system which has entries of the documents available even in extension or branch libraries.

मध्यवर्ती तालिकाकरण – **centralised cataloguing** - cataloguing of collection of group of libraries by a central agency to achieve uniformity.

मध्यवर्ती पंजीकरण – **centralized registration** - registration of library members at one place to use a library system.

मध्यवर्ती सोपस्कार विभाग – **central processing unit (CPU)** - primary data storage section of a computer which is regarded as a brain. It is a control unit which directs the sequence of operations. It receives and transfers data. Thus, it coordinates and controls data loading in first instance. It is a principle operating part of computer.

मध्यवर्ती सोपस्कार – **centralised processing** - a library staff unit works for purchase / acquisition/cataloguing/classification at one place to achieve economy and standardization in service.

मध्यवर्ती स्थान यादी – **central shelf list** - a shelf list developed for the holdings of the library.

मनोविकारतज्ञ – **psychiatrist** - a doctor trained in the study and treatment of diseases of the mind.

मर्यादांतर – **range** - the absolute difference between the highest value and the lowest value in a series of observations.

मर्यादित तालिकीकरण – **limited cataloguing** - implies reduction of bibliographical elements in an entry. Such treatment is given to documents which do not have sufficient bibliographic and reference utility.

मलपृष्ठ (ग्रंथाच्या वेष्टणाचे शेवटचे पान) – **fly-leaf** - last page of the wrapper or jacket of the document containing blurb or resume of the author.

मलपृष्ठावरील ग्रंथपरिचय - **blurb** - 1) jacket for hardbound books contain brief information about the book and its author. It provides a handy source for knowing the subject of the book.
2) description about a book published on jacket.

मसुदा/प्रारुप – **draft** - first level writing which undergoes modification and corrections.

महसूल जिल्हा – **revenue district** - the income from taxes, duties, etc. of a unit of government, as a district.

महसूल – **revenue** - income, especially total annual income of a state from taxes etc.

महाविद्यालय ग्रंथालय – **college library** - a library established, maintained and administered by a college to meet the needs of its students and faculty.

मागणी अंक – **call number** - notation used to identify and locate a book or document. It usually consists of the class number and the book number. It may also include a work number or a collection number also.

मागणी चिठ्ठी – demand slip - 1) slip used to ask for a document to be brought out form the stack room in the closed access system in library. 2) slip used to reserve a document issued out of a library.

मागणी पत्र – requisition card / slip - a card which is used to place demand for a document which is not available in a library.

मागणी शीर्षक – approach / access point - identified unique heading or a term, name, phrase, word or group of words under which a user of the library searches library collection to find out his or her information.

मागणी – demand - 1) reader's desire of readers for books or service they wish to issue or use. 2) the act of demanding, asking or seeking for what is due or claimed as due.

मागणीची लवचिकता - elasticity of demand - measuring the impact of change in price on the quantum of demand.

मातृक संघटन – metric organization - organization dealing with multiproducts or well defined projects, where the division of work and responsibility is organized on the basis of different products and projects.

मातृसंस्था – parent organization - main organization from which sister concerns are derived.

मानक आकार पत्र – standard size card - a card of commonly accepted size e.g. catalogue card of 5" x 3" is used in all libraries.

मानक ग्रंथ – standard book - published document having the contributions of permanent value.

मानक प्रत - standard copy - a copy evolved after observing guidelines available on the subject.

मानक प्रारूप – standard format - organization of information on accepted guidelines.

मानक – standard - the publication which provides specifications / details to achieve uniformity.

मानव संसाधने – human resources - human beings as carriers of information.

मानव–यंत्र तक्ते – man-machine charts - these are designed to analyze that work relationship between a man and one or more machines.

मानववंशीय/वंशीय/वंशदृष्ट्या – ethnic - related to a racial, national or tribal group.

मानवी संसाधने नियोजन – human resource planning - the process that helps organization to provide adequate human resources to achieve their current and future organizational objectives.

मानवी संसाधने विकास – **human resources development -** a process by which employees of an organization are helped to gain skills, competency in execution etc. and thereby achieve success through the involvement, commitment, motivation provided to give out the best etc.

मानवी संसाधने व्यवस्थापन – **human resource management -** a function performed in organization which facilitates effectiveness for the employees for the achieve organizational and individual goals.

मानवीय ज्ञान – **humanized knowledge -** devotion to studies which promotes knowledge of human culture, literary culture etc.

मानव्यविद्या – **humanities -** branch of knowledge which studies human nature, the condition of being a man or branches of learning concerned with human thought and relations, as distinguished from science; especially literature and philosophy and often fine arts, history etc.

मान्यता/ओळख – **recognition -** acceptance/approval for recognization or being recognized.

मापक्रम/मापप्रमाण – **scale -** the ratio of the distance on an architectural drawing map, globe model or vertical section, to the actual distances on earth surface they represent.

मापन – **scale -** series of marks used for measuring on a ruler, etc.

मार्क – **MARC (machine readable catalogue) -** 1) abbreviation for machine readable catalogue project. It was a piolet project started by Library of Congress in 1965. 2) abbreviation for machine readable catalogue project. A system, initially developed in the United States by the Library of Congress with the purpose of organizing and disseminating in machine readable form (and structured according to international cataloguing standards,) bibliographic data for incorporation into national and local records for the purpose of documentation.

मार्गदर्शक ग्रंथ – **guide book -** a handbook prepared for travellers and visitors which gives information about a country, region or places of interest, hotel etc.

मार्गदर्शक पत्र – **guide card -** a card with a projecting tab used in a card catalogue or file to indicate the arrangement and to facilitate reference.

मार्गनिश्चिती/सवयीचे – **routine -** the systematic circulation of serials among the members of the library in accordance with a prefixed routine precedure.

मालमत्ता कट्टा – **property counter -** 1) a counter at the entrance of a library where visitors can deposit belongings that are not allowed in the library.

2) a place in a library where user deposits his personal belonging before entering the library.

माला टिप्पण – **series note** - a note in catalogue entry to record name, number and editor of series to which document belongs.

माला नोंद - **series entry** - an added entry made to provide access for search through series approach.

माला विवरण – **series statement** - पहा– 'माला टिप्पण'

माला शीर्षक – **series title** - a title allotted to a series and entered in a catalogue entry.

माला संख्या/अंक – **series number** - a number assigned to each of the volume of the series.

माला – **series** - when publications are brought out under a collective title with an independent title allotted to each book with an individualising series number.

माळा – **tier** - floors of a structure placed one above the other.

माळे – **tiers** -rows of shelves in a library stack / rack.

मासिक कक्ष - **magazine room, periodical room.**

मासिक रॅक – **magazine rack** - furniture prepared for periodical display.

मासिक/नियतकालिक – **magazine** - a periodical publication which appears after a fixed interval, with district name with successive numbers.

माहिती बिट्स – **information bits** - in telecommunication, the bits that are generated by the data source solely as a function of the input information and not those used by the system for purpose of synchronization and error control.

माहिती वितरण– **information distribution**- distribution of information through different channels.

माहिती (संपत्ती) म्हणून – **information as wealth** - knowledge and information is stored and possessed as.

माहिती (सहभागीय) – **shareable information** - information used by two or more persons. or institutions without any loss in sharing.

माहिती अंकेक्षण/हिशेब – **information audit** - the process by which a physical verification and examination of the total information assets within an organization takes place to ensure that information resources which have been acquired by an organization can be accounted for and located. The information audit is a valuable management tool useful for reference and research and part of a continuous management review to assist in the process of achieving maximum effectiveness of information provision and use.

माहिती अदलाबदल/देवाणघेवाण – **information interchange** - exchange of information.

माहिती अधिकारी – **information officer** - one who is responsibile for providing information.

माहिती उद्योग/व्यवसाय – **information industry** - market place created by the convergence of computers, telecommunication and microelectronics.

माहिती उपभोक्ते – **information users** - persons using information.

माहिती कक्ष – **information desk** - a desk in a library or other building staffed by one or more persons whose function is to give information about the institution or section.

माहिती कार्य – **information work** - work developed as the result of various organised sets of information.

माहिती कार्यदल – **information workforce** - occupational force involved in information work.

माहिती केंद्र – **information centre** - 1) an organisation which collects and organizes information for dissemination among specialized users.

2) an organisation that;

(1) selects, acquires, stores and retrieves information in response to requests;

(2) announces, abstracts, extracts, indexes information;

(3) disseminates information in anticipation of and in response to requests.

(4) usually an office, or a section of bibliographical centre, research bureau or documentation centre, which gives information about books or on a subject with which the facilities of the centre are concerned. Staffing varies, but may include any or all of the following - research officers, librarians, bibliographers or trained information officers. It may include the functions of special library and extend its activities to include collateral functions such as technical writing, abstracting, SDI and library research for clients.

माहिती क्रांती – **information revolution** - information as a basic instrument of change bringing about major changes in society.

माहिती खंड – **information gap** - information missed due to unregulated collection or totally uncollected information.

माहिती ग्रंथपाल – **information librarian** - information officer working in a library.

माहिती ग्रंथालय – **information library** - a library which serves as the basis of an information service to its employees.

माहिती जाळे – **information network** - a network of libraries geographically scattered having connectivity through processors and terminals which gets interconnected using data communications facilities.

माहिती तंत्रज्ञान – **information technology** - technique of using machine for information processing and transmission to achieve efficiency and speed.

माहिती तत्त्व/घटक – **information element** - category of the information based on its characteristics. Unit of information which is also regarded as data element in cataloguing.

माहिती दलाल – **information broker** - 1) a specialist in database systems willing to sell his expertise in information handling for the advantage of a customer. 2) a self employed professional, expert in information retrieval and delivery, makes his research services commercially usually on a freelance basis.

माहिती धोरण - **information policy** - 1) set of rules / guidelines to carry out effective use of information framed by the Govt. /Govt. agency. 2) a set of decisions taken by government through appropriate laws and regulations. To orient the harmonious development of information transfer activities in order to satisfy the information needs of the country.

माहिती निर्माण – **information production** - industries or institutions involved in the production of information of various kinds.

माहिती निवडक्षमता – **information selectivity** - a process of finding expression which is representative of information in a database so as to retrieve desired information.

माहिती पद्धती – **information system** - data processing system operations and procedures.

माहिती पुरविणारी व्यक्ती/संस्था - **information provider** - a person or organization providing material for the database.

माहिती प्रक्रियक – **information processor** - a device that has stored information and instructions, receives input data or signals, processes its input and stores information.

माहिती प्रतिप्राप्ती पद्धत – **information retrieval system** - a system involved with the retrieval of information. In other words, matching the available information with an information need is the task of the information storage and retrieval system.

माहिती प्रतिप्राप्ती व्यवस्था/पद्धत – **information retrieval system** - a set of instructions programme used to retrieve information in desired manner.

माहिती प्रतिप्राप्ती शब्दसमूहकोश – **information retrieval thesaurus** - a tool designed for information storage and retrieval functions.

माहिती प्रतिप्राप्ती - **information retrieval** - 1) search of the desired information from the collection. The technique can be exercised manually or by application of machine. 2) the aspects of computer systems involved with recovering specific information from stored data for example from a database.

माहिती प्रतिसाद प्रणाली/पद्धत - **information feedback system** - an information transmission system that verifies accuracy of transmission by means of an echo check.

माहिती प्रधान समाज - **information society** - a society which is well informed about the latest developments taking place in its surroundings.

माहिती प्रवाह - **information flow** - information transfer through established channels.

माहिती मार्गदर्शक - **information guide** - a source of information which leads to secondary and / or primary literature.

माहिती मूल्य/किंमत - **information value / costs** - 1) importance; value of information. 2) information has a value, not always in terms of money but in relation to its use.

माहिती मूल्यमापन - **evaluation of information** - information about a single item or a series of items on a specific subject is submitted for critical appraisal by one or more specialists who determines its value in general or for a particular purpose.

माहिती युग - **information age** - a period characterized by domination of information.

माहिती विक्रेता - **information vendor** - person/ organization involved in obtaining machine readable databases through licensing agreements with different database producers and providing them to libraries and information centres through online information retrieval system or networks.

माहिती विज्ञान - **informatics** - the science of processing information / data.

माहिती विभाग - **information department** - a department of an organization the primary function of which is to provide information when requested. The department of any organization the primary function of which is to provide information when requested.

माहिती व्यवस्थापक जाळे - **information manager network** - network consists of a group of information managers each of whom is assigned responsibility for an information specific technical division while remaining organizationally linked.

माहिती व्यवस्थापन - **information management** - a skillful exercise of control over the acquisition to dissemination of information resources.

माहिती शास्त्रज्ञ - **information scientist** - a person who deals with information organisation by using computer technologies.

माहिती संग्रह घटक – **data element** - category of the information based on its characteristics. unit of information also regarded as data element in cataloguing.

माहिती संग्रह केंद्र – **data centre** - an organisation where information /data is acquired and processed for dissemination.

माहिती संग्रह क्षेत्र – **data field** - an area allocated to a data record in main memory of the computer.

माहिती संग्रह दोष – **data error** - a mistake in data.

माहिती संग्रह नमुना – **data format** - the way in which data is kept in a file.

माहिती संग्रह निर्विष्ट – **data input** - the process of recording data in computer device.

माहिती संग्रह नोंद निवेशकार – **data entry operator** - one who inputs data in computer.

माहिती संग्रह नोंदवही – **data register** - computer CPU where provision is available for the temporary storage.

माहिती संग्रह परिवर्तन – **data conversion** - the change of the data from one format to another.

माहिती संग्रह पेढी – **data bank** - unprocessed large store or organised information or a collection of information on a given subject.

माहिती संग्रह प्रवाह तक्ता – **data flowchart** - a flowchart showing the path of data through a system.

माहिती संग्रह रचना – **data design** - layout / format of information.

माहिती संग्रह व्यवस्थापक – **database manager** - a software component at the heart of a database manager which records changes to database files, translating the logical access requests issued by applications programme into terms of physical storage & ensures that the integrity & security of the data is maintained. The people closely involved with DBMS are referred to as managers & administrators.

माहिती संग्रह व्यवस्थापन प्रणाली – **database management system** - a collection of software that helps in managing database or comprehensive software system that builds, maintains and provides access to a database.

माहिती संग्रह संकलन – **data compilation** - the regular and systematic recording of information discovered in variety of miscellaneous collection.

माहिती संग्रह संकलन – **data collection** - compilation, organisation & collection of data / information according to requirements.

माहिती संग्रह संप्रेषण जाळे – **data communication network** - an-inter connected group of computer systems.

माहिती संग्रह संप्रेषण नियंत्रण संच – **data communication control unit** - the unit that scans the central terminal unit, buffers for messages and transfers them to the central processor.

माहिती संग्रह संप्रेषण प्रणाली – **data communication system** - a system of data processing in which terminal devices and special interfacing equipment is used.

माहिती संग्रह संप्रेषण – **data communication** - the transmission of data between points, generally by means of telecommunication system. Method of transferring data to processing site.

माहिती संग्रह संहिता – **data code** - a set of characters structured in such a way as to represent the data items of a data element.

माहिती संग्रह सारणी (पंजी) – **data file** - arranged order of various sets of data.

माहिती संग्रह सोपस्कार – **data processing** - generic term used for all operations carried out to use / handle data.

माहिती संग्रह – **data** - a term used for unprocessed or unorganized information in computer. It is a raw form of information. In its general sense it is a form of statistical profile. आणखी पहा – 'माहिती'

माहिती संग्रह – **database** - collection of structural and organised related information accessible to the user on demand through automatic search by using computer.

माहिती संचयिका/पेढी – **information bank** - a place where information is stored.

माहिती संचालन – **information handling** - activities concerning collection, processing & retrieval of information /data.

माहिती संसाधन/सोपस्कार/संस्करण – **information processing** - data processing. Activity related to distribution of literature and documents at the request. Notification of information and other documentation activities.

माहिती संस्था – **information institutions** - institutions that generate and store knowledge and information making them available to others.

माहिती सल्लागार – **information consultant** - a mediator implies a person who assists, guides, enables and intervenes in another person's information search process.

माहिती सादरीकरण – **information representation** - a series of action including gathering, processing, representing and storage of information in a database.

माहिती साधन नकाशा – **information source map** - document containing information about the scope, location, vocabulary and access conditions of database.

माहिती सिद्धान्त – **information theory** - scientific, technological and engineering disciplines and management techniques used in handling and processing information, their application on computers and their interaction with social economics matter.

माहिती सुरक्षितता – **information security** - information assurance.

माहिती सेवा - **information service** - 1) special service provided by a library which draws attention to information processed in the library. 2) information department in anticipation of demand. 3) It has been anticipated and will be of interest to potential users of the service.

माहिती स्रोत/साधने - **information resources** - all types of resources that provide information.

माहिती स्रोतांचे व्यवस्थापन – **information resources management** - a skillful exercise of control over the acquistion to dissemination of information resources.

माहिती स्थानांतर प्रक्रिया – **information transfer process** - movement of information generation to use with a series of intermediate links that connect each other to form a chain.

माहिती स्थानांतर – **information transfer** - the process of flow of information from generator to the user.

माहिती स्थानांतरण साखळी - **information transmission chain** - a linking chain that connects information from its generation to its use.

माहिती – **information** - 1) when a piece of data is processed, interpreted and presented in an acceptable form or gets related with existing relation, becomes information itself. 2) it is data which is used to generate knowledge. 3) In computer use, that property of signal / message whereby it something unpredictable is conveyed by and meaning to the receipt usually measured in BITS.

माहितीचा बाजार – **information markets** - markets that are trading information .

माहितीचा भुकेला – **information seeker** - a person who needs information for its use.

माहितीचा वापर – **information use** - applying knowledge and information for definite use.

माहितीचा स्फोट/परिस्फोट – **information explosion** - enormous growth of information in each discipline.

माहितीची गरज – **information need** - 1) the specific requirement (s) of information use. 2) it is mainly in idea form and consists of the process involving the identification analysis and satisfaction at conceptual level.

माहितीची चाळण/गाळण – **information filter** - an essential process between information sources and their users, for selecting partinent information.

माहितीची पुनर्बांधणी – **repackaging of information** - in this operation, the aim is to collect information obtained in different forms from different sources and present it in another form. Sometimes, on other carriers to facilitate the work of users.

माहितीचे एकत्रीकरण – **consolidation of information** - this consists of checking the validity or defining the limitations of information contained in the various documents and in confronting what is stated on a specific subject with other sources so as to arrive at cumulative and evaluated information. The outcome is generally recorded and disseminated in the form of a tertiary document. In most cases, consolidation calls for investigation into all the primary literature that has been collected.

माहितीचे ग्राहक – **information consumers** - readers who use information.

माहितीचे प्रसारण – **dissemination of information** - it is the service arranged with communication system to keep information within the reach of the user.

माहितीचे वितरण – **dissemination of information** - distribution or sending of information either specifically requested for or not, to members of an organisation by a librarian or information officer. The means used normally include news bulletins, abstracts,individual memoranda or letters and personal interview or, telephone calls, but may also include notes accompanying articles, memoranda, press clipping or reports.

माहितीचे विश्लेषण केंद्र – **information analysis centre** - 1) a formally structured organisational unit specifically (but not necessarily exclusively) established to acquire, select, store, retrieve,evaluate, analyse and synthesize a body of information and / or data in a clearly defined specialized field or pertaining to a specific mission with the intension of arranging and presenting the material in a most authoritative and useful form. 2) an organisation employing group of subject specialists & engaged in gathering information in well defined subject fields, analyzing and evaluating the information & consolidating & repackaging the information in the form of digests, extracts, critical reviews, state of the art reports etc.

माहितीचे विश्लेषण – **analysis of information** - describing the information contained in documents dealing with a specific field. The description has to respect a varying number of criteria that reflects the likely queries or points of view of user.

माहितीच्या उत्पादनाची मूल्यवृद्धी – **adding value to information products** - a key factor in the way that information professionals do their job today is the amount of added value they put into increasingly differentiated information products. Information professionals use a combination of skills and technology to process and value what it presents in order to meet highly specific needs.

माहितीच्या गरजा – **information needs** - individuals and groups looking for information support for their specific work.

माहितीपत्रक – **brochure** - a small publication containing announcement of current programmes regarding institution, association or programme.

माहितीपर सार – **informative abstract** - an abstract which gives important information about the main text. The information helps in deciding that the main text is required to see or not.

माहितीशास्त्र – **information science** - study of development and organisation of information.

मिश्र चिन्हांकन – **mixed notation** - a scheme of classification using more than one type of symbols as a notation.

मिश्र वर्ग - **complex class** - class framed by the combination of two or more basic or compound classes to express the relation between them, but excluding the case when one of the classes form an isolate of the other by subject device.

मिश्र वाचक – **mixed readers** - composite readers with various degree of specialization in a discipline or profession but having a common interest in a particular subject or profession.

मिश्र विषय - **complex subject** - a subject with one basic class and one or more isolate ideas, and more than one characteristics.

मिश्र/जटिल विषय – **complex subject** - a subject with multiple aspects. All class numbers obtained through synthesis are of complex subjects. DDC still is not able to provide complete (co-extensive) class numbers for many complex subjects, so one has to rely on characteristics to avoid cross classification.

मिश्र/संमिश्र पंक्ती उपांगे – **complex array isolate** - array isolate framed by the combination of two or more array isolate in one and the same array to express the relation between them but excluding the case of their superimposition.

मीमांसकवर्ग – **colloquium** - a series of lectures or seminars convened by a coordinator but featuring different speakers or leaders.

मुक्त पैलूयुक्त वर्गीकरण - freely faceted classification - classification scheme in which there is no rigid pre-determined facet formula for compound subjects going with a basic subject.

मुक्त कप्पा – discharging tray - a tray used to keep records of the documents operated at circulation desk.

मुक्त करणे – discharge - an act of cancellation of loan record of library documents when it is received back by the library.

मुक्त खरेदी – open purchase - when the purchase orders can be placed with any book distributor at any place.

मुक्त नोंद - open entry - an entry which can accept more information such as entries of periodicals, these are kept open to record new issues.

मुक्त पंक्ती – open array - an array of classes admitting extrapolation.

मुक्त प्रवेश – open access - when a library allows users to move around the shelves to get their information / documents.

मुखपत्र/संस्था पत्रिका – house organ - a bulletin or newsletter of an organisation describing its current activities.

मुखपत्र - official organ - a publication circulated by any institute or association to report its activities.

मुख्य आधार संगणक – main frame computer - the basic/essential portion of an assembly of computer hardware which has the capacity to support many powerful peripheral device. It may have multi user facilities and network of terminals.

मुख्य ग्रंथनाम पृष्ठ – main title page - a page which provides information about title and other details traced in catalogue.

मुख्य ग्रंथनाम – main title - the title which precedes the sub-title/alternative title. See also main heading.

मुख्य ग्रंथालय – main library - central library.

मुख्य तालिका नोंद – main catalogue entry - the entry in which all relevant information is traced to develop other added entries. See also main entry.

मुख्य तालिका – main catalogue - central catalogue which consists of entries for total holdings of a library.

मुख्य नोंद - main entry - an entry giving maximum information about a document.

मुख्य पंजी/संचिका – **master file** -a file containing permanent data.

मुख्य पत्र – **main card** - a catalogue card having the main entry for a work. It is also regarded as basic card/unit card.

मुख्य वर्ग - **main class** - 1) class enumerated in the array of order by using first level characteristic in scheme of classification for universal knowledge.
2) a theoretical subject accepted as subject from long time like mathematics, physics, economics, history etc.

मुख्य विषय – **main subject** - the subject which has a number of established branches and accepted aspects.

मुख्य शीर्षक – **main heading** - the first heading among multiple headings.

मुख्य संग्रह – **main store / principal store.**

मुख्यपत्र – **master card** - a card usually the first in its group containing informaion about other associated cards.

मुख्यालय - **head quarters** - location stating main controlling office.

मुदतीबाहेरचा ग्रंथ – **overdue book** - a book outstanding with member for more than the period it was allowed.

मुदतीबाहेरचे शुल्क – **overdue charges** - the charges collected from user for the return of library documents.

मुदतीबाहेरील सूचना – **overdue notice** - a request to call back the library document on expiry of its permitted period.

मुद्रक - **printer** - one who is responsible for printing with mechanical device, to produce printed copy, use output device for producing hard copies.

मुद्रण आणि प्रकाशन – **printing and publication** - an agency which prints and publishes document / book.

मुद्रण प्रत - **printout** - hard copy produced by a machine or paper, out put, gallyproof; final proof of the document available before actual printing.

मुद्रण - **printing** - process of printing typography; the way in which written material is arranged and prepared for printing.

मुद्रणातीत/मुद्रणास्व ग्रंथ – **In press** - book in printing process.

मुद्रित तालिका – **printed catalogue** - a catalogue printed and brought out in book form, also termed as book catalogue.

मुद्रित ग्रंथ सदृश तालिका – **printed book form catalogue** - it is a physical form of catalogue. Supplementary catalogues are issued to give updates.

मुद्रित ग्रंथ – **printed book** - a book produced in printed form by a mechanical method.

मुद्रित वाचक – **proof reader** - a person who corrects errors before final printout of a document/book is brought out.

मुलामा देणे/सोनेरी करणे – **gilding** - applying a layer of material with which things are gilded, generally such guilt is of golden or silver colour.

मूर्तीभंजक – **iconoclast** - a person who attacks popular beliefs or established customs.

मूलतत्त्वे/घटक – **elements** - the first of basic principles, rudiments, compound of elements or first principles.

मूलभूत घटक वर्गवारी– **fundamental category** - according to Dr. S.R.Ranganathan, there are only five fundamental categories Personality, Matter, Energy, Space and Time. Each facet of a subject is regarded as manifestation of one or other category of PMEST in their decreasing concreteness.

मूल्य अध्यवसाय – **value judgement** - estimate of the worth (of a statement in Delphi questionnaire) based on personal assessment.

मूल्य देय डाक – **VPP (value payable by post)** - a parcel to be delivered after receipt of the value mentioned, through postal service.

मूल्य फायदे विश्लेषण - **cost benefit analysis** - to explain relationship between cost involved and service generated by the programme.

मूल्यांकन अंक – **evaluation number** - part of the book number of a document, which is an appreciation, criticism, evaluation or review of or a reply to a pseudo classic, attached after a part taken from the book number of the host pseudo classic.

मूल्यांकन खरेदी पैलू – **evaluation acquisition facet** - part of the book number of a document, which is the evaluation acquisition number.

मूल्यांकन पैलू – **evaluation facet** - see 'evaluation acquisition facet.'

मूल्यमापन – **evaluation** - the process of measuring the performance of a service or system and assessing its effectiveness in meeting the established norms.

मूळ आवृत्ती – **original edition** - the first edition which has been published for sale to the public and implying that it was preceded by an edition printed afterwards.

मूळ ग्रंथ - **basic book** - a book in which fundamentals of the subject are discussed or appeared for the first time.

मूळ नोंद - **basic entry** - see 'main entry.'

मूळ पैलू - **basic facet** - first level division of an isolate.

मूळ रचना - **original work** - the work which refers as basic contribution of the author.

मूळ रचनेची चौकट - **infrastructure** - subordinate parts, installations, etc. that form the base of a system, an organization or an enterprise.

मूळ वर्ग - **basic class** - generic name for main or a canonical class in a scheme of classification for the universe of knowledge.

मूळ वर्गीकरण - **basic classification** - version of a scheme of classification prepared for the needs of macro thought and for libraries for general readers.

मूळ विषय - **basic subject** - see 'main class.'

मूळ संग्रह - **basic stock** - standard collection which is regarded, essential to the objectives of the library.

मूळाक्षर - **alphabet** - symbols with fixed value used in linguistics.

मृतपुस्तिका - **Book of the dead** - ancient Egyptians were obsessed with concerns with life after death. They wrote magical formulae on papyrus rolls and entombed these along with the coffins. These mortuary texts are collectively described as the Book of the dead. These provide the specimens of the earliest Egyptian writings on papyrus rolls.

मृत्यू दिनांक - **death date** - the year of death is entered in catalogue entry to highlight the period of the contributor.

मेगा बाइट - **mega byte** - this term is used as measure of the memory capacity of hard disks and tapes. A byte is 8 bits (binary digits) of information and is roughly synonymous with one character of data storage. (i.e. each character stored in memory will take up one byte of storage). A megabyte (MB) is 1048576 (220) bytes.

मेडलाईन - **MEDLINE (Medical Literature Network)** - a computerised service developed by the National Library of Medicine.

मेडलार्स - **MEDLARS (Medical Literature Analysis & Retrieval System)** - National Library of Medicine U.S.A. has created computer database in the field of medicine to provide a comprehensive bibliography of medical literature.

मेण – **bee's wax** - soft, sticky yellow substance produced by bees and used by them for making honey combs. This material is used for making surface smooth.

मेणीय कागद - **waxed paper** - paper impregnated or coated with wax. Used to interleave sheets undergoing wet repair, to prevent them from sticking together.

मेरिल ग्रंथांक – **Merrill book number** - a book number from a scheme devised by W.S. Merrill for arranging material in alphabetical order or by numbering or in chronological order by means of data abbreviations.

मेलविल डयुई – **Melvil Dewey** - an American library scientist who is regarded as father of library science, having basic contribution to preparation of Dewey Decimal Classification Scheme Published in 1876.

मोडपत्रक – **folder** - cover for holding loose papers etc. made of stiff material, especially card board, or thick card sheet.

मोडेम(राऊटर) – **Modem (Router)** - the acronym for modulator DEModulator. A device that can convert digital computer signals into analog telephone signals and can reverse the process at the other end on the line.

मोडेम – **MODEM** - the device which accepts digital wave form for transmission over an analog channel to develop a telecommunication channel.
2) a functional unit that modulates & demodulates signals, one of the functions of a modem is to enable digital data to be transmitted over analog transmission facilities.

मोनोग्राफ (एकविषयिका/प्रबोधिका) – **monograph** - a scholarly contribution on a specific subject.

मौखिक संप्रेषण - **oral communication** - transformation knowledge from one generation to the next, orally without being written down.

मौलिक/समर्थनीय संपादन - **substantive editing** - substantial changes advised or made by an editor to improve the language & presentation of a text, making it more interesting and easy to read.

य

यंत्र वाचनीय - **machine readable -** information in a form that can be directly assimilated by computer input equipment.

यंत्र सूचना (शोध) – **machine search -** search of information with the help of machine.

यंत्रचलित लाकडी कागद - **mechanical wood paper -** cheap paper made by grinding raw wood into pulp (newprint), all impurities and acid substances remain in the paper, using its early deterioration.

यंत्रचलित – **mechanical -** produced or operated by machinery or a mechanism.

यंत्रज्ञ - **mechanic -** a worker skilled in using tools or making, operating, and repairing machines.

यंत्रणा – **system mechanism -** mechanism of a set or arrangement of things so related or connected as to form a unity or organic whole.

यंत्रवाचनीय आधारसामग्री – **machine readable database -** data or information in a form which can be read or identified by a machine such as a computer or microform reader.

यजमान संगणक – **host computer -** the primary or controlling computer in a multiple computer operation or network.

यथार्थ मूल्य – **true value -** certain; as a proper value.

यथार्थ – **valid -** having legal force, properly executed with binding under the law.

यथार्थता – **authenticity** - the quality or state of being authentic; genuineness.

यथार्थदर्शन – **perspective** - person's total mental and conceptual vision with a foresight of ideas, facts, thoughts, actions etc. and their relationship with reference to the processes of growth, development and future shape and image of an organisation.

यदृच्छ – **random** - without predetermined sequence; haphazard; e.g. a random shot; a random guess, random sampling, etc.

यदृच्छ नमुना चाचणी – **random sampling** - samples at random without predetermined method or conscious choice.

यदृच्छ प्रवेश स्मृती - **RAM (random access memory)** - main memory of a personal computer where the data is not retained in case light goes off.

यदृच्छ स्मृती – **ROM (read only memory)** - a basic type of semiconductor memory used for permanent storage. Can only be read, not "written" that is, changed. Variations are Programmable Read Only Memory (PROM) and Erasable Programmable Read Only Memory (EPROM).

यदृच्छ/स्वैर/विनाधोरण प्रवेश – **random access** - access to database without predetermined rule that from where the next item is to be obtained.

यांत्रिक भाषा – **machine language** - code language in non-graphic physical symbols suited to the machine for heading them in accordance with prescribed programme, see also 'binary language.'

यांत्रिक अनुवाद – **mechanical translation** - translation work done using a computer which facilities selection and use of foreign language data, eventually by conjugation with the versatile character reading devices.

यांत्रिक क्रिया – **machine operation.**

यांत्रिक गणक – **calculating machine** - a machine especially designed for performing arithmetic operations.

यांत्रिक प्रतिप्राप्ती – **mechanized retrieval** - information that is connected with, produced by and operated by a machine or machines.

यांत्रिक वाचनीय माहिती – **machine readable database** - information /data stored on electronic device to use the same by machine.

यांत्रिक वाचनीय तालिका – **machine readable catalogue** - a library catalogue through computer is produced, in the form of tape, disk, floppy, CD ROM. etc.

यांत्रिक वाचनीय – **machine readable -** 1) that can be sensed by mechanical device such as disk, tape cassettes etc. 2) information stored in electronic media such as magnetic tape, disc and CD-ROM.

यांत्रिक शब्द – **machine word -** unit of information involving the standard number of distinct or primary code digits, which a computer regularly handles in each operation.

यांत्रिक संस्था – **mechanics institute -** the branch of physics that deals with motion and the phenomena of the action of forces on bodies.

यादी – **menu -** a technique whereby available options offered to a computer user are displayed on a visual display unit and can be selected by number.

यादृच्छीकरण – **randomisation -** selection of sample without predepermined sequence.

याप्रमाणे विभाजन करा - **divide like -** an instruction used in classification schedules to use the notation for a given subject which is already mentioned for another subject.

युक्ती/क्लृप्ती/तंत्र – **device -** it is a synoym for technique. An emblem or monogram used by a printer or publisher to identify his work. It is usually used as part of the printer's or publisher's name on the title page or spine.

युद्धशास्त्र - **military science -** science characteristics of for fit for soldiers or the armed forces.

युनिक्स – **UNIX-** in computing, a unit into which data can be entered, retained and later retrieved.

युनिमार्क - **UNIMARC - (Universal Machine Readable Catalogue)-** a system for the international communication format for the exchange of catalogue data.

युनिसिस्ट – **UNISIST (United Nations World Science Information System in Science and Technology)** 1) evolved by UNESCO 1971 to share information. 2) it is a programme evolved by UNESCO during 1971 towards a world science information system with the objective of advancing measures for sharing of information by the countries of the world through cooperative agreements among government international organisations and operating services.

युनेस्को – **UNESCO (United Nations Educational, Scientific and Cultural Organisation) -** an intergovernmental agency founded in 1946, since its inception, active in promotion, co-ordination and development of library, documentation and information services. It arranges seminars and meetings to extend advisory services.

येथे वर्ग/वर्गीक द्या टीप - **class here note** - instruction under a heading giving explicit instructions to class a topic under that class number where apparently it does not seem a part of that heading. Usually the subject to be classed here is broader than the heading under which this note appears.

योग्य/बरोबर यथादर्शन - **right perspective** - motivation or sense of purpose of the communicator, as well as that of audience.

योग्यता - **merit** - something deserving reward, praise or gratitude. Actual qualities or facts, good or bad; as to decide the question on its merits.

योजना/आखणी/बेत - **plans** - document giving a complete blueprint for executing an activity.

योजना - **plan** - a scheme for making, doing, or arranging something; a project; a programme; a schedule, to devise a scheme for doing, making or arranging.

योजनांतर्गत अनुदान - **plan grants** - 1) funds allotted to carry a project during a plan period. 2) funds made available for projects that go under annual plans, five year plans etc.

योजनेत्तर अनुदान - **non - plan grants** - budget allocation except the plan budget.

रंगनाथन्/एस. आर. - Ranganathan. S. R. - first Indian library science scientist who designed colon classification and also developed theories in various areas of the subject library science (B. 1892 D. 1972)

रंगमंदिर – theatre - a place where plays, operas, motion pictures etc. are presented; a building especially designed for such presentations.

रचना (क्रमसंयोगाने) - arrangement by combination of sequence - when the arrangement is not unitary and a self arrangement has a combination of characteristics for arrangement.

रचना (दाखल अंकाने) – arrangement by accession number - arrangement of documents as per accession numbers of a particular library.

रचना/क्रमरचना – arrangement - an enumeration of subjects according to the organizational principles.

रचनात्मक/सृजनशीलता - creativity - refers to the capacity of human beings to produce and understand an indefinitely large no. of ideas, most of which might not have been heard or used before. Ability of a person to propose new ideas.

रद्दबातल – withdrawl - the process of removing entries from the accession register catalogue and books from shelve.

रद्दबातल नोंदवही – withdrawl record / register - a record maintained in a library for the documents withdrawn from the library collections.

रस – **interest** - a feeling of intentness, concern, or curiosity about something. To excite the attention or curiosity of a person.

रसशास्त्र – **logistics** - the branch of military science dealing with moving, supplying, and quartering troops.

राखणदार/रक्षक – **custodian** - a person who is an incharge or who holds responsibility.

राजदूत – **ambassador** - the highest diplomatic representative that one sovereign power or state sends officially to another.

राजदूतवास - **embassy** - the official residence or offices of an ambassador in a foreign country : also called legation. An ambassador and his staff.

राजपत्र – **gazette** - to publish, announce decisions or lists official publication of a government intended of appointments to the public services.

राजस्व - **revenue** - an income earned through taxes.

राजाराम मोहन रॉय ग्रंथालय प्रतिष्ठान - **Raja Ram Mohan Roy Library Foundation (RRMRLF)** - It was established in May 1972 as an autonomous organization under Dept. of Culture of Govt. of India for promoting library services in India. It provides assistance under various schemes to develop public libraries and improve reading habits.

राज्य करणे/व्यवस्था पाहणे – **govern** - rule (a country etc.) control or direct the public affairs (a city, country etc.)

राज्य ग्रंथालय परिषद - **state library council** - a group of library professionals and others to look into the matters related to aided public libraries in the state.

राज्य ग्रंथालय सेवा - **state library service** - library services given by the state library service; library services provided in the state.

राज्य ग्रंथालय – **state library** - state level official /govt. library.

राज्य मध्यवर्ती ग्रंथालय – **state central library** - it is a respiratory of the publications published by the state, generally located at central place, it may also serve to provide information about the state to the government department.

राज्य मध्यवर्ती ग्रंथालयाचा ग्रंथपाल – **state librarian** - a person who is working as a librarian in a state central library.

राज्यपाल – **governor** - a person who governs; especially, a person appointed to govern a dependency, province, town, fort, etc; the nominated head of any state of the country.

रात्र विद्यालय/महाविद्यालय - **night school, college / academic institute -** where education is offered during night hours.

रायडरचे आंतरराष्ट्रीय वर्गीकरण – **Rider's international classification -** scheme of classification designed by Fremont rider and published for the first time in 1961.

राशी/रक्कम – **amount -** quantity of sum.

राष्ट्रकुल – **commonwealth -** the whole body of people in a state : the body politic; the public. The general welfare.

राष्ट्रीय ग्रंथालय – **National Library -** a library established by the government for acquisition and presentation of documents published in the country. It is a national repository for all documents. e.g. National Library, Kolkatta (India).

राष्ट्रीय माहिती केंद्र – **National Information Centre (NIC) -** the UGC has established three such centres one each at Mumbai, Baroda & Bangalore. Centre exclusively deals in science discipline whereas social science and humanity subjects are distributed among SNDT Women's University, Mumbai University and M.S. University, Baroda centre.

राष्ट्रीय उत्पन्न - **national income -** the total income of a nation, including all profits, rents, interest wages, salaries etc., during a specific period, usually a year.

राष्ट्रीय ग्रंथ न्यास – **(National Book Trust) -** national book trust of India is an autonomous organisation set up in 1957 to foster book mindedness among people of different ages and walks of life. It works to produce books in Hindi & English along with other eleven (now eighteen) regional Indian languages, besides, it organizes international, national and regional book fairs.

राष्ट्रीय ग्रंथालय व माहिती धोरण – **National library & information policy -** a set of guidelines for directing library & information activities of a country.

राष्ट्रीय माहिती धोरण - **National information policy -** a set of guidelines for directing information activities in country.

राष्ट्रीय माहिती पद्धत – **National information system -** 1) an information system evolved to disseminate information at national network. 2) set of discipline, mission, or function oriented information centres (or infrastructure) operating in a coordinated way and through the use of common techniques of information handling in accordance with the goals of the national information policy in order to satisfy the needs of the users at large.

राष्ट्रीय रसायनशास्त्र व रासायनिक तंत्रज्ञान माहिती केंद्र **NICHEM - (National Centre for Chemistry & Chemical Technology)** - NICHEM is an information centre developed under National Information System for Science & Technology (NISSAT), functional from 1986. The centre is operational with library & documentation services of National Chemical Laboratory (NCL) Pune. The centre has comprehensive collection in chemistry and chemical technology on mechanical retrieval system.

राष्ट्रीय विज्ञान व तंत्रज्ञान माहिती पद्धत - **National Information System for Sciences & Technology (NISSAT)** - NISSAT was set up to co-ordinate the resources of science & technology library so that the wasteful expenditure is avoided.

राष्ट्रीय शैक्षणिक संशोधन केंद्र - **NCERT (National Council for Education, Research and Training)** - A centre established by the central govenment in India at New Delhi in 1972 for undertaking educational research and training.

राष्ट्रीय सामाजिक शास्त्रे प्रलेख केंद्र - **National Social Sciences Documentation Centre (NASSCDOC)** - the centre is working in new Delhi under ICSR (Indian Council of Social Science Research). It is generating publication acquired in the field of social science.

राष्ट्रीय सूचना केंद्र – **National Informatic Centre** - centre is situated in Delhi. It has a computer communication network with district headquarters's to create database.

रिक्त आणि रिक्तकारक अंक - **empty and emptying digit** - a digit with ordinal value, without representing any specific formal idea, and depriving the preceding digit of focal idea. The concept is used in classification for giving equal status to classes.

रिक्तअंक - **empty digit** - a digit which has no semantic value, but it retains the ordinal value and generally used to expand notational capacity of other digits.

रिक्तकारक अंक – **emptying digit** - a digit with ordinal value and also depriving the preceding digit of its focal idea.

रिक्तकारक स्वतंत्र अंक – **emptying substantive digit** - a digit with ordinal values representing a focal idea, and depriving the preceding digit of its focal idea.

रीती/वळण – **mode** - frequent observation in the series.

रीती/कार्यपद्धती – **procedure** - regular order or way of doing things.

रीती/कार्यपद्धती निदेश पुस्तिका - **procedure manual** - work manual; a handbook describing the procedures to be adopted by a office.

रुग्णालय ग्रंथालय – **hospital library -** library collection maintained for patients, doctors and nurses.

रूढ लेखन – **spelling -** the act of forming words, etc. by putting letters together.

रूपरेखा लेखन – **scenario writing -** describing future possibilities / alternative descriptive technique in futuristic research.

रूपरेखा/बाह्यरेखा – **profiling -** user outline (individual, group / community) of information needs in conceptual terms.

रूपसरणी – **paradigm -** a pattern, example or model.

रुळविणे – **induction -** to give general knowledge of activities requirements, procedure adopted in a department to a newly joined employee.

रूप – **morpheme -** smallest meaningful morphological unit of a language that cannot be further divided e.g. in.

रूप – **form -** a general designator for a particular material, for example cinereal, sound recording microform, video recording CD ROM.

रूपरेषा – **profile -** a list of users with areas of their interest.

रूपरेषा – **synopsis -** a statement giving a brief, general review or condensation; summary, as of a story.

रूपावलीत्मक – **paradigmatic -** belonging to a set of linguistically associated or interchangeable forms.

रेक्झिन – **rexin -** strong unbleached cloth with a water resistant coating. It is then calendered to give proper grainings.

रेखांकन मापक्रम – **ranging scale -** numerical values assigned to precoded pairs of positive and negative replies.

रेखण – **chart -** a sheet giving information or facts, usually in tabular, diagrammatic, illustrative, or graphic form; as a genealogical, historical, or statistical chart. Such a table, diagram, graph etc.

रेखाकृती – **diagram -** figure which is marked out by lines, a diagram, a scale, from Latin word diagraphein, to mark out by lines, to draw; dia - through, across and graphein, to write.

रेल्वे खर्च मुक्त – **F.O.R. (free on rail) -** the condition stating that, the expenditure of transportation of parcels is to be borne by the supplier and not by the institution.

रैखिक व्यवस्था – **linear arrangement** -arrangement one after another, as in a line.

रॅम – **RAM (random access memory)** - 1) main memory of a personal computer. The data will not be retained in case light goes off. 2) the main memory of a computer. The acronym RAM can be used to refer either the integrated circuits that make up this type or memory or the memory itself. The computer can store values in distinct locations in RAM and then recall them, or it can alter and restore them if needed.

रोख मोबदला – **payment** - sum of money paid : paying or being paid.

रोजनिशी /दैनंदिनी – **diary** - personal daily record of events, thoughts, appointments, work done etc.

रोसेट्टा दगड – **rosetta stone** - it is a piece of ancient Egyptain stone bearing inscriptions. It is now preserved in the British Museum. It was found near that town of Rosetta or Rashid on the bank of river Nile. It was derived in 1999 A.D.

रॉम – **read only memory (ROM)** - the memory usually used to hold important programmes or data that must be available to the computer when power is first turned on. Information in ROM is placed during the process of manufacture and is unalterable. Informaiton stored in ROMs does not disappear when power is turned off.

रॉयल सोसायटी – **Royal Society -** a Society which the British government funded and supported for scientific investigation since 1662.

लक्षण मालिका - train of characteristics - series of characteristics used while preparing schedules of classification.

लक्षण/गुणविशेष – attribute / quality - any property, quality or characteristic that can be described to a person or thing; as strength and bravery are two of his attributes.

लक्षणांक/लक्षण - characteristic - an attribute by which concepts or things are assembled or divided in classification.

लक्षितार्थ – connotation - a term in classification indicating all the qualities conveyed by or comprised in a class name e.g. 'man' in connotation means the personality, colour, height etc.

लक्ष्य भाषा – target language - the language into which the translation is being made.

लक्ष्य वाचक- target readers - readers for whom a particular writing is meant.

लक्ष्य/केंद्र – focus - centre of attention.

लक्ष्य – foci - aim-target.

लक्ष्यशोध – focus finding - finding centre of activity, attention, etc.

लघु अनियतकालिके - little periodicals - irregular periodicals.

लघु तांत्रिक वाचक - low technique readers - readers who have a smattering knowledge of a subject or profession.

लघु तबकडी – **compact disk** - a storage device which uses optical laser storage techniques, ease of handling and greatly enhanced storage capacity.

लघु तालिकीकरण – **short cataloguing** - in such cataloguing, the entries provide author, main title and publisher only.

लघु शीर्षक/लघुग्रंथनाम - **fly title** - a short title of a document.

लघुआकारी/लघुआकार – **undersized** - document having size smaller than the normal one.

लघुकरण – **reduction** - action of reducing something.

लघुग्रंथनाम - **half title / partial title / false title / fly title / bastard title.**

लघुचित्र/लघुरूप – **miniature** - a small painting or illuminated letter, as in a medieval manuscript. A copy or model on a very small scale.

लघुनिबंध प्रकाशन – **monographic publication** - a publication of a scholarly written study of a single subject.

लघुनिबंध – **essay** - a short, literary composition dealing with a single subject usually from a personal point of view and without attempting completeness.

लघुपुस्तक – **brochure** - pamphlet, short descriptive booklet.

लघुरूपन – **miniaturization** - a copy of the document which is greatly reduced and usually read or reproduced by means of optical aids.

लघुलहरी उपग्रह – **microwave satellite** - Microwave transmission refers to the technology of transmitting information or energy by the use of radio waves whose wavelengths are conveniently measured in small numbers of centimetre; these are called microwaves.

ललित कला अकादमी – **Lalit Kala Akademy** - an institution established by Govt. of India in 1954 for development of Indian Art and Culture.

ललित साहित्य – **belle - letters** - polite literature or works of literary art showing grace and imagination as poetry, drama, criticism, fiction and essays. From the French; literally 'beautiful letters'.

ललितेतर वाङ्मय/ललितेतर – **non - fiction** - literary work except fiction, novels etc. or any other published material which is not fiction.

लवचिक अंदाजपत्रक – **flexible budget** - a budget that recognizes the difference and variable costs and is designed to change in relation to the level of activity actually attained.

लवचिक काळ - **flexitime** - a system allowing some flexibility as to working hours.

लवचिक चिन्हांकन – **flexible notation** - a notation which has the quality of allowing by addition one or more subject at any place in classification without dislocating the sequence of either notation or the classification schedule.

लवचिक तबकडी – **floppy disk** - a magnetic storage media of 5.25 inch size.

लवचिक बांधणी – **flexible binding** - any binding having material other than stiff boards in its cover, any binding that permits the book to open perfectly flat without damaging its pages.

लवचिकता/समायोजकता – **flexibility / elasticity** - ability to bend without breaking.

लवचिकपणा – **flexibility / elasticity** - the attribute is specially used for quality of classification scheme so as to accommodate newly emerged subject.

लवचिक वर्गीकरण – **flexible classification** - a classification scheme into which new subjects may be introduced without disturbing the logical arrangement of the system.

लवचिक – **elastic** - ability to recover readily from depression, adversity or like.

लागोपाठ येणारा – **consecutive** - following continuously, in sequence.

लाघव नियम – **law of parsimony** - law given by Dr. S. R. R. relating to selection of one the of alternatives which will save more and be more economic.

लिखित प्रतिसाद – **written response** - documentary response, which is put in black and white.

लिनन परिष्करण – **linen-finish** - paper, the surface of which is made to resemble linen by placing it between plates of zinc & sheets of linen under pressure.

लिनन कागद – **linen paper** - a paper made from rags, originally from linen rags.

लिननसदृश – **linen-faced** - paper with linen on one or both sides.

लिपी/लिखित – **script** - a form of printer's cursive type resembling handwriting. Any type face which is cut to resemble handwriting.

लिप्यंतर/प्रतिलेखन – **transcription** - an arrangement in which some liberty is taken for modification.

लिप्यंतर/अक्षरांतरण – **transliteration** - 1) transcription of a word written into corresponding letters of another language, for example, words written in Devanagari may be transcribed in Roman script, e.g. (AMAR).

2) to represent the work of one language in the script of another language phonetically, proper names are invariably transliterated and not translated.

लिप्यंतरण – **transliteration** - spelling the words of one language into other in form of earlier one.

लिलाव सूची - **auction catalogue** - list of the items available for sell through auction.

लेख - **article** - written work on a single subject.

लेख/दस्तऐवज/प्रलेख – **document** - anything written or printed to be used as record or proof.

लेखक अंक (ग्रंथकार नोंद) – **author number** - it is used for combination of letters and figures which has been assigned to each book for the purpose of preserving on the shelves with alphabetical arrangement by author under each class.

लेखक चिन्ह – **author mark** - symbols are used to represent authors and so individualize books having the same class, subject to simplify the arrangement of books and catalogue entries.

लेखक तालिका/ग्रंथकार तालिका – **author catalogue** - a catalogue in which entries are arranged by the names of authors.

लेखक शीर्षक पूरक नोंद – **author title added entry** - an added entry which involves two elements, placed in a tracing also at the top of a secondary entry. It would be given for author's name followed by the title of a book when adoption is involved or in a subject heading for a commentary on an individual work.

लेखक शीर्षक/ग्रंथकार शीर्षक – **author heading** - the heading under which an author entry is made.

लेखक /ग्रंथकार आवृत्ती – **author's edition** - writer's edition published with authors introduction, photograph, signature etc.

लेखक ग्रंथसूची – **author bibliography** - 1) A list of books, articles etc. by and about a particular author.
2) Bibliography on a subject arranged as per the alphabetical sequence of the names of the authors.

लेखक निर्देशन नोंद – **author index entry** - an index entry made under the name of an author.

लेखक नोंद/ग्रंथकार नोंद – **author entry** - an entry made according to the name of author.

लेखक व शीर्षक तालिका – **author and title catalogue** - a catalogue having author and title entries and sometimes entries for editors, translators but excluding subject entries.

लेखक विश्लेषणात्मक नोंद – **author analytical entry** - an entry which is made under author's name (for a part of work).

लेखक शीर्ष/लेखन शैली – **author style** - the usual combination of black capitals and lowercase letters which is used for author headings in a catalogue.

लेखक – **author / writer** - a person who can be considered as creator, originator of a work.

लेखनिक (लेखक) – **scribe** - a person engaged by the author to prepare script of a document.

लेखांची निर्देश सूची – **index to article** - an index of articles which are published in periodicals.

लेखाचित्रकार नोंद – **illustrator entry** - entry made in a catalogue under the name of illustrator.

लेखाचित्रकार – **illustrator** - a person who illustrates; especially, an artist who makes; illustrations for books, magazines, etc.

लेखाचित्रकाराचे नाव केलेली नोंद – **illustrator's entry** - a catalogue entry for an illustration whose work has been of sufficient importance to be catalogued.

लेखाचित्रित – **illustrated** - to furnish (books etc.) with explanatory or decorative drawings, designs, or pictures.

लेखाचित्रे/छायाचित्रे – **illustrationed** - a pictorial or other representation usually designed to elucidate the text.

लेखाच्या पूरक संदर्भासाठी दिलेले इतर संदर्भ – **reference** - supportive citations with keywords from text to footnotes or chapter notes.

लेखाधिकार/स्वामित्व – **copyright** - exclusive right granted by law for a certain number of years to make and sale copies of literary, musical or artistic work.

लेखापरीक्षण – **auditing** - an official examination of accounts & security of financial transactions of a government, or non-government body or institution.

लेखापरीक्षा/हिशेबतपासणी – **audit** - an inspection of an official accounts of a library.

लेखाशास्त्र – **accountancy** - system of maintaining account statement of receipts and payment.

लेबल काम/बोधचिठ्ठी काम – **labelling** - work of pasting and writing of labels.

लेबल/चिठ्ठी/खुणचिठ्ठी – **label** - tag. A small piece of paper fabric etc. attached to a book for giving information about call number.

लेव्हॅन्ट (चामडे) – **levant** - a high grade Morocco leather used for binding books, and made from the skin of the Angora goat.

लोकप्रिय आवृत्ती/स्वस्त आवृत्ती – **popular edition** - an edition which is sold at a cheaper price, because of the cheaper material used for its production.

लोकशाहीवादी नेता – **democratic leader** - a person who tries to do what the majority of subordinates desire.

लोकसंख्या – **population** - 1) an aggregate of individual units whether composed of things, having the characteristic under study. 2) all the inhabitants of a place.

लोकसंख्याशास्त्र – **demography** - the science of vital statistic, as of births, deaths, marriages, etc. of populations.

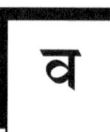

व

वंशावळीचा तक्ता – **genealogical table** - table concerned with tracing family descent. A diagram with branches showing a family ancestry.

वगळणे/गाळणे/पुसणे - **delete** - a command used in computer to remove a program, character from the memory of the computer.

वटवणी/निष्कासन/समाशोधन केंद्र – **clearing house** - an organization that collects and maintains records of research, development, and engineering being planned, currently in progress, or completed, it provides referral services to other sources for information relating to these activities.

वर्कशीट – **work sheet** - a sheet of paper containing working notes, preliminary formulations etc.

वर्ग मध्यंतर – **class interval** - in case of continuous data each observation may take a distinct but close value to another observation. Such observations are grouped and kept at a particular interval, for example, a case study may include all persons within the height of a 5 feet to 6 feet in one group. Such an interval is termed as class interval.

वर्ग – **class** - an original field of study which has common characteristics.

वर्गकार – **classifier** - a person who classifies the documents as per the given scheme of classification.

वर्गणी – subscription - the price at which periodical literature is available for a definite period.

वर्ग निर्देशी नोंद – class index entry - index entry in a classified catalogue giving the class number for a class.

वर्गवारी लावणे – classify - the process of grouping collections in their subject order or in any order which will suit to the user.

वर्गवारीचे काम – classifying - an act of grouping entities on the basis of characteristics.

वर्गांक – class number - 1) it is the translation of the subject embodied in a document from natural language to classificatory language or it is a symbol fixing the position of a subject document relating to other documents of the same subject and also with other subject.
2) the ordinal which fixes the place of a subject relative to other subjects in a scheme of classification.

वर्गीकरण (ग्रंथालय) – classification (library) - arranging books and other reading materials in a library primarily on the basis of their subject contents in a useful way. It is also called systematic or logical arrangement.

वर्गीकरण तक्ते – classification schedule / schedules of classification - 1) document specifying the subjects and sub-subjects alongwith the symbol i.e. assigned to each sub-subject.
2) that part of a classification system which lists subjects in a systematic way along with their notation given against each.

वर्गीकरण तज्ज्ञ – classificationist - a person who designs a scheme of classification.

वर्गीकरण पद्धत - classification system - a particular scheme/schedule of library classification, such as Dewey Decimal classification, Ranganathan's Colon classification, or Library of Congress classification, and many more.

वर्गीकरण विज्ञान – taxonomy - the science of classification.

वर्गीकरण संख्या – classification number - a specific number assigned to a particular subject.

वर्गीकरण संहिता – classification code - book explaining the rules and principles to be used for preparation of classification scheme, book explaining theory of classification.

वर्गीकरण – classification - a process of systematic arrangement of documents by applying common characteristics, or arrangement of things according to likeness and unlikeness.

वर्गीकरणकार – **classificationist -** a person responsible for preparation of the scheme of book classification.

वर्गीकृत क्रम – **classified arrangement -** arrangement in which documents are kept in their respective class identified by the classification scheme implemented. It is decided on the basis of characteristics which helps in arranging all the relevant subject documents at one place to facilitate.

वर्गीकृत ग्रंथालय – **classified library -** a library in which collection is arranged by using a scheme of classification.

वर्गीकृत तालिका संहिता – **classified catalogue code -** a catalogue code which contains rules for preparing classified subject entries. The code was formulated by Indian library scientist Dr. S.R. Ranganathan. First edition was published in 1934.

वर्गीकृत तालिका – **classified catalogue -** it comprises of two parts, classified and alphabetical. In classified part subject or number entries are arranged in subject order and in alphabetical order it forms a subject catalogue on the basis of subject classification adopted by the scheme implemented.

वर्गीकृत विषय तालिका – **classified subject catalogue -** forms part of library catalogue in which the entries are arranged alphabetically subjectwise.

वर्डस्टार – **wordstar -** a popular word processing package, frequently used in business.

वर्णक्रमानुसारी विषय दृष्टिकोन – **alphabetical subject approach -** there are different methods of providing subject approach to information contained in documents. One of them is known as alphabetical subject approach. As per this approach, items of information are first grouped under their specific subjects and then arranged according to alphabetical order so that specific subjects can be retrieved easily.

वर्णपट दृष्टिकोन – **spectrum approach -** approach of an appearance, image or specter.

वर्णानुक्रम युक्ती – **alphabetical device -** alphabetical plan. Use of first alphabet of popular name to suffix in a class number.

वर्णानुक्रम रचना शब्दानुसारी – **word - by - word alphabetization -** arrangement of information in alphabetical order. It may have letters or words as the basis for arrangement.

वर्तनवाद – **behaviourism -** social action or behaviour where interaction is the context in which personality develops.

वर्तुळाकार व द्विमार्गी प्रक्रिया – **circular and two way process -** involving or allowing exchange between the facilitator and the user of knowledge or information.

वर्तुळीय – **radial** - going from the centre outward or from the circumference inward along the radius.

वस्तुसंग्रहालय ग्रंथालय – **museum library** - a library having special collection of rare documents representing history and culture is maintained to facilitate the users.

वस्तुसंग्रहालय – **museum** - place where all items reflecting culture and history of the nation are preserved.

वस्तुसूची – **inventory** - detailed list. e.g. of goods, furniture, jobs to be done etc.

वांशिक तक्ता – **genealogical table** - a representation of the lineage of a person or persons in tabular or diagrammatical form.

वांशिक/राष्ट्रीय गट तक्ता – **racial / ethnic / national groups table** - a table of notations designating specific racial, ethnic, or national groups. It is applied to other notations in the schedules or in any auxiliary tables through use of add notes, or it is added to any class number in the schedules of its own through the ss-089 table 1, in DDC.

वाक्यरचना – **syntax** - a technical term in linguistics relating to the grammatical arrangement of words in a sentence.

वाक्यव्यवस्था/वाक्यविचारविषयक संबंध – **syntactic relationship** - syntactic relationship arise from the context of subjects in specific documents or syntax. They are less permanent as compared to semantic relationships. For an indexer, it is necessary to distinguish between these two types of relationships and to provide suitable mechanism in indexes to take care of them.

वाचक टीप – **reader's note** - a descriptive book annotation which has been intended to inform the reader about a book and to interest him in reading it.

वाचक मार्गदर्शन – **user guidance** - a guidance extended by the library staff for use of library.

वाचक सहयोगी – **user friendly** - a computer system which is easy to use, clear to understand and helpful to users.

वाचक खर्च – **user cost** - per user cost of providing services.

वाचक गट – **user group** - number of readers registered with a library.

वाचक गरजा पाहणी – **user need survey** - process of identifying requirements of users.

वाचक दुवा (ग्रंथपाल) - **user interface** - person making contact between informatione and user.

वाचक दुवा – **user interfaces** - establishment of direct contacts with users of an SDI service. This is one of the essential components of an SDI system which provides for direct interaction between the users and the SDI system. It helps in making the SDI service more purposive & efficient.

वाचक पत्र – **reader's card** - refers to the card issued to a reader while registering. It is an authority letter for reader to use a library.

वाचक रूपरेखा – **user profile** - 1) it is a statement of user's information requirements. The construction of user profiles in an exacting intellectual task.
2) a record of user with their subject interest.

वाचक लेखक नातेसंबंध – **reading writer relationship** - relation between writers and readers that implicitly or explicitly exist in a writing situation.

वाचक विश्लेषण – **reader analysis** - analyzing a target group with reference to a writing situation.

वाचक संक्षिप्त चरित्र – **user profile** - data on any type of readers as a guide for technical writing.

वाचक सल्ला सेवा – **RAS (reader's advisory service)** - formed at the end of 1973 by Science Associates International, and with the support of nearly 150 libraries and information centres throughout U.S.A. and Canada.

वाचक सहयोगी कार्यक्रम – **user friendly programme** - a program which is simple and can be used without much efforts.

वाचक सहयोगी – **User friendly** - a computer system or any system which is easy to use, clear to understand and helpful to users.

वाचक सेवा – **user services** - the service provided for making use of the holdings of the library.

वाचक स्मृती – **user memory** - central processing unit (CPU) memory which is able to be accessed and changed by the user. It usually refers to the portion of random access memory which is used by applicaiton programmes.

वाचक/उपयोक्ता गरज पाहणी – **user need survey** - a survey conducted for a systematic study of the information need of a specific group of people.

वाचक – **user / requester / reader** - 1) library user or in computer a device that accepts information in one form and converts it to another form, also called user.
2) the person who will ultimately use the retrieval information.

3) individual or a group of individuals who have potential for being exposed to and using and information product or service.

वाचकांचा वेळ वाचवा – **save time of the reader** - it is the fourth law of library science which is to improve/achieve accuracy in library services.

वाचकाची खूण – **reader's mark** - identification mark (user I D) registered for a user,

वाचन अभ्यासक्रम – **reading course** - a list of books selected for an individual or a group as a guide to systematic, consecutive reading on a definite subject.

वाचन आवड/रस – **reading interests** - topics that appeal to readers, especially to those of the same age, sex, occupation, income or cultural group.

वाचन कक्ष – **reading room** - a room in a library used by the readers to consult library collections.

वाचन मंडळ – **reading circle** - a group of people having a hobby of reading, a group of library users having interest in reading.

वाचन मार्गदर्शन – **reading guidance** - directing the choice of books by readers in accordance with their interests and abilities through personal advice or printed lists.

वाचन यादी – **reading list** - a list of documents which is required to study the given subject.

वाचन साहित्य – **reading material** - reading material which is required to study the given subject.

वाचन – **reading** - looking at & comprehending the meaning of printed matter.

वाचनीय प्रत – **readable copy** - copy of a book which is offered for sale in poor condition but the text of which is complete and legible.

वाचनीयता यार्ड काठी - **reading yardstick** - statistical measurement of use of library materials.

वाड्यांची ग्रंथालये – **hamlet libraries** - small village libraries.

वाढ/भार यादी – **list of additions** - a list of recently received documents in a library such as books, journals, reports etc. It may be in classified or alphabetical order.

वाढ/भार – **additions / acquisition** - acquisition is the continuous process for collection building of library records. It may be through purchase, gift, exchange etc.

वातविलेप – **aerosols** - an air pollutant which refers to the dispersion of solid or liquid particles of microscopic size in gaseous media, such as dust, smoke or moist.

वापर/परिपाठ/प्रथा – **usage -** manner of using some treatment, habitful or customary practice especially in the way words are used.

वारंवारिता वितरण – **frequency distribution -** it is a means of imposing a degree of structure and order on numerical research data.

वारंवारिता/पुन्हा पुन्हा – **frequency -** 1) rate of occurrence or repetition of some thing, usually measured over a particular period of time.
2) the number of times a recurring signal repeats itself within a given unit of time.
3) the number of times a particular value is observed is termed as the frequency of the particular value.

वार्ताशास्त्र/माहिती संगणकशास्त्र – **informatics -** 1) science of processing information/data.
2) science of information, a branch of computer science.

वार्षिक अंक – **year number -** ordinal number which is the translation of the year of publication of the document.

वार्षिक पैलू – **year facet -** part of the book number of a document which is its year number. It is used for construction of book number.

वार्षिकी अहवाल – **annual report -** a publication which gives account of the activities of the organisation during one year period. The information recorded in it is regarded as first hand authentic information.

वार्षिकी – **annual/yearbook -** 1) publication which appears once in a year.
2) yearbook is a document which covers events of a given year and is published to keep the earlier publication up to date.

वास्तव वेळ – **real-time -** in computing, pertaining to operations that are performed in conjuction with some external process or user and which are required to meet the time constraints imposed by that process or user. e.g. an online information service.

वास्तविक/खरा काळ (माहिती प्रतिप्राप्तीचा) – **real time (Information Retrieval) -** the technique of co-ordinating data processing with external related physical events on a time basis, thereby making possible the prompt reporting of conditions such as the airline reservation system which can report reservation openings almost instantly.

वास्तविक/खरे नांव – **real name -** a name of a person which has family recognition and recognition of law as well.

वाहतूक आकार/वाहणवळ - **freight -** the price paid for transporting goods or merchandise by hand, sea or air.

विंडोज – **windows** - in computer programming, pertaining to a software techniques that facilitates the movement of data between packages.

विकार – **inflections** - 1. suffix used to inflex a word (e.g.-ed, - ing).
2. the way that you speak, for example when you emphasise particular words.

विकेंद्रीकरण – **decentralization** - when duties, powers and authorities are delegated to another empolyee in an organisation.

विक्रीस उपलब्ध नसलेले साहित्य – **grey literature** - literature which is printed but not available for sale e.g. reports, office records, pamphlets, brochure etc.

विक्रेता – **vendor** - 1) a person who sales information sources.
2) the provider of online searching service.

विखुरलेला संदर्भ – **scattered reference** - a cross reference in the index not referring to a specific term but suggesting a variety of possibilities.

विगमन – **induation** - a formal process of introducing & training new employees on their job, position or office.

विगोपित – **exposed** - (of a place) not sheltered.

विचरण – **variance** - it is expressed as $0^2 = 1/n \ \text{fi}(xi - x)^2$

विचार/मोबदला – **consideration** - 1) a leader's act which implies supportive concern for the followers in a group. 2) remmuneration paid for the efforts or help extended.

विचारप्रणाली/मतप्रणाली - **school of thought.**

विजाणु प्रकाशक – **electronic publisher** - a publisher who brings out publication in various electronic media such as CD -ROM and WORM.

वितरण/वाटप वाहन – **delivery van** - a vehicle used for transporting documents of a library.

वित्त – **finance** - money; the capital involved in a project, especially the capital that has to be raised to start a new business.

वित्तीय अंदाज/अनुमान – **financial estimate** - estimate or tentative financial expenditure and requirement.

वित्तीय आकलन – **financial estimation** - estimating the amount of money required for running services of an institution.

वित्तीय नोंद/अभिलेख – **financial record** - 1) document, keeping record of financial expenditure and receipt etc.

2) documents which keep track of library expenditure, cash books ledger, salary bill register, allocation register etc.

वित्तीय वर्ष – **financial year (fiscal year)** - period of twelve months over which annual accounts and taxes are calculated. Generally it is from 1st April to 31st March of every year.

वित्तीय विवरण – **financial statement** - details of the finance distribution.

वित्तीय व्यवस्थापन – **financial management** - 1) management which deals with collection and tilization of funds.

2) management concerned with the planning, administration and control of financial resources in the accomplishment of organizational objectives.

3) an element of management dealing with acquisition, distribution and utilization of funds.

वित्तीय संसाधने – **financial resorces** - resources through which money is collected to run a library.

विदेशी चलन/हुंडावळ – **foreign exchange** - conversion of currency of one country with another.

विदेशी प्रकाशन – **foreign publication** - publication published in the countries other than the home country.

विदेशी माहिती केंद्र - **foreign exchange centre** - the information centre of the foreign agencies to disseminate information about their socio-cultural developments.

विद्यापीठ अनुदान आयोग – **university grants commission** - central autonomous body in a country providing grants and maintaining the standards of research, teaching and extension in universities / colleges.

विद्यापीठ ग्रंथालय – **university library** - the library maintained to support academic programmes of the university system.

विद्यापीठ/विश्वविद्यालय – **university** - an autonomous educational institution which imparts instructions in various disciplines and awards diploma / degrees.

विद्यार्थी पत्र – **student's card** - borrower card; reader ticket.

विद्याशाखा/ज्ञानशाखा – **discipline** - a branch of knowledge, subject of instructions.

विद्वत समाज – **learned society** - society having knowledge acquired by study. A group of knowledge scholarly people.

विद्वान – **erudite** - person having or showing great hearing scholarly.

विधान - **proposition** - generalized statement of a relationship among facts.

विधी अहवाल/निवेदन - **law reporter** - publication containing decisions of courts.

विधीग्राह्य – **valid upto** - letter of permission prepared and issued using the correct formalities.

विधीमंडळ - **legislature** - body of people with the power to make and change laws.

विनिमय प्रारूप – **exchange format** - an arrangement of data according to predefined rules (usually machine readable form) intended to facilitate the transfer of data between system and using tags or set position in the record for damnification of data elements.

विनिर्दिष्ट उलट संदर्भ – **specific cross reference** - a reference in a catalogue to a specific heading or headings.

विनिर्दिष्ट माहिती – **specific information** - a selected information on a identified topic.

विनिर्दिष्ट वर्गीकरण – **specific classification** - allocating a most specific class number when two or more options are available.

विनिर्दिष्ट/विविक्षित नोंद - **specific entry** - entry mentioning a specific approach.

विपणन तंत्र – **marketing technique** - the systematic gathering, recording and analysing of data about problems relating to marketing of goods and services.

विपणन लेखा – **marketing audit** - it is an independent examination of the entire marketing effort of an organisation covering objectives, programmes, implementation, organisation and control for the purpose of determining what is being done and recommending what would be done in the further.

विपणन – **marketing** - 1) theory and practice of commercial selling.
2) a planned approach to identify and gain support of users and develop appropriate services in a manner which benefits the user and further aims at objectives of the information centres.

विभाग माहिती केंद्र – **sectoral information centres** - information centres devoted for specific disciplines or mission or functions offering specialized services.

विभाग/अनुच्छेद – **section / department** - it is a section of the institution e.g. library has a periodical section.

विभागाचे ग्रंथालय – **department library** - 1) such library is maintained almost by all the ministries and subordinate departments 2) the library maintained as extension in the departments of university /college.

विभागीय केंद्र – **sectorial centres** - centres pertaining to a geographical sector.

विभागीय ग्रंथालय – **divisional library** - a collection attached to and administered by a division or a group of related section.

विभागीय तालिका – **departmental catalogue** - a catalogue consisting of entries for books possessed by a department for which it is developed.

विभागीय प्रकाशन - **departmental publication** - the publication generated by department. These are generally research /project reports.

विभागीय युक्ती – **sector/sectorial device** - sector device for forming an isolate or sharpening a host focus in the form of an isolate or an array isolate with the help of subject characteristics. This is one of the most important device in colon classification which provides much autonomy to classifier.

विभागीय संग्रह – **departmental collection** - a collection which is developed to satisfy the requirements of the department or collection of documents generated by the department.

विभाजक गुण – **divisional characteristic** - characteristic preferred as the basis for the division of the entities of a universe.

विभाजन (शिस्तीनुसार) – **division by discipline** - division of knowledge into broader areas of study like natural science, social science, humanities an so on. All the modern classification systems follow division of knowledge by discipline. J.D. Brown's subject classification follows the discipline reverse method of classification by topic, also called one place classification.

विभाजन – **division** - process of sorting the entities of a universe into sub-aggregates on the basis of a preferred characteristic, putting like entities into the same sub-aggregate and the unlike entities into different sub-aggregates.

विभेदन – **differentiation** - (from some thing) be a mark of difference between (people or things that distinguish)

विराम युक्ती/क्लृप्ती – **gap device** - device used to keep some gaps in numbers while denoting classification number so that in future if any new subject develops, it can be incorporated at proof place.

विरामचिन्हे - **punctuation mark** - literary symbols or (e.g. full stop, comma, question mark etc.) used in a written or printed text to separate sentences etc. and to make the meaning clear.

विरुद्धार्थक शब्द – **antonyms** - word that is opposite in meaning to another.

विरोधात्मक – **antithetic** - contract of ideas marked by the choice and arrangement of words.

विलंब शुल्क – **late fee / fine** - amount charged for defaulters who return documents late.

विल्हेवाट/वाटप – **allocation** - 1) distribution of grants for meeting the anticipated demand 2) in classification providing the relevant place to a class among other classes.

विवक्षा/प्रश्न – **problem** - 1) unknown fact or issue. 2) thing that is difficult to deal with or understand.

विवरण अनुच्छेद – **annotation section** - section in which a note added to any entry in a catalogue, reading list or bibliography, to elucidate, evaluate or describe the subject and centrents of a book; it sometimes gives particulars of the author.

विवरण – **description** - the detailed record.

विवरण/मानक – **specifications** - publications which provide details of preparation of a system or work standards to achieve uniformity.

विवरणकार – **descriptor** - a word or symbol used to represent the document.

विवरणपत्रिका फलक – **bulletin board** - an online message system which can post notices and general information on to the terminals of the users of a network.

विवरणपत्रिका – **bulletin** -1) a publication, generally a pamphlet, issued by a govt, society or other organization at regular intervals and in serial form.
2) a predicator occasional publication containing lists of books added to a library, and other library information.

विवरणात्मक ग्रंथसूची – **descriptive bibliography** - it is a type of bibliography in which information is covered in more detail.

विवरणात्मक घटक – **descriptive element** - terms added after the name of a person or a corporate body, inclusive of individualizing term, to denote the role played.

विवरणात्मक तालिकीकरण – **descriptive cataloguing** - type of library catalogue which has more concern with detailed physical description of a document.

विवरणात्मक संदर्भ – **explanatory reference** - reference that provides explanation.

विविधता – **multiplexing** - it is a system or device which takes a number of data communication channels and combines the signals into one common channel transmission.

विवेचक मार्ग पद्धत – **CPM (critical path method)** - a planning and control technique that involves the display of a complex project as a network with one time estimate used for each step in the project.

विवेचक मार्ग पद्धत – **critical path method** - an aspect of PERT; this is a method of network analysis that, by means of diagrams of the order in which jobs are to be accomplished is used for planning, estimating, scheduling and controlling, engineering, construction and related aspects.

विवेचन/वर्णनपद्धती – **treatment** - process or manner of treating subject.

विवेचनात्मक निबंध संग्रह – **treatise** - detailed work (on a literary work or other subject) dealing systematically with one subject.

विशिष्ट नोंद – **specific entry** - entry mentioning a specific approach.

विशिष्ट माहिती – **specific information** - a selected information.

विशिष्टी – **specifications** - a statement containing a detailed description of particulars as in the terms of a contract or directions on how to make or contract some thing.

विशेष अंक/संख्या – **special issue / number** - a special issue of the periodical brought out to meet the special occasions / purpose.

विशेष आवृत्ती – **special edition** - an edition brought out to fulfil certain identified objectives.

विशेष उपांग विचार – **special isolate idea** - isolate idea related to a basic class or to an isolate idea or to array isolate idea or to a small group of basic class, isolate idea and array isolate idea as the case may be.

विशेष ग्रंथालय– **special library** - a library developed by the various departments to achieve special objectives. The collections and services of these libraries are designed according to the specific purpose.

विशेष ग्रंथालये – **special libraries** - libraries that collect and store materials related only to the area of interest in addition to others, and serve the specialized requirements of specialist users in anticipation of and in response to specific demands.

विशेष नोंद – **specific entry** - entry mentioning a specific approach.

विशेष वर्गीकरण पद्धत – **special classification system** - 1) a classification developed only for a particular subject.
2) a scheme designed for depth classification of micro subjects going only with one and only specified subject field.

विशेष संग्रह – **special collection** - 1) a collection dealing with specific subject.
2) a collection of books connected with local history, celebrities, industries etc. or with one certain subject, period or collected for some particular reason, in a library which is general in character.

विशेष सूची – **special list** - a list prepared to meet some definite purpose.

विशेषज्ञ सत्ता/शक्ती/सामर्थ्य – **expert power** - an individual with this type of power has some technical expertise, skill or knowledge which are important in getting the job done.

विशेषज्ञ सल्ला – **specialist / expert advice** - advice given by a person having an expertise.

विशेषतादर्शक – **speciators** - for a special quality, feature, point, characteristic, etc.

विशेषत्व – **specificity** - in the testing of an information retrieval system, a measure expressing the ratio of the number of non-relevant documents not retrieved to the total number of non relevant documents in a file.

विश्लेषी–संश्लेषणात्मक वर्गीकरण – **analytico - synthetic classification** - पहा : विश्लेषक संश्लेषणात्मक वर्गीकरण

विश्लेषक संश्लेषणात्मक वर्गीकरण – **analytico-synthetic classification** - scheme of classification involving analysis of subject into its facets in the idea plane, transformation in the verbal plane, transformation from the focal terms in the verbal plane to the focal numbers in the notational plane, and synthesis of the focal numbers into class numbers in the notational plane.

विश्लेषक – **analyst** - a person who analyses / defines subject and develop solutions if desired.

विश्लेषण/पृथक्करण – **analysis** - study of a subject by examining its components and their relationship.

विश्लेषणात्मक ग्रंथसूची – **analytical bibliography** - a kind of bibliography which determines facts & data concerning a publication by examining the signatures, catchwords, cancels &water marks, and making a record in an approved form of the results also called 'critical' or 'historical bibliography'.

विश्लेषणात्मक टीप – **analytical note** - part of the analytical entry which gives information about the document that contains the work entered.

विश्लेषणात्मक विषय नोंद – **analytical subject entry** - specific added entry in dictionary catalogue, referring from the name of a subject forming a part of a document, to the host document and giving the place of occurrence of the subject in the host document.

विश्लेषणात्मक/अंशात्मक नोंद – **analytical entry** - entry supplementary to the main entry which is prepared for a part of the book/periodical contributions /such other works for separate authorship. It includes the reference of the document which contains it.

विश्लेषित निर्देश – **analysed index** - an alphabetical index under specific topics.

विश्लेषित शीर्षक – **analysed title** - title derived from Kernel title by adding after each kernel term. The symbol denoting the nature of its manifestation or a title comprised of focal terms identified with fundamental category.

विश्वकोश/ज्ञानकोश – **encyclopaedia** - a publication consisting of information on universe of knowledge or on all possible aspects of the branches of knowledge for which it is developed. It is usually arranged alphabetically. The publication may appear in number of volumes. It is kept upto date by publishing yearbooks.

विश्वसनीय/प्रामाणिक – **authentic** - 1) which is certified or works as per rules.
2) the one which can be believed.

विश्वसनीयता/अधिकृतता/विश्वासार्हता – **authenticity** - the quality or state of being authentic, genuine.

विषय ग्रंथसूची – **subject bibliography** - bibliography which consists entries on the subject for which it is developed.

विषय तालिका – **subject catalogue** - catalogue cards forming subject entries are strictly arranged in alphabetical order under subject headings.

विषय दृष्टिकोन – **subject approach** - users often approach information sources with a question that requires an answer or a topic for study. In other words they seek documents or information concerned with a particular subject. This method of seeking information by users, is known as subject approach to information. In order to make provision for this common approach, it is necessary to arrange documents & documents surrogates in library catalogues, indexes etc. in such a way that items of specific subject can be retrieved.

विषय निवड – **theme / topic selection** - selection of single idea/ thought for discussion through either testimony, reasoning, emotion, sensory reinforcement, analogy, illustration, example, facts and figures, and restatement.

विषय नोंद – **subject entry** - an added entry referring the subject of the document.

विषय पत्रिका/कार्यक्रम – **agenda** - a plan or subject item to be discussed for making decision on the given subject.

विषय युक्ती – subject device - 1) a class number used as an isolate number and joined to other to form class number.

2) according to Dr. S.R.Ranganathan the process is used for dividing whole classification by subject.

विषय वर्गीकरण – subject classification - scheme of classification designed by James Duff Brown and published for the first time in 1906.

विषय विभागणी वर्गीकरण – ramifying classification - branching classification.

विषय विभागणी – ramification - 1. part of a complex structure, secondary consequence, especially one that complicates.

2. branch of a subject, division extension sub-division.

विषय विशेषज्ञ – subject specialist - person who knows subject detail.

विषय विश्लेषणात्मक नोंद – subject analytical entry - specific added entry in dictionary catalogue, referring the name of a subject forming a part of a document, to the host document and giving the place of occurrence of the subject in the host document.

विषय व्यवस्था – subject arrangement - arrangement of books in their subject order.

विषय शीर्षक – subject heading - the terms reflecting the main aspect of the text. Thus these are the words or group of words which are used as search points.

विषय शीर्षक नामावली – list of subject headings - list of terms reflecting the main terms used in the text.

विषय संदर्भ – subject reference - an entry which refers as to other subject entry.

विषय – subject - 1) the theme/matter discussed in a document.

2) a theme or matter dealt within a document.

विषयव्याप्ती टिपण – scope note - a note explaining or illustrating the scope of the entry.

विषयांग युक्ती (अंकन तळ) – phase device (Notational plane) - device of prefixing a connecting symbol to digit representing a phase relation in the idea plane.

विषयांग युक्ती (विचार तळ) – phase device (Idea plane) - device for sharpening a host focus by the addition of a focus of the same species as a second phase.

विषयांग संबंध – phase relation - relation between the phases of a complex class or of a complex isolate or of a complex array isolate.

विषयांग १ – phase I - it is primary exposition of a complex class.

विषयांग २ - **phase II** - it is not the direct exposition but thereby affects the exposition of phase I.

विषयांग/अंग - **phase** - a component of a complex class or a complex isolate or a complex array isolate as the case may be.

विषयाची सखोलता/व्याप्ती - **intention & extension of the subject** - in a classification scheme, the extension of a term or class indicates all the different items included in the term. In other words, compass of the term intension indicates their qualities. Extension and intension vary conversely, in which one is great, the other is small.

विषयेतर लक्षणे - **non-subject characteristics** - features of a document representing aspects other than the core subject of the documents.

विसंकेतन - **decoder** - a logic circuit that changes a code from its encoded form back to its original form.

विसरण स्थानांतर - **diffusion transfer** - a photocopying method which produces a positive by chemical diffusion of the negative e.g. Agfa rapid, Gevacopy.

विसरण/अपस्करण - **dispersion** - reflection of the scatter of the data in a series, measures of dispersion are range, mean, deviation, standard deviation etc.

विस्तार क्षमता - **expansibility** - capacity of notation; expansion of thoughts.

विस्तार - **extension** - breadth and width of coverage of a subject.

विस्तृत वर्गीकरण - **broad classification** - arrangement of subjects in a classification scheme in broad general division with a minimum of sub-division.

विहित वर्ग - **canonical class** - further division of a class by terms expressing data or time.

वृत्त चयनक - **rapid selector** - machine designed to rotate film reel at high speed.

वृत्तपत्र कात्रण - **press clipping** - a printed paper piece clipped from a newspaper or magazine which contains some specific information on given subjects.

वृत्तपत्र चिन्ह - **press mark** - a symbol indicating the object fixed according to the requirement of press.

वृत्तपत्र विज्ञाप्ती - **press release** - official efforts to get information published for wider dissemination.

वृत्तपत्रिका - **newsletters** - publications issued by organizations, often simple in format and crisp in style, they provide speedy information for a definite public (audience).

वृत्तमाहितीपत्रक/विवरणपत्रिका – **bulletin** - a publication which appears at regular intervals as a serial publication.

वृत्तान्त – **annals** - a periodical record of events which generally appears in chronological order.

वृत्ती/दृष्टिकोन – **attitudes** - attitudes are structured psychological tendencies consisting of cognitive, affective (emotional feeling) and behavioural components each of which has its own content & structure. There can be wide variations in the content of an attitude, independently on an issue to which the attitude relates.

वृद्धी वाचन सवयींची – **promotion of reading habits** - the library has programmes like exhibition, extension lecture, essay competition etc. to create reading culture.

वृद्धी – **promotion** - 1) encouragement or aid to the progress of a cause.
2) advancement or encouragement on behalf of some cause, product, service or organisation.

वृद्धीची भूमिका – **promotional role** - activities related to raising the capacity of the library in relation to services to its users.

वेळ अभ्यास – **time study** - 1) the systematic measurement and analysis of the time required to do work.
2) technique used to determine the time required to carry out activity at a defined standard of performance.

वेष्टन/पुठ्ठा/आवरण – **cover** - paper or any other material like cloth, leather etc. to protect document.

वेष्टन – **jacket / wrapper** - the outer paper cover of the book which usually contains information about book (blurb) and its author (book jacket), on its last page.

वेष्टन/आवरण शीर्षक – **cover title** - short title is printed on the back or spine of the document to identify the document or title available on cover page.

वैदिक वर्गीकरण – **vedic classification** - scheme of classes implied in Upanishad and later adopted in the Puranas, the Bhagavat Geeta and the Tantras.

वैद्यकीय ग्रंथसूची – **medical bibliography** - bibliography for the documents available in the field of medical and allied sciences.

वैद्यकीय ग्रंथालय – **medical library** - library attached to the institution imparting instructions in health science education.

वैद्यकीय – **medical** - of the art of medicine of curing disease.

वैश्लेषिक/विश्लेपिक – **analytic** - of or using analysis.

व्यक्त प्रलेख – **known document** - a document about which user has some knowledge like writer, title, publisher and publication year and so on.

व्यक्तिगत संगणक – **personal computer** - a computer equipped with memory, languages, and peripherals and well suited for use in a home, office or school.

व्यक्तिचित्र/प्रतिमाचित्र – **portrait** - a representation of a person made from life, especially a picture or representation of the face.

व्यक्तित्व उपांग – **personality isolate** - the residue arising in the analysis of a subject into the fundamental categories after time, space, energy, matter and anteriorising isolates are separated out.

व्यक्तित्व दर्शन सामान्य (उपांग) – **personality common isolates** - the insolates preceded by when attached to a host class. Scheduled mnemonics based on subject device is used to devise common personality isolates. A common personality isolates should generally be added after space isolates. The schedule of common personality isolates includes profession, institution, laboratory, learning body, museum, educational institution, administrative departments, endowment, cultural organizations etc.

व्यक्तित्व मुख – **personality facet** - one of the five fundamental categories of classification stated by Dr.S.R. Ranganathan. It determines the degree of affinity of subjects, generally the wholes and organs. This fact has given status of soul by Dr. Ranganathan. Parts constituents etc. of the whole are regarded as the fundamental category personality.

व्यक्तित्व – **personality** - an image of the individual among others.

व्यक्तिबोली – **idiolect** - the linguistic system of an individual speaker i.e. her/his personal dialect.

व्यक्तिभावरहित – **impersonal** - not influenced by, showing or involving human feelings not referring to any particular personal objective.

व्यक्तिभेदकरण – **individual** - separation of an entity in a universe into a unitary class by the process of assortment.

व्यक्तिमत्त्व – **individuality** - all the characteristics that belongs to a particular person that make him/her different from others.

व्यक्ती तक्ता – **'persons' table** - a table of notations designating persons by specific occupational and other social classes. It is applied to other number in the schedules or auxiliary tables through the use of add notes, or it is added to any class number in the schedules of its own through the ss-088 in table 1, in DDC.

व्यक्तिगत तालिका – **personal catalogue** - a catalogue consisting of entries of one's collection and of collections about him.

व्यक्तिगत दैनंदिनी – **personal diary** - a record having personal feelings, details, accounts etc.,

व्यक्तिगत माहिती पद्धत – **personal system of information** - individual user's profile for modulated and planned independent study.

व्यक्तिगत लेखक – **personal author** - person as an author, the responsibilities for thought, expression contained in the work resting solely on his private capacity and not on the capacity of any office he may hold within and not 'on' the corporate body.

व्यक्तिगत संगणक – **personal computer (pc)** - low priced, more popular, widely used computers.

व्यक्तिगत संप्रेषण – **personal communication** - that which is communicated or imparted; information or intelligence imparted by word or writing; as, the general received an important personal communication.

व्यक्तिगत साहित्याचे उपविभाग तक्ता – **subdivisions of individual literature table** - it is a table primarily of form divisions of literature preceded by standard subdivisions applicable to the main class 800 literature. Table 3 is to be used only on instructions. The second part of table 3 is table 3-A consisting of recurring aspects, features or themes in liteature.

व्यक्तिगत सेवा – **personal service** - service when rendered directly person to person.

व्यक्तिगत – **personal** - affecting or belonging to a particular person.

व्यवसाय – **profession** - 1) paid occupation especially which requires advanced education and training e.g. architecture, law or medicine etc.
2) body of persons engaged in an occupation, requiring extensive education in branch of science, arts etc.

व्यवसायकर – **professional tax** - business tax, employment tax.

व्यवस्थापकीय कार्य – **managerial functions** - the major components of manager's job including planning, organization, motivating and controlling.

व्यवस्थापन तत्त्वे – **management principles** - guides for managerial action. They are fundamental truths of organization and management.

व्यवस्थापन नियंत्रण - **management control** - the process whereby resources are obtained & used effectively & efficiently in the accomplishment of the organization objectives.

व्यवस्थापन माहिती पद्धती - **management information system** - 1) computer based management in which automatic data processing is used by the user's of the programme.
2) a system designed to use all data collected by an organization to provide management with the information needed for decision making.

व्यवस्थापन - **management** - a combined process of planning, organizing and controlling to accomplish objectives.

व्याख्या - **definition** - stating the exact meaning of words etc. description of the word.

व्यापक दृष्टिकोन - **exhaustive approach** - approach tending to include maximum, especially leaving nothing out. complete thorough.

व्यापक वर्गीकरण - **expansive classification** - scheme of classification designed by Charles Ammi Cutter and published for the first time in 1893.

व्यापक संदर्भसेवा - **long-range reference service** -a reference service requiring more time and efforts.

व्यापकता - **generalization** - to draw general conclusion from particular example or evidence.

व्यापार - **trade** - process of purchase or sale of goods, manufactured by or sold by a firm.

व्यापारी तालिका - **trade catalogue** - catalogue of one or more publishers/distributors.

व्यापारी वाङ्मय (साहित्य) - **trade literature** -the publicity literature used to popularize goods, items of sale - catalogue of items showing specification and cost.

व्यापारी संकुल - **commercial complex** - building having business firm's offices etc. except residential one.

व्यापारी संस्था रूपरेषा - **company profile** - 1) a biographical account of a particular company combined with a description and assessment of its achievements.
2) a set of indexing terms, which characterize the interests of a particular, an SDI service.

व्यापारी नियतकालिक - **trade journal** - a journal which disseminates trade conditions and also used for publicity of initiatives in the field.

व्याप्तिलेख/प्रबंधिका – monograph - a separate treatise on a single subject or class of subjects, or on one person, usually detailed in treatment but not extensive in scope and often containing extensive bibliographies. Frequently published in series.

व्याप्ती (विस्तार) कट्टा extension counter - additional counter opened in the library or premises outside.

व्याप्ती (विस्तार) कार्य – extension activities - activities other than normal activities.

व्याप्ती (विस्तार) कार्य – extension work - when the existing equipment / service is extended to those who are not in direct service preview.

व्याप्ती (विस्तार) सेवा – extension service - service extended to a number of points where users are available.

व्याप्ती/मर्यादा – scope - range of matters being dealt with, studied etc. area covered for a study or research.

व्याप्ती/मर्यादा टीप – scope note - a note enumerating special restrictions generally applicable to a subject and its subdivisions.

व्यावसायिक लिखाण – professional writings - writings that deal with professional services.

व्यावसायिक सेवा – profession services - library and information services that need special skills.

व्यावसायिक साहाय्यक – professional assistant - an assistant who possesses some professional skill, and assists, the main person.

व्यावसायिक – professional - person who has undergone special training for a subject knowledge.

व्यावहारिकता – practicability - characteristic of practical nature.

व्यास – diameter - straight line connecting two ends across the centre of a circle or sphere or of the base of a cylinder, to two points on its sides.

व्यासपीठ - forum - place where important public issues can be discussed.

व्हाऊचर – voucher - written statement of payment / expenditure.

व्हेन आकृती – Venn diagram - graphic methods of sorting out the simple logical relationship between objects or classes of objects. they are named after the English logician John Venn (1834 - 1923).

श

शक्तिरेषा/सदिश – **vector** - quantity that has both magnitude and direction.

शक्तिशाली – **potent.**

शक्ती – **potency** - power; faculty.

शणपट – **canvas.**

शब्द अनुक्रमणिका नोंद – **word by word entry** - method of arranging entries considering one word as one entity.

शब्द नोंद – **word entry** - entry beginning with a word.

शब्द प्रक्रियक – **word processing** - the automated manipulation of text via a software package. Such a software package usually provides the ability to create edit, store and print documents easily.

शब्द विस्तार – **word length** - the number of characters / bits used to form a word.

शब्द समूह – **word group** - group of words functioning as a single unit and not separated by any punctuation mark other than a hypen.

शब्द सोपस्कार – **word processing** - 1) computer programme which is used for writing, editing, printing etc.
2) a technique used for composing text through computer software package.

शब्द – **word** - a group of letters which has some meaning and purpose. In computer, group of characters occupying one storage location.

शब्दकोश/शब्दसंग्रह – **thesaurus -** 1) compilation of words and phrases showing synonyms, hierarchical and other relationship and dependencies, the function of which is to provide a standard vocabulary for information storage and retrieval system. The object of the thesaurus is to exert terminology control in indexing and to aid in searching by alerting the searcher to the index terms that have been applied.

2) book containing list of words & phrases grouped according to their meaning.

शब्दकोश – **dictionary -** 1) the book containing the words of a language, arranged in alphabetical order with their explanation.

2) lexicon, vocabulary of a language.

शब्दनिहाय/अनुवर्ण तालिका – **dictionary catalogue -** catalogue in which all word entries (i.e. author, title, places, subjects) are arranged in alphabetical order. This comprises one part of catalogue.

शब्दभांडार/शब्दसंग्रह – **vocabulary -** 1) a list of words used in subject heading list either as a preferred or a forbidden term.

2) book containing list of words and phrases grouped according to their meaning.

शब्दसंग्रह/निर्देश भाषा – **vocabulary / index language -** the language used in the subject index which is part of an information retrieval system. It may be an alphabetical or classified arrangement of terms, or a variation of these.

शब्दांच्या वापराची पद्धत – **usage -** use of a language usually not governed by grammatical rules.

शब्दानुक्रमणिका – **concordance -** an alphabetical index for the words in a document.

शब्दानुसारी मुळाक्षररचना – **word-by-word alphabetisation -** items/ concepts which have the same first alphabet are arranged in alphabetical order of the subsequent word. Here word (not the letter) is considered as unit. It is also called nothing before something method. This method is also recommended by the British Standards Institution.

शब्दार्थ मूल्य – **semantic value -** the ordinal value which fixes the place of a subject relative to other subjects in a scheme of classificaiton.

शब्दसंग्रह/शब्दार्थ संग्रह – **glossary -** an alphabetical list of abstruse or technical terms concerned with any specific subject, together with their definitions or elucidations.

शब्दार्थविचार नातेसंबंध – **semantic relationship -** semantics generally means the study of meaning of words. But, in the context of subject indexing, semantic relationships are relationships between the subjects, which are stable, and reflect the consensus of opinion concerning the connections between the subjects. For examples, the component of the building is roof and not vice versa, physics is a branch of science and not the reverse.

शब्दावडंबर – **rhetoric -** art of writing.

शब्दिक क्षेत्र/पातळी – **verbal plane -** the plane of expression of a concept in a natural language or a stage when thoughts are assigned suitable terms before assigning it appropriate notation.

शब्दिक – **verbal -** 1) relating to or in the form of words. Attending to words only as distinguished from facts or ideas. 2) dealing with words or terminology.

शहर मध्यवर्ती ग्रंथालय – **city central library -** the main monitoring city library of the system or a library which has number of branches.

शाखा ग्रंथालय – **branch library -** branch of the main library.

शाखा – **discipline -** an organised field of study or branch of learning dealing with specific kinds of subjects and / or subjects considered from specific points of view.

शाब्दिक स्मरणसुलभ – **verbal mnemonics -** first alphabet of the word is used as a notational part of class number which makes it easy to remember.

शारीरिक शिक्षण – **physical education.**

शासकीय ग्रंथालय – **government library -** library established and maintained by government funds and functions under government policies.

शासकीय प्रकाशन/प्रलेख – **government publication / document -** the publication brought out by government agency.

शासन/सरकार – **government -** body of persons governing a state, having power to govern.

शासन – **government.**

शास्त्र – **science -** organized knowledge, especially when obtained by observation & testing of facts about the physical world, natural laws & society; study leading to such knowledge.

शास्त्रशुद्ध व्यवस्थापन – **scientific management -** 1) management of an institute, by applying scientific principles.
2) a style of management in which scientific management principles are applied to production, control, distribution and other activities in an organization. This style does not give the right place to employer's participation in management.

शास्त्रीय व्यवस्थापन - **scientific management.**

शास्त्रीय कार्यपद्धती – **scientific procedure** - procedure in research based on theories & principles.

शास्त्रीय चौकशी – **scientific enquiry** - inquiry in research made systematically or methodologically.

शास्त्रीय चौकशी/अध्ययन – **scientific investigation** - systematic/methodological investigation in research.

शास्त्रीय जिज्ञासा – **scientific curiosity** - curiosity in research made systematically or methodologically.

शास्त्रीय दर्जा – **scientific status** - status based on science.

शास्त्रीय पद्धत – **scientific method** - a systematic method which is based on science.

शास्त्रीय संज्ञा – **scientific term** - term which are used in science education.

शिकलगार/झिलईचा दगड – **agate stone** - type of very hard semiprecious stone with bands or patches of colour.

शिक्षण (ग्रंथपालनासाठी) – **education for librarianship** - science in which systematic study of library services and education is covered.

शिक्षण – **education** - it is to promote full awareness of social and human values, so thatone can develop a strong character and live better life and can function as responsible member of the society.

शिडीपाट आधार – **shelf support** - a small fitting which fits into slots in the up rights and actually supports a shelf. It may be brackets.

शिडीपाट क्षमता – **a book shelf capacity** - capacity of holding number of volumes on a shelf.

शिडीपाट चिन्ह – **shelf mark** - a symbol showing the location of a shelf.

शिडीपाट दर्शक – **shelf guide** - an indicator displaying class number and description of documents belonging to the indicated class available on a particular shelf.

शिडीपाट यादी – **shelf list** - a list of library holdings arranged in order as these are available on shelves. For each document one entry with full details is arranged and used only by library staff.

शिडीपाट संख्या – **shelf number** - a number assigned to a shelf to fix its location.

शिडीपाट संशोधन – **shelf rectification -** the process of restoring order of the scheduled documents on the shelves.

शिडीपाट – **book stack or shelf -** an equipment for holding library collections.

शिफारस पाठ्यक्रम/अभ्यासक्रम – **recommended curricula -** curriculum which is approved for a particular certificate or degree.

शिफारस – **recommendation -** the act of recommending some action.

शिरस – **glue -** thick, sticky liquid used for joining things in the process of book binding.

शिल्प – **art / craft.**

शिल्पकला – **sculpture.**

शिल्पकारी/कारागिरी – **craftsmanship -** a system wherein employees control the work system cycle and the management provides the resources for raw material, equipment, finance & training

शीघ्र संदर्भसेवा – **quick /ready reference service -** a quick service based generally on reference documents which is completed in less time, quickly.

शीघ्रतम – **expeditous -** done with speed & efficiency.

शीर्ष ओळ – **headline -** a first line of the front page or top of the page focusing subject. Usually the title or the heading of the chapter is used as headline.

शीर्षक अनुच्छेद/विभाग – **heading section -** a part of catalogue card on which heading of the entry is written.

शीर्षक शब्द – **title word -** any word figuring in a source article title and is considered for premature subject index.

शीर्षक – **title.**

शीर्षक/नोंदशीर्षक – **heading -** word or group of words appearing on the top of the entry and used as access point. It represents the entire work.

शुद्ध चिन्हांकन – **pure notation -** simple base notation of classification in which only one type symbol is used to represent all classes.

शुद्धिवादी – **purist -** one who insists on preserving what she/he considers the 'correct' form of language, and is against language variation and language change.

शृंखला प्रक्रिया – **chain procedure -** procedure for determining the class index entries, the specific subject entries and subject entries of a document from its class number and the class number of the cross reference entries provided for it, or it is a systematic method of driving class index entries from a given class number.

शृंखला – **chain** - 1) it is a sequence of subordinate classes of decreasing extension and increasing intention achieved by successive divisions of any universe chain, can be derived from its immediate class.

2) a sequence of hierarchy consisting of a generic class and a succession of subordinate classes.

शेवटचा उपयोक्ता – **end user** - in communications, a person who is the ultimate recipient of information flowing through the system.

शेवटचा भाग/हात फिरवणे – **finishing** - the part of binding concerned with the book after the cover is fixed over it. Includes tooling, lettering & polishing.

शेवटचे कागद (आंतरपृष्ठे) – **end papers** - a sheet of paper at end of a book inserted by the binder to help fasten the sewn sections to the cover.

शेवटचे पृष्ठ/आंतरपृष्ठ – **end page** - the thick blank sheet of paper sewn into either sides (ends) of a book with one part of it pasted on to the inside cover.

शेष – **remainder/residual** - a copy or copies of a book still held by a publisher when the sale has fallen off, or having outdated knowledge hence usually disposed off very cheaply.

शैक्षणिक ग्रंथालय - **academic library** - 1) library of school, college, university and all other academic institutions forming part of, or associated with, institutions of edcuation.

2) the library established by an educational institution such as university college, school etc. falls in this category. The kind of academic library may be ascertained on the nature of the institution to which it is attached.

शैक्षणिक तंत्रज्ञान – **educational technology** - the development application and evaluation of system techniques and aids to improve the process of human learning.

शैक्षणिक – **academic** - 1) associated with education; matter related with education as a subject.

2) related to schools or colleges and their learning; scholastic; scholarly.

शैली नियमपुस्तिका – **style manual** - a text that guides the editor's decisions on punctuation, use of numbers, abbreviations and other mechanics to achieve consistency of presentation in a manuscript. e.g. Chicago style.

शैली संपादन – style editing - in particular publications, consistent use of the mechanics of writing following approved conventions i.e. use of any particular system of abbreviations, symbols, numbers, punctuation, spelling (American or English) etc.

शैलीत्मक विभेदन – stylistic differentiation - refers to the level of formality which speakers adopt in situations i.e. formal / colloquial, informal style.

शोध उपकरण – access tool - a tool, generally a hard copy which consists access points to locate stored information.

शोध निबंध – dissertation - an original work brought out by the researcher.

शोध पद्धती – search method - the technique used to perform a search.

शोध बिंदू – search point - identified unique heading or a term, name, phase, word or group of words under which a user of the library searches library collection to find out information needed.

शोध व्यूहतंत्र – search strategy - the plan adopted for answering a particular enquiry or more specifically the search statements used to answer an enquiry.

शोध संज्ञा/शब्द – search term - 1) a search term is an expression, a sequence of signs, letters and /or figures relevant to specific query. A search term in a profile can be a single word. A sequence of words in a string an author's name, the name of an institution, a descriptor, a subject heading, a classification code etc.
2) a term used as an approach point.

शोध सहायता – search aid - devices used to perform a search.

शोध सेवा – search service - service involved in retrieving information.

शोध – search - an effort to locate the selected piece of information.

शोध/अन्वेषण अनुच्छेद – tracing section - the section which records all the added entries.

शोधकर्ता – searcher - the person who actually searches the database.

शोधन – act of writing tracing - preparation of record of entries made for a document which is generally traced in one paragraph in accordance with cataloguing rules. This helps to edit all entries in future.

शोभित हस्तलिखित – iIlluminated manuscript - many religious manuscripts and some of the others were ornamented in the early days by patterns and pictures done in gold paint and brilliant blues and reds. These are known as illuminated manuscripts.

श्रद्धावाद/श्रद्धता – dogmatism - positiveness in the assertion in matters of opinion.

श्रृंखला निर्देशीकरण – **chain indexing** - a mechanical process of achieving index through analysis of class number into its digits representing subjects. It was originated by Dr. S.R. Ranganathan.

श्रेणी / श्रेणीबंध – **hierarchy** - 1) the order of the terms showing their relation with each other in a scheme of classification.
2) the arrangement of subjects moving from general to specific.

श्रेणीनुक्रम – **hierarchical order** - an arrangement according to the level / position of the subject.

श्रेणीय जाळे – **hierarchical network** - a network where unsatisfied needs are passed on to the next greater resource centre.

श्रेणीय संबंध – **hierarchical relation** - higher and lower level relationship between ideas. e.g. Zoology - birds - crows. Medicine - respiratory organs - lungs.

श्रेणीयुक्त – **graded** - to arrange in degrees, ranks, classes or steps, according to order, series, quality, size, etc.

श्रेणीवार अंकन / चिन्हांकन – **hierarchical notation** - a notation designed to show that two terms are in the same array of the same chain.

श्रेणीवार दाब – **hierarchical force** - the property by which headings and certain notes apply to all subdivisions of the topic described & defined.

श्रेणीवार शोध – **hierarchical search** - refers to an examination of entries in a subject catalogue under heads which constitute a chain; it has been conducted in an upward direction from the most to the least, specific heading.

श्रेणीवार / श्रेणीय माळे – **hierarchical tiers** - any system of organizational set up ranked one above the other.

श्रेष्ठ पुस्तक (ग्रंथ) – **best book (document)** - a selected book on a subject giving comprehensive account.

श्रोतावृंद विश्लेषण – **audience analysis** - grouping of audience into highly educative, non technical, mixed type, international, or single group or public at large.

स

संकरित जाळे – **hybrid network -** combination of star, ring and bus concept network.

संकलक (संगणक) – **compiler -** software form that translates a complete program into machine language or checks errors of the program.

संकलक – **compiler -** a person who collects matter from various sources and puts it in order to use.

संकलक – **compiler -** a piece of software that translates a complete program into machine language. As it performs this translation process, it also checks for any errors that might have been made by the programmer.

संकलन – **compilation -** a work developed by collecting relevant material from available words.

संकरित संगणक – **hybrid computer -** the combination of digital and analog computers. These are specially designed computers by combining the advantage of analog and digital computers.

संकल्पनात्मक सूचना – **conceptual instruction -** an integrated system of concepts in a logically closed system.

संकीर्ण वर्ग – **generalia class -** section of a classification scheme specifying class numbers for documents of general nature.

संकेतन – **coding -** process of assigning symbols, usually numeric to each entity.

संकेतन – **coding** - the digital representation of the characters.

संकेतन – **encoder** - a logic circuit that changes data into a code suitable for machine entry.

संकेतमान्य नांव – **conventional rate** - name other than real name.

संक्षिप्त आवृत्ती – **abridged edition** - a summarized edition of the original form or the work developed by taking essential features of the original work.

संक्षिप्त – **annotate** - an art of preparing summary of the work.

संक्षिप्तकरण/लघुकरण – **reduction** - reduced reproduction of the document.

संक्षिप्तीकरण – **annotation** - a brief statement added at the end of an entry of a document, explaining/evaluating its contents.

संक्षिप्तन/संद्रवण – **condensation** - the act of making a book, speech, report etc. in a shorter form.

संक्षेप/सार – **abstract** - the brief summary of the work. It is of two types; indicative & informative.

संक्षेप/सारपत्रिका – **abstract bulletin** - a bulletin containing abstract of currently published articles and works added to the library. It may appear after fixed intervals.

संक्षेपन – **abridgement** - reduced form of a work, produced by removing details or by keeping main sense of the original work.

संक्षेपाक्षर – **abbreviation** - shortened form of a word, phrase, etc. acronym - a word formed from the first (or in some cases first few) letters of a series of words.

संक्षेपाक्षरे – **acronyms** - word formed from the intital letters of a group of words e.g. IGNOU. (Indira Gandhi National Open University).

संक्षेपित तालिका नोंद – **abbreviated catalogue entry** - catalogue entry which contains selected information or an entry for selected information.

संक्षेपित तालिका पत्र – **abbreviated catalogue card** - a catalogue card containing less information than the main card.

संक्षेपित नांव – **abbreviated name** - the name in which initial letters or words are used. The method may be used for whole of the name or for a portion of it.

संख्या – **number** - a numerical digit.

संख्यात्मक विश्लेषण – **quantitative analysis** - analysis based on quantification.

संख्याशास्त्र – **statistics** - collection of information shown in numbers, science of collecting, classifying and analyzing such information.

संगणक उत्पादन युक्ती – **computer output device** - in computer, pertaining to the action, or the result, of transferring data from the internal storage of a computer to an external device or user.

संगणक उपयोजन/प्रयोग – **computer applications** - use of computers for various sources and operations.

संगणक केंद्र – **computer centre** - a computer equipped location.

संगणक चालक – **computer operator** - one who makes use of computer.

संगणक जाळे – **computer network** - 1) set of computers connected through communication lines from a computer network.
2) system of two or more computers interconnected by communication channels.

संगणक निवेश युक्ती – **computer input device** - in data processing, a device by which data can be entered into a computer system.

संगणक परिणाम – **computer output** - the results achieved with the application of mechanical process.

संगणक प्रणाली – **computer system** - total unit of the computer which includes number of machine parts such as CPU, monitor and keyboard etc.

संगणक भाषा – **computer language** - language used to establish communication lines, forms network for computer.

संगणक योजना – **computer programme** - a set of instruction organised to deal with the work performance of the computer.

संगणक विज्ञान – **computer science** - the subject dealing with the design and use of computers.

संगणक शब्द – **computer word** - a series of bits or characters that is treated as an unit and which in particular, occupies a single storage location.

संगणक संप्रेषण प्रणाली – **computer communication system** - any form of communication aided and abetted by computers, including, but not limited to e-mail, chat, and conference.

संगणक सुलभ भाषा – **low-level computer language** - low-level languages are often hardware specific and are not necessarily portable between computers.

संगणक – **computer** - a machine capable of accepting data and processing it by the application of mathematical and / or logical operations.

संगणकाधिष्ठित उपार्जन नियंत्रण – computer based acquisition control - it helps to reduce clerical support & ease decision making, helps to generate financial & statistical information, periodic reports of fund status, minimises paper work and contributes to the development of integrated library system.

संगणकाधिष्ठित सूचनासंग्रह/संगणकीकृत आधारसामग्री – computerised database - 1) the information collection in machine readable form or information storage in computer. 2) datafiles produced, maintained and accessed with the aid of computer.

संगणकीकृत आधारसामग्री – computerised database - data files produced, maintained and accessed with the aid of computers.

संगणकीय उपार्जन पद्धती – computerised acquisition systems - they are evolved beyond the fundamental ordering and receiving functions with the advent of integrated systems, external interfaces with suppliers and control through micro-computer based support.

संगणकीय उपार्जन व कालिके नियंत्रण – computerised acquisitions & serials control - they often regulate as separate units, but both share an important function. The acquisition of library material.

संगणकीय कालिके नियंत्रण काम – computerised serials control tasks - to support the acquistion of serial publications (viz journals, magazines, periodicals, etc.)

संगणकीय भाषांतरकार – assembler - the programme which converts the symbolic language programme, written by the programmer, to a machine-language programme.

संगीत ग्रंथालय – music library - the collection comprises of music records, tapes CD's DVD's, VCD's cassettes etc.

संग्रह (ग्रंथ) विकास – collection development - process of collecting documents for library.

संग्रह (ग्रंथ) - collection - number of documents acquired by a library.

संग्रह (ग्रंथ) अंक/संग्रहांक/ग्रंथांक – collection number - a number used to represent library holdings. आणखी पहा– दाखल अंक

संग्रह नोंदवही – stock register - a register in which entries are made for those items which are in possession of the organisation.

संग्रह पडताळणी/ग्रंथपरिगणन – stock taking / stock checking / stock verification - physical check up of library documents / holdings.

संग्रह युक्ती – storage device - in computing, a unit into which data can be entered, retrieved and later retrieved.

संग्रह वही – **stock book** - register in which available material is recorded.

संग्रह संख्या – **stock number** - a number assigned to item on the basis of the stock entry.

संग्रह/साठवण आणि प्रतिप्राप्ती – **storage and retrieval** - the recording of the holdings of library material of various kinds & information recorded in such material & the means of ascertaining the whereabouts of the material of information by means of catalogues, indexes and mechanised methods.

संग्रह – **holds** - books that are kept on reserve for users which are already on issue.

संग्रह – **stock** - book collection available in a particular library.

संग्रहस्थळ ग्रंथालय – **depository library** - a library in which less used documents are shifted or a library which receives documents free of cost under the provision of law.

संग्रहस्थळ/भांडार – **repository** - store of a library or group of libraries.

संग्रहांक – **collection number** - 1) a symbol denoting the collection, other than the general where the document belongs.
2) number indicative of a document as belonging to a particular distinctive collection in the library.

संघ/संयुक्त तालिका – **union catalogue** - a merged listing of the contents of two or more libraries or a record of group of libraries, usually arranged in an alphabetical order, showing the name of the library where a document is physically available.

संघटन – **organizing** - it is the process through which the efforts of people are directed and coordinated towards the achievement of set goals. It refers to the formal relationship or individuals of an organisation working together to achieve the objectives of the organization.

संघटन/संगठन/संघटना – **organization** - grouping of activities in desired manner.

संघटनात्मक आराखडा – **organizational structure** - the formal relationship among groups and individuals in the organization.

संघटनात्मक संस्कृती – **organizational culture** - it is a subculture that identifies working philosophies, designs and practices peculiar to an individual organization. The effect of this process is to generate appropriate values, ideas and practices, as per the level of circumstances in a particular organization. The notion philosophy is concerned with abstract values & ideas, not directly with concrete methods and techniques which may serve to guide and structure concrete action.

संच – **set** - group of similar things that belongs together in some way.

संचय – **storage -** device to keep information for future use. See also memory.

संचयन – **cumulation -** 1) progressive indexing of entries in a predetermined order circulated for use after a fixed period.
2) the progressive inter-filling of items arranged in a predetermined order and usually published in periodical form, the same order of arrangement being maintained.

संचयी क्षमता – **storage capacity -** in computer it is memory capacity or in case of store it is a holding capacity of collections.

संचयी निर्देश – **cumulative index -** 1) one which is built up from time to time by combining separately published indexes into one sequence.
2) an index resulted by combining separately published indexes.

संचयी यादी – **cumulative list -** a list developed by merging separately prepared lists.

संचारण – **transmission -** transfer of information from one end to another.

संचालक – **director -** the chief executive head of the institution.

संचालनालय – **directorate -** a separate administrative section of government.

संचिका/पंजी सोपस्कार – **file processing -** updating the file.

संची/पंजी निर्देश – **file index -** a table or list of files.

संची/पंजी व्यवस्थापन पद्धती – **file management system -** a system used to control the files available in any database or computer software to define specified records and files to make use on demand.

संची/संचायिका/पंजी – **file -** it is an organised, named collection of information for some particular purpose, or a collection of related records as one unit.

संचीकरण/पंजीकरण खण – **filing cabinet -** a steel or wooden cabinet used to hold files in helpful arrangement.

संचीकरण/पंजीकरण – **filing -** arrangement of related items.

संज्ञा – **term truncation -** specific name of an item.

संज्ञा – **term -** any word or phrase having a limiting and definite meaning in some science, art, etc. Any word or phrase used in a definite or precise sense, expression.

संज्ञाकोश/शब्दकुल कोश – **thesaurus -** a book of words that shows explicitly the relationship among the words it contains. It is an introduction to indexing system to control vocabulary in mechanized way.

संतुलित संग्रह - **balanced collections -** the collections developed on some principles and having almost all important and relevant documents available in the field.

संदर्भ कक्ष/खोली - **reference room -** room in which reference collection is stored for use.

संदर्भ कार्य - **reference work -** work created to meet reference service requirement.

संदर्भ ग्रंथ - **reference books -** 1) books which are kept for reference only and are not allowed to carry outside the building of library. These are compiled to supply definite pieces of information varying extent, and intended to be referred to rather than read thoroughly e.g. Encyclopaedia, Dictionaries, Year book etc.

2) the books which supply definite piece of information and are not required for thorough reading. Such books are generally not loaned for outside use and are kept in reading room for consultation.

संदर्भ ग्रंथपाल - **reference librarian -** the incharge of the work for the reference department.

संदर्भ ग्रंथालय - **reference library -** the library which has exclusive collections and which are also not available commonly in other libraries. These collections are not loaned.

संदर्भ नोंद - **reference entry -** an entry which refers to another entry by using the terms such as, i.e. see/see also, etc.

संदर्भ मुलाखत - **reference interview -** that part of the reference process in which the inquirer and the searcher interact to stabilise the enquiry.

संदर्भ विभाग - **reference department /section -** a section of the library in which reference service is arranged.

संदर्भ साहाय्यक - **reference assistant -** an assistant who retrieves reference.

संदर्भ साधन - **reference sources -** any document / individual used to obtain information.

संदर्भ सेवा - **reference service -** service vide which reply is arranged for the query.

संदर्भ - **reference -** directing users to the source of information.

संदर्भरहित मुख्य शब्द - **KWOC (key word out of context) -** key words are separated from the title to act as subject heading in index.

संदर्भसंबंधी - **context -** words that come before and after a word, phrase, statement, etc. helping to show what its meaning is.

संदर्भासहित मुख्य शब्द - **KWIC (key word in context) -** a method of achieving index with the help of keywords.

संदर्भासाठी – referral - directing users to source of information rather than providing the information itself.

संदर्भित प्रारूप – contextualised model - a model based on the text jointly arrived at by an informatician and a user.

संदिग्ध ग्रंथनाम – ambiguous title - a title which is not clear & creates confusion in understanding the work to which it belongs.

संदिग्धता – ambiguity - presence of more than one meaning.

संद्रवण/संक्षिप्तन – condensation - the act of making a book, speech, report etc. in a shorter form.

संपादक संदर्भ – editor reference - information about editor traces in catalogue card.

संपादक – editor - a person who prepares contributions for publication and the contributions are not his own. He makes changes and corrections wherever necessary.

संपादकीय प्रती – editorial copies - copies of new publication sent out by the publisher for review, notice or record.

संपादकीय – editorial - a statement in which current matters are presented by the editor or the point of view of the work.

संपादन – edit - adjustment of information / data into required format.

संपादन – editing - it is an activity of incorporating correction of a work or selection of relevant material in its sequence.

संपादित – edited - the work prepared for publication by the person other than author.

संप्रेषण उपग्रह – communication satellite - an orbiting artificial earth communication satellite that relays radio, television and other signals between ground terminal stations thousands of miles apart.

संप्रेषण तारा – communication star - expert approached by others within the organisation for advice on technical matters due to his perceived knowledge and experience, having professional & personal links with significant people outside the organisation.

संप्रेषण मार्ग – communication channel - a channel which is used for transmitting information from main point to other.

संप्रेषण - communication - 1) convergence of communication and computer technology. 2)transfer of information between two or more points.

संबंधानुसार अनुक्रम – **filiatory sequence** - sequence of documents on the basis of relationship of subjects.

संबंधित ग्रंथ – **associated book** - a book written about another book and also known as critique.

संभाव्यता – **probability** - something which may be expected to happen or to be so.

संमिश्र/संयुक्त ग्रंथ – **composite book** - a book with two or more contributions, not forming a continuous exposition, and often though not necessarily by different authors. These are of two types-ordinary composite book and artificial composite book.

संमिश्र/संयुक्त लेखक – **composite author** - an author responsible for the contributions included as a part of composite book.

संमिश्र/संयुक्त वर्गीकरण - **composite classificaiton** - a classificaiton scheme which is used by mixing more than one scheme.

संमेलन/परिषद कक्ष – **conference room** - a room used to arrange conference.

संमेलन/परिषद – **conference** - a meeting to discuss certain identified issues.

संयुक्त आडनाव – **compound surname** - a name which is made of two or more proper names and generally connected by a hyphen, conjuction or preposition.

संयुक्त आधार/पाया – **compound base** - class with a basic facet and one or more isolate facets.

संयुक्त खंड – **compound volume** - a bound volume which is made up of two or more separately published works, such as pamphlets.

संयुक्त ग्रंथकारी – **shared authorship** - a work which is produced by the collaboration of two authors, compilers, editors, translators, collectors, adapters, etc.

संयुक्त तालिकीकरण – **shared cataloguing** - a group of libraries when share cataloguing works to achieve uniformity and efficiency.

संयुक्त नाव – **compound name** - a proper name formed from two or more single word proper names after connected by a hyphen, a conjuction or a preposition.

संयुक्त वर्ग – **compound class** - class with a basic facet and one or more isolate facets.

संयुक्त वर्गीकरण – **compound classification** - a classification scheme which is used by mixing more than one scheme.

संयुक्त विषय शीर्षक – **compound subject heading** - a subject name which is used as a heading in a catalogue and consisting of more than one word.

संयुक्त विषय – **compound subject** - a subject closely associated with another subject or which is the result of combination of more than one subjects.

संयोग वेळ – **connect time** - in computer, the time when a user logs in.

संयोग – **cluster** - the group of related documents.

संयोजक/संबंधकचिन्ह – **connecting symbol** - any symbol used in a class number to add to facet to back class or with other facets.

संयोजन/संबंधक अंक – **connecting digit** - a digit used as a connector in a class number, that is as a conjuction in a classificatory language.

संरक्षण – **preservation** - process of protection of items, documents.

संरक्षणशास्त्र/माहिती आणि प्रलेखन केंद्र (डेसिडॉक) – **DESIDOC (Defence Science Information and Documentation Centre)** - the centre is functional under the Defence Research and Development Organisation to serve the requirement of HRD scientists. It connects information from published and unpublished soures to disseminate it to defence establishments. It has official organs like newsletter and bulletin to provide current information in the field of defence, science and technology.

संरचना – **nomenclature** - a set or system of names in a subject.

संरचनात्मक प्रश्न/शंका – **structured query** - a query having syntax, standardized terminology and formulated so as to have compatibility with the database.

संलग्न/संबंधित महाविद्यालय – **affiliated college** - the college which follows the guidelines framed by the university to run the courses through it functions with its own management.

संलग्नित/संबंधित विद्यापीठ – **affiliating university** - university which runs its course programmes through its various affiliated institutions.

संवर्ग – **cadre** - small permanent group of trained workers, soldiers etc. having hierarchial position.

संविधिक/संविधिमान्य/कायदेशीर – **statutory** - required, permitted or enacted by statute.

संविधी/अधिनियम – **statute** - an enactment made by a legislative body and expressed in a formal document, a permanent rule established by an organisation to govern its internal affairs.

संवेदनक्षम – **perceptual** - process by which one becomes aware of changes.

संशोधक – **researcher** - one who is engaged in a process of enquiry of new facts and knowledge.

संशोधन कक्ष/खोली – **research carrel** - siting arrangement for researchers in the library.

संशोधन ग्रंथालय – **research library** - the library which has selected material on the subject which is useful for in depth studies. It has sufficient number of journals / reference books.

संशोधन प्रतिवृत्ते/अहवाल – **research reports** - reports containing information about research carried out in any subject.

संशोधन प्रबंध – **research monograph** - these are published research reports.

संशोधन – **research** - research is different from the studies which rely upon speculation, belief, prayers & instrumentations. Research is a systematic, controlled empirical & critical investigating of hypothetical propositions about the presumed relations among phenomenon.

संशोधित आवृत्ती – **revised edition** - corrected and enlarged edition based on previous work.

संश्लेषण – **synthesis** - combining separate parts, elements etc. to form a complex whole.

संश्लेषित ग्रंथनाम – **synthesized title** - title abridged after using eight steps of classification process.

संसाधन सहभागी – **resources sharing** - a sort of implied agreement amongst participating libraries wherein each participant is willing to spare its resources with other members and in turn is privileged to share the resources of its partners as and when the need arises.

संस्करण/आवृत्ती विवरण – **edition statement** - an information pertaining to the edition on the document generally made in a catalogue card.

संस्करण/आवृत्ती – **edition** - copies of the document published first time.

संस्कृती – **culture** - state of intellectual development of a society.

संस्था पत्रिका/मुखपत्र – **house organ / journal** - a journal for disseminating current activities of any organisation which has more concern within the department.

संस्था – **institution** - 1) an organisation, establishment, foundation or the like, devoted to the promotion of a particular object.
2) society or organization for a special (usually social, professional or educational) purpose.

संस्थात्मक साधने/स्रोत – **institutional resources** - institutions that serve as sources of information.

संस्थावाद/संस्थापरता – **institutionalization -** development of stable patterns of social interaction based on formalized rules, laws, customs and rituals.

संस्थेचे ग्रंथालय – **institutional library -** a library run by the institution.

संस्थेचे सभासदत्व – **institutional membership -** extension of right to participate in the activities of the institution.

संस्वरूप/धारणी – **configuration -** a particular grouping of hardware/software elements designed to meet a particular requirement.

संहिता कोश **- code dictionary -** dictionary giving code symbols of the technical terms usually occurring in learned papers and their abstracts.

संहिता – **code -** a set of rules or symbols specifying their use in particular situation.

सकल गुणवत्ता व्यवस्थापन – **total quality management -** style of management in which the best principles and practices of scientific management and participative management are blended appropriately to achieve success for the organization.

सखोल वर्गीकरण – **depth classification -** the version of a scheme of classification expressing the complex treatment of subject in documents.

सचेतित साहित्य – **sensitized material -** material used in documentary reproduction which is coated with an emulsion sensitive to light or heat as used in a thermographic process.

सजातीय संगणक जाळे – **homogeneous computer network -** a network of similar computers or of particular model.

सत्ता/शक्ती – **power -** ability to exercise influence or control over others.

सत्ताशास्त्र – **ontology -** the science or study of being.

सत्यशोधन – **fact finding / verification effort -** a process of checking the holdings or facts.

सदस्यता यादी – **membership list -** a list consisting names of the members of a library.

सदस्यता – **membership -** permission for using the library.

सदृश्य अंक – **quasi digit -** group of digit to be treated as it they together form a single digit.

सदृश्य उपांग विचार – **quasi isolate idea -** a characteristic enumerated in an array as if it were an isolate idea.

सदृश्य वर्ग – **quasi-class -** work, such as a secret work, a classic, a literary work or a periodical publication or a bibliography treated in a scheme of a classification as if it were a class in the universe of knowledge.

सदृश्य संदर्भ सेवा – **quasi reference service** - reference service is given in least possible time see also ready reference service.

सद्य:स्थिती दर्शक अहवाल – **state-of-art-report** - an exhaustive, systematic and sometimes critical review of (mostly) published and unpublished material (largely periodical articles) on a specific subject report.

सन्निध केंद्र - **approach point** - term or word under which the information is searched.

सन्निध संज्ञा – **approach term** - the word which a catalogue-user seeks in a catalogue, in anticipation that it will lead him to a statement in subject heading language of a required compound subject.

सन्निध सामग्री – **approach material** - the material which is used to understand the subject.

सभा – **congress** - a formal meeting or assembly of representative individuals for discussion, arrangement or promotion of some matter of common interest.

सभा/मेळावा – **congress** - formal meeting or series of meetings for discussion between representatives.

सभागृह/सभाभवन – **auditorium** - a portion of the building used by the audience.

सभासद (पंजी) – **borrower's file** - membership forms are arranged in alphabetical order in this file. It is also recognised as registration file.

सभासद अभिलेख – **borrower's record** - record of registered users in a library.

सभासद नोंदवही – **borrower's register** - a register containing particulars and addresses of the borrowers.

सभासद पत्र – **borrower's card / ticket** - the membership card or cards permitting the holders carrying books from the library. May also be known as library card.

सभासद संख्या – **borrower's number** - the registration number assigned to the individual member of the library.

सभासद – **patron / member/ borrower** - classed users of the library.

सभासद/उपभोक्ता – **borrower** - a user who is allowed library books outside the premises. See also 'user' or 'reader'.

समतुल्य अनुदान – **matching grant** - grants to suit; to correspond; to be equal, smiliar, suitable, or corresponding in some way; where equal share is of institute.

समनाव – **homonym** - a word which is similar in spelling & used in different meaning.

समन्वय – **co-ordination** - action of co-ordinating ability to control one's movements properly.

समन्वित निर्देशीकरण – **co-ordinate indexing** - an indexing scheme whereby the inter relations of terms are shown by coupling individual words.

समन्वित वर्ग – **co-ordinate classes** - classes with same order of specification and grade of division in a classification.

समन्वित/समपदस्थ संबंध – **co-ordinate relation** - the relation between terms which are subordinate to the same term.

समरूप शब्द – **homonym** - words with the same or different spellings but pronounced in the same way and having different meaning.

समरूप/एकरूप – **congruent** - agreeing or corresponding in character, accordant.

समष्टी ग्रंथकार – **corporate author** - corporate authorship is an effort where group of persons are identified by a particular common name and associated for common cause. The authorship lies with institution or other such body.

समष्टी नोंद – **corporate entry** - an entry which is rendered under a corporate body.

समष्टी मंडळ - **corporate body** - a group of individuals associated together as an organised unit with common objectives.

समष्टीवादी/व्यूहगुण – **gestalt** - a technical term in psychology. It is something that you see or think of that has particular qualities when you consider it as a whole, which are not apparent when you consider only the separate parts of it.

समांतर क्रम – **parallel sequence** - two or more collections classified according to one and the same scheme displaying uniform sequence of classes.

समांतर ग्रंथनाम/शीर्षक – **parallel title** - 1) a title appearing in more than one language / script.
2) the title proper of an item in another language or script.

समांतरता – **parallelism** - the state or quality of being parallel.

समांतरीत संचयन – **lateral filing** - equipment which consists of packets of tough paper, or linen which are suspended (and usually move laterally within limits).
From two rails placed one behind the other and running from left to right.

समाकर्षण/संलग्नता – **cohesion** - piece of writing where parts and ideas are fitted well so that they form a unified whole.

समाकलित मंडल – **integrated circuit** - a small (less than the size of a finger nail and also as thin as thin layer of glassy material (usually silicon) into which an electronic circuit has been etched. A single IC can contain 10 to 10,000 different electronic components.

समाकार विश्लेषण – **configurational analysis** - the relative distribution of the parts or elements of a library network.

समान उपांग विस्तार – **common isolate idea** - isolate idea that can be attached to several host classes, but is denoted by the same isolate terms, and represented by the same isolate number, whatever be the host class.

समान पैलू – **common facet** - a facet which can occur in any of the class in a scheme of classification.

समान संप्रेषण प्रारूप / नमुना – **common communication format** - it is a standard format to exchange bibliographic records.

समान साहाय्यकारी – **common auxiliaries** - auxiliary tables are provided with the classification schemes.

समानार्थी शब्द – **synonyms** - words or phrase with the same meaning as another in the same language, through perhaps with a different style, grammar or technical use.

समानुभूती – **empathy** - the ability to identify with the various feelings and thoughts of another person.

समान्वित/समपदस्थ – **co-ordinate** - specific terms subordinated to the same genus.

समावेशन टीप – **inclusion note** - a note instructing the classing of some topics (listed after the term) 'including' under a given number on ad-hoc basis.

समावेशन युक्ती – **interpolation device** - the insertion of a new topic at any point in a scheme of classification.

समाशोधन केंद्र – **clearing house** - an organisation that collects & maintains records of research, development and other activities being planned currently in progress or completed; it provides documents derived from these activities and referral services to other sources for information relating to these activities.

समाश्रेयण रेषा – **regression line** - the estimated equation expressing linear relationship between the variables e.g. $Y = a^\wedge + b x^\wedge$

समाश्रेयणांक – **regression coefficient** - in the equation $Y = a + b X$, b is the regression coefficient. it implies the amount of change in Y given at unit change in X.

समास – **margin** - blank space on the side of a page (side of written text) of the written text.

समासांतर – **indention** - 1) the distance from the left of catalogue card to plot information on fixed layout to make a new paragraph.
2) typographical setting in which subheadings are printed leaving a space to the left of the line on the first letter of the main heading.

समिती – **committee** - group of people appointed (usually by a large group) to deal with a particular matter.

समीक्षण प्रत – **review copy** - a copy of the publication used for preparing review.

समीक्षण/समीक्षा/परिक्षण – **review** - critical analysis or method of introducing contents of a documents.

समीक्षणात्मक आवृत्ती – **critical edition** - a scholarly text of a work established by an editor after original research and the comparison of manuscripts, documents, letters and earlier texts.

समीक्षणात्मक ग्रंथसूची – **critical bibliography** - the comparative and historical study of the physical form of books.

समीक्षणात्मक नियतकालिक – **reviewing periodical** - a periodical giving narrative form, an account of the contribution bearing on a stated subject and appearing in the fascicles of periodicals and the books published during its period provides review on a particular subject.

समीक्षणात्मक वर्गीकरण – **critical classification** - the exercise of the classifier's personal opinion when classifying a book; if care is not taken to avoid bias or prejudice, this may result in wrong shelving.

समीक्षणात्मक/टीकात्मक पैलू – **critical facet** - facet used in main class literature to show that it is a thoughtful analysis, interpretation and evaluation of an artistic or literary work of the author who has produced it.

समीक्षा/टीका – **criticism** - looking for faults, pointing out faults.

समुपदेशन – **counselling** - helping the employee to grow and develop in the organisation.

समूर्तता वृद्धी – **increasing concreteness** - concreteness that goes on increasing.

समूह/समाज – **society** - system whereby people live together in organized communities; social way of living.

समोच्च रेषा – contours - 1) outward curve of something (e.g. a coast, mountain range body)

2) lines drawn on a map to join all places at the same height about sea level. The intervals between contours may represent height differences from 50 to several thousand feet depending on the scale of map. On physical maps the areas between contours are often shown in different colours.

सर्व–करा वर्गीकरण – do-all classification - a general classification which can meet all the requirements of the special classification in different subjects irrespective of their extension as well as depth of intension.

सर्वव्यापी (जागतिक) दशांश वर्गीकरण पद्धती – UDC (universal decimal classification) system/scheme - scheme of classification sponsored by the International Institute of Bibliography and its success or body, the International Federation for Documentation published for the first time in 1896.

सर्वव्यापी ज्ञान – universe of knowledge - known knowledge of the world.

सर्वसमावेशक कार्य – comprehensive work - the work (literery or any type of) having the quality of comprehending well; understanding much.

सर्वसमावेशक ग्रंथसूची – comprehensive bibliography - 1) a bibliography prepared for every thing brought out in a subject.

2) a bibliography which lists, as far as possible, everything published on the subject.

सर्वसमावेशक बाजार संशोधन/विश्लेषण – market research/analysis - collecting together all information at every level in the marketing process. It is putting into order the information that enables management to make better decisions.

सर्वसमावेशक संग्रह – comprehensive collection - the collections in a particular library, which are sufficient to meet the requirements of the users.

सर्वसमावेशक सार – comprehensive abstracting - an abstracting of documents covering, involving much; inclusive.

सर्वसमावेशक सारकारी सेवा – comprehensive abstracting service - an abstracting service in which all important contributions of a given subject are covered.

सर्वाधिकार आरक्षित – all rights reserved - it is a statement recorded on every document to reserve copyright or right of permitting reproduction of the work. The right generally remains with author or publisher.

सर्वानुमते/सार्वमत - **consensus** - a relative agreement as to what the major classes of knowledge are, their scope and essential relations between them.

सल्लागार मंडळ - **advisory board** - committee of experts and prominent scholars to recommend or advice new methods to achieve efficiency in library services.

सल्लागार समिती - **advisory committee** - the committee which is constituted to frame policies or to suggest guidelines to achieve efficiency in services. The librarian of the institution works as member secretary to it. Such committee is also appointed by government to study the service needs and also to know status of library services during a particular period.

सल्लागार - **consultant** - an expert who gives professional advice usually on payment basis.

सल्लामसलत (संस्था) - **consultancy** - an organisation that provides professional or organization expert advice on payment basis.

सह-शिक्षण - **co-education** - education of girls & boys together.

सह-तालिका - **joint catalogue** - catalogue of two or more libraries.

सह-निर्देश नोंद - **joint index entry** - index entry generated by merging one or more indices.

सह-नोंद - **joint entry** - entry which is made for associated document.

सह-लेखक नोंद - **joint-author entry** - leading section used to record the name of joint author. It is always an added entry.

सह-लेखक - **joint-author** - a person or a corporate body sharing responsibility with another / other for the thought and expression contained in a work, each of the author is responsible being neither specified nor separable.

सह-संज्ञा - **co-term** - a term figuring in the source article title and subordinated to a primary term in the permuterm subject index.

सह-संपादक - **joint editor** - an editor who is associated with another editor.

सह-समिती - **joint committee** - a committee composed of representatives of various committees of various libraries.

सह-सल्लागार समिती - **joint consultation committee** - committee formed by taking members from two committees.

सह/संयुक्त सहयोगक - **joint collaborator** - person who is associated with another, or others, especially in the writing of books, being responsible for some aspect of, or contribution to, a work, but not responsible for the content as a whole.

सहकार बाह्य ग्रंथालय – outlier libraries - a library of a research institution or one devoted to a particular subject, which does not generally participate in the work of a regional bureau, but whose stock is available to other libraries through the National Central Library.

सहकारी तालिकीकरण – co-operative cataloguing - 1) collective efforts by a group of libraries to achieve economy and uniformity. Manpower and expenditure is also shared by participating libraries. It avoids duplicate working.
2) the sharing by a number of libraries the cost and labour of cataloguing to avoid the duplication of effort common to each.

सहकारी संकलन – co-operative acquisition - joint approach for achieving effective collections with limited funds.

सहकारी साठवण – co-operative storage - it is an effort to improve the quantum of information without hinderance of space and distance.

सहगामी – concomitant - accompanying; conjoined; concurrent, attendant. An accompanying or attendant condition, circumstance, or thing.

सहगुणक/गुणक/गुणांक – co-efficient - quantity placed before and multiplying another quantity. Measure of a particular property of a substance under specific conditions.

सहजात परिणाम – synergetic effect - an effect produced as a result of combination of two or more forces representing more than their mere summation.

सहभाग/अंशदान/वर्गणी – contribution - a work of forming a part of composite book periodical / serial / thought embodied in a host document in the form of an article in a periodical or of a section or a paragraph in a book, or a portion of the amount of service.

सहभागात्मक व्यवस्थापन – participative management - a style of management in which employees take appropriate part in every activity of the organization.

सहभागी लेखक - collaborator - a person who associates with another person or other persons to produce a work.

सहभागी/सहभागात्मक नेता – participative leader - a person who involves subordinates in decision making but may retain the final authority.

सहयोगी ग्रंथ – associated book - a book written about another book and also known as criticism.

सहयोगी वर्गीकरण – associate classification - groups of classes displaying only associations with a common factor. e.g. Chemical of gold Gold-chem. Chemical technology Gold-chem. Tech of Gold.

सहयोगी संबंध – **associative relation** - a type of relationship between ideas, the first suggesting the other and vice versa e.g. road traffic and accidents.

सहयोगी/सहयोजन – **collaborator** - one who gets associated with another or others, especially in the writing of books being responsible for some aspect of or contribution to a work, but not responsible for the content as a whole.

सहसंबंध/सहनिर्देशक – **coordinate relation** - headings of equal ranking e.g. rice, wheat, pulses under crop in agriculture.

सहस्थापन – **collocation** - placing closely related subjects in close proximity.

सहाध्यायी – **subordinate** - narrower divisions of a subject.

साहाय्य/मदत – **aid** - a help extended or provided by a person or a document or a component of a documents that helps in locating the desired information from an information sources.

साहाय्यक अनुदान – **grant in aid** - grant of funds by the federal govt. to a state or by a foundation to a writer, scientist, artist, etc. to support a specific programme or project.

साहाय्यक ग्रंथपाल – **assistant librarian** - a library professional who assists the chief librarian and generally performs the specific duties assigned by the librarian.

साहाय्यक – **assistant** - person who performs duties on direction of his supervisor.

साहाय्यकारी अंक – **auxiliary number** - one placed after the class number in order to group the books by some method, such as alphabetically or chronologically.

साहाय्यकारी ग्रंथनाम – **auxiliary title** - refers to the title that co-relates and helps the full meaning of the title /supplement.

साहाय्यकारी तक्ते – **auxiliary tables** - 1) in the UDC tables of secondary aspects of subject which may be applied to primary aspects to show point of nature and are distinguished by a special symbols, or 'facet indicator'.
2) a sequence of dependent notations indicating special concepts used repeatedly in several subjects and disciplines. A list of features common to all of main classes.

साहाय्यकारी परिशिष्ट व तक्ते – **auxiliary schedules and tables** - tables of sub-divisions which are appended to schedules of all scheme of classification. They consist of items of relationship, time, locality, etc. and then symbols of the different items can be added to book classification numbers.

साहाय्यकारी प्रकाशन – **auxiliary publication -** the process of making data available by means of specially ordered microfilm or photocopies.

साहाय्यकारी संग्रह – **auxiliary storage -** a storage that supplements the primary internal storage of a computer.

साहाय्यकारी सत्यस्थिती – **auxiliary data -** data related to other data, but not part of it, for example, back up data.

सांख्यिकी माहिती – **statistical data -** information in numerical form.

सांघिक लेखन – **corporate writing -** technical writing in corporate bodies such as government and its agencies, institutions, learned societies, professional associations & others.

सांधणे – **articulate -** to connect, as by joint.

सांरचनिक प्रश्न – **structured questions -** multiple choice questions in a questionnaire.

सांस्कृतिक साहित्य – **cultural materials -** literary contributions in the form of prose, poetry, drama, fiction or contributions in fine arts like music, dance, drawing, painting and sculpture or contributions in philosophy, religion, history etc.

सांस्कृतिक स्थानांतरण – **cultural transmission -** property of human 'language' whereby the ability to speak a language is transmitted from generation to generation by a process of learning, and not genetically.

साकल्य दृष्टिक्षेन – **holistic approach -** interrelationship between concepts, subjects and disciplines involving complete approach. Analyzing the relation between parts and wholes.

साकार अस्तित्व - **concrete entity -** entity existing physically in space time, means outside the mind of the knower, as it is commonly understood. It is either recognizable with the aid of the primary senses or inferable from data obtained with the aid of primary senses.

साक्षर – **literate -** person capable of reading & writing.

साथ अभिसरण प्रारूप – **epidemic model of diffusion -** diffusion process examined on the analogy drawn from the spread of diseases.

साधन/सामग्री – **source -** the mode of communicating messages through signs, symbols. texts or graphics.

साधन/सामग्री/साधनसंपत्ती केंद्र – **resource centre -** place where documents are available for use.

साधन/सामग्रीचा वापर – **resource sharing -** sharing of collections and services of group of libraries to achieve economy.

साधा ग्रंथ/पुस्तक – simple book - a book which is not composite and which embodies continuous exposition of the subject matter.

साधा पाया/आधार – simple base - a base consisting only one conventional set of digits.

साधारण ग्रंथनाम – general title - a title of a document.

साधारण ग्रंथालय – general library - a library which is not limited to a special subject or a special user and is the main library of any institution.

साधारण तालिका – general catalogue - list of items arranged in desired sequence.

साधारण वाचक – general reader - a user who has no requirement for special materials.

साधारण विषय – general subject - subject of common interest.

साधारण संकीर्ण वर्ग – general class - a class in which the documents of general nature are kept.

साधारण संगणक – general computer - computer system.

साधारण संबंध अवस्था – general phase relation - second phase of a complex class or of a complex isolate or of a complex array isolate as the case may be.

साधारण संबंध – general relation - more or less comprehensive or non-descriptive relation between two phases.

साधारण/सामान्य ग्रंथ – general book - when a book gives general exposition of a subject.

साधे/सरळ शीर्षक – simple heading - heading consisting of a single block.

सान्निध बिंदू/संपर्क – approach point - a term, name, phrase or word group under which a user searches a library catalogue to find his document.

सापेक्ष निर्देश – relative index - 1) an alphabetical index to a classification scheme. 2) an alphabetical index to a classification scheme in which all relationships and aspects of subjects are brought together under each index entry. s.a - abbreviation for see also note. It refers to the related topics scattered in the index under different terms.

सापेक्ष वर्गीकरण – relative classification - classification which shows the relationship between subjects as most modern schemes propose to do.

सापेक्ष स्थान – relative location - arrangement of document in relation to one another.

सापेक्षआर्द्रता – relative humidity - the quantity of water vapour in the air relative to the temperature of the atmosphere.

साप्ताहिक – weekly - publication which is brought out once in a week e.g. India Today, Current Contents, Time, Newsweek etc.

सामग्री – material - it includes all items which are in possession. The term is also used for literature in libraries.

सामाजिक ज्ञान – social knowledge - the knowledge possessed collectively by a society or a social system and available freely and equally to all members of society.

सामाजिक संपत्ती – social wealth - a wealth available freely to all the members of society e.g.park, street lights, roads, information etc.

सामान्य उपविभाग – standard sub-division - sub-divisions in a classification schedule are used to attach the form characteristic of the document, in main class number.

सामान्य उपांग कल्पना – common isolate idea - isolate ideas that can be attached to several host classes, but denoted by the same isolate term and represented by the same isolate number, whatever be the host class.

सामान्य उपांगे – common isolates/auxiliaries - 1) known by different names in different systems, these are usually non-subject but recurring aspects of knowledge presentation as embodied in documents. These are not required in knowledge classification 2) an isolate which can be attached to several host numbers (subject numbers).

सामान्य नियंत्रण भाषा – common command language - set of commands or instructions used for searching several online systems.

सामान्य पत्र – ordinary letter - a letter of routine nature.

सामान्य पैलू – common facet - an idea which can occur in any of the class in a classification.

सामान्य प्रकाशन – ordinary publication - a publication on traditional pattern.

सामान्य वर्गीकरण पद्धती – general classification system - a classification whose area of purview extends to the entire domain of the universe of knowledge for classifying documents in all media. In contrast, the special classification schemes are limited by subject area.

सामान्य वाचक – lay readers - readers using general knowledge not related to any specialized subject or profession.

सामान्य संप्रेषण नमुना प्रारूप – common communication format - 1) a standard format to exchange bibliographic records.
2) bibliographic exchange format useful for libraries and information centres developed by UNISIST.

सामान्य संयुक्त ग्रंथ – **ordinary composite book** - a composite book with a single generic title to denote all the contributions collectively.

सामान्य साहाय्यकारी – **common auxiliaries** - auxiliary tables provided with classification scheme.

सामान्य साहित्य नामनिर्देश – **GMD (general material designation)** -

सामान्यीकरण – **generalizations** - formulation of general statement on the basis of specific observations.

सामावून घेणारी रचना (कपाटावरील) – **adjustable shelving** - shelves which can be raised or lowered by adjusting nuts and bolts to accomodate the books of various sizes.

सामावून घेणारे वर्गीकरण – **adjustable classification** - scheme of classification designed by James Duff Brown for smaller English libraries with a notation of letters and numbers allowing for later insertions.

सार पत्रिका/पत्र – **abstract bulletin /journal / periodical** - a bulletin containing abstract or currently published articles and works added to the library. It may appear after fixed intervals.

सार/संक्षेप – **abstract** - brief summary of a work. It is of two types, indicative & informative.

सारकरण – **abstraction** - 1) the process of separation of achieving grouping in classification. 2) the quality or process of dealing with ideas eathar than events.

सारकर्ता/संक्षेपकार – **abstractor** - a person who develops summary of the work of contribution.

सारकारी नियतकालिक – **abstracting periodical** - 1) a periodical on a stated subject appearing in the current fascicles of periodicals, each entry being provided with an abstract of the article described by it. It may also include annotated entries of books currently published.
2) a periodical containing the abstracts of articles with bibliographical details.

सारकारी सेवा – **abstracting services** - 1) of organisation or individual who extends activity to provide abstracts.
2) preparation of abstracts usually in a limited field, by an individual, an industrial organisation, or a commercial organisation. The abstracts are published and supplied regularly to subscribers. Also, the organisation producing the abstracts. Such services may be either comprehensive or selective.

सारकारी – **abstracting** - method /art of preparing abstract.

सारणी/तक्ता विषय – **table of contents** - list of the table headings with page number. In case of a periodical, it is a list of title of contributions along with the name of contributors and page number.

सारणी/तक्ता – **table** - a layout of written numerical statement or words.

सारपत्रिका/सारसंग्रह – **digest** - 1) a publication consisting of verious information related to a topic in every condensed form.
2) a condensation of descriptive text of information and an orderly presentation of core ideas in brief.
3) a complication or summary of naterial or information.
4) a publication consisting of summaries of information on a single topic or a number of related topics.

सारांश सूचना – **abstract instruction** - an instruction having selected parts of an information into a specified location.

सारांश – **abstract** - selected part of a subject issued as separate work.

सारांश/गोषवारा – **synopsis** - a brief outline of the plot setting, or important points of a play, book or serial.

सारांश/संक्षिप्त – **summary** - 1) brief account selected from detailed text.
2) major outline of the division of knowledge in the DDC. There are three summaries of increasing details in the DDC.

सार्वजनिक अभिलेख – **public record** - records which are in access of the public.

सार्वजनिक ग्रंथालय – **public library** - a library wholly or partly run with public funds, it remains open for all without reservation regarding caste, creed, sex, colour, religion etc.

सार्वजनिक ग्रंथालय अधिनियम – **Public Library Act.** - legistative Act passed to establish a chain of public libraries.

सार्वजनिक ग्रंथालय जाहिरनामा – **Public Library Manifesto** - a document on the subject was first published by UNESCO in 1949. It includes guidelines for the future development of public libraries.

सार्वजनिक ग्रंथालय प्रणाली – **public library system** - public libraries with extension.

सार्वजनिक ग्रंथालयाची निर्देशिका – **directory of public libraries** - an alphabetical list of the libraries with brief information about each library included in it, such directories are brought out by ILA and RRMRLF

सार्वजनिक ग्रंथालयाचे संचालक – **Director of public libraries** - chief officer of government who gives directions to public libraries.

सार्वजनिक संबंध – **public relation** - systematic promotion of mutual understanding between organisation and information user.

सार्वमत – **consensus** - opinion reached through mutual agreement.

साहचर्य/सहयोग/संघ/संस्था ग्रंथालय – **association's library** - a library which is maintained by the association to update its members in the areas of its working.

साहाय्यकारी अनुक्रम – **helpful sequence** - sequence of classes in a classification which is according to the requirement of the user. Thus like things and unlike things are grouped in separate sequences.

साहाय्यकारी क्रम – **helpful order** - order in a classification which provides all related information close to each other.

साहाय्यकारी – **synergism** - the cooperative action between two or more persons working together to accomplish more than they could by working separately.

साहित्य निर्मिती प्रमाण – **literary warrant** - an amount of literature published or to be published on any subjects.

साहित्य मार्गदर्शक – **literature guide** - a publication which helps in knowing the literature on a particular subjects. It may be a particular subject. It may be a reference document.

साहित्य शोध – **literature search** - 1) systematic and intensive search for desired information on a given subject.
2) a systematic search for literature in any form on a particular topic.
3) searching current literature on a given topic through bibliographical tools.

साहित्य प्रकार/प्रारूप – **form (form of literature)** - it is a mode of literary expression of literature such as poetry, drama fiction, essays, etc. Each of the forms has been divided into varieties e.g. lyrical peotry, epic poetry, short stories, science fiction etc.

साहित्य – **literature** - writings that are valued as work of art, especially fiction, drama and poetry (as contrasted with technical books & journalism)

साहित्यशैली – **stylistic** - style of writing.

साहित्यिक कार्य – **literary work** - creative work in the form of poetry, drama, fiction, prose etc. of which the outstanding qualities are taken to be beauty of form and emotional appeal, and which is of instinctive or trans-intellectual origin.

साहित्यिक ग्रंथनाम – **literary title** - in library classification literary titles are translated to their actual theme. These are the titles which do not speak about subject directly.

सिद्धान्त/तत्त्व/वाद/उपपत्ती/मीमांसावाद/नियम – **theory** - 1) written statement 2) an idea that is intended to explain something.

सिद्धान्त/तत्त्व (डावे ते उजवे) – **principle of left to right** - if the isolate in an array occur roughly along a horizontal line, they should be arranged from left to right.

सिद्धान्त/तत्त्व उत्क्रांतीनुसार – **principle of later in evolution** - if the isolate in an array belongs to different stages of evolution they should be arranged parallel to the course of evolution.

सिद्धान्त/तत्त्व घड्याळाच्या दिशेने - **principle of clockwise arrangement** - the isolates in an array can be taken to those occuring roughly in a circle, they should be arranged in clockwise direction.

सिद्धान्त/तत्त्व जटिलता वृद्धीचे – **principle of increasing complexity** - if the isolate in an array shows different degrees of complexity, it is helpful to arrange them in the sequence of increasing measure of their complexity.

सिद्धान्त/तत्त्व प्रमाणमापानुसार वृद्धीचे – **principle of increasing quantity** - if the characteristic used as the basis of classification admits of quantitative measurement, the sequence of the isolate should be in the ascending order of the measures in which the characteristic is shared by the isolate.

सिद्धान्त/तत्त्व मूर्तता वृद्धीचे – **principle of increasing concreteness** - if two classes X & Y are such that X can be said to be more abstract and less concrete than Y, X should precede Y.

सिद्धान्त/तत्त्व वर्गीकरणाचे – **principle of classification** - rules of classification which are formulated by classifiers by which a scheme of classification is made. See canon of classification.

सिद्धान्त/तत्त्व विशेष सान्निध्यानुसारचे – **principle of special contiguity** - if the isolates in an array occur continuously in space, they should be arranged in a parallel spatial sequence.

सिद्धान्त/तत्त्व व्यापारी क्रमाने – **principle of commercial sequence** - when the isolate in an array is traditionally mentioned in specific sequence.

सिद्धान्त/तत्त्व व्युत्क्रमाचे – **principle of inversion** - the facets in the facet formula of a basis class should be in the decreasing order of their concreteness in each of the rounds.

सिद्धान्त/तत्त्व साहित्य निर्मितीचे - **principle of literary warrant** - the isolates in an array may be arranged in the decreasing sequence of literary warrant.

सिद्धान्त/तत्त्व/तल उर्ध्वमुखाचे - **principle of bottom upward** - if the isolate in an array can be taken to be those occurring regularly along with a vertical line, then they should be arranged from bottom upward.

सिद्धांत/तत्त्वे अनुवर्ण क्रमाने - **principle of alphabetical sequence** - the isolate having international accepted current names. They may be arranged alphabetically by those names.

सिद्धान्त/तत्त्व स्थितीपासून दूर - **principles away from position** - if the isolate in an array can be taken to start from a certain point and diverge away from it roughly along a line, they should be arranged from the starting point along the diverging line.

सिद्धान्त/तत्त्व - **principle** - a fundamental truth, law, doctrine, or motivating force, upon which others are based.

सी.डी. रॉम - **CD-ROM** - a shortened version of Compact Disk Read Only Memory, an optical storage media having high storage capacity.

सी.डी.एस/आय.एस.आय.एस. - **CDS/ISIS (computerised documentation service/ integrated set of information system)** - it is a computer used software conceived and developed by UNESCO for managing documentary databases. It is especially designed programme for storage and retrieval of information called from textual records. In India distribution is available from NISSAT.

सीमांत उपयोगिता - **marginal utility** - additional satisfaction received from consumption of an additional unit of a commodity.

सीमांत किंमत - **marginal cost** - the change in total cost of production which results when output is varied by one unit.

सुगावा पृष्ठ - **clue page** - 1) a secrete page chosen and uniformly used in all documents belonging to a library for writing the Accession Number. This will be unnoticed by readers but could be used in identifying the document in case of theft, etc., even if the title page has been removed.
2) page indicating by or as by a clue e.g. secret page on which accession number and library stamp is compulsorily given.

सुधारित आवृत्ती - **corrected edition** - a new edition after incorporating corrections.

सुलभ चलन - **soft currency** - a currency in plentiful supply on the foreign exchange market as a result of the country concerned being inclined to import more than it exports.

सुविधा – **facility -** circumstances, equipment, etc. that make it possible or easier to do something.

सुशिक्षितावस्था – **civilization -** culture and way of life of a people, nation or period regarded as a stage in the development of organised society.

सुसंगतता – **consistency -** quality of being consistent.

सुसंगती/सुसंवाद – **coherence -** (of ideas, thoughts, speech, reasoning etc.) connected logically or consistently, easy to understand, clear being coherent.

सूक्ष्म पट – **microfilm -** a film containing information in reduced size as compared with paper form. A fine gained film of 16mm or 35 mm width used for making very small photographs of documents.

सूक्ष्म पत्र – **microcard -** a term trade mark of the microcard corporation which is covered by an American patent, which refers exclusively to 5 x 5 inch cards with images arranged in a specific manner.

सूक्ष्म प्रलेख – **micro-document -** document embodying micro thought.

सूक्ष्म प्रारूप वाचन कक्ष – **micro-form reading room -** a specially designed room equipped with electronic gadgets.

सूक्ष्म फॅसिमाईल – **micro-facsimile -** a copy of an original reproduced in micro size.

सूक्ष्म विचार – **micro-thought -** a subject of great intention and small extension, deliberations on specialised topics, generally appears in periodicals/newspapers.

सूक्ष्म–अपारदर्शक – **micro-opaque -** the microform through which light cannot pass.

सूक्ष्म–पारदर्शिका – **micro transparency -** the microform through which light can be transmitted.

सूक्ष्म–पारिपथ – **integrated circuit -** very small electronic circuit, made of a single small piece of semiconductor material (e.g. a silicon chip,) designed to replace a conventional electric circuit of many parts.

सूक्ष्म–प्रलेख – **micro-documents -** small documents such as articles in periodical publications, pamphlets, micro-films, micro-cards etc.

सूक्ष्म–फिच/सूक्ष्मपृष्ठ – **micro-fitch -** a flat sheet of standard pictographic film used to record information. The record may be in rows and columns.

सूक्ष्म–लहरी – **micro-wave -** very short wavelength radio waves which are used for high capacity terrestrial point-to-point satellite links.

सूक्ष्म–संगणक – micro-computer - these are the smallest, cheapest and commonly used computer machines in modern age.

सूक्ष्म–संगणकाचे कार्य – micro-computer function - these computers have four basic units, CPU, control, memory and input/output.

सूक्ष्मपत्र – microcard - an opaque micro form of size 3 x 5.

सूक्ष्मप्रक्रियक – micro-processor - it is one of the principal components which consists of the arithmetic logic unit and the control logic unit etc.

सूक्ष्मप्रत – microcopy - a copy in microform.

सूक्ष्मप्रतिमा – micrograph - a graphic record of the image formed by a microscope of an object.

सूक्ष्मप्रारूप/स्वरूप – micro-form - 1) hard copy of document when reduced/ transferred to photographic sheet for using it with mechanical device to achieve efficiency and also to reduce bulk. This includes role film and microfiche.
2) any material on which somethings can be produced by highly reduced form.

सूक्ष्मरूप - microform - a greatly reduced photographic copy of a printed page or the like.

सूचक – menu - set of instructions / message required to handle operation.

सूचक/दर्शक अंक – indicator digit - a symbol used to differentiate / highlight the used digits.

सूचक/दर्शक – indicator - a device used in computer to visualize display place. Proposer one who proposes some action, thought.

सूचनात्मक तंत्रज्ञान – instructional technology - hardware software and /or telecomm unications which are used to assist the learner in engaging in an educational activity.

सूचनात्मक लेखन – instructional writing - writings that aid the process of learning, teaching, application, operations. etc.

सूचनात्मक साहित्य – instructional materials - writings that are meant to provide guidance in learning & using a system.

सूचनापटकार/आज्ञावलीकार – programmer - a specialist who designs, writes, and maintains the computer programmes.

सूचीकरण/निर्देशन – indexing - an art/technique of preparing an index.

सूत्र अनुवर्ण क्रमाचे – Principle of Alphabetical Sequence - When no other sequence of the classes in an array is more helpful, they are arranged alphabetically by their names current in international usage.

सूत्र अपरिवर्तनाचे – **canon of modulation** - a chain of classes should be divided from the universe with the use of correct resolving power at each stage of division.

सूत्र अपवर्जकतेचे – **canon of exclusiveness** - classes in an array of classes should be matually exclusive.

सूत्र अभिजात ग्रंथाचे – **canon of classics** - a scheme of classification should have a device to bring together all the editions, translations and adoptions of a classic, and next to them all the editions etc. of the different commentaries of it, those of a particular commentary coming together and next to each commentary all the editions etc. of the commentaries on itself.

सूत्र उपवर्गांचे (गौण) – **canon of sub ordinate classes** - all the sub-ordinate classes of a class in whatever chain they may occur should immediately follow it without being separated from it or among themselves by any other class.

सूत्र एकतेचे – **canon of uniformity** - the number of digits in a class number should be constant whatever be the order of the class it represents.

सूत्र ग्रंथांकाचे – **canon of book number** - a scheme of document classification should be provided with a scheme of book numbers to individualize the documents having the same class of knowledge as their ultimate class.

सूत्र तक्त्यांर्गत स्मरणसुलभतेचे – **Canon of Scheduled Mnemonics** - A scheme of classification should include a preliminary set of schedules of divisions based on characteristics likely to recur in an array of some order or other of all or many classes, or refer any recurrent array of divisions to the one schedule of them giving in connection with an appropriate class.

सूत्र नात्यानुसारी अनुक्रम – **canon for filiatory sequence** - a sequence that respects the degree of mutual relation between subject.

सूत्र नि:शेषतेचे – **canon of exhaustiveness** - classes in an array of classes should be totally exhaustive of their immediate universe.

सूत्र निर्धारणाचे – **canon of ascertainability** - each characteristic used as the basis for the classification of a universe should be definitely ascertainable.

सूत्र पंक्तीविषयक आतिथ्यशीलतेचे – **canon of hospitality in array** - the construction of a class number or an isolate number should admit of an infinite number of new co-ordinate classes or isolate being added at the end of its chain without disturbing the existing class numbers or isolate numbers in any way.

सूत्र पदक्रम नसलेले चिन्हांकनाचे – **canon of non-hierarchical notation -** in the class number there should not be a digit to represent each of the characteristics used in constructing the class number.

सूत्र पारंपरिक अनुक्रमाचे – **canon for canonical sequence -** not derived on the basis of any definite characteristic or traditional arrangement of subjects, no underlying principle of discoverable.

सूत्र प्रगणनाचे – **canon of enumeration -** the denotation of term in a scheme of classification should be determined in the light of or through the sub classes (lower links) enumerated in the various chains having the class denoted by the term in questing as their common link.

सूत्र प्रचलिततेचे – **canon of currency -** the terms used to denote a class in a scheme of classification should be one currently accepted by those specializing in the universe to which the scheme is applicable.

सूत्र बीजभूत/बीजमूलक स्मरणसुलभता – **canon of seminal mnemonics -** a scheme of classification should use one and the same digit to represent seminally equivalent concepts in whatever array of whatever facet of whatever class they may be denoted by different terms in different contexts of arrays.

सूत्र मिश्र चिन्हांकनाचे – **canon of mixed notation -** the notation of a scheme of classification should be a mixed one.

सूत्र मुग्धतेचे – **canon of reticence -** the term used to denote a class in a scheme of classification should not be critical, that is should not express any opinion of the classification.

सूत्र लक्षणविषयक/साम्यगुणविषयक – **canon of characteristics -** two canons dealing with characteristics viz. a) canon of differentiation and b)canon of permanence.

सूत्र वर्गांच्या पंक्तीविषयक – **canon for arrays of classes -** each array of classes in a scheme of classification has to satisfy four canons viz. canon of exhaustiveness, canon of exclusivenes, canon of helpful sequence and canon of consistent sequence.

सूत्र वर्गीकरणासाठीचे – **canon for classification -** canons dealing with book classification.

सूत्र विभिन्नतेचे – **canon of distinctiveness -** in a scheme of library classification the number of class, book and the collection, should be written quite distinctly or apart from another.

सूत्र विभेदनाचे – **canon of differentiation -** a characteristic used as the basis for the classification of a universe should differentiate some of its entities, that is it should give rise to at least two classes.

सूत्र विस्तार-आकुंचनाचे - canon of decreasing extension - while moving down a chain of classes, from its first link to last, the intention of the class should increase and their extension should decrease at each step.

सूत्र व्यवस्थित स्मरणसुलभतेचे - canon of systematic mnemonics - a scheme of classification should use one and the same sequence of digits to represent the isolate in an array arranged according to each one of the principles such as later in time, special contiguity.

सूत्र शाब्दिक स्मरणसुलभतेचे - canon of verbal mnemonics - the alphabetical device may be used to represent any isolate or array isolate, when arrangement on the basis of any characteristic other than the name is not more helpful.

सूत्र शुद्ध चिन्हांकनाचे - canon of pure notation - the notation of a scheme of classification should be a pure one.

सूत्र श्रृंखला विषयक आतिथ्यशीलतेचे - canon of hospitality in chain - the construction of a class number or an isolate number should admit of an infinite number of new class numbers or isolate numbers being added at the end of the chain to which it belongs, without disturbing the existing class numbers or isolate numbers in any way.

सूत्र संग्रहकांचे - canon of collection number - A Scheme of Book Classification may be provided with a Schedule of Collection Numbers to individualise the various collections of special documents to be formed on the basis of the peculiarities of their gross bodies, or their rarity, or service exigency of facilitate use by readers. The collection numbers based on physical peculiarity may be of use in bibliographies also.

सूत्र संज्ञाविषयकाचे - for terminology canon - the terms used in a schedule of classification must be one approved & used by the subject experts.

सूत्र संदर्भाचे/पूर्वापार संबंधाचे - canon of context - in a classification scheme each term should be decided in the lights of different classes of lower order belonging to the same primary chain as the class denoted by the term.

सूत्र संबंधाचे - canon of contact - the denotation of a term in a scheme of classification should be determined in the light of different classes of lower order (upper links) belonging to the same primary chain as the class denoted by the term in question.

सूत्र समपदस्थ वर्गाचे - canon of co-ordinate classes - 1) among the classes no class with less identity should come between two classes or arrays with greater altinity.
2) among the classes in an array no class with less identity should come.

सूत्र समर्पक अनुक्रमाचे – canon of relevance sequence - characteristic used as the basis for the classification for a universe should be used successively in a sequence relevant to purpose of the classification.

सूत्र समर्पकताचे – canon of relevance - a characteristic used as the basis for the classification of a universe should be relevant to the purpose of the classification.

सूत्र सहगामित्वाचे – canon of concomitance - no two characteristics used in succession as the basis for the classification of a universe should be concomitant, that is they should not give rise to the same array of classes.

सूत्र सापेक्षताचे – canon of relativity - the number of digits in a class number should be proportional to the order of the class it represents.

सूत्र साहाय्यक अनुक्रमाचे – canon of favoured sequence - 1) in arrangement precedence should be given to a class, whatever be its natural position in the normal sequence so as to be of greater help to those for whom it is intended.
2) of helpful sequence - classes in array should be helpful to those to whom it is intended.

सूत्र सुव्यक्ततेचे – canon of expressiveness - in a class number there should be a digit to represent each of the characteristics used in constructing the class number. A class number should be expressive of the relevant characteristics of the class represented by it.

सूत्र सुसंगतीक्रमाचे – canon of consistent sequence - if similar classes occur in different arrays, the sequence should be parallel in all the arrays, unless there is a positive difference in purpose and helpfulness.

सूत्र सुसंगतीचे – canon of consistency - characteristics used as the basis for the classification of a universe, should be used successively in the same sequence, so long there is no charge in the purpose of classification,

सूत्र स्थानिक फेरबदलाचे - canon of local variation - the notational system of a book classification should provide for variation due to special interests.

सूत्र स्थायित्वाचे – canon of permanence - a characteristics used as the basis for the classification of a universe should continue to be unchanged so long as there is no change in the purpose of classification.

सूत्र स्मरणसुलभतेचे – canon of mnemonics - digit or digits used to represent a specified concept in a class number should be the same in all class numbers having that concept represented in them.

सूत्र - cannon - guiding principles framed by Dr. S.R. Ranganathan for the help of classification and cataloguing.

सूत्र - formula - fixed guidelines.

सूत्रबद्ध अनुक्रम - canonical sequence - traditional arrangement of subjects which is not derived on the basis of any definite characteristic.

सूत्रबद्ध क्रम - canonical order - the order in which sub classes of a main class are arranged. The order in which sequence of canon is followed.

सूत्रबद्ध वर्ग canonical class - traditional sub-class of a main class, enumerated as such in a scheme of classification for the universe of knowledge, and not derived on the basis of definite characteristics.

सूत्रे - canons - principles of classification used in this sense first by W. C. Sayers.

सृजनशील/निर्माण लेखन - creative writing - writing that is built mainly on institution feelings and imagination. The writers in this area should have a flair for writing.

सृजनशील - creative - having power to create intelligence and imagination not merely mechanical skill.

सेंद्रिय संज्ञा - organic terms - in relation to a part of the whole, arising and developing like plants or animals.

सेल्यूलोज ॲसीटेट - cellulose acetate - 'safety' film stock introduced around 1930, does not burst into flame in normal environmental condition, but does shrink and separates from the emulsion (image).

सेल्यूलोज नायट्रेट - cellulose nitrate - film stock used prior to the introduction of 'safety' stock (see cellulose acetate). It decomposes and can spontaneously burst into flame.

सेल्यूलोज - cellulose - organic substance that forms the main part of all plants and trees and is used in making plastics, paper etc.

सेवक/कर्मचारी खोली - staff room - a room reserved for the common use of the staff.

सेवक/कर्मचारी वर्ग व्यवस्थापन/मानव संसाधन व्यवस्थापन - personnel management - planning, organising, directing and controling the procurement, development, compensation, integration, maintenance and separation of human resources to the end that individual organisational and societal objectives are accomplish. -Edward Flipp.

सेवक/कर्मचारी - staff - group of people working in a library.

सेवक/कार्यमार्गदर्शन संहिता – **staff manual** - a guide book for day to day working of the staff.

सेवा – **services** - literature search, supply of current reference on a topic, supply of a copy of a journal article, translation etc.

सेवांतर्गत प्रशिक्षण – **in service training** - 1) training to up keep knowledge while a person is working.
2) training of the staff members while in service.

सेवानिवृत्ती – **superannuation** - completion of the service period under the rules.

सोपस्करण आणि संघटन – **processing and organisation** - classification, cataloguing documents in a library & displaying them properly for use, includes tools like library catalogues and similar others for public use.

सोपा/सुलभ करणे – **facilitate** - make something easy or less difficult.

सोय/फायदा – **advantage** - advantageous position.

सौंदर्यशास्त्र – **aesthetics** - theory of fine arts and philosophy of mind and emotions in relation to it, that branch of philosophy which deals with the beautiful, the doctrines of taste.

सौदा – **bargain** - discuss prices, terms of trade, etc. with the aim of buying or selling goods or changing conditions or terms that are favourable to oneself.

सौम्य शब्दप्रयोग – **euphemism** - the use of pleasant, less direct name for something thought to be unpleasant.

सौम्य – **euphemistic** - speech or word containing euphemism i.e. use of pleasant, mild or indirect words or phrases in place of more accurate or direct ones.

स्तर – **level** - position on a scale of quantity, strength, value etc.

स्तरण – **lamination** - cover of a thin transparent layer on the reading papers for providing protection or combination of more than one formulation of a compound class.

स्रोत भाषा – **source language** - the language by which the translation is being translated.

स्रोत/साधन बाब – **source item** - a document, i.e. a research paper, a review paper, a short communication, etc. that has the potentiality of being cited. (synonym - source document).

स्रोतीय तालिकीकरण – **cataloguing in source** - cataloguing books before they are published, the entries being compiled from proof copies made available by the publisher, the work being carried out by a centralized agency so that full cataloguing information is printed in the books concerned.

स्थल (भौगोलिक) – **geographical space** - in classification the term is used to represent geographical area.

स्थल उपांग – **space isolate** - conventional division of the inside and outside surface of the earth.

स्थल संलग्नता – **spatial contiguity** - contiguity of or relating to space. Contiguity of happening or existing in space.

स्थळवर्णन कोश **gazetteers** - document especially designed to keep information about nation, cities, districts, etc. with details of social, cultural and economic conditions. These also give geographical details.

स्थान खूण – **location mark** - a letter, word, group of words or symbols used for catalogue entry, book list or bibliography, sometimes in conjuction with the call number.

स्थान निर्देश – **location index** - a record used in country libraries for tracing the whereabouts of particular books.

स्थान निर्धारण - **location** - the place on the shelves or elsewhere in which required material may be found.

स्थान पंजी – **location register** - a collection, or list of records of books, documents or other items, arranged by the fixed location method or in a classed access library.

स्थान यादी – **shelf list** - a list of books in a library, the entries being brief and in card form arranged in the same classified sequence as the books on the shelves.

स्थानपत्र/सूचीस्थान यादी – **shelf list** - a catalogue of library holdings arranged in such order as on shelves. For each document one entry with full details is arranged and used only by library staff.

स्थानांतरण किंमती – **transfer pricing** – where responsibility centres or profit centres exist & one centre provides products or services to another centre, an intra-organization pricing is established & transfer price of such products or services is determined based on i) full cost, ii) variable cost, iii) market price or iv) a negotiated price.

स्थानिक अधिकारी – **local authority** - the unit of administration in Britain which is responsible for providing, certain services within the area of its geographical boundaries, either on its own behalf and as it is entitled to do by law, or on behalf of the central government.

स्थानिक ग्रंथपाल – **local librarian** - a voluntary worker at a village or other centre of a country library.

स्थानिक ग्रंथसूची – **local bibliography** - a bibliography of books and other forms of written record related to a geographical area smaller than a country.

स्थानिक प्रवेश – **local access** - access to the information stored on number of computers for their own use or use of the local database directly.

स्थानिक यादी – **local list** - list of books relating to a particular locality.

स्थानिक संग्रह – **local collection** - collections of specific locality, local language, local history and culture etc.

स्थानिय क्षेत्र जाळे – **local area network (LAN)** - 1) a network of communication links / computers available in a particular compact area.
2) a communication facility that covers a limited topology and interconnects in an effective manner different types of servers and work stations, particularly personal computers.

स्थानीय निर्देशिका – **local directory** - a directory related to specified locality, it may be limited in scope in any way e.g. to telephone address or business.

स्थापत्यकला/वास्तुकला – **architecture** - art & science of designing and constructing buildings.

स्थायी आदेश – **standing order** - an order with understanding that a new publication / new edition or addition should be supplied without further communication.

स्थायी समिती – **standing committee** - the committee which assists in continuing functions. Such committee can also be regarded as important committee, being next to the executive one.

स्थूल प्रलेख – **macro document** - document embodying macro thought. Document elaborated to discuss concept in detail. See also macro thought.

स्थूल वर्गीकरण – **broad classification** - arrangement of subjects in a classification system in broad general divisions with minimum of sub-divisions.

स्थूल विचार – **macro thought** - a subject of great extension usually embodied in the form of a book.

स्पष्टीकरणात्मक संदर्भ – **explanatory reference** - a reference which gives the detailed guidance for the effective use of the concerned headings.

स्पेन्सर वर्गीकरण – **Sponsor classification** - scheme of classes given in the classification of science (1864) of Herbert Spensor.

स्मरणशील – **mnemonic** - any acronym or other symbol used in place of something more difficult to remember.

स्मरणसुलभता युक्ती – **mnemonics device** - device in which same digit is used to represent the same concept wherever it occurs.

स्मरणसुलभता – **mnemonics** - 1) An effort of replacing all the terms used for one concept in entire text by one term, symbol or synonym to aid memory or in computer it is an art of improving the efficiency of the memory.

2) Aids to memory. The use of a symbol or symbols representing a given concept consistently in all classes in which that concept is present.

3) The meaning of the word is to assist memory. In a scheme of classification a digit is used to represent a specific concept in all class numbers having that concept. Uniform representation of a concept.

स्मृती – **memory** - capacity of machine to store information. The capacity once fixed cannot be increased. It is an essential part of the computer.

स्वतंत्र अभ्यास – **independent study** - cognitive capabilities of users to access library resources and services independently.

स्वतंत्र चल – **independent variable** - also called explanatory variable; these are assumed to vary exogenously i.e. not influenced by other variables in the equation.

स्वयंचलन कार्यक्रम – **automatic programming** - technique in which computer is used to perform exercise in preparation of program.

स्वयंचलन नोंद/अभिलेख – **automatic record** - record of any phenomenon - natural or social unmediated and uninterrupted by human intellect e.g. instrument or photographic record, electronic record or telerecord.

स्वयंचलन – **automation** - 1) the term automation applies more correctly & narrowly to automatic process control and this was historically the first use of the term.

2) the organisation of machine handling of routines or operations, requiring minimal human intervention.

स्वयंचलित कार्यालय – **automated office** - an office which makes use of electronic devices and telecommunication technology for its functioning.

स्वयंचलित ग्रंथसूची – **automated bibliography** - a bibliography stored in computer. Also known as database.

स्वयंचलित परिभाषा कोश – **automated glossary** - a glossary stored in computer for automatic use.

स्वयंचलित वितरण प्रणाली – **automated circulation system** - a computer used system for arranging the circulation of library information collections.

स्वयंचलित शब्दकोश – **automated dictionary** - a dictionary maintained as computer database.

स्वयंचलित – **automatic** - working by itself without direct human control; self-regulating.

स्वयंसेवक – **volunteer** - person who offers service without being compelled and without remuneration.

स्वरूप अंक – **form number** - a symbol used to indicate the literary form in which a work is written.

स्वरूप नोंद – **form entry** - an entry in a catalogue under the name of the form in which a book is written.

स्वरूप पत्र पद्धत – **feature card system** - a method of information renewal in which a card is reserved for features such as 'aspect', 'dimension', 'facet', characteristic, or piece of information.

स्वरूप विभाग – **form division** - adjuncts to a classification which enable books to be arranged (with their subject) according to the form in which they are written.

स्वरूप शीर्षक – **feature heading** - the verbal part of a subject heading used in the systematic file of a classified catalogue i.e. that part which is a translation into words of the last element of a classification symbol.

स्वरूप शीर्षक – **form heading** - a heading used in a catalogue for a form entry. A heading describing the category of document.

स्वरूप – **form** - a classification term applied to the manner in which the text of a book is arranged as a dictionary, or the literary form in which it is written, as drama, poetry etc.

स्वरूप उपशीर्षक – **form sub-heading** - a sub-heading used for sub-arranging in a catalogue entries for books on the same subject by their literary or practical form.

स्वरूप चित्रफीत (चित्रपट) - **feature film** - a term used by exhibitors to define the film or films used mainly in cinema programme and filling over 3000 feet of 35 mm film.

स्वरूप पत्र – **feature card** - a plain or punched card allocated to a 'feature' in co-ordinate indexing.

स्वरूप/वैशिष्ट्य – **feature** - a characteristic of a thing indexed.

स्वस्त आवृत्ती – **cheap edition** - an edition of a document brought out on cheaper price than original, which is generally in paper back.

स्वातंत्र्यवाद – **libertarianism** - principles of doctrines of the freedom of will.

स्वामित्व ग्रंथालय – **copyright library** - a library which is entitled to receive a free copy of every published document under Copyright Act.

स्वामित्व चिन्ह – **ownership mark** - it may be a stamp or printed stationary pasted on document to ascertain ownership. e.g. © author, publisher etc.

स्वामित्व दिनांक – **copyright date** - the date on which copyright of a book is extended, generally printed on the back of title page.

स्वामित्व – **copyright** - right of an author / publisher / any other body under rule on a contribution.

स्वामित्व हक्क/लेखाधिकार – **copyright** - means to protect the exclusive right of an author and/or publisher or any other person or body by the government by law so that nobody else is permitted to reproduce the original literary, musical or artistic work, for a specified number of years.

स्वायत्तता – **autonomy** - the degree to which the job provides substantial freedom, independence, and discretion to the individual in scheduling the work and in determining the procedures to be used in carrying it out.

ह

हंगामी फेरबदल/विभिन्नता – **seasonal variation** - periodical fluctuation in the data, spanning less than a year, caused by seasonal changes.

हकीकत/अहवाल – **reporting** - keeping the executive authorities informed of the activities and progress.

हक्क – **right** - the privileges of entitlement to permit the publication, performance, or adoption of authorship and receive payment of same.

हस्त स्तरण – **hand lamination** - the process which gives a coat of shiffon and fixes cellulose acetate foil to it by means of acetone.

हस्तपुस्तिका/हस्ताध्याय – **handbook** - a concise reference book devoted to a particular topic capable of being carried conveniently. Usually, it provides all such information as is often required by the working professionals.

हस्तलिखित ग्रंथ विज्ञान – **manuscriptology** - science / study of manuscripts.

हस्तलिखित ग्रंथपाल – **manuscript librarian** - a librarian who deals with handwritten books, documents.

हस्तलिखित ग्रंथालय – **manuscript library** - a library which has collection of handwritten books on various discipline.

हस्तलिखित तालिका – **manuscript catalogue** - a catalogue based on the entries prepared exclusively for manuscripts.

हस्तलिखित – **manuscript** - a document written by hand.

हस्तांतरण – **delegation** - the process of assiging responsibility along with required authority

हस्ताक्षर कला – **calligraphy** - the art of beautiful writing.

हस्ताक्षर – **autograph** - handwriting; the signatures given by a person himself / herself.

हस्ताक्षरित आवृत्ती – **signed edition** - an edition of the document signed by the author.

हस्ताक्षरित पृष्ठ – **signed page** - page signed by the author.

हातपोथी / निर्देश पुस्तिका – **manual** - a helping book or guideline on the subject for which it has been prepared see also 'handbook'.

हार्ड डिस्क - **hard disk** - a hard disk is made up of a stack of metal plates (disks) on which data is recorded in concentric circles or 'tracks' : A read / write head reads or records (writes) information on the tracks. Two heads, one for each surface of the disk, reads and writes data as the disk spins. Each read or write operation requires that data be located, which is an operation called seek. A hard disk can be categorized as a disk pack or a Winchester Disk depending on the way it is packed.

हार्डवेअर – **hardware** - the physical aspect of computers, telecommunications, and other information technology devices. The term is collectively used for computers along with connectors, cables, power supply units and peripheral devices like mouse, keyboard, printer etc.

हास्यके/चित्रके – **comics** - writing /pictures etc. which makes laugh.

हिशोब तपासणी/लेखा परिक्षण – **audit** - method of authentic examination or the service to check the correctness of expenditures and income records of an organisation.

हेगेल वर्गीकरण – **Hegel classification** - scheme of classes implied in the logic (1812) of Hegel.

हेतु/प्रस्ताव – **preamble** - a statement recording objectives of the contribution.

हेतू/उद्दिष्ट – **intention** - depth of the subject.

हॉवर्थॉर्न अभ्यास – **Hawthorn study** - the effect of making people feel very special by changing their perception.

क्षेत्र – **sector -** 1) a set of isolate achieving on the basis of single characteristic. 2) broad areas devoted to subject / discipline / mission.

क्षेत्र युक्ती – **sector device -** device using a sectorising digit, that is, to form another sector or sketch co-ordinate digits by adding the successive digits of the species and deeming the resulting double digit numbers as diffused into a single digit, and repeating this process to form successive sectors.

क्षेत्र आराखडा/संरचना – **field structure -** layout of data in a field and its identifier.

क्षेत्र – **1) zone -** a portion of an array in which all the array isolates are formed by one and the same device, division of surface of the earth.

2) field - the smallest piece of information in a database. A patron's last name, the title of a book, or a call number are all examples of fields.

क्षेत्रीय उपांग/उपविभाग – **zonal isolate -** sub/ division of a physiographic feature based on some characteristic intrinsic to it.

क्षेत्र सारणी – **area table -** a table of class numbers used to represent a geographical area.

क्षेत्र सिद्धान्त – **field theory -** a method of analysis in behavioural science that describes actions or events as a result of dynamic interplay among sociocultural and motivational forces.

क्षेत्रीय/प्रादेशिक ग्रंथालय – **regional library -** a library catering to the needs of a region.

क्षेत्र तक्ता – **area table -** an auxiliary table enlisting geographical areas & their respective notations. Area of the world are arranged in a systematic way. It is to be used with the class numbers in the schedules.

ज्ञान आधार/ज्ञानार्थी – **knowledge base -** in computing a database containing the codified knowledge of a human expert or experts.

ज्ञान वर्ग – **knowledge class -** subject ranked along other subjects of the universe of knowledge in a scheme of classification.

ज्ञान वर्गीकरण – **knowledge classification -** classification which is used for any branch of knowledge.

ज्ञान विस्फोट/ज्ञानस्फोट – **knowledge explosion -** the huge mass of printed material being produced currently due to extensive scientific research and other intellectual activities.

ज्ञान शाखा – **discipline -** an organised field of learning.

ज्ञान संपादन/ज्ञानार्जन – **learning -** the act of obtaining knowledge or skill. Acquired knowledge or skill; especially, knowledge related to a specific topic/subject : erudition.

ज्ञान – **knowledge -** it is the result of assimilation process of the information. The volume of information can not be used until one knows the elements of analysis, selection of information and also use it in adequate manner. See also information.

ज्ञानमीमांसा – **epistemology -** methods of scientific procedure which lead to the acquisition of sociological knowledge.

ज्ञानाधारित/ज्ञान उद्योग – **knowledge industry -** industry that produces records of knowledge and information in print as well as non-print.

ज्ञानेंद्रिय – **sense organ -** an organ or structure which receives specific stimuli and transmits them as sensations to the brain; any organ of sense, as the ear, eye or nose; a receptor.

ज्ञापनपत्र (संस्थेचे) – **memorandum of association -** in business, a statement, made by the consignor, of the goods and terms of consignment sent with the privilege of return. In law, a short written statement of terms of an agreement, contract, or transaction.

इंग्रजी – मराठी

abbreviated – संक्षेपित – शब्दाचे पदबंधाचे संक्षिप्त रूप.

abbreviated catalogue card – **संक्षेपित पत्र/तालिका पत्र** – अशा तालिकापत्रात ग्रंथाबाबतची माहिती संक्षेपित रूपात दिलेली असते.

abbreviated catalogue entry – **संक्षेपित तालिका नोंद** – ग्रंथांची त्रोटक माहिती असणारी नोंद.

abbreviated catalogue name – **संक्षेपित तालिका नाव.**

abbreviations – **संक्षेपाक्षरे** – संस्था अथवा शब्दसमूह यांच्या आद्याक्षरांचा समूह.

aberrant copy – **सदोष मजकुरी प्रत** – बांधणीमध्ये किंवा जुळणीमध्ये काही त्रुटी आढळून येणारी प्रत. यातील चुका सहज दृष्टिक्षेपात येण्यासारख्या असून बहुतेकवेळा सुधारणा समजून येण्यासारख्या असतात.

abnormal book – **असाधारण ग्रंथ** – ग्रंथाच्या बाह्याआकारामुळे किंवा विशिष्ट स्वरूपातील मजकुरामुळे असाधारण असा ग्रंथ. काहीवेळा हा जतन करण्यायोग्य व विशेष दुर्मिळ ग्रंथ म्हणून महत्त्वाचा असतो. उदा. ग्रंथ उघडल्यावर संगणकाच्या आकाराची प्रतिकृती समाविष्ट केलेली दिसते.

abnormal book – **असाधारण आकाराचा ग्रंथ** – सर्वसाधारण ग्रंथाच्या आकारापेक्षा खूप मोठा अथवा अत्यंत लहान आकार असलेला ग्रंथ.

abort – **स्थगिती** – संगणकातील माहितीबरोबर चालू असलेली प्रक्रिया तात्पुरती थांबविण्याची कृती.

abort timer – **संगणकातील स्थगितीकार्य कालमापक** – संगणकातील माहितीचे विशिष्ट कालावधीमध्ये प्रसारण झाल्यास संगणकाचे कार्य थांबविण्याचे काम हा भाग करतो.

abridged – संक्षिप्त/गोषवारा/थोडक्यात/संक्षेपाने.

abridged classification – **संक्षिप्त वर्गीकरण** – ग्रंथाच्या विषयाचे ढोबळ वर्गीकरण करून तयार केलेली वर्गांक सारणी.

abridged decimal classification – **संक्षिप्त दशांश वर्गीकरण** – लहान ग्रंथालयांसाठी तयार केलेले दशांश वर्गीकरणाचे संक्षेपीकरण.

abridged edition – **संक्षिप्त आवृत्ती** – लेखकाच्या मूळ लेखनाची लांबी कमी करून काढलेली आवृत्ती. ही आवृत्ती मूळ लेखनाचे संक्षिप्तरूप दर्शविते.

abridgement – **संक्षेपीकरण** – मूळ रचना न बदलता महत्त्वाचे मुद्दे घेऊन तयार केलेले सार. मूळ लेखनातील काही भागाचे विशिष्ट हेतूने सारांशलेखन करून संक्षेपीकरण केले जाते. मूळ कृतीतील आवश्यक भाग त्यात तसाच घेतला जातो.

absolute address / machine address – **स्वयंस्थान** – संगणकाच्या स्मरणिकेत विशिष्ट माहितीसाठी दिलेले निश्चित स्थान.

absolute data – **स्वयंस्थान माहिती** – संगणकातील आलेखन करण्यासाठी लागणारी आधारसामग्री.

absolute location (fixed location)– **(ग्रंथाचे) निश्चित स्थान** – ग्रंथाचे ग्रंथमांडणीतील स्थान निश्चित करण्यासाठी ग्रंथामध्ये कपाट क्रमांक, कप्पा क्रमांक यांचा उल्लेख ग्रंथांकाबरोबर केला जातो. यामुळे ग्रंथ चटकन् मिळविणे सहज शक्य होते.

absolute size (exact size) – **(ग्रंथाचा) अचूक आकार** – ग्रंथाच्या आकाराचे चिन्हात्मक स्वरूप देण्याऐवजी सेंमी. किंवा इंच या मापांद्वारे दिलेला ग्रंथाचा अचूक आकार.

abstract – **संक्षेप/गोषवारा/सारविवरण/संक्षिप्त/अमूर्त/तत्त्वांश/सारांश/सारलेख**– एखाद्या प्रलेखाचा सारांश किंवा सारनियतकालिकातील एक नोंद ग्रंथसूचीमध्ये ग्रंथातील मजकुराविषयी दिलेला सारांश.

abstract index – **सार निर्देश** – मूळ लेखाचा सारांश देणारी सूची.

abstracting – **सारलेखन** – सार तयार करण्याच्या पद्धती.

abstracting coard – **सारलेखन मंडळ** – लेखांचे सारांश तयार करणारे मंडळ.

abstracting culletin – **सारदर्शक पत्रक.**

abstracting journal – **सारदर्शक पत्रिका** – लेखांचे सारांश प्रकाशित करणारे नियतकालिक.

abstracting periodical – **सारदर्शक नियतकालिके** – विविध लेखांच्या सारांशाचा समावेश करून प्रकाशित केलेले नियतकालिक.

abstraction service (secondary service) – **सारलेखन सेवा** – एखाद्या व्यक्तीने, संस्थेने विशिष्ट उपयोगिता लक्षात घेऊन सारलेख तयार करणे. हे सारलेख प्रकाशित करून सभासदांना नियमितपणे पुरविले जातात. या 'सारलेख सेवा' निवडक विषयापुरत्या अथवा सर्वंकष असतात.

abstraction – **पृथक्करण** – माहितीचे विभाजन करून गट करण्याची मानसिक प्रक्रिया. (वर्गीकरणप्रक्रियेत अभिप्रेत असलेली प्रक्रिया.)

abstractor – **सारकर्ता/संक्षेपकार** – सारांश तयार करणारी व्यक्ती.

academic – **शैक्षणिक/शिक्षणासंबंधी**.

academic libraries – **शैक्षणिक ग्रंथालये** – विद्यापीठ, महाविद्यालय, शाळा यांसारख्या शैक्षणिक संस्थांची ग्रंथालये.

academic publication – **शैक्षणिक प्रकाशन** – शिक्षणविषयक चर्चा करणारे प्रकाशन.

academic year – **शैक्षणिक वर्ष** – विद्यापीठ, महाविद्यालये; शाळा यांसारख्या शैक्षणिक संस्थांमधील कामाचे वर्ष. भारतात जे साधारणत: जून ते मे असते.

academy – **अकादमी** – विशिष्ट ज्ञानासंबंधी विविध कामे करणारी संस्था.

academy publication – **अकादमी प्रकाशन** – विशिष्ट विषयासाठी वाहिलेल्या संस्थेने प्रकाशित केलेले प्रकाशन.

acceleration time – **प्रवेगकाल** – संगणकातील आधारसामग्रीचे वाचन किंवा लेखन यांचा वेग वाढविण्यासाठी लागणारा कालावधी.

access – **माहिती प्रतिप्राप्तीसाठी प्रवेश** – ज्या कार्यपद्धतीने माहितीपर्यंत पोहोचता येते, ती संगणकीय क्रिया –
(१) प्रलेख किंवा माहिती मिळविण्यासाठी आवश्यक क्लृप्ती किंवा पद्धती.
(२) प्रलेख वापरण्याची परवानगी आणि संधी.
(३) कोणत्याही प्रकारे (निर्देश, ग्रंथसूची, संगणक) माहितीसंचय करण्याचा दृष्टिकोन.
(दफ्तर) सरकारी बखरी किंवा दफ्तरखान्यातील दुर्मिळ ग्रंथ लोकांना उपलब्ध होणे.

access point – **शोधशीर्षक माहितीचे प्रवेशद्वार/शोधशीर्षक निर्देशातील एखादे विशिष्ट शीर्षक** – या शीर्षकाद्वारे संगणकीय फाइल वापरण्यास प्रवेश मिळविला जातो. ग्रंथाचा ज्या शीर्षकाखाली तालिकेमध्ये शोध केला जातो त्यास 'शोधशीर्षक' म्हणतात. ग्रंथालय तालिकेत, ग्रंथ शोधण्यासाठी, वाचकांनी उपयोगात आणलेले नाव, शीर्षक, संज्ञा किंवा शब्दसमूह. (आणखी पाहा – मागणीशीर्षक)

access time – **परिप्राप्ती कालावधी** – माहिती उपलब्ध होण्यासाठी किंवा मिळविण्यासाठी लागणारा कालावधी.

access tool – **परिप्राप्ती साधन** – एखादा लेख, ग्रंथ शोधण्यासाठी त्या ग्रंथाची ग्रंथसूची, माहिती, वर्णन (जसे ग्रंथकार, वर्ष) मिळण्यासाठी साहाय्यक ठरणारे साधन.

accession – **पटांकन/दाखलनोंद** – दाखलअंकानुसार दाखलनोंद करणे, ग्रंथालयात ग्रंथ दाखल होण्याच्या क्रमाने नोंद करणे किंवा संगणकामध्ये दाखलअंकानुसार दाखलनोंदीत प्रवेश मिळविणे.

accession arrangement – **दाखलनोंद संख्याक्रम व्यवस्था**.

accession book – **दाखलनोंदवही** – ज्यात ग्रंथाच्या दाखलनोंदी केल्या जातात अशी वही. (आणखी पहा – Accession Register)

accession date – **दाखलनोंदीचा दिनांक** – ज्या दिवशी दाखलनोंद केली जाते त्या दिवसाचा दिनांक.

accession department – **दाखलनोंद विभाग** – दाखलनोंदीचे कामकाज चालविणारा ग्रंथालयाचा विभाग.

accession list – **दाखलनोंद यादी/सूची** – ग्रंथसंग्रहाची दाखलअंकानुसार केलेली यादी किंवा सूची.

accession number/code – **दाखल अंक** – ग्रंथ अथवा प्रलेख ग्रंथालयात दाखल झाल्यावर त्याला ओळखक्रमांक देऊन दाखलअंक असे संबोधले जाते. या अंकाची नोंद दाखलनोंद वहीमध्ये केली जाते.

accession number section – **दाखलअंक अनुच्छेद** – ग्रंथालय तालिकेतील मुख्य नोंदीत ग्रंथाचा दाखलनोंद अंक देणाऱ्या शेवटच्या अनुच्छेदाला 'दाखलअंक अनुच्छेदन' असे म्हणतात.

accession order/arrangement/system – **दाखलनोंदीनुसार रचना** – ग्रंथालयात दाखलअंकानुसार विशिष्ट वर्गांकामध्ये एका कप्प्यात केलेली ग्रंथमांडणी.

accession register – **दाखलनोंदवही** – ग्रंथपट अथवा दाखलनोंदवही ही कोणत्याही ग्रंथालयाची मूळ/मुख्य अभिलेख/नोंदवही असते.

accession stamp – **दाखलनोंद शिक्का** – दाखलनोंद दर्शविणारा शिक्का.

accessioning – **दाखलनोंदणी** – दाखलनोंद करण्याची क्रिया.

accompanying material – **ग्रंथाबरोबर मिळणारे पूरक साहित्य** – उदा. नकाशा, ध्वनिचित्रफीत, सीडी रॉम, इत्यादी.

accounting – **लेखाकर्म** – जमा आणि खर्च यांची पद्धतशीरपणे करावयाची नोंद.

accreditation – **अधिस्वीकृती** – शैक्षणिक अभ्यासक्रम घेणाऱ्या संस्थांची अधिकृतता व दर्जा विषयक मूल्यमापन. विशेषत: अमेरिकन लायब्ररी असोसिएशनची ग्रंथालयशास्त्र शिक्षण संस्थांविषयीची मूल्यमापन भूमिका. उदा. भारतात नॅक (National Assessment & Accreditation Council) ची अधिस्वीकृती.

accuracy – **अचूकता/परिशुद्धता** – निर्दोष माहिती.

accumulator – **संचायक** – संगणकातील संग्राहक नोंदफाईल; गणिती प्रक्रियांसाठी वापर करता येतो. गणिती प्रक्रिया पूर्ण झाल्यावर परिणामनोंदी येथेच धारण केल्या जातात.

acknowledgement – **ऋणनिर्देश** – ग्रंथनिर्मितीसाठी मदत करणाऱ्या व्यक्ती, संस्थांबाबत आभार व्यक्त करणारे ग्रंथाचे पृष्ठ.

acoustic coupler – **श्रवणीय/ध्वनिक भाग** – दोन संगणकांमध्ये दूरसंचार यंत्रणेद्वारा माहिती पाठविण्याचे कार्य करणारा संगणकाचा भाग. दूरसंचार सूचनेचे ध्वनीसूचनेत रूपांतर करण्यासाठी याचा उपयोग होतो. या उपकरणाच्या साहाय्याने इतर संगणकाशी संपर्क साधणे शक्य होते.

acquisition – **ग्रंथोपार्जन/उपार्जन/अर्जन/संपादन** – ग्रंथालय माहितीकेंद्र किंवा दप्तरखाना यासाठी ग्रंथ व इतर साहित्य मिळविण्याची प्रक्रिया.

acquisition department – **ग्रंथोपार्जन विभाग** – खरेदी, देणगी, अदलाबदल, ग्रंथालयाचा संग्रह विकसित करणारा विभाग.

acquisition of books – **ग्रंथोपार्जन** – खरेदी, देणगी किंवा अदलाबदलीने सातत्याने ग्रंथालयाचा संग्रह वाढविणे.

acquisition officer – **ग्रंथोपार्जन अधिकारी** – ग्रंथोपार्जन विभागाचे कामकाज पाहणारा अधिकारी.

acquisition number – **ग्रंथोपार्जन अंक** – वाचनसाहित्यास दिलेला अनुक्रमांक.

acquisition record – **ग्रंथोपार्जन नोंद** – ग्रंथसंग्रहात समाविष्ट होत असलेले ग्रंथ व ग्रंथेतर वाचनसाहित्य यांची नोंद.

acquisition system – **ग्रंथोपार्जन पद्धती** – ग्रंथालयात सर्व वाचनसाहित्याचे उपार्जन करण्यासाठी वापरली जाणारी विशिष्ट पद्धती. यात वाचकाने वाचनसाहित्याची शिफारस करण्यापासून नवे वाचनसाहित्य खरेदी करून ग्रंथ देवघेवी उपलब्ध करून देण्यापर्यंतच्या सर्व क्रिया/पायऱ्या अंतर्भूत आहेत.

acquisition work – **ग्रंथोपार्जन कार्य** – ग्रंथालयात सर्व वाचनसाहित्याचे उपार्जन करण्यासाठी केले जाणारे सर्व कामकाज.

acronym – **संक्षेपाक्षर/आद्याक्षरी नाव** – संयुक्त संज्ञेच्या प्रत्येक विभागाच्या किंवा प्रमुख विभागाच्या आद्याक्षरांनी बनलेला शब्द किंवा व्यक्तीच्या किंवा संस्थेच्या आद्याक्षरांचा गट तयार करून केलेले नाव. उदा. UGC (University Grants Commission)

acrophony – **चित्रध्वनिलेखन** – चित्राकृती अथवा लेखनामध्ये नावाच्या आद्याक्षराचा चिन्ह म्हणून उपयोग करून ते चिन्ह म्हणजेच ते मूल्य गृहीत धरले जाते. उदा. b of beta, g of gamma.

acting edition – **रंगकर्मी आवृत्ती/रंगावृत्ती** – रंगकर्मींना हावभाव, अभिनय, नेपथ्य याविषयी विशेष सूचना देणारी नाटकाची प्रत.

action – **कृती** – क्रिया व प्रतिक्रिया, कार्य व प्रतिकार्य.

active documentation – **कार्यप्रवण प्रलेखन** – एखाद्या विषयावरील माहितीची विचारणा केली जाईल हे ओळखून त्याविषयी प्रलेखन तयारी करणे. (उदा. वर्ष २००० संगणक समस्या)

active file – **कार्यप्रवण पत्रिका** – संगणकावर वापरात असलेली फाईल. या फाईलमधील माहिती उपयोजक केव्हाही बदलू शकतो.

adaptation – **अनुकूलन/अनुयोजन/अनुयोजना/समायोजन/रूपांतरण** – रूपांतरित ग्रंथ संपादन करून रूपांतरण केलेला ग्रंथ. उदा. मुलांना वाचण्यासाठी किंवा नाट्यवाचन करण्यासाठी मूळ पुस्तकात आवश्यक बदल करून तयार केलेले पुस्तक. संक्षेपीकरणापेक्षा वेगळे.

add instructions – **पूरक सूचनासंच** – दशांश वर्गीकरण ग्रंथाच्या १८,१९,२०,२१व्या आवृत्तीत मूळ वर्गांकाबरोबर क्रमांक समाविष्ट करण्यासाठी दिलेल्या पूरक सूचना.

add to note – **पूरक टीप/भर घाला टीप** – एखाद्या नोंदीसाठी दिलेली सूचना. यानुसार डी.डी.सी.च्या खंड २ अनुसूचीमधून अथवा खंड १ टेबल्स क्रमांक २ ते ६ मधून क्रमांक घेऊन तो मूळ वर्गांकाला जोडता येतो. त्यामुळे सविस्तर वर्गांक तयार करता येतो.

added copies – **अधिक प्रती** – संग्रहात असलेल्या जास्तीच्या ग्रंथप्रती.

added edition – **पूरक आवृत्ती** – ग्रंथालयात असलेल्या आवृत्तीशिवाय समाविष्ट केलेली वेगळी आवृत्ती.

added entry – **पूरक नोंद** – मुख्य नोंदीव्यतिरिक्त केलेली पूरक दुय्यम तालिकानोंद. उदा. विषयनोंद, संपादन नोंद, मालानोंद. थोडक्यात, मुख्य नोंद सोडून इतर नोंदीस 'पूरक नोंद' असे म्हणतात.

added title entry – **पूरक शीर्षक नोंद** – मुख्य नोंदीशिवाय केलेली ग्रंथशीर्षक नोंद.

addenda addendum – **ग्रंथ पूर्ण छापल्यानंतर वाढीव मजकुरासाठी येणारी पुरवणी अनुबंध** – ग्रंथाचे लेखन पूर्ण झाल्यावर काही भाग समाविष्ट केला जातो. अशावेळी ग्रंथांच्या सुरुवातीला किंवा शेवटी पृष्ठांचा समावेश केला जातो. परंतु ही पुरवणी असते.

additional – **अतिरिक्त/जादा किंवा वाढीव.**

additional librarian – **अतिरिक्त ग्रंथपाल.**

additional copy – **अतिरिक्त प्रत** – एका ग्रंथालयातील एका ग्रंथापेक्षा अधिकच्या प्रती.

additions – **समावेशन/वाढ/भर** – असलेल्या संग्रहात वाढ.

additions list – **समावेशन यादी** – नव्याने दाखल झालेल्या ग्रंथांची यादी.

address – **पत्ता/स्थान** – संगणकाच्या स्मरणिकेमध्ये माहितीचे स्थान कोणते आहे हे दर्शविणारे नाव, क्रमांक किंवा खूण.

address number – **स्थानदर्शक अंक/संख्या** – जागा दर्शविणारी संख्या किंवा अंक.

address register – **स्थान/पत्ता नोंदवही.**

adjunct – **गुणवाचक** – काहीतरी प्रासंगिक, परंतु महत्त्वाच्या भागाशी जोडण्याची आवश्यकता नसलेले.

adjustable – **संयोजनक्षम** – पुनर्रचना करता येण्याजोगे.

adjustable classification – **संयोजनक्षम वर्गीकरण** – जेम्स ब्राऊन यांनी १८९७ मध्ये तयार केलेली वर्गीकरण पद्धती. ही पद्धती ब्राऊन यांच्या विषयवर्गीकरण पद्धतीपेक्षा अप्रचलित राहिली.

adjustable shelving – **संयोजनक्षम कपाटरचना** – कपाटाची अशी रचना की ज्यात कप्प्यांची उंची कमी/जास्त करता येते.

administration – **प्रशासन** – कार्यालयीन कारभार करण्याची प्रक्रिया, प्रशासन पद्धती.

administrative office – **प्रशासनिक कार्यालय/प्रशासकीय कार्यालय.**

administrative building – **प्रशासनिक/प्रशासकीय इमारत.**

admission – **प्रवेश.**

admission card – **प्रवेश पत्र** – ग्रंथालयात प्रवेश करण्यासाठी असलेले ओळखपत्र.

admission record – **प्रवेश नोंद** – प्रवेश घेतल्याचे दर्शविणारा अभिलेख.

admission slip – **प्रवेश चिठ्ठी.**

adobe acrobat reader – **ॲडोब ॲक्रोबॅट वाचक** – संगणकीय कार्यक्रमाचा एक प्रकार; ज्याचा वापर डीटीपीसाठी प्रामुख्याने केला जातो.

adolescent library – **प्रौढांसाठीचे ग्रंथालय.**

adult education – **प्रौढ शिक्षण** – ३५ ते ५० वयोगटातील व्यक्तीसाठीचे शिक्षण.

advance copy – **आगाऊ प्रत** – प्रकाशन दिनांकाच्या अगोदर मिळालेली ग्रंथांची प्रत किंवा ग्रंथप्रकाशनापूर्वी सुट्या पृष्ठस्वरूपातील किंवा बांधणी केलेली ग्रंथाची कच्ची प्रत. त्याचा उपयोग बांधणीकाराला किंवा ग्रंथ परीक्षण, जाहिरात यासाठी करता येतो.

advance payment – **अग्रिम अदायगी/आगाऊ रक्कम** – देय दिनांकापूर्वी घेतलेला पगार, वेतन.

advertisement file – **जाहिरात संचिका** – अनेक वर्तमानपत्रे/मासिके इत्यादी मधून एखाद्या विशिष्ट पदाच्या/संस्थेच्या जाहिरातींची संचिका; ज्याची रचना शक्यतो कालक्रमाने असते.

ad verbum – **मुळाबरहुकूम** – जसेच्या तसे शब्द.

advisory board – **सल्लागार मंडळ** – संस्थेला मार्गदर्शन करणारे मंडळ

advisory committee – **सल्लागार समिती.**

advisory services – **सल्लागार सेवा.**

advocate – **अधिवक्ता** – बाजू मांडणारा, वकील.

aerial map – **हवाई नकाशा** – हवाई पाहणीतून काढलेल्या एक किंवा अनेक छायाचित्रांचा वापर करून तयार केलेला नकाशा.

aerial photograph – **हवाई चित्र** – अवकाशातून घेतलेले छायाचित्र.

affiliated – **संलग्नित** – शाखारूप शाखा केलेला, (सख्यसंबंधाने) जोडलेला, स्वयंसंबंधी केलेला उपकृष्ट.

affiliated college – संलग्नित महाविद्यालय – शिखर संस्थेशी जोडलेले / मान्यता असलेले महाविद्यालय.

affiliated university – संलग्नित विद्यापीठ.

affiliated library – संलग्नित ग्रंथालय – प्रमुख ग्रंथालयाचा भाग असलेले परंतु स्वतंत्रीत्या कामकाज करणारे ग्रंथालय.

agate stone – अकीक दगड – जिल्हईचा दगड.

agency – कारकत्व/प्रतिनिधी संस्था – एखाद्या उद्योजकाने/प्रकाशकाने नेमलेला अधिकृत विक्रेता किंवा प्रतिष्ठान/संस्था.

agent – प्रतिनिधी – अडत्या किंवा गुमास्ता जो एखाद्या कंपनीचा/संस्थेचा प्रतिनिधी असतो. ग्रंथालयाला आवश्यक साहित्य मिळवून देण्यासाठी प्रकाशक व ग्रंथपाल यांच्यातील मध्यस्थ म्हणून काम करणारी व्यक्ती किंवा संस्था.

agenda – कार्यसूची/विषय पत्रिका – सभेपुढे विचारार्थ ठेवावयाची, प्रश्नांची, योजनांची, प्रस्तावांची, कार्यक्रमांची इ. यादी.

aggregate – एकूण/समग्र/समष्टि/साकल्य – समुदाय, एकूण रक्कम.

agris – ॲग्रिस – इंटरनॅशनल सिस्टिम फॉर ॲग्रिकल्चरल सायन्सेस ॲण्ड टेक्नॉलॉजी, प्रचलित कृषी आणि तंत्रज्ञान साहित्यावरील सहकारी जागतिक माहिती पद्धती.

agriculture college – कृषी विषयाचे शिक्षण देणारे महाविद्यालय.

agricultural engineering – कृषी अभियांत्रिकी – कृषी अवजारांवर संशोधन करणारे विज्ञान.

agricultural library – कृषीविषयक ग्रंथालय – कृषीविषयक माहितीची सेवा देणारे ग्रंथालय.

agricultural school – कृषी शाळा/विद्यालय.

agricultural university – कृषी विद्यापीठ – कृषी विषयात संशोधन/प्रशिक्षण देणारे विद्यापीठ.

aided library – अनुदानित ग्रंथालय– ग्रंथालयसेवा पुरविण्यासाठी सरकार किंवा इतर संस्था यांच्याकडून अनुदान मिळणारे ग्रंथालय.

airtight – हवाबंद – हवा आत शिरणार नाही अशा रीतीने तोंड बंद केलेले वेष्टण.

ajoure binding – अजूर बांधणी – व्हेनिस येथे १५व्या शतकात प्रचलित असलेली ग्रंथबांधणी पद्धती.

album – संग्रहिका – कोरी पाने असलेले पुस्तक त्यात साहित्यातील उतारे, सुविचार, कविता, चित्रे, छायाचित्रे, सह्यांचे नमुने, वृत्तपत्र कात्रणे, तिकिटे, चलन इ. लिखाण किंवा चिकटविण्याचे काम केले जाते.

alcove / carrel / cubicle / study – अभ्यासिका – कृत्रिम भिंती तयार करून बसण्यासाठी तयार केलेला मोठ्या खोलीतील कक्ष.

alert box – **सतर्क चौकट/सूचना कप्पा** – संगणकाला दिलेली सूचना खरोखरच अंमलात आणावयाची किंवा नाही याबाबत सावधानतेने विचारणा करणारा सूचना कप्पा.

algebraic sub grouping – **बैजिक उपगट** – बीजगणितात केल्या जाणाऱ्या उपगटांप्रमाणे वर्गीकरणात केलेले उपगट, काही चिन्हांच्या साहाय्याने हे उपगट तयार होतात. दोन किंवा अधिक घटकांना/ उपविषयांना संमिश्र अंक जोडून एक संयुक्त अंक तयार करावा लागतो.

algorithum – **नियतरीती/गणनविधी** – आज्ञावली तयार करण्यापूर्वी संगणकास द्यावयाच्या आज्ञा सरळ वाक्यात (इंग्रजी मातृभाषा) लिहून काढण्याच्या क्रियेस 'ॲल्गोरिदम' म्हणतात. अशी सरळ वाक्ये नंतर उच्चस्तरीय भाषेमध्ये बदलणे सोपे जाते किंवा संगणक संयोजनामध्ये येणाऱ्या समस्या सोडविण्यासाठी दिलेल्या सूचनांचा संग्रह.

alien region – **परकीय/अन्यदेशीय प्रदेश** – संबंधित नसलेले प्रदेश.

alien subject – **परकीय विषय** – पूर्णत: विषयाला धरून नसलेले विषय.

alienation – **दूरीभवन/अनन्यसंक्रमण** – दफ्तरखान्यातील काही ग्रंथ व प्रलेख हे कार्यालयाशी संबंधित नसलेल्या व्यक्ती किंवा संस्थेकडे सुपूर्द करण्याची प्रक्रिया.

alignment – **संरेखन/स्तरबद्धता** – ग्रंथाच्या पृष्ठावरील मजकुरामध्ये राखलेले योग्य समासांतर.

all along binding – **एकधागी बांधणी** – हाताने किंवा यंत्राच्या साहाय्याने केलेली एकधागी बांधणी.

all published – ज्याचे प्रकाशन सुरू झाले परंतु पूर्ण झाले नाही अशा प्रकाशनाची तालिकानोंद यात नियतकालिकाचे सुटे अंग किंवा स्थगित झालेल्या प्रकाशअंकांचा समावेश होतो.

all rights reserved – **स्वामित्व** – सर्वाधिकार सुरक्षित, मालकी, लेखक, प्रकाशक इ.चे स्वामित्व (मालकी) अधिकार राखून ठेवणेबाबतची सूचना. हा संदेश ग्रंथाच्या शीर्षकपृष्ठाच्या मागे दिला जातो. या संदेशाद्वारे ग्रंथाचे भाषांतर, गायन, नाट्यरूपांतर, अनुवाद इ. विषयीचे हक्क कोणाचे आहेत यांचा उल्लेख केला जातो. याकरिता © हे चिन्ह वापरतात.

all through alphacetisation – **सरसकट वर्णानुक्रमरचना** – सरसकट वर्णानुक्रमाला अनुसरून केलेली रचना.

allocate to – ग्रंथालयाच्या कोणत्या विभागात कोणती पुस्तके ठेवावीत याचा निर्णय घेऊन गटवारी करताना द्यावयाची सूचना.

allocation – **वाटप/वाटणी/विभाजन.**

allotment – **वाटप/वाटून/विभागून देणे.**

pseudonym – **टोपणनाव** – आपली ओळख पटू नये म्हणून लेखकाने घेतलेले नाव.

allusion book – **निर्देश संदर्भ ग्रंथ** – एखाद्या लेखकाच्या नाम–माहात्म्यामुळे नावारूपाला आलेला ग्रंथ.

almanac / ephemeris – पंचांग – ज्यामध्ये दैनंदिन अथवा खगोलशास्त्रीय माहिती समाविष्ट असते असे प्रकाशन. पुढील वर्षातील महिने, तिथी, दिवस, नक्षत्र, योग व यासंबंधी विस्तृत माहिती व गणितीय महत्त्व यांची माहिती देणारे वार्षिक नौकानयन क्षेत्राकरिता अशी माहिती देणारे प्रकाशन.

alphabet – मुळाक्षर/अक्षरमाला/वर्णमाला – एखादी भाषा लिहिण्यासाठी वापरण्यात येणारे वर्ण.

alphabetical – वर्णक्रमानुसार – अनुवर्णानुसार, अक्षरमालेतील अक्षरांच्या क्रमानुसार, वर्णानुक्रम, विल्हेवार.

alphabetical arrangement–वर्णानुक्रमानुसार रचना – (१) ग्रंथसूची, तालिका, निर्देश यांमधील वर्णक्रमानुसार रचना केलेल्या सुरचित नोंदी. (२) ग्रंथालयातील कपाटांमध्ये लेखकांची नावे, ग्रंथविषयाप्रमाणे वर्ग वा इतर लक्षणे वापरून वर्णानुसार रचना केलेली मांडणी.

alphabetical catalogue – वर्णानुक्रमानुसार/अनुवर्णात्मक तालिका – तालिकेतील नोंदी पहिल्या अक्षराच्या वर्णानुक्रमानुसार लावून तयार केलेली तालिका.

alphabetical code – अनुवर्णानुसार संहिता – तालिकापत्रे अनुवर्णानुसार लावण्याचे नियम.

alphabetical device – अनुवर्ण युक्ती/आद्याक्षर क्लृप्ती – चिन्हांकनातील अतिथ्यशीलता वाढविण्यासाठी वापरण्याची युक्ती. एखाद्या विषयाचे वैशिष्ट्य त्या विषयाच्या आद्याक्षराने दर्शविणे. उदा. ००५.१३३ या संगणक भाषेसाठी दिलेल्या चिन्हांकनापुढे संगणकीय भाषेचे आद्याक्षर लिहिले जाते.

alphabetical index – वर्णानुक्रम निर्देश – एकापेक्षा अधिक ग्रंथांची वर्णनिहाय केलेली यादी.

alphabetical order – वर्णानुक्रम – वर्णानुसार केलेली रचना.

alphabetical sequence – वर्णानुक्रम – वर्णानुसार लावलेला अनुक्रम.

alphabetical subject catalogue – अनुवर्ण विषय तालिका – विषयांची आद्याक्षरानुसार मांडणी करून पुन्हा उपविषयानुसार वर्णानुक्रम अनुसरून तयार केलेली तालिका.

alphabetical subject index – अनुवर्ण विषय निर्देश – विषयनिहाय पण अनुवर्णासह तयार केलेला निर्देश.

alphabetico–classed catalogue – अनुवर्ण वर्ग तालिका – प्रमुख वर्गांची वर्णानुक्रमानुसार मांडणी करून त्या प्रत्येक विषयांमधील वर्गांची पुन्हा वर्णक्रमानुसार मांडणी करून तयार केली जाणारी तालिका.

alphabetico–specific – अनुवर्ण विविक्षित.

alphabetico subject catalogue – अनुवर्ण विषय तालिका – विषयांची आद्याक्षरानुसार मांडणी करून पुन्हा उपविषयानुसार वर्णानुक्रम अनुसरून तयार केलेली तालिका.

alphabetisation – वर्णानुक्रम रचना – वर्णानुक्रमानुसार माहितीची रचना, नावे, शब्द, संज्ञा, वाक्प्रचार यांची आद्याक्षरानुसार अनुक्रमे रचना करून यादी करणे.

alphanumeric – **अक्षरांक/अंकाक्षररचना** – अक्षरे व अंक या दोन्हींचा समावेश असलेला संगणकाचा कळफलक. बहुतेक सर्व संगणकांचे कळफलक अंकाक्षररचना असलेले असतात.

alternate key (Alt key) – **एकांतर कळ/एकांतरित कळ** – बऱ्याचशा संगणक कळफलकावर असलेली पर्यायी कळ. ही कळ इतर कार्यवाही कळांबरोबर वापरली जाते.

alternative title – **पर्यायी शीर्षक/ग्रंथनाम** – एखाद्या ग्रंथनामाचे दोन भाग असतात. दोन्हीही ग्रंथनामे असतात. हे दोन्ही भाग किंवा या शब्दाने अथवा इतर भाषेतील त्याच्या समतुल्य शब्दाने जोडलेले असतात किंवा ग्रंथशीर्षकाच्या दुय्यम भागात समाविष्ट केलेले शीर्षक. पर्यायी शीर्षक/पर्यायी ग्रंथनाम, 'or' किंवा 'म्हणजे' अशा शब्दांचा वापर असलेले शीर्षक.

amateur – **उमेदवार** – शिकाऊ माणूस.

ambiguity – **संदिग्धता/दुटप्पीपणा/अपूर्णता.**

ambiguous title – **संदिग्ध शीर्षक/ग्रंथनाम** – ग्रंथशीर्षकावरून अर्थाचा निश्चित बोध होत नसेल किंवा द्रव्य या अर्थी ग्रंथशीर्षक असेल तर ही संज्ञा वापरली जाते.

amendment – **दुरुस्ती/सुधारणा.**

American Library Association – **अमेरिकन ग्रंथालय संघ** – इ.स. १८७६ मध्ये स्थापन झालेला ग्रंथालय संघ. सर्वांत जुना व मोठा ग्रंथालय संघ ज्याचे कार्यालय शिकागो येथे आहे.

amount – **राशी/रक्कम/प्रमाण.**

ampere classification – **ॲम्पिअर वर्गीकरण (पद्धती)** – ॲन्ड्री मेरी ॲम्पियर (१७७५-१८३६) यांनी तयार केलेली ज्ञानवर्गीकरण पद्धती.

ampersand – **& चिन्ह** – इंग्रजी 'and' – या शब्दाऐवजी वापरले जाणारे चिन्ह. संगणक कळफलकावर हे चिन्ह काढलेले असते. उदा. (&)

analistic arrangement – लेखकाच्या प्रकाशन क्रमानुसार रचना असलेली ग्रंथसूचीची रचना.

analog computer – **अंकीय संगणक** – तक्ते, आलेख स्वरूपातील नोंदी ज्या यंत्रांद्वारे केल्या जातात त्यांचे नियंत्रण करण्यासाठी वापरावयाचा संगणक. उदा. E.C.G. हृदयावरील परिणाम मोजण्यासाठी वापर करतात.

analysed index – **विश्लेषित निर्देश** – विश्लेषण करणारा निर्देश.

analysed title – **विश्लेषित शीर्षक** – शीर्षकाचे विश्लेषण करून तयार झालेले शीर्षक.

analysis – **विश्लेषण/पृथक्करण** – एखाद्या गोष्टीचे विश्लेषण करून केलेला अभ्यास.

analytical – **अंशात्मक/विश्लेषणात्मक/विश्लेषिक.**

analytical entry – **अंशात्मक नोंद** – ग्रंथातील काही महत्त्वाचा मजकूर वाचकांच्या निदर्शनास आणून देण्याकरिता केलेली नोंद.

analytical bibliography – **विश्लेषणात्मक ग्रंथसूची** – प्रकाशनातील माहिती व अंतर्भूत गोष्टी याबाबत परीक्षण करून अपेक्षित नोंदीद्वारे केलेली विश्लेषणात्मक ग्रंथसूची.

analytical entries – **विश्लेषणात्मक नोंदी** – एका पुस्तकाच्या वेगवेगळ्या विषयांच्या अगर प्रकरणांच्या नावाने अथवा उपविषयांवर केल्या जाणाऱ्या नोंदी.

analytical index – **विश्लेषणात्मक निर्देश** – सरसकट वर्णक्रमानुसार नोंदी न करता वेगवेगळ्या उपविषयांनुसार वेगवेगळ्या नोंदी करून तयार केलेला निर्देश किंवा उल्लेखसूची.

analytical method – **विश्लेषणात्मक पद्धती** – वर्गीकरण करताना एखाद्या विशिष्ट विषयांमधील छोट्या शीर्षकांचे दिलेल्या सूत्रानुसार भाग पाडले जातात. नंतर अधिकाधिक सोयीप्रमाणे पुन्हा जोडणी करून उपयुक्त रचना केली जाते.

analytical note – **विश्लेषणात्मक टीप** – तालिकीकरण करताना ग्रंथांचे एखादे वैशिष्ट्य वाचकाच्या निदर्शनास आणून देण्याकरिता नोंदीत लिहिली जाणारी माहिती.

analytical subject entry – **विश्लेषणात्मक विषय नोंद.**

analytico–synthetic classification – **विश्लेषण** - **संश्लेषणात्मक वर्गीकरण** – ग्रंथाच्या विषयातील घटकांचे दिलेल्या पैलूनुसार विश्लेषण केले जाते. त्या पैलूस असणारे चिन्ह निर्धारित केले जाते. वेगवेगळ्या पैलूंवर विषयाच्या विश्लेषणावर आधारित वर्गीकरण पद्धती. पैलू अंकांच्या शेवटी योग्य अशा संयोजन चिन्हांच्या साहाय्याने संश्लेषणाने वर्गांक तयार केले जातात. नियमावलीमध्ये समाविष्ट विषयांच्या सखोल वर्गीकरणासाठी वर्गीकरणकाराला जास्तीत जास्त स्वातंत्र्य देणारी वर्गीकरण पद्धती. डॉ. रंगनाथन यांची द्विबिंदू वर्गीकरण पद्धती ही या स्वरूपाची पहिली पद्धती आहे.

and others – **आणि इतर** – जेव्हा तीनपेक्षा अधिक सहलेखकांचा सहभाग ग्रंथामध्ये असेल तेव्हा तालिकानोंद करताना पहिल्या लेखकाचे नाव लिहून 'आणि इतर' असा उल्लेख केला जातो.

angle – **कोन** – संयोग करणाऱ्या दोन रेषांच्या मधली जागा, कोन.

angle bracket – **चौकोनी कंस** – [ ] द्विबिंदू वर्गीकरणामध्ये डॉ. रंगनाथन यांनी वापरलेले एक चिन्ह.

Anglo American Cataloguing Rules (AACR) – **अँग्लो–अमेरिकन तालिकीकरण नियम** – १९६६ मध्ये पहिली व १९७८ मध्ये दुसरी आवृत्ती, ब्रिटिश आणि अमेरिकन ग्रंथालय संघाने प्रकाशित केलेले तालिकीकरणाचे नियम. पहिल्या आवृत्तीस AACR-I तर दुसऱ्या आवृत्तीस AACR-II म्हटले जाते.

animation – **सचेतनीकरण** – संगणकाच्या साहाय्याने चित्र, आकृती यांच्या हालचालींमध्ये आलेला जिवंतपणा. उदा. व्यंगचित्र.

annals – **वृत्तान्त** – ऐतिहासिक कागदपत्रे, बखरी इ. वृत्तान्त किंवा घटनांचा प्रतिवार्षिक वृत्तान्त.

anniversary issue – **वर्धापन अंक/वर्षारंभदिन अंक** – एखाद्या व्यक्ती/संस्था यांच्या जयंतीनिमित्त किंवा संस्थेच्या वर्धापन दिनानिमित्त काढलेला अंक.

annobium domestieum – ग्रंथास उपद्रवी असणारा एक कीटक.

annotated bibliography – टिप्पणीसह ग्रंथसूची – यामध्ये ग्रंथवर्णनाशिवाय ग्रंथावरील माहितीची टिपणी दिली जाते.

annotate – संक्षिप्त – लिखाणाचे सार तयार करण्याची कला.

annotated document list – टिप्पणीसह प्रलेखन यादी.

annotation – टिप्पणी/विवरण टीप – तालिकेमध्ये शिफारस ग्रंथयादी किंवा ग्रंथसूची यामधील नोंदीमध्ये नमूद केलेली पूरक टीप. ही टीप सामान्यत: ग्रंथाचा विषय आणि आशय विशद करण्यासाठी त्याचे मूल्यमापन किंवा वर्णन करण्याच्या उद्देशाने देतात. तालिकापत्रात ग्रंथविषयी अधिक माहिती देणारी (उदा. संदर्भसूची, मूल्यमापन, ग्रंथसूची) विशेष नोंद टीप.

annotation section – विशिष्ट विवरण अनुच्छेद – तालिकेत समाविष्ट केलेल्या ग्रंथाचे विशिष्ट विवरण अथवा गोषवारा देणाऱ्या मुख्य नोंदीतील अनुच्छेदाला 'विशिष्ट विवरण अनुच्छेद' असे म्हणतात.

annual / yearbook – वार्षिक – प्रत्येक वर्षी किंवा वर्षातून एकदा प्रकाशित होणारे प्रकाशन. अहवाल, निर्देशिका यांचे वार्षिक प्रकाशन.

annual report – वार्षिक अहवाल – संस्थेच्या शैक्षणिक किंवा वित्तीय वर्षात केलेल्या कामाचा आढावा घेणारे प्रकाशन, ज्यात त्या संस्थेतील त्या वर्णनातील घटनांची माहिती सविस्तर दिली जाते.

anonymous works (book) – अनामिक ग्रंथ/निनावी ग्रंथ – ज्या ग्रंथावर ग्रंथकाराचा उल्लेख नाही असा ग्रंथ. ग्रंथाच्या आतील पृष्ठांवर किंवा मुखपृष्ठावर कोठेही ग्रंथकाराच्या मूळ नावाचा उल्लेख नसलेला ग्रंथ.

anonymous classic – अनामिक/अभिजात ग्रंथ – अनामिक ग्रंथकाराचा अभिजात ग्रंथ. उदा. वेदग्रंथ.

anteriorising common isolates – अग्रवर्ती/पूर्ववर्ती सामान्य उपविभाग – मुख्य वर्गाला रचनाक्रमानुसार प्रथम जोडले जाणारे चिन्हांकन किंवा कोणत्याही मुख्य वर्गास वा उपवर्गास कोणत्याही संयोजन चिन्हांशिवाय जोडता येणारे उपविभाग. उदा. द्विबिंदू वर्गीकरणामध्ये साहित्यप्रकार दर्शविताना मुख्य वर्गाला जेव्हा जोडचिन्ह न देता उपवर्ग जोडला जातो तो अग्रवर्ती सामान्य उपविभाग.

anteriorising digit – अग्रवर्ती अंक.

anteriorising idea – अग्रवर्ती कल्पना/विचार.

anteriorising value – अग्रवर्ती मूल्य – मूल्य नसणाऱ्या वा अंकांच्या वापरामुळे मूल्य असलेल्या अंकांना प्राप्त होणारे नवे मूल्य.

anthology – स्तबक/संग्रह – निवडक विषयांवरील एका किंवा अनेक लेखकांच्या कार्याचा संग्रह. बरेचदा कविता किंवा पुरातन साहित्याचा असा संग्रह केला जातो.

anticipatory documentation list – उद्दिष्ट्यपेक्षी/अपेक्षामूलक/अपेक्षित प्रलेखन यादी.

anticipatory service – अपेक्षित/विचारणापूर्व सेवा – मागणी येईल या अपेक्षेने दिलेली माहितीसेवा, यामध्ये वाचकांची गरज काय आहे याचे सर्वसाधारण मूल्यमापन करतात. ही सेवा वाचकांच्या गटांना दिली जाते, एक व्यक्तीला नाही.

antithetic – विरोधात्मक – विसंगती किंवा विचारातील विरोध, साधारणपणे दोन वाक्प्रचारातील किंवा वाक्यांतील.

antonym – विरुद्धदर्शक शब्द – विरुद्ध अर्थाचे शब्द.

antonymous catchword – विरुद्ध अर्थाचे सूचकशब्द – निर्देशन प्रक्रियेमध्ये उपयुक्त.

apex – अग्र/शिखर/शिरोबिंदू.

apocryphal book – अनिश्चित आधाराचा ग्रंथ – लेखकाविषयी माहिती नसलेला किंवा अधिकृततेविषयी शंका असलेला ग्रंथ.

apograph – नक्कल – मूळ हस्तलिखिताची प्रत.

appendix – परिशिष्ट – साधारणतः ग्रंथ पूर्ण करण्यासाठी शेवटी जोडण्यात येणारी पुस्ती किंवा ग्रंथाच्या शेवटी काही पाने समाविष्ट करून त्यावर ग्रंथातील विषयासंबंधी अधिक, अद्ययावत माहिती देणाऱ्या टीपा, नोंदी, गणिती तक्ते दिले जातात. ती माहिती कोणत्या पानावर आलेली आहे याचा पृष्ठांक दिलेला असतो.

application – उपयोजन/अर्ज – संगणकामध्ये विशिष्ट कार्य पार पाडण्यासाठी योजलेली आज्ञावली.

application file – अर्जाची संचिका/नस्ती.

application form – अर्जाचा नमुना.

application oriented language – उपयोजित आज्ञावली भाषा – उपयोजित आज्ञावली लिहिण्यासाठी वापरली जाणारी आज्ञावली भाषा. उदा. C++ and pascal

application program – उपयोजन आज्ञावली – विशिष्ट काम संगणकाकडून करून घेण्यासाठी लिहिलेल्या विविध आज्ञांच्या साखळीला उपयोजन आज्ञावली म्हटले जाते. ग्रंथालयात ग्रंथखरेदीचे काम संगणकाकडून करून घ्यायचे झाल्यास ज्या आज्ञावली लिहिल्या जाऊ शकतात त्या या प्रकारात मोडतात.

applied science – उपयोजित विज्ञान – मानवी जीवनातील प्रश्न सोडविण्यासाठी उपयुक्त असे शास्त्र.

applied research – उपयोजित संशोधन – मानवी प्रश्नांची उत्तरे शोधण्यासाठी केले जाणारे संशोधन.

appraisal – छाननी मूल्यमापन – विषयाचे प्रतिनिधित्व करणाऱ्या ग्रंथांमध्ये त्या ग्रंथाच्या मूल्यात्मक सहभागाविषयी दिलेला अंदाज.

approach document – अभिगत साहित्य/प्रलेख.

approach material – अभिगत सामग्री.

approach point – **अभिगत शीर्षक** – ग्रंथाचे एकत्व सिद्ध करण्यासाठी किंवा तो शोधण्यासाठी तालिका नोंदींच्या अग्रभागी वापरलेली संज्ञा, नाव किंवा वाक्प्रयोग.

approval – **मान्यता/मंजुरी** – पसंत न पडल्यास कोणतेही शुल्क न देता परत करावयाचे ग्रंथ वगैरे.

arabic figures/numbers – **अरेबिक अंक** – अरेबिक पद्धतीने लिहिले जाणारे अंक. उदा. 1,2,3....

architect – **वास्तुशास्त्रज्ञ/वास्तुशिल्पविशारद**.

architecture – **स्थापत्य कला/वास्तुकला**.

archaeological museum – **पुराण वस्तुसंग्रहालय**.

archetypal novel – **जुन्या काळातील प्रेमकथा** – गोष्टी, ललित इ. लिहिलेली कादंबरी.

archive – **दफ्तर**.

archives – **अभिलेखागार/पुराभिलेख** – ऐतिहासिक महत्त्व असलेल्या कागदपत्रांचा संग्रह. दफ्तरखाना.

archives department – **पुराभिलेख विभाग** – शासकीय दफ्तरखाना.

archives service – **पुराभिलेख सेवा** – ऐसिहासिक महत्त्व असलेल्या कागदपत्रांची व्यवस्था पाहून ती उपयोजकांना उपलब्ध करून देण्याची सेवा.

archivist – **अभिलेखापाल** – दुर्मिळ ग्रंथ संग्रहांची देखभाल करणारी व्यक्ती.

area – **क्षेत्र/क्षेत्रफळ** – उदा. (१) ग्रंथालयात वाचनासाठी उपलब्ध असलेले क्षेत्र. (२) तालिकापत्रावर विशिष्ट नोंद करण्यासाठी उपलब्ध असलेले क्षेत्र.

area search – **क्षेत्र शोध** – (संगणकामध्ये) विशिष्ट वर्ग वा उपविषयांवरील प्रलेखांचा स्थानविषयक परीक्षण करून शोध लावणे.

area table – **भू क्षेत्र सारणी** – दशांश वर्गीकरण पद्धतीमध्ये भौगोलिक स्थानानुसार वर्गीकरण करण्यासाठी दिलेला क्षेत्रानुसार तक्ता.

aristonym – **पदवी नाव** – पदवी दाखल मिळालेले नाव किंवा पदवीचा आडनाव म्हणून केलेला वापर. उदा. पाटील, कुळकर्णी, देशमुख.

armoury – **शस्त्रागार/शस्त्रसंभार**.

arrange – **क्रमाने लावणे** – क्रमवार रचना करणे.

arrangement – **रचना** – क्रमरचना, गरजेनुसार विषयांची/नोंदींची रचना करणे किंवा विशिष्ट हेतूने केलेली ग्रंथांची मांडणी. उदा. अनुवर्ण, अनुवर्णाप्रमाणे.

arrangement by accession number – **दाखलअंकानुसार केलेली रचना**.

arrangement by classification number – **वर्गांकानुसार केलेली रचना**.

arrangement by a combination of sequences – क्रम संयोगाने केलेली रचना.

array – **पंक्ती** – साम्यगुणाच्या साहाय्याने एखाद्या विषयाच्या/वर्गांच्या उपविभागांचा पहिल्या दर्जाचा संच. उदा. खेळणी (वापरलेल्या कच्च्या मालाच्या/साहित्याच्या अनुरोधाने मातीची लाकडी, धातूची, कागदी, प्लास्टिकची इ.).

array isolate idea – **पंक्ती उपांग विचार.**

array telescoping point – **पंक्ती दूरदर्शी केंद्र.**

arrester – **समाप्तिचिन्ह** – द्विबिंदू वर्गीकरणामध्ये विषयपैलू क्रमांक पूर्ण करताना द्यावयाचे चिन्ह.

arrow – **बाण** – उदा. (→) वर्गीकरण पद्धतीत वापरली जाणारी एक खूण, चिन्ह.

arrow backward – **उलटा बाण** – उदा. ←

arrow downward – **उतरता बाण** – उदा. ↓

arrow forward – **सुलटा बाण** – उदा. →

arrow upword – **उभा बाण** – उदा. ↑

art – **कला.**

artifacts – **मानवनिर्मित वस्तू** – मानवी संस्कृतीचे अवशेष, उदा. फर्निचर.

artist – **कलाकार.**

artefactual value of a document – **मानवनिर्मित मूल्य असलेला प्रलेख** – ज्यास त्यातील विषय किंवा माहिती व्यतिरिक्त बाह्यस्वरूप वा इतर कारणांमुळे मूल्य असते. असे प्रलेख वा मूळ स्वरूपात जतन करण्याचा प्रयत्न केला जातो.

article – **लेख** – ग्रंथात अथवा नियतकालिकांमध्ये प्रसिद्ध करण्यासाठी एक किंवा अनेक व्यक्तींनी मिळून लिहिलेला लेख.

article database – **लेख माहितीसंग्रह.**

art–gallery (art museum) – **कलादालन** – चित्रे, वस्तू, छायाचित्रे, पेन्टिंग्ज इ.चे प्रदर्शन भरविण्याची जागा किंवा ठिकाण.

artificial characteristic – **कृत्रिम लक्षण** – वर्गीकरणासाठी गृहीत धरलेला कृत्रिम लक्षणगुण.

artificial classification – **कृत्रिम वर्गीकरण** – कृत्रिम लक्षणे विचारात घेऊन केलेले वर्गीकरण.

artificial composite book – **कृत्रिम समासित ग्रंथ.**

artificial digit – **कृत्रिम अंक.**

artificial intelligence – **कृत्रिम बुद्धिमत्ता** – आधुनिक संगणक विकसित करण्याचे शास्त्र, मानवी विचारांप्रमाणे कार्य करण्यासाठी या संगणकाला प्रशिक्षण दिले जाते.

artificial language – **कृत्रिम भाषा.**

artificial classification – **कृत्रिम वर्गीकरण.**

arithmetic unit – **अंकगणितीय घटक.**

artistic map – **कलात्मक नकाशा** – नकाशाऐवजी कलाकाराकडून पुरवणी किंवा जाहिरात म्हणून वापरण्यासाठी नकाशा तयार करवून घेतला जातो.

as if filing – **पूर्ण शब्दरचनेनुसार संक्षेपाने केलेल्या माहितीची रचना.**
उदा. St. as Saint. Mr. as Mister

as issued – दुय्यम वापरातले पुस्तक पुन्हा विक्रीसाठी आणताना मूळ स्वरूपातील आहे हे दर्शविणारा संदेश.

as new – दुय्यम वापरातले पुस्तक पुन्हा विक्रीसाठी आणताना त्याचे बाह्यस्वरूप बदलले आहे हे दर्शविणारा संदेश.

ascender – **आरोहक** – मुळाक्षरांपैकी खालच्या बाजूला मुख्य भाग असलेली इंग्रजी अक्षरे. उदा. c, d, k

ascending order – **चढता क्रम/चढती भाजणी.**

aspect classification – **दृष्टिकोन वर्गीकरण** – दृष्टिकोनानुसार विषय वर्गीकरण करणे, जसे कोळशाच्या खाणी या विषयाचा अंतर्भाव खाणी याखाली होईल तर कोळशाचे रसायनशास्त्र हा विषय रसायनशास्त्र या विषयामध्ये समाविष्ट केला जाईल.

aspects – **दृष्टिकोन.**

assembler – **संगणकीय भाषांतरकार** – कार्यसुलभ भाषेतील सांकेतिक शब्द. संगणकास कळणाऱ्या यंत्रभाषेमध्ये लिहिलेल्या आज्ञावलींना 'असेम्ब्लर' असे म्हणतात. संगणकीय आज्ञावली भाषेत रूपांतरित करणारा संगणकातील भाग.

assembly language – **कार्यसुलभ भाषा** – मशीन लँग्वेजच्या रचनेसारखीच परंतु स्मरणसुलभतेसाठी सांकेतिक इंग्रजी शब्दांचा मोठ्या प्रमाणात वापर केलेली भाषा. या भाषेत लिहिलेल्या आज्ञावली मानवास समजणे मशिन लँग्वेजमध्ये लिहिलेल्या आज्ञावलीइतके अवघड नसते किंवा संगणक आज्ञावली तयार करण्यासाठी वापरण्यात येणारी साधी भाषा यात लक्षात ठेवण्यास सोप्या सूचना, चिन्हे यांचा उपयोग केला जातो. या आज्ञावली भाषेचे रूपांतर संगणकाच्या भाषेमध्ये केले जाते.

assistant – **साहाय्यक** – मदतनीस म्हणून काम करणारी व्यक्ती.

assistant librarian – **साहाय्यक ग्रंथपाल** – साहाय्यक ग्रंथपालाचे काम करणारी व्यक्ती.

associated – **संबंधित** – सख्य-सहवास-संगत केलेला.

associated book – **संबंधित ग्रंथ** – एखाद्या ग्रंथाविषयी लिहिलेला सहयोगी ग्रंथ. उदा. समीक्षाग्रंथ.

association – **साहचर्य/सहयोग संस्था/संघ** – एखाद्या (विशिष्ट) कारणासाठी एकत्र आलेल्या लोकांचा गट.

Association of Government Librarians & Information Specialists (AGLIS) – सरकारी ग्रंथपाल व माहिती तज्ज्ञांचा संघ (अग्लीस) – १९३३ मध्ये स्थापन झालेला संघ याचे वरील नामकरण १९७७ मध्ये झाले.

Association of Special Librarians & Information Bureaux – अस्लिब – १९२६ मध्ये स्थापन झालेला आंतरराष्ट्रीय संघ.

association library – संघ ग्रंथालय.

associative relation – सहयोगी संबंध – एकामुळे दुसऱ्याची कल्पना येते व दुसऱ्यामुळे पहिल्यासंबंधी कल्पना येते असे दोन कल्पनांमधील एक प्रकारचे संबंध. उदा. वृत्तपत्र आणि बातम्या.

asterisk (*) – ताराचिन्ह/तारांकित – तळटीपांसाठी संदर्भचिन्ह म्हणून वापरले जाते.

astronomical map /star map – ग्रह/तारे चिन्हांचा नकाशा.

asyndetic catalogue – प्रतिसंदर्भ न दिलेली तालिका.

atlas – नकाशासंग्रह/नकाशापुस्तक – अनेक नकाशांचे एकत्रित पुस्तक म्हणजे नकाशासंग्रह.

attendant – परिचर – एखाद्या सार्वजनिक ठिकाणी सेवा करणारा सेवक, नोकर.

attendance – उपस्थिती – एखाद्या कामासाठी हजर राहणे, हजेरी.

attention interruption – लक्षवेधी कळ – संगणक कळपट्टीवरील लक्षवेधी कळ कार्यरत केल्यामुळे मिळालेली व्यत्ययसूचना.

attention note – लक्षवेधी टीप – उपाययोजकांना रस असलेल्या लेखामध्ये नियतकालिकाच्या अंकात विशिष्ट खूण म्हणून ठेवलेली टिपणचिठ्ठी.

attributed author / presumed author / supposed author – संदिग्ध ग्रंथकार – लेखनाविषयी संदिग्धता असल्यामुळे ग्रंथाचे श्रेय ज्याला दिले जाते तो ग्रंथकार.

audio – श्राव्य – ऐकू येणारी, ऐकण्यायोग्य.

audio cassette – श्राव्यफीत/ध्वनीफीत.

audio library – श्राव्य ग्रंथालय – ध्वनिफितींचा संग्रह करणारे ग्रंथालय.

audio–visual aids / audio visual material – दृक्-श्राव्य साधने – दृक्-श्राव्य माध्यमांसाठी वापरली जाणारी साधने.

audio–visual library – दृक्-श्राव्य ग्रंथालय – दृक्-श्राव्य साधनांचा संग्रह करणारे ग्रंथालय.

audio–visual apparatus / audio visual equipment – दृक्-श्राव्य उपकरणे (साधन/यंत्र) – चित्रे पाहणे, ध्वनी ऐकणे यासाठी उपयुक्त असणारी उपकरणे.

audio–visual system – दृक्-श्राव्य प्रणाली.

audio-visual centre – दृक्-श्राव्य केंद्र.

audio-visual communication – दृक्-श्राव्य संप्रेषण – चित्र व ध्वनीद्वारे संदेश.

audio-visual education – दृक्-श्राव्य शिक्षण – दृक्-श्राव्य माध्यम वापरून दिले जाणारे शिक्षण.

audit – हिशेब तपासणी – जमा-खर्चाच्या हिशेबाची, नोंदीची व इतर आर्थिक व्यवहारांची तपासणी. ग्रंथालयाच्या जमा-खर्चाबाबतची हिशेबतपासणी.

auditing – लेखा परीक्षण – लेखा परीक्षणाचे कार्य व पद्धती.

auditor – लेखा परीक्षक – लेखा परीक्षणासाठीची अधिकृत व्यक्ती.

auditorium – सभागृह/सभाभवन – सभा, संमेलन, परिषद, कार्यशाळा इ. साठीचे दालन.

authentic – विश्वसनीय – खरा, सत्य म्हणून ज्ञात असलेला.

authentication – खरेपणा आणणे/शाबीत करणे.

authenticity – सत्यता/खरेपणा/विश्वसनीयता/अधिकृतता.

author / writer – ग्रंथकार/लेखक – लिखित साहित्यासाठीची जबाबदार व्यक्ती प्रकाशनांमध्ये लेखन किंवा संपादन करणारी एक वा अनेक व्यक्ती/संस्था.

author abstract – लेखक सार – लेखकाच्या नावानुसार रचना केलेला सार.

author analytic entry – ग्रंथकार विश्लेषणात्मक नोंद – लेखकाच्या नावाची विश्लेषणात्मक नोंद. मूळ ग्रंथात असणाऱ्या ग्रंथकाराच्या आणि त्यांच्या नोंद ग्रंथाच्या नावावरून संबंधित ग्रंथालयातील त्याच्या स्थानाची माहिती देणारी जी विशिष्ट पूरक नोंद असते तिला 'ग्रंथकार विश्लेषक नोंद' असे म्हणतात.

author bibliography – लेखक ग्रंथसूची/ग्रंथकार ग्रंथसूची – लेखकाच्या नावानुसार वर्णानुक्रमे तयार केलेली लेखक ग्रंथसूची. एका लेखकाची एकत्रित ग्रंथसूची.

author card – लेखकपत्र – तालिकीकरण करताना लेखकाच्या नावाने तयार केलेले तालिकापत्र. ग्रंथकारनाम पत्र.

author catalogue – लेखक तालिका/ग्रंथकार तालिका – लेखांची नावे वर्णनानुसार क्रमाने लावून तयार केलेली तालिका.

author copy – लेखकाची प्रत – लेखकाने तयार केलेली मूळ प्रत.

author index – लेखक निर्देश/ग्रंथकार निर्देश.

author entry – लेखक नोंद – लेखकाच्या नावाला प्राधान्य देऊन त्यानुसार केलेली नोंद.

author index entry – लेखक निर्देश नोंद – लेखकांच्या निर्देशामध्ये केलेली नोंद.

author mark – लेखकांक/लेखक चिन्ह – विशिष्ट लेखकाचे साहित्य ओळखण्यासाठी वापरलेले चिन्ह किंवा खूण, यामुळे ग्रंथमांडणीमध्ये सुलभता आणता येते.

author number – **लेखक ग्रंथसंख्या** – लेखकाने लिहिलेल्या ग्रंथांची संख्या दर्शविणारे चिन्ह.

author-published – **लेखक-प्रकाशित** – स्वत:चे लेखन स्वत:च प्रकाशित करणारा लेखक.

author statement – **लेखक विवरण** – प्रलेखांचे लेखक, सहलेखक यांच्याविषयीचे विवरण.

author search – **लेखकाच्या नावानुसार घेतलेला साहित्य शोध.**

author title index – **लेखक-शीर्षक निर्देश** – लेखकांच्या नावानुसार व शीर्षकानुसार वर्णानुक्रम लावून तयार केलेला निर्देश.

author's binding – **लेखकासाठी खास ग्रंथ बांधणी** – ग्रंथाची खास पद्धतीने केलेली बांधणी. या प्रतींचा उपयोग लेखक भेट देण्यासाठी करतो.

author's correction – **लेखक अंतिम मुद्रिते** – ग्रंथाच्या आराखड्यामध्ये लेखक स्वत: सुधारणा करतो. नंतरच ग्रंथाची प्रत्यक्ष अंतिम छपाई केली जाते.

author's edition – **लेखक आवृत्ती** – एखाद्या विशिष्ट लेखकाचे संपूर्ण लेखनसाहित्य एकत्रित बांधणी करून शीर्षक पृष्ठावर तसा उल्लेख करून काढलेली आवृत्ती.

authority – **प्राधिकरण/प्राधिकारी** – आज्ञा देण्याची सत्ता, अधिकार, हुकमत असणारे मंडळ.

authority card – **अधिकार पत्र.**

authority code / authorised code / authorization code – **अधिकृत संकेत** – उपयोजकाला हवी ती माहिती मिळण्यासाठी संगणकाला द्यावयाचा संकेत.

authority file – **अधिकृत प्रमाण पंजिका** – यादी, नोंद, वर्गीकरण आणि तालिकीकरण करताना वर्गीकरण पद्धतीतील आणि तालिकासंहितेतील सर्वच नियमांचे तसेच्या तसे पालन करणे शक्य होत नाही. स्थानिक गरजेनुसार बदल करावे लागतात. काही वेळेस नवीन वर्गांची विषय शीर्षकांची भर घालावी लागते. या सर्व बदलांची आणि भरीची अधिकृत नोंद ज्या पंजिकेमध्ये केली जाते त्या पंजिकेस 'अधिकृत प्रमाण पंजिका' असे म्हणतात.

autoanswer – **स्वयंप्रतिसाद** – दूरध्वनीला संगणकाद्वारे आपोआप प्रतिसाद देण्याची पद्धती.

auto acstract – **यांत्रिक सारलेख** – संगणकाद्वारे प्रमुख शब्द निवडून सारलेख तयार करण्याची प्रक्रिया.

auto-bias device – **दुय्यम छाया/पडछाया क्लृप्ती** – वर्गीकरण करताना ग्रंथातील एका विषयाचा त्याच मुखातील दुसऱ्या विषयाशी संबंध येणे म्हणजे एका विषयाची छाया दुसऱ्या विषयावर पडणे. अशा वेळी पहिल्या विषयाचे बोधचिन्ह लिहिल्यावर आडवी रेघ (–) हे चिन्ह लिहून त्यानंतर दुसऱ्या विषयाचे बोधचिन्ह लिहावे. उदा. स. ११–३१ ग्रामीण बालक.

auto-index – **स्वयंनिर्देश** – संगणकाद्वारा तयार केलेला निर्देश किंवा उल्लेखसूची.

autobiographer – **आत्मचरित्रकार** – स्वत:च्या जीवनाचा वृत्तांत लिहिलेली व्यक्ती.

autobiography – **आत्मचरित्र** – स्वत:च्या जीवनाचा वृत्तांत लिहिणे.

autodialer – **स्वयंचलित तबकडी** – स्वयंचलित दूरध्वनी तबकडी असलेला संगणक. एखाद्या ठिकाणी नियमितपणे माहिती पाठवायची असेल तेव्हा असा संगणक स्वत:च दूरध्वनी क्रमांकाशी संपर्क साधून माहिती पाठवितो.

autograph – **हस्ताक्षर/स्वाक्षरी** – व्यक्तीने स्वत: केलेली स्वाक्षरी/हस्ताक्षर.

autographed edition – **स्वाक्षरीत आवृत्ती** – एखाद्या प्रकाशनाच्या प्रतींवर लेखकाची सही असलेली आवृत्ती.

autography – **स्वहस्ताक्षर शास्त्र,कला** –(१) लेखकाचे स्वत:चे हस्ताक्षर, (२) स्वाक्षरीविषयक अभ्यास करणारी शाखा, (३) ठसामुद्रणाची कला.

autolithography – **स्वयंशीला मुद्रणाची कला** – यासाठी दगडावर किंवा दुसऱ्या माध्यमांवर बरोबर उलट्या दिशेने कलाकार चित्रे, आवृत्ती वा लेखन करतो.

automated bibliography – **संगणकीय ग्रंथसूची** – संगणकामध्ये माहिती साठवून केलेली ग्रंथसूची.

automated dictionary – **संगणकीय शब्दकोश** – संगणकामध्ये जतन केलेला शब्दकोश.

automatic – **स्वयंचलित** – मानवाच्या नियंत्रणाविना राहणारे चालणारे/कार्यरत.

automatic abstracting – **संगणकीय सारलेखन.**

automatic book charging – **संगणकीय ग्रंथ देव-घेव पद्धती** – देव-घेव नोंद संगणकामध्ये करण्याची पद्धती.

automatic data processing – **स्वयंचलित/संगणकीय माहिती संस्करण** – संगणकाच्या साहाय्याने माहितीवर केलेली संस्करण प्रक्रिया.

automatic programme – **स्वयंचलित कार्यक्रम** – संगणकाद्वारे आपोआप चालणारा कार्यक्रम.

automatic record – **स्वयंचलित नोंद/अभिलेख** – संगणकाद्वारे आपोआप निर्माण होणारी नोंद/ अभिलेख.

automatic hyphenation – **स्वयंचलित विभाजन** – संगणकाला माहिती समाविष्ट करताना एका ओळीत शब्द मावत नसेल तर संगणक स्वत:च शब्द विभागण्याचे किंवा संपूर्ण शब्द खालच्या ओळीवर लिहिण्याचे काम करतो ती क्रिया.

automatic indexing – **स्वयंचलित निर्देशन** – निर्देशनासाठी नोंदी करताना प्रमुख शब्दांची निवड संगणकाद्वारे करून केलेली निर्देशन प्रक्रिया.

automatic pagination – **स्वयंचलित पृष्ठांकन** – संगणकामध्ये एका पानावर मजकूर पूर्ण लिहिल्यानंतर पुढचा मजकूर पडद्यावर नंतरच्या पानावर आपोआप दाखविला जातो.

automation – **संगणकीकरण/स्वयंचलन** – ग्रंथालयातील शक्य तेवढी कामे संगणकाकडून करवून घेण्यासाठी ग्रंथालयाचे केलेले संगणकीकरण.

autonym – **स्वनाम** – लेखकाचे मूळ नाव.

autosave – **स्वयंचलित सुरक्षितता** – काही आज्ञावली संयोजनांमध्ये संगणकातील माहिती जतन करण्यासाठी स्वयंचलित सुरक्षितता देण्याची सोय उपलब्ध असते.

auxiliary – **साहाय्यक उपांगे** – मदतनीस घेतलेला, पुरवणीसाठी.

auxiliary number – **साहाय्यक अंक** – वर्गांकाबरोबरच सुलभ ग्रंथरचनेसाठी दिलेला साहाय्यक अंक. उदा. कटर पद्धतीनुसार लेखकचिन्ह लिहिणे.

auxiliary publication – **साहाय्यक प्रकाशन** – अप्रकाशित साहित्यातील माहिती मायक्रोफिल्म व छायाप्रतींद्वारा उपलब्ध करणे.

auxiliary storage – **साहाय्यक संग्रह/साठा मदतीसाठीचा साहाय्यक संग्रह** – संगणकातील माहिती मुख्य स्मरणिकेशिवाय साहाय्यक माध्यमांद्वारे (उदा. फ्लॉपी डिस्क, चुंबकीय फीत/इतरत्र साठविण्याची प्रक्रिया.)

auxiliary tables – **साहाय्यकारी तक्ते** – मूळ वर्गीकरण पद्धती सोबत दिले जाणारे साहाय्यक तक्ते ज्यातील चिन्हे मूळ सारणीतील सर्व चिन्हांकनाला जोडता येतात.

auxiliary title – **साहाय्यकारी ग्रंथनाम.**

Bachelor in Library & Information Science (BLIS) – बी.एल.आय.एस. – ग्रंथालय आणि माहितीशास्त्रातील पदवी.

back – कणा/पाठ – ग्रंथाचा कणा किंवा बांधणी केलेली बाजू, ज्यावर काही वेळा ग्रंथकार व शीर्षक दिलेले असते.

back-cover – मलपृष्ठ/ग्रंथ आवरण – ग्रंथाच्या पाठीमागची वेष्टनाची बाजू.

back-file – पूर्वी प्रकाशित झालेल्या साहित्याची संचिका.

back-issue – मागचा अंक – नियतकालिकाचा प्रकाशित झालेला जुना अंक.

back-list – छपाईसाठी घेतलेल्या ग्रंथशीर्षकांची प्रकाशकाकडील यादी.

back-margin – मागचा समास.

back-matter – ग्रंथातील मजकुराच्या शेवटी छापलेली पाने – उदा. परिशिष्ट, ग्रंथसूची, निर्देश इ.

back-number – मागचा अंक – पूर्वीच्या नियतकालिकाची क्रमसंख्या.

back-order – पूर्वीचा आदेश.

back-page – मलपृष्ठ – ग्रंथाचे मागचे पृष्ठ, ग्रंथपानाची वेष्टणाच्या मागची बाजू.

back title / binder's title / cover title – पृष्ठाच्या मागील पृष्ठ – ग्रंथाच्या कण्यावर छापलेले ग्रंथशीर्षक.

back-space – **मागील जागा** – संगणकाच्या/टंकलेखनाच्या कामात मागील अक्षरावर जाण्यासाठी वापरावयाची कळ.

back-up – **संगणकातील माहितीची जादा प्रत** – सुरक्षिततेचा उपाय म्हणून संगणकामध्ये जतन केली जाते.

back-up services – **पूरक संदर्भ सेवा** – ग्रंथालयातून दिल्या जाणाऱ्या पूरक संदर्भ सेवा. उदा. संदर्भ यादी, प्रलेखयादी इ.

background – **पार्श्वभूमी/पृष्ठभूमिका.**

back-approach – **पार्श्वभूमी दृष्टिकोन.**

back-printing – **पार्श्वमुद्रण** – संगणकावरील माहितीची छपाई चालू असताना इतर काम संगणकावर कार्यरत ठेवणे.

back-processing – **पार्श्वसंस्करण** – उपयोजकाच्या कृतीशिवाय चालू/सुरू राहणारे संगणकाचे संस्करणकार्य.

backing – **गोलाई ठोकणे/काढणे** – ग्रंथबांधणी करताना गोलाई काढणे, ठोकणे.

backboards – **ग्रंथबांधणीसाठी वापरण्यात येणाऱ्या गोलाईच्या पट्ट्या.**

back machine – **गोलाई यंत्र** – ग्रंथात गोलाई करण्याचे यंत्र.

backtracking – **संगणकावरील यादी उलट्या क्रमाने पाहण्याची प्रक्रिया.**

Baconian classification – **बेकन वर्गीकरण** – फ्रान्सिस बेकन यांनी सुचविलेली वर्गीकरण पद्धती. स्मरण, कल्पना व कार्यकारणभाव या त्रयींवर आधारित वर्गीकरण पद्धती.

balance – **बाकी/शिल्लक** – समतोल संतुलन करणे, समतोल असणे.

bandwidth – **पट्टविस्तार.**

banned book – **बंदी घातलेला ग्रंथ** – आक्षेपार्ह असल्यामुळे शासनाने बंदी घातलेले प्रकाशन.

barcode – **दंडरेषांचा गट** – संगणकाच्या वापरात ग्रंथावर लिहिलेली दंड संकेत पट्टी – संगणकाला सांकेतिक माहिती पुरविणाऱ्या लहान–मोठ्या समांतर दंडरेषांचा गट.

bar lacel – **दंडरेषागट चिठ्ठी.**

bar number – **दंडरेषागट अंक/क्रमांक.**

bargain – **सौदा/व्यवहार** – एखादी गोष्ट करण्यासाठी, विकण्यासाठी, विकत घेण्यासाठी केलेली पैशांची घासाघीस.

base – **आधार** – चिन्हांकनात वापरलेला चिन्हांचा संपूर्ण गट.

base line – **आधाररेषा** – तालिकापत्रावर इंग्रजी अक्षरे लिहिताना मानलेली काल्पनिक आधाररेषा.

base of a notation – **चिन्हांकनाचा आधार/पाया** – वर्गीकरण पद्धतीमधील चिन्हांकन ज्या चिन्हावर आधारलेले असते ती चिन्हे. उदा. दशांश वर्गीकरण पद्धतीमध्ये 0 ते 9 हे अंक वापरून चिन्हांकन तयार केले आहे.

base of number – **अंकाचा आधार/पाया.**

base number – **आधार अंक** – सुरुवातीचे चित्रांकन (मूळ विषयाची वर्गदर्शक खूण) हा पुढे दुसऱ्या अन्य अंकांनी वाढविता येतो.

basic class / summum genus – **मूळ/नि:श्रेयस वर्ग** – ग्रंथवर्गीकरण पद्धतीतील मुख्य वर्ग; वर्गीकरण पद्धतीची रचना अशा वर्गांनी केली जाते. वर्गीकरण करताना विचारात घेतलेला प्रलेखाचा (मूळ दर्शकचिन्हाचा) समूह.

basic classes – **वर्गीकरण पद्धतीतील मूळ विषय.**

basic classification – **मूलभूत/प्राथमिक वर्गीकरण.**

basic entry – **मूळ नोंद** – या नोंदीवरून अन्य नोंदी केल्या जातात.

basic facet – **मूळ पैलू.**

basic stock – **मूलभूत/आधारभूत ग्रंथसंग्रह.**

basic subject – **मूलभूत विषय/रूढीविषयक** – द्विबिंदू वर्गीकरणामध्ये हे आधारतत्त्व मानले जाते. मूळ विषय, मूळ वर्ग, मूळ पैलू हे समानार्थी शब्द म्हणून वापरले जातात.

batch file – **सूचनागट** – संगणकाद्वारे एका सूचनेद्वारा अमलात आणता येईल असा सूचनागट.

batch number – **माहितीक्रम अंक** – माहितीचा क्रम दर्शविणारा अंक.

batch processing – **संगणकावर माहिती आणि आज्ञावली एकाच वेळी नोंदवून संस्कारित माहिती मिळविण्याची एक पद्धत** – यात एकदा आज्ञावलीवर हुकूम काम सुरू झाले की, मानवाला मध्येच हस्तक्षेप करता येत नाही. सुरुवातीपासून शोध प्रक्रियेत आणि आता एस.डी.आय. सेवेत हीच पद्धत रूढ आहे; संस्करण करायचा माहितीगट एकत्रित करण्याचे तंत्र.

battered – **झिजलेला** – न ओळखता येणारा मजकूर.

bay – **दालन/रांग** – विशिष्ट कारणासाठी वापरली जाणारी जागा किंवा इमारतीचा भाग. ग्रंथकक्षातील कपाटांच्यामध्ये सोडण्यात येणारी मोकळी जागा.

bay guide – **दर्शक फलक** – ग्रंथसंग्रह दालनातील ग्रंथांची रांग व त्यात समाविष्ट असणारे विषयदर्शक फलक.

beach wood – **वृक्षाचा/वनस्पतीचा एक प्रकार.**

bespoke books – **प्रकाशनापूर्वी मागणी केलेली पुस्तके.**

bee's wax – **मेण** – मधमाश्यांच्या पोळ्यापासून तयार केलेले मेण.

Beginners All-Purpose Symbolic Instruction Code (BASIC) – **बेसिक** : नावातील सुरुवातीची अक्षरे घेऊन बनवलेला शब्द. हा संगणक नवसाक्षरांसाठी आज्ञावली लिहिण्याकरिता वापरलेल्या अतिशय सोप्या उच्च श्रेणी (Hyper Text) भाषेचा एक प्रकार आहे. या भाषेच्या नव्या, अभिनव आवृत्तीस 'बेसिक-ए' म्हणतात.

bestseller – **उत्तम खप असलेला ग्रंथ** – अशा ग्रंथाचे वारंवार मुद्रण करावे लागते.

bettle – **बेटल** – पुस्तकाला लागणाऱ्या एक प्रकारच्या किड्याची जात.

bi-annual / half yearly / semi-annual – **अर्धवार्षिक/सहामाही/षण्मासिक** – वर्षातून दोनदा प्रकाशित होणारे प्रकाशन.

bi-annual – **द्वैवार्षिक** – दोन वर्षांतून एकदा प्रकाशित होणारे प्रकाशन.

bi-monthly – **द्वैमासिक** – दोन महिन्यातून एकदा प्रकाशित होणारे प्रकाशन.

bias – **पूर्वग्रहदूषित.**

bias device – **कलदर्शक युक्ती/क्लृप्ती.**

bias number device – **कलदर्शक अंक युक्ती.**

bias phase – **कल प्रावस्था** – वर्गीकरण करताना ग्रंथाचा वाचक लक्षात न घेता ग्रंथाचा विषय लक्षात घेऊन कलप्रावस्था पद्धतीने वर्गीकरण केले जाते. उदा. 'गृहिणींसाठी अर्थशास्त्र' हा ग्रंथ अर्थशास्त्र शाखेत मांडला जातो. रंगनाथन् यांनी वापरलेली संज्ञा.

bias phase relation – **कल उपांग संबंध** – याचा वापर द्विबिंदू वर्गीकरणात केला आहे.

bibelot – **अत्यंत छोट्या आकाराचा ग्रंथ** – त्याचा आकार व दुर्मिळतेमुळे उत्सुकतेचा विषय बनलेला ग्रंथ.

bibliogony – **ग्रंथउत्पादन.**

bibliographer / bibliographee – **ग्रंथसूचीकार** – ग्रंथसूची तयार करण्याचे कौशल्य अवगत असलेली व्यक्ती.

bibliographic – **ग्रंथसूचीत्मक.**

bibliographic centre – **ग्रंथसूची केंद्र.**

bibliographic citation – **ग्रंथसूचीत्मक उद्धरण.**

bibliographic classification system – **ग्रंथसूची वर्गीकरण पद्धती** – ग्रंथ वर्गीकरणाची एक पद्धती जिची निर्मिती एच.ई. ब्लिस यांनी अमेरिकेत १९३५ मध्ये केली.

bibliographic database – **ग्रंथसूचीय माहिती/संकलन** – संगणकावर संग्रहित केलेली सूचिबद्ध माहिती.

bibliographic description – **ग्रंथवर्णन** – ग्रंथाचा तपशील.

bibliographic index - ग्रंथसूचींचा निर्देश - प्रचलित ग्रंथसूचींचा विषय निर्देश. अमेरिकेतील एच.डब्ल्यू.विल्सन कंपनीतर्फे वर्षातून तीन वेळा प्रकाशित होतो.

bibliographic instruction - ग्रंथसूचीय सूचना.

bibliographic information - ग्रंथांबाबत आवश्यक तेवढी माहिती.

bibliographic information network - ग्रंथसूचीय माहितीचे जाळे - विशिष्ट विषयातील माहितीवर आधारित सूचिबद्ध माहितीच्या डेटाबेसच्या निर्मितीच्या उद्देशाने निर्मिलेले नेटवर्क.

bibliographic record - ग्रंथाची नोंद/अभिलेख.

bibliographic record format - ग्रंथ अभिलेख प्रारूप - ग्रंथविषयक नोंदीचे प्रारूप, एखाद्या पुस्तकाच्या नोंदी संगणकीकृत तालिकेमध्ये नोंदविण्यासाठी तयार करण्यात आलेला नमुना, आराखडा, साचा.

bibliographic reference - ग्रंथसूचीय संदर्भ.

bibliographic description - ग्रंथसूचीविषयक वर्णन - वाङ्मयीन ग्रंथ किंवा रचना यांचे वर्णन, यामध्ये लेखकाचे ग्रंथकर्तृत्व आणि अन्य ज्या कोणी मूळ मजकूर सादर करण्यात लेखनसाहाय्य केले असेल (उदा. संपादक, अनुवादक इ.) यांचा तपशील, ग्रंथनाम, आवृत्ती, प्रकाशन वर्ष, तसेच प्रकाशनवृत्तांताही (प्रकाशन स्थळ/प्रकाशकाचे नाव इ.) तपशील दिलेला असतो; ज्यायोगे पाहिजे असलेला ग्रंथ मिळविता येतो.

bibliographical centre - ग्रंथसूचीय केंद्र - ग्रंथसूचीचा संग्रह करून त्याचे तालिकीकरण करणे. ग्रंथसूचीविषयक माहिती एकत्र करणे, जतन करणे हे काम करणारे केंद्र.

bibliographical classification - ग्रंथसूचीय वर्गीकरण - ग्रंथसूचीमध्ये तसेच तालिकीकरण करताना नोंदी करण्यासाठी वापरलेले वर्गीकरण.

bibliographical control - ग्रंथसूचीय उपलब्धी - ग्रंथालयात असलेल्या साहित्याची नोंद तयार करणे, ते विकसित करणे, त्याचे योग्य व्यवस्थापन करून अशा नोंदी वाचकांना उपलब्ध करून देण्याची प्रक्रिया.

bibliographical coupling - ग्रंथसूचीय जोडी/विश्लेषण - विशिष्ट विषयांवरील पुस्तके व लेख यामधून मिळालेल्या माहितीचा तुलनात्मक अभ्यास करणे.

bibliographical data - ग्रंथवर्णनाची माहिती - पुस्तकाचा लेखक, ग्रंथनाम, प्रकाशन, प्रकाशनाचे स्थळ व वर्ष, पृष्ठे, आकृत्या इ. बद्दलचे वर्णन.

bibliographical database - ग्रंथसूचीय आधारसामग्री - ग्रंथसूचीय माहितीची नोंद असलेली आधारसामग्री.

bibliographical description - ग्रंथसूचीय वर्णन - प्रकाशित साहित्याचे सखोल वर्णन. यामध्ये लेखक, संपादक, अनुवादक, रचनाकार याविषयी तसेच ग्रंथशीर्षक, आवृत्ती, प्रकाशनवर्ष, प्रकाशनस्थळ, प्रकाशकाचे नाव, मुद्रकाचे नाव यांचा उल्लेख केला जातो.

bibliographical index – **ग्रंथसूचीय निर्देश** – फक्त ग्रंथसूचीय संदर्भ असलेल्या प्रकाशनांचा किंवा नियतकालिकांमधील लेखांचा निर्देश.

bibliographical information – **ग्रंथसूचीय माहिती** – मागणी नोंदविण्यासाठी आवश्यक माहितीचा उल्लेख त्यात पुढील गोष्टींचा उल्लेख असतो. लेखक, शीर्षक, प्रकाशक, आवृत्ती, प्रकाशनवर्ष, प्रकाशनस्थळ, माला नोंद, खंड नोंद, भाग, किंमत याशिवाय काही वेळा संपादक, अनुवादक यांची माहिती दिली जाते.

bibliographical instruction – **ग्रंथसूचीय सूचना** – उपलब्ध माहितीचा उपयोग कसा करवून घ्यावा याबाबत ग्रंथालय कर्मचाऱ्यांनी वाचकांना प्रशिक्षण देण्यासाठी केलेल्या सूचना.

bibliographical item – **ग्रंथसूचीय घटक** – नियतकालिकांतील लेख, तांत्रिक अहवाल, पेटंट यांची ग्रंथसूची किंवा तालिकेमध्ये समाविष्ट होऊ शकेल अशी ग्रंथसूचीय वेगळी नोंद.

bibliographical note – **ग्रंथसूचीय टीप** – ग्रंथातील किंवा लेखाच्या मजकुराला संदर्भ म्हणून वापरलेल्या साहित्याची ग्रंथसूचीय वर्णन करणारी टीप.

bibliographical reference – **ग्रंथसूचीय संदर्भ** – ग्रंथ, ग्रंथाचे भाग, नियतकालिके, लेखमाला याविषयी माहिती देणारे संदर्भ.

bibliographical scatter – **ग्रंथसूचीय विस्कळीतता** – एखाद्या विषयावरील लेख अगदी वेगळ्या विषयावरील नियतकालिकामध्ये अंतर्भूत केल्याचे लक्षात येणे.

bibliographical section – **ग्रंथसूची/ग्रंथशरीर** – **रूपदर्शक अनुच्छेद** – ग्रंथाच्या मुख्य नोंदीत ग्रंथाचा आकार, त्याचे खंड, पृष्ठे, चित्रे, नकाशे, प्रकाशनाचे स्थान, प्रकाशक, प्रकाशनवर्ष ही माहिती ज्या अनुच्छेदात देण्यात येते त्याला 'ग्रंथशरीर-रूपदर्शक अनुच्छेद' असे म्हणतात.

bibliographical service – **ग्रंथसूचीय सेवा** – आवश्यकतेनुसार उपलब्ध करून दिलेल्या ग्रंथसूचीविषयक सेवा.

bibliographical tool – **ग्रंथसूचीविषयक साधन** – प्रकाशनांच्या यादीसारखी ग्रंथसूची तयार करण्यासाठी ग्रंथसूचीकाराने वापरण्याचे साधन.

bibliographical unit – **ग्रंथसूचीविषयक कार्यसमूह** – ग्रंथसूचीविषयक काम करणाऱ्या लोकांचा गट.

bibliographical volume – **ग्रंथसूचीय खंड** – इतर खंडांपेक्षा वेगळा, वेगळ्या शीर्षकावरून अर्धशीर्षक असलेला ग्रंथसूचीविषयक माहिती देणारा खंड.

bibliography – **ग्रंथसूची** – प्रकाशित ग्रंथ अथवा अन्य साहित्याची विशिष्ट पद्धतीनुसार तयार केलेली वर्णनात्मक यादी किंवा ज्ञानसाहित्याची व्यवस्थितरीत्या मांडणी केलेली यादी. ग्रंथविषयक सखोल व सर्वांगीण माहिती विशिष्ट तत्त्वानुसार क्रमाने देणारी सूची. ग्रंथसूची एका लेखकाची, एका विषयाची, विशिष्ट प्रदेशातील, विशिष्ट कालावधीतील वाचनसाहित्य किंवा ग्रंथसंपदा समाविष्ट केलेली असू शकते.

bibliography of bibliographies – **ग्रंथसूचींची ग्रंथसूची** – ग्रंथसूचींची सर्वंकष यादी.

bicliology – **ग्रंथकोश/पुस्तकांचा कोश** – ग्रंथाच्या प्रगतीविषयक ऐतिहासिक माहिती व शास्त्रशुद्ध वर्णन असलेली परिपूर्ण यादी.

bibliomania – **ग्रंथछंद** – ग्रंथाचा संग्रह करण्याचे व संग्रहाची मालकी राखण्याचे वेड.

bibliometrics – **प्रलेखगणनशास्त्र/ग्रंथ उपयोगिता मापनशास्त्र** – एखाद्या विषयावरील उपलब्ध वाङ्मयाचे संख्याशास्त्रीय व गणितीय प्रमेयातून केलेले विश्लेषण किंवा ग्रंथालयामध्ये ग्रंथ व इतर साहित्याचा वापर किती प्रमाणात केला जातो याचा अभ्यास करण्यासाठी गणितीय व संख्याशास्त्रीय पद्धतींचे उपयोजन करून ग्रंथ उपयोगिता मापन करण्याचे शास्त्र.

bibliometry – **प्रलेखीय सांख्यिकी** – प्रलेखित माहितीचे संख्याशास्त्रीय विश्लेषण.

bibliophile – **ग्रंथसंग्रह जाणकार** – चांगल्या आणि वाईट आवृत्तींमध्ये फरक कसा ओळखावा याचे ज्ञान असणारा ग्रंथसंग्रह प्रेमी. ग्रंथसंग्रह करण्याचा छंद असणारी व्यक्ती.

bibliophile edition – **ग्रंथसंग्रहप्रेमी आवृत्ती** – चांगल्या, वाईट आवृत्तीविषयक ज्ञान असलेल्या ग्रंथसंग्रह प्रेमींसाठी खास छापून बांधणी केलेली आवृत्ती.

bibliophobia – **ग्रंथविषयक भयगंड** – ग्रंथविषयक नावड, ग्रंथवाचन न आवडणाऱ्या व्यक्ती.

bibliopole – **ग्रंथ विकणारा** – दुर्मिळ व दुर्लभ ग्रंथविषयक व्यवहार करणारी व्यक्ती, संस्था, विक्रेता.

bibliopsychology – **ग्रंथमानसशास्त्र** – ग्रंथ, वाचक, लेखक आणि त्यांचे सहसंबंध याविषयीचा अभ्यास.

bibliothecal classification – **ग्रंथस्थानीय वर्गीकरण.**

bibliotherapy – **ग्रंथोपचार पद्धती** – मानसिक आरोग्य व प्रत्यक्ष औषध योजना म्हणून निवडक वाचन व इतर योजना म्हणून निवडक वाचन व इतर साधनांचा उपयोग करून वापरलेली उपचार पद्धती.

bilingual dictionary – **द्विभाषिय शब्दकोश** – एका भाषेतील शब्दाचा अर्थ दुसऱ्या भाषेत देणारा शब्दकोश. उदा. इंग्रजी-मराठी शब्दकोश.

bill / invoice – **देयक** – माल आणि सेवा यासाठी देय असलेली रक्कम दर्शविणारा कागद, देयक.
(१) कायदाविषयक लिहिलेली टीप. (२) देयक – ग्रंथकिंमत मागणीपत्रक.

binary – **द्विअंकी/द्विक्रम** – केवळ १ आणि ० यांचा आधार घेऊन तयार केलेली अंकपद्धती.

binary code – **द्विअंकी संहिता.**

binary digit – **द्विअंकी अंक** – ० अथवा १ यापैकी एक अंक.

binary number – **द्विअंकी संख्या** – संगणकाची आज्ञावली दर्शविणारी संख्या/अंक.

binary number system – **द्विअंकी क्रमपद्धती** – अनेक संगणकांमध्ये वापरलेली शून्य व एक अंकधारित क्रमपद्धती.

binary search – **द्विअंकी शोध** – संगणकीय चिन्हांचा शोध.

binary digit (Bit) – **बिट** – नावातील बी.आय. व टी. ही अक्षरे घेऊन तयार केलेला शब्द. ० आणि १ ही दोनच चिन्हे वापरून संगणकात माहिती साठवावयाची असते. यापैकी एकमेव चिन्हास बिट असे म्हटले आहे. ही चिन्हे वापरून संगणकास समजणारा शब्द (बाईट) तयार होतो.

bind – **बांधणी** – हस्तलिखिते किंवा छपाई कागद जुळणी करून एका वेष्टनात बांधून दिलेले ग्रंथस्वरूप.

binder – **बांधणीकार** – ग्रंथाची बांधणी करणारी व्यक्ती.

binder's title / back title – **ग्रंथाच्या कण्यावर लिहिले जाणारे ग्रंथशीर्षक**

bindery – **ग्रंथबांधणी विभाग/दुकान** – ग्रंथांची बांधणी व पुनर्बांधणी केली जाते ती जागा, ठिकाण, दुकान.

binding – **ग्रंथबांधणी** – ग्रंथाचे/खंडाचे संरक्षणात्मक आवरण.

binding department – **ग्रंथबांधणी विभाग** – ग्रंथबांधणीचे कामकाज चालविणारा विभाग.

binding edge – **ग्रंथबांधणी काठ/कडा/किनारा.**

binding record – **ग्रंथबांधणीबाबतची नोंद.**

binding slip (sheet) – **ग्रंथबांधणी चिठ्ठी.**

binding spiral (sheet) – **सर्पिल ग्रंथबांधणी** – यामध्ये बांधणीसाठी दोऱ्याऐवजी प्लास्टिक रिबन वापरतात.

binding variations – **ग्रंथबांधणी विविधता** – ग्रंथाच्या आवृत्तीची एकाच वेळी बांधणी न झाल्यामुळे काहीवेळा रंगामध्ये किंवा वेगळ्या प्रकारे झालेली ग्रंथबांधणी.

bio–bibliography – **चरित्रग्रंथसूची** – लेखकांच्या चरित्रविषयक छोट्या नोंदी देणारी ग्रंथसूची. अनेक व्यक्तींच्या संक्षिप्त चरित्रविषयक तपशिलाचा अंतर्भाव असलेली ग्रंथसूची.

biographee – **चरित्र** – व्यक्तीचरित्र दर्शविणारा ग्रंथ.

biographee entry – **चरित्रनायक नोंद** – चरित्रनायकाच्या नावाखालील तालिकेतील (नामतालिका किंवा विषयतालिका) नोंद.

biographer – **चरित्रकार** – अन्य व्यक्तींचे चरित्र लिहिणारी व्यक्ती.

biographical dictionary – **चरित्रकोश** – अनेक व्यक्तींच्या चरित्रांचा, वर्णानुक्रमे रचना असलेला संग्रह.

biographical sources – **चरित्र साधने.**

biography – **चरित्र** – (१) व्यक्तीच्या जीवनाचा लिखित वृत्तान्त, (२) लोकांच्या जीवनाशी संबंधित असलेली ललित वाङ्मयाची शाखा.

biography file – **चरित्र पंजिका** – व्यक्तींची माहिती देणारी पत्रस्वरूपातील किंवा कात्रणांची संचिका किंवा एखाद्या व्यक्तीच्या आयुष्यातील घटना, प्रसंग, व्यक्तीविशेष यांचा समावेश असलेला ग्रंथ. उदा. हूज हू

biological enemies of the book – **ग्रंथ खराब करणारे जैविक शत्रू.**

birchcark leaf – **भूर्जपत्र** – प्राचीन काळी लिखाणासाठी वापरण्याचे साधन.

birth date – **जन्मदिनांक** – एखाद्या व्यक्तीचा/लेखकाचा जन्मदिनांक.

bit – **चित्रबिंदू** – माहितीचे लहानात लहान एकक 'शून्य', 'एक' Y, N (Yes, No)

bit error rate – **संगणकातील एकक चुकांचा वेग** – माहितीचे प्रक्षेपण करताना मूळ माहिती लेखनापेक्षा किती चुका झाल्या हे दर्शविणारे एकक.

bit map – **बिंदुयुक्त नकाशा (चित्र/आकृती)** – संगणकावरील एक आविष्कार.

biweekly / semi-monthly / fortnightly / half monthly – **पाक्षिक** – दर दोन आठवड्याने प्रकाशित होणारे प्रकाशन.

blank book – **कोरे पुस्तक** – नोंदी, टीपा, हिशेब लिहिण्यासाठी वापरण्याची कोरी पाने असलेले पुस्तक.

blank cover – **कोरे वेष्टन** – ग्रंथाच्या सजावटीसाठी राखून ठेवलेले कोरे वेष्टनपृष्ठ.

blank leaves – **ग्रंथाच्या शेवटी असणारी कोरी पाने.**

blanket order – **एक प्रत (प्रत्येकाची) घेण्याचे आदेश.**

bleach – **खळ वगैरे असलेला.**

bleed illustration – **समास नसलेले लेखाचित्र.**

blind reference – **अपुरा संदर्भ** – ग्रंथसूची किंवा तालिकेत नोंद नाही असा संदर्भ.

block – **ठसा/गट** – (१) संस्करण प्रक्रियेसाठी निवड केलेला माहितीचा गट. (२) छपाईसाठी वापरला जाणारा ठसा.

block arrangement – **ग्रंथांची कपाटवार रचना/मांडणी.**

block books – **ठोकळमुद्रित ग्रंथ** – लाकडी ठोकळ्यावर कोरीव काम करून छपाई केलेले ग्रंथ. नेदरलँड्स, जर्मनी येथे इ.स. १४१०च्या सुमारास असे ग्रंथ आढळले.

block letters – **रोमन मोठ्या लिपीतील अक्षरे** – उदा. **A, B, C.**

block printing – **लाकडी व धातूच्या साहाय्याने केलेले मुद्रण.**

blue-books – **निळी पुस्तके** – ब्रिटिश सरकारचा पांढऱ्या कागदांवर मजकूर असलेला, निळ्या रंगाच्या वेष्टनातील शासकीय अहवाल ग्रंथ. पार्लमेंट रिपोर्ट वगैरेंची पुस्तके.

blurb – **मलपृष्ठावर प्रकाशकाने दिलेला ग्रंथपरिचय.**

body – **मंडळ** – एकत्रितपणे काम करणाऱ्या लोकांचा गट, मंडळ.

book – **ग्रंथ (पुस्तक)** – अनियतकालिक नसून ज्यात कमीत कमी ४९ पृष्ठे मुद्रित करून आवरण घातले आहे असा ग्रंथ.

book acquisition – ग्रंथोपार्जन – ग्रंथालयासाठी, ग्रंथ मिळविण्यासाठी अंतर्भूत असलेल्या प्रक्रिया.

book availability – ग्रंथाची उपलब्धता – हवा असलेला ग्रंथ बाजारात किंवा ग्रंथालयात आहे किंवा नाही याची पडताळणी.

book band – ग्रंथपट्टी – ग्रंथाची जाहिरात करण्यासाठी तयार केलेली ग्रंथवेष्टनावर लावलेली छोटी पट्टी.

book bank – ग्रंथ पेटी/पुस्तक पेढी – विद्यार्थ्यांना वर्षभर वापरावयास दिल्या जाणाऱ्या ग्रंथाबाबतची योजना.

book binder – ग्रंथ बांधणीकार.

book budget – ग्रंथासाठीचे अंदाजपत्रक.

book card – ग्रंथपत्र – ग्रंथाची ओळख पटविण्यासाठी आवश्यक माहिती लिहिलेले पत्र जे ग्रंथासोबत ठेवले जाते.

book care – ग्रंथनिगा/ग्रंथाची काळजी.

book catalogue – पुस्तक रूपातील ग्रंथ तालिका.

book case – ग्रंथ कपाट – ग्रंथ ठेवण्यासाठी काचेचे दार असणारे कपाट.

book charging slip – ग्रंथ देव-घेव चिठ्ठी.

book charging system – ग्रंथ देवघेव पद्धती – ग्रंथालयाच्या वाचकांना ग्रंथ देणे व परत घेण्याची पद्धती.

book classification – ग्रंथ वर्गीकरण – ग्रंथ कपाटात ठेवण्यापूर्वी ग्रंथाचे विशिष्ट विषयातील स्थान ठरविण्यासाठी वर्गांक तयार करण्याची प्रक्रिया.

book club – ग्रंथमंडळ – ग्रंथवाचन अथवा खरेदीसाठी निर्माण झालेली हौशी मंडळ.

book condition – ग्रंथाची उपलब्धता/अवस्था.

book cover – ग्रंथाचे आवरण/कागदी वेस्टन.

book collection – ग्रंथ संग्रह – एखाद्या ग्रंथालयातील एकूण वाचनसाहित्य.

book conservation – ग्रंथनिगा –ग्रंथ टिकावा यासाठी घेतलेली काळजी.

book deposit centre – ग्रंथाचे ठेव केंद्र – ग्रंथ जमा करण्याचे ठिकाण.

book display (exhibition) – ग्रंथ प्रदर्शन.

book detection system / detection system – ग्रंथ देवघेव निदान पद्धती – ग्रंथालयातून वाचक बाहेर जाण्यापूर्वी त्याच्याकडील पुस्तके विशिष्ट उपकरणात ठेवली जातात तसेच परत आलेली पुस्तके या उपकरणात ठेवली जातात. पुस्तके नियमित/नियमानुसार देवघेव पद्धतीने घेतली नसतील तर गजर वाजतो व ग्रंथालयाचे दार बंद होते.

book distributor – **ग्रंथ वितरक** – प्रकाशकाकडील ग्रंथ, व्यक्ती, संस्था व ग्रंथालये यांना उपलब्ध करून देणारी मध्यस्थ संस्था.

book drop – **ग्रंथ सोडून जाण्याची सुविधा** – ग्रंथालय बंद असताना ग्रंथालयाच्या प्रवेशद्वाराजवळ ग्रंथ परतीसाठी बसवलेली पेटी किंवा कप्पा.

book end / support – **ग्रंथ टेकू** – ग्रंथमांडणीमध्ये ग्रंथ ताठ सरळ रहावेत म्हणून ग्रंथओळीच्या शेवटी लावलेले लाकडी किंवा धातूचे इंग्रजी **L, T** आकाराचे आधारस्तंभ.

book exchange – **ग्रंथाची अदलाबदल** – एका ग्रंथालयातील अतिरिक्त ग्रंथ दुसऱ्यास देऊन त्याऐवजी उपयुक्त ग्रंथ स्वीकारणे.

book exhibition / fair – **ग्रंथजत्रा/ग्रंथप्रदर्शन** – ग्रंथ प्रकाशक, विक्रेते, वाचक यांना एकत्र आणणारा ग्रंथमेळा, वाचकांना नवीन ग्रंथाविषयी माहिती उपलब्ध करून देण्यासाठी भरवलेला ग्रंथ आणि वाचक यांचा मेळावा किंवा ग्रंथविक्रेत्यांनी आयोजित केलेले ग्रंथविक्रीचे प्रदर्शन.

book form index – **ग्रंथस्वरूप दिलेला निर्देश.**

book catalogue – **ग्रंथरूप तालिका** – ग्रंथालयातील ग्रंथांच्या नोंदी ग्रंथरूपात केलेली तालिका.

book fund – **ग्रंथ निधी** – ग्रंथ खरेदीसाठी उपलब्ध असलेला निधी.

book hand – (छपाईतंत्र माहीत होण्यापूर्वी) ग्रंथासाठी आकर्षक सजावटपूर्ण हस्ताक्षर लिहिण्याचे तंत्र.

book holder – पुस्तकाची छायाप्रत काढताना ग्रंथ सरळ राहण्याच्या दृष्टीने ग्रंथ उघडून ठेवण्याची जागा.

book hunter – ग्रंथाच्या दुय्यम विक्री बाजारात विशिष्ट ग्रंथ शोधून त्याची माहिती पुरविण्याचा व्यवसाय करणारी व्यक्ती.

book index entry – **ग्रंथ निर्देशी नोंद** – ग्रंथाच्या माहितीने (जसे ग्रंथनाम) सुरू होणारी तालिकेतील नोंद.

book illustration – **ग्रंथ सुशोभन** – ग्रंथातील मजकुराला सजावट करण्यासाठी चित्रे, आकृत्या यांचा वापर.

book issue – **वाचकास ग्रंथ वाचावयास देण्याची क्रिया.**

book jacket / dust cover / dust wrapper – **ग्रंथवेष्टन** – प्रकाशकाने ग्रंथसंरक्षण व ग्रंथाकर्षण या हेतूने ग्रंथाला लावलेले वेष्टन. यावर लेखक, शीर्षक यांचा उल्लेख करून आतील बाजूस लेखक परिचय, लेखकाचा फोटो, ग्रंथाला मिळालेली पारितोषिके, लेखकाची इतर प्रकाशने यांची माहिती दिली जाते.

book jobber – **ग्रंथ पुरवठा करणारा.**

book label – **ग्रंथचिठ्ठी** – ग्रंथालयातील ग्रंथाचे स्थान दर्शविणारी ग्रंथसंस्करण प्रक्रियेत ग्रंथालयाने चिकटवलेली खूणचिठ्ठी.

booklet – **पुस्तिका** – कमी पृष्ठसंख्या असलेले पुस्तक.

book lifter – **ग्रंथ उदवाहक** – ग्रंथालयात ग्रंथांची ने–आण करणारा सेवक किंवा ग्रंथाची ने–आण करण्यासाठी वरच्या मजल्यावरून खाली किंवा खालून वर ग्रंथवहन करण्याकरिता असलेली सोय.

book list – **ग्रंथ यादी** – विशिष्ट विषयाची लेखकाच्या नावानुसार किंवा वर्गवारीनुसार तयार केलेली यादी.

book mark – **ग्रंथखूण** – ग्रंथवाचन करताना खूण म्हणून वापरण्याचे साधन. काही वेळा प्रकाशक ग्रंथबांधणीमध्येच रिबन, कागद, धातूची पट्टी यांवर आकर्षक लिखाण, नक्षीकाम करून ग्रंथवाचन खूण ग्रंथाबरोबर पुरवितात.

book maker – **ग्रंथकर्ता/ग्रंथनिर्माता/लेखक.**

book number – **ग्रंथांक** – ग्रंथालयात विषयानुसार मोजणीमध्ये ग्रंथाचे स्थान ठरविण्यासाठी दिलेला वर्गीकृत अंक. ग्रंथांक हा वर्गीकरण पद्धतीनुसार अंक, अक्षरे व चिन्हे यांचा वापर करून तयार केला जातो.

book of hours / mass book / missal – **बहुजन समाजासाठी तयार केलेला ग्रंथ.**

book on approval – **पसंतीसाठी ग्रंथ** – ग्रंथालयात खरेदीपूर्वी वाचकांच्या पसंतीसाठी आलेला ग्रंथ.

book on loan – **उधार ग्रंथ** – ग्रंथालयात ग्रंथ उपलब्ध नसल्यामुळे वाचकांची गरज तात्पुरती भागविण्यासाठी दुसऱ्या ग्रंथालयाकडून उसनवारीने मागितलेला ग्रंथ.

book on order – **आदिष्ट ग्रंथावली.**

book order list – **ग्रंथआदेश यादी.**

book ordering section – **ग्रंथ आदेशन विभाग** – ग्रंथखरेदीसाठी ग्रंथमागणी प्रक्रिया करणारा विभाग.

book paper – **केवळ ग्रंथछपाईसाठी वापरण्याचा कागद.**

book piracy – **ग्रंथचौर्य** – मूळ ग्रंथकाराच्या परवानगीशिवाय प्रकाशित केलेल्या ग्रंथांच्या प्रती.

book plate – **ग्रंथमुद्रा** – ग्रंथावर लावलेला शिक्का.

book pocket – **ग्रंथकप्पा/ग्रंथपाकीट/ग्रंथखिसा** – ग्रंथाच्या पुढील किंवा मागील बाजूस शेवटच्या पानावर ग्रंथपत्र ठेवण्यासाठी चिकटविलेला कप्पा, पाकीट.

book post – **पुस्तप्रेष** – फक्त छापील मजकूर सवलतीच्या दराने टपालाद्वारे पाठविण्याची सोय. पुस्तप्रेष.

book processing – **ग्रंथसंस्करण** – ग्रंथखरेदी झाल्यानंतर ग्रंथमांडणी करण्यापूर्वी ग्रंथालयात पूर्ण करण्याची प्रक्रिया. यामध्ये दाखलक्रमांक, वर्गीकरण, तालिकीकरण इ. समावेश होतो.

book preservation – **ग्रंथनिगा/ग्रंथसंरक्षण.**

book processing centre/section – **ग्रंथसोपस्कार/ग्रंथसंस्करण केंद्र** – अनेक ग्रंथालयाच्या सहकार्यासाठी एकत्रितरीत्या ग्रंथसंस्करण करण्याचे केंद्र.

book production – **ग्रंथोत्पादन** – ग्रंथछपाई, सजावट, नक्षीकाम, बांधणी यांचा समावेश.

book purchase – ग्रंथखरेदी.

book rack – **ग्रंथमांडणी कपाट** – ग्रंथ ठेवण्यासाठीचे ग्रंथदालनातील दरवाजे नसलेले कपाट.

book record – ग्रंथनोंद/ग्रंथ अभिलेख.

book repaire – **ग्रंथाची दुरुस्ती** – ग्रंथाची किरकोळ दुरुस्ती.

book replacement – **बदली ग्रंथ** – वाचकाने ग्रंथ हरविल्यास, खराब, गहाळ केल्यास त्याच्याकडून त्याच ग्रंथाची घेतलेली प्रत.

book rest – **ग्रंथ कपाटात सरळ रहावेत म्हणून दिलेला आधार.**

book return – **ग्रंथ परती.**

book room – **ग्रंथकक्ष** – ग्रंथसंग्रह असलेली खोली.

book review – **ग्रंथपरीक्षण.**

book sale – **ग्रंथविक्री** – ग्रंथालयातील अधिक प्रती व जुनी पुस्तके यांची ग्रंथालयाने केलेली विक्री.

book selection – **ग्रंथनिवड** – ग्रंथालयातील ग्रंथसंग्रहाची समतोल वाढ होण्याच्या दृष्टीने केलेली ग्रंथनिवड.

book selection card – **ग्रंथनिवडपत्र.**

book seller – **ग्रंथविक्रेता.**

book sellers catalogue – **ग्रंथविक्रेता तालिका** – ग्रंथ विक्रेत्याकडे उलपब्ध असलेल्या ग्रंथाची, वाचन साहित्याची यादी.

book shelf – **ग्रंथकप्पा** – ग्रंथ साठवण्याचा एक खण.

book size – **ग्रंथआकार** – ग्रंथाची लांबी, रुंदी, जाडी.

book slip – **ग्रंथचिठ्ठी** – ग्रंथ देवघेवीसाठी पूर्वी वापरात असलेली एक पद्धती.

book stack / room – **ग्रंथ संग्रह खोली** – ग्रंथालयातील ग्रंथ ठेवण्याची खोली.

book stamp – **ग्रंथशिक्का/ग्रंथठसा** – ग्रंथाची मालकी दर्शविणारा शीर्षक पानावर किंवा शेवटच्या पानावर उमटवलेला ठसा.

book stand – **ग्रंथ ठेवण्याचे/प्रदर्शित करण्याचे साहित्य, उपकरण.**

book stock – **ग्रंथसंग्रह** – ग्रंथालयातील एकूण वाचनसाहित्य.

book supporter (end) – **ग्रंथटेकू** – ग्रंथास आधार देणारा कपाटात ग्रंथ ताठ उभे रहावेत म्हणून देण्याचा आधार.

book talk – **ग्रंथवार्ता** – ग्रंथांची माहिती देणारे भाषण.

book trade – ग्रंथव्यापार – ग्रंथांची खरेदी-विक्री व्यवहार.

book trade journal – ग्रंथाची व्यापारी पत्रिका.

book tray – ग्रंथकप्पा.

book trolley – ग्रंथवाहिनी – ग्रंथालयात ग्रंथ ने-आण करण्यासाठी वापरायचे वाहन. ग्रंथांच्या वाहतुकीसाठीची ढकलगाडी.

book week – ग्रंथसप्ताह – ग्रंथालयात ग्रंथ, विक्रेते व वाचक यांच्यामध्ये चर्चा, मेळावे, भाषणे यांचे आयोजन केलेला सप्ताह. भारतात हा सप्ताह ७ ते १४ नोव्हेंबर (बालकदिन) या काळात साजरा केला जातो.

book work – ग्रंथाविषयीचे काम.

book worm – ग्रंथकिडा/वाळवी – ग्रंथास लागणारी कीड, किडा, कीटक किंवा अतीप्रमाणात वाचन करणारी व्यक्ती.

book van (bus) – फिरत्या ग्रंथालयाची सेवा देणारे ग्रंथवाहन.

books, documents, informations are for use – ग्रंथ उपयोगासाठी आहेत – ग्रंथालयशास्त्राचे पहिले सूत्र.

books in print – छापील ग्रंथांची सूची – उदा. इंडियन नॅशनल बिब्लिओग्राफी.

boolean operators (terms) – विशिष्ट प्रचालक/कारक. उदा. And, or and not.

boolean searching – संगणकाद्वारे विशिष्ट शोध घेण्याचा मार्ग – And, or and not अशासारख्या शब्दांमुळे येणाऱ्या माहितीचा मूळ माहितीमधून घेतलेला शोध.

boot – संगणककार्याला प्रारंभ करणे.

borrow – उसनवारीने घेणे – एखादी वस्तू/ग्रंथ परत करण्याच्या उद्देशाने उसनवारीने घेणे.

borrower / reader / user / clientele / patron / member / customer – सभासद/वाचक/ ग्राहक – ज्या वाचकाला ग्रंथालयाचे ग्रंथ परिसराबाहेर तात्पुरते नेण्याची परवानगी देण्यात आली आहे असा सभासद.

borrower's card (ticket) – सभासद पत्र – ज्यावर सभासदत्वाचा मजकूर लिहिला जातो.

borrower's file – सभासदाची माहिती असणारी संचिका/धारिका.

borrower's number – सभासद अंक/क्रम – सभासदास ग्रंथालयातर्फे देण्यात आलेला संकेतांक.

borrowers record – सभासद नोंद/अभिलेख – वाचकाने घेतलेल्या वाचनसाहित्याची माहिती देणारी नोंद.

borrower's register – ग्रंथवाचक नोंदवही – ग्रंथ देव-घेवीच्या नोंद ठेवण्याची एक पद्धती.

bound – बंध/बद्ध.

bound term / collateral term / generic term – **सहसंबंधित संज्ञा** – निर्देशन करताना वापरलेली एकापेक्षा अधिक शब्द असलेली संज्ञा.

bound periodical/ journal – **बंध/बद्ध/नियतकालिक** – बांधीव नियतकालिक.

bound volume – **बांधीव खंड** – नियतकालिकांचे सुटे अंक एकत्रित करून बांधणी केलेला खंड.

brackets – **कंसचिन्हे** – आयताकार चिन्हांमध्ये तालिकाकाराने समाविष्ट केलेला मजकूर लिहिला जातो. उदा. [ ]

branch library – **शाखा ग्रंथालय** – मुख्य ग्रंथालयाशिवाय असणारी ग्रंथालयाची शाखा.

Braille – **ब्रेल** – लुईस ब्रेल या अंध व्यक्तीने शोधून काढलेली अंधांच्या ग्रंथवाचनासाठी उपयुक्त लिपी.

Braille Script library – **ब्रेललिपी ग्रंथालय** – ब्रेल लिपीतील पुस्तकांचे ग्रंथालय.

branching classification / ramifying classification – **दोन किंवा अधिक उपवर्गांचे विभाजन पुन: पुन्हा उपवर्गांमध्ये करून केलेले वर्गीकरण** – काहीवेळा तक्ता स्वरूपात वर्गांची मांडणी केली जाते.

brief cataloguing – **संक्षिप्त तालिकीकरण** – काही पुस्तकांच्या तालिकेतील नोंदींमध्ये सुलभता आणण्यासाठी निवडक नोंदी केल्या जातात.

brightness – **चकाकी/चकचकीतपणा.**

british library – **ब्रिटिश ग्रंथालय** – इंग्लंडचे राष्ट्रीय ग्रंथालय.

broad classification – **स्थूल वर्गीकरण** – मुख्य विषय दर्शविणारे वर्गीकरण.

broader term (BT) – **स्थूल संज्ञा** – माहितीची प्रतिप्राप्ती करताना विशिष्ट अर्थापेक्षा सर्वसामान्य अर्थ दर्शविणारी संज्ञा. उदा. विज्ञान ही संज्ञा पदार्थविज्ञान पेक्षा स्थूलसंज्ञा.

brochure – **लघुपुस्तक/विवरणिका/माहितीपुस्तिका** – एखाद्या संस्थेची थोडक्यात माहिती देण्यासाठी तयार केलेले पुस्तक.

broken order – **भग्नक्रम/खंडितक्रम/ग्रंथरचनेचा एक प्रकार** – विशिष्ट विषयावरील ग्रंथ त्यांच्या वर्गीकरण नियम ग्रंथमांडणीतून वेगळे काढून वाचकांना उपलब्ध करून देणे.

browne's classification – **जेम्स डी. ब्राऊन यांची विषय वर्गीकरण पद्धती.**

browne's book changing system / pocket cover charging system – नीना इ. ब्राऊन या अमेरिकन ग्रंथपालांनी १८९५ मध्ये विषद केलेल्या ग्रंथपत्र नोंदीद्वारे ग्रंथ देवघेव करावयाची पद्धती.

browse – **विचयन/विचरण करणे**– ग्रंथसंग्रहातील विशिष्ट ग्रंथ वा प्रलेख प्रत्यक्ष किंवा संगणकाद्वारे पाहणी करून शोधून काढणे.

browser – **विचयक/विचरक** – ग्राफिक्स किंवा टेक्स्ट स्वरूपातील माहिती पाहण्यासाठीची आज्ञावली. ह्यामध्ये नेटस्केप ब्राऊझर व इंटरनेट एक्सप्लोरर या नावाने ब्राऊझर्स उपलब्ध आहेत.

buckram – ग्रंथबांधणीसाठी उपयोगात आणलेले मजबूत व कडक कापड.

budget – **अर्थसंकल्प/आर्थिक तरतूद** – आर्थिक वर्षातील जमाखर्चाचे अंदाजपत्रक ग्रंथालयातील एकूण खर्चासाठी उपलब्ध असलेली तरतूद.

budget allocation register – **अनुदान वाटप नोंदवही.**

budget allotment – **नियत रक्कम** – अर्थसंकल्पात शीर्षकनिहाय रकमेचे नियोजन.

budget estimate – **अर्थ अंदाजपत्रक** – वर्षभरातील जमा-खर्चाचे अंदाजित विवरण.

budget provision – **अर्थविषयक तरतूद** – वर्षभरातील खर्चासाठी केलेली अर्थसंकल्पातील तरतूद.

budgeting – **अर्थसंकल्पन.**

buffer – **उपधान/चयक** – संगणकामध्ये माहितीची तात्पुरती साठवण करण्यासाठी असलेला भाग

bug / error – **दोष** – संगणकाच्या आज्ञावलीमधील समस्या, त्रुटी. हार्डवेअरमधील न सापडणाऱ्या दोषांनाही 'बग' म्हणतात.

bulky – **अवजड** – हलविण्यास अवघड.

bulky volume – **अवजड खंड** – अनेक पृष्ठांचा ग्रंथ.

bulletin – **वृत्तपत्रिका/विवरण पत्रिका** – जे प्रकाशन ठराविक कालावधीमध्ये प्रकाशित होते.

bulletin board service (BBS) – **वृत्तपत्रिका विवरण सेवा.**

business / industrial library – **व्यावसायिक/औद्योगिक ग्रंथालय** – व्यावसायिक, औद्योगिक क्षेत्रांत काम करणाऱ्या लोकांसाठीचे ग्रंथालय.

bye–laws – **उपअधिनियम** – मार्गदर्शक मुद्यांचा, नियमांचा संच.

byname – **उपनाव** – खऱ्या नावांशिवाय येणारे इतर नाव.

byte – **अष्टमान/अष्टमान एकक** – संगणकाच्या स्मरणिकेतील एका माहिती एककाने व्यापलेली जागा. संगणकाच्या स्मृती, संग्रहण व्यवस्था, फाईलसचा आकार, मोजण्याचे परिमाण. एक बाईट कमीत कमी ८ बिट्सचा असतो. नव्या संगणकात तो १६, ३२, ६४ बिट्सचाही आहे.

cabinet – **कपाट**.

cadre – **संवर्ग** – कर्मचाऱ्यांची वर्गदर्शक श्रेणी.

calculating machine – **गणकयंत्र/परिगणनयंत्र/परिगणक** – गणितीय कार्य करण्यासाठी तयार केलेले यंत्र किंवा अंकांमधील परस्पर संबंध समजून घेण्यासाठी अनेक सुविधा असलेले परिगणन किंवा मोजणीस उपयुक्त यंत्र.

calendar – **दिनदर्शिका** – विशिष्ट वर्षाचे दिवस, आठवडे आणि महिने दर्शविणारे पत्रक. किंवा (१) महिना, वार, दिनांक, तिथी इ.नोंदी असलेले पंचांग, (२) संग्रहातील प्रलेखांची सुसंगत यादी. यादीतील प्रत्येक नोंदीवर आशय, दिनांक यांचा उल्लेख.

calligraphy – **हस्तलेखनकला/सुलेखनकला/रुचिराक्षरकला/हस्ताक्षरकला** – सुंदर लिखाण करण्याची कला.

call number – **बोधांक** – विशिष्ट ग्रंथालयातील ग्रंथांचे एकत्व सिद्ध करण्यासाठी आणि तो शोधण्यासाठी वापरलेले अंक. बोधांक हा किमान वर्गांक, ग्रंथांक आणि दाखल अंक यांचा मिळून बनलेला असतो. याशिवाय त्यात संग्राहक किंवा कृती क्रमांकसुद्धा असू शकतो.

call entry – **बोधांक नोंद**.

call section – **बोधांक उपविभाग**.

call slip / recommendation slip / requisition slip – **विनंती चिठ्ठी** – ग्रंथालयातून मागितलेल्या ग्रंथाविषयीची माहिती या चिठ्ठीवर लिहिली जाते.

campus – प्रांगण/परिसर – शाळा, महाविद्यालय किंवा विद्यापीठ यांची जमीन, परिसर.

cancellation – रद्द करणे/काढून टाकणे.

canon – सूत्र/नियम/उपसूत्र/मार्गदर्शक तत्त्व.

canon of alphabetical sequence – अनुवर्ण क्रमाचे सूत्र/तत्त्व – अनुवर्णानुसार रचना करण्यासाठी वापरायचे सूत्र.

canon of ascertainability – निश्चितपणाचे/निर्णायकतेचे/निर्धारणाचे सूत्र – तत्त्वतः तालिकेतील नोंदीमध्ये लिहिण्यासाठी ग्रंथविषयक माहिती विश्वसनीय आणि निश्चित स्वरूपाची असावी असे हे सूत्र सांगते.

canon of booknumcer – ग्रंथांकाचे सूत्र – ग्रंथ व तालिकापत्रे यांची रचना ग्रंथांकातील घटकानुसार करण्याबाबतचे सूत्र.

canon of canonical sequence – तत्त्वांच्या अनुक्रमाचे सूत्र – वर्गीकरण करताना मुख्य विषयांच्या किंवा उपविषयांच्या पंक्तीत विषयांचा पारंपारिक क्रम कायम ठेवावा असे हे सूत्र सांगते.

canon of classics – अभिजात ग्रंथांचे तत्त्व/सूत्र – ग्रंथकक्षात अभिजात ग्रंथ व त्यावरील समीक्षा एकत्र ठेवण्यात येण्यासाठी करावयाच्या रचनेचे सूत्र.

canon of collection number – संग्रहकांचे सूत्र.

canon of concomitance – सहगामित्व/सहगामित्वाचे तत्त्व, सूत्र – वर्गीकरण करताना वापरायच्या दोन लक्षणांमध्ये सहगामित्व असू नये म्हणजे दोन अथवा अधिक लक्षणांच्या वापरामुळे मूळ विषयाचे विभाजन एकाच उपवर्गात होऊ नये. उदा. 'वय' आणि 'जन्मतारीख' या दोन लक्षणांच्या आधारे समूहाच्या एकाच उपगटात वर्गीकरण होईल; अशा लक्षणांचा वापर वर्गीकरणाकरता केला जाऊ नये असे हे सूत्र सांगते.

canon of consistency – सुसंगतीचे/सुसंगतीसूत्र/सातत्यत्वाचे तत्त्व/सूत्र – तालिकीकरण करण्यासाठी उपलब्ध नियमावलीमध्ये नियम तयार करताना ते कायमस्वरूपी राहतील असे दूरदृष्टीने तयार केलेले असावे असे हे सूत्र सांगते.

canon of consistent sequence – सुसंगतीक्रमाचे तत्त्व/सूत्र – तालिकीकरण क्रियेमध्ये करावयाच्या नोंदी अशा सुसंगत क्रमाने कराव्यात की वाचकांना योग्य विषयानुरूप माहिती मिळाली पाहिजे असे हे सूत्र सांगते.

canon of co-ordinate classes – समपदस्थ वर्गांचे तत्त्व/सूत्र – एकाच दर्जाच्या विषयांना देण्यात येणारे चिन्हांकन समान चिन्हे वापरून तयार व्हावे असे हे सूत्र सांगते.

canon of context – संदर्भाचे/पूर्वापार संबंध तत्त्व/सूत्र – तालिकेमध्ये नोंद करताना ग्रंथाची प्रमाणित नोंद करणे आवश्यक आहे. तसेच आवश्यक तेव्हा नियमावलीतही बदल करता आले पाहिजेत असा या सूत्राचा हेतू आहे.

canon of currency – प्रचलिताचे/अद्ययावतपणाचे प्रचलिततेचे तत्त्व/सूत्र – वर्गीकरण करताना नोंद करण्याची विषयशीर्षके जास्तीत जास्त अद्ययावत असावी असे हे सूत्र सांगते.

canon of decreasing extension – विस्तार आकुंचन अवगामित्वाचे तत्त्व/सूत्र – वर्गीकरण करताना शृंखलेच्या पहिल्या दुव्यापासून शेवटच्या दुव्याकडे विभाजन प्रक्रिया गतिमान होत असता विषयाची प्रखरता वाढत गेली पाहिजे व विस्तार कमी कमी होत गेला पाहिजे असे या सूत्रात सांगितले आहे.

canon of differentiation – विभाजनाचे, विभेदन तत्त्व/सूत्र – वर्गीकरण करताना असे लक्षण वापरावे की ज्यामुळे विषयाचे किमान दोन वा अधिक गट निर्माण होतील. उदा. 'उडणारे पक्षी' असे लक्षण वापरता येणार नाही तर 'देशादेशांतील पक्षी' वा इतर लक्षणे वापरावी असा या सूत्राचा अर्थ आहे.

canon of distinctiveness – विभिन्नतेचे तत्त्व/सूत्र – वर्गीकरणाद्वारे तयार होणारे गट निश्चितपणे एकमेकांपासून एका लक्षणाने ओळखता यावेत असे हे सूत्र सांगते.

canon of enumeration – प्रगणन, प्रगणनाचे तत्त्व/सूत्र – वर्गीकरण पद्धतीच्या तक्त्यात वापरलेल्या संज्ञेची निश्चित अर्थव्याप्ती किती आहे हे अजमावण्यासाठी शृंखलेत वापरलेल्या संज्ञांची गणना व्हावी असे हे सूत्र सांगते.

canon of exclusiveness – अपवर्जकतेचे, समावेशकतेचे तत्त्व/सूत्र – वर्गीकरणाद्वारे तयार होते.

canon of exhaustiveness – नि:शेषता, नि:शेषतेचे तत्त्व/सूत्र – वर्गीकरण करताना एखादे लक्षण असे वापरावे की ज्यामुळे नि:शेष वर्गवारी केली जाईल. वर्गांमध्ये आणखी भर पडणे अशक्य ठरले पाहिजे असे हे सूत्र सांगते.

canon of expressiveness – सुव्यक्तता, सुव्यक्ततेचे तत्त्व/सूत्र – वर्गांत वापरलेल्या चिन्हांकनाचे स्वरूप हे वापरलेल्या लक्षणांना अनुसरून असावे असे या सूत्रात प्रतिपादन केले आहे.

canon of favoured sequence – आवडत्या अनुक्रमाचे तत्त्व/सूत्र – ग्रंथवर्गीकरण पद्धतीतील विषयांचा क्रम त्या विषयामधील अनुरूपतेनुसार ठरवावा असे हे सूत्र सांगते.

canon of helpful sequence – साह्यकारी अनुक्रमाचे तत्त्व/सूत्र – वर्गीकरण करताना पंक्तीमधील अनुक्रम साह्यकारी असावा असे हे सूत्र सुचविते.

canon of hospitality in array – पंक्ती विषयक अतिथ्यशीलतेचे तत्त्व/सूत्र – एका पंक्तीमधील विषयांना चिन्हांकन ठरविताना अतिथ्यशीलता राखावी असे हे सूत्र सांगते.

canon of individualisation – व्यक्ती वैशिष्ट्याचे तत्त्व/सूत्र – तालिकेमध्ये विविध प्रकारच्या शीर्षकांचा वापर करताना व्यक्ती, समष्टी, ग्रंथकार, स्थलनाम, मालानाम, भाषा याविषयक संज्ञा लिहिताना ती संज्ञा एक म्हणजे एकच आहे हे समजण्यासाठी आवश्यक तेवढी व्यक्ती वैशिष्ट्ये वापरून तिचे विशेषीकरण झाले पाहिजे असे हे सूत्र सुचविते.

canon of local variation – **स्थानिक फेरबदलाचे तत्त्व/सूत्र** – ग्रंथ वर्गीकरणात देण्यात आलेल्या चिन्हांकनाने समाधानकारक ग्रंथरचना करता येत नसल्यास स्थानिक स्तरावर किरकोळ फेरबदल करण्याबाबत हे सूत्र सुचविते.

canon of mixed notation – **मिश्र चिन्हांकनाचे तत्त्व/सूत्र** – वर्गीकरण पद्धतीच्या चिन्हांकनात, अनेक प्रकारची चिन्हे वापरलेली असावीत. म्हणजेच ते मिश्र असावे. अंक, रोमी लहान व मोठी वर्ण व इतर चिन्हे वापरल्यास अनेक समपदस्थ वर्गांना, मुख्य वर्गाच्या एकाच पंक्तीत स्थान मिळू शकते.

canon of mnemonics – **स्मरणसुलभतेचे, स्मृतीसुलभता तत्त्व/सूत्र** – तालिकेमध्ये नोंद करताना सहजत: स्मरणात राहिल असे नोंदशीर्षक वापरावे. यामुळे वाचकांना ग्रंथ उपलब्ध करताना अधिक सुलभता येईल.

canon of modulation – **अपरिवर्तन, अपरिवर्तनाचे तत्त्व/सूत्र** – वर्गीकरण करताना शृंखलेतील सर्व दुवे एकमेकांशी संगतवार साधले गेले पाहिजेत. पहिल्यातून दुसरा, दुसऱ्यातून तिसरा, तिसऱ्यातून चौथा या क्रमानेच उत्क्रांत होत गेले पाहिजेत.

canon of mutual exclusiveness – **अपवर्जकता तत्त्व/सूत्र** – मोठ्या विषयाचे वर्गीकरण करताना यातील उपविषय हे कोणत्यातरी एकाच उपवर्गात वर्गीकृत केले जावे.

canon of non–hierarchical notation – **अश्रेणीय चिन्हांकनाचे तत्त्व/सूत्र**– ग्रंथवर्गीकरणातील चिन्हांकनाच्या संज्ञांना श्रेणीय अर्थ नसतो असे हे सूत्र सांगते.

canon of permanence – **स्थायित्वाचे, कायमतेचे, चिरकालीनतेचे तत्त्व/सूत्र** – कोणत्याही नोंदीचे शीर्षक तयार करताना सर्व संभाव्य गोष्टींचा विचार करून शीर्षकस्थानी दिली जाणारी माहिती चिरकाल टिकेल अशा पद्धतीने नोंदशीर्षक तयार करावे असे हे सूत्र सुचविते.

canon of prepotence – **महत्त्वक्रम तत्त्व/सूत्र** – तालिकेच्या नोंदीमध्ये अतिमहत्त्वाची माहिती आधी देऊन त्यानंतर महत्त्वानुसार क्रमाने माहिती द्यावी, असे या सूत्राचे स्पष्टीकरण आहे.

canon of pure notation – **शुद्ध चिन्हांकनाचे तत्त्व/सूत्र.**

canon of recall value – **पुनर्मागणी मूल्य तत्त्व/सूत्र** – तालिकेमध्ये नोंद करताना दिलेल्या माहितीवरून वाचकाला वाचनसाहित्य मिळणे सोयीचे होईल अशा प्रकारे महत्त्वाचा शब्द शीर्षकस्थानी असावा असे हे सूत्र सांगते.

canon of reticence – **मुग्धतेचे, मतनिरपेक्षता तत्त्व/सूत्र** – वर्गीकरण करताना वैयक्तिक मताचा प्रभाव न पाडता शास्त्रीय दृष्टिकोनातून संज्ञांकन करावे.

canon of relativity – **सापेक्षता, सापेक्षतेचे तत्त्व/सूत्र** – वर्गीकरण पद्धतीमधील वर्गांकाची लांबी, विषयाची व्याप्ती व प्रखरता याला अनुसरून असावी.

canon of relevance – **समर्पकतेचे, संबंधसूत्र/तत्त्व** – तालिकेच्या नोंदीमध्ये दिली जाणारी माहिती ही वाचकांच्या हेतूशी पूरक व तालिकेचे उद्देश साध्य करणारी असावी असे हे सूत्र सुचविते.

canon of relevant sequence – **समर्पक अनुक्रमाचे अनुक्रम तत्त्व/सूत्र** – वर्गीकरणासाठी एकापेक्षा अधिक लक्षणांचा वापर करताना वर्गीकरणाच्या उद्दिष्टाला समर्पक असा लक्षणक्रम असावा.

canon of scheduled mnemonics – **तक्त्यांतर्गत स्मरण सुलभतेचे तत्त्व/सूत्र** – ग्रंथ वर्गीकरणात विविध उपविषयात वापरलेल्या संज्ञा एकाच अर्थाने वापराव्यात असे हे सूत्र सांगते.

canon of seminal mnemonics – **बीजमूलक स्मरणसुलभतेचे तत्त्व/सूत्र** – ग्रंथ वर्गीकरण तक्त्यात समान गुणधर्म असणाऱ्या विविध विषयांना एकच चिन्ह वापरावे असे हे सूत्र सुचविते.

canon of sought heading – **समर्पक मथळासूत्र** – तालिकेमध्ये नोंद करण्यासाठी वर्गांकाचे विश्लेषण करून नोंदशीर्षके तयार केली जातात. येथे वर्गांकातील प्रत्येक घटकाचा अर्थ देता आला पाहिजे. अशा पद्धतीने समर्पकरीत्या मथळा देण्याविषयी हे सूत्र मार्गदर्शक ठरते.

canon of subordinate classes – **उपवर्गांकाचे (गौणवर्गांचे) तत्त्व/सूत्र** – एका विषयातील उपविषयाच्या चिन्हांकनाद्वारे त्याच्या मुख्य विषयाची कल्पना आली पाहिजे असे हे सूत्र सांगते.

canon of systematic mnemonics – **व्यवस्थित स्मरण सुलभतेचे तत्त्व/सूत्र** – वर्गीकरण करताना वापरलेला संज्ञांचा क्रम असा असावा की ज्यामुळे स्मरण सुलभता साधली जाईल असे हे सूत्र सांगते.

canon of uniformity – **एकतेचे तत्त्व/सूत्र** – ग्रंथवर्गीकरण पद्धतीतील विषय–उपविषय मांडणीत एकसूत्रता असावी असे हे सूत्र सांगते.

canon of vercal mnemonics – **शाब्दिक स्मरणसुलभतेचे तत्त्व/सूत्र** – विशिष्ट उपविषयातील उपगटाकरिता शाब्दिक रचनेचा वापर करून उपगट तयार केले जातात. मात्र, त्यासाठीचा निवडलेला शब्द स्मरणसुलभ असावा असे हे सूत्र सांगते.

canon for arrays of classes – **वर्गांच्या पंक्तीविषयक तत्त्व/सूत्र** – एकाच लक्षणगुणावर आधारित, समान योग्यतेच्या वर्गांचा हा समूह असतो. आपसातील संबंधानुसार त्यांची रचना असते, या योजनेला 'पंक्ती' म्हणतात. प्रत्येक वर्गीकरण पद्धतीत मुख्य वर्गांची पहिली पंक्ती असते. प्रत्येक मुख्य वर्गांचे विभाग ही दुसरी पंक्ती व उपविभाग ही त्यापुढील पंक्ती असते.

canon for classification – **वर्गीकरणासाठीचे तत्त्व/सूत्र.**

canon for filiatory sequence – **नात्यानुसार अनुक्रमाचे तत्त्व/सूत्र** – ग्रंथ वर्गीकरणातील उपविषयांची रचना करताना त्यातील नातेसंबंध विचारात घेतले पाहिजेत असे हे सूत्र सुचविते.

canon for terminology – **संज्ञाविषयकतेचे तत्त्व/सूत्र** – ग्रंथवर्गीकरणात वापरल्या जाणाऱ्या संज्ञा प्रमाणित व वापरातील असाव्यात असे हे सूत्र सांगते.

canonical – **सूत्रबद्ध/सुसंगत.**

canonical class – **सुत्रबद्ध वर्ग/पारंपरिक वर्ग** – वर्गीकरण सूत्रानुसार ग्रंथाचा वर्ग मुख्य वर्गांची सूत्रबद्ध/ रूढ नियमानुसार केलेली विभागणी.

canonical order – **सूत्रबद्ध/प्रचलित/रूढ विषयाचा क्रम** – नोंदींचा गट असेल तेव्हा नोंदींची रचना करण्यासाठी अनुवर्णाव्यतिरिक्त निवडलेला क्रम.

canonical sequence – **विषयांचा सूत्रबद्ध अनुक्रम.**

capitals – **आद्याक्षरे** – इंग्रजी वर्णमालेतील मुख्य लिपीतील आद्याक्षरे.

caps lock – **मोठ्या लिपीतील अक्षरे उमटविण्यासाठी संगणक फलकावरील कळ.**

caption – **मथळा/सूचक शीर्षक** – मथळा, लेख, चित्र, आकृती यांना दिलेले सूचक शीर्षक.

card – **पत्र** – ग्रंथालयात वापरले जाणारे आयताकार नोंदपत्र.

card cabinet – **पत्र खण/कप्पा** – पत्रांची रचना करावयासाठी असलेले कपाट/खणांचा समूह.

card catalogue – **पत्रतालिका** – ग्रंथालयातील तालिका, ज्यामधील नोंदी विविध पत्रावर केल्या जातात.

card charging system – **पत्र देवघेव पद्धती** – ग्रंथपत्रांचा वापर करून तयार केलेली ग्रंथ देवघेवीची पद्धत.

card drawer – **पत्र ठेवण्यासाठीचा खण.**

card form catalogue – **पत्ररूप तालिका** – पत्रकांवर नोंदी करून, त्यांची क्रमवार रचना केलेली तालिका.

card index – **पत्ररूप निर्देश** – पत्रकांद्वारे तयार केलेला निर्देश.

card issue system – **पत्ररूप देवघेव पद्धती.**

card number – **ग्रंथपत्रक क्रमांक.**

card set – **पत्ररूप संच.**

card tray – **ग्रंथपत्र/तालिकापत्र तबक** – ग्रंथपत्र अथवा तालिकापत्र ठेवावयाचे तबक.

care – **निगा/संरक्षण/काळजी.**

carrel / cubicle / alcove / study – **संशोधनकक्ष** – ग्रंथालयातील छोटी अभ्यासिका.

cardinal value – **संख्यावाचक मूल्य** – अशी संकल्पना की ज्यांचे १,२,३,४ इत्यादी प्रकारे गणितीय मूल्य दर्शविता येते.

carry forward – **पुढच्या भागात घेणे.**

cartobibliography – **नकाशांची सूची.**

cartography – **नकाशाविद्या** – नकाशा तयार करण्याचे शास्त्र व कला.

case – **पुस्तके ठेवण्यासाठी छोटे खोके** – बरेचदा खंड प्रकाशन करताना खंड एकत्र मावतील असे खोके तयार करून एकत्र खंड विक्रीस ठेवला जातो.

cassette – चुंबकीय फीत.

cassette (audio) – ध्वनिफीत – ज्यावर आवाज नोंदविता व ऐकता येतो.

cassette (video) – चित्रफीत – ज्याद्वारे चित्र नोंदविता व पाहता येते.

catalogue – तालिका – वर्णाच्या अथवा वर्गांकाच्या किंवा योजनाबद्ध नियमावलीनुसार केलेली आशयदर्शक रचना म्हणजे तालिका.

catalogue drawer/tray – तालिकाकप्पा – ग्रंथालयात तालिकापत्र रचना करण्यासाठी असलेला खण, कप्पा.

catalogue entry – तालिकापत्र नोंद.

cataloguer – तालिकाकार – तालिकेतील नोंदी तालिका संहितेनुसार/नियमावलीनुसार तयार करणारी व्यक्ती.

cataloguing – तालिकीकरण – तालिका नोंदी करण्याची कला, प्रक्रिया.

cataloguing department/section – तालिकीकरण विभाग – तालिकीकरणाचे काम पाहणारा ग्रंथालयातील विभाग.

cataloguing in publication / cataloguing in source – प्रकाशनपूर्व तालिकीकरण – ग्रंथ छपाईपूर्वी ग्रंथविषयक माहिती तालिकीकरण संस्थेकडे सोपविली जाते. ही संस्था तालिकापत्र तयार करून प्रकाशकाला पाठविते. यानंतर हे तालिकापत्र ग्रंथाच्या शीर्षकपृष्ठाच्या मागील बाजूस छापले जाते.

cataloguing rules – तालिकीकरण नियम – तालिका तयार करण्याचे नियम.

cataloguing technique / art – तालिकीकरणाचे तंत्र/कला.

catalogues catalogurum– ग्रंथतालिकांची तालिका.

catchword – सूचकशब्द/पर्यायी शब्द –

(१) प्रत्येक पानावरील मजकूर संपल्यावर खाली एक शब्द लिहिला जातो. हा शब्द पुढील पानावर पहिला शब्द असतो. ही पद्धत ग्रंथबांधणीसाठी पाने जुळविताना फार उपयुक्त ठरते. परंतु, ही पद्धत १९व्या शतकात बंद पडलेली दिसते.

(२) ज्ञानकोश, विश्वकोश यांमध्ये प्रत्येक पानाच्या मजकुराच्या वर किंवा स्तंभाच्या वरच्या बाजूस असलेला शब्द.

(३) निर्देशन करताना, निर्देशातील नोंदीचे स्थान ठरविणारा शब्द.

catchword entry – सूचकशब्द नोंद/पर्यायी शब्द नोंद/लक्ष्यवेधीशब्द नोंद – ग्रंथशीर्षकातील लक्ष्यवेधी शब्दांची तालिकेतील ग्रंथसूची किंवा निर्देशातील नोंद.

catchword title – ग्रंथाचे लक्ष्यवेधी शीर्षक – सहज लक्षात राहण्यासारखा शब्द वा वाक्प्रचार असलेले शीर्षक.

category – प्रवर्ग – वर्गवारीमध्ये एखाद्या नोंदीची मुख्य गट/प्रकार.

category – favoured category – प्राधान्य वर्ग.

category – fundamental category – मूलभूत प्रवर्ग.

caution money / deposit – अनामत रक्कम/ठेव – ग्रंथालय सभासदत्व मिळविण्याच्या प्रक्रियेचा एक भाग म्हणून ग्रंथालयाने घेतलेली अनामत रक्कम जी सभासदत्व रद्द झाल्यानंतर परत करण्यात येते.

ceased puclication – स्थगित केलेले प्रकाशन – अनेक खंडांमधले प्रकाशन अपूर्ण असताना स्थगिती दिलेले प्रकाशन.

censorship – प्रसारबंदी – सरकारने बंदी घातलेल्या प्रकाशनाचे उत्पादन, वितरण, प्रचलन, विक्री इ. करण्यास शासनाने केलेला मज्जाव.

central catalogue – केंद्रीय तालिका – अनेक ग्रंथालयांनी मिळून तयार केलेली तालिका.

central library – केंद्रीय/मध्यवर्ती ग्रंथालय.

central processing unit – संगणकातील मध्यवर्ती भाग – यामध्ये संगणकाला दिलेल्या सूचना अमलात आणण्यासंबंधीचे संस्करण केले जाते.

central registration – मुख्य पंजीकरण.

central shelf list – प्रमुख स्थान यादी.

centralised cataloguing – केंद्रीभूत/मध्यवर्ती तालिकीकरण – एक मध्यवर्ती संघटना वा ग्रंथालयाद्वारे तालिकीकरण करण्यात येते व त्यापासून छापील अगर संगणकीकृत तालिकापत्रांचे सभासद ग्रंथालयांना वितरण करण्यात येते.

centralised processing – मध्यवर्ती/केंद्रीय संस्करण – अमेरिकेमध्ये ग्रंथखरेदी, तालिकीकरण, वर्गीकरण या प्रक्रिया ग्रंथ, ध्वनिफिती व इतर ग्रंथालयसाहित्य याबाबत संस्करण क्रिया मध्यवर्ती केंद्रामध्ये केल्या जातात.

centralised registration – केंद्रीय मध्यवर्ती सभासद नोंदणी – ग्रंथालय पद्धतीतील प्रत्येक ग्रंथालयाच्या वाचकांची मध्यवर्ती नोंदणी.

centred entry/heading – केंद्रस्थान शीर्षक/नोंद – एखाद्या सर्वसमावेशक विषयाला जेव्हा स्वतंत्र वर्गांक देता येत नाही त्यावेळी सलग क्रमांकांनी दाखविलेला वर्गांक.

cess – कर – नागरिकांनी विशिष्ट प्रमाणात विकासासाठी शासन अथवा स्थानिक स्वराज्य संस्थांना द्यावयाची रक्कम.

cess library – कराद्वारे चालविण्यात येणारे ग्रंथालय.

chain – शृंखला/साखळी – वर्गीकरण करताना उपवर्गाची केलेली साखळी.

chain indexing – निर्देशन पद्धती/शृंखला निर्देशन – डॉ. एस. आर. रंगनाथन् यांनी सांगितलेली.

chain mark – शृंखला चिन्ह.

chain of classes – वर्गशृंखला – वर्गांची साखळी.

chain procedure – शृंखला पद्धती – डॉ. रंगनाथन् यांनी चिन्हांकापासून तालिकाशीर्षक प्राप्त करण्याकरिता नमूद केलेली पद्धती.

changed name – बदललेले नाव.

changed title – बदललेले शीर्षक.

change of title note – परिवर्तित शीर्षक टीप – बदललेल्या ग्रंथशीर्षकाची तालिकापत्रातील माहिती.

change of record – नोंद/अभिलेखातील परिवर्तन.

chapter – धडा/प्रकरण/विभाग/अध्याय.

chapter heading – प्रकरणाचे शीर्षक.

character – एकक – एक अक्षर, संख्या किंवा चिन्ह.

character code – अक्षरचिन्ह संकेत – उदा. & = and

character count – मजकुरातील एकूण एक अक्षर/चिन्ह/संख्या यांची मोजणी.

character set – अक्षरचिन्हांचा संच.

characteristics – लक्षणे/गुणधर्म – वर्गीकरणासाठी निवडलेला गुणधर्म.

characteristic of a classification – वर्गीकरणाचे लक्षण – ग्रंथांचे विषयानुसार वर्गीकरण करताना वर्गीकरणकाराला विषयाची वैशिष्ट्य किंवा लक्षणगुण आधारभूत मानावा लागतो. त्यानुसार वर्गीकरणकाराने निवडलेला गुणधर्म.

charge – (१) किंमत/वसुली/ग्रंथाचा मोबदला. (२) ग्रंथ वाचनासाठी देणे-घेणे.

charges (collection) – वसुली/जमा.

charging and discharging – ग्रंथ देवघेव – ग्रंथालयातील ग्रंथ उसनवारीने देतांना/घेतांना केलेल्या नोंदी.

charging department – देवघेव विभाग.

charging desk – देवघेवीच्या कामकाजासाठी वापरण्यात येणारे मेज.

charging file – देवघेव संचिका.

charging method/ system – वाचनसाहित्य देवघेवीची पद्धत.

charging record – देवघेवीची नोंद.

charging slip – देवघेव चिठ्ठी.

charging tray – ग्रंथ-देवघेव पत्रे ठेवावयाचा कप्पा/तबक.

chart – तक्ता – तक्तारूपातील माहिती.

cheap edition – **स्वस्त आवृत्ती** – स्वस्त किमतीत उपलब्ध करून दिलेली आवृत्ती ज्यास 'पेपर बॅक आवृत्ती' म्हणतात; कारण त्याची बांधणी पुठ्ठ्याऐवजी जाड कागदाची असते.

check card – तपासणी पत्र.

check digit – **तपासणी अंक** – प्रत्येक ग्रंथाला दिलेल्या क्रमांकामधील (ISBN) मधील शेवटचा अंक हा तपासणी अंक होय.

check list – तपासणी यादी.

check marks – **तपासणी खुणा** – तालिकाकाराने तालिकेत नोंदी करण्यासाठी शीर्षक पत्रावर पेन्सिलने केलेल्या खुणा.

check out / charge out – तपासून बाहेर पाठविलेले साहित्य.

checking – **तपासणी** – चूक किंवा बरोबर हे पडताळून पाहण्याची क्रिया.

chemist – रसायनतज्ज्ञ.

Chicago style manual – संशोधनपर लिखाणात वापरावयाची शैली.

chief librarian – प्रमुख ग्रंथपाल.

chief source of information – **माहितीचे प्रमुख साधन** – ग्रंथाच्या तालिकीकरण नोंदी करण्यासाठी आवश्यक ती माहिती देणारे साधन.

children's library / junior library / junior department –**बालग्रंथालय** – केवळ बालकांसाठी पुस्तके व इतर साहित्य यांचा केलेला संग्रह. यामध्ये ग्रंथालयाची मांडणी व साहित्य बालकांना उपयुक्त होईल (कमी उंचीचे) अशी रचना केली जाते.

chip – **पटलिका** – इंटिग्रेटेड सर्किटसाठी अमेरिकनांनी वापरलेला शब्द. विशिष्ट प्रक्रिया केलेल्या सिलिकॉनच्या छोट्या तुकड्यावर प्रचंड माहिती/आज्ञा साठवण्यासाठी तयार केलेली एक इलेक्ट्रॉनिक तबकडी.

chirograph – औपचारिक हस्तलिखित प्रलेख.

chiroxylographic book – **ठसेमुद्रण केलेले हस्तलिखित** – चित्रे, आकृत्यांचे ठसेमुद्रण करून मजकूर हाताने लिहिलेला ग्रंथ.

chorographic map – **फार मोठा प्रदेश** – देशाचे क्षेत्र छोट्या प्रमाणात दर्शविणारा नकाशा.

chorestomathy – **परकीय भाषेतील लेखांचा संग्रह** – विशिष्ट भाषेचा किंवा साहित्याचा नमुना म्हणून वापर केला जातो.

chronical literature – **बखर वाङ्मय.**

chronogram – **कालगणना, संकेत** – लेखनकाल निदर्शक शब्द.

chronological – **अनुकाळ (काळानुसार)** – कालानुक्रमे.

chronological class – **निर्मितीक्रमानुसार रचना केलेला ग्रंथवर्गीकरण पद्धतीतील वर्ग/विषय.**

chronological device – **कालक्रम/अनुकाळ क्लृप्ती** – द्विबिंदू वर्गीकरणपद्धतीमध्ये कालखंड दर्शविण्यासाठी वापरण्याची क्लृप्ती. उदा. मानसशास्त्रातील 'मनोविश्लेषण पद्धती' – **YMgs** म्हणजे १९००

chronological division – **कालक्रमानुसार विभाजन.**

chronological facet – **कालदर्शक पैलू.**

chronological order – **अनुकाळ क्रम/कालक्रमानुसार रचना** – कालक्रमानुसार रचना केलेला क्रम किंवा वर्गीकरण पद्धतीत अथवा तालिकेतील क्रमाला (प्रकाशनाचा दिनांक, प्रकाशन वृत्त किंवा कॉपीराइट) किंवा प्रत्यक्ष त्या साहित्याला (ग्रंथपुस्तिका किंवा कात्रणे) यांना ही युक्ती लागू पडते.

chronology – **कालगणनाविद्या** – कालनिश्चिती करण्याचे शास्त्र.

chrysography – **सुवर्णाक्षरांनी लिहिण्याची कला.**

circa – **शिरस** – ग्रंथबांधणीसाठी वापरण्यात येणारा चिकट पदार्थ.

circular – **परिपत्रक** – बऱ्याच लोकांना पाठवावयाचे छापील पत्रक, जाहिरात वगैरे.

circular crackets – **गोल कंस** – ज्याचा वापर काही वर्गीकरण पद्धतीत केला जातो. उदा. (   )

circulating – **आवर्त/पुनरावर्तक/पसरणारा.**

circulation – **देवघेव/अभिसरण/परिवहन/प्रसार/खप/परिचलन.**

circulation control system – **ग्रंथ देवघेव नियंत्रण पद्धती** – वाचकाने घेतलेले पुस्तक रीतसर नोंदणी करून घेतले आहे किंवा नाही यावर नियंत्रण ठेवणारी पद्धती.

circulation department – **ग्रंथालयातील ग्रंथ देवघेव विभाग.**

circulation desk – **ग्रंथ देवघेव कट्टा/टेबल** – ग्रंथ देवघेव करावयाचे मेज.

circulation record – **देवघेव नोंद/अभिलेख.**

circulation statistics – **ग्रंथ देवघेव सांख्यिकी** – ग्रंथालय वाचकांची मागणी अभ्यासण्याच्या दृष्टीने अशी आकडेवारी ठेवली जाते.

circulation work – ग्रंथ देवघेव कार्य – ग्रंथालयातील वाचनसाहित्य तात्पुरते वाचण्यासाठी देणे व परत घेण्याचे कार्य.

citation – उद्धरण/प्रासिसंदर्भ/उल्लेख/अवतरणे – संशोधन अहवालात त्यापूर्वीच्या संशोधनाबाबत दिलेले संदर्भ.

citation analysis – उद्धरण विश्लेषण – वैज्ञानिक लिखाणातील पूर्वीच्या उद्धृत लिखाणाचे विश्लेषण.

citation index – उल्लेख निर्देश/सूची – मूळ लेख प्रसिद्ध झाल्यावर अन्य लेखात त्या लेखाचा संदर्भ दिलेला असतो किंवा काही मजकूर उद्धृत केलेला असतो, ज्या लेखातून संदर्भ/उद्धरण दिलेले असते अशा लेखांची सूची.

citation order – उद्धरण रचना – विशिष्ट प्रलेखाला वर्गांक देण्यासाठी विभाजनसूत्रांची केलेली उपयोजक रचना.

citation style – उद्धरण शैली– पूर्वीच्या लिखाणाचा दाखला देताना ग्रंथ वर्णनासाठी वापरावयाची पद्धत.

cite – उतारा करणे, घेणे – इतरांचे लिखाण उद्धृत करणे.

cited article – उद्धृत लेख – पूर्वी प्रकाशित लेखाचा केलेला उल्लेख.

cited author – उद्धृत लेखक – पूर्वीच्या लेखकाचा केलेला उल्लेख.

city central library – शहर/नागरी मध्यवर्ती ग्रंथालय.

city library – नागरी ग्रंथालय.

civilization – सभ्यता/सुधारणा/संस्कृती.

claim – दावा/मागणी – सत्य आहे असे म्हणणे, आग्रही प्रतिपादन.

claim for book by the reader – ग्रंथवाचकाचा मागणीहक्क – पुस्तक ग्रंथालयातून अन्य वाचकास दिले असल्यास त्या वाचकाने परत केल्यावर प्रथम पुस्तक घेण्याविषयीचा हक्क.

clandestine literature / secret literature / underground literature – गोपनीय साहित्य – युद्धप्रसंगी किंवा राजकारणदृष्ट्या महत्त्वाचे साहित्य.

clandestine press / underground press / secret press – गोपनीय छापखाना –गोपनीयरीत्या चालविलेला छापखाना.

class – वर्ग – काही समान गुणधर्म असलेल्या संकल्पना किंवा वस्तूंचा गट.

class elsewhere note – अन्यत्र वर्गांक द्या – शीर्षकाखाली दिलेली अशी नोंद जी संबंधित विषयास किंवा त्याच्या उपविषयात वेगळा वर्गांक दर्शविते.

class entry – वर्गांक नोंद – तालिकेच्या शीर्षक रेषेवर वर्गांक असणारी नोंद.

class guide – वर्गांक मार्गदर्शक – ग्रंथकक्षातील वर्गांकनिहाय रचना दर्शविणारे मार्गदर्शक फलक.

class here-notes – 'येथे वर्गांक द्या'/'येथे वर्गीकरण करा', अशी सूचना देणारी टीप – ज्या उपविषयाचे वर्गीकरण करावयाचे तो विषय सकृतदृष्ट्या या उपविषयाचा भाग असतो. सामान्यपणे ज्या विषयाला वर्गांक द्यावयाचा तो ज्या शीर्षकाखाली ही टीप दिलेली असते त्यापेक्षा विस्तृत असतो.

index entry – निर्देशांमध्ये केलेली विशिष्ट वर्गाची नोंद.

class mark – वर्गदर्शक खूण.

class number – वर्गांक – विशिष्ट वर्गीकरण पद्धतीनुसार पुस्तकाला दिलेला वर्गदर्शक अंक.

classed catalogue / classified catalogue – वर्गीकृत तालिका – विषयाच्या वर्गवारीनुसार क्रमाने नोंदींची रचना केलेली तालिका.

classics – चिरसाहित्य/अभिजात ग्रंथ – लोकप्रिय आणि उत्कृष्ट दर्जाचा ग्रंथ किंवा इतर कलाकृती जी अनेक वर्षांपासून लोकप्रिय असते.

classics device – अभिजात क्लृप्ती/ग्रंथ युक्ती – ग्रंथवर्गीकरणातील एक चिन्हांकन सूत्र ज्यामुळे सर्व अभिजात ग्रंथ व त्यावरील सर्व साहित्य, आवृत्या, समालोचन एकत्र आणले जाते. द्विबिंदू वर्गीकरणामध्ये 'x' हे अक्षर वर्गांकाच्या पुढे वापरून अभिजात क्लृप्तीचा वापर केला जातो.

classical – अभिजात/प्रतिष्ठित/शास्त्रीय/सरस/सर्वोत्कृष्ट.

classical author – अभिजात/लोकप्रिय लेखक – अभिजात ग्रंथ लिहिणारा लेखक.

classical school – तत्त्वज्ञानातील एक संप्रदाय/विचारप्रवाह.

classical theory – अभिजात ग्रंथाचा सिद्धान्त.

classification – वर्गीकरण – कल्पित वा प्रत्यक्ष दिसणाऱ्या कल्पना, वस्तू इत्यादींची त्यातील साम्यानुसार करावयाच्या मांडणीची कला अथवा शास्त्र.

classification chart – वर्गीकरण तक्ता – वर्गीकरण करण्यासाठी विषय-उपविषय मार्गदर्शक तक्ता.

classification code – वर्गीकरण संहिता – वर्गीकरण करण्याची नियमावली किंवा संहिता.

classification schedule – वर्गीकरण परिशिष्ट – ग्रंथ वर्गीकरण करण्यासाठी मुख्य विषयांची व त्यांच्या उपविषयांची एका विशिष्ट पद्धतीने त्यांच्या समवेत चिन्हांकन दर्शविणारे हस्तलिखित अथवा छापील यादी (तयार वर्गांकाचे कोष्टक).

classification scheme (system) – वर्गीकरण पद्धत – ग्रंथाचे वर्गीकरण करण्यासाठी वापरण्याची वर्गीकरण पद्धती.

classificationist – वर्गीकरणकार/ग्रंथवर्गीकरण पद्धतीचा रचनाकार – निरनिराळ्या विषयांसाठी तंत्रशुद्ध वर्गीकरण पद्धती तयार करणारी व्यक्ती.

classified – वर्गीकृत – वर्गांकानुसार.

classified arrangement – **वर्गीकृत रचना** – ग्रंथालयातील ग्रंथांची विशिष्ट वर्गीकरण पद्धतीनुसार केलेली रचना.

classified catalogue – **वर्गीकृत तालिका** – ज्यातील तालिकापत्रे वर्गांच्या चढत्या क्रमानुसार आयोजित केली जातात.

classified catalogue code – **वर्गीकृत तालिका संहिता** – डॉ. एस. आर. रंगनाथन् यांनी १९३४ मध्ये तयार केलेली तालिका तयार करण्याची नियमावली.

classified documentation list – **वर्गीकृत प्रलेखन यादी** – सूक्ष्म विषयांवरील लेखांच्या नोंदी असलेली यादी.

classified index – **वर्गीकृत निर्देश** – विषय शीर्षकानुसार नोंदी करून तयार केलेला निर्देश.

classified library – **वर्गीकृत ग्रंथालय** – ज्यातील ग्रंथ अधिकृत वर्गीकरण पद्धतीनुसार रचना केलेले आहेत असे ग्रंथालय.

classified material – **वर्गीकृत साधने** – वर्गीकृत रचना केलेली ग्रंथेतर साधने. उदा. ध्वनिफिती यांची यादी.

classified order – **वर्गीकृत रचना** – विशिष्ट वर्गीकरण पद्धतीनुसार केलेली ग्रंथरचना.

classified subject catalogue – **वर्गीकृत विषय तालिका** – वर्गीकृत तालिकेमध्ये विषयनोंद दिलेली तालिका.

classified subject index – **वर्गीकृत/विषयनिर्देश** – वर्गीकृत विषयानुसार नोंद केलेला निर्देश.

classify – **वर्गीकृत रचना करणे** – समान गुणधर्मांच्या नोंदी एका शीर्षकाखाली आणण्याचे कार्य.

clay tablet – **इष्टिका/मृत्तिकापट्टी** – प्राचीन काळात लिखाणासाठी वापरात असलेले मातीपासून बनविण्यात येणारे लेखनसाहित्य.

clearing – **वटवणी/निष्कासन/समाशोधन.**

clearing house – **समाशोधन केंद्र/संग्रह गृह** – संशोधन आणि प्रगती याविषयी माहिती व नोंदी यांचा संग्रह करणारी संस्था.

click – **संगणकाच्या मूषकाची (माऊस) कळ दाबून प्रक्रिया चालू करणे.**

clinical librarian – **ग्रंथोपचारासाठी नेमलेला ग्रंथपाल.**

clip art – **संगणकात उपलब्ध असलेली चित्रे/आकृत्या यांचा संच.**

clipping / cutting – **कात्रण** – वृत्तपत्र, मासिक इत्यादींतील मुद्रित लेख. त्यात एखाद्या विषयावर विशेष माहिती असते.

clipping bureau – **कात्रणसेवा गृह** – वृत्तपत्रे व मासिके यांमधील कात्रणे कापून सभासदांना पाठविणारी व्यापारी संस्था.

clipping file – **कात्रण वही/संचिका.**

clipping service – **कात्रण सेवा** – विशिष्ट विषयावरील कात्रणे, मासिके व वर्तमानपत्रातून कापून रोजच्या रोज सभासदांना पाठविण्याची सोय/सेवा.

cloak room – **अनामत गृह** – प्रवासी/वाचक यांचेकडील साहित्य तात्पुरते ठेवण्यासाठीची खोली.

clone – **(संगणकाच्या हार्डवेअरची) हुबेहूब प्रतिकृती.**

closed access – **नियंत्रित प्रवेश** – बंद प्रवेश पद्धती ज्यात वाचकांना ग्रंथाच्या कपाटाजवळ जाऊन ग्रंथ हाताळण्यास परवानगी नसते. ग्रंथालयातील कर्मचारी वाचनसाहित्य कपाटामधून काढून त्यांना आणून देतात.

closed array – **मर्यादित पंक्ती** – वर्गीकरण पद्धतीत उपलब्ध सर्व चिन्हे वापरलेली असतील अशा पंक्ती

closed bibliography – **पूर्ण झालेली ग्रंथसूची.**

closed entry – **बंदिस्त/बद्ध नोंद** – माला प्रकाशनातील सर्व खंडांची पूर्ण नोंद असलेली तालिका नोंद.

closed file – **बंद संचिका** – सर्व प्रक्रिया पूर्ण केलेली संचिका.

closed indexing system – **बंदिस्त निर्देशन पद्धती** – ज्यात नवीन विषयांची नोंद सहजपणे समाविष्ट करता येत नाही.

closed library – **मर्यादित प्रवेश असलेले ग्रंथालय.**

closed shelves – **बंदिस्त कपाटे/अलमारी** – या कपाटांना दरवाजे/कुलूप लावण्याची सोय असते.

closed sequence – **बंदिस्त/बद्ध क्रम.**

closed stack – **प्रवेशबंदी असलेला संग्रह.**

closing file – **समारोप संचिका** – संगणकामध्ये माहितीचा गट पडद्यावरून तात्पुरता काढून टाकणे.

cloth binding – **कापडी बांधणी** – ग्रंथाची बांधणी पुठ्ठ्यावर कापड वापरून करणे ज्यामुळे वेष्टण टिकाऊ बनते.

clue page – **सुगावा पृष्ठ** – ग्रंथालयाने निश्चित केलेले असे पृष्ठ वा पृष्ठे की ज्यावर ग्रंथालयाचा शिक्का उमटविला जातो आणि दाखलअंक लिहिला जातो. या पृष्ठावरील माहितीमुळे ग्रंथाची सुरुवातीची अथवा शेवटची पृष्ठे गहाळ झाली तरीही ग्रंथालयाची मालकी सिद्ध करता येते.

cluster – **संगणक तबकडीवरील एक भाग, (संबंधित प्रलेखांचा संच)**

co–author/joint author – **सहलेखक/सहग्रंथकार** – ग्रंथाचे लेखन दोन अथवा अधिक लेखकांनी केले असेल तेव्हा पहिला लेखक वगळून इतर लेखकांना सहलेखक म्हणून संबोधले जाते.

cob paper – **कागदाचा एक प्रकार.**

COBOL (Common Business Oriented Language) – सूचनापट तयार करण्यासाठी तयार केलेली व्यावसायाभिमुख आज्ञावली.

code – संहिता/नियमावली/संकेत – विशिष्ट परिस्थितीत उपयोगात आणण्यासाठी तयार केलेली मान्यताप्राप्त नियमावली.

code area – संगणकामध्ये संकेतचिन्हासाठी राखीव क्षेत्र.

code of conduct – आचारसंहिता – पाळावयाची आदर्श नियमावली.

codex – पोथीरूप हस्तलिखित.

co-editor / joint editor – सहसंपादक.

co-education – सहशिक्षण – यामध्ये स्त्री-पुरुष एकाच अध्ययन कक्षात अध्ययन करतात.

co-effibient – गुणांक/गुणक/सहगुणक.

co-extensiveness – समव्यापकता – ग्रंथवर्गीकरण करताना सहयोगी ग्रंथ विषय लक्षात घेऊन वर्गीकरण करण्याचे तत्त्व.

coherence – सुसंगती/सुसंवाद

coil binding / spiral binding – सर्पिल बांधणी – या प्रकारच्या बांधणीत प्लास्टिकच्या साखळीद्वारे ग्रंथाची पृष्ठे एकत्र बांधली जातात.

collation – खंड पृष्ठादिवृत्तान्त – तालिकीकरण करताना ग्रंथाचे प्राकृतिक वर्णन न देता त्यामध्ये खंडांची संख्या, पृष्ठसंख्या, रकाने, लेख, चित्रे, छायाचित्रे, नकाशे, बांधणी, आकार इत्यादी तपशील नमूद केलेला असतो.

collaboration – सहयोग/सहकार्य.

collaborator – सहयोगक/सहयोगी/साहाय्यक – प्रदान/मुख्य ग्रंथकारास ग्रंथनिर्मितीमध्ये मदत करणारी व्यक्ती म्हणजेच सहयोगी (साहाय्यक) ग्रंथकार होय.

collaborator entry – सहयोगी लेखकाची नोंद.

collage – कोलाज – चित्रे, फोटो, कागद, कापड इत्यादींचा वापर करून तयार केलेले चित्र.

collated term / bound term / generic term – सहसंबंधित संज्ञा – निर्देशनामध्ये वापरली जाणारी सहसंबंधित संज्ञा.

collected edition / omnibus edition – समग्र आवृत्ती – लेखकाच्या एक/अनेक खंडातील प्रकाशनांची समरूप बांधणी, आवृत्ती.

collected works – संकलित साहित्य – एखाद्या लेखकाचे आतापर्यंत प्रकाशित व अप्रकाशित साहित्य एक किंवा अनेक खंडांमध्ये समरूप बांधणी करून प्रकाशित केले जाते.

collection – **संग्रह/ग्रंथालयाचा संग्रह** – एका लेखकाच्या अनेक लेखांचे/कृतींचे किंवा अनेक लेखकांच्या लेखांचे/कृतींचे केलेले संकलन म्हणजेच संग्रह होय.

collection development – **संग्रह विकास** – ग्रंथसंग्रहामध्ये नवीन ग्रंथ मिळविणे, प्रक्रिया करणे, ग्रंथ सांभाळणे व या सर्वांचा अभ्यास करण्यासाठी पुढील ग्रंथयोजना आखण्याची प्रक्रिया.

collection management – **संग्रह व्यवस्थापन** – ग्रंथसंग्रहाची एकूण व्यवस्था पाहण्याची प्रक्रिया.

collection number – **संग्रहांक** – ग्रंथ ग्रंथालयातील ज्या दालनात (संग्रहात) ठेवावयाचा आहे तो संग्रह दर्शविणारा अंक. उदा. संदर्भ विभाग, दुर्मिळ ग्रंथ विभाग, नियतकालिक विभाग, पाठ्यपुस्तके विभाग इत्यादी.

collective biography – **व्यक्तिचरित्रांचा संग्रह** – अनेक विषयक्षेत्राशी संबंधित व्यक्तींच्या चरित्रांचा संग्रह.

collective cataloguing – **संग्रहित तालिकीकरण** – ग्रंथेतर किरकोळ साहित्य एकत्र करून त्याला संग्रहित शीर्षकाखाली रचना करणे अशा सर्व शीर्षकांची नोंदतालिका करणे.

collective entries – **संग्रहित नोंदी** – निवडक तालिकीकरण करताना एकाच ठिकाणी एका विषयाच्या किंवा संबंधित विषयांच्या नोंदी आणल्या जातात. विशेषत: हस्तपुस्तिकांसाठी ही पद्धत वापरली जाते.

collective title – **सामूहिक शीर्षक** – एकाच शीर्षकाखाली वेगवेगळ्या लेखकांचे लेख एकत्रितरीत्या प्रकाशित केले जातात.

collective via direct cataloguing – **संग्रहित/अंतर्भूत प्रत्यक्ष तालिकीकरण** – एकाच लेखकाची अनेक पुस्तके विविध टोपणनावांनी प्रसिद्ध करण्याचे तत्त्व. उदा. शिरवाडकर वि.वा./कुसुमाग्रज/ विशाखा.

college – **महाविद्यालय** – उच्च शिक्षण देणारी संस्था.

college library – **महाविद्यालयीन ग्रंथालय** – महाविद्यालयाच्या शिक्षक व विद्यार्थ्यांना उपयुक्त असे महाविद्यालयाने चालविलेले ग्रंथालय.

collocation – **संज्ञांचे सहस्थापन** – वर्गीकरणातील उपवर्गांची रचना करण्याची प्रक्रिया.

colon – **द्विबिंदू (:)** – डॉ. रंगनाथन् यांनी ग्रंथवर्गीकरण पद्धतीत वापरलेले एक चिन्ह.

colon abbreviations – **द्विबिंदू संक्षिप्त नामकरण** – सी. ए. कटर यांनी सांगितलेली पद्धती. ग्रंथलेखकाचे पूर्ण नाव लिहिण्याऐवजी पहिले अक्षर लिहून त्यापुढे द्विबिंदू दिला जातो. पुरुष लेखक असेल तर उभ्या पातळीत व स्त्री लेखिका असेल आडव्या पातळीत द्विबिंदू दिला जातो. उदा. H : (Henry) M .. (Mary)

colon book number – **द्विबिंदू ग्रंथांक** – द्विबिंदू वर्गीकरण पद्धती वापरून तयार केलेला ग्रंथांक.

colon classification – **द्विबिंदू वर्गीकरण** – डॉ. एस. आर. रंगनाथन् यांनी १९३३ साली प्रकाशित केलेली विशेषत: भारतीय ग्रंथांसाठी उपयुक्त अशी वर्गीकरण पद्धती.

colon notation – **द्विबिंदू चिन्हांकन** – डॉ. रंगनाथन् यांच्या वर्गीकरण पद्धतीमध्ये वापरलेली चिन्हांकन पद्धती.

colophon – **समाप्तिलेखन** – पूर्वी प्रकाशित झालेल्या ग्रंथांच्या शेवटच्या पानांवर मुद्रकाचे नाव, मुद्रणस्थळ, मुद्रणदिनांक, शीर्षक, लेखक व इतर माहिती दिलेली असे.

colophon date – **समाप्तिलेख दिनांक** – समाप्तिलेखात उल्लेख केलेला दिनांक हा तालिका व ग्रंथसूचीसाठी संदर्भ म्हणून घेतला जात असे.

column – **स्तंभ/रकाना** – नियतकालिकाच्या छपाईतील किंवा संगणकातील स्तंभ.

comics – **हास्यके/चित्रके** – बालकांसाठी तयार केलेल्या चित्राद्वारे गोष्टी सांगणारे मासिक, चित्रकथा मासिक, चित्रकथांक.

COM (Computer Output Microfilm) – **संगणक कार्योत्पादन सूक्ष्मपट** – सूक्ष्मपटावर माहितीची नोंद करणारा संगणकातील एक भाग.

comma – **स्वल्पविराम** (,) – वर्गीकरणात वापरण्याचे एक चिन्ह.

command – **आज्ञा** – संगणकाला दिलेली आज्ञा.

command–drive – **आज्ञावली** – आज्ञेवर चालणारा संगणकीय कार्यक्रम.

command line interpreter – **संगणकातील आज्ञापालन करणारा दुभाषा** (आज्ञेद्वारे चालणाऱ्या सूचना–पटांमध्ये याची गरज असते.)

commemoration volume – **स्मृतिग्रंथ** – व्यक्ती वा घटना, संस्था यांच्या स्मृत्यर्थ ग्रंथ.

comment – **भाष्य/टीका** – संगणक संयोजनातील एक संदेश.

commentary – **वर्णनात्मक भाष्य/टीका** – एखादे पुस्तक.भाष्य, वृत्तान्त, टीका इ.

commentator – **टीकाकार/भाष्यकार** – मूळ ग्रंथावर टीका/समीक्षा लिहिणारा लेखक.

commercial complex – **व्यापारी/उद्योग संकुल.**

commercial / industrial / business library – **व्यापारी/औद्योगिक ग्रंथालय** – व्यापारविषयक ग्रंथसंग्रह करणारे ग्रंथालय.

commission – **अडत/दलाली/बट्टा/मंडळ/आयोग/सूट** – एखाद्या विषयाची चौकशी करून त्यावर अहवाल देण्यासाठी अधिकृतपणे नेमलेले मंडळ; आयोग.

commitment – **बांधिलकी/कार्यनिष्ठ/वचन.**

committee – **समिती** – एखाद्या विशिष्ट हेतूच्या पूर्ततेसाठी नेमलेला व्यक्तींचा गट.

committee-adhoc – **तदर्थ समिती.**

committee-executive – **कार्यकारी समिती.**

committee-expert – **तज्ज्ञ समिती** – एखाद्या विषयावर सल्ला देण्यासाठी नेमलेले मंडळ.

committee-inquiry – **चौकशी समिती** – विशिष्ट घटनेची माहिती घेण्यासाठी नेमलेले मंडळ.

committee-joint – **सहसमिती.**

committee-standing – **स्थायी समिती.**

common – **सामान्य/सर्वसामान्य/सामाईक/सार्वजनिक/नेहमीचा/सर्वसाधारण.**

CCF (Common Communication Format) – **सामान्य संप्रेषण प्रारूप** – चे संक्षिप्त रूप. संगणकामध्ये वाचनसाहित्याच्या माहितीचा संग्रह करताना आवश्यक त्या घटक आणि उपघटकांची यादी. यात प्रत्येक उपघटकाला विशिष्ट टॅग क्रमांकही दिला आहे. माहितीच्या संग्रहाचा आराखडा तयार करताना वापरलेच पाहिजे असे उपयुक्त आंतरराष्ट्रीय स्तरावरील युनेस्कोने तयार केलेले सर्वमान्य मानक.

common auxiliaries – **सहयोगी सारणी** – स्वरूप विभागाची सारणी, तक्ते, यातील क्रमांक मूळ वर्गांकाला जोडता येतात.

common facets – **सामान्य पैलू** – सर्वसाधारण वर्गीकरण करताना वारंवार दिसून येणारे पैलू.

common isolates – **सामान्य उपविभाग/स्वरूप विभाग** – कोणत्याही वर्गांकास जोडता येणारे उपविभाग.

common sub-divisions – **सामान्य उपविभाग** – वर्गीकरण पद्धतींमध्ये एखादा विषय उपविषयांमध्ये विभागण्यासाठी उपलब्ध असलेले उपविभाग.

common sucdivision device – **स्वरूप/विभाग युक्ती/क्लृप्ती.**

common title – **सामान्य ग्रंथनाम** – खंडात्मक ग्रंथाच्या संचातील सर्व खंडांना दिलेले सामाईक ग्रंथनाम.

communication – **संप्रेषण/संभाषण/संदेशवहन** – एकापेक्षा अनेक व्यक्तिंपर्यन्त विचार पोहोचविणे.

communication channel – **संप्रेषणाचे मार्ग.**

communication of information – **माहितीचे संप्रेषण** – माहितीचे एका ठिकाणाहून दुसरीकडे वाहून जाणे/येणे.

communication network – **संप्रेषण जाळे** – संगणकामध्ये मदत करणाऱ्या साधनांचा संच.

communication link – **संप्रेषण दुवा/संभाषण जोड** – माहितीची देवाणघेवाण करण्यासाठी वापरण्याचे साधन.

communication system – **संप्रेषण पद्धती** – माहितीच्या दळणवळणामध्ये अंतर्भूत साधने.

community characteristic – **जाती विभाजन गुण** – वर्गीकरण करताना वापरण्याचे तत्त्व.

community library – **नागरी ग्रंथालय** – बरेचदा ग्रंथालयशाखा सल्ला केंद्र म्हणून काम करते. स्थानिक माहिती पुरविण्याचे काम येथे केले जाते.

compact disc (CD) – **लघुतबकडी/कॉम्पॅक्ट डिस्क** – १२ सें. मी. परीघ असलेली संगणक कार्यासाठी उपयुक्त तबकडी.

compact storage – **संकुचित साठा** – फिरणाऱ्या किंवा झुलत्या मांडणीमध्ये पुस्तके ठेवून संकुचितरीत्या साठा केला जातो. अशी मांडणी ग्रंथकक्षामध्ये आढळते.

comparative librarianship – **तौलनिक ग्रंथपालन** – विविध देशांमधील ग्रंथपालन व्यवसाय, शिक्षण सेवांचा तुलनात्मक अभ्यास.

comparison phase – **तुलनात्मक/तुलना प्रावस्था** – डॉ. रंगनाथन् यांची संज्ञा. वर्गीकरण करताना दोन वा अधिक विषयांशी संबंधित ग्रंथ असेल तेव्हा विषयांचा तुलनात्मक पातळीवर विचार करून केलेले वर्गीकरण.

comparision phase relation – **तुलना विषयांग संबंध.**

compendium – **सारसंग्रह** – अतिशय मोठ्या ग्रंथप्रकल्पाचा आढावा घेणारा छोटासा सारसंग्रह.

compilation – **संकलन** – इतर ग्रंथांमधून माहिती घेऊन ती विशिष्ट पद्धतीने जुळविण्याची, रचना करण्याची प्रक्रिया.

compilation of bibliography – **ग्रंथसूचीचे संकलन.**

compiler – **संकलक/संगणकीय भाषांतर आज्ञावली**– (१) अनेक लेखकांचे किंवा एकाच लेखकाचे विविध लेख/कृती (ग्रंथ) एकत्र करून नवीन ग्रंथ निर्माण करणारी व्यक्ती, (२) संकलनाचे काम करणारी व्यक्ती, (३) संगणकातील संयोजनभाषेचे यांत्रिक संकेतात रूपांतर करणारी आज्ञावली, (४) ही एक आज्ञावली आहे. उपयोजनमूलक भाषेत लिहिलेल्या आज्ञावली संगणकास समजणाऱ्या यंत्रभाषेत बदलण्याचे कार्य ही आज्ञावली करते. हे काम करीत असताना उपयोजनमूलक भाषेमध्ये लिहिलेल्या आज्ञावलीतील वाक्यरचनेच्या (syntax) शब्दांच्या चुका ही आज्ञावली निदर्शनास आणण्याचे कार्य करते.

compiler entry – **संकलक नोंद** – संकलकाच्या नावे केली जाणारी तालिकेतील नोंद.

complementary copy – **भेटप्रत** – (१) ग्रंथकाराने भेट म्हणून देण्यासाठी वापरलेली प्रत. (२) मोफत दिलेली प्रत जी कार्यमूल्यमापन किंवा लोकप्रियतेसाठी दिलेली असते व तिची विक्री करणे अपेक्षित नसते.

complex – **संयुक्त/अवघड/संमिश्र.**

complex array isolate – **संमिश्र पंक्ती उपांगे.**

complex book – **मिश्र ग्रंथ** – एकाहून अधिक विषयावरील साहित्य एकत्रित आणलेला ग्रंथ.

complex class – **संमिश्र वर्ग** – ग्रंथवर्गीकरणात याचा वापर केला जातो.

complex subject – **संमिश्र विषय** – दोन अथवा अधिक मूळ विषयांचा समावेश असणारा विषय.

component – **घटक**.

composer – **रचनाकार**.   उदा. संगीतकार.

composite – **संमिश्र/संयुक्त** – विविध घटकांनी बनलेला, संयुक्त.

composite authors – **संयुक्त/संमिश्र लेखक** – एका ग्रंथामध्ये अनेकांचा सहभाग असेल तेव्हा त्यांना संयुक्त लेखक म्हटले जाते. परंतु हे सहलेखक नव्हेत, कारण संपूर्ण ग्रंथलेखनात सर्वांचा सहभाग नसतो.

composite book – **संयुक्त ग्रंथ/संमिश्र ग्रंथ** –
  (१) संपादकाने एकाच खंडात अनेक लेखकांचे लेख एकत्र आणून तयार केलेला ग्रंथ.
  (२) एकापेक्षा अधिक विषयांची माहिती देणारा ग्रंथ.
  (३) संयुक्तरीत्या लेखन केलेला ग्रंथ.

composite classification – **संयुक्त वर्गीकरण** – वर्गीकरण नियमावलीमधील दोन वा जास्त संज्ञा वापरून विशिष्ट विषय दर्शविण्याची वर्गीकरण हातोटी.

composite heading – **संयुक्त शीर्षक** – तालिकीकरण करताना असे शीर्षक अवतरण चिन्हांद्वारा दर्शविले जाते; यामुळे नोंद रचनेचे काम सोपे होते.

composite subject – **संयुक्त विषय** – वर्गीकरण करताना एखादा विषय हा इतर अनेक विषयांना अंतर्भूत करून घेतो तेव्हा तो संयुक्त विषय होतो.

composite work – **संयुक्त कार्य** – दोन वा अधिक लेखकांनी एकाच विषयावर संयुक्तरीत्या केलेले लेखन.

compound – **मिश्र** – दोन किंवा अधिक घटक समाविष्ट असलेला.

compund case – **संयुक्त पाया/आधार**.

compound catchword – **मिश्र वेचक शब्द** – निर्देशन करताना जोडरेषेने दर्शविलेला शब्द जोडरेषा नाही असे समजून वापरावा लागतो.

compound class – **मिश्र/संयुक्त वर्ग** – दोन किंवा अधिक प्रमुख विषय असणारा वर्ग.

compound heading – **मिश्र शीर्षक** – माहितीची प्रतिप्रासी करताना मिश्रशीर्षक असणाऱ्या विषयांची विशिष्ट रचना केली जाते.

compound name – **जोडनाम/संयुक्तनाम** – दोन घटकांनी बनलेले नाव. उदा. ग्रामीण अर्थशास्त्र.

compound subject – **मिश्र विषय** – (१) तालिकीकरण करताना मिश्रविषयक स्पष्ट होण्यासाठी विषयशीर्षक देताना एकापेक्षा अधिक शब्द वापरावे लागतात. (२) वर्गीकरण करताना एका मिश्र विषयात अधिक विषय अंतर्भूत झालेले दिसून येतात. (उदा. तयार कपडे, लोकरीचे, सुती इ. विषय)

compound subject heading – **मिश्र विषयशीर्षक** – (१) दोन वा अधिक शब्द जोडून तयार झालेले शीर्षक, (२) वाक्प्रचार म्हणून वापरले जाणारे शीर्षक, (३) नेहमीच एकमेकांशी संबंधित वापरले जाणारे विषय.

compound surname – **मिश्र आडनाव** – उदा. पेंडसे-नाईक.

comprehensive – **बहुसमावेशक/सर्वसमावेशक**.

comprehensive abstracting – **सर्वसमावेशक सारनिर्मिती**.

comprehensive bibliography – **सर्वसमावेशक ग्रंथसूची** – एका विषयावर प्रकाशित झालेल्या जवळ जवळ सर्व साहित्याचा समावेश असलेली ग्रंथसूची.

comprehensive collection – **परिपूर्ण/सर्वसमावेशक संग्रह**.

comprehensive indexing system – **सर्वसमावेशक निर्देशन पद्धती** – सर्वसमावेशक नोंदी असलेली निर्देशन पद्धती.

comprehensive work – **बहुआयामी कार्य** – संपूर्ण आढावा घेणारा वृत्तान्त.

computer – **संगणक** – माहितीचे संकलन, संस्करण आणि कार्योत्पादन प्रदान करणारे एक इलेक्ट्रॉनिक साधन. यात नवीन/वेगळी माहिती आणि आदेश ग्रहण करून त्याप्रमाणे कार्य करण्याची क्षमता असते.

computer applications – **संगणकाचा वापर/उपयोजन**.

computer based training – **संगणकाविषयी मूलभूत प्रशिक्षण**.

computer centre – **संगणक केंद्र** – संगणक वापरासाठी उपलब्ध केलेली जागा, ठिकाण.

computer communication – **संगणकाद्वारे संप्रेषण**.

computer game – **संगणकीय क्रीडा प्रकार/खेळ**.

computer language – **संगणक आज्ञावलीतील भाषा**.

computer library – **संगणक आज्ञावलीतील फाईलींचा संग्रह**.

computer literacy – **संगणक साक्षरता** – संगणकाचा वापर करण्याची किमान क्षमता.

computer network – **संगणक जाळे** – दोन अथवा अधिक संगणक एकमेकांना जोडून तयार केलेले परस्पर पूरक माहिती दळणवळणाचे जाळे.

computer networks – **संगणकाची जाळीदार रचना** – परस्पर संबंधित कार्य करू शकणाऱ्या संगणकांची जाळीदार रचना.

computer operator – **संगणक चालक**.

computer output – **संगणकाने आज्ञावलीनुसार केलेले कार्य**.

computer programme – संगणकासाठी तयार केलेली आज्ञावली.

computer science – संगणकशास्त्र.

computer security – **संगणक सुरक्षितता** – संगणकातील माहिती व तिची रचना यामध्ये अनधिकृतरीत्या बदल करता येऊ नये म्हणून वापरावयाची सावधानता सुविधा.

computer system – **संगणकपद्धती** – मुख्य संगणक व माहिती दळणवळणासाठी आवश्यक साधनांची एकत्र गटसंज्ञा.

compression – संकोच/संकोचन/संपीडन/पीडन.

CAM – **कॅम** – Computer Aided Microform साठी वापरलेला संक्षिप्त शब्द. यात मायक्रोफीच आणि मायक्रोफिल्म ही दोन्ही रूपे येतात.

computerised data case – **संगणकाधिष्ठित माहिती संचय/आधारसामग्री** – संगणकाच्या साहाय्याने तयार करून संगणकाच्याच साहाय्याने अद्ययावत ठेवली जाणारी व संगणकाच्याच साहाय्याने वापरली जाणारी माहिती.

CDS/ISIS – **सी.डी.एस./आय.एस.आय.एस.** (Computerised Documentation System/ Integrated Set of Information Systems) – हे **याचे विस्तारित रूप** – युनेस्कोने विकसित करून उपलब्ध केलेले सॉफ्टवेअर. टेक्सट्युअल टाइप सॉफ्टवेअरचे त्याच्या गुणांमुळे अनेक ग्रंथालयात याचा वापर होतो.

COMPENDEX – **कॉम्पेनडेक्स** (Computerised Engineering Index) – **याचे संक्षिप्त रूप** – इंजिनियरिंग इंडेक्सचे यंत्रद्वारा वाचण्यासाठी रूपांतर, स्थापत्यशास्त्रातील व्यापक क्षेत्रातील नियतकालिकांचे सारलेखन व निर्देशन करणारे प्रमुख प्रकाशन.

concept co-ordination – **संकल्पना सहसंबंध** – एका संकल्पनेचे बहुविध प्रकारे निर्देशन करून विशिष्ट प्रलेख ओळखण्यासाठीची पद्धती.

concept indexing – **संकल्पना निर्देशन** – विषय निर्देश करताना एक विशिष्ट प्रलेखात कोणकोणत्या संकल्पना महत्त्वाच्या ठरतात हे ठरविण्याची प्रक्रिया.

conceptual hierarchy – **संकल्पनात्मक श्रेणीरचना/विचारांची श्रेणीबद्धता** – तार्किक दृष्टीने विचारांची रचना करणे.

concise description, principle of – **संक्षिप्त वर्णनाचे तत्त्व** – तालिकापत्रात नोंद करताना अनावश्यक माहिती किंवा दोनदा माहिती देण्याचे टाळण्यासाठी वापरावयाचे तत्त्व.

conclusion – निष्कर्ष.

conclusion stage – निष्कर्ष स्थिती.

concordance – **शब्दानुक्रमणिका** – प्रलेखातील/ग्रंथातील लेखकाने वापरलेल्या सर्व महत्त्वाच्या शब्दांची सूची/निर्देश.

concrete – साकार/सादृश्य/निश्चित.

concrete entry – निश्चित घटक/नोंद.

condition survey – स्थितीसर्वेक्षण – ग्रंथालयातील ग्रंथांचे बाह्यस्वरूप तपासण्याच्या दृष्टीने केलेले सर्वेक्षण. यानंतर ग्रंथाच्या टिकाऊपणासाठी प्रक्रिया केल्या जातात.

conference – परिषद सभा – विचारविनिमय किंवा चर्चेकरिता आयोजिलेली संघटना सदस्यांची सभा.

conference paper – परिषदेतील सादरीकृत व्याख्यान/लिखाण.

conference proceedings – परिषदांची इतिवृत्ते – याद्वारे आधुनिक व नवी माहिती पहिल्यांदा मिळते, एक प्राथमिक माहिती साधन.

confidential room/hall – गोपनीय सभाकक्ष/खोली.

confidential file – गोपनीय संचिका – अतिमहत्त्वाचे कागदपत्र असलेली संचिका, जिचा उपयोग अधिकृत व्यक्तीच करू शकतात.

confidential report – गोपनीय अहवाल – कार्याध्ययातील सर्व घटकांना सांगावयाची नाही अशी माहिती, नोकरीतील व्यक्तीच्या कार्याचे मूल्यमापन करणारा वार्षिक अहवाल.

cojoint authorship – सहलेखकत्व.

connecting digit – संयोजक अंक – दोन पैलू जोडण्याकरिता वापरलेले संयोजक चिन्ह.

connecting symbol – संबंधक चिन्ह (संकेतचिन्ह) संयोजक चिन्ह – वर्गांक तयार करताना निरनिराळ्या पैलूंतील घटक विषयांची चिन्हे/संज्ञा एकमेकांना जोडण्यासाठी वापरण्यात येणारी चिन्हे.

connotation – लक्षितार्थ – वर्गीकरण करताना लक्षात घेण्याची संज्ञा.

consensus – सर्वमान्य मत/मतैक्य – सर्वसाधारण संमती.

conserve – रक्षण/जतन – दुखापत, अपव्यय यांपासून संरक्षण करणे.

conservation – (साहित्याचे) दीर्घकाल जतन – ग्रंथ व इतर साहित्याचे कीड लागणे, फाटणे व इतर हानी होण्यापासून संरक्षण.

consistant order – सुसंगत क्रम.

consistency – सुसंगतता – सुसंगत असण्याचा गुण, सातत्य.

consolidated catalogue – एकत्रित तालिका – अनेक ग्रंथालयांची मिळून तयार झालेली, एकत्रित तालिका.

consolidated entry – एकत्रित नोंद – दोन किंवा जास्त नोंदी एकत्रित करणे.

consolidated general entry – एकत्रित साधारण नोंद.

consolidated index – **एकत्रित निर्देश** – अनेक खंड, मालाप्रकाशन, नियतकालिके यांचा एका विशिष्ट क्रमाने तयार केलेला निर्देश.

consolidated specific entry – **एकत्रित विशिष्ट नोंद.**

consolidated system – **एकत्रित ग्रंथालयपद्धती** – अनेक पालिका सदस्य, मतदार, विश्वस्त मंडळाच्या निर्णयाने कार्य करीत असलेली ग्रंथालयपद्धती प्रत्येक ग्रंथालय शाखाग्रंथालय म्हणून काम करते.

consortia – **कॉनसोरशिया** – ग्रंथालयांनी एकत्रित येऊन सर्वांच्या हिताकरिता केलेला सामंजस्य करार.

conspectus – **दिग्दर्शन/सार/टांचण/मसुदा** – हे ग्रंथालयांना ग्रंथसंग्रहाबाबत निर्णय घेण्याचे एक साधन आहे. ग्रंथालयांची सध्याची ग्रंथसंख्या तसेच नजीकच्या काळातील ग्रंथ खरेदीचे धोरण, लायब्ररी ऑफ काँग्रेसच्या विषय वर्गणीनुसार सोप्या अक्षर व अंकांच्या सांकेतिक भाषेत लिहून देता येतो. १९७९ मध्ये सहकारी ग्रंथपालनाचे (Research Libraries Group in United States) RLG चे प्रयत्न यशस्वी करण्यासाठी प्रथम याचा वापर झाला.

constitute – **मिळून बनलेले.**

constitution – **घटना** – संस्थेचे कार्यविश्लेषण करणारी नियमावली.

consultation service – **सल्लामसलत सेवा.**

consulting librarian – **ग्रंथालय सल्लागार/सल्लागार ग्रंथपाल** – काही व्यक्ती ग्रंथालय सल्लागाराचे काम करतात.

content analysis – **आशय विश्लेषण** – ग्रंथात, नियतकालिकांत समाविष्ट असलेल्या विषयाचे/ विषयातील घटकांचे पृथक्करण. विषय सूचित करणाऱ्या विधानाच्या आधारेच त्या विषयाचे विविध पैलू समजायला मदत होते.

content page – **अनुक्रमणिका पृष्ठ** – ग्रंथातील प्रकरणांची यादी छापलेले पृष्ठ.

contents – **अनुक्रमणिका** – धडे, पाठ यांची शीर्षक यादी.

contents list – **अनुक्रमणिकांची यादी.**

contents list bulletin – **अनुक्रमणिका यादी पत्रिका** – अनेक नियतकालिकांच्या अनुक्रमणिका याद्या एकत्रित करून तयार केलेली पत्रिका.

contents note – **अनुक्रमणिका टीप/आशयटीप** – तालिकेनंतर दिली जाणारी टीप. यात प्रकरणशीर्षके, भाग, खंड यांचा उल्लेख केला जातो.

context – **संदर्भ** – (१) जेथे एखादा शब्द वापरला गेला असेल ते वाक्य, पदबंध वगैरे. (२) निर्देशन करताना शीर्षक किंवा मजकुराचा जो भाग वेचकशब्द म्हणून घेतला जातो त्याचा अर्थ सूचित करणारा भाग.

continuation – **(क्रमशः) पूरक/सातत्य** – (१) एखाद्या ग्रंथाचा काही भाग मूळ लेखकाने लिहिला असेल व उरलेला भाग इतर व्यक्तीने पूर्ण केला असेल असा ग्रंथ.

continued card / continuation card – संततपत्र – नियतकालिकांच्या नोंदणीसाठी संततपत्र वापरले जाते. खंडात्मक प्रकाशनांना उपयुक्त.

continuation file – संतत संचिका.

continuing education – निरंतर शिक्षण – नोकरी-व्यवसायात असलेल्या व्यावसायिकांचे ज्ञानकौशल्य वाढीस लागून त्यांना फायदा व्हावा या हेतूने अनौपचारिक सहभाग घेणे/नोंदविणे.

continuing resource – निरंतर साधनसामग्री.

continuity – सलगता/संलग्नता.

continuous feed – सलग पुरवठा – छपाईयंत्राला होणारा सलगपणे कागद पुरवठा.

continuous revision – सतत पुनर्आढावा – अनेक खंडांचा मोठा ग्रंथ. जसे विश्वकोशात्मक ग्रंथ संपूर्ण आढावा न घेता नवीन आवृत्ती म्हणून प्रकाशित केले जातात. यामुळे ते प्रकाशन अद्ययावत राहते.

continuous stationary – संगणकाच्या छपाईयंत्राला वापरण्याचा कागद – अनेक मीटर लांब असून ठराविक अंतरावर कागद फाडण्याची खूण केलेली असा असतो.

contours / contour lines – समोच्च रेषा – (१) नकाशांमध्ये समुद्रपातळीपासून समान उंचीवर असलेल्या ठिकाणांना जोडणाऱ्या रेषा. (२) समुद्र पातळीवर एकच उंची असलेली सर्व स्थाने जोडणाऱ्या नकाशामध्ये काढल्या जाणाऱ्या रेषा. या कंटूर रेषांमधील मध्यंतराने ५० ते कित्येक हजार फूट असणारा उंचीतील फरक दाखविला जातो. मात्र, हे नकाशात वापरलेल्या मापनावर अवलंबून असते. प्राकृतिक नकाशांमध्ये या कंटूर रेषांमधील भू-क्षेत्रे नेहमी निरनिराळ्या रंगाने दाखविली जातात.

contract – करारपत्र – दोन व्यक्ती किंवा संस्था यांनी एकमेकांबरोबर काम करताना पाळावयाच्या अटी दर्शविणारा दस्तऐवज.

contrast – भेद/व्यतिरेक/वैधर्म्य/विरोधाभास – दोन विरुद्ध टोकांमधला फरक संगणकाच्या पडद्यावरील गडदपणा, छपाईतील गडद-फिकेपणा यामधील फरक.

contribution – सहभाग/लेखनातील सहभाग.

contributor – सहभागी (लेखक) – अनेक लेखकांनी लिहिलेल्या ग्रंथाचा एक लेखक.

contributor index entry – सहभागी लेखकाची निर्देशातील नोंद.

control – पर्यवेक्षण/नियंत्रण.

control character – संगणकातील नियंत्रक अंकाक्षर.

control field – नियंत्रित क्षेत्र – यंत्रवाचनीय नोंदीमधील विशिष्ट माहितीचा भाग ओळखणारे क्षेत्र.

control key – नियंत्रण कळ – संगणकाच्या कळपट्टीवरील नियंत्रण कळ.

control unit – **नियंत्रण एकक** – संगणकातील नियंत्रण एकक.

controlled circulation serial – **नियंत्रित प्रचलनमालिका** – प्रकाशनात सहभागी झालेल्या व्यक्तींना विनामूल्य पाठविले जाणारे प्रकाशन.

controlled indexing – **नियंत्रित निर्देशन** – निर्देशन करताना संबंधित विषय विस्कळीत होऊ नयेत म्हणून परिभाषेची काळजीपूर्वक निवड करावी लागते.

controlled term list – **नियंत्रित संज्ञांची यादी** – तालिकीकरणातील अधिकृत यादीमध्ये समाविष्ट असलेल्या संज्ञेला समांतर अशी संज्ञा माहितीची प्रतिप्राप्ती करताना वापरली जाते.

controlled vocabullary – **निश्चित/नियंत्रित संज्ञासंग्रह** – विषयांच्या नावास योग्य अशा संज्ञांची केलेली यादी.

convenience file – **सोईस्कर संचिका** – दप्तर किंवा बखरी यांसारख्या जुन्या कागदपत्रांची दुसरी प्रत काढून ती सुलभपणे उपलब्ध करण्यासाठी तयार केलेली दुसरी संचिका प्रत.

conventional – **संकेतमान्य/पारंपरिक/परंपरागत** – रितीवर आधारित, चाली पाळणारा, रूढ.

conventional documents – **परंपरागत प्रलेख** – हस्तलिखिते, ग्रंथ, नकाशे, नियतकालिके यांसारखे पूर्वापार प्रचलित प्रलेख.

conventional name – **पारंपरिक नाव/प्रचलित नाव.**

conventional title – **रूढ ग्रंथनाम** – ग्रंथविषय व स्वरूपाला अनुसरून असे दिलेले ग्रंथशीर्षक संगतीविषयक ग्रंथांचे तालिकीकरण करताना याचा वापर अधिक प्रमाणात होतो.

conversion – **रूपांतरण** – लिखित माहितीचे रूपांतरण यंत्रवाचनीय स्वरूपात केले जाते.

conversion programme – **रूपांतरण आज्ञावली** – संगणकामध्ये माहिती रूपांतरणासाठी वापरावयाची आज्ञावली.

co-operation – **सहकार** – अनेक ग्रंथालयांनी एकत्र येऊन सर्वांसाठी ग्रंथालयीन प्रक्रिया एकत्रितरीत्या करणे. उदा. सहकारी तालिकीकरण.

co-operative acquisition – **सहकारी ग्रंथोपार्जन** – सहकारी तत्त्वावर ग्रंथ मिळविण्याची प्रक्रिया.

co-operative cataloguing – **सहकारी तालिकीकरण** – तालिकीकरणाच्या समान कामांमधील पुनरावृत्ती टाळण्याकरिता काही ग्रंथालये एकत्र येऊन सहकारी पद्धतीने तालिकीकरण करतात. त्यामुळे तालिकीकरणासाठी करावयाच्या खर्चाची व श्रमांची बचत होते.

co-operative storage – **सहकारी पद्धतीने साठवण.**

co-operative training – **सहकारी प्रशिक्षण** – अनेक संस्थांचे मिळून प्रशिक्षण.

co-ordinate – **समपदस्थ (समन्वित)** – प्रकल्प पूर्ण करण्यास सर्व प्रयत्नांत सुसूत्रता आणणे.

co-ordinate classes – **सहसंबंधित वर्ग/समपदस्थ वर्ग** – (१) वर्गीकरण रचनेमध्ये एकापुढे एक येणारे सहसंबंधित वर्ग. (२) एका पंक्तीमध्ये असणारे वर्ग.

co-ordinate indexing – **समन्वित निर्देशन/संबंधदर्शक निर्देशीकरण** – संज्ञांचा सहसंबंध दर्शविणारी समन्वय पद्धतीने निर्देशन करण्याची पद्धती.

co-ordinate relation – **समपदस्थ संबंध** – समान अंतरावरील शीर्षके. उदा. भात, गहू, ज्वारी, बाजरी इ. धान्ये.

co-ordination – **समन्वय** – माहिती पद्धतीतील घटकांची आशावादी साधनांसमवेत सुसंगत आंतरक्रिया.

co-ordination of terms – **संज्ञा समन्वय** – वर्गीकरण करताना एका संज्ञेकडून दुसऱ्या संज्ञेकडे जाण्याचा विशिष्ट क्रम.

co-processor – **सहसंस्कारक** – संगणकाची प्रक्रिया वेगाने होण्यासाठी उपयुक्त असा भाग.

copy – **नक्कल/प्रत/प्रतिलिपी/प्रतिकृती** – (१) प्रलेख, मासिके इ.ची मूळ किंवा प्रतिरूप प्रत. (२) संगणकामध्ये एक माहिती दोन प्रतींमध्ये साठविणे.

copy filing – **प्रतींचे पंजीकरण.**

copy number – **प्रत अंक** – (१) प्रत्येक प्रतीला दिलेला क्रमांक. (२) ज्याचा वापर डॉ. रंगनाथन् यांनी ग्रंथांक ठरविण्यासाठी केला आहे.

copy & paste – **संगणकातील मजकुराची प्रत करून ती अन्य ठिकाणी समाविष्ट करणे.**

copy protection – **प्रतसंरक्षण** – संगणकामध्ये माहिती प्रतीचे संरक्षण करणे.

copying maching – **प्रतिलिपीयंत्र** – झेरॉक्स अथवा तत्सम.

copying technique – **प्रतिलिपीतंत्र.**

copyright / all right reserved – **स्वामित्व/मालकी हक्क/प्रतहक्क** – (१) एखाद्या वाङ्मयीन, सांगीतिक किंवा कलात्मक कलाकृतीच्या प्रती तयार करण्याचा काही विशिष्ट वर्षांच्या मर्यादिपर्यंत झालेला कायदेशीर अधिकार. (२) प्रकाशनाविषयी लेखकाकडे/प्रकाशकाकडे/अन्य व्यक्तीकडे/ संस्थेकडे कायद्याने असलेला विशिष्ट कालखंडापुरता एकमेवाधिकार. या एकमेवाधिकारामुळे त्या कालखंडात कोणत्याही लेखनकृतीच्या/कलाकृतीच्या/सांगीतिक कृतीचे एकमेवाधिकारकाच्या अनुमतीशिवाय निर्माण व वितरण करता येत नाही.

copyright Act – **स्वामित्व कायदा** – प्रकाशित मजकुराच्या लेखकाचे हक्क जपणारा कायदा.

copyright date – **मालकीहक्क दिनांक** – हा दिनांक ग्रंथशीर्षकाच्या मागील पानावर लिहिलेला असतो.

copyright deposit – **मालकीप्रत ठेव** – कायद्यानुसार प्रकाशित झालेल्या प्रत्येक ग्रंथाची मोफत प्रत ठेव म्हणून अधिनिक्षेप ग्रंथालयात ठेवली जाते.

copyright fee – **मालकीहक्क शुल्क** – रचनेच्या मालकाला रचना वापरण्याबद्दल दिलेला मोबदला.

copyright library – **स्वामित्व ग्रंथालय** – ज्या ग्रंथालयास प्रकाशित/निर्माण केलेल्या साहित्याची प्रत पाठविणे स्वामित्व कायद्यान्वये बंधनकारक असते असे ग्रंथालय.

copyright list – **मालकीहक्क कायद्यानुसार ग्रंथालयात जमा झालेली ग्रंथांची यादी.**

copy writer – **प्रत लेखक** – प्रत तयार करणारा.

coranto – फार पूर्वी वापरात असलेल्या वृत्तपत्राचा प्रकार. एकाच पानावर दोन स्तंभांमध्ये दोन्ही बाजूस मजकूर लिहिलेला असे.

core journal – **आवश्यक नियतकालिक** – एखाद्या विषयशाखेचे सर्वांत महत्त्वाचे नियतकालिक. याचे वाचन आवश्यक समजले जाते.

corporate author – **समष्टी ग्रंथकार** – शासनाचा एखादा विभाग किंवा एखादी संस्था किंवा स्वतंत्र अस्तित्व असलेली संघटना एखादे प्रकाशन करते तेव्हा लेखक म्हणून या विभागाचे वा संस्थेचे नाव दिले जाते.

corporate cody – **समष्टी/सहकारी समिती/प्रतिष्ठान** – समष्टी ग्रंथकार म्हणून नाव असलेली समिती.

corporate entry – **समष्टी नोंद** – समष्टी ग्रंथकाराची तालिकेतील नोंद.

corporate name – **समष्टी नाम** – समष्टी समितीचे नाव.

corrected edition – **सुधारित आवृत्ती** – चुका दुरुस्त करून अथवा मूळ आवृत्तीत बदल करून काढलेली नवी आवृत्ती.

correlation of properties – **वर्गीकरण करताना लक्षण गुणांमधील परस्परसंबंध.**

correlative index – **परस्परसंबंधित निर्देश** – प्रलेखांची निवड त्यातील संबंधित शब्द, अंक वा इतर चिन्हांनुसार करता येईल असा निर्देश.

corrigendum – **शुद्धीपत्र/दुरुस्तीपत्र** – छपाईनंतर लक्षात आलेल्या त्रुटी व चुकांची पृष्ठक्रमांक संदर्भासह तयार केलेली छापील यादी. ही यादी ग्रंथाच्या पानांमध्ये चिकटविली जाते वा नंतर समाविष्ट केली जाते.

corrupted data – **सदोष प्रक्षिप्त माहिती** – हस्तक्षेपामुळे सदोष झालेली माहिती.

cost benefit / cost effectiveness analysis – **मूल्य फायदे/मूल्यपरिणाम विश्लेषण** – एखादे कार्य, सेवा अथवा साधन यावर केलेला खर्च आणि त्यापासून होणारे आर्थिक वा अन्य फायदे यांचा समन्वय प्रस्थापित करण्यासाठी किंवा फायदा/तोटा तपासण्यासाठी विकसित केलेली शास्त्रीय पद्धती.

council – **परिषद/मंडळ.**

counter – **कट्टा/देवघेवकट्टा.**

country characteristic – **देश विभाजनगुण** – वर्गीकरण करताना देशानुसार वर्गांक दिला जातो.

country library – **प्रांतिक ग्रंथालय.**

coupon – **नोंद चिठ्ठी** – एखादी गोष्ट करण्याचा किंवा मिळण्याचा अधिकार देणारे तिकीट, प्रतिपत्र.

course reserves – **अभ्यासक्रम आरक्षित साहित्य.**

cover – **वेष्टन** – ग्रंथाच्या संरक्षणासाठी लावलेले कागद, कपडा, चामडी इ.चे आवरण.

cover jacket – **ग्रंथास घातलेले आवेष्टन.**

cover title – **वेष्टनावरील ग्रंथशीर्षक** – आवेष्टनावर लिहिलेले ग्रंथनाम शीर्षक.

cover to cover translation – **शब्दश: संपूर्ण भाषांतर** – परभाषीय मालाप्रकाशनातील संपूर्ण वा मोठा भाग भाषांतरीत केलेले माला प्रकाशन.

coverage – **वृत्तान्त** – दिलेले वृत्त.

crabs – विक्री न झाल्यामुळे ग्रंथविक्रेत्यांनी प्रकाशकाकडे पाठविलेला ग्रंथ.

craft – **हस्तकला** – हाताचे कौशल्य असलेला धंदा – उदा. कोरीव काम, मातीकाम, कुंभाराचे काम.

craft paper – **खाकी रंगाचा कागद.**

craftsmanship – **हुन्नर/कला** – कारागिरीचे कसब.

craftsman – **कुशल कारागीर.**

crash / hang – **भंजन/स्तब्ध होणे** – संगणक प्रक्रियेत अचानक निर्माण झालेला बिघाड.

credibility – **विश्वासार्हता.**

credit line – **निर्माता श्रेय रेषा** – चित्रे, आकृती, लेखन, छायाचित्र यांच्या निर्मात्याला श्रेय देणारा उल्लेख.

criterion – **कसोटी/निकष/निर्णायक लक्षण** – एखादी गोष्ट मोजण्याचे मानक, प्रमाण.

critical – **चिकित्सक/टीकात्मक/चिंताजनक.**

critical analysis – **चिकित्सक/टीकात्मक मूल्यमापन** – साहित्य, कला वगैरेंबाबत मूल्यमापन.

critical bibliography – **सटीप विश्लेषक ग्रंथसूची** – ग्रंथांची तुलनात्मक ऐतिहासिक माहिती देणारी ग्रंथसूची.

critical edition – **चिकित्सक/टीकात्मक आवृत्ती** – मूळ संशोधनानंतर अतिशय अभ्यासपूर्ण संपादन करून तयार केलेली आवृत्ती.

CPM (Critical Path Method) – **परिणमकारक मार्गपद्धती** – कार्यमूल्यमापन आणि अवलोकन तंत्र (PERT) चा हा एक भाग आहे. यात पार पाडावयाच्या सर्व कार्याचा विशिष्ट पद्धतीने आकृतिबंध तयार केला जातो. कार्य पार पाडण्याकरिता त्यातून योग्य मार्ग अवलंबिला जातो.

criticism – **टीका/समीक्षा** – साहित्य, ग्रंथ वगैरेचे परीक्षण करण्याची कला.

criticism facet – **समीक्षा पैलू** – पैलूचा वर्गांक मूळ वर्गांकास जोडल्यामुळे मूळ ग्रंथ आणि त्यावरील समीक्षा कपाटात जवळ येतात.

criticism number – **समीक्षांक/टीकांक** – ज्याचा वापर डॉ. रंगनाथन् यांनी ग्रंथांक तयार करताना केला आहे.

crooked cracket – **वक्र कोष्टक/कंस.**

chronological – **कालानुक्रमानुसार.**

chronological order – **अनुकाल क्रम** –उदा. इसवीसन निहाय क्रम.

cross classification – **छेदक वर्गीकरण** – एका विभाजनाचे वेळी एकापेक्षा जास्त लक्षणगुण विचारात घेऊन केलेले वर्गीकरण.

cross index – **छेदक निर्देश** – अनेक शीर्षकांखाली निर्देशनोंद केलेला निर्देश.

cross reference – **उलट संदर्भ** – उदा. 'पाहा' 'आणखी पाहा.'

cross reference entry – **उलट संदर्भदर्शक नोंद** – अनुवर्ग सूचीतील विशिष्ट पूरक नोंदीला 'उलट संदर्भ नोंद' असे म्हणतात.

cross reference index entry – **उलट संदर्भ निर्देशी नोंद** – एक शब्द अथवा शब्द समुच्चयापासून दुसऱ्या समानार्थ शब्दाकडे अथवा शब्द समुच्चयाकडे निर्देश करणारी जी नोंद असते तिला 'उलट संदर्भ निर्देशी नोंद' असे म्हणतात.

cryogetic store – **महासंगणकासाठी विकसित केलेली स्मरणिका.**

crucial – **निर्णायक/खडतर** – कठीण, निर्णायक स्वरूपाचा.

crucked – **बेढब/वेडीवाकडी.**

cryptonym – **गुप्तनाम/संकेतनाम.**

cryptonymous book – **संकेतनाम/ग्रंथकाराचा ग्रंथ.**

cubicle / alcove / carrel / study – **अभ्यासिका.**

culture – **संस्कृती** – कला, साहित्य वगैरे (जगण्याचा आस्वाद घेण्याची पद्धती.)

cultural library – **सांस्कृतिक ग्रंथालय** – नागर ग्रंथालय येथे सर्व प्रकारचे ग्रंथ असतात.

cumulated volume – **क्रमसंचयी ग्रंथ/खंड** – पूर्वी प्रकाशित झालेल्या मजकुराची जुळणी करून पुन: प्रकाशित केलेला ग्रंथ.

cumulation – **क्रमसंचय/क्रमसंचयी** – (१) ताज्या घडामोडींच्या नियतकालिकांच्या अंकास निर्देश असतो. अनेक अंक प्रसिद्ध झाल्यावर या निर्देशातील नोंदीमध्ये नवीन निर्देशातील नोंदीचा समावेश

करतात. याला 'क्रमसंचयी' म्हणतात. यामुळे निर्देश अद्ययावत राहतो. प्रत्येक अंकाबरोबर नवीन विषयाचा/बाबींचा समावेश होतो. त्यांचा जो रचनाक्रम अगोदर ठरलेला असेल त्यानुसार त्या माहितीच्या बाबींचे योग्य जागी अंतर्वेशन करणे. हे सामान्यत: नियतकालिकाच्या स्वरूपात प्रकाशित होतात आणि यामध्ये एकच रचनाक्रम राखला जातो. (२) विशिष्ट क्रमाने नोंदी करून नियतकालिकाच्या स्वरूपात प्रसिद्ध केली जाणारी पद्धती.

cumulation encyclopaedia – **क्रमसंचयी ज्ञानकोश** – विशिष्ट क्रमाने नोंद केलेला ज्ञानकोश.

cumulative index – **संचयी/क्रमसंचयी निर्देश** – स्वतंत्रपणे प्रकाशित झालेले निर्देश एकत्रित करून आणि एकाच अनुक्रमानुसार लावणे.

cuneiform writing – **कीलाकार लेखन.**

curator – **ग्रंथालयाधिपती/अभिरक्षक** – साहित्याचे, वस्तूंचे जतन करण्याची जबाबदारी दिलेला अधिकारी.

currency – **चलन.**

currency rate – **चलनविनियमाचा दर** – एका देशातील चलनाचा दुसऱ्या देशातील चलनाशी विनिमय दर.

current approach – **प्रचलित दृष्टिकोन** – अधिकाधिक नवीनतम माहिती मिळविण्याचा दृष्टिकोन.

current awareness journal – **प्रचलित जागरूकता नियतकालिक** –वेगवेगळ्या नियतकालिकातील अनुक्रमणिकांच्या प्रती देणारे नियतकालिक.

current awarness publication – **प्रचलित जागरूकता प्रकाशन.**

current awareness service (CAS) – **प्रचलित जागरूकता सेवा** – (१) विशिष्ट विषयाच्या प्रचलित किंवा अद्ययावत नियतकालिकांमध्ये प्रकाशित झालेल्या लेखासंबंधीची ग्रंथवर्णनविषयक माहिती किंवा अनुक्रमणिका पृष्ठासंबंधी माहिती देणारी सेवा. (२) वाचकाची गरज व प्रचलित साहित्य यांची सांगड घालून पुरविलेली सेवा.

current bibliography – **प्रचलित/ताजी ग्रंथसूची.**

current contents – **सद्य:स्थितीची अनुक्रमणिका.**

current directory – **प्रचलित निर्देशिका.**

current information – **प्रचलित माहिती.**

current journal / periodical – **प्रचलित नियतकालिक.**

current list – **सध्याची/प्रचलित यादी.**

current number – **सध्याचा/प्रचलित अंक.**

current records – **प्रचलित साहित्याच्या नोंदी.**

current reviews – नवीन साहित्याची समीक्षा.

currently reveived – नुकतेच प्रकाशित/प्राप्त झालेले.

curriculum resource centre – अभ्यासक्रम संसाधन केंद्र.

cursor – स्थान बिंदू (संगणकातील कर्सर) – संगणक पडद्यावरील स्थान दर्शविणारा दर्शक. जो सहसा बाणाने दर्शविला जातो.

cursor control keys – स्थानबिंदू नियंत्रक कळ.

custodian – राखणदार – ज्या व्यक्तीवर संग्रहाची निगा राखण्याची व जतन करण्याची जबाबदारी असते.

cutter classification / expansive classification – कटरचे वर्गीकरण – कटर यांची विस्तारशील वर्गीकरण पद्धती.

cutter number – कटर अंक – चार्ल्स् एमी कटर यांनी सुचवलेली गुणांक पद्धती.

cutting / clippings – कात्रणे – वर्तमानपत्रातील कात्रणे काढून ती ग्रंथालयात जतन केली जातात.

cybernetics – अध्ययनशास्त्र – प्राण्यांमधील संभाषणशास्त्र या शास्त्राचा उपयोग संगणकामध्ये केला जातो.

cycle story – कथामाला – विशिष्ट विषयावरील क्रमशः कथा प्रकाशन.

cyclopedia / encyclopaedia – ज्ञानकोश/विश्वकोश – सर्वांगीण माहिती उपलब्ध करून देणारा कोश.

cyclostyle – चक्रमुद्रण – एकावेळी अधिक प्रती तयार करण्याकरिता मेण लावलेल्या कागदावर मजकूर लिहून अथवा टंकलिखित करून प्रती तयार करण्याची क्रिया.

cylinder press – दंडगोल मुद्रणयंत्र.

dagger – कट्यार चिन्ह – (†) तळटिपांमध्ये ताराचिन्हांनंतर येणारे दुसरे संदर्भ चिन्ह.

daily – दैनिक, दैनिक वृत्तपत्र/वर्तमानपत्र – नवीन/प्रचलित बातम्या प्रसारित करण्यासाठी दररोज प्रकाशित होणारे वृत्तपत्र.

damaged book – खराब झालेला ग्रंथ – वापरासाठी, वाचनासाठी उपयुक्त नसलेला ग्रंथ.

damp – ओलसर/दमट.

dash – जोडरेषाचिन्ह – दोन अक्षरे, शब्द, संज्ञा यांना जोडण्यासाठी वापरले जाणारे चिन्ह (–)

data – डेटा/मूलभूत माहिती/सत्यस्थिती व वस्तुस्थिती–
(१) तुटक, असंघटित माहितीचे तुकडे/कण.
(२) संगणकामध्ये जतन करण्यासाठी अंक, अक्षरे व आकृत्या यांच्या स्वरूपात असलेली मूलभूत माहिती.
(३) 'डेटम्' या संज्ञेचे बहुवचन. तिचा अर्थ 'घटना, आकडेवारी किंवा माहिती' असा आहे.

data acquisition – माहिती उपार्जन – संगणकाच्या कार्यासाठी उपयुक्त स्वरूपात माहिती मिळविण्याची प्रक्रिया.

data archives – माहिती जपणूक – यंत्रवाचक स्वरूपातील मूलभूत माहितीची जपणूक करणारे केंद्र.

data bank – माहिती पेढी – माहिती संचिका, मूलभूत माहितीची संचयिका.

database – **आधारसामग्री संच** – (१) संगणकावर संग्रहित केलेली माहिती. या माहितीचे स्वरूप सतत बदलते असू शकते. त्यात वाढ/घट होते. ही माहिती पूर्वी नमूद केलेल्या आराखड्यामध्ये समाविष्ट केली जाते. यामुळे यातील विशिष्ट माहिती चटकन् शोधणे आणि हवी तेव्हढीच परत मिळविणे शक्य होते किंवा आधारसामग्रीचा संग्रह किंवा संगणकाच्या संचिकेमध्ये संग्रहित केलेली माहिती जी दूरस्थ संगणक आणि दूर संप्रेषणाच्या साखळीद्वारे प्राप्त करता येते. (२) संगणकात केलेला माहितीचा संचय व त्या माहितीबाबत दिलेली व्यवस्थित माहिती. ती सर्व माहिती दूरच्या संगणकावरूनही उपलब्ध होऊ शकते; कारण ते सर्व संगणक दूरसंचार यंत्रणेच्या दुव्याने सांधलेले असतात. (३) माहितीच्या परस्परांशी संबंध असलेल्या बाबींचा समूह ज्या एकत्रित मिळून एका वेगळ्याच बाबीची/बाजूची नोंदणी होते. सामान्यत: संगणकाचे उत्पादन.

Database Management System (DBMS) – **आधारसामग्री व्यवस्थापन पद्धत** – संगणकीय सॉफ्टवेअरचा एक प्रकार, वाचनसाहित्य/आधारसामग्री व्यवस्थापन एक पद्धती.

data capture – **आधारसामग्री प्रग्रहण करणे** – मूलभूत माहितीची संगणकातील समावेशनप्रक्रिया.

data centre – **आधारसामग्री केंद्र.**

data code – **आधारसामग्री संहिता.**

data collection – **आधारसामग्री संग्रह** – जमा प्रतिसाद वा तत्सम अशा मूलभूत माहितीचा संग्रह. (१) अनेक संचिकेतून माहिती एकत्रित करून त्याचे उपयोजन करणे. (२) साधनसामग्री/प्रतिसाद जमा करण्याचे काम.

data communication – **मूलभूत माहितीचे संप्रेषण** – आधार सामग्रीचे अनुग्रहण व प्रसारणकार्य.

data compilation – **आधारसामग्रीचे संकलन.**

data compression – **मूलभूत/आधारसामग्रीचे संकोचन** – मूलभूत माहितीमधील रिकाम्या जागा काढून, त्रुटी कमी करून माहितीचे संकोचन करण्याचे काम/तंत्र.

data control – **आधारसामग्रीचे नियंत्रण** – संगणक कार्यामध्ये समाविष्ट होणारी व बाहेर पडणारी माहिती नियंत्रित करण्याची प्रक्रिया.

data conversion – **आधारसामग्रीचे रूपांतरण** – मूलभूत माहितीचे स्वरूप बदलण्याचे तंत्र.

data corruption – **आधार सामग्री नष्ट होणे** – माहिती साठवणुकीत हस्तक्षेपामुळे मोठ्या प्रमाणात त्रुटी व चुका निर्माण होऊन संगणककार्यात निर्माण होणारा व्यत्यय.

data design – **आधारसामग्री/माहिती आकृतिबंध.**

data dictionary – **आधारसामग्री/माहिती शब्दकोश** – मूलभूत माहितीमधील शब्दांचा अर्थ, परस्परसंबंध, मूळ शब्द, उपयोगिता याविषयी संगणकात एकत्र साठविलेला माहितीकोश.

data element – **माहितीतील घटक.**

data entry / input – **माहिती नोंद** – मूलभूत माहिती संगणकामध्ये नोंद करण्याची प्रक्रिया.

data entry operator – **माहिती नोंद निवेशकार.**

data error – **माहितीतील चूक.**

data library – **आधारसामग्री ग्रंथालय** – संगणकातील परस्परसंबंधित माहिती संचाचा किंवा फाइल्सचा संग्रह केलेला माहितीगट.

data field – **माहिती क्षेत्र** – संगणकात माहिती साठविण्यासाठी एका घटकास दिलेली जागा.

data file – **माहितीची संचिका.**

data flowchart – **माहितीचा प्रवाहतक्ता** – करावयाची कार्ये/पायऱ्या क्रमाने एकानंतर एक नोंदविणे.

data format – **माहितीची संरचना/आराखडा/प्रारूप.**

data processing / information processing – **माहितीवरील सोपस्कार/संस्करण** – मूलभूत माहितीची हाताळणी, एकत्रीकरण, गटविभाजन, संगणकीकरण इ.चा समावेश.

data protection – **माहिती संरक्षण** – मूलभूत माहितीचे संरक्षण करणारी यंत्रणा.

data reduction – **–माहिती कपात** – ढोबळ माहितीतील अनावश्यक भाग गाळून माहितीचे अधिक उपयुक्त स्वरूपात रूपांतरण करणे.

data register – **माहितीची नोंदवही.**

data retrieval – **माहितीची पुनर्प्राप्ती** – संगणकातील उपलब्ध माहितीमधून हवी तेवढीच माहिती शोधून, निवडून पुन्हा मिळविणे.

datamation – **स्वयंचलित मूलभूत माहितीचे संकलन करण्याची प्रक्रिया.**

DBS III (Database III) – संगणक प्रणालीचा एक प्रकार.

date – **दिनांक** – ग्रंथ/प्रलेख प्रकाशित झाल्याचा दिनांक.

date card – **दिनांक पत्र** – ग्रंथदेवघेव पद्धतीत वापरले जाणारे पत्र.

date due / due date – **देयदिनांक/ग्रंथपरतीचा दिनांक.**

date guide – **दिनांक मार्गदर्शक** – ग्रंथ परतीचा दिनांक दर्शविणारे मार्गदर्शक. (ब्राऊन देवघेव पद्धतीमध्ये वापर.)

date label / date slip – **दिनांक चिठ्ठी** – ग्रंथ ग्रंथालयात कधी परत करावयाचा याची नोंद असलेली चिठ्ठी.

date line –**दिनांक रेषा** – नियतकालिकांवरील प्रकाशन दिनांक लिहिलेली रेषा.

date of accession – **दाखलनोंदीचा दिनांक** – वाचनसाहित्य ग्रंथालयात नोंदविल्याचा दिनांक.

date of birth – **जन्मदिनांक** – द्विबिंदू वर्गीकरणामध्ये वाङ्मयाचे वर्गीकरण करताना लेखकाचे जन्मवर्ष लिहावे लागते.

date of issue – ग्रंथ देवाण दिनांक – वाचकास ग्रंथ दिल्याचा दिनांक.

date of puclication – ग्रंथ प्रकाशनाचा दिनांक.

date of return – ग्रंथपरतीचा दिनांक.

date stamp – दिनांकाचा शिक्का – ग्रंथाचा देयदिनांक दर्शविणारा शिक्का.

dater – दिनांकाचा ठसा/शिक्का.

day to day work – दैनंदिन काम.

dead stock – अनुपयोगी भांडवली वस्तू/शिलकी सामान/भांडार साहित्य/जड संग्रह.

dead stock register – जड वस्तू सामग्रीची/भांडार साहित्य नोंदवही.

death date – मृत्यू दिनांक.

debug – दोषमार्जन – संगणकातील माहिती निर्दोष करण्याची प्रक्रिया.

decennial – दशवार्षिक प्रकाशन.

decimal – दशांश.

decimal classification – दशांश वर्गीकरण – दशांश वर्गीकरण म्हणजेच ड्युई डेसिमल वर्गीकरण. मेलविल ड्युई या अमेरिकन ग्रंथपालाने सन १८७६ मध्ये प्रसिद्ध केलेली दशांश वर्गीकरण पद्धती.

decimal fraction device – दशांश अपूर्णांक युक्ती/क्लृप्ती.

decimal notation – दशांश चिन्हांकन – वर्गीकरण पद्धतीतील विषय शोधून काढण्यासाठी वापरले जाणारे चिन्हांकन.

decimal number – दशांश अंक – दशांश चिन्हाचा वापर करून लिहिलेला क्रमांक.

decipher – अक्षर आकलन/अक्षर लावणे – सांकेतिक अर्थ लावणे, उलगडा करणे.

decision support system / management information system – माहिती व्यवस्थापन पद्धत – आधारित माहितीमधून निर्णयात्मक अनुमान काढण्यासाठी व्यवस्थापकाला मदत करणारी व्यवस्थापन माहितीपद्धतीची उपशाखा.

deck – पोटमाळा – ग्रंथालयातील स्टॉकरूममध्ये याचा वापर केलेला असतो.

declassify – बाद/निष्कासन वर्गीकरण – एखादा खासगी प्रलेख सुरक्षित वर्गीकरणातून अधिकृतरीत्या काढून घेणे.

decoder – संगणकातील दुभाषायंत्र – याच्या साहाय्याने सांकेतिक माहितीचे रूपांतर वाचकाला योग्य स्वरूपात केले जाते.

decorate – सुशोभित करणे.

decorated cover – ग्रंथाचे अलंकृत वेष्टन.

decorative arts museums – शोभिवंत कला वस्तुसंग्रहालये.

decreasing concreteness, prinbiple of – वर्गीकरणासाठी विचारात घेण्याच्या लक्षणगुणांची रचना कशा पद्धतीने करावी याविषयीचे तत्त्व. डॉ. रंगनाथन् यांनी यासाठी **'PMEST'** असे सूत्र सांगितले आहे. हे घटक पुढीलप्रमाणे आहेत. –
(1) Personality (2) Matter, (3) Energy, (4) Space, (5) Time

decreasing extension – **संकोची व्याप्ती** – वर्गीकरणासाठी वापरायचे तत्त्व. वर्गीकरण करताना मुख्य विषयाचे चिन्हांकन आधी देऊन कमी महत्त्वाच्या विषयाचे चिन्ह क्रमाने देत चिन्हांकनाची व्याप्ती संकुचित करण्याचे तत्त्व.

dedicate – **अर्पणपत्रिका** – एखाद्याविषयी आदर व्यक्त करून साहित्यकृती त्यास अर्पण करणारे लेखकाचे विवरण.

dedication – कर्तव्य परायणता/कामातील एकरूपता.

dedication page – **अर्पणपत्रिका पृष्ठ** – ग्रंथ अर्पण केल्याचा उल्लेख असलेले पृष्ठ.

dedication copy – **ग्रंथ अर्पणप्रत** – लेखकाने व्यक्तीला वा संस्थेला अर्पण करण्यासाठी वापरलेली प्रत.

default – **संगणकाचे स्वसंस्करण** – जेव्हा स्पष्टीकरण दिले नसेल तेव्हा संगणकाकडून पर्यायी मूल्याचा वापर करून संस्करण केले जाते.

default value – **संगणकाचे गृहीतमूल्य** – उपयोजकाने स्पष्ट केलेले नसेल तेव्हा संगणकाने वापरलेले पर्यायी मूल्य.

defaulter – **कसुरदार/थकबाकीदार/दोषी व्यक्ती** – (१) दिलेल्या मुदतीत ग्रंथालयाचा ग्रंथ परत न करणारी व्यक्ती, (२) ग्रंथ वेळेवर परत न केलेली व्यक्ती.

defective copy – **दोषयुक्त प्रत** – मुद्रण किंवा बांधणीत दोष असलेली ग्रंथाची प्रत.

DESIDOC (Defence Science Information & Documentaion Centre) – **डेसिडॉक** – संरक्षणशास्त्र माहिती आणि प्रलेखन केंद्र. संरक्षणविषयक संशोधन व विकासाला माहितीविषयक पूरक कार्य करणारे केंद्र.

deferred cataloguing – **स्थगित तालिकीकरण** – ग्रंथालयातील कमी महत्त्वाच्या साहित्याचे संपूर्ण तालिकीकरण पुढे ढकलले जाते. संक्षिप्त नोंदी करून असे साहित्य बाजूला ठेवले जाते.

definition – **व्याख्या** – शब्दाचा अर्थ स्पष्ट करणारे विधान.

definitive edition – **प्रमाणभूत आवृत्ती** – लेखकाच्या मूळ लेखनाची अधिकृत आवृत्ती. बरेचदा लेखकाच्या मृत्यूनंतर संपादित केलेली आवृत्ती या प्रकारची असते.

delegation of powers – **अधिकार हस्तांतरण** – ठराविक पातळीवर अधिकारांचे हस्तांतरण करणे.

delete – **वगळणे** – (१) संगणकाच्या स्मृतीतून अनावश्यक माहिती वगळणे/गाळणे यासाठी द्यावयाची सूचना. (२) संगणकातील माहिती काढून टाकणे. एखादे एकक, नोंद, फाईल वा माहितीगट काढून टाकणे/वगळणे.

delivery of books Act – **ग्रंथप्रेषणाचा अधिनियम.**

delivery station – **ग्रंथ वितरण/वाटप केंद्र** – प्रकाशकाने आपण प्रकाशित केलेल्या ग्रंथांच्या काही प्रती शासनाकडे देण्याबाबतचा कायदा.

delivery van – **वितरणाचे वाहन** – फिरत्या ग्रंथालयात वाचनसाहित्य नेणारे वाहन.

delphi techniques – **तज्ज्ञ मतधारणावर आधारित तंत्रे** – एखाद्या कार्याच्या नियोजनासाठी त्या कार्याचे नजीकच्या भविष्यकाळातील स्वरूप जाणून घेणे आवश्यक असते. हे तंत्र जाणून घेण्याचे तंत्र म्हणजे डेल्फी टेक्निक्स होय. या तंत्रात या कार्यातील अधिकारी व्यक्तींची मते अजमावून त्यावरून निष्कर्ष काढले जातात.

deluxe binding – **उत्कृष्ट बांधणी** – कलात्मकरीत्या केलेली ग्रंथाची आकर्षक बांधणी.

deluxe edition – **उत्कृष्ट आवृत्ती** – कागद, छपाई, बांधणीच्या दृष्टीने उत्कृष्ट दर्जा असलेला ग्रंथ.

demand – **मागणी/आवश्यक/जरुरी असणे.**

demand slip – **ग्रंथमागणी चिठ्ठी** – ग्रंथमागणी करण्यासाठी सविस्तर ग्रंथमाहिती दिलेले शिफारसपत्र.

demonstration library – **प्रायोगिक तत्त्वावर चालविलेले ग्रंथालय.**

demy – **डेमी** –छपाईसाठी वापरला जाणारा प्रमाणित कागदाचा आकार. याचा आकार ($१७\frac{१}{२}×२२\frac{१}{२}$ इंच) असतो.

denudation – **व्याप्ती संकोच** – वर्गीकरण करताना विशिष्ट वर्गांची शृंखला तयार करणे.

department – **विभाग** – एखाद्या संस्थेचा विभाग.

department of library and information science – **ग्रंथालय व माहितीशास्त्र विभाग.**

departmental – **विभागीय.**

departmental catalogue – **विभागीय तालिका.**

departmental collection – **विभागीय/शाखा संग्रह** – एखाद्या विषयापुरते/ज्ञानशाखेपुरते ग्रंथ उपलब्ध असलेला वाचनसाहित्य संग्रह.

departmental library – **विभागीय ग्रंथालय/विभाग ग्रंथालय.**

departmental puclication – **विभागांची प्रकाशने** – विशिष्ट विभागाने प्रकाशित केलेले प्रकाशन.

department auxiliary – **अवलंबित साहाय्यकारी** – यु.डी.सी.मधील सामान्य साहाय्यकारी उपविभाग: यांचा उपयोग फक्त प्रमुख अंकाबरोबरच होतो. जसे, दृष्टिकोन साहित्य, व्यक्ती.

deposit / caution money – **अनामत रक्कम/ठेव** – एखादी गोष्ट तात्पुरत्या वापरासाठी घेण्यापूर्वी द्यावयाची रक्कम.

deposit collection – **अनामत संग्रह** – विशिष्ट लेखक वा प्रकाशन याजकडून मिळालेले साहित्य ग्रंथालयात वेगळे ठेवून वाचकांना उपलब्ध करून देणे.

deposit copy – **ठेवप्रत** – ठेव ग्रंथालयात जमा केलेली नवीन प्रकाशित झालेल्या ग्रंथाची प्रत.

deposit library – **ठेव ग्रंथालय** – शासनाने ठरविलेल्या नियमानुसार प्रकाशित होणाऱ्या प्रत्येक ग्रंथाची प्रत या ग्रंथालयात ठेवली जाते.

deposit room – **अनामत कक्ष/खोली.**

depository – **संग्रह स्थळ** – सुरक्षिततेसाठी वस्तू/ग्रंथ ठेवण्याची जागा.

depository library – **संग्रह ग्रंथालय.**

depository catalogue – **ठेवप्रतीची तालिका.**

depth classification – **सखोल वर्गीकरण** – प्रत्येक विशिष्ट विषयाला वर्गीकरणामध्ये स्थान मिळवून देणे.

depth indexing – **सखोल निर्देशन** – मजकुरातील महत्त्वाच्या शक्यतो प्रत्येक संज्ञा, व्यक्ती, स्थाने, विषय यांची नोंद करणे.

deputy librarian – **उपग्रंथपाल** – (१) प्रमुख ग्रंथालयाच्या खालोखाल अधिकार असणारी व्यक्ती. (२) ग्रंथपालाच्या गैरहजेरीत ग्रंथपाल म्हणून व इतर वेळी ग्रंथालयासोबत समन्वित कार्य करणारी व्यक्ती.

descender – **अवरोही अक्षरमुद्रा,** उदा. g, j, p, q, y

description – **वर्णन.**

descriptive – **वर्णनात्मक.**

descriptive bibliography / physical bibliography – **वर्णनात्मक ग्रंथसूची** – (१) ग्रंथसूचीचा एक प्रकार ज्यात विस्तृतरीत्या माहिती दिलेली असते. (२) ग्रंथाचे संपूर्ण वर्णन – लेखकाचे संपूर्ण नाव, निश्चित शीर्षक, प्रकाशन वर्ष व स्थळ, प्रकाशक व मुद्रकाचे नाव, ग्रंथाचे स्वरूप, पृष्ठांकन,चित्रे, किंमत यांचा उल्लेख ग्रंथसूचीमध्ये केला जातो.

descriptive cataloguing – **वर्णनात्मक तालिकीकरण** – ग्रंथाचे संपूर्ण वर्णन असलेली नोंद केलेले तालिकीकरण.

descriptive element – **वर्णनात्मक घटक** – वर्णनाचा घटक.

descriptive list – **वर्णनात्मक यादी** – जतनसंग्रहातील साहित्याची संक्षिप्त वर्णन असलेली यादी.

descriptors – **वर्णनकारके/वर्णनाचे शीर्षक** – माहितीची प्रतिप्राप्ती करताना वापरलेली ग्रंथविषयक दर्शक संज्ञा.

desiderata – ग्रंथलेखकाला हव्या असलेल्या विषयांची सूची.

desiderata file – आदिदीक्षित ग्रंथ संचिका.

design – आकृती/नकाशा/नक्षी/आराखडा – एखादी गोष्ट बनविण्यासाठीचा आराखडा, आकृतिबंध.

desk copies – जास्त मागणी असलेल्या ग्रंथाच्या वितरण कक्षातील प्रती.

destination slip – इष्टस्थान चिठ्ठी – ग्रंथालयानुसार विभागणी केलेली ग्रंथाची रंगीत चिठ्ठी. या चिठ्ठीच्या रंगानुसार ग्रंथ, ग्रंथालयातील मागणी विभाग वा तालिकीकरण विभागात पाठविला जातो.

destruction schedule – बाद ग्रंथांची यादी – ग्रंथालयाच्या संग्रहातून बाद करायच्या ग्रंथांची यादी तयार करून अधिकृतरीत्या संमत करून घेणे.

detached copy – सुटी पाने असलेली प्रत.

detection system / book detection system – ग्रंथ देवघेव निदान पद्धती – ग्रंथालयातून वाचक बाहेर जाण्यापूर्वी पुस्तके विशिष्ट यंत्रामध्ये ठेवून देवघेव नोंदद्वारा तपासणी केली जाते.

deterioration – प्रकृती ढासळणे/कागदपत्र खराब होणे/ठिसूळ होणे.

device – क्लृप्ती/युक्ती – (१) वर्गीकरण किंवा इतर कार्यांमध्ये वापरण्याचे तंत्र. (२) संगणकावर माहिती साठविण्याचे साधन. (३) एका उपविषयाचे अनेक उपविषय होऊ शकतात. या सर्वांची स्वतंत्र यादी करून प्रत्येकास स्वतंत्र क्रमांक देण्याऐवजी एखाद्या विशिष्ट योजनेचा वापर करतात. उदा. कालक्रमानुसार योजना, विषयानुसार योजना, वर्णक्रमानुसार योजना इ. यामुळे स्मरणसुलभता वाढते. तक्त्यांची लांबी कमी होते व तक्त्यांतील पृष्ठसंख्या कमी होते. तसेच एखाद्या उपविषयाचे सखोल वर्गीकरण करता येते.

device of enumeration – प्रगणन/मोजणी/गणती युक्ती/क्लृप्ती – वर्गीकरणासाठी वापरावयाचे तत्त्व, डॉ. रंगनाथन् यांनी विशिष्ट विषयांकरिता या युक्तीची योजना केली. जे उपविभाग एखाद्या वर्गाच्या उपान्त्य अष्टकांत समाविष्ट करण्याजोगे आहेत परंतु ज्यांना कालक्रम युक्तीने अथवा विषय युक्तीने वर्गांक तयार करता येत नाही अशा उपविभागांचे वर्गांक तयार करण्यासाठी या युक्तीचा उपयोग केला जातो.

Dewey decimal classification – ड्युईचे दशांश वर्गीकरण – (पहा decimal classification)

diacritic – उच्चार भेददर्शक/ध्वनिभेददर्शक – एकाच अक्षराचे निरनिराळे उच्चार दाखविणारी खूण.

diacritical marks – उच्चारचिन्ह – एखाद्या अक्षराचा दुसऱ्या सारख्या अक्षरामधील भेद दर्शविण्यासाठी आणि त्याला ठराविक ध्वनिमूल्य देण्यासाठी एखादे चिन्ह. उदा. बिंदू जोडलेला असतो. अशी चिन्हे संस्कृत भाषेत प्रचलित आहेत.

diagram – रेखाकृती/आकृती – वस्तू किंवा विषयाची अभिव्यक्ती.

diameter – व्यास/वर्तुळाची मध्यरेषा – वर्तुळ मध्यातून काढलेली आणि वर्तुळाच्या दोन्ही बाजूंना स्पर्श करणारी रेषा.

diary – **रोजनिशी** – एखाद्याच्या जीवनात दररोज घडणाऱ्या घटनांची नोंदवही दैनंदिनी.

diazo printing – **डायझो मुद्रण** – मुद्रणाचा एक प्रकार.

dichotomy – **द्विविभाजन पद्धतीचे वर्गीकरण.**

Dickman's charging system – **डिकमन्स् देवघेव पद्धती.**

dictionary – **शब्दकोश** – (१) विशिष्ट भाषेतील शब्द वा संज्ञांची अनुवर्णानुसार यादी करून त्याचा अर्थ, उच्चार, उत्पत्ती यांची माहिती दिलेली असते. (२) एखाद्या भाषेतील अथवा विषयातील शब्दांची वर्णानुक्रमे रचना करून अर्थ दर्शविणारा ग्रंथ.

dictionary catalogue – **कोशतालिका/आद्याक्षरानुसारी तालिका** – शब्दकोशाप्रमाणे प्रत्येक शब्दाचा क्रम लावून नोंद केलेली तालिका.

dictionary documentation list – **कोशस्वरूपाची प्रलेखन यादी.**

dictionary part of the classified catalogue – **वर्गीकृत तालिकेतील कोश विभाग/अनुवर्ण विभाग.**

difference – **फरक.**

difference phase relation – **विभेदन विषयांग संबंध.**

differentation – **विभेदन.**

diffusion transfer – **विसरण स्थानांतर.**

digest – **सारपत्रिका/सारसंग्रह/लेखसंग्रह** – एखाद्या विषयाविषयी अथवा विषयासंबंधी एखाद्या विषयाशी संबंधित शाखेविषयी लेखांचे सारांश देणारी पत्रिका/मासिक.

digit – **अंक** – (१) चिन्हांकनात असणारा स्वतंत्र असा एकच अंक. (२) द्विबिंदू वर्गीकरणामध्ये ग्रंथांकामधील प्रत्येक चिन्ह. (३) वर्गीकरणातील चिन्ह.

digital computer – **अंकसंगणक** – अंकस्वरूपात साठविणारा संगणक.

digital signal – **अंकीय संकेत.**

dilapidated condition – **जीर्णावस्था (ग्रंथाची).**

dime novel – **सवंग कादंबरी.**

diplomatics – **राजदप्तरविद्या** – पुरातन लेख, प्रलेख यांची सत्यता स्वत:कडे राखण्याचे शास्त्र.

direct sub-division – **थेट उपविभाजन** – कोशतालिकेतील नोंदी करताना विषयशीर्षक ठरविण्यासाठी विशिष्ट स्थानाशी संबंधित ग्रंथ असेल तेव्हा स्थानानुसार उपविभाजन केले जाते.

direct tax – **प्रत्यक्ष कर** – आयकर, विक्रीकर.

direction line – **मार्गदर्शक रेषा** – प्रारंभिक बांधणी चिन्हानुसार बांधणीकार पानांची जुळणी करतो.

directional question – दिशादर्शक/मार्गदर्शक प्रश्न.

director – संचालक – एखाद्या संस्थेचा मुख्य/प्रमुख.

director of archives – अभिलेखाधिकारी/संचालक/अभिलेखागार प्रमुख.

director of libraries – ग्रंथालय संचालक.

directorate of libraries – ग्रंथालय संचालनालय – ग्रंथालयांची व्यवस्था पाहणे, अनुदान देणे यासाठी शासकीय विभाग.

director of public instructions – लोकशिक्षण संचालक.

director of public libraries – सार्वजनिक ग्रंथालयांचे संचालक.

director of national library – राष्ट्रीय ग्रंथालयाचे संचालक.

directory – निर्देशिका – अनुवर्णाप्रमाणे व्यक्ती, नावे, ठिकाण, संस्था, शहरे, क्रमांक, देश इ.ची थोडक्यात माहिती देऊन तयार केलेली यादी/सूची.

directory of libraries – ग्रंथालयांची निर्देशिका.

directing section – दर्शक अनुच्छेद – ग्रंथाकडे, वर्गाकडे, वर्गाच्या नावाकडे अथवा अवांतर नावाकडे लक्ष वेधणाऱ्या पूरक नोंदीच्या अनुच्छेदाला 'दर्शक अनुच्छेद' असे म्हणतात.

disaster plan – आपत्कालीन योजना (ग्रंथालयासाठी).

disbursing – व्यय/देऊन टाकणे.

disbursing authority – खर्चाची/व्यय प्राधिकरण.

discard – काढून टाकणे/टाकून देणे.

discharge – मुक्त करणे/होणे, सुटका – ग्रंथ परत घेण्याची प्रक्रिया.

discharge tray – ग्रंथ देवघेवीकरिता वापरला जाणारा, ग्रंथपत्राचा कप्पा.

discipline – ज्ञानशाखा/शिस्त – ज्ञानविश्वाचे मोठे विभाजन.

discography – ध्वनिमुद्रणाची तालिका – गुंडाळी, तबकडी, फीत इ. स्वरूपात असलेली तालिका. यात शीर्षक, गीतकार, दिनांक, सादरकर्ते यांविषयी संपूर्ण माहिती उपलब्ध केली जाते.

discount – सूट/कसर/बट्टा/सवलत/वजावट – ग्रंथाच्या किंमतीमध्ये ग्रंथालयांना मिळणारी सूट.

discontinued number – वर्गीकरणातील स्थगित क्रमांक, या क्रमांकाने विषय दर्शविलेला नसतो.

discussion lists – चर्चा यादी – ठरावीक विषयावर चर्चा करणाऱ्यांची यादी.

disk – तबकडी.

disk drive – संगणकातील तबकडी विभाग – येथे तबकडीच्या हालचालींवर नियंत्रण विभाग.

disk map – तबकडीवरील माहितीदर्शक नकाशा.

disk mirroring – तबकडीवरील माहिती एकावेळी दोन ठिकाणी साठविण्याची प्रक्रिया.

display / exhibition of books – ग्रंथप्रदर्शन – दर्शन, पडद्यावर दाखविणे, प्रदर्शन.

display board – काचफलक.

display case – काचपेटी.

display of books – ग्रंथप्रदर्शन.

display stand – माहिती प्रदर्शित करावयाचा फलक किंवा चौकट.

disposal list – ग्रंथालयातील साहित्य रद्दबातल/बाद करण्याची यादी.

disposition – निंदा – ग्रंथसंग्रहातून साहित्य काढणे. काही वेळा जतनसंग्रहात ठेवण्यासाठी, पुनर्निर्माण, सूक्ष्मफीत तयार करण्यासाठी तर काहीवेळा पूर्णत: बाद केले जाते.

dissection – विच्छेदन – वर्गीकरण करताना सहसंबंधित वर्गाची पंक्ती तयार करणे.

dissemination – प्रसारण/प्रसार करणे.

dissemination of information – माहितीचे प्रसारण – (१) ग्रंथालयाकडून केले जाणारे माहितीचे प्रसारण. (२) एखाद्या संघटनेतील सभासदांना ग्रंथपालाने किंवा माहिती अधिकाऱ्याने माहितीचे वितरण करणे किंवा माहिती पाठविणे, मग ती मुद्दाम मागविलेली असो किंवा नसो. यासाठी वापरल्या जाणाऱ्या साधनांमध्ये सामान्यत: वृत्तपत्रिका (News Bulletin) सार, व्यक्तिगत टिपण किंवा पत्रे आणि व्यक्तिश: मुलाखती किंवा दूरध्वनी/भ्रमण ध्वनीवर संपर्क यांचा समावेश असतो. परंतु, लेखाबरोबरची टाचणे, कात्रणे किंवा अहवाल यांचाही समावेश असू शकतो.

dissertation – लघुशोधनिबंध – (१) संशोधकाने तयार केलेल्या प्रबंधापेक्षा कनिष्ठ स्वरूपाचे लिखाण/ कार्य. (२) पदवी किंवा पदविकेसाठी तयार केलेला शैक्षणिक लघु शोधनिबंध.

distributed facet – वितरित पैलू – माहितीची प्रतिप्राप्ती करताना वर्गीकरणामध्ये मिश्र विषयांमधील समाविष्ट असलेले परंतु रचनेमध्ये विखुरलेले पैलू किंवा संज्ञा.

distance education – दूरशिक्षण/दूरस्थ शिक्षण – अशा शिक्षणात नियमित व दररोज अध्यापन केंद्रात जाणे अपेक्षित नसते.

distribution – वितरण (ग्रंथवितरण) – प्रकाशक व ग्रंथविक्रेते यामधील ग्रंथवितरणाची व्यवस्था.

district – जिल्हा – शासनाचा महसुली भौगोलिक विभाग.

district central library – जिल्ह्याचे केंद्रीय ग्रंथालय.

district library – जिल्हा ग्रंथालय – विशिष्ट जिल्ह्यासाठी सेवा देणारे ग्रंथालय.

district revenue – जिल्ह्यातून जमा होणारा महसूल.

divide like – **याप्रमाणे विभाजन करा** – एका विषयाचे सखोल वर्गीकरण करून ते क्रमांक दुसऱ्या विषयाकरिता वापरण्यासाठी दिलेली वर्गीकरण सारणीतील सूचना.

divided catalogue – दोन वा अधिक अनुक्रमामध्ये विभागून नोंदी केलेली तालिका. मोठ्या कोश तालिकेमध्ये संदर्भ घेणे, फायलिंग करणे सोपे करण्यासाठी अशी तालिका तयार केली जाते.

divider – **छेदक** – रेषा, कोन वगैरेंचे मोजमाप करण्याचे साधन, द्विभाजक.

division – **विभाग** – (१) मोठ्या संघटनेचा किंवा संस्थेचा विभाग. (२) ग्रंथालयातील विशिष्ट प्रकारचे काम करणारा विभाग. उदा. देवघेव विभाग (३) वर्गीकरण करताना विषयाचे अनेक उपवर्ग, उपविभाग केले जातात.

division characteristic – **विच्छेदनाचा गुण**.

divisional library – **विभागीय ग्रंथालय**.

divisional title – **विभागीय ग्रंथनामपृष्ठ** – ग्रंथातील मजकूर विविध विभागानुसार दिला असेल तेव्हा विभागाचे शीर्षक वेगळ्या पृष्ठावर दिले जाते.

document/documents – **प्रलेख** – ग्रंथ, लेख, आलेखस्वरूप, अक्षरअंकस्वरूप, नकाशे, हस्तलिखिते, ध्वनिफिती इ. ज्या ज्या साहित्याचा माहितीसाठी उपयोग केला जातो किंवा सर्व प्रकारच्या वाचनसाहित्यासाठी वापरले जाणारे सामूहिक नाव.

document address – **प्रलेखस्थान** – संगणकामध्ये विशिष्ट माहितीचे स्थान दर्शविणारे प्रलेखस्थान.

document bibliography – **प्रलेख/प्रलेखांची सूची**.

document case – **प्रलेख ठेवण्यासाठी खोके/खण**.

document delivery – **प्रलेख वितरण/उपलब्धी–** (१) उपयोजकास हवे असलेले, माहिती असलेले साहित्य पुरविणे. (२) एखादे वाचनसाहित्य (मुख्यत्वेकरून लेख) वाचकास किंवा ग्रंथालयास त्यांच्या विनंतीनुसार (छायाप्रत, संगणकावरील संचिका, पुनर्मुद्रण इ. प्रकारात) पाठवण्याच्या क्रियेस दिलेले नाव.

document delivery service – **प्रलेख प्रदान सेवा/प्रलेख वितरण सेवा/प्रलेख उपलब्धी सेवा**.

document management – **प्रलेखांचे व्यवस्थापन** – व्यवसायासाठी आवश्यक अशा प्रलेखांची उपलब्धी, हाताळणी, साठवण इ. व्यवस्था पाहणे.

document profile – **प्रलेख रूपरेखा** – संदर्भसूची असलेली संगणकावरील फाईल (थोडक्यात माहितीसंग्रह) ही विशिष्ट शोध समीकरणे वापरून शोधता येते. CDS/ISIS मध्ये ही संज्ञा माहिती संग्रहासाठी वापरली जाते.

document retrieval system – **प्रलेख प्रतिप्राप्ती पद्धत** – संगणकाद्वारे केवळ संदर्भ, उल्लेख मिळविण्यापेक्षा संपूर्ण प्रलेख मिळविण्याची पद्धत.

document store – **प्रलेख संचय** – माहिती प्रतिप्राप्ती पद्धतीमध्ये प्रलेखांची साठवण केलेले स्थान.

document supply centre – **प्रलेख पुरवठा केंद्र** – मोठ्या ग्रंथालयाच्या वाचकांना प्रत्यक्ष वाचनसाहित्य पुरविणारा विभाग.

documentalist – **प्रलेखक/अभिलेखक/प्रलेखतज्ञ** – केवळ ग्रंथपालनापेक्षा प्रलेखनशास्त्रात पारंगत असलेली व प्रलेखनविषयक कार्य सांभाळणारी व्यक्ती.

documentary information – **प्रलेखांविषयी/प्रलेखबद्ध माहिती** – प्रलेखांमध्ये नोंद केलेली किंवा प्रलेखविषयी माहिती.

documentary reproduction – **प्रलेखांची पुनर्निमिती** – प्रलेखांची जादा प्रत काढणे.

documentation – **प्रलेखन/अभिलेखन** – (१) पुरावा म्हणून वापरलेली कागदपत्रे. प्रलेखन केंद्र, विशेषत: वैज्ञानिक अहवाल, अप्रकाशित साहित्य, सांख्यिकी माहिती याविषयी साहित्य मिळविणे, हाताळणे, माहितीसंप्रेषण याविषयीचा अभ्यास.

documentation centre – **प्रलेखन केंद्र** – (१) प्रलेखन केंद्रामध्ये साहित्य मिळविणे, संस्करण, जतन यांबराबेरच सारांशलेखन, निर्देशन केले जाते. वाचकांना उपयुक्त विषयांच्या माहितीपत्रिकांचे वितरण केले जाते.

documentation list – **प्रलेखन यादी.**

documentation science – **प्रलेखन विज्ञान.**

documentation service – **प्रलेखन सेवा** – प्रलेखनकेंद्राने संस्कारित केलेल्या प्रलेखविषयक सेवा.

documentation work – **प्रलेखन कार्य.**

DRTC (documentation research & training centre) – **प्रलेखन संशोधन आणि प्रशिक्षण केंद्र** – बंगलोर स्थित ग्रंथालय व माहितीशास्त्रातील प्रगत संशोधन व प्रशिक्षण देणारे व डॉ. रंगनाथन् यांनी १९६२ला स्थापन केलेले बंगलोर येथील केंद्र.

dog-ear (page) – **कोपरा दुमडलेले पृष्ठ.**

domain – **सत्ता/अधिकार/ताबा/मालकी.**

domain name – **मालकी नाव.**

donation – **देणगी/भेट** – ग्रंथालयाला भेट म्हणून मिळणारे ग्रंथ/रक्कम/साहित्य इ.

donation receipt – **देणगी पावती.**

donation record – **देणगीची नोंद/अभिलेख.**

donor – **देणगीदार/दाता.**

dormitory library – **सुप्त ग्रंथागार** – अमेरिकन महाविद्यालये वा संस्थांमध्ये बरेचदा करमणुकीसाठीची पुस्तके अथवा कमी मागणी असणारी पुस्तके मुख्य संग्रहालयापासून दूर ठेवली जातात. काहीवेळा कालबाह्य पाठ्यपुस्तकाच्या जुन्या आवृत्त्यांचा यात समावेश असतो.

dot – बिंदू – द्विबिंदू वर्गीकरणातील एक चिन्ह.

dot map – बिंदू नकाशा – बिंदूच्या साहाय्याने दर्शविलेला ग्रंथवितरणस्थिती दर्शविणारा नकाशा.

double acting card catalogue – द्विमुखी पत्रतालिका.

double book – अर्धपृष्ठावर छपाई केलेला ग्रंथ.

double click – दुहेरी क्लिक – संगणकमूषकाची कळ दोन वेळा दाबून संगणक पडद्यावरील कृतीपर्याय निवडण्याची प्रक्रिया.

double columned – दोन स्तंभात लेखन केलेले पृष्ठ.

double dagger – दुहेरी कट्यारचिन्ह – ग्रंथ पृष्ठावरील तिसऱ्या क्रमांकावरील चिन्ह (‡)

double entry – दुहेरी नोंद – तालिकेमध्ये एकच नोंद दोन विषयांखाली किंवा विषय आणि स्थान, सहलेखकांच्या नावाने करणे.

double numeration – दुहेरी अंकन – ग्रंथातील चित्रे, तक्ते यांना प्रकरणानुसार संबंधित क्रमांक देणे.

double plate – द्विपृष्ठी चित्र – दोन पृष्ठांवर मिळून असलेले.

double quotes – दुहेरी अवतरणचिन्ह (".........")

double space – दुहेरी अंतर – टंकलेखनातील दोन ओळींत सोडली जाणारी नेहमीपेक्षा दुप्पट जागा.

double title page – द्विशीर्षक पृष्ठ – ग्रंथाच्या डाव्या-उजव्या दोन्ही पृष्ठांवर शीर्षक लिहिले जाते. बरेचदा डाव्या बाजूला माला प्रकाशनातील इतर शीर्षके व उजव्या बाजूस विशिष्ट खंडाचे शीर्षक लिहिले जाते.

doubtful authorship – साशंक लेखकत्व – विशिष्ट ग्रंथाचे लेखन संबंधित लेखकाचेच असल्याचा पुरावा उपलब्ध नसेल तेव्हा ग्रंथ तालिकेत साशंकता दर्शविली जाते.

download – उतरवण – संगणकाद्वारे माहितीची प्रत तयार करणे.

downloading – उतरवणे – (१) संगणकातील माहिती स्थानिक संगणकात अथवा अन्य प्रतिलिपी साधनात उतरवून घेण्याची प्रक्रिया. (२) दूरवरच्या संगणकात साठविण्यात आलेली माहिती 'ऑन लाईन' प्रकियेद्वारा मिळवून ती स्वतंत्र अशा वेगळ्या संगणकात साठविण्याची व वापरण्याची क्रिया.

downloading time – उतरवण काल – संगणकातून माहितीची प्रतिलिपी करणाऱ्या प्रक्रियेसाठी लागणारा वेळ.

draft – मसुदा/प्रारूप – लिखाणाची पहिली पायरी ज्यात नंतर सुधारणा केल्या जातात.

dramatic work – नाट्यलेखन/नाट्यकाम.

dry-run – पूर्व परीक्षण – आज्ञावली लिहून झाल्यावर प्रत्येक पायरीपायरीने वापरल्यास काय होईल हे संगणक न वापरता मानवी साहाय्याने तपासण्याची पद्धत.

DTP (Desk Top Publishing) – संगणकीय प्रकाशन – मजकूर, आकृत्या, चित्रे यांची प्रकाशनपूर्व मांडणी.

due book – देयपुस्तक/देयग्रंथ – प्रकाशकाने ठेवलेले प्रकाशनपूर्व मागणीचे पुस्तक.

due date / date due – नियत दिनांक/देयदिनांक – ग्रंथ परतीचा दिनांक.

dues – दंड – ग्रंथालयात वेळेवर परत न आलेल्या पुस्तकांसाठी आकारलेली रक्कम.

dummy – प्रतिवस्तू – मूळ ग्रंथाच्या ऐवजी तो ग्रंथ ग्रंथालयाबाहेर कोणाला दिला आहे हे दर्शविणारी त्या ग्रंथाची प्रतिनिधी म्हणून ठेवलेली दुसरी वस्तू, पुठ्ठा किंवा लाकडी फळी. नक्कल, मुळाबरहुकूम.

dummy system – ग्रंथदेवघेवीची एक पद्धत– यामध्ये ग्रंथ दिल्यानंतर त्या जागी त्यादाखल नोंद क्रमांकाचा ठोकळा ठेवला जात असे.

dump – संगणकावर माहिती सुरक्षित साठविणे.

duplicate – दुसरी/नक्कल प्रत – प्रतिलिपीमुळे प्रतीची हुबेहूब नक्कल.

duplicate entry – द्वितीय नोंद / दुबार नोंद – निर्देशनातील एकाच विषयाची दोन वेळा केलेली नोंद. ही नोंद दोन वेगळ्या विषयशीर्षकाखाली केलेली असते.

duplicate paging – दुबार पृष्ठांकन – ग्रंथाची दुबार प्रत डाव्या बाजूस (मूळ ग्रंथपृष्ठाची प्रत) तर उजव्या बाजूस भाषांतरित मजकुराची प्रत असे पृष्ठांकन केलेले असते.

duplicate ticket – दुबार परवानापत्रक – ग्रंथ वापरण्यासाठी दिलेले ग्रंथपत्र गहाळ झाल्यानंतर देण्यात येणारे ग्रंथपत्र.

duplicate title – दुबार शीर्षक/दुहेरी शीर्षक – पुन: मुद्रितांसाठी मूळ शीर्षकाबरोबरच दुहेरी शीर्षक दिले जाते.

duplication – प्रतिलिपीकरण – मूळ प्रतींपासून अनेक प्रती मिळविण्याची पद्धती/क्रिया.

duplication centre – प्रतिलिपीकरण केंद्र.

duplicating machine / xerox machine – प्रतिलिपीयंत्र – दुबार प्रत काढण्यासाठीचे यंत्र.

duplicating technique – प्रतिलिपी तंत्र – दुबार प्रत काढण्याविषयीचे तंत्र.

duplicator – प्रतिलिपीयंत्र – मूळ माहितीच्या अनेक प्रति यंत्रांच्या साहाय्याने मिळवितात ते यंत्र.

dust cover / dust wrapper / book jacket – ग्रंथवेष्टन/मलपृष्ठ.

dust wrapper / dust cover / book jacket – ग्रंथवेष्टन.

dynamic map – हालचालदर्शक नकाशा – बाण, तुटक रेषा वापरून वाहतूक, स्थलांतर दर्शविणारा नकाशा.

econometrics – **अर्थगणनशास्त्र** – अर्थविषयक बाबींचे संख्याशास्त्रीय सिद्धान्ताचा उपयोग करून केलेले विश्लेषण.

edge-notched / marginal hole / punched cards – **खाचा/कडा/खाचयुक्त पत्रे** – कडांना खाचा असलेली पत्रे.

edit – **संपादन** – (१) संपादन करणे. (२) संगणकामध्ये माहिती समाविष्ट करणे, बदलणे.

edited – **संपादित** – (१) अनेक व्यक्तींनी लिखाणात सहभाग घेऊन प्रकाशित केलेले साहित्य. (२) एक किंवा अनेक लेखकांच्या वेगवेगळ्या लेखनाचे संपादन करणे.

editing – **संपादनाची कार्यवाही.**

edition – **आवृत्ती** – (१) एकावेळी छापलेल्या व प्रकाशित झालेल्या ग्रंथाच्या प्रती. (२) एकावेळी एका ग्रंथाच्या एकाच स्वरूपात काढलेल्या समरूप प्रती.

edition binding / publisher's binding – **मूळ, प्रकाशक बांधणी** – प्रकाशकाने प्रकाशनप्रक्रियेत ठरवून केलेली व प्रकाशकाने मोबदला देऊन करवून घेतलेली बांधणी.

edition statement – **आवृत्तीविषयक उत्तरदायित्वाचे विवरण** – हे विवरण तालिकापत्रात नोंदविले जाते.

editor – **संपादक** – (१) अनेक लेखकांचे लेख वा कृती एकत्र करून नवीन ग्रंथ निर्माण करणारा अशा ग्रंथामध्ये स्वतःचे योगदान म्हणून टिपा, प्रस्तावना किंवा टीकात्मक लिखाणांचा समावेश करणारी व्यक्ती किंवा विविध ग्रंथकारांनी लिहिलेले लेख, ग्रंथ इ. एकत्र करून ग्रंथनिर्मिती करणारी व्यक्ती म्हणजेच संपादक. (२) संगणकामध्ये माहितीत बदल करून सुधारणा करणारा सूचनापट.

editor entry – **संपादक नोंद** – तालिकेमध्ये संपादकाच्या नावाने केलेली नोंद.

editor reference – **संपादकीय संदर्भ** – तालिकेमध्ये संपादकाच्या नावाने नोंद केलेली माहिती.

editorial – **संपादकीय** – ताज्या घटनांसंदर्भात नियतकालिकांची स्वत:ची भूमिका विशद करणारा लेख.

editorial direction – **संपादकीय कार्यदर्शन** – संपादकीय मार्गदर्शनाखाली तयार केलेला ग्रंथ – ही एक सामूहिक साहित्यकृती असते.

education – **शिक्षण**.

education for librarianship – **ग्रंथपालनासाठीचे शिक्षण**.

educational library – **शैक्षणिक ग्रंथालय** – शाळा, महाविद्यालय, विद्यापीठ इ.चे ग्रंथालय.

elasticity – **लवचिकपणा/स्थितिस्थापकत्व**.

electic bibliography – **मतसंग्रही ग्रंथसूची** – अनेक मतांच्या संदर्भात निवडलेल्या ग्रंथांची सूची.

elective bibliography – **ऐच्छिक/वैकल्पिक ग्रंथसूची** – ग्रंथालयाने पसंत केलेल्या ग्रंथांची सूची.

electronic book – **विद्युत/विजाणु ग्रंथ** – परमाणूंच्या साहाय्याने तयार केलेला ग्रंथ. उदा. CD-ROM

electronic database – **विजाणु/विद्युतीय माहितीसंग्रह**.

electronic document delivery system – **विद्युत/विजाणु प्रलेख प्रदान पद्धती** – ग्रंथालयाकडून किंवा प्रकाशकाकडून वाचकाला यंत्राद्वारे पुरविलेली माहिती. उदा. e-mail, CD-ROM चा वापर.

electronic information resources – **विजाणु माहिती साधने**.

electronic journal – **विजाणु पत्रिका/मासिक** – यंत्राद्वारे, संगणकाद्वारे प्रसिद्ध केले जाणारे नियतकालिक. विद्युत परमाणूंच्या साहाय्याने दृश्य तबकडीवर माहिती उपलब्ध करून देणारे नियतकालिक.

electronic library – **विजाणु ग्रंथालय** – संगणकाद्वारे वापरावयाचे वाचनसाहित्य उपलब्ध असलेले ग्रंथालय.

electronic mail / e-mail – **विजाणु परमाणू टपाल** – संगणकाद्वारे पाठविलेले टपाल, पत्रव्यवहार, माहितीचे आदान-प्रदान.

electronic media – **विजाणु माध्यम** – माहितीचा संचय आणि प्रतिप्राप्तीसाठी वापरली जाणारी संगणकाधिष्ठित माध्यमे.

electronic ordering – **विजाणु आदेशन** – संगणकाद्वारे वाचनसाहित्याचे आदेशन.

electronic publishing – **विजाणु प्रकाशन** – संगणकाच्या साहाय्याने केलेले माहितीचे प्रकाशन व प्रसारण.

electronics – **विजाणुतंत्र** – इलेक्ट्रॉनिक साधनांचे शास्त्र किंवा त्याचा विकास.

elements – मूलतत्त्वे/घटक – (१) संपूर्णातील एक भाग, अवयव (२) वर्गीकरण करताना गृहीत धरलेले तत्त्व.

elision – अंत्यस्वरलोप/पदलोप – उदा. २००७–८, २००८–९ असे लिहिणे.

ellipsis – ommission marks – गाळलेल्या शब्दांसाठी चिन्हे – उदा. (...........)

embossed book – उमट रेखित/कोरीव ग्रंथ – कोरून अक्षरे काढलेला ग्रंथ. उदा. ब्रेल लिपीतील ग्रंथ किंवा उमट रेखनतंत्राने तयार केलेला ग्रंथ.

embossing – उमटरेखन – कागदावर दाबून अक्षरे आत उमटविण्याची क्रिया.

embroidered binding – कशिदाबांधणी – नक्षी कामासह ग्रंथबांधणी.

embroidered covers – कशिदा/बेलबुट्टी काढलेली आच्छादने.

empty digit – रिक्तअंक/निरर्थक संकेत चिन्ह/रिकामा अंक – (१) असा अंक ज्यास क्रमवाचक मूल्य असते पण चिन्हांकनदर्शक मूल्य नसते. (२) वर्गीकरण करताना वापरावयाची चिन्हे. उदा. अवतरण चिन्हे. अशा चिन्हाचा वापर वर्गीकरण पद्धतीत केला जातो.

emptying digit – निरर्थक अंक/रिकामा करणारा अंक – आधार विषयातील असा अंक किंवा उपांगातील असा अंक जो आपल्या नंतरच्या अंकास त्याच्या शब्ददर्शक मूल्यापासून वंचित करतो परंतु क्रमवाचक संख्या कायम ठेवतो; अशा अंकाचा वापर द्विबिंदू वर्गीकरण पद्धतीत केला आहे.

empty / emptying digit – रिकामा करणारा अंक – वर्गीकरण पद्धतीत वापरलेला असा अंक जो रूढार्थाने मूल्यहीन पद्धतीत एकापेक्षा जास्त समपदस्थ वर्ग निर्माण करण्यासाठी नऊ हा अंक या अर्थाने वापरला आहे.

encode – संकेतन – संगणकातील माहितीचे तात्पुरते सांकेतिक रूपांतर करणे. ही माहिती हवी तेव्हा मूळ स्वरूपात मिळविता येते.

encryption – सांकेतिक जतन – संगणकातील माहिती सांकेतिक स्वरूपात रूपांतरित करण्याची यंत्रणा. ही माहिती फक्त अधिकृत उपयोजकांना पाहता येते, वापरता येते.

encumbering – गुंता/अडचण/अडथळा/पायगुंता/खोडा/बोजा लादणे.

encyclopaedia / cyclopaedia – विश्वकोश/ज्ञानकोश – सर्वांगीण माहिती किंवा विशिष्ट विषयावरील माहिती वर्णानुक्रमानुसार रचना करून तयार केलेला माहितीकोश. बरेचदा अनेक खंडात प्रकाशित होतात. याच्या अद्ययावततेसाठी वार्षिक पुरवणी खंड पुरविला जातो.

encyclopaedia – general – सामान्य विश्वकोश/ज्ञानकोश – एक अथवा सर्व विषयातील ज्ञानाची ढोबळमानाने माहिती देणारा ग्रंथ.

encyclopaedia special – विशेष/विषय ज्ञानकोश – यामध्ये केवळ विशिष्ट विषयांबाबतची माहिती समाविष्ट असते.

end key – अंत्य कळ – संगणकाच्या कळपटावरील एक कळ ज्यामुळे ओळीच्या शेवटी स्थानबिंदू (कर्सर) पोहोचतो.

endowment – देणगी/धर्मार्थ – विशिष्ट कार्याकरता दिलेली कायमची देणगी.

end matter – समाप्ती संदर्भपृष्ठे – यात टीपा, ग्रंथसूची इ. समाविष्ट असतात.

endowment fund – वर्षासन निधी/रक्कम.

end user – प्रत्यक्ष उपयोजक – उत्पादने व ग्रंथालय सेवांचा प्रत्यक्ष उपयोग करणारी व्यक्ती.

end papers – आंतरपृष्ठे समाप्ती पृष्ठे (शेवटचे कागद) – पुस्तकाच्या सुरुवातीस आणि शेवटी बांधणीकाराने ग्रंथाची शिवलेली बांधणी पक्की राहण्यासाठी वापरलेले कागद.

end user searching – प्रत्यक्ष उपयोजकाने संगणकाद्वारा माहितीचा शोध घेणे.

end notes – समाप्ती नोंद – प्रकरणाच्या किंवा ग्रंथाच्या शेवटी छापलेल्या नोंदी.

ends – पुस्तकाच्या बाजू/कडा.

energy – ऊर्जा – जोमाने किंवा उत्साहाने काम करण्याची शक्ती, ताकद.

energy facet – ऊर्जा पैलू/ऊर्जा मुख – (द्विबिंदू वर्गीकरणातील पैलू) (१) द्विबिंदू वर्गीकरण पद्धतीत वापरलेला विभाजक घटक. (२) द्विबिंदू वर्गीकरणाच्या विशिष्ट वर्गातील निगडित प्रश्न, पद्धती किंवा कार्य दर्शविणारा पैलू. मुख्य वर्गातील महत्त्वाचा गुणधर्म दर्शविणारा पैलू उदा. ग्रंथालय शास्त्र या मुख्य वर्गात वर्गीकरण, तालिकीकरण यांसारख्या क्रिया दर्शविल्या जातात. ऊर्जा मुखाद्वारे एखादी क्रिया दर्शविली जाते.

energy isolate – ऊर्जा उपांग – ज्याचा वापर द्विबिंदू वर्गीकरण पद्धतीत केला आहे.

engineering drawings – अभियांत्रिकी रेखाचित्रे – हे माहितीचे प्राथमिक स्रोत होत.

engraving – कोरीव काम – लाकूड, धातू वा इतर पदार्थ यावर अक्षरे किंवा संकल्पचित्रे कोरण्याची कला. यासाठी कागदावर किंवा अन्य साहित्यावर इन्टॅग्लिओ प्रोसेसने मुद्रणासाठी किंवा ठसा उमटविण्यासाठी कापून किंवा आम्लीकरण करून कोरीव काम केले जाते.

enhanced local area network – स्थानिक संगणक जाळे अधिकाधिक सुविधायुक्त करणे.

enlarged edition – विस्तारित आवृत्ती – ग्रंथाच्या मूळ आवृत्तीत भर घालून नवीन आवृत्ती प्रकाशित करणे.

enliven – सजीव करणे/जिवंतपणा आणणे/तरतरी आणणे.

enter key – संगणकाच्या कळपटावरील एक कळ – संगणकाला दिलेल्या सूचना अमलात आणण्यासाठी वापरावयाची अंतिम सूचनाकळ.

entity – अस्तित्व – (१) स्वतंत्र अस्तित्व असलेली वस्तू अथवा घटक.

entry – नोंद – ग्रंथालयामध्ये ग्रंथ वा इतर साहित्य यांविषयी लिहिलेली माहिती.

entry element – **नोंदघटक** – ज्या शब्दाखाली किंवा शब्दसमूहाखाली नोंद केली जाते तो शब्द किंवा शब्दसमूह.

entry word – **नोंद प्रथम पद/शब्द** – (१) नोंदीतील पहिल्या शब्दाला नोंद प्रथम पद असे म्हणतात. (२) तालिकेमध्ये ज्या शब्दाची शीर्षक म्हणून नोंद झाली आहे असा अनुक्रम निर्देशन शब्द. (३) तालिकेमध्ये त्या विशिष्ट नोंदीचे स्थान ठरविणारा शब्द.

enumeration – **प्रगणन/मोजणी** – ग्रंथवर्गीकरण करताना प्रगणन क्लृप्ती वापरली जाते.

enumeration device – **प्रगणन युक्ती.**

enumerative – **प्रगणनीय/परिगणनात्मक** – सविस्तर वर्णन केलेला/वर्णिलेला.

enumerative bibliography – **प्रगणनीय ग्रंथसूची** – संकलकाने ठरविलेल्या मर्यादित नोंदींची सूची. ही भौगोलिकदृष्ट्या, क्रमानुसार किंवा विषयानुसार असू शकते.

enumerative classification – **प्रगणात्मक वर्गीकरण** – (१) वर्गीकरण तक्त्यात पद्धतशीरपणे सर्व विषयांचे केलेले विस्तृत प्रगणन/यादीकरण. (२) विशिष्ट विषयांची सूची करण्याचा प्रयत्न करणारे वर्गीकरण निवडक वर्गीकरण करण्याची प्रक्रिया.

enumerative indexing language – **प्रगणनीय निर्देशन भाषा** – निर्देशनामध्ये विशिष्ट विषयांबरोबर मिश्र विषयांसाठी वापरल्या जाणाऱ्या संज्ञांची बंदिस्त पद्धती. उदा. दोन संज्ञांच्यामध्ये कोणतीही संज्ञा समाविष्ट करता येणार नाही. अशी संज्ञांची यादी.

envelop – **वेष्टण/पाकीट** – संगणकातील संदेशजतन कप्पा.

environment – **पर्यावरण** – सभोवतालची परिस्थिती.

environmental science – **पर्यावरण शास्त्र.**

environmental technology – **पर्यावरण तंत्रज्ञान.**

entropy – **अवक्रममाप.**

ephemera – **अल्पकाळ महत्त्वाचे असणारे साहित्य/कार्यक्रमपत्रिका/पत्रके.**

ephemeris / almanac – **पंचांग** – भौगोलिक वैशिष्ट्यपूर्ण दैनंदिन माहिती देणारे प्रकाशन.

epigraph – **पुरालेख** – अवतरणदर्शक नोंद. ग्रंथातील प्रकरणाचे सुरुवातीला किंवा ग्रंथांची सुरुवातीची मजकुराविषयी संकल्पना देणारी नोंदपृष्ठे.

epithet – **पुरवणीनाम** – ग्रंथकाराचे विशिष्ट पर्यायी नाव. ज्या नावाने नोंद केली असेल असे ग्रंथकाराचे नाव लिहिले जाते.

epitome – **संक्षेपग्रंथ** – उदा. ज्ञानेश्वरी/गीताध्याय यांचे संक्षेप ग्रंथ.

eponym – **एखाद्या स्थानाला/कालखंडाला दिलेले व्यक्तीचे नाव.** उदा. पहिला बाजीराव पेशवा कालखंड.

erase – **वगळणे** – संगणकातील चुकीची माहिती काढून टाकण्याची क्रिया.

erotica – **शृंगारिक साहित्य.**

errata – **शुद्धिपत्र** – ग्रंथातील चुकीच्या मजकुराचा संदर्भासहित उल्लेख करून सुधारणा सुचविणारे पृष्ठ. हे पृष्ठ बहुधा ग्रंथाच्या शेवटी समाविष्ट केले जाते.

error / bug – **चूक** – (१) चुकीसाठी वापरली जाणारी संज्ञा, (२) संगणक पडद्यावर दिसणारा चुकीची आज्ञा दिल्याचा संदेश.

erudite – **विद्वान** – सखोल ज्ञान असलेला.

escape – **रद्द सूचना संदेश** – संगणकाला दिलेली आज्ञा रद्द करण्याची सूचना.

escapist literature – **हलके-फुलके साहित्य** – गूढकथा, शौर्यकथा, प्रेमकथा यांसारखे केवळ मनोरंजनासाठी उपलब्ध साहित्य.

et al – **आणि इतर** – तळटीप देताना पूर्वी उल्लेखसूचीमध्ये दिलेल्या दोन किंवा अधिक सहलेखकांबाबत उल्लेख करण्यासाठी हा संक्षेप वापरला जातो.

et alia – **आणि इतर गोष्ट.**

et alibi – **आणि इतरत्र.**

etc. – **इत्यादी.**

ethernet – **जोडलेल्या संगणकांसाठी सर्वमान्य नियम.**

etching – **कोरीव काम** – काच, तांबे, लोखंड, जस्त यांसारख्या धातूंवर विशिष्ट सुईने कोरून नक्षी वा मजकूर काढण्याची प्रक्रिया.

ethics – **नीतीशास्त्र/नीतीमूल्ये** – विशिष्ट समूहाच्या मान्यतेने, परंपरेने रूढ असलेली आचारसंहिता.

ethnic number / linguistic number – **वंशांक** – वर्गीकामध्ये भाषा किंवा वंशानुसार समाविष्ट केला जाणारा अंक. या अंकानुसार ग्रंथरचना केली जाते.

eurotra – **स्वयंचलित भाषांतर पद्धती** – केंद्रीय सांकेतिक भाषेचा आधार घेऊन इतर अनेक भाषांमध्ये वापरण्यास उपयुक्त पद्धती. ही सध्या विकासात्मक अवस्थेत असून त्याचा उपयोग अनेक भाषांमध्ये वेगाने लेखप्रकाशन करण्यासाठी होऊ शकेल.

evaluation – **मूल्यांकन/मूल्यमापन** – सेवांची परिणामकारकता मोजण्याचे साधन.

evaluation number – **मूल्यांक.**

evaluation facet – **मूल्यमापन पैलू.**

even page – **ग्रंथाचे समअंकी पृष्ठ** – ग्रंथाचे डाव्या बाजूचे पृष्ठ.

everyday approach – **दैनंदिन दृष्टिकोन.**

every book its reader – प्रत्येक ग्रंथाला वाचक – ग्रंथालयशास्त्राचे तिसरे सूत्र.

every reader his/her book – प्रत्येक वाचकाला ग्रंथ – ग्रंथालयशास्त्राचे दुसरे सूत्र.

evolutionary order – उत्क्रांतिक्रम – वर्गीकरण करताना उत्क्रांतिक्रमानुसार किंवा इतिहासानुसार विषयरचना करणे.

exact size / absolute size – अचूक आकार (ग्रंथाचा) – ग्रंथाच्या आकाराचे चिन्हात्मक स्वरूप देण्याऐवजी सेंमी किंवा इंच या मापांद्वारे दिलेला ग्रंथाचा अचूक आकार.

excerpt – उतारा – ग्रंथातील मजकुराचा काही भाग.

exchange – अदलाबदल/विनिमय – (१) एखाद्या वस्तूची चलनाऐवजी दुसऱ्या वस्तूद्वारे किंमत. (२) ग्रंथालय सहकार करताना दोन वा अधिक ग्रंथालयांमध्ये नियतकालिके वा इतर अधिक प्रतींची अदलाबदल केली जाते.

exchange department – विनिमय/अदलाबदल विभाग.

exchange rate – विनिमय दर – आंतरदेशीय चलनाचा दर.

exclusive – अपवर्जक/निवडक/विशिष्ट/वगळून.

exclusiveness – अपवर्जकता.

execute – अंमलबजावणी करणे – योजनेनुसार कार्यान्वित करणे.

executive director – कार्यकारी संचालक.

executive order – कार्यकारी/अंमलबजावणी आदेश.

exhausted edition / out of print – अनुपलब्ध/छपाईबाह्य आवृत्ती – सर्वसमावेशक आवृत्ती/ नि:शेष आवृत्ती.

exhaustive – व्यापक – सर्वसमावेशक.

exhaustive approach – व्यापक दृष्टिकोन/सर्वसमावेशक दृष्टिकोन.

exhaustive bibliography – सर्वसमावेशक ग्रंथसूची – नि:शेष ग्रंथसूची.

exhaustiveness – नि:शेषता – विभागणीनंतर काहीही शिल्लक न रहाणे.

exhibition – प्रदर्शन.

exhibition of book – ग्रंथांचे प्रदर्शन.

exit permit – (पुस्तके) बाहेर नेण्यासाठीचा परवाना.

expansibility – विस्तारक्षमता.

expansive classification / Cutter classification – विस्तारशील वर्गीकरण – सी.ए. कटर यांची सर्वसाधारण ग्रंथालयांसाठी उपयुक्त अशी वर्गीकरण पद्धती इ.स. १८९३ मध्ये तयार केली. सध्या ती वापरात नाही.

expeditious – शीघ्रतम/त्वरेने/लवकर.

expert – विशेषतज्ज्ञ – एखाद्या विषयातील तज्ज्ञ व्यक्ती.

expert advice – तज्ज्ञाचा सल्ला.

expert system – तज्ज्ञ पद्धती – विशिष्ट विषयाची सर्वांगीण माहिती जतन करणारी संगणकपद्धती.

explanatory reference – विवरणात्मक संदर्भ – संबंधित शीर्षकाच्या उपयोगासाठी सविस्तर मार्गदर्शन करणारा संदर्भ.

explicit – समाप्तीपत्र – हस्तलिखिते किंवा जुन्या ग्रंथाच्या शेवटी दिलेली समाप्सीनोंद.

exponential growth – गुणित वृद्धी – गुणित प्रमाणात झालेली संख्यात्मक वाढ.

exposed – विग्रेपित/उघडणे.

expound – उघड/स्पष्ट करणे – तपशिलाने (एखादी गोष्ट) स्पष्ट करणे किंवा विशद करणे.

expressed thought – अभिव्यक्त विचार – भाषा, चित्र, चिन्ह किंवा इतर माध्यमांच्या साहाय्याने संप्रेषित केलेले विचार.

expressive notation – अर्थवाहक चिन्हांकन – डॉ. रंगनाथन् यांच्या चिन्हांकन सूत्रांमधील एक सूत्र. दोन संज्ञा या एकाच पंक्तीमधील वा शृंखलेतील आहेत हे दर्शविणारे चिन्हांकन.

expurgated edition – आक्षेपार्ह मजकूर वगळून तयार केलेली संक्षिप्त आवृत्ती.

extension – व्याप्ती/विस्तार – (१) वर्गीकरण करताना वर्गविस्तार किंवा संज्ञाविस्तार हा समाविष्ट असलेल्या संज्ञा दर्शवितो. (२) एखाद्या विषयाची व्याप्ती.

extension activities – विस्तार कार्ये – मूळ कार्यास पूरक असणारी कामे.

extension cards – पूरक पत्र.

extension counter – मर्यादित सेवा देण्यासाठीचा कट्टा.

extension service – विस्तार सेवा.

extension work – विस्तार कार्य – ग्रंथालयातील कामाव्यतिरिक्त संबंधित कार्य. उदा. चर्चासत्र, वाचकसभा इ.

external – बाह्य/बाहेरचा.

external back-up – बाह्य/बहि:स्थ स्थळप्रत – संगणकाच्या मुख्य संचयाव्यतिरिक्त राखला जाणारा माहितीसंचय. उदा. तबकडीच्या साहाय्याने.

external reader – बहि:स्थ वाचक – (१) ग्रंथालयाचा नोंदणीकृत नसलेला वाचक. (२) ग्रंथालयामध्ये तात्पुरती वाचनाची परवानगी दिलेला वाचक.

extra binding – विशेष बांधणी.

extranet – अतिरिक्त संगणक जाळे.

extract – सारांश/सार – (१) दुसऱ्या ग्रंथातील भाग समाविष्ट असलेला ग्रंथ. (२) सारांशरूपाने घेतलेला उतारा.

extract note – सार टीप.

extrinsic – बाह्य/बाहेरचा.

F

facet – पैलू – (१) प्रमुख वर्ग किंवा मूळ वर्ग. साम्य गुणाच्या आधारे निश्चित केलेला एक उपांगाचा गट. उदा. रसायनशास्त्राच्या वर्गीकरणातील पैलूंपैकी पदार्थ (मूलद्रव्य) हे एक उपांग आहे. (२) वर्गीकरण करताना एखादा विषय एकाच लक्षणगुणानुसार वर्गीकृत केला जातो तेव्हा विशिष्ट पैलूचा विचार केला जातो.

facet analysis – पैलू विश्लेषण – (१) ग्रंथबद्ध – ग्रंथनिविष्ट असलेल्या विषयाचे त्याच्या वैशिष्ट्यांनुसार विविध पैलूंमध्ये केलेले विश्लेषण. (२) वर्गीकरण करताना पात्र मूलभूत पैलूंचा विचार करून कोणता पैलू वर्गीकरण करण्यासाठी वापरावा हे ठरविण्यासाठी विश्लेषण करावे.

facet common – सामान्य पैलू.

facet criticism – टीका पैलू.

facet device – पैलू व्यक्ती.

facet distributed – वितरीत पैलू.

facet formula – पैलू परिसूत्र – वर्गीकरण करताना विषय विभाजनासाठी पैलूसूत्र वापरावे लागते.

facet indicator – पैलूदर्शक चिन्ह – द्विबिंदू वर्गीकरण पद्धतीमधील चिन्हांकनामध्ये चिन्हांकनाचे भाग दर्शविणारे व कोणता पैलू वापरावा हे दर्शविणारे चिन्ह.

facet relation – पैलूमधील संबंध – एखाद्या विषयाच्या विविध अंगांचे परस्पर संबंध.

facet synthesis – पैलू संश्लेषण.

facet telescoping point – पैलूतील दूरस्थ बिंदू.

faceted – पैलूबद्ध.

faceted classification scheme – **पैलूबद्ध/पैलूयुक्त वर्गीकरण पद्धती** – वर्गीकरण पद्धतीमध्ये पैलूंचा वापर करण्याची सुविधा असलेली पद्धती. आधुनिक वर्गीकरण पद्धतीमध्ये काल व स्थान हे पैलू वापरता येतात.

faceted notation – **पैलूयुक्त/पैलूबद्ध चिन्हांकन** – ग्रंथ वर्गीकरणामध्ये ग्रंथविषयाचे पैलू दर्शविणारे चिन्हांकन.

facetiae – अश्लील साहित्य.

facilitate – सोपा/सुलभ करणे.

facility – **सुविधा** – विशिष्ट कारणासाठी पुरविलेली सेवा.

facsimile – **प्रतिरूप** – मूळ ग्रंथानुरूप हुबेहूब प्रत.

facsimile binding – **मूळ बांधणीरूप बांधणी/प्रतिरूप बांधणी.**

facsimile catalogue – **प्रतिरूप तालिका** – नकाशा, चित्रे, नक्षी यांची प्रतिरूपे वापरून नेहमीच्या तालिकेपेक्षा मोठ्या आकाराच्या तालिकापत्रावर केलेल्या नोंदी.

facsimile edition – **प्रतिरूप आवृत्ती** – छायाचित्रण वा छायाप्रतींद्वारे काढलेली हुबेहूब आवृत्ती. बहुधा छपाईबाह्य पुस्तकांबाबत पुन्हा खर्च करण्याऐवजी अशी आवृत्ती काढली जाते.

facsimile reprint – **प्रतिरूप पुनर्मुद्रण.**

facsimile transmission – **प्रतिरूप प्रसारण/स्थानांतरण** – एखादा माहितीसंच दूरसंचार प्रसाराद्वारे दुसऱ्या यंत्रावर हुबेहूब प्रतिरूप करणे.

fact – **वस्तुस्थिती/सत्य.**

fair copy – **स्वच्छ/चांगली प्रत** – मजकुराचा मसुदा पाहून अतिशय काळजीपूर्वक तयार केलेली बिनचूक प्रत. अशी प्रत हस्तलिखित किंवा टंकलिखित असू शकते.

fair use – **योग्य वापर** – उदा. संशोधन, अध्ययन व अध्यापनासाठीचा वापर.

fairy tale – **परिकथा.**

false – **चूक.**

false combinations – **माहितीची प्रतिप्राप्ती करताना माहितीसंचाद्वारे होणारा आवाज.**

false date – **चुकीचा दिनांक** – हेतूपूर्वक वा अनवधानाने चुकीचा दिनांक दिला जातो. तालिकेमध्ये काहीवेळा विशेष नोंद करून कंसात योग्य दिनांक दिला जातो.

false drop – माहितीची प्रतिप्राप्ती करताना आढळून आलेला चुकीचा उल्लेख. उल्लेख केलेल्या प्रलेखात प्रत्यक्षात संदर्भ उपलब्ध नसणे.

false first edition – **चुकीची प्रथमावृत्ती** – दुसऱ्या प्रकाशकाने आधी आवृत्ती प्रसिद्ध केली असताना काहीवेळा ग्रंथामध्ये प्रथम आवृत्ती असा उल्लेख केला जातो.

false link – **अर्थहीन दुवा** – वर्गीकरण क्रियेमध्ये उपयुक्त शृंखला निर्देशनामध्ये योग्य संज्ञा दिल्याशिवाय चिन्हांकन शृंखला वाढविली जाते ती पायरी डॉ. रंगनाथन् यांच्या साखळी पद्धतीत वापरलेली संज्ञा.

false name – **बनावट नाव/टोपण नाव.**

family – **कुल/घराणे** – समान गुणधर्म असलेला ग्रंथसंग्रह.

family name – **कुलनाम/परिवार/कुटुंब नाव** – आनुवंशिकता दर्शविणारे नाव.

fanciful title – **कल्पनारम्य ग्रंथनाम/ग्रंथशीर्षक** – ग्रंथनाम वाङ्मयीन अभिरुचीने उच्च तथापि रूपक गोष्टीद्वारे अर्थ सूचित करते असे ग्रंथनाम.

farmington plan – **फर्मिंग्टन योजना** – या योजनेनुसार ६० अमेरिकन ग्रंथालयांनी एकत्र येऊन परदेशी ग्रंथ एकत्रितरीत्या खरेदी करण्यास मान्यता दिली होती. संशोधकांना त्यांच्या छायाप्रती उपलब्ध करून दिल्या गेल्या.

fassicle / fascicule – **पृष्ठसंच** – छपाई व प्रकाशनाच्या सोयीसाठी ग्रंथाचे छोटे भाग केले जातात.

fault – **दोष** – संगणकाच्या कार्यवाहीमध्ये आलेला अडथळा/व्यत्यय.

favoured – **अनुग्रहित/आवडता.**

favoured category – **प्राधान्य वर्ग** – वर्गीकरणामध्ये प्रवर्गाद्वारे वर्गांक देताना वापरण्याचे तत्त्व.

favoured category device – **प्राधान्य प्रवर्ग क्लृप्ती** – प्राधान्य प्रवर्गानुसार वर्गांक तयार करण्याची पद्धती.

favoured country – **प्राधान्यदेश/इष्टदेश** – वर्गीकरण करताना देशानुरूप वर्गांक देताना वापरण्याचे तत्त्व.

favoured focus number – **प्राधान्य मुख्य अंक.**

favoured language – **आवडती भाषा/मातृभाषा/प्राधान्यभाषा/इष्टभाषा** – वर्गीकरणामध्ये भाषेनुरूप वर्गांक देताना वापरण्याचे तत्त्व.

favoured script – **प्राधान्यलिपी/इष्टलिपी** – वर्गीकरणामध्ये लिपीरूप वर्गांक देताना वापरण्याचे तत्त्व.

fax machine – **फॅक्स यंत्र** – उपग्रह संदेशवहनाद्वारा संदेश देण्याचे एक साधन.

featherweight paper – **पिसाप्रमाणे वजनाला हलका कागद.**

feather work – **ग्रंथ अलंकरणाचा एक प्रकार** – १८व्या शतकात आयर्लंडमध्ये अतिशय कलात्मक ग्रंथसजावटीची ही पद्धत सुरू झाली.

feature – **लक्षणगुण** – निर्देशन केलेल्या नोंदीचा लक्षणगुण.

feature cards – लक्षण पत्रे.

feature card system – **वैशिष्ट्य पत्र पद्धती** – माहितीची प्रतिप्राप्ती करण्याची एक पद्धती.

feature heading – **वैशिष्ट्यपूर्ण शीर्षक** – वर्गीकरण परिशिष्टामध्ये अचूक चिन्हांकन दिलेले नाही असा शीर्षकाचा वैशिष्ट्यपूर्ण भाग.

features – स्वरूप/वैशिष्ट्ये.

feedback – **प्रतिसाद** – (१) पुरविलेल्या माहितीबद्दल प्रतिक्रिया देणे, अभिप्राय देणे. (२) घटनेच्या परिणामांचा प्रत्यक्ष वापर. उदा. वाचकांच्या सूचनेनुसार ग्रंथालय सेवांमध्ये बदल वा सुधारणा घडवून आणणे.

feeder service – **पूरक सेवा** – ग्रंथालयाची पूरक सेवा.

felicitation volume – **गौरवग्रंथ** – (१) स्मरणार्थ म्हणून किंवा गौरवार्थ प्रकाशित केलेला ग्रंथ. यामध्ये ख्यातनाम व्यक्तींचे लेख असतात. यामध्ये पुष्कळदा त्या व्यक्तीचे विद्यार्थी आणि सहव्यवसायी, जोडीदार यांच्या लेखांचा समावेश असतो. असा ग्रंथ एखाद्या व्यक्तीच्या सन्मानार्थ प्रकाशित केला जातो. (२) व्यक्ती किंवा संस्थेच्या गौरवपर विशेष प्रसंगी प्रकाशित केलेला ग्रंथ.

festschrift/commomoration volume – **स्मृतिग्रंथ** – एखाद्या विशिष्ट व्यक्तीच्या सन्मानार्थ प्रकाशित ग्रंथ. या ग्रंथात गौरविलेल्या व्यक्तीचे चरित्र आणि त्यासंबंधी इतरांचे लेख असतात.

fibre optics – **प्रकाश तंतू** – विद्युतभारित संदेशाचे प्रकाशकिरणांमध्ये रूपांतर करून संदेशवहन करू शकणारी काचसदृश माध्यमाची केबल.

fiction – **कादंबरी/कल्पितकथा** – वाङ्मय साहित्याचा एक प्रकार.

fictious name – **काल्पनिक नाव** – लेखनकार्यासाठी धारण केलेले काल्पनिक नाव.

field – **नोंदक्षेत्र/रकाना** – (१) डेटाबेसमधील नोंदीचा/नोंद लिहिण्याचा एक भाग – उदा. पु. ल. देशपांडे यांच्या 'बटाट्याची चाळ' या पुस्तकाच्या नोंदीत 'ग्रंथकार' या फिल्डमध्ये देशपांडे पु.ल. ही माहिती नोंदली जाईल. (२) तालिकीकरणामध्ये विशिष्ट माहितीसाठी विशिष्ट नोंदक्षेत्र उपलब्ध असते. (३) वर्गीकरण करताना विशिष्ट गुणवैशिष्ट्यांनुसार नोंद केली जाते. (४) माहितीसंचामधील अगदी छोटासा रकाना. (५) माहिती भरण्यासाठीची जागा.

field chart – घटक/रकाना/तक्ता.

field searching – घटकांचे शोधन.

field specific search – घटकांचा विशेष शोध.

field data field – घटकांची माहिती.

fields – अनेक घटक.

figure – **आकृती/संख्या** – ग्रंथातील मजकूर काहीवेळा चित्रे, नकाशे, आकृत्या, आलेख यांनी अधिक स्पष्ट केला जातो.

file – संचिका/पंजिका – (१) ग्रंथालयातील नोंदी एकत्रित ठेवण्यासाठी नोंदवही. (२) संगणकातील माहिती संच. (३) डेटाबेसमध्ये व्यवस्थितपणे माहिती नोंदविण्याची जागा – एखाद्या डेटाबेसमध्ये अनेक फाईल्स (एक माहितीसाठी दुसरी सूचीसाठी, तिसरी आज्ञावलीसाठी इ.) असतात. रूढार्थाने, संगणकात कुठलीही माहिती नोंदविण्यासाठी एक संचिका सुरू करावी लागतेच. कालांतराने पुन्हा ती माहिती वाचायची असेल तर प्रथम एका संचिकेचे नाव देऊन उघडावी लागते.

file extention – संचिका विस्तार – माहितीसंचाला दिलेले संगणकातील विस्तारनाम.

file insertion – संचिका समावेशन – संगणकामध्ये एका माहितीसंचातील माहिती दुसऱ्या माहितीसंचामध्ये समाविष्ट करणे.

file index – संचिका निर्देश.

file item – संचिकेमधील नोंद करण्याचा मजकूर.

file management system – संचिका व्यवस्थापन पद्धती.

file protection – संचिका संरक्षण – संगणकातील माहिती सुरक्षित ठेवण्यासाठी केलेली व्यवस्था.

file processing – संचिकेवरील सोपस्कार.

file server – संस्थेतील इतर संगणकांसाठी माहिती धारण करणारा संगणक.

file transfer – माहितीगटाच्या संगणकातील स्थानबदल.

filiatory – नात्यानुसार संबंध.

filiatory arrangement – नात्यानुसार रचना/क्रमरचना – वर्गीकरण पद्धती तयार करताना वापरण्याचे तत्त्व.

filiatory order – नात्यानुसार क्रम – (१) संबंध दर्शविला जाईल असा क्रम. (२) ग्रंथवर्गीकरण पद्धतीत विषयांचा क्रम ठरविण्याचे तत्त्व.

filiatory sequence – संबंधानुसार अनुक्रम.

filing – क्रमानुगत संचिकरण – (१) क्रमानुसार ग्रंथांची, तालिकापत्रांची रचना करणे. (२) संबंधित वस्तूंची/नोंदींची रचना, व्यवस्था.

filing cabinet – तालिकापत्रे अथवा ग्रंथपत्रे ठेवावयाचा खण/कप्पा.

filing rules – क्रमरचना/क्रमानुगत नियम – अधिकृत नियमावलीनुसार क्रमरचनेसाठी नियम पाळले जातात.

filing significance – क्रमरचना महत्त्व – फायलिंगसाठी अतिशय महत्त्वाचा मानला जाणारा नोंदीतील मजकूर.

filing title – क्रमरचना शीर्षक – ज्या शीर्षकाखाली नोंद केली जाते व त्यानुसार क्रमरचना केली जाते ते शीर्षक.

film library – **चित्रफीत ग्रंथालय** – चित्रफितींचा संग्रह असलेले ग्रंथालय.

film script – **पटकथा** – चित्रफीत ग्रंथालयांमध्ये पटकथांचाही संग्रह केला जातो.

film strip – **चित्रपट्टी** – १६ मिमी. किंवा ३५ मिमी. किंवा ७०मिमी.ची चित्रफीत.

finance – **वित्त/अर्थ/निधी/अर्थपुरवठा/वित्तव्यवस्था.**

financial – **वित्तीय/आर्थिक.**

financial estimate – **जमाखर्चाचे अंदाज/अनुमान.**

financial management – **वित्तीय व्यवस्थापन.**

financial record – **वित्तीय नोंद/अभिलेख.**

financial resources – **आर्थिक संसाधने.**

financial statement – **जमाखर्चाचे विवरण.**

finding aids – **ग्रंथ साहित्य मदतसाधने** – ग्रंथालयातील साहित्य हवे तेव्हा मिळविण्यासाठी मदतसाधने. उदा. वर्गीकरण पद्धती, तालिका, निर्देश इ.

finding list – **अतिसंक्षिप्त शोधसूची** – ग्रंथालयातील साहित्याची अतिसंक्षिप्त सूची.

fine / overdue charges / late fee – **दंड/द्रव्यदंड/विलंबशुल्क** – ग्रंथपरतीला उशीर झाल्याबद्दल शिक्षा म्हणून घेतलेला मोबदला.

finish – **समाप्ती** – ग्रंथाच्या शेवटी वापरलेले समाप्तीचिन्ह.

finishing – **अंतिम सफाई** – ग्रंथबांधणी करताना ग्रंथाला आवरण बसविल्यानंतर त्यावर करण्याची अंतिम प्रक्रिया. यात कोरीव काम, अक्षरलेखन व उठाव आणण्याचे काम अंतर्भूत आहे.

firm order books – **निश्चित ग्रंथ आदेश.**

first – **प्रथम/पहिला.**

first edition – **प्रथमावृत्ती** – ग्रंथाची प्रथमच प्रकाशित झालेली आवृत्ती. वाचकांना खरेदीसाठी उपलब्ध असलेली पहिली प्रकाशित आवृत्ती.

first impression – **प्रथम मुद्रण.**

first indentation – **प्रथम समासांतर.**

first line index – **प्रथमचरण निर्देश** – या निर्देशामध्ये कविता, गीत, सुविचार यांची पहिली ओळ वर्णानुक्रमानुसार लावलेली असते.

first link – **प्रथम कडी** – ग्रंथावलीसाठी घ्यावयाचा शोधशब्दातील प्रथम अहवालाचा शब्द.

first name / forename / personal name – **व्यक्तिनाम.**

first proof – प्रथम पुरावा.

first series –प्रथम ग्रंथमाला – प्रथम प्रकाशित झालेली ग्रंथमाला.

first summary – प्राथमिक कोष्टक/गोषवारा – वर्गीकरणासाठी प्राथमिक कोष्टक.

first search – प्राथमिक शोध.

first word entry – आद्यपद नोंद – ग्रंथशीर्षकाच्या पहिल्या शब्दाखाली असलेली तालिकेतील नोंद.

fiscal – राजकोषीय.

fiscal policy – राजकोषीय धोरण.

fiscal year – राजकोषीय वर्ष – एप्रिल ०१ ते मार्च ३१चा कालावधी असणारे वित्तीय वर्ष.

five fundamental catagories – पाच मूलभूत घटक – द्विबिंदू वर्गीकरण पद्धतीतील पाच मूलभूत घटक (PMEST) Personality, Matter, Energy, Space & Time.

five laws of library science – ग्रंथालयशासनाची पाच सूत्रे – डॉ. रंगनाथन् यांनी सांगितलेली ग्रंथालयप्रशासनाची पाच सूत्रे.

fixed location / absolute location – निश्चित स्थान – ग्रंथांक आणि वर्गांक चिन्हांद्वारे ग्रंथाचे ग्रंथसंग्रह मांडणीमध्ये स्थान निश्चित करणे.

flat – चपट्या आकाराचा/समतल.

flat back – सपाट कणा असलेला ग्रंथ.

flat display – ग्रंथाचे मुखपृष्ठ दर्शनी ठेवलेली मांडणी.

flat rate – सरसकट दर.

flexible – लवचिक – सहजपणे वाकविता येण्याजोगा.

flexible binding – लवचिक बांधणी – ग्रंथ उघडल्यावर दोन्ही बाजूंची पाने पृष्ठभागाला सपाट राहू शकतील अशी बांधणी.

flexible classification – लवचिक वर्गीकरण – वर्गीकरणाच्या विषय रचनेमध्ये बदल न करता दोन विषयांमध्ये नवीन विषय सहजपणे समाविष्ट केला जातो.

flexible notation – लवचिक चिन्हांकन – वर्गीकरणातील चिन्हांकनाचा क्रम न बदलता नवीन विषय समाविष्ट करून सहजपणे चिन्हांकन करता येते ते लवचिक चिन्हांकन.

flexibility – लवचिकपणा – लवचिकतेचा गुणधर्म.

flexitime – लवचिक काळ – ग्रंथालयसेवा जास्तीत जास्त काळ उपलब्ध असण्यासाठी ग्रंथालय कर्मचाऱ्यांच्या कार्यालयीन वेळामध्ये लवचिकता आणणे.

floating library service – अस्थायी ग्रंथालयसेवा.

floppy disk – **माहितीसंचय तबकडी** – चुंबकीय लेप लावलेली पातळ तबकडी ही एक पूरक संग्रह साधनांचे उदाहरण आहे. सर्वसाधारणत: या तबकडीचा आकार ९x९ सेंमी. असतो व १.४४ MB ची क्षमता असते. याहून मोठ्या आकाराची व १.२२ MB क्षमतेची तबकडीही उपलब्ध असते. या तबकडीवर माहिती/आज्ञावली नोंदवून दुसऱ्या संगणकावर वापरण्यासाठी नेणे सोयीचे असते.

flochart / flow / line map – **चित्ररूप तक्ता/नकाशा** – (१) आज्ञावलीचे टप्पे दर्शविणारे चित्ररूप. यामुळे आज्ञावलीतील आज्ञांचा क्रम कळणे सोयीचे जाते आणि आज्ञावली लिहिणे सोपे जाते. (२) रेल्वेमार्ग किंवा पाण्याचा मार्ग जाड रेषांद्वारे दाखवून हालचाल दर्शविलेला नकाशा. रेषेची जाडी ही जाणाऱ्या मार्गाचे (पाण्याचे) प्रमाण दर्शविते.

flyleaf / end papers – **मलपृष्ठ** – (१) ग्रंथनाम पृष्ठाच्या बाजूस दर्शनी बाजूला अथवा ग्रंथातील अंतिम मजकुरानंतर असलेले कोरे पृष्ठ. (२) ग्रंथाच्या आरंभीचे व शेवटचे कोरे पान.

fly title / half title – **लघुग्रंथनाम** – ग्रंथाच्या पृष्ठाच्या आधी असलेल्या पृष्ठावरील ग्रंथनाम.

focal point – **केंद्रबिंदू** – केंद्रीय किंवा मध्यवर्ती किंवा मुख्य संघटनेचे कार्य किंवा लक्ष्य.

focus – **केंद्रबिंदू.**

folded book / gate fold – ग्रंथातील चित्र, नकाशा दर्शविणारे लांबीला जास्त असल्यामुळे दुमडलेले पृष्ठ.

folder – **घडीपत्रक** – एखाद्या विषयाची थोड्या/अल्प प्रमाणात माहिती देणारे व घडी घातलेले पत्र, माहितीपत्रक.

foliated – **पत्रांकित** – हस्तलिखिताच्या पानांना क्रमांक दिलेले पृष्ठ.

folio – **दुडा** – कागदाची एक घडी. पोथीप्रमाणे रचना असलेले पुस्तक.

folio edition – **द्विपत्री आवृत्ती** – पोथीप्रमाणे रचना असलेली आवृत्ती.

follow copy – **यथामूळपत्र** – नमुनाप्रत तयार करून जुळणीकाराला या प्रतीनुसार हुबेहूब प्रती काढण्याची सूचना दिली जाते.

follow-up – **पाठपुरावा** – कोणतेही कार्य यशस्वी करण्यासाठी अथवा निर्णयाची अंमलबजावणी करण्यासाठी करावयाची कार्यवाही. ज्यामध्ये अनेक उपकामांचा समावेश असतो.

font – **अक्षरसंच** – संगणकामध्ये शीर्षक किंवा इतर महत्त्वाच्या मजकुरासाठी वेगवेगळ्या तसेच लहान– मोठ्या आकारात अक्षरे लिहिण्याची सोय असते. उदा. Times New Roman font.

footline – **तळपंक्ती** – ग्रंथपृष्ठातील शेवटची ओळ.

footnote – **तळटीप** – ग्रंथपृष्ठावरील खूण केलेली संकल्पना स्पष्ट करणारी नोंदवजा टीप.

fore edge / front edge – **दर्शनी कडा/टोक** – पुस्तकाची पुढील बाजू.

fore edge painting – **कडाचित्रण** – ग्रंथपृष्ठाच्या सुट्या बाजूवर केलेले चित्रण.

fore edge title – **कडाशीर्षक** – ग्रंथपृष्ठांच्या सुट्या बाजूवर हाताने लिहिलेले शीर्षक.

foreign – परदेशी/परदेशातील/परकीय.

foreign exchange – परकीय चलन/विदेशी हुंडावळ.

foreign information centre – परदेश माहिती केंद्र – परकीय देशाने चालविलेले माहिती केंद्र.

foreign puclication – परकीय/परदेशीय प्रकाशन – परदेशात प्रकाशित होणारे प्रकाशन.

forename / personal name / first name – प्रथम नाम/व्यक्तिनाम – (१) कुलनाम, वर्गनाम किंवा आडनाव ह्यापूर्वी येणारे नाव – नामकरण (ख्रिश्चन पद्धतीने) केलेले अगर व्यक्तिनाम हे नाव अगर नावाचा भाग विशिष्ट व्यक्ती दर्शविते. तसेच समान कुलनाम, वर्गनाम अगर आडनाव धारण करणाऱ्या इतर व्यक्तींपासून भेद दर्शविते. नावाचा हा भाग व्यक्तिनाम म्हणूनही ओळखला जातो.

forename entry – प्रथमनाम नोंद – ग्रंथकाराच्या आडनावाची नोंद करण्याऐवजी प्रथम नावाने केलेली नोंद.

form – प्रपत्र – आवेदनपत्र, आकृतिबंध, ललित वाङ्मयातील विषयाचे स्वरूप.

form of catalogue – तालिका प्रारूप – तालिकेचे बाह्य स्वरूप.

form class – स्वरूप वर्ग – वर्गीकरणासाठी स्वरूपानुसार (ललित साहित्यानुसार) केलेला वर्ग. उदा. कविता, नाटक, कादंबरी, कथा, निबंध, पत्रलेखन इ. या स्वरूपांना स्वतंत्र विषयाचा दर्जा दिला जातो.

form division – स्वरूप विभाग – (१) सामान्य पोटविभाग, जे वर्गांकास जोडावयाचे असतात, कारण यांचा वापर सर्व विषयात करता येतो.
(२) विशिष्ट विषयाची पुस्तके मांडणी करताना बाह्यस्वरूप विभाग किंवा अंत:स्वरूपविभाग यानुसार मांडणी केली जाते. उदा. ग्रंथ हा निबंध, ग्रंथसूची की नियतकालिकाप्रमाणे आहे हे ठरविले जाते. तसेच त्या विषयाचा तो इतिहास आहे, तत्त्वज्ञान आहे, विवेचन आहे हे पाहिले जाते.

form entry – स्वरूप नोंद – ग्रंथस्वरूपानुसार तालिकेमध्ये केलेली नोंद.

form feed – संगणकाद्वारे छपाईयंत्राला देण्याची सूचना.

form heading –स्वरूप शीर्षक – तालिकेमध्ये ग्रंथरूप नोंद करण्यासाठी वापरलेले शीर्षक. उदा. विश्वकोश.

form number – स्वरूप दर्शविणारा अंक – ग्रंथरूपानुसार अंक. साहित्यातील ज्या प्रकारानुसार वर्गांक दिला जातो तो अंक. उदा. नाटक.

form phase – स्वरूप प्रावस्था – (१) विषयाचे विशिष्ट अंग दर्शविणारा वर्गीकरण पद्धतीतील विभाग.
(२) डॉ. रंगनाथन् यांची संज्ञा. ग्रंथातील मजकूर हा गुंतागुंतीच्या विषयांशी संबंधित असेल तेव्हा वर्गीकरण करताना प्रत्येक विषयाच्या मांडणीचे स्वरूप लक्षात घेऊन केलेले वर्गीकरण.

form sub-heading – ग्रंथस्वरूप उपशीर्षक – तालिकेमध्ये विषयाखाली उपविषयानुसार नोंदी करण्यासाठी वापरले जाणारे शीर्षक. उदा. ग्रंथालयशास्त्र–ग्रंथसूची.

formal – औपचारिक/शिष्टसंमत.

formal communication – औपचारिक संप्रेषण.

formal education – औपचारिक शिक्षण.

format – प्रारूप/नमुना/रूपरेषा/नमुनाबद्ध रचना – आराखडा माहितीची साठवण करताना त्यात सुसूत्रता यावी म्हणून ठरवलेला नमुना. नोंदीतील माहितीचा आराखडा; यंत्राद्वारा वाचनीय नोंदीमध्ये द्यावयाच्या माहितीचा आराखडा.

format control – माहितीच्या साच्याचे नियंत्रण.

format storage – माहिती नियंत्रण नमुन्यांचा संग्रह.

format of records – अभिलेखांचा/नोंदीचा नमुना.

formula – सूत्र/परिसूत्र.

FORTRAN (Formula Translator) – संगणकासाठी तयार केलेली त्यातील प्रथम अक्षर वापरून तयार केलेल्या भाषेचे संक्षेपाक्षर. या संगणकाच्या उच्चस्तरीय भाषेचा वापर मुख्यत्वेकरून गणितीय पद्धती अंतर्भूत असणाऱ्या आज्ञावलीसाठी करण्यात येतो.

forthcoming book – आगामी ग्रंथ – लवकरच प्रकाशित होणारे ग्रंथ.

forthnightly / bi-weekly – पाक्षिक – महिन्यातून दोन वेळा प्रसिद्ध होणारे प्रकाशन.

forum – व्यासपीठ – विशिष्ट समूहाला सर्वसामान्य बाबींसाठी चर्चा करण्याकरिता उपलब्ध करून दिलेला सार्वजनिक मंच.

forward arrow – सुलटा बाण/अभिमुख बाण.

forwarding – प्रस्तावित/अग्रेषण.

foundry – ओतशाळा – छपाईअक्षरे तयार करण्याची जागा.

frame – चौकट.

free access – मुक्त प्रवेश (ग्रंथालयात).

free endpaper – मुक्त आधारपृष्ठ.

free indexing – मुक्त निर्देशन – निर्देशकाने ठरविलेल्या शब्द वा वाक्याच्या आधारे निर्देशन केले जाते. तो शब्द किंवा वाक्य हे विशिष्ट प्रलेखामध्ये उल्लेख केले असेलच असे नाही.

free text – मुक्त मजकूर.

freelance – स्वायत्त (लेखन) – कोणत्याही संस्थेची वा इतर बांधिलकी नसताना केलेले काम.

freelance journalist – स्वायत्त पत्रकार.

free on rail (F.O.R.) – रेल्वे खर्च न आकारता साहित्य पुरविण्याची अट.

freight – वाहतूक आकार/वाहणावळ/वाहतूक खर्च.

french joint / open joint – (बांधणीसाठी) विशिष्ट फ्रेंच पद्धतीचा जोड.

frequency – वारंवारिता – नियतकालिक प्रकाशनांचा प्रकाशित होण्याचा कालावधी. उदा. सामाहिक, मासिक, त्रैमासिक इ.

front board – ग्रंथाचा वरचा पुठ्ठा.

front edge / fore edge – दर्शनी कडा.

front matter – आरंभिक सामग्री.

front piece – ग्रंथारंभ चित्र.

fugitive literature – दुष्प्राप्य/अप्राप्त साहित्य.

full binding – संपूर्ण बांधणी.

full cataloguing – संपूर्ण/सविस्तर तालिकीकरण – तालिकीकरण नियमावलीनुसार संपूर्ण माहितीची नोंद तालिकेमध्ये करण्याची पद्धत.

full cloth binding – संपूर्ण कापडी बांधणी.

full leather binding – संपूर्ण चामडीची बांधणी.

full name – संपूर्ण नाव – कुलनाम, व्यक्तीनाम व वडिलांचे नाव.

full point / full stop – पूर्णविराम.

full size – संपूर्ण आकृती/पूर्ण चित्र.

fulltext retrieval/searching – संपूर्ण माहितीचा प्रत्येक शब्द.

fulltext article – संपूर्ण माहितीपर लेख.

fulltext database – संपूर्ण माहितीसंग्रह.

full title – पूर्ण शीर्षक.

fumigation – धुरीकरण/धुरी – ग्रंथास कीटकांचा उपद्रव झाल्यास त्यापासून बचाव करण्यासाठी करावयाची क्रिया.

fumigator – धुरी देण्यासाठी वापरण्यात येणारे रसायन.

function – कार्य – एखाद्या संस्थेचे हेतू.

function key – कार्यवाही कळ – संगणकाच्या कळफलकावरील कार्यवाही कळ.

fund – निधी/रोख रक्कम – विशिष्ट हेतूसाठी असलेला निधी.

fundamental – मूलभूत/मूलतत्त्व/मौलिक रूप/महत्त्वाचा/अत्यावश्यक/जरुरीचा.

fundamental category – मूलभूत प्रवर्ग/श्रेणी/अंग – डॉ. रंगनाथन् यांनी सांगितलेले वर्गीकरणाचे मूलभूत प्रवर्ग (PMEST)

fundamental science – मूलभूत विज्ञान.

fundamentals – मूलतत्त्वे.

futurologists – भवितव्य शास्त्रज्ञ – सामाजिक भवितव्याबद्दल शास्त्रीय भाकीत करणारे शास्त्रज्ञ.

furniture – सामान/चीजवस्तू साहित्य – संग्रह ठेवण्यासाठी, बसण्यासाठी प्लास्टिक, लाकूड, स्टील इ.पासून बनविलेले साहित्य.

fused link – प्रज्वलक कडी.

fused number – प्रज्वलक अंक.

fusion – एकीकरण/संयोग/विलयन – अनेक गोष्टींचा मिलाफ.

G

gallary - **कलादालन/कलाभवन** - चित्र, मूर्ती, ग्रंथ इत्यादींच्या प्रदर्शनासाठी असलेला मोठा कक्ष.

galley proof - **पाटमुद्रित** - जुळणीकाराने जुळणी करून छपाईसाठी दिलेला कच्चा मसुदा.

gangway guide - **मार्गिका फलक** - ग्रंथदालनातील कपाटांची रचना दर्शविणारे फलक.

gap card - **खंड अभाव दर्शविणारे पत्र** - तालिकेमध्ये मालिकेतील नसलेल्या खंडाचे अभावदर्शक नोंदपत्रक लावले जाते.

gap device - **विराम क्लृप्ती** - वर्गीकरण पद्धतीमध्ये अंकांचा वापर पूर्णांक म्हणून करताना भविष्यकाळातील ज्ञानशाखांचा विचार करून दोन पूर्णांकामध्ये मोकळी जागा म्हणजेच विराम ठेवण्याची क्लृप्ती; ही पद्धत लायब्ररी ऑफ काँग्रेस वर्गीकरण पद्धतीमध्ये वापरली जाते.

garbage - **कचरा/निरुपयोगी/टाकाऊ वस्तू** - संगणकातील अनावश्यक माहितीचा संचय.

gate fold / folded leaf - **दुमडलेले पृष्ठ** - ग्रंथामध्ये समाविष्ट केलेले एखादे चित्र, आकृती, नकाशा, दर्शविणारे पृष्ठ. ग्रंथापेक्षा मोठ्या आकाराचे असेल तेव्हा ते दुमडले जाते.

gate pass - **परवानापत्र** - ग्रंथालयातून ग्रंथ बाहेर नेण्यासाठी दिलेले प्रपत्र.

gate register - **प्रवेशद्वार नोंदवही** - (१) ग्रंथालय प्रवेश नोंदवही. (२) ग्रंथालयाच्या प्रवेशद्वाराजवळ ठेवलेली वाचक उपस्थिती नोंदवही - यामध्ये ग्रंथालयाचे वाचक अथवा भेट देणारे, भेटीचा दिनांक, स्वतःचे नाव, पत्ता, भेटीची वेळ, भेटीचा हेतू आणि स्वाक्षरी इ.माहिती नोंदवितात.

gate way - **प्रवेशद्वार** - संगणक जाळ्यांमधील एक संगणक दुसऱ्या संगणक जाळ्यामधील संगणकाबरोबर काम करण्यासाठी असलेले प्रवेशद्वार.

gazette – **राजपत्र** – शासनाचे समाचारपत्र.

gazetteer – **स्थलवर्णनकोश** – एखादे राज्य, जिल्हा, तालुका किंवा गाव याविषयी भौगोलिक, सामाजिक, अर्थशास्त्रीय, ऐतिहासिक, लोकसंख्याविषयक, सांस्कृतिक, प्रशासकीय इ. स्वरूपाची माहिती देणारा कोश.

gelatine – **जिलेटिन** – सरसाचा एक प्रकार.

genealogical table – **वंशावळीचा तक्ता** – व्यक्तींची आकृतीच्या स्वरूपात दाखविलेली वंशावळ.

general added entry – **साधारण पूरक नोंद** – ग्रंथाबाबत विशिष्ट माहिती दाखविणारी साधारण पूरक नोंद असे म्हणतात.

general classification – **सर्वसाधारण/सामान्य वर्गीकरण.**

general entry – **तालिकेतील सर्वसाधारण नोंद.**

general phase relation – **सामान्य विषयांग संबंध.**

general reference – **सर्वसाधारण संदर्भ** – कोणताही विशिष्ट संदर्भ न दर्शविता 'आणखी पाहा' या शीर्षकाखाली सर्व संबंधित वर्गांक दर्शविले जातात.

general secondary – **सर्वसाधारण दुय्यम नोंद** – एखादी व्यक्ती किंवा संस्था यांची नोंद कोणत्याही शीर्षकाखाली (उदा. संपादक, संयोजक) करता येत नसेल तेव्हा सर्वसाधारण दुय्यम नोंद केली जाते.

general title – **सर्वसाधारण शीर्षक/संकीर्ण शीर्षक** – पूर्वी प्रकाशित झालेले विविध शीर्षकांचे लेख एकत्रितरीत्या एखाद्या ग्रंथामध्ये असतील तेव्हा अशा ग्रंथाला सर्वसाधारण शीर्षक दिले जाते. प्रत्येक लेखाच्या शीर्षकाला 'विभागीय शीर्षक पृष्ठ' असे म्हटले जाते.

GMD (General Material Designation) – **सामान्य साहित्य नामनिर्देश** – तालिकीकरण केलेल्या साहित्याचे बाह्यस्वरूप अथवा प्रकार याचा तालिका नोंदीत केलेला उल्लेख. उदा. मोशन पिक्चर्स, साऊंड, रेकॉर्डिंग, मायक्रोफिल्म, कॅसेट इत्यादी.

general subject entry – **साधारण विषय नोंद** – विषयाच्या नावावरून त्याच्या वर्गांकाकडे निर्देश करणारी अथवा एका विषयाच्या नावावरून दुसऱ्या विषयाच्या नावाकडे निर्देश करणारी जी नोंद असते तिला 'साधारण विषय नोंद' असे म्हणतात.

generalia class – **संकीर्ण वर्ग/सर्वसाधारण वर्ग**– दशांश वर्गीकरणामधील पहिला वर्ग बहुविषय मजकूर असलेले ग्रंथ या वर्गामध्ये वर्गीकृत केले जातात.

generally recurrent – **सामान्य आवर्ती** – सर्व विषयांना लागू असणारे पोटविभाग. उदा. साहित्याचे प्रकार, भाषा, इत्यादी हे सामान्य साहाय्यकारी पोटविभागांच्या यादीत फक्त एकदाच दिले जातात.

generic coding – **सर्वसमावेशक संकेतन/जाति संकेतन** – वर्गीकरण करताना चढत्या क्रमाने वर्गांक असलेल्या वर्गांचे संकेतन करणे.

generic relation – जाति संबंध – वर्गीकरण करताना मुख्य विषयक आणि उपविषय यांचा सहसंबंध.

generic searching – जाती संकेतन शोधन.

generic term / bound term / collateral term – सहसंबंधित संज्ञा – निर्देशन करताना मुख्य संज्ञेमध्ये सहभागी असलेली संज्ञा.

generic title – जाती/वर्गदर्शक शीर्षक.

genus – जाती/प्रजाती – समान ढोबळ गुणधर्म असणारा प्राणी अथवा वनस्पतींचा गट.

geographical device – भौगोलिक युक्ती – वर्गांकामध्ये भूप्रदेश (खंड, देश, राज्य इत्यादी) दर्शविण्यासाठी या युक्तीचा वापर केला जातो.

geographical area – भूक्षेत्र – वर्गीकरणासाठी आवश्यक लक्षणगुण.

geographical characteristic – भौगोलिक लक्षणगुण/सामान्यगुण – वर्गीकरण करताना ग्रंथात उल्लेख केलेल्या भौगोलिक क्षेत्राचा वैशिष्ट्यगुण लक्षात घेतला जातो. उदा. अमेरिकेतील विद्यापीठ ग्रंथालय.

geographical contiguity – भौगोलिक संलग्नता – एकमेकांस लागून असलेले भौगोलिक प्रदेश. उदा. उत्तरप्रदेश आणि बिहार हे भौगोलिक दृष्ट्या संलग्न प्रदेश आहेत.

geographical division – भौगोलिक विभाग – ज्याचा वापर वर्गीकरण पद्धतीत दर्शविलेला असतो.

geographical entry – भौगोलिक नोंद – स्थानानुसार केलेली नोंद.

geographical facet – भूपैलू/भौगोलिक पैलू – भौगोलिक स्थानानुसार वर्गीकरणासाठी वापरण्याचे तत्त्व.

geographical number / geographical code – भूअंक/स्थलअंक – वर्गीकरण चिन्हाबरोबर भौगोलिक स्थानानुसार दिलेला अंक.

geographical order – भौगोलिक क्रम – भौगोलिक स्थानानुसार क्रमरचना.

geographic filing method – भौगोलिक स्थानानुसार नोंदींची क्रमरचना करण्याची पद्धती.

Gestalt alphabetisation – गेस्टॉल्ट यांनी सुचविलेली अक्षरक्रमरचना.

Gestalt theory – गेस्टॉल्ट पत्ररचनापद्धती.

gift binding – मानार्थ/भेट बांधणी – भेटवस्तू म्हणून देण्याकरिता ग्रंथाची केलेली विशेष बांधणी.

gift plate – मानार्थ पट्टिका.

gift slip – मानार्थ चिठ्ठी.

gigabyte (g byte) – संगणकाच्या स्मृती मापनाचे एकक.

gilding – मुलामा देणे/सोनेरी करणे.

gild edges – सोनेरी कडा – ग्रंथबांधणी करताना सजावट म्हणून ग्रंथाच्या कडा सोनेरी रंगाच्या केल्या जातात.

gilt top – सोनेरी शीर्षकडा – ग्रंथबांधणीमध्ये ग्रंथाची वरच्या बाजूची कड सोनेरी केली जाते.

girdle book – मेखलाबद्ध पुस्तक – काही ग्रंथांना अधिक संरक्षण म्हणून जास्तीचे कातडी वेष्टन घालून त्याला दोरी लावली जात असे.

gist – मथितार्थ – लेखाचा मथितार्थ दिलेला परिच्छेद.

glaze – तकाकी – पातळ चकाकदार असा मुलामा देणे, झळाळी.

glaze morcco – चमकदार मोरोक्को कातडे.

glocal information system – जागतिक माहिती पद्धती – जागतिक सहकारी स्तरावरील वाचक/ संशोधकांना कमीत कमी पैशांत आणि कमी प्रयत्नात विभिन्न सेवा आणि निर्मिती करण्यासंदर्भात माहिती देणारी पद्धत.

gloce – पृथ्वीगोल – ग्रंथालयामध्ये जगाची भौगोलिक माहिती मिळविण्याचे महत्त्वाचे साधन.

gloss – चकाकी/झिलई/तकाकी – एखाद्या पृष्ठभागावरची चकाकी, झिलई.

glossarial index – पारिभाषिक निर्देश – निर्देशामध्ये उल्लेख केलेल्या संज्ञेचे वर्णन व पृष्ठक्रमांक देणारा निर्देश.

glossary – शब्दावली/पारिभाषिक शब्दकोश – अनुवर्णक्रमाने वर्णनासह संज्ञा देणारा शब्दकोश.

glue – सरस/गोंद – वस्तू चिकटविण्याचा चिकट, घट्ट द्रवपदार्थ.

gold tooling – सोनेरी सुशोभन.

goffer – नक्षीदार पुस्तक.

govern – राज्य करणे/व्यवस्था पाहणे.

governance – अभिशासन/शासन/राज्य कारभार/अंमल.

governing body – नियामक संस्था/मंडळ.

government – शासन/सरकार – राज्य किंवा देशावर शासन करणारा वर्ग.

government document – शासकीय प्रलेख.

government library – शासकीय ग्रंथालय – राज्य सरकारच्या निधीद्वारे व प्रशासनाद्वारे चालणारे ग्रंथालय.

government publications – शासकीय प्रकाशने – शासकीय विभागाने प्रकाशित केलेली प्रकाशने.

gradation – प्रतवारी – एखाद्या वस्तूची प्रत/दर्जा ठरविणे.

grants – अनुदान – (१) ग्रंथालय खर्च भागविण्यासाठी दिलेली आर्थिक मदत. (२) विशेषतः सरकारकडून प्राप्त होणारा आर्थिक निधी.

gramophone library – ध्वनिमुद्रकांचे ग्रंथालय.

gramophone record / phonograph record – ध्वनिमुद्रिका – ध्वनीचे मुद्रण करण्यासाठी वापरलेली तबकडी.

grant in aid – परिरक्षणात्मक अनुदान.

grant-in-aid-library – अनुदान प्राप्त ग्रंथालये.

graph – आलेख.

graphics – आलेखिकी – चित्रे, आकृत्या, नक्षी स्वरूपातील माहिती.

graphic abstracts – आलेखिकी सार – चित्रे किंवा आकृती स्वरूपातील सारांश माहिती.

graphical crowser – चित्रमय विषयक – चित्रे, आकृती, नक्षी स्वरूपातील माहिती घेऊ शकणारा.

graphics mode – आलेखिकी अवस्था – संगणकामध्ये चित्र, आकृत्या, यांच्या साहाय्याने माहिती दर्शविणारा मार्ग.

grey literature – **विक्रीस उलपब्ध नसलेले साहित्य** – मुद्रित झालेले परंतु विक्रीस उपलब्ध नसलेले साहित्य. उदा. वार्षिक वृत्तान्त संस्थांतर्गत अभिलेख, कार्यालयातील फाईलमधील अभिलेख इ.

grid – वृत्तजाळी – एखाद्या प्रक्षेपणावरील मोजलेल्या अंतराचा उपयोग करून देणारी संदर्भदायी पद्धती.

group – गट (समुच्चय) – माणसांचा किंवा वस्तूंचा गट.

group characteristic – गटलक्षण/गटवैशिष्ट्ये – वर्गीकरणासाठी वापरण्याचा वैशिष्ट्यगुण.

group notation device – गट चिन्हांकन युक्ती.

guard book catalogue – ग्रंथरूप चिट्ठी तालिका.

guarding – सुरक्षण.

guide – मार्गदर्शक – मार्गदर्शन करणारी व्यक्ती, वाटाड्या.

guide board – मार्गदर्शक फलक – ग्रंथालयामध्ये वेगवेगळे विभाग दर्शविणरा फलक.

guide books – मार्गदर्शिका/प्रवासी मार्गदर्शिका.

guide card – मार्गदर्शक पत्र – तालिकेमधील मार्गदर्शक नोंदपत्र किंवा तालिकापत्रांचा क्रम दर्शविणारे मार्गदर्शक तालिकापत्र.

guide letter – अलंकृत आद्याक्षर.

guide to reprints – पुनर्मुद्रण साहित्याची मार्गदर्शिका.

guided scheme – मार्गदर्शकयुक्त पद्धती.

hachures – उठावरेषा – (१) पृथ्वीच्या पृष्ठभागाच्या उंचीची दिशा आणि त्यातील उंचीतील चढामधील तफावत दाखविणाऱ्या नकाशातील उभ्या आणि आडव्या रेषा. त्यांची लांबी आणि त्यातील निकटता यावरून दिशा व उंचीचा अंदाज घेता येतो. (२) नकाशामध्ये चढ-उतार दर्शविणाऱ्या उठावरेषा.

half binding – अर्धबांधणी.

half cloth binding – अर्धी कपडा बांधणी – ज्यामध्ये ग्रंथाच्या काठास आणि कण्यास कपडा लावला जातो.

half leather binding – अर्ध कातडी बांधणी.

half monthly / fortnightly / bi-weekly / semi-monthly – पाक्षिक – महिन्यातून दोन वेळा प्रसिद्ध होणारे नियतकालिक.

half see face – ग्रंथविक्रेत्याने प्रकाशकाला दिलेली सूचना. ग्रंथविक्रेता प्रकाशकाकडे मागणी नोंदविताना विक्री न झाल्यास अर्ध्या प्रती परत करून त्याऐवजी दुसरे प्रकाशन प्रतींमध्ये देण्याविषयी सूचना करतो.

half title – अर्धशीर्षक/उपग्रंथनाम.

half title page – अर्धशीर्षक पृष्ठ – ज्यावर ग्रंथाचे फक्त उपग्रंथनाम लिहिलेले असते.

half-title / bastered title / fly title – अर्धशीर्षक/लघुशीर्षक – ग्रंथाच्या शीर्षकपृष्ठानंतरच्या पृष्ठावर दिलेले संक्षिप्त शीर्षक.

half yearly / bi-annuel – अर्धशीर्षक/षण्मासिक – वर्षातून दोन वेळा प्रकाशित होणारे नियतकालिक.

hamnlet libraries – पाडा/वाड्यांची ग्रंथालये – लहान/कमी लोकवस्ती असलेल्या ठिकाणचे ग्रंथालय.

hand bills – हस्तपत्रके – मोफत वाटला जाणारा छापील एकपानी मजकूर.

hand book – हस्तपुस्तिका/निर्देश ग्रंथ – हस्ताध्यायी दैनंदिन कार्यासाठी लागणारी माहिती असलेला ग्रंथ.

hand composition / hand setting – हातजुळणी – छपाईसाठी छपाईयंत्रावर हाताने केलेली जुळणी.

hand made paper – यंत्राशिवाय–हाताने बनविलेला कागद.

hand–shaking – दूरसंचार संभाषण – संगणकाच्या साहाय्याने आज्ञावली तयार करताना माहितीची अदलाबदल करण्यासाठी तयार केलेला नकाशा.

hand viewer / film viewer – सूक्ष्मवाचनी भिंग.

hand writing – हस्ताक्षर.

hang – crash – बिघाड/संगणकप्रक्रियेतील व्यत्यय.

hanging indention – आलंबित समासांतर – परिच्छेदाची पहिली ओळ डाव्या समासापासून सुरू झालेली असते. दुसरी व त्यानंतरच्या ओळी डाव्या समासापासून अधिक अंतरावर लिहिल्या जातात. या ओळी दर्शविणारी रेषा.

hard board – बांधणीचा कठीण पुठ्ठा.

hard cound / hard cover – कठीण पुठ्ठा बांधणी – पुठ्ठा बांधणी असलेले पुस्तक.

hard copy / printed copy – छापील प्रत.

hard currency – रोख रक्कम – रोखीने अदा केलेले चलन.

hard disk – संगणकातील संग्रहण साधन/तबकडी – (१) संगणकामध्ये अनेक चुंबकीय तबकड्या एका मजबूत आवरणात ठेवलेल्या असल्याने याची माहिती साठविण्याची क्षमता मेगाबाईट्समध्ये आणि गीगाबाईट्समध्येही मोजली जाते. (२) संगणकामध्ये बसविलेली माहिती संचय तबकडी.

hard space – संगणकातील माहितीमध्ये दोन शब्दांमधील रिकामी जागा.

hardware – यंत्रसामग्री – (१) संगणकाच्या दृश्य भागांना त्याचे हार्डवेअर म्हटले जाते. यात सी.पी.यू., आय/ओ युनीट्स आणि पूरक स्मृतिसाधने (external memories) येतात. (२) संगणकामधला माहितीच्या संस्करणाचे कार्य करणारा विभाग.

hardware compatibility – संगणक यंत्रातील समानता.

Harvard style – हार्वर्ड शैली – संशोधनपर लिखाणात उद्धरण देण्याची एक शैली.

Harvard system – हार्वर्ड पद्धत – वैज्ञानिक पुस्तके व नियतकालिकांमधील लेखांची उल्लेखसूची करण्याची विशिष्ट पद्धती.

head – (१) पृष्ठाच्या शीर्षभागातील मोकळी जागा. (२) संगणकातील माहिती वाचणे, लिहिणे, सुलभ करणारा दर्शक.

head and tail – ग्रंथाची वरची व खालची कडा.

head margin – वरचा समास – पृष्ठाच्या वरच्या बाजूस सोडलेली रिकामी जागा.

head ornament / head piece – पृष्ठशीर्षांचे अलंकरण.

head title – शीर्ष ग्रंथनाम – पृष्ठाच्या वरच्या भागावर लिहिलेले शीर्षक.

heading – शीर्षक/नोंदशीर्षक/मथळा – (१) तालिकापत्रावरील नोंदीच्या शीर्षक विभागात लिहिलेले संज्ञानाम, शब्द वा शब्दसमूह म्हणजेच नोंदशीर्षक. (२) निर्देशन करताना निवडलेला शब्द.

heading section – शीर्षक अनुच्छेद/अनुविभाग.

headline – शीर्षरेषा/ओळ – (१) मुख्य पृष्ठावरील दिलेल्या बातमीचे/माहितीचे शीर्षक. (२) ग्रंथातील पानावर मजकुराची सुरुवात केली जाते ती रेषा.

headqurters – मुख्यालय/प्रधान कार्यालय – नियंत्रण करणारे मुख्य कार्यालय.

health science library – आरोग्य विज्ञान ग्रंथालय – आरोग्य विज्ञानविषयक ग्रंथालय.

Hegel classification – हेगेलचे वर्गीकरण – १८१२ मध्ये हेगेल याने तर्कशास्त्रासाठी तयार केलेली वर्गीकरण पद्धती.

help – मदत – संगणकातील साहाय्यकारी सूचना कप्पा.

help desk – मदत मेज/बाक.

helpful – साहाय्यकारी.

helpful order / helpful sequence – साहाय्यकारी/उपयुक्त अनुक्रम मांडणी – (१) विविध विषयांची, त्यांच्या पैलूंची, उपांगांची एक तर्कशुद्ध अशी मांडणी जिच्या आधारे ग्रंथालयातील विविध ग्रंथ वाचकांच्या नजरेस आणणे शक्य होते. (२) वर्गीकरण तक्त्यामधील नोंदीचा क्रम साहाय्यकारी विषयाकडे वळण्यासाठी मदत होईल अशा प्रकारचा वर्गीकरण वापरलेला अनुक्रम.

herald – जाहीरपणे माहिती देणारा – (१) एखाद्या विषयाची जाहीर माहिती देणे. (२) आगाऊ सूचना/ माहिती देणारा.

hidden file – न दिसणारी/अप्रत्यक्ष फाईल – संगणकामध्ये तयार झालेल्या अशा फाईल्समधल्या माहितीमध्ये बदल करता येत नाही.

hierarchical – श्रेणीय/अधिकार श्रेणीनुसार.

hierarchical chain – श्रेणीयुक्त साखळी.

hierarchical classification – **पायरीनुसार वर्गीकरण** – कमी-अधिक पायरीच्या स्थानानुसार संज्ञांची रचना असलेली वर्गीकरण पद्धती. उदा. दशांश वर्गीकरण पद्धती.

hierarchical database – **पायरीप्रमाणे रचना असलेला माहितीसंच.**

hierarchical force – **वर्गीकरण करताना वापरावयाचा वैशिष्ट्यगुण.**

hierarchical notation – **श्रेणीबद्ध चिन्हांकन** – पायरीप्रमाणे रचना असलेले चिन्हांकन.

hierarchical relation – **श्रेणीवर आधारित संबंध** – एखाद्या विषयामधील वेगवेगळ्या स्तरांवरील कल्पनांचे परस्परसंबंध. उदा. प्राणीशास्त्र – पक्षी-कावळे, वैद्यकशास्त्र-श्वसनेंद्रिये-फुप्फुसे इ.

hierarchical structure – **श्रेणीय संरचना** – वर्गीकरणात्मक संरचना जी वर्गांची श्रेणी, पातळी, दर्जा दर्शविते. ज्यात कोणत्याही पातळीवरील वर्ग त्याच्याखाली असलेल्या वर्गापेक्षा वरच्या दर्जाचा आणि त्याच्या खालच्या वर्गापेक्षा वरिष्ठ दर्जाचा असतो. श्रेणीतील कोणत्याही पातळीवरील वर्ग सामान्य वैशिष्ट्यांवर आधारित पण आपापसात वेगवेगळे असतात.

hierarchy – **अधिकारश्रेणी/सोपानश्रेणी** – (१) विषयांचे किंवा वस्तूंचे समन्वय स्पष्ट करणारी किंवा दर्जानुसार केलेली क्रमवार मांडणी किंवा सामान्याकडून विशिष्टाकडे असा क्रम दर्शविणारी विषयमालिका. (२) वर्गीकरण पद्धतीतील श्रेणी.

hieroglyphics – **चित्रलिपी** – दगडावर अंकित चित्रलिपी (प्राचीन कालखंड) मध्ये याचा वापर सूचना किंवा विचार व्यक्त करण्यासाठी केला जात असे.

high level language – **उपयोजनामूलक भाषा** – (१) इंग्रजी भाषेतील निवडक शब्दांचा वापर करून तयार केलेली भाषा. संगणकास समजण्यासाठी ती बदलली जाते. (२) संगणकाची उच्चस्तरीय संयोजनभाषा. उदा. BASIC, COBOL, FORTRAN

highlight – **स्पष्ट करणे/माहितीद्वारे प्रकाश टाकणे/उठाव देणे** – संगणकातील विशिष्ट माहिती उठावदर्शक करणे.

high speed printer – **वेगवान मुद्रणयंत्र** – वेगाने मुद्रण करणारे मुद्रणयंत्र.

historiated initial – **सार्थ चित्राक्षर** – प्राण्याचे, मानवाचे चित्र, आकृती काढलेले पुस्तक.

historical – ऐतिहासिक.

historical / analytical / applied / critical / descriptive / external / merterial bibliography – ऐतिहासिक/ग्रंथशास्त्रेतिहास ग्रंथसूची/अभ्याससूची – (१) ग्रंथ उत्पादन, छपाई, बांधणी, कागद बनविणे, सजावट, प्रकाशन यांविषयी इतिहास अभ्यासणारी सूची.

historical method – **ऐतिहासिक पद्धती** – संशोधनात वापरली जाणारी एक संशोधन पद्धत.

history card – **इतिहास पत्र** – समष्टी ग्रंथकार संदर्भपत्र.

history entry – **इतिहास नोंद** – तालिकेमध्ये ग्रंथकार, ग्रंथशीर्षक वा इतर नावांमध्ये झालेला बदल तारखेनिशी देणारी नोंद.

hit rate – **वेगदर** – संगणकातील माहितीचा शोध घेताना केल्या जाणाऱ्या नोंदींचा वेगदर – संगणकावरील वेबसाईट पाहणाऱ्या दर्शकांची संख्या.

holds / books reserved – **आरक्षित ग्रंथ** – ग्रंथालयाबाहेर वाचकास दिलेली पुस्तके अन्य वाचकांना देण्यासाठी राखून ठेवणे.

holding – **साहित्य संग्रह** – ग्रंथालयातील एकूण वाचनसाहित्य संग्रह.

holdings of periodicals – **नियतकालिकांचा संग्रह** – ग्रंथालयातील नियतकालिकांचे जुने खंड.

holdings statement – **वाचनसाहित्य निवेदन/विधान/विवरणपत्र.**

holiday issue – **सुटीच्या दिवशीची देवघेव.**

hollow back / loose back – **ग्रंथाचा पोकळ कणा** – ग्रंथाचे वेष्टन व बांधणी यांमधील पोकळी.

holograph – **संपूर्ण आलेख** – हस्तलिखिताची छायाप्रतीत नोंद करण्याची प्रक्रिया.

home bindery – **ग्रंथालयांतर्गत बांधणी विभाग.**

home / door delivery service – **घरपोच वितरण सेवा.**

home key – **मूलस्थान कळ** – संगणकाच्या कळपटावरील विशिष्ट कळ. याच्या साहाय्याने स्थानकबिंदू सुरुवातीला येतो.

home libraries – **गृहग्रंथालये** – व्यक्तिगत संग्रह असलेली ग्रंथालये.

home page – **मुख्यपृष्ठ** – वेबसाईटचे मुख्य पृष्ठ.

home reading department / lending department – **ग्रंथ देवघेव विभाग.**

homework – **गृहपाठ.**

homeograph – इंग्रजी स्पेलिंग सारखे असणारे परंतु अर्थ वेगवेगळे असलेले शब्द. असे शब्द शीर्षक म्हणून नोंदी करण्यासाठी शक्यतो टाळावे. अन्यथा प्रत्येकाचा अर्थ देऊन नोंद करावी. उदा. Birmingham (Alacama) Birmingham (England)

homology – **सजातीयता** – वर्गीकरण सारणी तयार करताना समान गुणधर्माचे विषय जवळ आणण्यासाठी वापरायचे तत्त्व.

homonym – **समनाम/सारखे नाव** – (१) समान अक्षरांचे शब्द किंवा वेगवेगळी अक्षरे असलेले शब्द ज्यांचा उच्चार सारखा व अर्थ मात्र वेगळा असू शकतो.(२) उच्चार सारखाच पण स्पेलिंग वेगळे असा शब्द.

homophone – उच्चार एकच पण अर्थ व स्पेलिंग वेगवेगळे असलेले शब्द.

hog machine – **भोके पाडण्याचे यंत्र.**

honorific title – **सन्मानदर्शक शीर्षक/नाव.**

    उदा. रॅंलर र. पु. परांजपे,

    सर एडमंड हिलरी,

    महात्मा गांधी,

    पंडित जवाहरलाल नेहरू

horn book – **शृंगी ग्रंथ** – (सोळाव्या शतकात प्रचलित असलेला मुलांसाठी पुस्तकाचा प्रकार.)

hospital library – **रुग्णालय ग्रंथालय** – रुग्णालयातील रुग्णांसाठीचे ग्रंथालय.

hospitality – **आतिथ्यशीलता/स्वागतशीलता/समावेशकता** – (१) ग्रंथ वर्गीकरण पद्धतीमध्ये नवीन विषय/उपविषयांचा समावेश योग्य ठिकाणी करण्याची क्षमता, नवीन विषयात सामावून घेणारा.

(२) वर्गीकरणपद्धतीमध्ये चिन्हांकनासाठी वापरावयाचे तत्त्व.

hospitality in array – **पंक्तीतील/पंक्तिरचनेतील आतिथ्यशीलता** – एखाद्या ज्ञानशाखेचे विभाजन केल्यावर मिळणाऱ्या पंक्तीमध्ये भविष्यकाळात निर्माण होणाऱ्या ज्ञानशाखांना स्थान मिळण्याची पंक्तीतील क्षमता.

hospitality in chain – **शृंखलेतील/साखळीतील अतिथ्यशीलता** – शृंखलेतील ज्ञानशाखांमध्ये नवीन उपविभाग तयार होतात तेव्हा साखळीमध्ये नवीन दुव्यांची भर पडते. अशा नवीन दुव्यांना सामावून घेण्याची क्षमता म्हणजे साखळीतील आतिथ्यशीलता.

hospitality in notation – **चिन्हांकनातील आतिथ्यशीलता** – ज्ञानशाखांचे उपविषय चिन्हांमध्ये दर्शविताना नवीन उपविषयाला सामावून घेण्यासाठी चिन्हांकन पद्धतीमध्ये असलेली क्षमता.

host – **यजमान** – संगणक जाळ्यातील माहितीधारक यजमान संगणक.

host book – **यजमान ग्रंथ** – द्विबिंदू वर्गिकरणसंदर्भात ज्या ग्रंथाबद्दल लिखाण केले आहे (उदा. समीक्षा, टीका इ.) तो ग्रंथ.

hot key – **शीघ्रक कळ** – संगणकामध्ये त्वरित आज्ञापालनासाठी उपयोजित कळ.

house journal / house periodical / house magazine – **संस्थापत्रिका/संस्थेचे प्रकाशनकालिक** – मर्यादित वितरण असलेले व संस्थेच्या कार्याची माहिती असणारे प्रकाशन.

house organ – **संस्थापत्रिका/मुखपत्र** – संस्थेच्या कार्याची माहिती देणारे वार्तापत्र अथवा पत्रिका.

house paper – **संसदीय कागदपत्रे.**

house keeping – (१) ग्रंथालयातील दैनंदिन कामकाज. (२) संगणकातील माहिती काळजीपूर्वक जतन करण्याचे दैनंदिन कार्य. (३) ग्रंथालय सेवा व्यवस्थित देता यावी या उद्देशाने करावी लागणारी

पडद्यामागील कामे – ग्रंथोपार्जन, तालिकीकरण, नियतकालिकांची नोंद, देवघेव विभागातील कामे इत्यादी.

humanities – **मानव्यविद्या** – मानवी जीवनाशी प्रत्यक्ष संबंधित शास्त्राचा अभ्यास.

hypothesis – **प्रावकल्पना/गृहीतक** – वास्तविकांची संभाव्य कारणमीमांसा करणारी कल्पना.

hybrid computer – **संकरित संगणक** – अॅनालॉग व डिजीटल या दोन्ही प्रकारच्या संगणकाचे मिश्रण.

hyphen – **जोडरेषा** – (१) दोन शब्द जोडण्यासाठी वापरण्यात येणारे चिन्ह (–)

ibidem (abbre, ib or ibid) – **कित्ता** – तळटीप लिहिताना संदर्भनोंदींची पुनरावृत्ती असेल तेव्हा संपूर्ण लेखाचे नाव व संदर्भ देण्याऐवजी 'पूर्वीप्रमाणे' या अर्थी दिलेली सूचना.

icon – **बोधचिन्ह/प्रतीक** – एखाद्या सॉफ्टवेअरचे किंवा फाईलचे बोधचिन्ह यामुळे टंकलेखनाद्वारे सूचना देण्याऐवजी बोधचिन्हाला सूचना देताच विशिष्ट फाईलला प्रवेश मिळतो.

idea plane – **वैचारिक/कल्पना क्षेत्र/स्तर** – वर्गीकरणामध्ये एखाद्या संज्ञेला दिलेले काल्पनिक स्वरूप म्हणजे वैचारिक स्तर होय.

identification card – **ओळखचिन्ह पत्र.**

identity card – **ओळखपत्र** – शाळा, महाविद्यालय, विद्यापीठ व इतर शैक्षणिक ग्रंथालयांचे सभासदत्व मिळविण्यासाठी आवश्यक.

ideograph – **भावार्थ चित्र** – चित्र, आकृती, नक्षी याद्वारे कल्पनाविस्तार.

illuminated binding – **अलंकृत बांधणी** – रंगीत कडा, नक्षी यांचा बांधणीमध्ये वापर केला जातो.

illuminated book – **अलंकृत ग्रंथ** – सोनेरी कडा किंवा इतर प्रकारे सजविलेला ग्रंथ.

illuminated initial – **अलंकृत आद्याक्षर** – शब्द, ओळ, परिच्छेद यातील अलंकृत आद्याक्षर.

illustration – **चित्रमय साहित्य/लेखचित्रे** – ग्रंथातील मजकूर अधिक स्पष्ट करण्यासाठी ग्रंथामध्ये समाविष्ट केलेली छायाचित्रे, चित्रे, नकाशे, सारण्या, आकृत्या इ.

illustrations collection – **लेखचित्रांचा संग्रह.**

illustrative matter – लेखचित्रांचे साहित्य/वाचनसाहित्य.

illustrator – लेखचित्रकार – जी व्यक्ती प्रलेखातील चित्रे, नकाशे, तक्ते इ. काढते.

illustrator entry – लेखचित्रकाराच्या नावे केलेली नोंद.

image – प्रतिमा/आकृती.

image building – प्रतिमा बांधणी – जनमानसातील प्रतिमा.

immitation foil – नकली वर्ख.

imperfect copy / defective copy – सदोष प्रत – ग्रंथातील पाने गहाळ झालेली, फाटलेली, चुकीच्या क्रमाने किंवा उलटी लावली गेली असतील अशी प्रत.

impersonal – व्यक्तिभावविरहित.

import – आयात – (१) दुसऱ्या देशातून आयात केलेला ग्रंथ. (२) दुसऱ्या संगणकाकडून माहिती आयात करणे.

imposition – पृष्ठसंयोजने – ग्रंथातील पानांची अचूक मागणी.

impression – मुद्रितप्रत – ग्रंथाच्या शीर्षकपृष्ठाच्या मागील बाजूस उल्लेख केला जातो.

imprint – प्रकाशनवृत्त (१) प्रकाशन स्थळ, प्रकाशक, प्रकाशन वर्ष – ग्रंथाच्या प्रकाशनासंबंधी किंवा मुद्रणाविषयी ग्रंथामध्ये नमूद केलेले निवेदन.

imprint date / date of publication / year of publication – ग्रंथाचे प्रकाशनवर्ष/ प्रकाशनदिनांक.

inclusion note – समावेशक टीप – एखाद्या नवीन उपविषयाला हंगामी स्वरूपात येथे वर्गांक द्यावा अशी टीप.

increasing complexity – जटिलता वृद्धी.

increasing complexity order – जटिलता वृद्धी क्रम.

increasing concreteness – समूर्तता वृद्धी.

increasing concreteness – समूर्तता वृद्धी क्रम.

increasing quantity – प्रमाणवाचक वृद्धी.

in print – आगामी प्रकाशन – प्रकाशकाकडे प्रकाशन प्रक्रियेत असलेला ग्रंथ.

in progress – प्रगतावस्थेचा ग्रंथ – अनेक खंडांमधील प्रकाशन अजूनही चालू/सुरू असल्याची नोंद.

in stock – ग्रंथविक्रेत्यामुळे विक्रीसाठी संग्रहात असलेला ग्रंथ.

inclusive edition – सर्वसमावेशक आवृत्ती.

inclusive notation – **सर्वसमावेशक चिन्हांकन** – वर्गीकरणामध्ये ग्रंथविषयाची सर्व वैशिष्ट्ये सामावून घेणारे चिन्हांकन.

income tax – **आयकर** – उत्पन्नावरील शासकीय कर.

incunabula – **दोलामुद्रिते** – (१) इ.स. १५०० पूर्वी छापलेली पुस्तके. (२) मुद्रणाच्या प्रारंभावस्थेत निर्माण झालेला ग्रंथ.

incunabulist – **दोलामुद्रितकार** – दोलामुद्रितांविषयी सर्व माहिती असलेली तज्ज्ञ व्यक्ती.

idea plane – **वैचारिक स्तर** – वर्गीकरण पद्धती तयार करतानाचा पहिला स्तर.

indention – **समासांतर** – (१) छपाई करताना वापरलेली अक्षरे आणि त्यांची मांडणी, उपशीर्षकाची मांडणी आणि प्रमुख शीर्षकाखाली छपाई करताना सोडलेली जागा. (२) मजकुरातील ओळीपूर्वी किंवा परिच्छेदापूर्वी सोडलेले अंतर.

indentions – **अंतरे** (तालिकापत्रातील) – तालिकापत्रावर दोन उभ्या रेषा असतात. पहिल्या उभ्या रेषेपासून नोंदीतील घटकांची सुरुवात केली जाते. यालाच पहिला समास असे म्हणतात. दुसऱ्या उभ्या रेषेपासून नोंद घटकातील राहिलेली माहिती लिहितात, त्याला दुसरा समास म्हणतात.

independent auxiliaries – **सामान्य साहाय्यकारी** – युडीसीमध्ये असे सामान्य साहाय्यकारी पोटविभाग आहे की ज्यांचा वापर वर्गांक म्हणूनही केला जातो. उदा. क्षेत्रीय अभ्यास, या विषयासाठी स्थल अंकाचा वापर करून अंकबांधणी करणे शक्य होते. येथे स्थल पैलू हा स्वतंत्र साहाय्यकारी पोटविभाग आहे. (आणखी पाहा अवलंबित साहाय्यकारी पोटविभाग.)

independents – स्वतंत्रीत्या प्रकाशित झालेली; परंतु नंतर एकत्रित बांधलेली पत्रके, पुस्तके.

index – **निर्देश/सूची/उल्लेखसूची/निर्देशांक/अनुक्रमणिका** – (१) एखाद्या ग्रंथातील ग्रंथकारनामे, विषयनामे, उपविषयनामे इत्यादी उल्लेखांची वर्णानुक्रमानुसार केलेली यादी. त्यामध्ये तो उल्लेख सूचीमध्ये, ग्रंथामध्ये नक्की कोठे आहे त्याचे स्थान दाखविलेले असते. (२) संगणकामध्ये फाइल्स किंवा प्रलेखांची त्यांच्या स्थानाच्या उल्लेखांसह केलेली यादी.

index code – **सूची संकेतांक**.

index entry – **निर्देशी नोंद** – उल्लेख सूचीमध्ये समाविष्ट केलेली नोंद.

index language – **निर्देशभाषा/संकेतभाषा** – उल्लेखसूचीमध्ये विषयनिर्देशासाठी वापरलेली संकेतभाषा.

index map – **निर्देश नकाशा** – नकाशांच्या सूचीचा निर्देशक नकाशा.

index number section – **निर्देशांक विभाग/निर्देशी अंक अनुच्छेद** – तालिकापत्रातील नोंदीमधील निर्देश अंक दर्शविणारा अनुच्छेद.

index – relative – **सापेक्ष निर्देश** – यामध्ये एका विषयाचे अन्य विषयाशी असलेले संबंध आणि त्याचे चिन्हांकन दर्शवितात.

index specific – **विनिर्दिष्ट निर्देश** – यामध्ये विषय आणि त्याचे चिन्हांकन दर्शवितात.

index term – **निर्देशसंज्ञा** – निर्देशामध्ये नोंद करण्यासाठी वापरलेली संज्ञा.

index to article – **लेखांची निर्देशसूची** – लेखांच्या नोंदी असलेली सूची.

index to periodical – **नियतकालिकांसाठी लेखांची सूची** – नियतकालिकांमधील लेखांची नोंद असलेली सूची.

index translationum – **अनुवाद निर्देशसूची** – अनुवादांच्या नोंदी असलेली सूची.

index verborum – **शब्दानुसारी निर्देशसूची** – शब्दानुसार नोंदी असलेली सूची.

indexer – **निर्देशसूचीकार** – नोंदी करणारी व्यक्ती.

indexing – **निर्देशन** – (१) उल्लेखसूची संकलित करण्याची प्रक्रिया. (२) निर्देश तयार करण्याची कला किंवा तंत्र.

indexing language – **निर्देशनासाठी वापरलेली संकेतभाषा** – विशिष्ट प्रतिप्राप्ती पद्धतीनुसार वापरला जाणारा विशिष्ट निर्देशसंज्ञांचा संच.

indexing periodical – **निर्देशात्मक नियतकालिक** – (१) नियतकालिकातील लेखांची सूचीविषयक माहिती पद्धतशीरपणे मांडणी/यादी प्रकाशित करणारे नियतकालिक. (२) लेखांचा उल्लेख संदर्भासहित नोंद करणारे नियतकालिक.

indexing service – **निर्देशन सेवा** – नियतकालिकांच्या अनुक्रमणिकांचे निर्देश तयार करून नियमितपणे प्रकाशित करणारी नियतकालिक सेवा.

IASLIC (Indian Association of Special Libraries and Information Centres) – **भारतीय विशेष ग्रंथालये व माहिती केंद्र** – कोलकाता येथे १९५५ मध्ये स्थापन झालेली संस्था जी विशेष ग्रंथालयांच्या विकासासाठी काम करते.

Indian ink – कायमस्वरूपी लिखाण अपेक्षित असेल तेव्हा वापरली जाणारी दीर्घकाळ टिकणारी शाई.

ILA (Indian Library Association) – **भारतीय ग्रंथालय संघ** – १९३३ मध्ये स्थापन झालेली ग्रंथालय संघटना जी ग्रंथालये व ग्रंथालयशास्त्राच्या विकासासाठी काम करते.

INB (Indian National Bibliography) – **भारताची राष्ट्रीय ग्रंथसूची** – राष्ट्रीय संदर्भ ग्रंथालयाद्वारे प्रकाशित होणारी ग्रंथसूची. या सूचीमध्ये भारतात विशिष्ट वर्षात प्रकाशित झालेल्या ग्रंथांचे ग्रंथवर्णन दिले जाते.

INSDOC (Indian National Scientific Documentation Centre) – **भारतीय राष्ट्रीय वैज्ञानिक प्रलेखन केंद्र** – दिल्ली स्थित संस्था देशपातळीवरील विज्ञानविषयक संदर्भाचा संग्रह करून संशोधकांना काही प्रमाणात बहुविध प्रकारची सेवा ही संस्था देते. काही प्रमाणात आंतरराष्ट्रीय क्षेत्रातील संशोधनाची माहिती ही संस्था देते. (आता NISCAIR नावाने प्रचलित)

Indian names – **भारतीय नावे** – मूळ भारतीय नागरिकांची नावे.

indicative abstract – **निर्देशक सारलेख** – मूळ विभागाचा निर्देश करणारा सारलेख.

indicator – निर्देशफलक – ग्रंथसंग्रहाविषयी सद्य:स्थिती दर्शविणारा फलक.

indicator digit – सूचक चिन्ह/मूलभूत प्रकार दर्शक अंक – अंकाच्या पूर्वी असलेले चिन्ह. याला पूर्वी संयोजन चिन्ह म्हटले जात असे.

indicators – सूचके – विषयाचे पृथक्करण करून आशय दर्शविणारे चिन्हे.

indicography – निर्देशांचे संकलन करण्याची प्रक्रिया.

icon – चिन्ह/प्रतीक – संगणकाच्या पडद्यावर असणारे उपलब्ध संचिकेचे चिन्ह.

indirect subject heading – अप्रत्यक्ष विषयशीर्षक – दुसऱ्या विषयशीर्षकाचा निर्देश करणारे विषयशीर्षक. उदा. 'पाहा' नोंद केलेले विषयशीर्षक.

indirect tax – अप्रत्यक्ष कर.

individual entry – स्वतंत्र नोंद – वस्तूनाम किंवा व्यक्तिनाम, स्थलनामाने केलेली नोंद.

individualisation – व्यक्तिभेदकरण.

individuality – व्यक्तित्व विशेष.

indo-arabic numerals – इंडो अरेबिक अंकसंग्रह

indology – भारतीय कटिबंधातील विधी अथवा विषयांची माहिती असणारे ग्रंथ.

induction – रुळविणे – नवीन संस्थेतील/ग्रंथालयातील कामासंबंधी माहिती देऊन ते काम करण्यासाठी व्यक्तीस संस्थेमध्ये रुळविणे, नव्या कामांची ओळख करून देणे.

industrial / commercial / business / trade library – औद्योगिक ग्रंथालय/औद्योगिक संस्थेचे ग्रंथालय.

in edita – अप्रकाशित साहित्य.

in edited – संपादकीय संस्कार न करता प्रकाशित केलेले साहित्य.

influence phase relation – प्रभाव विषयांग संबंध.

influenbing phase – प्रभावी प्रावस्था – डॉ. रंगनाथन् यांनी विशद केलेल्या विषयांच्या नातेसंबंधामधील एक प्रावस्था. प्रत्येक प्रलेखाला किंवा ग्रंथाला विषयाच्या प्रभावानुसार अचूक वर्गात वर्गीकृत करण्याची प्रक्रिया.

informal – अनौपचारिक – अप्रत्यक्षपणे सांगणे.

informal communication – अनौपचारिक संप्रेषण/संदेशन.

informal education – अनौपचारिक शिक्षण – शिक्षण संस्थेशिवाय मिळणारे शिक्षण.

infix – अंतर्भाव होणारा – एखाद्या वस्तूघटक किंवा अंक जो दुसऱ्या अंकामध्ये समाविष्ट करतो, ज्यामुळे अधिक अर्थवाही वर्गांक तयार करता येतो.

informatics – **माहितीसंगणकशास्त्र** – माहितीविषयक हाताळणी संगणकाद्वारे कशी करावी याविषयीचे शास्त्र.

information – **माहिती** – सत्य परिस्थिती, ज्ञान किंवा संप्रेषणासाठी योग्य अशा स्वरूपातील माहिती.

information and referral service – **माहिती आणि संदर्भित सेवा** – अमेरिकन संस्था केंद्राद्वारे उपयोजकांकडून दूरध्वनी वा इतर संपर्क माध्यमांद्वारे विचारलेली माहिती व तत्काळ त्या प्रकारची माहिती पुरविणाऱ्या केंद्राला माहिती पोहोचविण्याची सेवा.

information age – **माहितीयुग** – माहितीविषयक ज्ञानामुळे प्रभावित झालेला काळ.

information audit – **माहितीचे अंकेक्षण** – संस्थेतील उपलब्ध माहितीची प्राप्तीसाधने, माहितीसेवा व उत्पादनांचे मूल्यांकन करून अधिक उपयुक्त परिणामकारकतेसाठी अभ्यास केला जातो.

information bank – **माहिती संचयिका** – माहितीची जपणूक करून योग्यवेळी माहिती पुरविणारी पेढी.

information bits – **माहिती कण**.

information broker – **माहिती दलाल** – वैयक्तिकरीत्या व्यावसायिक तत्त्वावर माहितीसेवा देणारी व्यक्ती अथवा संस्था.

information bulletin – **माहिती पत्रिका**.

information centre – **माहितीकेंद्र** – (१) माहितीचे संकलन, संग्रहण, हाताळणे, संरक्षण आणि प्रसारण करणारी संघटना अथवा संस्था. (२) माहितीसंबंधी सर्व प्रकारच्या सेवा पुरविणारे केंद्र.

information communication – **माहिती संप्रेषण**.

information communication chain – **माहिती संप्रेषण साखळी** – माहिती निर्मितीपासून माहिती उपयोगात येईपर्यंत येणाऱ्या दुव्यांनी जोडलेली साखळी.

information consultant – **माहिती सल्लागार** – माहितीविषयक सेवा देण्यासाठी किंवा माहिती मिळविण्यासाठी व्यावसायिक तत्त्वावर मार्गदर्शन करणारी व्यक्ती वा संस्था.

information costs – **माहिती खर्च** – संगणकामध्ये माहिती साठविणे, प्रक्रिया करणे, सुरक्षितता राखणे यासाठी लागणारा वेळ व या सर्व प्रक्रियेसाठी येणारा एकूण खर्च.

information department/section – **माहिती विभाग** – एखाद्या संस्थेतील माहितीविषयक कार्य करणारा विभाग.

information desk – **माहिती कक्ष** – (१) माहिती पुरविणारा कक्ष (२) ग्रंथालयातील वा इतर संस्थेतील विशिष्ट कर्मचाऱ्यांद्वारे माहिती पुरविणारा कक्ष/विभाग.

information element – **माहितीचा घटक**.

information explosion – **माहिती विस्फोट/परिस्फोट**– (१) दिवसेंदिवस वाढत चाललेला माहितीचा ओघ. (२) माहितीची प्रचंड प्रमाणावरील निर्मिती.

information file – **माहितीसंचय/माहितीसंचिका**– (१) माहिती मिळण्याची संभाव्य प्राप्तीस्थाने. (२) उतारे, चित्रे, सारलेख, हस्तपुस्तिका यांचा संग्रह तत्काळ संदर्भासाठी विशिष्ट क्रमाने ठेवणे.

information handling – **माहितीचे सूत्रसंचलन** – मिळविलेल्या माहितीची साठवण, प्रक्रियाकरण, प्रतिप्राप्ती यांची उपयोजकासाठी सूत्रबद्ध हाताळणी.

information interchange – **माहितीची अदलाबदल** – एका संगणकाकडून माहिती पाठविणे व दुसऱ्या संगणकाने ती स्वीकारणे यामध्ये माहितीमध्ये कमी–जास्त बदल न होता तिची देवाणघेवाण करण्याची प्रक्रिया.

information librarian – **माहिती पुरविणारा ग्रंथपाल/संदर्भ ग्रंथपाल.**

information library – **माहिती देणारे ग्रंथालय/संदर्भ ग्रंथालय.**

information literacy – **माहिती साक्षरता** – माहितीची उपलब्धता वाचकांना सांगणारा कार्यक्रम.

information management – **माहितीचे व्यवस्थापन** – माहिती मिळविण्यापासून ती उपयोजकाला उपयोगासाठी पुरविण्यासाठी केल्या जाणाऱ्या सर्व प्रक्रिया तज्ज्ञांची मदत घेऊन यशस्वीरीत्या पार पाडण्याची प्रक्रिया.

information mapping – **माहितीचे नकाशाकरण** – माहिती सहजपणे व तत्काळ मिळविण्यासाठी माहितीचे ग्रंथालयातील स्थान निश्चित करण्याचे तंत्र.

information officer – **माहिती अधिकारी** – संस्थेतील माहितीविषयक सेवेचे व्यवस्थापन व सेवा याविषयी देखरेख करणारी अधिकारी व्यक्ती.

information organisation – **माहिती संरचना/संघटन** – माहिती हाताळणे, समाविष्ट करणे, स्वरूप बदलणे यासारखी पद्धतशीर प्रक्रिया.

information policy – **माहितीचे धोरण.**

information processing – **माहिती सोपदृक्कार/माहितीसंदृक्करण** – संगणकातील माहिती उपयोजकाला अधिकाधिक उपयुक्त होण्यासाठी माहितीवर विविध प्रक्रिया करण्याची क्रिया. उदा. निर्देश तयार करणे.

information provider – **माहिती पुरविणारी व्यक्ती/संस्था** – माहिती प्राप्तीस्थान तयार करण्यासाठी माहिती पुरविण्यास जबाबदार असलेली व्यक्ती वा संस्था.

information products – **माहितीची उत्पादने/प्रकाशने** – लेखसूची/निर्देश, सारांश, डायजेस्ट आणि इतर प्रकाशने.

information resource management – **माहिती स्रोतांचे व्यवस्थापन.**

information retrieval – **माहितीची प्रतिप्राप्ती** – संगणकाच्या माहितीसंचयातील हवी असलेली माहिती शोधण्याची प्रक्रिया.

information science – **माहिती विज्ञान** – माहितीची उपयोगिता, प्राप्तीस्थाने व विकास यांचा अभ्यास करणारे विज्ञान.

information scientist – **माहिती शास्त्रज्ञ** – माहितीविज्ञानाचा अभ्यास केलेली तज्ज्ञ व्यक्ती.

information security – **माहितीची सुरक्षितता** – माहितीचे अचानक किंवा हेतूपूर्वक अनधिकृतरीत्या प्रसारण, अदलाबदल, रूपांतरण किंवा नुकसान होण्यापासून संरक्षण करणे.

information service – **माहिती सेवा** – विशेष ग्रंथालयांकडून दिली जाणारी सेवा. यामध्ये वाचकांच्या मागणीपूर्वीच माहितीसंदृकरण केले जाते.

information society – **माहिती प्रधान समाज** – माहितीविषयक कार्यामुळे प्रभावित झालेला समाज.

information system – **माहिती पद्धती/संचलनपद्धती** – एखाद्या कार्यातील संपर्क साधनांचे संगणकजाळे.

information technology – **माहिती तंत्रज्ञान** – संगणक व दूरसंचार यंत्रणेद्वारे विविध प्रकारची माहिती मिळविणे, प्रक्रिया करणे व प्रसारण करणे.

information theory – **माहिती सिद्धान्त** – माहितीचे मोजमाप करण्याची तसेच गुणधर्मांविषयी अभ्यास करण्याची अभ्यासशाखा.

information work – **माहिती कार्य** – माहिती मिळविणे, अवलोकन करणे, प्रसार करणे इ. सांगोपांग कार्य.

information abstract – **माहितीपर/माहितीपूर्ण सार** – (१) विषयाच्या मूळ गाभ्याविषयी माहिती देणारे सार. (२) मूळ लेखातील प्रमुख मुद्यांचा आढावा घेऊन मुख्य आधारसामग्री विषयक माहिती देणारा सारलेख.

infrastructure – **पायाभूत घटक** – मूळ रचनेची चौकट, पायाभूत सोयी, आंतररचना, भौतिक सुविधा संस्थांमध्ये असलेली माहितीची साधने आणि इमारत, फर्निचर, इलेक्ट्रिक फिटिंग्ज, टेलिफोन इ.सोयी.

initial letter – **अलंकृत आद्याक्षर** – एखाद्या शब्दाचे, ओळीचे वा परिच्छेदाचे सुरुवातीचे अक्षर मोठ्या लिपीत व अलंकारिक पद्धतीने लिहिले जाते.

inlay – ग्रंथाच्या आतील भागाचे अलंकरण पुनर्बांधणी करताना काहीवेळा केले जाते.

input / data entry – **निर्विष्टी** – संगणकाच्या स्मृतिपटलावर माहिती संग्रहित करणे.

input area – **माहिती संग्रहण क्षेत्र.**

input device – **संग्रहण/समावेशन साधने/युक्ती** – (१) संगणकाच्या स्मृतीपटलावर माहिती संग्रहित करण्याचे साधन. (२) संगणकामध्ये माहिती समाविष्ट करण्यासाठी उपयुक्त अशी कळपट, मूषक यांसारखी उपकरणे.

input equipment – **माहिती संग्रहाचे साधन/उपकरण.**

input / output – **आदान/प्रदान** – संगणकात माहिती समाविष्ट करण्यासाठी तसेच संगणकातून माहिती मिळविण्यासाठी कार्य करणारे संगणकाचे भाग.

in-press/to be published – आगामी प्रकाशन.

in-process card – ग्रंथोपस्काराधीन पत्र.

in-process material – ग्रंथोपस्काराधीन वाचनसाहित्य.

inscribed copy – लेखकाने स्वाक्षरी केलेली भेट प्रत.

in-service training – सेवान्तर्गत प्रशिक्षण – नोकरी स्वीकारल्यानंतर अद्ययावत ज्ञान राखण्यासाठीचे सेवान्तर्गत प्रशिक्षण.

insert – समावेश करणे/समावेशन क्रिया – संगणकाच्या माहितीतील दोन ओळी किंवा दोन शब्द यामध्ये माहिती समाविष्ट करणे.

insert key – अंतर्भाव कळ – संगणकातील समावेशनासाठी उपयुक्त कळपटावरील विशिष्ट कळ.

insertion – उत्तर समावेशन,अंतर्वेशन – मूळ मजकुरामध्ये नंतर समाविष्ट केलेली माहिती.

inset map – ग्रंथामध्ये बांधणी करताना समाविष्ट केलेल्या नकाशामध्ये छापलेला छोटा नकाशा.

installation programme – प्रस्थापना कार्यक्रम – संगणकामध्ये सॉफ्टवेअरचा समावेश करण्यासाठीचे संयोजन.

installation time – प्रस्थापना काल – हार्डवेअर किंवा सॉफ्टवेअर संगणकास स्थापित करण्यास लागणारा वेळ. एखाद्या संगणकामध्ये मूळ कार्यक्रमाच्या संचिका समाविष्ट करण्यासाठी व चाचणी घेण्यासाठी लागणारा वेळ.

institute – institution – संस्था – एखाद्या विशिष्ट ध्येयाच्या प्रगतीसाठी वाहून घेतलेली संस्था, आस्थापना, पीठ किंवा तत्सम.

INSPECC (Information Services for Physics Electro-Technology, Computer and Controls) – इन्स्पेक – इन्स्टिट्यूट ऑफ इलेक्ट्रॉनिक इंजिनियर्सच्या इन्फर्मेशन डिव्हिजनच्या वतीने प्रसारित होणाऱ्या 'इन्फर्मेशन सर्व्हिसेस फॉर फिजिक्स, इलेक्ट्रो-टेक्नॉलॉजी, कम्प्यूटर्स ॲन्ड कंट्रोल्स' या माहिती सेवेच्या नावाची आद्याक्षर संज्ञा.

institutional – संस्थेचा/संस्थेची/संस्थेबाबत.

instituional library – संस्थेचे ग्रंथालय.

institutional membership – संस्थेचे सभासदत्व/सदस्यत्व.

instruction – सूचना.

instruction area – अनुदेश क्षेत्र – संगणकाच्या स्मरणिकेतील सूचना धारण करणारे क्षेत्र.

instruction set – सूचना संच – संगणकातील आज्ञावली पद्धतीतील भाषांमधील सूचनांचा संच.

integer notation – पूर्णांक असलेले चिन्हांकन.

interal notation – **अविभाज्य चिन्हांकन** – दशांशचिन्हाचा वापर न करता केलेले चिन्हांकन. उदा. लायब्ररी ऑफ काँग्रेस पद्धतीचे चिन्हांकन.

integrating resource – **अखंडित संसाधने.**

integrity – **अखंडता** – एका संगणकाकडून दुसऱ्या संगणकाकडे माहिती पाठविल्यानंतर माहितीची अचूकता व पूर्णत्व यांची तपासणी.

integrity of numbers – **अंकांची एकात्मता/अखंडता.** (१) वर्गीकरण पद्धतीत एखाद्या विषयासाठी अंक निश्चित करण्याची पद्धती. संकल्पनेशी कायमस्वरूपी संबंधित असल्याने मूळच्या वर्गाशी संमिलित. (२) वर्गीकरण नियमावलीच्या पुरवणीमध्ये एखाद्या विषयाचे चिन्ह किंवा वर्गांक फार मोठ्या प्रमाणावर संकुचित केलेला नसावा, असे सुचविणारे तत्त्व.

intensive reference service – **सखोल संदर्भसेवा** – वाचकाला हवी असलेली माहिती सखोलरीत्या संदर्भ उपलब्ध करण्याची ग्रंथालयसेवा.

interdisciplinary – **आंतरशाखीय** – दोन किंवा अधिक विद्याशाखांशी संबंधित असलेला विषय/ संकल्पना.

inter leaf – **ग्रंथाचे अंत:पान** – ग्रंथाच्या मुख्य पानांबरोबर जास्तीचे पान बांधणी करताना समाविष्ट केले जाते. याचा उद्देश काहीवेळा टीपा लिहिण्यासाठी, छायाचित्र संरक्षित करण्यासाठी होतो.

interfile – **क्रमरचना** – वर्गीकरणानुसार एखादा विषय अनुक्रमानुसार येथे बसविणे/घालणे इष्ट आहे. तेथे पूर्वी असलेल्या विषयाचा क्रम न बदलता अंतर्भाव करणे.

inter-government – आंतरराष्ट्रीय संघटन ज्यामध्ये अनेक राष्ट्रांची सरकारे सभासद असतात.

inter library co-operation – **आंतरग्रंथालयीन सहकार्य** – अनेक ग्रंथालयांनी एकत्र येऊन सहकारी वृत्तीने ग्रंथालयीन कार्य संयुक्तरीत्या पार पाडणे.

inter library loan / inter library lending – **आंतरग्रंथालयीन देवघेव/उसनवारी** – दुसऱ्या ग्रंथालयाला सभासद मानून ग्रंथ देवघेव करणे.

integrated circuits – **सूक्ष्म परिपथ** – संगणकातील एक भाग – लहान आणि पातळ आकाराच्या सिलिकॉनच्या तुकड्यांवर लॉजिक गेट्स कोरलेली असतात. १० ते १०,००० इलेक्ट्रॉनिकी लॉजिक गेट्स एका इंटिग्रेटेड सर्किटवर (आय.सी.वर) असू शकतात.

intention – **लक्ष्य/रोख/हेतू/उद्देश.**

interactive access – **संगणक आणि उपयोजक यांच्यातील प्रत्यक्ष संपर्क.**

interactive information system – **प्रत्यक्ष संपर्क माहिती पद्धती** – यात संगणकावर एखादी आज्ञावली वापरून काम सुरू असेल तेव्हा तो वापरणाऱ्याला मध्ये हस्तक्षेप करता येतो किंवा विशिष्ट कामाचा भाग संपल्यावर पुढील काम कोणते असावे हे संगणक वापरणारा एकूण कामाचा आढावा घेऊन निर्णय घेऊ शकतो.

intercalation – अंतर्वेशन – ज्यायोगे 'अंतर्भाव होणारा' Infix या संज्ञेमध्ये नमूद केल्याप्रमाणे कार्य करता येते अशी क्लृप्ती.

interdependent – परस्परावलंबी.

interdisciplinary approach – आंतरशाखीय दृष्टिकोन – दोन विषयांशी संबंध असणारा दृष्टिकोन.

interdisciplinary research – आंतरशाखीय संशोधन – दोन विषयांशी संबंधित संशोधन.

interdisciplinary system – आंतरशाखीय पद्धत.

interdisciplinary work – आंतरशाखीय कार्य.

interface – दुवा/मध्यस्थ – दोन भिन्न उपकरण साधनांमधील अथवा माध्यमातील दुवा. उदा. दूरध्वनी आणि संगणक यांना जोडणारा दुवा (modem) किंवा अभ्यासक आणि वाचनसाहित्य यांना जोडणारा दुवा (user interface) ग्रंथपाल अथवा ग्रंथालय कर्मचारी.

internal audit – अंतर्गत अंकेक्षण – कर्मचाऱ्याने करावयाची लेखा तपासणी.

internal examination – अंतर्गत परीक्षा – संबंधित शिक्षकाने घेतलेली व गुणदान केलेली परीक्षा.

internal research reports – अंतर्गत शोध प्रतिवृत्ते – संस्थेतील संशोधनाचा अहवाल.

international – आंतरराष्ट्रीय – दोन अथवा अधिक राष्ट्रांमधील.

international bibliography – आंतरराष्ट्रीय ग्रंथसूची – सर्व देशातील वाचनसाहित्याची सूची.

International Federation for Documentation and Information (FID) – प्रलेखन व माहितीसाठी आंतरराष्ट्रीय संघ.

IFLA (International Federation of Library Association) – जागतिक स्तरावरील ग्रंथालयशास्त्र व ग्रंथपाल यांचा संघ. ज्याची सुरुवात १९२४ मध्ये झाली.

international library – आंतरराष्ट्रीय ग्रंथालय.

ISBN (International Standard Book Number) – आय.एस.बी.एन. – (१) विशिष्ट ग्रंथ ओळखता यावा तसेच यासाठी देवाणघेवाण सुलभ व्हावी यासाठी आंतरराष्ट्रीय संघटना हा संकेत क्रमांक देत असते. हा क्रमांक त्या ग्रंथाची ओळख खूण असते. (२) प्रकाशनापूर्वी प्रत्येक ग्रंथाला दिलेला आंतरराष्ट्रीय प्रमाणित ग्रंथ क्रमांक ० ते ९ या अंकाचा वापर करून दहा अंकी क्रमांक दिला जातो.

ISSN (International Standard Serial Number) – आय.एस.एस.एन. – (१) जगातील नियतकालिके/सातत्याने प्रकाशित होणाऱ्या प्रकाशनासाठी विशिष्ट संकेतांक दिला जातो. (२) नियतकालिकांच्या प्रत्येक अंकासाठी दिलेला तयार आंतरराष्ट्रीय प्रमाणित माला क्रमांक (७ अंकी)

internet – आंतरराष्ट्रीय संगणकजाळे/माहिती महाजाळे.

interpolated note – अंतर्वेशित टीप – तालिकेतील किंवा ग्रंथसूचीतील नोंदीमध्ये संकलकाने दिलेली स्पष्टीकरणात्मक किंवा वर्णनात्मक टीप. ही बहुधा चौकोनी कंसामध्ये लिहिली जाते.

interpolation – अंतर्वेशन/समावेशक – वर्गीकरण करताना वर्गीकरण पद्धतीमध्ये कोणत्याही ठिकाणी नवीन विषय समाविष्ट करणे.

interpolation device – समावेशन क्लृप्ती – वर्गीकरण करताना विषयांचे समावेशन करून चिन्हांकन देण्याची क्लृप्ती.

interpolation number – समावेशन अंक.

interprete – अर्थनिर्वचन – अर्थ सांगणे, उलगडा करणे, विवरण किंवा स्पष्टीकरण करणे.

interpreter – संगणकातील दुभाष्या – (१) माहितीचे आकलन होण्यासाठी तयार केलेली संगणक आज्ञावली. (२) कडाछिद्रित पत्रांचे संस्करण करताना छिद्रांनुसार छपाई करणारा संगणकाचा भाग.

interogation mark / question mark – प्रश्नचिन्ह (?)

inter subject – आंतरविषय.

interrupt – अंतरायन – संगणकाचा स्थगिती इशारा. संगणकाचे काम तात्पुरते स्थगित करणे.

interrupted publication – खंडित प्रकाशन – माला अथवा नियतकालिक प्रकाशनातील काही खंड प्रकाशित झाले असताना व्यत्यय आल्यामुळे थांबलेले प्रकाशन.

intra – अंतर्गत – आत (पैलू किंवा पंक्ती अंतर्गत).

intra aray – पंक्तीमधील.

intra facet – पैलूमधील.

intra facet relation – आंतरपैलू संबंध.

intranet – आंतरजाळे – संस्था अंतर्गत असणारे जाळे.

introduction – प्रस्तावना/परिचय – (१) ग्रंथाच्या सुरुवातीला दिलेली परिचयात्मक टीप. (२) कार्याची ओळख होण्यासाठीचे प्राथमिक लिखाण, त्यात विषय, पद्धती आणि वापरलेली साधने यांचा उल्लेख असतो.

introductory note – परिचयात्मक टीप.

inventory – अस्तित्वपत्र/वस्तूसूची – (१) वस्तूंची दीर्घ अगर वर्णनात्मक यादी. (२) ग्रंथालय जतनसंग्रहातील (Archieves) ग्रंथाचे स्थान दर्शविणारे पत्र.

inversion of title – ग्रंथशीर्षकातील शब्दांची अदलाबदल – शब्दकोशांची नोंद करताना विशेषत: हवा तो शब्द सुरुवातीला आणून विषयाकडे लक्ष वेधले जाते.

inverted comma – अवतरण चिन्ह (' ')

inverted entry – **स्थानबदल नोंद** – महत्त्वाचा शब्द सुरुवातीला आणणारी उल्लेखसूचीमधील नोंद.

inverted heading – **स्थानबदलात्मक मथळा** – महत्त्वाचा शब्द सुरुवातीला घेण्यासाठी केलेले तालिकेतील स्थानबदलात्मक शीर्षक.

inverted pages – **द्विमुखी ग्रंथ** – अशा ग्रंथाची छपाई पोथीप्रमाणे असते.

inverted title / inversion of title – **विषयरचित ग्रंथनाम** – मुख्य शब्द सुरुवातीला आणण्यासाठी शब्दांचा स्थानबदल केलेले शीर्षक.

invisible colleges – **अदृश्य महाविद्यालये** – निरीक्षणाद्वारे मिळणारे शिक्षण.

invoice / bill – **देयक** – पुरविलेल्या वस्तूंची किंमत दर्शविणारी यादी. ज्याआधारे किंमत अदा केली जाते.

irregular periodical – **अनियतकालिके** – प्रकाशनकाल निश्चित नसलेले नियतकालिक.

irregular serial – **अनियमित कालिक.**

irreversicle relation – **उलटे न करता येणारे संबंध.**

isolate – **विभक्त/उपविभाग** – (१) मुख्य विषयाबरोबर जाणारी एक संकल्पना, घटक, विषय, उपविषय – एखाद्या मुख्य विषयाशी निगडित अशी एक संकल्पना. (२) द्विबिंदू वर्गीकरणामध्ये सांगितलेल्या तीन पातळींना मिळून दिलेली संज्ञा यामध्ये काल, स्थल, भाषा हे उपविभाग वर्गीकरणासाठी विचारात घेतले जातात.

issue – **अंक** – नियतकालिकाच्या ठरावीक कालावधीने प्रसिद्ध होणाऱ्या प्रत्येक भागास 'अंक' म्हणतात. प्रत्येक अंकास क्रमांक दिलेला असतो. यामुळे प्रत्येक अंकाची स्वतंत्रपणे दखल घेता येते. वर्षभरातील अंक एकत्रित केल्यास खंड बनतो.

issue system/method / circulation system – **ग्रंथ देवघेव पद्धती** – ग्रंथालयातील ग्रंथ उसनवारीने वाचकांना देताना करावयाची नोंद पद्धती.

issue counter – **ग्रंथ देवघेव कट्टा/कक्ष.**

issue date – **वाचकाला ग्रंथ दिल्याचा दिनांक.**

issue register – **देवघेव नोंदवही** – उसनवारीने दिलेल्या ग्रंथांची ग्रंथालयातील नोंदवही.

issue number – **देवघेव क्रमांक/अंक क्रमांक** – नियतकालिकाच्या प्रत्येक प्रकाशनास दिला जाणारा क्रमांक.

italics – तिरपी अक्षरे असलेली इंग्रजी लिपी.

item – **बाब/एक भाग** – वस्तू घटक.

item size – **एक भाग/बाब/आकार.**

iternative searching – **पुनरावृत्तीय शोध.**

jacket – वेष्टन/मुख्य ग्रंथावरील कागदी आवरण – ग्रंथकारनाम दर्शविणारे कागदाचे सैल आवरण.

jail library / prison library – कैदी/कारागृह ग्रंथालय.

JAVA – जावा – संगणकासाठी उपयुक्त एक आज्ञावली भाषा.

job – सोपविलेले काम – संगणकाला दिलेल्या कामाचे विश्लेषण करणारा आधारसामग्री संच.

job analysis – कार्य पृथक्करण – विविध कामे, कार्य आणि कार्यक्रम यांचे पृथक्करण करणे.

job description – कार्य वर्णन – विशिष्ट पदावरील व्यक्तीच्या करावयाच्या कामांचा तपशील.

job valuation – कार्य मूल्यमापन –इतर कामांच्या संबंधात करावयाच्या कामाचे मूल्यमापन करणे.

jobber – ग्रंथ पुरवठाकार.

joint author / co-author – सहग्रंथकार/सहलेखक/संयुक्त ग्रंथकार – (१) संयुक्त जबाबदारीने ग्रंथाच्या लिखाणात सहभागी होणारा लेखक. (२) दुसऱ्या एखाद्या किंवा अनेक लेखकांबरोबर लेखन करणारा लेखक.

joint author entry – सहग्रंथकार नोंद/सहलेखक नोंद – तालिकेमध्ये सहलेखकाच्या नावाने केलेली नोंद.

joint author index entry – सहलेखक निर्देशनोंद – निर्देशातील सहलेखकाच्या नावाने केलेली नोंद.

joint catalogue – संयुक्ततालिका/एकत्रिततालिका – दोन किंवा अधिक ग्रंथालयांची मिळून तयार केलेली तालिका.

joint committee – **संयुक्त समिती** – दोन संख्याअथवा अधिकार मंडळातील काही सदस्यांची मिळून बनविलेली समिती.

joint corporate author – **सहसमष्टी ग्रंथकार नोंद** – शासकीय किंवा तत्सम समष्टिग्रंथकार दोन किंवा अधिक असल्यास त्यांच्या नावे केलेली नोंद.

joint editor – **सह संपादक** – दोन वा अधिक व्यक्तींनी केलेले संपादनाचे कार्य.

joint editor entry – **सहसंपादकाची नोंद** – दोन वा अधिक संपादकांच्या नावे तालिकेमध्ये केलेली नोंद.

joint index entry – **सहनिर्देशी नोंद**.

joint collaborator – **सह–सहयोगक** – सहयोगक वेगवेगळ्या प्रकारचे असू शकतात. उदा. संपादक, भाषांतरकार, संक्षेपक, टीकाकार इ.

journal – **पत्रिका/रोजनामा/ज्ञानपत्रिका** – (१) विशिष्ट विषयाबाबत प्राथमिक माहिती प्रकाशित करणारे नियतकालिक. (२) एखाद्या संस्थेने प्रकाशित केलेले ठरावीक प्रकाशनकाल असलेले कालिक. निश्चित कालावधी, प्रत्येक अंकाला स्वतंत्र क्रमांक व प्रकाशनाचे सातत्य, एकच नाव, ही वैशिष्ट्ये.

journalese – **वृत्तपत्रशैली**.

journalism – **पत्रकारिता/वृत्तपत्रव्यवसाय** – वृत्तपत्र विद्या.

journalist – **पत्रकार/वृत्तपत्रकार** – जी व्यक्ती नियतकालिके/वृत्तपत्रे प्रकाशित करण्याच्या कामात सहभागी असते.

junior assistant – **कनिष्ठ साहाय्यक** – वरिष्ठ व्यक्तीच्या हाताखाली काम करणारी परंतु तांत्रिक कामाची क्षमता धारण करणारी व्यक्ती.

junior book – **बालसाहित्य ग्रंथ**.

junior department/children's library/junior library – **बालवाचनालय**.

junior librarian – **कनिष्ठ ग्रंथपाल**.

justification – **स्पष्टीकरण** – (१) तालिकीकरणामध्ये नोंद करताना सर्व अत्यावश्यक व अधिक माहितीची नोंद केली वा नाही याचे समाधानकारक स्पष्टीकरण तालिकाकाराला करावे लागते.
(२) छपाई करताना साधलेले कागदावरील पंक्तिसमकरण.

juvenile book – **कुमारांसाठी ग्रंथ**.

juvenile edition – **कुमारांसाठी तयार झालेली विशेष आवृत्ती**.

juvenile library – **बाल/कुमारांसाठी ग्रंथालय**.

juvenilla – **बाल/कुमारांसाठी रचना**.

juxtapose – **एकमेकांजवळ ठेवणे/तुलना करणे**.

k – **किलो** – या संकल्पनेसाठी वापरलेले त्या शब्दाचे आद्याक्षर. किलो म्हणजे हजार. किलोबाईट हे परिमाण सर्वसाधारणपणे संगणकाच्या स्मृती/संग्रहण साधने मोजण्यासाठी वापरतात. संगणक परिभाषेतील एक किलो हा २१० म्हणजेच १०२४ बाईट्सचा असतो.

kent classification – **केन्टचे वर्गीकरण** – १७८१ मध्ये इम्युअल केन्ट यांनी तयार केलेली वर्गीकरण पद्धती.

key – **कळ/चावी** – संगणकाच्या कळपट्टीवरील कळ. यामुळे संगणकाची अपेक्षित कार्यवाही साधता येते.

key author – **प्रमुख लेखक** – संपादित ग्रंथाचा प्रमुख लेखक.

keyboard – **कळफलक** – (१) संगणकास माहिती पुरविण्यासाठी वापरलेले एक उपकरण. सर्वसाधारणपणे आता १०१ कळांचे फलक मिळतात. टंकलेखनासाठी वापरलेल्या विशिष्ट कामासाठी वापरलेल्या आणि अंकासाठी असणाऱ्या अशा तीन भागांत यावरील कळा विभागलेल्या असतात. (२) संगणकाला कार्यवाहीत करण्यासाठीच्या कृतीसाधनांचा फलक.

key note – **प्रमुख शब्द टीप** – महत्त्वाची टीप.

key title – **प्रमुख ग्रंथनाम.**

key word – **कळशब्द/प्रमुख शब्द** – प्रलेखाच्या शीर्षकातील विषय दर्शविणारा प्रमुख शब्द.

KWIC (Key Word in Context) – संदर्भासहित मुख्य शब्द/दुव्यांचे शब्द – संगणक आज्ञावली शीर्षकानुसार प्रमुख शब्द. वर्णरचनेप्रमाणे क्रम असलेल्या आज्ञावलींची यादी. हा निर्देश तयार करताना प्रमुख शब्द शीर्षकापुढे उठावदारपणे लिहिला जातो. तसेच सर्व शीर्षकांमधील शब्दांची वर्णक्रमानुसार उभी रचना केली जाते.

KWIC (Key Word in Context Indexting) – मुख्यशब्दाधारित सूचीकरण – दुव्यांच्या शब्दांनी निर्देश मिळविण्याची पद्धती.

key words – कळ शब्द – दुव्यांचे शब्द, पारिभाषिक शब्द, मुख्य शब्द.

key word index – मुख्य शब्द निर्देश – प्रमुख शब्दांचा तयार केलेला निर्देश.

KWOC (Key Word Out Of Context) – संदर्भरहित प्रमुख शब्द – अनेक प्रमुख शब्दांच्या खाली पूर्ण शीर्षकाची नोंद केली जाते. प्रमुख शब्द हे शीर्षकातील किंवा इतर शीर्षक याद्यांमधून घेतले जातात. प्रमुख संदर्भ शीर्षकामध्ये असेलच असे नाही.

keyword search – प्रमुख शब्दाद्वारा माहितीशोध – माहितीचा शोध घेताना प्रमुख शब्दांचा संदर्भ देऊन साहित्य मिळविण्याची प्रक्रिया.

kyle classification – कायल वर्गीकरण.

knowledge – ज्ञान – माहितीचे सुसंघटित स्वरूप.

knowledge class – ज्ञानवर्ग – ज्ञानाची विषयवार विभागणी दर्शविणारे मुख्य वर्ग.

knowledge classification / philosophical classification – ज्ञान वर्गीकरण/तत्त्वज्ञानात्मक वर्गीकरण – उपलब्ध अनेकविध माहितीचे विषयानुसार केलेले वर्गीकरण.

knowledge commission – ज्ञान आयोग – सॅम पित्रोदा यांच्या अध्यक्षतेखाली भारत सरकारने २००६ मध्ये स्थापन केलेला राष्ट्रीय ज्ञान आयोग.

knowledge explosion – ज्ञान विस्फोट/परिस्फोट – प्रचंड प्रमाणात होणारी ज्ञान निर्मिती.

known document – ज्ञात प्रलेख/व्यक्त प्रलेख – वाचकांस लेख, शीर्षक, प्रकाशक इ. संबंधी माहिती असलेला प्रलेख.

label / tag – खूणचिट्ठी – (१) वस्तूची माहिती, मालकी वगैरे दर्शविणारा व वस्तूवर चिकटविलेला कागद. (२) पुस्तकामध्ये ठेवलेली ग्रंथनाम, प्रकाशक, लेखक यांच्या नावाचा उल्लेख करणारी खूणचिट्ठी. (३) संगणकातील आधारसामग्री संचाबद्दल माहिती देणारी बोधाक्षरे.

label field – खुणांनी व्यक्त केलेले क्षेत्र.

labelled notation – खूणचिट्ठी चिन्हांकन – द्विबिंदू वर्गीकरणामध्ये प्रत्येक मुख्य वर्ग एका अक्षराने दर्शविला जातो. नंतरचा वर्ग पैलूयुक्त चिन्हांकन देऊन संज्ञा या अंकांनी दर्शविल्या जातात.

labelling – खूणचिट्ठी लावण्याचे काम – ग्रंथचिट्ठी चिकटविण्याचे कार्य.

laboratory manual – प्रयोगशाला पुस्तिका.

laboratory notes – प्रयोगशाळेतील टिपणे.

lacuna (pl. lacunae) – उणीव/कमतरता/दोष.

Lalit Kala Akademy – ललित कला अकादमी – इ.स. १९५४ मध्ये भारताच्या केंद्र शासनाने भारतीय संस्कृती व कला परंपरा जतन व संवर्धन व्हावे यासाठी स्थापलेली संस्था.

lamination – स्तरण/पटलीकरण – (१) कागदावर पारदर्शक प्लास्टिक चिकटविण्याची क्रिया. (२) जुने दुर्मिळ ग्रंथ अधिक काळ टिकविण्यासाठी ग्रंथातील पृष्ठाला सलग पातळ कागद लावून पुन्हा बांधणी करण्याची प्रक्रिया.

land revenue – जमीन महसूल.

landscape – आडवे पुस्तक – लांबीपेक्षा रुंदी जास्त असलेला ग्रंथ.

landscape page - ग्रंथामध्ये आलेख, नकाशा, चित्रे दर्शविणारे आडवे पान.

language – **भाषा** – विचार आणि भावना व्यक्त करणारी भाषा.

language classification – **भाषा विषयाचे वर्गीकरण.**

language division – **भाषाविभाग** – (१) ग्रंथाची भाषा दर्शविणारा वर्गांकातील चिन्हसमूह. (२) वर्गीकरण करताना भाषेनुसार विभाजन अंक दिलेला सारणीतील विभाग.

language engineering – **भाषा अभियांत्रिकी.**

language facet – **भाषा पैलू** – वर्गीकरण करताना भाषेनुसार वर्गांक देण्यासाठी लक्षात घेतलेले विषय वैशिष्ट्य.

language interpreter – **दुभाषा** – संगणकाला एका संगणकभाषेतून दिलेल्या सूचना स्वीकारून त्याचे दुसऱ्या संगणकभाषेत रूपांतरण करणारा दुभाषी घटक.

language number – **भाषांक** – ग्रंथाच्या मजकुराची भाषा असेल त्यानुसार अंक, मूळ वर्गांकामध्ये समाविष्ट केला जातो.

language processor – **भाषा प्रक्रियक** – (१) संगणकातील भाषा ओळखून त्यावर क्रिया करणारा घटक. (२) विशिष्ट आज्ञावली भाषेवर भाषांतर स्पष्टीकरण इ. प्रक्रिया करणारी संगणक आज्ञावली.

language sub-division – **भाषा/उपविभाग** – याद्वारे वर्गीकरण करताना मूळ वर्गांनंतर ग्रंथाच्या भाषेनुसार उपविभाग करून वर्गांक तयार केला जातो.

laptop – **अंकतळ संगणक** – स्वत:बरोबर बाळगण्यायोग्य छोटा वैयक्तिक संगणक.

large paper copy / large paper edition – ग्रंथाची बृहदाकार आवृत्ती.

large print – **बृहद्मुद्रण** – दृष्टी अधू असलेल्यांसाठी बनविलेला ग्रंथ.

laser printer – **लेसर छपाई/मुद्रण यंत्र** – लेसर किरणांचा वापर करून छपाई करणारे संगणकाला जोडता येणारे यंत्र.

late fee / fine / overdue charges – **विलंबशुल्क/दंड** – ग्रंथालयातील ग्रंथ वेळेवर परत न केल्याबद्दल आकारली जाणारी प्रतिदिनाची रक्कम.

later in evolution – **उत्क्रांतिनुसार** **केलेली रचना.**

later in time – **कालक्रमानुसार केलेली रचना.**

lateral filing – **समान्तरित संचयन.**

latest edition – **नवीन आवृत्ती** – नुकतीच प्रकाशित झालेली आवृत्ती.

law – **कायदा** – शासनाने केलेला कायदा, विधी.

law / legal library – **विधी/कायदा ग्रंथालय.**

law of parsimony – **काटकसर सिद्धान्त** – ह्या तत्त्वानुसार जर एखाद्या गोष्टीसाठी दोन पर्याय असतील तर ज्या पर्यायामुळे जास्तीत जास्त काटकसर होईल तोच पर्याय स्वीकारावा असे तत्त्व सांगितले आहे.

law of scattering – **विस्तारशीलता सूत्र** – डॉ. ब्रॅडफोर्ड यांनी सांगितलेले सूत्र. नियतकालिकांमधील लेखांच्या संदर्भाबाबत सांगितलेले सूत्र.

law report – कायदेविषयक अहवाल/निवेदन.

leader writer – **अग्रलेखकार** – वृत्तपत्रातील अग्रलेख लिहिणारा लेखक, संपादक.

leaderette – संपादकीय स्फुट.

leading article – अग्रलेख.

leading line – **अग्ररेषा** – (१) तालिकापत्रावरील पहिली आडवी ओळ. या ओळीवरील मजकूर नोंदीतील प्रमुख मजकूर असतो. (२) तालिकीकरणाची नोंद करण्यासाठी वापरावयाची पहिली रेषा.

leading section – **अग्र/अग्रेसर विभाग** – (१) तालिकेमधील नोंदीचा प्रमुख भाग. ज्याच्यामुळे त्या नोंदीची तालिकेमधील जागा ठरते. (२) तालिकानोंद करताना नोंद करण्यासाठीचा मुख्य विभाग.

leaf – ग्रंथाचे पाठपोठ पृष्ठ.

leaflet – माहितीपत्रिका.

learned – **विद्वत्** – विषयाची भरपूर माहिती असलेली व्यक्ती.

learned periodical / journal – **ज्ञानप्रधान नियतकालिक/पत्रिका** – अभ्यासू माहिती प्रकाशित करणारी पत्रिका.

learned society – **विद्वत् समाज** – सुशिक्षित लोकांचा समाज.

learning resources – **ज्ञानाची प्राप्तिस्थाने** – ग्रंथालये, दृक्श्राव्य साधने, संगणकसुविधा व इतर शैक्षणिक प्राप्तिस्थानांच्या संदर्भात एकत्रित वापरलेली संज्ञा.

leather – चामडे/कातडे.

leather binding – चामडी/कातडी बांधणी.

lecture – व्याख्यान.

lecturer – व्याख्याता.

lecture series – **व्याख्यानमाला** – एका विशिष्ट ठिकाणी आयोजित केलेली व्याख्यानांची मालिका.

ledger – **खातेवही/खतावणी** – आर्थिक शीर्षकनिहाय खर्च दाखविणारी वही.

ledger catalogue – खतावणी तालिका.

ledger charging system – **खतावणी देवघेव पद्धती** – ग्रंथ देवीघेवीसाठी वापरली जाणारी खतावणी, देवघेवपद्धती.

left justify – संगणकावरील एक सुविधा – माहितीसंच डावीकडे सरकविण्याची सूचना.

legal deposit – कायदेशीर ठेवग्रंथप्रत – कायद्यानुसार प्रत्येक ग्रंथाची एक प्रत शासनाच्या ठेवग्रंथ ग्रंथालयात जमा करणे आवश्यक असते.

legend – दंतकथा/अख्यायिका – दंतकथा वाङ्मय (पुराण). नाणी, बिल्ला इत्यादी वरील कोरीव शब्द किंवा वाक्ये.

legislature – विधिमंडळ – कायदे करण्याचा आणि बदलण्याचा अधिकार असलेली शासकीय संस्था.

lending – उसनवारी/प्रदानशील.

lending department / lending division / home reading / lending section / issue section – ग्रंथ देवघेव विभाग – ग्रंथालयातील साहित्य उसनवारीने देणारा विभाग.

lending library – प्रदानशील ग्रंथालय – उसनवारीने ग्रंथ देणारे ग्रंथालय.

letter – अक्षर – ध्वनीचे प्रतिनिधिक असे लेखन किंवा छपाईत वापरले जाणारे चिन्ह, पत्र.

letter-by-letter alphabetization – मुळाक्षरानुसार क्रमरचना.

letter-by-letter arrangement – अक्षरानुसार क्रमरचना.

letter-by-letter filing – अक्षरक्रम संयोजन/वर्णानुक्रमे रचना.

lettering – अक्षरलेखन.

letterpress – अक्षरमुद्रण.

level – स्तर – (१) वर्गीकरण करताना एखाद्या संज्ञेची, संकल्पनेची वा वर्गाची संमिश्रता, संकीर्णता मोजण्याची पातळी. (२) अधिकाराची किंवा श्रेणीची पातळी.

lexicographer – शब्दकोशकार.

lexicography – शब्दकोश संपादनाची कला.

lexicon – शब्दकोश.

librachine / mobile library / travelling library / van library – चलित, फिरते ग्रंथालय/ चल ग्रंथालय.

librametry – ग्रंथालय गणनशास्त्र – गणितशास्त्रीय व सांख्यिकी पद्धतीच्या साहाय्याने ग्रंथालयातील विविध कार्यांचा अभ्यास करणारे शास्त्र.

library – ग्रंथालय/वाचनालय/संग्रहालय/पुस्तकालय – (१) माहितीचे वितरण करणारी, सेवा देणारी संस्था जी आपल्या संस्कृती व इतिहासाचा ठेवा असते.

library accounts – ग्रंथालयीन लेखाकर्म.

library act – ग्रंथालय अधिनियम – ग्रंथालय मान्यता, अनुदान याबाबत शासनाचा कायदा.

library activites – ग्रंथालयाची कार्ये.

library administration – ग्रंथालय प्रशासन – ग्रंथालय सेवेचे व्यवस्थापन.

library advisory committee – ग्रंथालय सल्लागार समिती – ग्रंथालयाच्या कामकाजाबाबत सल्ला देणारी समिती.

library association – ग्रंथालय संघ/संघटना.

library attendant – ग्रंथालयाचे परिचर – ग्रंथालयातील एक अर्धव्यावसायिक पद.

library authority – ग्रंथालयासाठीचे प्राधिकरण.

library binding – ग्रंथालयासाठीची ग्रंथबांधणी.

library broucher – ग्रंथलयीन माहितीपत्रक – ग्रंथालयाची माहिती देणारे पत्रक.

library budget – ग्रंथालयाचे अंदाजपत्रक/अर्थसंकल्प – ग्रंथालयातील खर्चाच्या बाबी व खर्चाची तरतूद यांची योजनाबद्ध मांडणी.

library card – ग्रंथालयाचे सभासदपत्र.

library catalogue – ग्रंथालय तालिका – ग्रंथालयातील वाचनसाहित्याची तालिका.

library cess / levy / tax – ग्रंथालय कर – ग्रंथालयासाठीची कर आकारणी.

library classification – ग्रंथालय वर्गीकरण.

library clerk – ग्रंथालय लिपिक – ग्रंथालयातील कामकाज करणारा लिपिक.

library collection / holdings / resources – वाचनसाहित्य संग्रह – ग्रंथालयातील वाचनसाहित्य संग्रह.

library committee – ग्रंथालय समिती – ग्रंथालय सेवा पुरविण्यासाठी जबाबदार असलेली यंत्रणा.

library consultant – ग्रंथालयासाठीचा सल्लागार – ग्रंथालयाच्या प्रकारानुसार विविध सेवा पुरविण्याबाबत देणारी व्यावसायिक व्यक्ती.

library co-operation – ग्रंथालय सहकार – दोन वा अधिक ग्रंथालयांनी एकत्र येऊन ग्रंथालयाची कामे एकत्रितरीत्या करणे.

library discount – ग्रंथ खरेदीवर मिळणारी सूट/सवलत.

library document – ग्रंथालयातील प्रलेख.

library economy – ग्रंथालयाची अर्थव्यवस्था.

library edition – ग्रंथालय आवृत्ती – पक्की बांधणी केलेली ग्रंथाची आवृत्ती.

library education – ग्रंथालय शिक्षण – ग्रंथालयशास्त्राचे शिक्षण.

library equipment – ग्रंथालयातील उपकरण.

library expenditure – ग्रंथालय खर्च – ग्रंथालयीन व्यय.

library extension – ग्रंथालय इमारतीचा विस्तार.

library extension activities – ग्रंथालयातर्फे आयोजित विस्तार कार्यक्रम.

library fees – ग्रंथालय शुल्क/फी.

library finance – ग्रंथालयातील वित्त व्यवस्था/पुरवठा.

library fine – ग्रंथालयाचा दंड – ग्रंथालयाने आकारलेला दंड.

library functions – ग्रंथालयाची कार्ये.

library fund – ग्रंथालयाचा निधी.

library hours – ग्रंथालयाच्या कामकाजाच्या वेळा.

library holding / collection / resources – वाचनसाहित्याचा उपलब्ध संग्रह.

library materials – ग्रंथालयाचे साहित्य.

library movement – ग्रंथालय चळवळ – ज्ञान व माहिती जनतेला सहज उपलब्ध करून देण्यासाठी, ग्रंथालयाच्या विकासाची कार्यवाही.

library organisation – ग्रंथालय संघटन – ग्रंथालयशास्त्रातील एक तात्त्विक विषय.

library planning – ग्रंथालय नियोजन – ग्रंथालय वाढीसाठी नियोजनाचे कार्य.

library policy – ग्रंथालयविषयक धोरण.

library records – ग्रंथालयाचे अभिलेख – ग्रंथालयीन दस्तऐवज.

library repositories – वाचनसाहित्याची संग्रहालये.

library service – ग्रंथालय सेवा – ग्रंथांचा उपयोग करण्यासाठी व माहितीच्या प्रसारणासाठी ग्रंथालयात उपलब्ध असलेल्या सुविधा.

library software – ग्रंथालय आज्ञावली – ग्रंथालयात वापरण्याजोगी संगणकाची आज्ञावली.

library stack – ग्रंथालय कपाटे – ग्रंथ ठेवण्यासाठी विशिष्ट आकाराची कपाटे.

library ticket – ग्रंथालयाचे सभासदपत्र.

library–Act / library Law – ग्रंथालय अधिनियम/कायदा – विशिष्ट देशामध्ये अस्तित्वात असलेला ग्रंथालय कायदा.

library administration – ग्रंथालय प्रशासन – ग्रंथालयाचे प्रशासकीय कार्य सांभाळण्याचे तंत्र.

library and information science – ग्रंथालय व माहितीशास्त्र.

library assistant - ग्रंथालय साहाय्यक - ग्रंथालय कर्मचारी वर्गातील एक व्यावसायिक श्रेणी.

library association (LA) - ग्रंथालय संघ - ग्रंथपालन व्यवसायाचे नियमन करण्याच्या उद्देशाचे काम करणारी लंडन येथील संस्था.

library associations - ग्रंथालय संघ/संघटना - ग्रंथपालांना एकत्र आणण्यासाठी विविध पातळीवर काम करणाऱ्या संघटना.

library authority - ग्रंथालय प्राधिकरण - सार्वजनिक ग्रंथालय सेवा सुरळीत चालण्यासाठी जबाबदार असलेली शासकीय यंत्रणा.

library automation - ग्रंथालयाचे संगणकीकरण/यांत्रिकीकरण - उत्कृष्ट ग्रंथालय सेवा देता यावी यासाठी आणि सेवेत अचूकता, वेळेचा अपव्यय टाळण्यासाठी संगणक आणि इतर यंत्रे वापरून केलेली कामे.

library classification - ग्रंथालय वर्गीकरण - ग्रंथालयशास्त्रातील एक तात्त्विक आणि प्रात्यक्षिक विषय, ज्यामुळे ग्रंथांचे विषयनिहाय ग्रंथालयातील स्थान निश्चित केले जाते.

library copy - ग्रंथालयाची स्थळप्रत.

library cost - ग्रंथालयाची एकूण किंमत - याचा उपयोग विमा संरक्षणासाठी होतो.

library design - ग्रंथालय संकल्पचित्र.

library development plan - ग्रंथालय विकास योजना.

library hand - ग्रंथालय सुलेखन - ग्रंथालयातील नोंदी सुवाच्य अक्षरात करणारी व्यक्ती.

library heating and air conditioning - ग्रंथालयीन वातानुकूलन व्यवस्था.

library lacks - ग्रंथालयात अनुपलब्ध (असलेले साहित्य).

library legislation - ग्रंथालय विधिविधान.

library management - ग्रंथालय व्यवस्थापन - ग्रंथालयाचे दैनंदिन कार्य व ग्रंथालय सेवेची उत्तम व्यवस्था राखण्याचे कौशल्य.

library of congress classification - अमेरिकन काँग्रेस ग्रंथालयानुसार वर्गीकरण.

library of congress MARC-II records - अमेरिकन काँग्रेस ग्रंथालयाद्वारे Machin Readacle Catalogue - II नमुन्याप्रमाणे तयार करण्यात आलेल्या तालिका नोंदी. हे आंतरराष्ट्रीय स्तरावर ग्रंथसूचीविषयक माहितीचे आदान-प्रदान करण्यासाठी आधारसामग्री यंत्राद्वारे वाचनीय प्रारूपामध्ये उपलब्ध करून देण्यासाठी १९६७ मध्ये विकसित करण्यात आले. याची सुधारित आवृत्ती १९७४ मध्ये प्रकाशित करण्यात आली; जी MARC- II या नावाने ओळखली जाते.

library resources - ग्रंथालय साधनसंपत्ती - ग्रंथालयाकडील मंजूर रक्कम, वाचनसाहित्य, प्रकरणे, सेवक, इमारत म्हणजेच ग्रंथालय साधनसंपत्ती.

library rules – **ग्रंथालय नियम** – ग्रंथालयात वाचकांनी पाळण्याचे नियम.

library stamp – **ग्रंथालय शिक्का** – ग्रंथालयाच्या मालकीच्या साहित्यावर उमटविण्यासाठी तयार केलेला ग्रंथालयाच्या नावाचा शिक्का.

library statistics – **ग्रंथालयाची आकडेवारी** – विविध सेवांची ग्रंथालयातील अंकदर्शक माहिती.

library supplier – **ग्रंथालय पुरवठाकार** – ग्रंथालयाला आवश्यक साहित्य पुरविणारा विक्रेता. उदा. वितरक, मुद्रक इ.

library technical assisant – **ग्रंथालय तंत्रसाहाय्यक** – ग्रंथालय कर्मचारी वर्गातील तांत्रिक साहाय्यक.

library user / reader / clientele / patron / customer – **ग्रंथालय उपभोक्ता** – ग्रंथालयाचा वापर करणारी व्यक्ती वा संस्था.

liliput edition / miniature edition – छोटेखानी आवृत्ती.

librarian – **ग्रंथपाल** – ग्रंथालय सेवा देणारी ग्रंथालयातील जबाबदार व्यावसायिक व्यक्ती.

librarianship – **ग्रंथपालन** – ग्रंथालय कर्मचाऱ्यांचा व्यवसाय.

limited cataloguing – **मर्यादित तालिकीकरण** – लायब्ररी ऑफ काँग्रेसने जलद तालिकीकरण करण्याच्या उद्देशाने वापरलेली संज्ञा.

limited edition – **मर्यादित आवृत्ती** – विशेष कागदावर छापलेली, विशेष बांधणी केलेली आणि ठराविक संख्येने प्रसिद्ध केलेली आवृत्ती. काहीवेळा लेखकाची स्वाक्षरी या आवृत्तीवर असते.

linear arrangement – **ओळीनुसार रचना** – एखाद्या ओळीप्रमाणे एकानंतर दुसरी अशी मांडणी.

linear programming – **गणितशास्त्रावर आधारित अशी प्रतिभास पद्धती** – याचा उपयोग एखाद्या कार्यप्रणालीचे मूल्यमापन करून त्या कार्यप्रणालीस सुयोग्य पद्धतीचे निर्देशन केले जाते. ही माहिती सर्वसाधारणपणे समीकरणाच्या स्वरूपात दिली जाते.

line – **रेषा/रघ** – संगणकावर एका ओळीत समाविष्ट असलेला अक्षरसंच.

line art – रेखांकनकला.

line block – रेखाचित्र ठसा.

line division mark – पंक्तिविभाजन चिन्ह.

line drawing – रेखाचित्र.

line engraving – रेखाउमटन कला.

line number – **रेखांक** – संगणकातील माहितीसंचाला दिलेला रेषाक्रमांक.

line number editing – **रेखा संख्या संपादन** – संगणकातील माहितीसंचात नोंदी किंवा रेषा समाविष्ट करणे, रूपांतर करणे, काढून टाकणे इ. प्रक्रियांचे संपादन.

line printer – **पंक्ति छपाईयंत्र** – एकाचवेळी एक संपूर्ण ओळ छापणारे यंत्र.

line by line index – **एका ओळीत एक अशी नोंद केलेला निर्देश.**

linguistic bibliography – **भाषानुसार ग्रंथसूची** – एका भाषेतील ग्रंथांची एकत्रित सूची.

linguistic numbers – **भाषांक**– ग्रंथांची मांडणी भाषेनुसार करण्यासाठी वर्गांकामध्ये, ग्रंथाच्या मजकुराची भाषा असेल त्यानुसार भाषांक समाविष्ट केला जातो.

link – **दुवा** – संगणक संयोजनामध्ये दुवा साधणे. डॉ. रंगनाथन् यांच्या साखळी पद्धतीत वापरलेली संज्ञा.

linked books – **दुवाबद्ध ग्रंथ** – वेगवेगळी बांधणी केलेली परंतु दुवा साधणारी पुस्तके काहीवेळा माला – ग्रंथनाम, क्रमश: पानांकन/पृष्ठांकन केलेले असते. अनुक्रमणिका किंवा पहिल्या काही पानांमध्ये समान दुव्याचा उल्लेख केलेला असतो.

list – **यादी/सूची** – विशिष्ट नोंदीची.

list of additions –**समावेश यादी** – ग्रंथालयात नव्याने भर पडलेल्या ग्रंथांची यादी/सूची.

list of contents – **अनुक्रमणिका.**

list of illustrations – **ग्रंथातील समाविष्ट चित्रे वा आकृत्यांची यादी/सूची.**

list of subject headings – **विषय नामावली** – उदा. सिअर्स लिस्ट ऑफ सब्जेक्ट हेडिंग्ज व Library of Congress list of subject headings.

literary – **साहित्यविषयक.**

literary agent – **ग्रंथकाराचे ग्रंथविक्रीसाठी प्रकाशकांशी व्यवहार करणारा प्रतिनिधी/मध्यस्थ** – विशिष्ट लेखनाचे नाट्यरूपांतर, प्रसारण यासंबंधी व्यवहार ही व्यक्ती ठरविते.

literary manuscript – **साहित्यिक हस्तलिखित** – मजकुरापेक्षा साहित्यिक महत्त्व असलेले हस्तलिखित.

literary property – **साहित्यिक संपत्ती** – लेखकाचे हस्तलिखित व प्रकाशित ग्रंथांना आर्थिकदृष्ट्या असलेले मूल्य.

literary search – **साहित्यविषयक शोध** – विशिष्ट विषयावरील प्रकाशित, अप्रकाशित साहित्याचा शोध.

literary title – **वाचनसाहित्याचे शीर्षक.**

literary warrant – **साहित्यनिर्मिती प्रमाण** – ग्रंथवर्गीकरण पद्धतीमध्ये ज्या विविध सोयी/तरतुदी (म्हणजेच विविध विषयांचा समावेश) केलेल्या आढळतात, त्यांचे समर्थन केवळ तत्त्वसिद्धान्तावर आधारित नसते तर त्याला प्रत्यक्ष ग्रंथाच्या उपलब्धतेचा/ग्रंथ अस्तित्वाचा आधार असतो.

literary work – **साहित्यविषयक कार्य/साहित्यकृती.**

literature – **वाङ्मय/साहित्य.**

literature guide / guide to literature – **वाङ्मय मार्गदर्शक.**

literature review – वाङ्मय परीक्षण.

literature search – **साहित्य शोध** – अनुरूप माहितीचा घेतलेला आढावा.

literature survey – **वाङ्मय साहित्याचे सर्वेक्षण** – विशिष्ट विषयावरील झालेल्या साहित्याची प्रयत्नपूर्वक तयार केलेली ग्रंथसूची.

literate – **साक्षर** – जी व्यक्ती भाषा वाचू, लिहू व समजू शकते.

lithography – **शीळामुद्रण** – दगडावर छपाई करण्याचे यंत्र.

load – **प्रभार** – संगणकातील माहितीयंत्रामध्ये अधिक माहितीची भर घालणे.

loan – **उसनवारी** – ठरावीक काळाकरिता साहित्य देणे.

loan of books – ग्रंथांची उसनवारी.

loan period – **उसनवारी कालावधी** – वाचन साहित्य उसनवारीने द्यावयाचा कालावधी.

loan system – ग्रंथ उसनवारीची पद्धती.

lobby – उपकक्ष/व्हरांडा.

local – स्थानीय/परिसरातील.

local area network (LAN) – **क्षेत्रीय संगणकजाळे** – (१) एखाद्या भूक्षेत्रापुरते संगणक व इतर दूरसंचार माध्यमांमध्ये दुवा साधणे. यामुळे आंतरकार्यालयीन कामांमध्ये सुसंगती आणता येते व इतर क्षेत्रीय संगणक जाळ्यांशी संपर्क साधता येतो. (२) सर्वसाधारणपणे एकाच इमारतीतील अनेक लघुसंगणक एकमेकांशी संदेशवहन करणाऱ्या तारांनी जोडलेले असतात. अशा जोडणीमुळे एका संगणकावरील माहिती दुसऱ्या संगणकावर वाचणे, त्यावर प्रक्रिया करणे आणि उपकरणांचा (उदा. प्रिंटर) सामाईक उपयोग करणे शक्य होते.

local access – सामान्य/स्थानीय प्रवेश.

local bibliography – **स्थानीय ग्रंथसूची** – विशिष्ट भूभागापुरती मर्यादित ग्रंथांची सूची. यात बहुधा या भूभागाविषयी, तेथील प्रसिद्ध व्यक्ती, ठिकाणे, इतिहास यांसारखे ग्रंथ समाविष्ट केले जातात.

local collection – **स्थानीय ग्रंथसंग्रह** – विशिष्ट माहिती असणारे नकाशे, आकृत्या, चित्रे यांचा संग्रह.

local directory – **स्थानीय निर्देशिका** – विशिष्ट स्थानापुरती मर्यादित निर्देशिका.

local documentation list – स्थानिक प्रलेखन यादी.

local library authority – स्थानिक ग्रंथालय प्राधिकरण.

local variation – **स्थानिक फेरबदल** – (मूळ संहितेमध्ये) ग्रंथालयाच्या सोयीसाठी केलेले फेरबदल.

location – **स्थान निर्धारण** – ग्रंथसंग्रहातील विशिष्ट ग्रंथाची जागा.

location index – **स्थाननिर्देश सूची** – ग्रंथाचे स्थान निर्देशित करणारी सूची. वर्गांकानुसार ग्रंथाचे स्थान समजणे सुलभ ठरते.

locations mark / locations symbol – **स्थानांक** – ग्रंथसंग्रहातील ग्रंथाचे स्थान दर्शविणारे अक्षर, शब्द, शब्दसमूह, चिन्हे यांचा तालिकेतील नोंदीमध्ये किंवा ग्रंथसूचीमध्ये केलेला वापर.

location register – **ग्रंथाची स्थानदर्शक नोंदवही** – मर्यादित प्रवेश ग्रंथालयातील यादी किंवा निश्चित स्थानपद्धतीमध्ये रचना केलेल्या ग्रंथाची यादी. (Fixed Location Method)

location symbol / location mark – **स्थानचिन्ह** – ग्रंथालयातील ग्रंथाचे स्थान किंवा संगणकातील माहितीचे स्थान दर्शविणारे चिन्ह.

locus section – **संदर्भस्थान विभाग** – व्यापक ग्रंथातील किंवा यजमान ग्रंथातील भागाच्या प्रकरणाच्या स्थानाची माहिती देणारा विभाग.

logical arrangement / logical sequence – **तार्किक रचना** – (१) अक्षरानुसार क्रम वगळून विषयाच्या आशयाशी संबंधित विचारांनुसार अथवा नोंदीच्या प्रकारानुसार नोंदीचा क्रम. उदा. कालक्रमानुसार, अधिकार श्रेणीनुसार, संख्यांकानुसार. (२) विशिष्ट हेतूने केलेली तालिकेतील नोंदीची तर्कसिद्ध रचना.

logical notation – **तर्कसिद्ध चिन्हांकन** – वर्गीकरण पद्धतीतील एखादे चिन्ह अनेक वेळा सारख्याच स्वरूपात विभागले जाते. परंतु, प्रत्येकवेळी उपविभाजन करताना ती वर्गीकरणाची पुढची पायरी म्हणून वापरली जाते.

log in/log on – **प्रवेश प्राप्ती** – संगणक वापर प्रक्रियेत प्रवेश करणे.

log off / log out – **सत्र समाप्ती** – संगणक वापर प्रक्रियेतून बाहेर पडणे.

logogram – **संक्षेपाक्षरे** – संक्षेप करण्यासाठी वापरलेले आद्याक्षर किंवा आद्यक्रमांक.

logograph – **संक्षेप चिन्ह** – संपूर्ण शब्दासाठी वापरलेले चिन्ह. उदा. गणिती संज्ञेत 'म्हणून' या शब्दासाठी "---" हे चिन्ह.

long range reference service – **विलंबित संदर्भसेवा/व्यापक संदर्भसेवा** – दीर्घकाळ चालू राहणारी संदर्भसेवा.

loose back / hollow back – **ग्रंथाचा पोकळ भाग** – ग्रंथाचे वेष्टन व बांधणी यामधील जागा.

loose leaf binding – **काढण्या-घालण्यास सोपी अशी बांधणी** – पाने/पृष्ठे समाविष्ट करणे वा काढून घेणे केव्हाही सुलभ होईल अशी गोलाकार बांधणी.

loose leaf catalogue – **सुट्या पानांची तालिका.**

loose leaf service – **मला प्रकाशनामध्ये सतत पुरवणी** – पुनरावृत्ती, निर्देशन हे सुट्या पानांच्या स्वरूपात केले जाते. सतत नवीन माहिती पुरविली जाते.

lower link – **खालची कडी** – डॉ. रंगनाथन् यांच्या साखळी पद्धतीतील एक संज्ञा.

low level language – **संगणक सुलभ भाषा** – संगणकास कुठलेही अनुवादक अथवा जोडचिन्हे वापरता समतोल अशी भाषा. विशिष्ट खुणांनी [(0) आणि (1)] ने ती बनलेली असते.

machine aided translation / machine translation – संगणकाच्या साहाय्याने केलेले मजकुराचे भाषांतर.

machine address / absolute address – संगणकाच्या स्मरणिकेत विशिष्ट माहितीसाठी दिलेले निश्चित स्थान.

machine code / machine language – संगणकीय सांकेतिक भाषा.

machine indexing – **यांत्रिक निर्देशन** – संगणकाच्या साहाय्याने केलेले निर्देशन.

machine language / machine code – **यंत्रास समजेल अशी भाषा** – (१) संगणकास फक्त हीच भाषा कळते. ० ते १ हे दोनच आकडे वापरून ती लिहिलेली असते. (२) संगणकाच्या नोंद माध्यमांसाठी संयोजनसूचनांची नोंद करताना वापरण्याची संगणकीय सांकेतिक भाषा.

machine literature searching – **संगणकीय साहित्यशोध** – संगणकाच्या साहाय्याने हव्या त्या माहितीचे प्राप्तीस्थान शोधणे.

machine readable catalogue (MARC) – **यंत्रवाचनीय / संगणक वाचनीय तालिका** – लायब्ररी ऑफ काँग्रेसने १९६५ मध्ये सुरू केलेला प्रकल्प.

MARC format – **मार्क प्रारूप** – ग्रंथाची संगणकात नोंद घेण्यासाठी अमेरिकन लायब्ररी ऑफ काँग्रेसने सर्वप्रथम तयार केलेल्या आणि जगभर मान्यता पावलेल्या प्रारूपाचे नाव Machine Readable Catalogue Format.

machine readable database – यंत्रवाचनीय/संगणक वाचनीय आधारसामग्री – संगणक किंवा इतर यंत्राच्या साहाय्यानेच वाचता येणारी माहिती.

machine readable format – यंत्र वाचनीय स्वरूप – ह्या प्रकारचा ग्रंथ वाचण्यास संगणक अगर मायक्रोफॉर्म वाचनयंत्र अशा प्रकारच्या एखाद्या यंत्राचे साहाय्य घ्यावे लागते.

machine search – संगणकाद्वारे घेतला जाणारा माहितीचा शोध.

machine word – संगणकीय भाषेतील शब्द.

machine translation / machine aided translation / machine mechanical translation – संगणकीय भाषांतर.

macro – स्थूल/ढोबळ.

macro abstract – स्थूल सारलेख – मूळ प्रलेख वाचल्यानंतर स्थूल स्वरूपात लिहिलेला सारलेख.

macro description – वाचनसाहित्याचे स्थूलवर्णन.

macro document – स्थूल/प्रमुख/मोठे प्रलेख.

made up copy – सदोष ग्रंथामध्ये त्या ग्रंथाच्या इतर प्रतींमधून सुधारित मजकूर घेऊन समाविष्ट केलेली प्रत.

made up set – सुधारित प्रत – एकापेक्षा अधिक आवृत्त्यांमधील खंड एकत्र ठेवून तयार केलेला संच. तालिकेमध्ये संच म्हणून नोंद केली जाते. वेगवेगळ्या आवृत्त्यांचा उल्लेख या नोंदीमध्ये केला जातो.

magazine / periodical / journal – नियतकालिक – (१) जे ठरावीक कालावधीने एकाच नावाने पण वेगवेगळ्या मजकूरासह प्रकाशित होते. (२) नियमित प्रकाशनकाल असलेल्या संख्येचे प्रकाशन. याच्या प्रत्येक खंडास व अंकास सलग क्रमांक दिलेले असतात.

magazine rack – नियतकालिके ठेवण्याचे/साठविण्याचे कपाट.

magazine room – नियतकालिकांची खोली/कक्ष.

magnetic – चुंबकीय.

magnetic card – चुंबकीय पत्र – माहितीच्या चुंबकीय नोंदीसाठी विशिष्ट चुंबकीय पृष्ठभाग असलेले पत्र.

magnetic core – चुंबकीय केंद्र – माहितीसंचयासाठी वापरला जाणारा अर्धवर्तुळाकार चुंबकीय तुकडा.

magnetic disc – चुंबकीय तबकडी – चुंबकीय पृष्ठभाग असलेली सपाट वर्तुळाकार तबकडी. याचा उपयोग माहिती साठविण्याकरिता केला जातो.

magnetic drum – चुंबकीय नळकांडे – चुंबकीय नोंदीद्वारे माहिती साठविण्याचा चुंबकीय दंडगोल.

magnetic records – चुंबकीय अभिलेख – चुंबकीय क्षेत्राचा वापर करून तयार केलेले अभिलेख.

magnetic storage – माहितीची चुंबकीय साठवण – विशिष्ट साधनांचे चुंबकीय गुणधर्म वापरून केलेला माहितीसंच.

magnetic tape – **चुंबकीय फीत** – चुंबकीय नोंदी करण्याची चुंबकीयपृष्ठ असलेली फीत.

mail – टपाल/संदेश/पत्र.

mail merge – **टपाल विलय/विलीनीकरण** – संगणकातील माहितीसंचयात उपलब्ध असलेले पत्र व ते पाठवावयाचे पत्ते यांचा मेळ घालून संगणकाद्वारे तयार केला जाणारा संदेश.

mailing list – **टपालयादी** – ग्रंथालयाची प्रकाशने पाठविण्यासाठी तयार केलेली यादी.

main – **मुख्य/प्रमुख**.

main card – **मुख्य पत्र** – (१) तालिकेतील प्रमुख नोंद असलेले पत्र.(२) तालिकेतील मुख्य नोंदीचे तालिकापत्र.

main class – **मुख्य वर्ग/प्रमुख वर्ग** – (१) वर्गीकरण पद्धतीचे प्रमुख विभाजक. उदा. दशांश वर्गीकरण – तत्त्वज्ञान, धर्म, सामाजिक शास्त्रे, भाषा. (२) वर्गीकरण पद्धतीत दिलेले प्रमुख वर्ग.

main catalogue – **मुख्य तालिका** – यातील तालिकापत्रावरून इतर नोंदी केल्या जातात.

main catalogue entry – **मुख्य/प्रमुख तालिका नोंद**.

main entry – **प्रमुख नोंद** – ग्रंथाची परिपूर्ण माहिती देणारी नोंद.

main heading – **प्रमुख शीर्षक/ग्रंथाचे शीर्षक** – (१) निर्देशन करताना निवडलेले मुख्य शीर्षक. (२) तालिकीकरण करताना नोंदी करण्यासाठी निवडलेले मुख्य शीर्षक.

main library / central library – **प्रमुख/मध्यवर्ती ग्रंथालय**.

main subject – **मुख्य विषय** – ग्रंथामध्ये अनेक विषय हाताळले जातात. वर्गीकरणकार व तालिकाकार अनेक विषयांचे प्रतिसंदर्भ देऊ इच्छितो. परंतु, ग्रंथामध्ये ज्या विषयाला प्राधान्य दिले जाते तो विषय.

main title – **प्रमुख शीर्षक** – ग्रंथाच्या उपशीर्षकापूर्वी येणारे मुख्य शीर्षक.

main title page – **ग्रंथाचे शीर्षक पृष्ठ/मुख्य ग्रंथनाम पृष्ठ** – ग्रंथाच्या तालिकेतील नोंदीसाठी संदर्भ म्हणून वापरलेले ग्रंथपृष्ठ.

mainframe – **मोठ्या क्षमतेचा संगणक**.

maintenence – **परीक्षण** – व्यवस्था/पद्धती कार्यरत राहण्यासाठी केलेले काम.

management – **व्यवस्थापन** – पूर्वानुमान करणे, नियोजन करणे, आदेश देणे व नियंत्रण ठेवणे ही कार्ये म्हणजे 'व्यवस्थापन' होय.

management information system / decision support system – **व्यवस्थापन माहिती पद्धती** – (१) व्यवस्थापनाच्या विविध अंगांना, विशेषत: निर्णय घेणे, नियोजन आणि कामावरील नियंत्रण याकरिता आवश्यक असलेली माहिती पुरविण्यासाठी निर्माण केलेली संरचना. यात माहितीचे विविध प्रकारे केलेले संकलन, संचयन, विश्लेषण, अंतिमत: विशिष्ट कार्यसिद्धीसाठी केलेली पुनर्मांडणी आणि संप्रेषण यांचा समावेश होतो.

manifestation – अभिव्यक्ती/प्रकटीकरण – अस्तित्व उघडपणे दाखविणे.

manifesto – जाहीरनामा/घोषणापत्र – पक्षाचा, व्यक्तीचा अगर संस्थेचे हेतू/धोरण स्पष्ट करणारा कार्यक्रम.

manual – निर्देशग्रंथ/निर्देशपुस्तिका/हस्तपुस्तिका/मार्गदर्शिका – एखाद्या विशिष्ट क्षेत्रातील कामाची पूर्तता करण्यासाठी मार्गदर्शन करणारी पुस्तिका.

manual input – मानवी कृतीने केलेला निवेश.

manual operation – मानवाच्या साहाय्याने केलेली क्रिया.

manuscript – हस्तलिखित – (१) हस्ताक्षरात लिहिलेला ग्रंथ, प्रलेख इ.
(२) हाताने लिहून तयार केलेली माहिती. छपाईचा शोध लागण्यापूर्वीपासून प्रचलित प्रकार.

manuscript catalogue – हस्तलिखितांची तालिका – हस्ताक्षरात असलेली तालिका.

manuscript librarian – हस्तलिखितांचा ग्रंथपाल – (१) हस्तलिखितांची देखभाल करणारी तज्ज्ञ ग्रंथपाल व्यक्ती.
(२) हस्तलिखितांचे व्यवस्थापन करणारा ग्रंथपाल.

manuscript library – हस्तलिखितांचे ग्रंथालय.

manuscriptology – हस्तलिखित ग्रंथ विज्ञान – हस्तलिखितांचा अभ्यास करणारे शास्त्र/विज्ञान.

map – नकाशा – एखाद्या भूभागाची प्रमाणित आकृती.

map cabinet – नकाशांचे कपाट/खण – (१) नकाशांसाठीचे कपाट. (२) नकाशे संग्रहित करण्यासाठी बनविलेले कपाट/खण.

map endpapers – नकाशा असलेले समाप्तीपृष्ठ.

map file – नकाशांची पंजी – विशिष्ट रचना केलेला नकाशांचा संच.

map projection – नकाशा प्रक्षेपण.

map room / section – नकाशा दालन.

margin – समास – लिखित पृष्ठाच्या डाव्या बाजूस सोडलेली मोकळी जागा.

marginal figure / runner – समासांक.

marginal heading – समासामध्ये छापलेले शीर्षक.

marginal hole punched card / edge notched cards – निर्देशन करताना तयार केलेली कडाछिद्रित पत्रे.

marginal note – समासात दिलेली टीप.

marine library – जहाजावरील ग्रंथालय.

mark of interrogation / question mark – प्रश्नचिन्ह (?)

mark of omission – मजकूर वगळण्यासाठीचे चिन्ह (d)

mark of reference – संदर्भचिन्ह.

marketing – विपणन – विक्रीचे शास्त्र व कला.

marketing technology – पणन तंत्रज्ञान – अपेक्षित ग्राहकासंबंधी सर्व प्रकारची माहिती पद्धतशीरपणे गोळा करून एखाद्या मालाचे अगर सेवेचे योग्य वितरण करण्याकरिता आखलेली व्यूहरचना.

mass book / missal / book of hours – बहुजनसमाजासाठी तयार केलेला ग्रंथ.

master – मूळ/मुख्य – सर्वसमावेशक.

master card – मूळ पत्र – यात सविस्तर माहिती समाविष्ट असते.

master catalogue – सर्वसमावेशक प्रमुख तालिका.

master copy – मूळ/मुख्य प्रत – ज्या प्रतीवरून अनेक प्रती बनविता येतात अशी प्रत.

master file – सर्वसमावेशक माहितीसंच – विशिष्ट संगणककार्यामध्ये अधिकृत मानलेली संचिका.

master piece – साहित्यातील सर्वोत्कृष्ट कृती.

matching grant – समतुल्य अनुदान – यामध्ये निधी देणाऱ्या व निधी घेणाऱ्या संस्थांचा समान हिस्सा असतो.

material – सामग्री/साहित्य/साधनभूत पदार्थ/पुरवठा.

material facet / matter facet – साधन पैलू/वस्तूपैलू – द्विबिंदू वर्गीकरण पद्धतीतील एक विभेदक गुणधर्म.

material matter facet – द्विबिंदू वर्गीकरण पद्धतीतील सामग्री वस्तुमुख.

mathematical order – गणितीय क्रम – इ.सी. रिचर्डसन यांची संज्ञा. वर्गीकरण करताना पंक्तीतील संज्ञांचा चिन्हांकानुसार क्रम लावल्यामुळे सहसंबंधित वर्गांची तयार होणारी रचना.

matrix – प्रमाणके – (१) समचतुष्कोनाकृती आकृती, जिच्यामध्ये विविध संकल्पना काही रांगा आणि स्तंभ यांच्या मदतीने विशद केलेल्या असतात. (२) संगणकातील माहितीच्या ओळी व स्तंभ मिळून झालेली आयताकार पंक्तिरूप मांडणी.

matter – पदार्थ (द्रव्य)/लिखित मजकूर/वस्तू.

matter facet / material facet – पदार्थ/वस्तू पैलू – (१) द्विबिंदू वर्गीकरण पद्धतीमधील एक पैलू. (२) वर्गांक द्यावयाची वस्तू कशापासून बनली आहे हे दर्शविण्यासाठी या पैलूचा वापर करता येतो. या पैलूचे संयोगचिन्ह अर्धविराम (;) हे आहे.

mechanical – यंत्रचलित.

mechanical translation / machine aided translation / machine translation - संगणकाच्या साहाय्याने केले जाणारे भाषांतर.

mechanics institute - यांत्रिक संस्था.

mechanized retrieval system - यंत्रित प्रतिप्राप्ती पद्धती - माहितीची संगणकाच्या साहाय्याने माहितीची प्रतिप्राप्ती करण्याची पद्धती.

media - प्रसारमाध्यम - जनसंपर्काचे माध्यम.

media centre - प्रसारमाध्यम केंद्र - प्रसारमाध्यमांसाठी आवश्यक माहिती केंद्र.

media file - प्रसारमाध्यम पंजी - जाहिरातदारांसाठी प्रसारमाध्यमांनी तयार केलेला माहितीसंच. यात प्रचलन, स्तंभ, मुद्रणप्रकार, दरपत्रक याविषयी माहिती दिलेली असते.

media school - प्रसारमाध्यम संकुल.

media science - प्रसारमाध्यम विज्ञान - माध्यमशास्त्र.

media studies - प्रसारमाध्यमे अभ्यास.

mediated searching - प्रत्यक्ष उपयोजकांसाठी ग्रंथालय कर्मचाऱ्यांनी माहिती शोधणे.

medical - वैद्यकीय.

medical bibliography - वैद्यकविषयक ग्रंथसूची.

medical board - वैद्यकीय मंडळ.

medical library - वैद्यकीय ग्रंथालय - वैद्यकशास्त्रावरील वाचनसाहित्य असणारे ग्रंथालय.

medical literature, analysis and retrieval system (MEDLARS) - मेडलार्स् - 'मेडिकल लिटरेचर ॲनालिसिस ॲण्ड रिट्रिव्हल सिस्टिम' याची आद्याक्षर संज्ञा - ही संस्था नॅशनल लायब्ररी ऑफ मेडिसिन, यूएसए येथून कार्य करते.

medium - माध्यम.

megabyte (Mb or mbyte) - (१) संगणकाच्या स्मरणिकेतील मापनासाठीचे एकक. (२) दशलक्ष संख्या नोंदवण्याचे परिमाण. संगणकाची स्मृती आणि पूरक संग्रहण साधने या परिमाणात मोजली जातात. एमबी या चिन्हाने ती संबोधली जातात.

member / borrower / user / reader / clientele / patron - सभासद   (ग्रंथालयाचा) - संस्थेतील सहभागासाठी वापरासाठी आवश्यक अटी पूर्ण केलेली व्यक्ती.

membership - सभासदत्व - संस्थेचे/ग्रंथालयाचे दिलेले सदस्यत्व.

membership card - सभासदत्व पत्र.

membership record - सभासदाविषयक नोंद.

membership list – सभासद यादी.

memories – स्मरणनोंदी – लेखकाची निरीक्षणे, अनुभव यांची यादी

memorial volume / festschrift – गौरवग्रंथ/स्मरणग्रंथ – एखादी व्यक्ती किंवा घटना यांच्या सन्मानाप्रीत्यर्थ अनेक व्यक्तींनी लेखन करून तयार केलेला ग्रंथ.

memory – स्मरणिका (संगणकाची)/स्मृती – संगणकातील माहितीसंचय वेगाने करण्यासाठी उपयोजित भाग.

memory map – स्मरणिका/स्मृती नकाशा (संगणकातील)

memory unit – स्मृतीघटक/मंजुषा – (१) संगणकातील स्मरणिकासंच (२) माहिती साठविण्याची क्षमता.

menu / pull down menu – सूचक (संगणकातील) सुविधा तक्ता – सूचना/संदेश हाताळण्यासाठी बनविलेला संच.

merge – विलीन करणे – माहितीची प्रतिप्रासी करताना केलेले दोन वेगळ्या माहितीसंचाचे एकत्रीकरण.

Merrill book number – मेरिल ग्रंथांक – डब्ल्यू. एस. मेरिल यांनी तयार केलेली ग्रंथांक पद्धती/योजना.

message – संदेश – (१) माहिती पोहोचविण्यासाठी संगणकामार्फत तयार केलेली अक्षरसाखळी. (२) अक्षरे व चिन्हे यांचा वापर करून एका संगणकाकडून दुसऱ्या ठिकाणी संगणकामार्फत दिलेला डाटा.

meta data – यंत्राच्या साहाय्याने वापरावयाचे माहितीसाधन.

meta documents – यांत्रिक प्रलेख – यंत्राच्या साहाय्याने तयार केलेले प्रलेख. उदा. उपग्रहाद्वारे मिळविलेली छायाचित्रे, हवामानविषयक अहवाल इ.

metasearch engine – अनेकविध/बहुविध शोध यंत्र.

method matter facet – पद्धती वस्तुमुख (वस्तूपैलू).

Metropolitan Area Network (MAN) – मॅन – एखाद्या शहरातील महत्त्वाची ठिकाणे व परिसर यांना जोडणारी संगणक यंत्रणा.

micro – सूक्ष्म/अतिशय लहान.

micro abstract – सूक्ष्म सारलेख – मूळ लेखकाचे अतिशय सूक्ष्म स्वरूपात म्हणजे २/३ ओळीत आढावा घेणारा सारलेख.

micro card – सूक्ष्मपत्र.

micro computer / personal computer –वैयक्तिक संगणक – लहान प्रमाणातील कार्य पार पाडण्यासाठी उपयुक्त असलेले संगणक. उदा. लॅपटॉप कंप्यूटर.

micro copy – सूक्ष्म प्रत – (१) कमी माहिती असणारी प्रत. (२) मूळ आवृत्तीपेक्षा सूक्ष्म स्वरूपात असलेली प्रत.

micro document – सूक्ष्म प्रलेख.

microfiche – सूक्ष्मपृष्ठ/मायक्रोफिच – माहितीची लघुप्रतिमा धारण करू शकेल असे सूक्ष्मपृष्ठ.

microfilm – सूक्ष्मपट/मायक्रोफिल्म – (१) लघुप्रतिमा धारण करू शकेल असा सूक्ष्मपट. (२) १६ किंवा ३५ मिलीमीटर रुंदीच्या चित्रफिती, वृत्तपत्रे, नियतकालिके, अहवाल, मुद्रणातीत किंवा दुर्मिळ ग्रंथांच्या प्रती काढण्यासाठी सूक्ष्मपटांचा उपयोग करतात.

microfilm reader – सूक्ष्मपट वाचनयंत्र – सूक्ष्मप्रतिमा वाचू शकेल असे वाचनयंत्र.

microcard – प्रकाशबंद सूक्ष्मपत्र.

micro from – सूक्ष्म प्रारूप – कोणतीही सूक्ष्म स्वरूपातील माहिती.

micro graph – सूक्ष्म आलेख – वस्तूच्या सूक्ष्मप्रतिमेवरून तयार केलेली नोंद.

micro graphics – सूक्ष्म आलेखिकी – सूक्ष्म स्वरूपातील माहितीसंच तयार करण्याचे तंत्र.

micro image – सूक्ष्मप्रतिमा – सामान्य दृष्टीद्वारे वाचता न येणारा मजकूर. मोठे स्वरूप दिल्याशिवाय वाचता येणार नाही एवढी सूक्ष्म प्रतिमा.

micro opaque – सूक्ष्म अपारदर्शिते – सूक्ष्म छायाचित्रणाच्या साहाय्याने तयार केलेली लेखाची अपारदर्शित प्रतिमा.

microphotography – सूक्ष्मछायाचित्रण – या तंत्राने मायक्रोफिच व मायक्रोफिल्म तयार केली जाते.

micro processor – सूक्ष्म प्रक्रियक – संगणकाच्या यंत्ररूप भाषेमधील आज्ञावली समजावून घेण्याची आणि त्या बरहुकूम काम पार पाडण्याची क्षमता असलेली इंटिग्रेटेड सर्किट्स.

microscopic edition – छोटेखानी आवृत्ती – साधारणत: ३ इंच वा कमी उंचीची पुस्तके.

micro thought – सूक्ष्म विचार – एखाद्या नियमाचा बारकाईने केलेला अभ्यास.

micro transparancies – सूक्ष्म पारदर्शिका/सूक्ष्म पारदर्शिते.

miniature book/lilliput edition – छोटेखानी आवृत्ती – ३ इंच वा कमी उंचीची पुस्तके.

mini computer – छोटा संगणक – कमी स्मृतीक्षमता असलेला संगणक.

minor series – उपमाला (ग्रंथप्रकाशन).

mint book – छोटे पण करकरीत पुस्तक.

minute book – कार्यवृत्ताची/सभावृत्त नोंदवही.

minutes – कार्यवृत्त – बैठकीत बोललेल्या किंवा घेतलेल्या निर्णयांचे वृत्त.

minutes of meeting – सभेचा वृत्तान्त/सभावृत्त.

miscellany - **संकीर्ण लेखसंग्रह** – अनेक लेखकांनी लिहिलेला किंवा अनेक विषयांची माहिती असलेला ग्रंथ.

misleading title - **भ्रामक शीर्षक** – ज्या शीर्षकाद्वारे त्यातील विषयाचा अंदाज येत नाही, असे ग्रंथनाम.

misprint - **मुद्रणदोष** – ग्रंथ छापताना मुद्रकाकडून झालेल्या मजकुरातील चुका.

missal / mass book / book of honours - **बहुजन समाजासाठी तयार केलेला ग्रंथ.**

misses - **उणीव ग्रंथ** – माहितीची प्रतिप्राप्ती करताना न सापडलेला समर्पक ग्रंथ, उदा. year 2000 हा ग्रंथ y_2k हा कळशब्द न दिल्यास प्रतिप्राप्ती y_2k शीर्षकाखाली होणार नाही.

missing – सुटलेला/चुकलेला/हरवलेला/लुप्त.

missing isolate – लुप्त उपांग.

missing link – **लुप्त कडी** – ग्रंथ वर्गीकरणात चिन्हांवरून ठरविताना आढळणारा घटक.

mistake – चूक.

mixed notation – **मिश्र चिन्हांकन** – (१) ग्रंथ वर्गीकरण पद्धतीत दोन किंवा जास्त प्रकारची चिन्हे वापरली जातात असे चिन्हांकन. (२) दोन किंवा अधिक प्रकारच्या चिन्हांचा वापर करून तयार केलेले चिन्हांकन.

mixed responsibility – **मिश्र जबाबदारी** – ग्रंथाच्या निर्मितीमध्ये ग्रंथकार, चित्रकार, भाषांतरकार, संपादक इ. विविध व्यक्तींचा वा संस्थांचा सहभाग असेल तर त्या ग्रंथास मिश्र जबाबदारीने तयार केलेला ग्रंथ असे म्हणतात.

mixed subject heading – **मिश्र विषयशीर्षक** – निर्देशन करताना मुख्य विषयशीर्षकाशिवाय नोंद केलेले शीर्षक. उदा. 'आणखी पाहा' नोंद असलेले शीर्षक.

mnemonic – **स्मरणसुलभ** – स्मरण, वाचन, उच्चारण यासाठी सोपे असणारे.

mnemonic device – **स्मृतिसुलभ क्लृप्ती** – वर्गीकरण करताना वापरण्याचे एक तत्त्व. सहजत: स्मरणात राहील असा वर्गांक तयार करण्याची क्लृप्ती/युक्ती, स्मृतीसुलभता.

mnemonic quality – **स्मरणसुलभतेचा दर्जा/गुण.**

mnemonic terms – **स्मरणसुलभ संज्ञा** – लांबलचक शब्द लक्षात ठेवण्यासाठी अवघड असलेल्या बार्बींसाठी स्मरणसुलभ असे छोटे सुटसुटीत नाव. 0 ते 1 ही किचकट चिन्हे वापरून यंत्रभाषेमध्ये आज्ञावली लिहिण्याऐवजी त्यांना काही स्मरणसुलभ इंग्रजी शब्दार्थाशी निगडित संज्ञा संगणकासाठी वापरल्या गेल्या, त्यांना 'स्मरणसुलभ संज्ञा' म्हणतात.

mnemonics - **स्मरणसुलभता/स्मृतिसाधके** – स्मरणशक्तीला साहाय्य करणारे, ग्रंथवर्गीकरण पद्धतीतील वर्गांकामधील सारखीच संकल्पना ज्यांच्यामुळे स्पष्ट होते अशा अंकांचा एक गट. थोडक्यात, त्याच त्या संकल्पनांचे पुनर्प्रगटीकरण करणारे शब्दसमूह.

mnemonics seminal mnemonics / unscheduled mnemonics – अनुसूची बाह्य स्मृतिसाधके
– वर्गीकरणामध्ये नियमांना संज्ञा/चिन्हांकन ठरविताना त्याद्वारे सहज अर्थबोध होईल अशी चिन्हे निवडण्याची क्रिया. उदा. त्रिकोण, चौकोन या संकल्पनांसाठी अनुक्रमे ३ व ४ ही चिन्हे वापरणे.

mobile librarian – फिरत्या ग्रंथालयाचा ग्रंथपाल.

mobile library / travelling library / librachine – फिरते ग्रंथालय – दारोदर सेवा देत फिरणारे ग्रंथालय.

model – आदर्श/प्रतिरूप/प्रतिकृती.

model library act – आदर्श ग्रंथालय कायदा/अधिनियम.

model plan – आदर्श आराखडा/योजना.

modem – मोडेम – (१) संगणकावरील संख्यारूपातील माहिती दळणवळणाच्या साधनांवरून वाहून नेण्यासाठी सांकेतिक रूपात बदलावी लागते त्याचे साधन. इ-मेल सारख्या सेवेत हे वापरले जातात. हा संगणक आणि टेलिफोन यामधील दुवा आहे. (२) इंटरनेटमधील सूचनांची देवाण-घेवाण करणारा संगणकीय महत्त्वाचा भाग.

modification – अपरिवर्तन/परिवर्तन – सुधारित बदल – (१) तालिकीकरण करताना नोंदीमध्ये आवश्यक परिवर्तन करणे. उदा. समान शीर्षकाचा वापर उत्पादनसंस्थेचे नाव नोंदीच्या सुरुवातीला घेणे. भूप्रदेश दर्शविणारा भाग नोंदीतून वगळणे इ. (२) निर्देशन करताना नोंदीचे उपविभाजन टाळण्यासाठी माहितीचे समावेशन करणे.

modulation of terms – संज्ञांचे फेरनियमन – वर्गीकरणामध्ये संज्ञा किंवा शीर्षकाचे फेरनियमन.

moduler construction – चौकोनात्मक इमारत बांधणी – अशा बांधकामात अंतर्गत बदल सहजपणे करणे शक्य असते, कारण अंतर्गत बांधकाम बदलण्यायोग्य असते.

monitor – प्रबोधक – संगणकाचा पडदा ज्यावर रंगीत किंवा कृष्णधवल स्वरूपात माहिती दिसते.

monograph – विनिबंध – (१) एकाच विशिष्ट विषयावरील विद्वत्तापूर्ण प्रकाशन. (२) एकाच विषयावरील प्रबंध. व्याप्ती कमी असते परंतु सखोल माहिती दिली जाते.

monograph series – निबंधमाला – एका मालाशीर्षकाखाली लिहिलेला ग्रंथ.

monographic publication – लघुनिबंध प्रकाशन – माला शीर्षकाखाली नसलेले लघुनिबंधाचे प्रकाशन एकाच खंडामध्ये किंवा विशिष्ट खंडामध्ये प्रकाशित होणारे लघुनिबंध.

monolingual dictionary – एकभाषीय शब्दकोश – शब्दाचा अर्थ त्याच भाषेत समजावून सांगणारा कोश. उदा. आपटेकृत मराठी रत्नाकर.

monthly – मासिक/नियतकालिक – (१) दर महिन्याला प्रकाशित होणारे कालिक.
(२) प्रत्येक महिन्याला ठरावीक दिवशी प्रकाशित होणारे नियतकालिक.

monthly progress report – मासिक प्रगती अहवाल.

moon type – **मून छपाई ठसा** – अंध व्यक्तींसाठी तयार केलेल्या ग्रंथांमध्ये वापरलेला डॉ. विल्यम मून यांच्या नावाने प्रसिद्ध असलेला छपाईठसा. मोठेपणी अंधत्व आलेल्या व्यक्तींना तसेच ब्रेललिपी शिकणे अवघड जात असलेल्या व्यक्तींना उपयुक्त.

morgue – वर्तमानपत्रांच्या कार्यालयात तयार केलेला अद्ययावत ख्यातव्यक्तिचरित्र संदर्भ माहितीसंच.

morocco – **मोरोक्को कातडे** – ग्रंथबांधणीसाठी वापरले जाणारे कातडे.

mosaic map – **मोझाइक नकाशा** – पृथ्वीवरील उंचसखल भाग दर्शविणारी छायाचित्रे जोडून तयार केलेला नकाशा.

motivation – प्रेरणा/प्रेरकता/अभिप्रेरणा.

MS-DOS (Microsoft Disk Operating System) – आयबीएमपीसी आणि तत्सम लघुसंगणकासाठी वापरली जाणारी कार्यपद्धती.

multi – बहु/अनेक.

multicountry library – बहुप्रादेशिक ग्रंथालय.

multicultural librarianship – बहुसांस्कृतिक ग्रंथपालन – सार्वजनिक ग्रंथालयांद्वारे अनेक भाषांमध्ये अनेक संस्कृतींसाठी दिलेली ग्रंथालयसेवा.

multi – dimensional classification – **बहुविध वर्गीकरण** – अनेक दृष्टिकोनातून एका ग्रंथाचे केलेले वर्गीकरण. अनेक प्रती उपलब्ध असतील तर प्रत्येक वर्गामध्ये प्रत्यक्ष स्थान देणे शक्य होते.

multifaceted – **अनेक पैलू असणारे** – ग्रंथवर्गीकरणास उपयुक्त ठरतील असे.

multifocal work – **बहुकेंद्रीय कार्य** – अनेक घटक समाविष्ट असणारे.

multi level indexing – **बहुस्तरीय निर्देशन** – निर्देशन करताना प्रलेखाची नोंद सर्वसमावेशक **(generic)** संज्ञेद्वारे तसेच संकोची **(narrower)** संज्ञेद्वारे करण्याची प्रक्रिया.

multilingual dictionary – बहुभाषिक शब्दकोश – दोन किंवा अधिक भाषांतून अर्थ स्पष्ट करणारा शब्दकोश.

multimedia – बहुविध प्रसारमाध्यमे.

multiple – अनेक/बहुविध.

multiple approach, principle of – **बहुविध दृष्टिकोनतत्त्व** – तालिकाकाराने नोंदी करताना ग्रंथाची मागणी किती प्रकारच्या दृष्टिकोनातून (उदा. लेखकाचे नाव, ग्रंथनाम, माला विषय) होऊ शकते, ते लक्षात घेऊन तालिकीकरण करण्याचे तत्त्व.

multiple card system – **अनेक पत्र-पद्धती** – ग्रंथ देवघेव, ग्रंथालयीन नोंदी करताना याचा विचार होतो.

multiple class – **बहुविध वर्ग** – दोनपेक्षा जास्त विषयांचा समावेश असणारा वर्ग.

multiple copies – अनेक प्रती – एका ग्रंथाच्या अनेक प्रती.

multiple entry – बहुविध नोंद – एकाच प्रलेखाच्या बहुविध दृष्टिकोनातून केलेल्या नोंदी.

multiple group – संमिश्र गट.

multiple heading – संमिश्र शीर्षक – दोन किंवा अधिक प्रमुख विषयांचा समावेश असणारे ग्रंथनाम.

multi volume publication – बहुखंड प्रकाशन – माला प्रकाशन नसलेले परंतु अनेक खंडात केलेले प्रकाशन.

multiplier – गुणकांक/गुणक – ज्यामुळे विशिष्ट कृती पुन्हा होते व त्याद्वारे विकासाचा मार्ग दाखविला जातो.

multi-volumed books – बहुखंडात्मक ग्रंथ – अनेक भागांमध्ये प्रकाशित झालेल्या व प्रत्येक भागाचा स्वतंत्र खंड असणाऱ्या किंवा प्रकाशित होणार असलेल्या ग्रंथास 'बहुखंडात्मक ग्रंथ' म्हणतात.

multi-volume publication – बहुखंड प्रकाशन – माला प्रकाशन नसलेले परंतु अनेक खंडात केलेले प्रकाशन.

municipal library – नगरपालिका ग्रंथालय – नगरपालिका/महानगरपालिकेमार्फत चालविले जाणारे ग्रंथालय.

monument room – पुराभिलेख दालन – पुराभिलेख (Archives) ठेवलेले दालन.

museum – वस्तुसंग्रहालय – राष्ट्राचा इतिहास संस्कृती जतन करण्यासाठी वस्तूंचे संरक्षण करून त्यांचे प्रदर्शन व जतन करण्याचे ठिकाण.

museum music library – संगीत विषयाच्या वाचनसाहित्याचे ग्रंथालय – कॅसेट, ध्वनिमुद्रिका इ.चा संग्रह असलेले ग्रंथालय.

mutually exclusive – परस्पर वर्जक – एकमेकांत सामावला जाणारा.

Mysore public library act, 1965 – म्हैसूर सार्वजनिक ग्रंथालय अधिनियम १९६५ – २२ एप्रिल १९६५ मध्ये पारित झालेला कायदा. १९७३ पासून यास कर्नाटक सार्वजनिक ग्रंथालय अधिनियम म्हणून ओळखले जाते.

name – नाव/नाम – (१) अस्तित्व म्हणून ओळख. (२) संगणकातील माहितीसंचाला दिलेले नाव.

name authority file / authority list / subject / authority file – **अधिकृतनाम माहितीसंच** – दिलेल्या तालिकेतील नामशीर्षकांची यादी आणि दुसऱ्या माहितीसंचातील संदर्भ यांची संचिका.

name catalogue / personal catalogue – **नामतालिका** – व्यक्तीनाम, स्थलनाम यांची स्वतंत्र वा वर्णक्रमानुसार रचना केलेली तालिका.

name entry – **नामनोंद/नामदर्शक नोंद** – निर्देशन करताना व्यक्ती, स्थळ किंवा संस्थेच्या नावाने केलेली नोंद.

name heading – **नामशीर्षक** – एखाद्या नोंदीत लेखक, संस्था इ.चे नाव शीर्षक म्हणून वापरणे.

name index – **नामनिर्देश** – लेखक वा इतर व्यक्तींच्या नावाचा.

name reference – **नामसंदर्भ** – पर्यायी नाम उपलब्ध असेल तेव्हा तालिकेतील नोंदीसाठी शीर्षक निवडलेल्या नावाचा संदर्भ.

napthalene ball – **डांबर गोळी** – ग्रंथाचे झुरळ अथवा तत्सम कीटकापासून संरक्षण करण्याकरिता वापरण्यात येणारे रसायन.

narrower term (NT) – **संकोची/सुस्पष्ट संज्ञा** – माहितीची प्रतिप्रासी करताना वापरली जाणारी अधिक स्पष्ट संज्ञा. (उदा. खुर्ची ही संज्ञा फर्निचर या संज्ञेपेक्षा संकोची संज्ञा आहे.)

nascent – **नवीनतम** – नवीन विचारांना वाव देणारे. ताजी माहिती देणारे.

nascent document – **नवीन माहितीने युक्त प्रलेख.**

nascent information – नवीनतम माहिती.

nascent thought – नुकताच निर्माण झालेला विचार.

national – राष्ट्रीय.

national archieves – राष्ट्रीय पुराभिलेखागार – केंद्र सरकारची पुराभिलेख, जतनपत्रके यांची व्यवस्था पाहणारी संस्था.

national bibliography – राष्ट्रीय ग्रंथसूची – एखाद्या देशात प्रकाशित झालेल्या सर्व साहित्याची सूची.

national biography – राष्ट्रीय चरित्रग्रंथ – राष्ट्रीय नेत्यांचा, प्रसिद्ध, नामांकित व्यक्तींचा चरित्रग्रंथ.

National Book Trust (NBT) – राष्ट्रीय ग्रंथ न्यास – १९५७ मध्ये स्थापन झालेली भारताची ग्रंथप्रसार करणारी संस्था जी भारतीय भाषांमध्ये ग्रंथ प्रकाशित करते व ग्रंथ प्रदर्शने/यात्रा देशभर भरविते.

national catalogue / national bibliography – राष्ट्रीय ग्रंथ सूची/राष्ट्रीय ग्रंथ तालिका.

national council for education research training (NCERT) – शैक्षणिक अनुसंधान.

national documentation list – राष्ट्रीय प्रलेखन यादी.

national educational research centre – राष्ट्रीय शैक्षणिक शोध केंद्र.

national film archive – राष्ट्रीय चित्रफीत पुराभिलेख कार्यालय.

national gallery – राष्ट्रीय कलाभवन.

National Informatic Centre (NIC) – राष्ट्रीय माहिती /सूचना केंद्र.

National Informational Centre – राष्ट्रीय माहिती केंद्र.

National Information System – राष्ट्रीय माहिती पद्धती – सध्या अस्तित्वात असलेल्या माहिती संस्थांचे जाळे (नेटवर्क) आणि आढळून आलेल्या उणिवा भरून काढण्यासाठी द्यावयाच्या सेवा यांच्यातील समन्वय साधणारा दुवा ज्यामुळे प्रत्येक घटकाच्या कार्यामध्ये वाढ होते.

National Information Centre for Chemistry and Chemical Technology (NICHEM) – निकेम – निसाट (आता निसकेअर) ICSR संस्थेच्या अधिपत्याखाली १९८५ पासून कार्यरत असणारी संस्था.

National Information System for Science Technology (NISSAT) – मे १९७७ मध्ये स्थापन झालेली संस्था. विज्ञान आणि तंत्रज्ञान या क्षेत्रासाठीची राष्ट्रीय स्वरूपाची माहिती ही संस्था पुरविते. (आता NISCAIR)

National Informatics Centre Network (NICNET) – निकनेट – दिल्ली येथील राष्ट्रीय माहिती केंद्राद्वारे विकसित करण्यात आलेले जाळे/नेटवर्क.

National library – राष्ट्रीय ग्रंथालय – विशिष्ट देशाचे मुख्य ग्रंथालय म्हणून कार्य करणारे ग्रंथालय.

National Social Science Documentation Centre (NASSDOC) – **राष्ट्रीय समाजविज्ञान प्रलेखन केंद्र** – राष्ट्रीय समाजविज्ञान संशोधन परिसंस्थेच्या अधिपत्याखाली नवी दिल्ली येथे माहिती केंद्र म्हणून कार्य करणारी संस्था.

national translation centre – **राष्ट्रीय भाषांतर केंद्र** – याद्वारे वाचकांना परभाषांमधील अप्रकाशित भाषांतरे उपलब्ध करून देण्यासाठी मदत केली जाते. विशेषत: वैज्ञानिक, तांत्रिक व सामाजिक शास्त्रे या विषयातील भाषांतरासाठी विशेष मदत दिली जाते.

national union catalogue – राष्ट्रीय संघ तालिका.

natural – नैसर्गिक/स्वाभाविक/प्राकृतिक.

natural characteristic – नैसर्गिक लक्षण/गुण.

natural classification – **स्वाभाविक वर्गीकरण** – ग्रंथांची विषय वैशिष्ट्ये लक्षात घेऊन केलेले वर्गीकरण.

natural language – **प्रचलित/नैसर्गिक भाषा** – (उदा. हिंदी, मराठी, इंग्रजी) प्रलेखांचे निर्देशन ज्या भाषेत केले आहे ती भाषा.

natural language search – प्रचलित/नैसर्गिक भाषा शोध.

natural material – नैसर्गिक संपदा/साहित्य.

natural science – प्राकृतिक/नैसर्गिक विज्ञानशास्त्रे.

nautical almanac – **नौकानयन विषयक मार्गदर्शन** – विशिष्ट दिवशी सूर्य, चंद्र, तारे यांचे स्थान दिवसा व रात्री कोठे असेल, तसेच भरती, ओहोटी विषयक वाचकांना आवश्यक असणारी माहिती दिलेले प्रकाशन.

nautical chart – नौकानयन विषयक तक्ता.

neat line – नकाशातील कडा दर्शविणारी रेखीव ठळक सीमारेषा.

need to know – **नीड टू नो** – सुरक्षिततेचे मूलभूत तत्त्व. विशिष्ट व्यक्तींनाच माहितीविभागात प्रवेश करण्यास दिलेला परवाना.

needlework binding / embroidered binding – **कशिदा बांधणी** – भरतकाम केलेले वेष्टण असणारी ग्रंथबांधणी.

negative selection / weeding / withdrawal – **निंदणी/निष्कासन** – ग्रंथसंग्रहातून ग्रंथ काढून टाकणे.

neo conventional document / ultra micro document – **नवपरिचित प्रलेख** – पेटंट्स, प्रमाणके, वर्तमानपत्रातील कात्रणे यासारखे नव्याने प्रचलित होणारे प्रलेख.

net – जाळे.

net book agreement – **निव्वळ ग्रंथमूल्य करार** – इंग्लंडमध्ये १९२९ मध्ये प्रकाशन, ग्रंथविक्रेते, ग्रंथालय संघ यांनी एकत्र येऊन केवळ प्रकाशकाने छापलेल्या किमतीलाच ग्रंथ विकला जाण्यासाठी केलेला करार.

net book price – **ग्रंथाचे निव्वळ मूल्य.**

netiquette – इंटरनेट सुविधा वापरताना पाळावयाचे शिष्टाचार.

netizen – इंटरनेट सुविधांचा वापर करणारे नागरिक.

netscape – एक प्रकारचे वेब ब्राऊजर सॉफ्टवेअर.

network – **जाळे/संगणकजाळे** – (१) दोन अथवा अधिक संस्थांमधील आंतरजुळणी केलेली संकुल रचना. (२) अंतर्गत जोडणी केलेली संगणकाची जाळीरचना.

network analysis – **जाळ्यांचे विश्लेषण** – व्यवस्थापन पद्धतीने नियोजन, वेळापत्रक तयार करणे, कार्यवाही आणि मूल्यमापन करण्याचे तंत्र वापरणे.

networked database – **जाळीय आधारसामग्री** – सर्व्हरवर उपलब्ध असलेला माहिती संग्रह.

neutrality – **तटस्थता** – विषयानुसार तालिकीकरण करताना प्राधान्यविषय लक्षात न घेता नोंद केली जाते. विशेषत: सार्वजनिक ग्रंथालयांमध्ये तालिकीकरण करताना तटस्थता दृष्टिकोन ठेवला जातो.

new additions / new arrivals – **नवीन भरती** – (१) एखाद्या ग्रंथालयात दाखल झालेले नवीन वाचनसाहित्य. (२) ग्रंथालयात नवीन आलेले ग्रंथ.

new edition / latest edition – **नवीन आवृत्ती** – आधीच्या आवृत्तीतील चुका सुधारून प्रकाशित केलेली आवृत्ती.

newark charging system – **नेवार्क देवघेव पद्धती** – ग्रंथपत्रावर सभासदक्रमांक व दिनांक लिहून देवघेव नोंद ठेवण्याची अमेरिकन पद्धती.

news – **वृत्त बातम्या** – दैनंदिन घडामोडींचा वृत्तान्त, वार्ता.

newsbook – बातम्या, वृत्ते छापलेला छोटा २४ पानांपर्यंत पृष्ठे असलेला ग्रंथ. १६२२ मध्ये प्रथम छापला.

news bulletin – **वार्तापत्रिका.**

news clipping – **वृत्तपत्र कात्रण.**

news letter – **वृत्तपत्रिका/वार्तापत्र** – संस्था, व्यावसायिक व्यवस्थापन यांचे अहवालात्मक प्रकाशन.

newspaper – **वर्तमानपत्र/वृत्तपत्र** – रोज घडणाऱ्या घटना, नवी माहिती, ताज्या बातम्या देणारे, रोज प्रसिद्ध होणारे प्रकाशन.

newspaper index – **वृत्तपत्र निर्देश.**

newspaper library – वर्तमानपत्र/वृत्तपत्र ग्रंथालय – वृत्तपत्रांसाठी लागणारे अहवाल, छायाचित्रे, संदर्भग्रंथ, हस्तपुस्तिका इ.चा संग्रह करणारे ग्रंथालय.

newspaper stand – वृत्तपत्र प्रदर्शक.

newsprint – वृत्तपत्रासाठी वापरला जाणारा कागद.

news room – ग्रंथालयांमध्ये वृत्तपत्रांसाठी वापरले जाणारे दालन.

news series – वृत्तमाला.

nibble – संगणकातील स्मरणिका मापनाचे एकक.

nickname – टोपणनाव – व्यक्ती/संस्था/स्थान यांचे इतरांनी ठेवलेले टोपणनाव.

nickname index – टोपणनाव सूची – यात प्रसिद्ध व्यक्ती, स्थान, अधिकृत अहवाल, कायदे, संस्था यांच्या टोपणनावांची अनुवर्णक्रमानुसार यादी करून त्यांची अधिकृत नावे व इतर तपशील दिला जातो.

noble – अभिजात/उदात्त/थोर/प्रगल्भ.

noble prize – नोबेल पुरस्कार – अल्फ्रेड नोबेल यांच्या नावाने आंतरराष्ट्रीय स्तरावर दिला जाणारा पुरस्कार.

no conflict policy – समायोजन तत्त्व – अस्तित्वात असलेल्या विषय शीर्षकांमध्ये अडचण येत नसेल तेव्हा तालिकीकरणाचे नवीन नियम स्वीकारण्याविषयीचे धोरण.

no date [abbr n.d.] – प्रकाशन वर्ष माहीत नाही. ग्रंथसूची किंवा तालिकेतील नोंदीमध्ये चौकोनी [ ] कंसात उल्लेख केला जातो.

no dues certificate – बेबाकी प्रमाणपत्र – वाचकाला दिलेले ना देय प्रमाणपत्र. ग्रंथालयाचे सभासदत्व सोडताना 'ना देय प्रमाणपत्र' घेणे आवश्यक असते; त्यामुळे वाचकाकडे ग्रंथालयाचे (पुस्तकाचे/पैशांचे) येणे नाही हे स्पष्ट होते.

nomenclature – नाव/संज्ञा/नामपद्धती – (१) विषयांतर्गत नावाचा एक गट किंवा पद्धती. (२) वर्गीकरण करताना वापरण्याची संज्ञांची परिभाषा.

nominated – नियुक्त/नामनिर्देशित.

no more published – आणखी प्रकाशन नाही – प्रकाशकाने दिलेली सूचना.

non–aided library – विनाअनुदान तत्त्वावर चालविलेले ग्रंथालय.

non–book material – ग्रंथेतर साहित्य – ग्रंथालयात संग्रही असलेल्या ग्रंथांव्यतिरिक्त ध्वनिफिती, चित्रफिती, सूक्ष्मचित्रफिती, संगणक इ. साहित्य.

non–circulating material – वितरणासाठी उपलब्ध नसलेले साहित्य.

non–conventional document – अपारंपरिक प्रलेख – माहितीपेक्षा बाह्यस्वरूपाला महत्त्व असलेले मायक्रोफिल्मस्, टेप्स यांसारखे प्रलेख.

non-current records - अप्रचलित नोंदी.

non-documentary sources of information - प्रलेखविरहित माहितीस्रोत किंवा साधने - माहितीची साधने जी प्रलेखविरहित आहेत. उदा. तज्ज्ञ, संस्था, शासकीय विभाग इत्यादी.

non-fiction - ललितेतर साहित्य.

non-formal education - अनौपचारिक शिक्षण - स्वयंअध्ययनाने अनौपचारिकरीत्या शिक्षण घेता येते.

non periodical - अनियतकालिक - एकदाच वा अनेक खंडांमध्ये केलेले प्रकाशन. खंडांची संख्या आधी ठरविली जाते.

non-plan grants - योजनेतर अनुदान - अर्थसंकल्पामध्ये विशिष्ट कालावधींसाठी तरतूद केलेली रक्कम.

non-print - ग्रंथेतर - अमुद्रित छपाईव्यतिरिक्त असणारे वाचनसाहित्य. उदा. CD-ROM

non-recurring expenditure - अनावर्ती खर्च - जो खर्च पुन: पुन्हा केला जात नाही असा खर्च. जसे इमारत, बांधकाम, साधनसामग्री, यंत्रे, फर्निचर खरेदी इत्यादी.

non-volatile memory - संगणकांची स्थिर स्मरणिका.

norm - प्रमाणक/मानक - एक नियम, आदर्श किंवा एक प्रमाणित मानदंड.

not available - अनुपलब्ध - ग्रंथ उपलब्ध नाही.

not in stock - ग्रंथ सध्या संग्रहात नाही.

not tracable - ग्रंथ सापडत नाही.

not transferable notation - अहस्तांतरणीय/चिन्हांकन - वर्गीकरण पद्धतीत एखादा विषय किंवा उपविषय दर्शविणारी वर्ण किंवा अंक/चिन्हपद्धती.

notation system - चिन्हांकन पद्धती - असे रचनाक्रम दर्शक अंक ज्यांचा उपयोग वर्गीकरण पद्धतीतील वर्ग दर्शविण्यासाठी होतो.

notational plane - चिन्हांकन पातळी/स्तर - डॉ. रंगनाथन् यांच्या द्विबिंदू वर्गीकरण पद्धतीतील संज्ञा.

note - टिपण/टिप्पणी - प्रलेख, प्रकरण, ग्रंथ यांच्या शेवटी किंवा पानाच्या शेवटच्या ओळीवर मजकुराचे दिलेले स्पष्टीकरण.

note area - टीप क्षेत्र - तालिकापत्रात टीप अनुच्छेद दर्शविणारा विभाग.

note book - टिपणवही.

notebook computer - नोटबुक संगणक - नोटबुकाच्या आकाराचा संगणक.

notepad - संगणकाच्या स्मरणिकेतील एक भाग.

note section – टीप अनुच्छेद/टीपा विभाग – मालेचे नाव अथवा संबंधित ग्रंथाचे नाव देणाऱ्या मुख्य नोंदीच्या अनुच्छेदाला 'टीप अनुच्छेद' असे म्हणतात.

nothing before something arrangement – शब्दनिष्ठ वर्णक्रम.

notification – अधिसूचना.

novel – कादंबरी – वाङ्मयाचा/साहित्याचा एक प्रकार.

novelist – कादंबरीकार.

num lock key – संगणकाच्या कळपट्टीवरील एक कळ.

number – चिन्हांक/अंक – संख्या व्यक्त करणारा शब्द किंवा चिन्ह.

number building – चिन्हांक बांधणी – 'ला जोडा' टिपेनुसार अंकांची पुढील संश्लेषण प्रक्रिया किंवा अचूक वर्गांक तयार करणे.

number building note – वर्गांक बांधणी टीप– वर्गांकाचा विस्तार करण्यासाठी ही टीप देतात.

numbered and signed edition – संख्यांकित व स्वाक्षरीत आवृत्ती – आवृत्तीच्या प्रतींना क्रमांक दिले जातात व लेखकाने स्वाक्षरी केलेली असते.

numbered copy –अंकन प्रत – मर्यादित प्रमाणात छापलेल्या आवृत्तीच्या क्रमांक दिलेल्या प्रती.

numbered entry – छापील ग्रंथसूची किंवा तालिकेतील क्रमांक दिलेल्या नोंदी.

numeral – संख्यावाचक शब्द – ग्रंथाच्या कण्यावर वर्गांक लिहिणे.

numerals – अंक.

numeration – क्रमांकन –तालिकीकरण करताना संख्यावाचक अंक नोंदीला दिला जातो. यामुळे शीर्षकाचा अनुक्रम समजणे सुलभ होते.

numeric keypad – अंकरूप कळफलक– केवळ अंक असलेला छोटा कळफलक.

numerical order – संख्याक्रम.

numbering – अंकन/क्रमांकन – क्रमवारीनुसार अंक निश्चित करण्याची क्रिया.

obcjective classification – **वस्तुनिष्ठ वर्गीकरण** – संबंधित विज्ञानशाखांचे वस्तुनिष्ठ वर्गीकरण.

objective – **ध्येय/उद्दिष्ट** – विशिष्ट काम, प्रयोगाद्वारे प्राप्त करावयाचे ध्येय किंवा लक्ष्य.

oblique – **तिरपी रेघ** (/) – एक चिन्ह 'किंवा' या शब्दासाठी वापरण्यात येणारे पर्यायी चिन्ह.

oblong – **आडवे पुस्तक** – उंचीपेक्षा रुंदी अधिक असणारे पुस्तक.

observation – **निरीक्षण** – संशोधनात वापरली जाणारी एक पद्धती.

observation stage – **निरीक्षण स्थिती.**

obserse cover / front cover – (ग्रंथाचे) मुखपृष्ठ.

octave – **अष्टक** – आठांचा समुदाय.

octave device – **अष्टक कलृप्ती/युक्ती** – डॉ. रंगनाथन् यांनी दिलेली संज्ञा. चिन्हांकातील अंक वापरताना १ ते ८ हे अंक वापरून ९ अंक वापरला जात नाही त्याऐवजी प्रत्येक क्रमांकाबरोबर १ ते ८ अंक वापरून आठ विषयांचा गट निर्माण होतो. यामुळे अनेक विषयांना एकपदस्थ दर्जा देता येतो.

octroi – **जकात** – आयात-निर्यातीवरचा स्थानिक स्वराज्य संस्थेचा कर, महसूल.

odd folios – ग्रंथामध्ये पृष्ठांना दिलेले विषम अंक. उजव्या बाजूचे पानांक.

odd page – **ग्रंथाचे विषम पान/उजवे पान** (उदा. पान १,३,५)

office – **कार्यालय.**

office information system – **कार्यालय माहिती यंत्रणा** – कार्यालयातील आधुनिक पद्धतीने संगणकाच्या साहाय्याने चालविलेली प्रशासकीय यंत्रणा.

office library – **कार्यालयीन ग्रंथालय** – यामध्ये कार्यालयीन कामकाजाकरिता लागणारे ग्रंथ ठेवले जातात.

official – **कार्यालयीन/अधिकृत.**

official catalogue – **अधिकृत तालिका.**

official gazette – **शासकीय राजपत्र** – शासन, विद्यापीठ यांचे निर्णय, अहवाल प्रसिद्ध करणारे नियतकालिक.

official organ – **मुखपत्र/अधिकृत पत्र** – विशिष्ट समूहाचे जसे संस्था, संघटना यांचे प्रतिनिधित्व करणारे नियतकालिक, वर्तमानपत्र किंवा अन्य प्रकाशन.

official name – **संस्थेचे अधिकृत नाव.**

official puclication – **संस्थेचे अधिकृत प्रकाशन.**

off-line – **मार्गबाह्य** – माहिती प्राप्तीच्या क्रियेमध्ये जेव्हा उपकरण किंवा संयंत्र हे प्रेषण साखळी किंवा संगणकाच्या मध्यवर्ती प्रक्रिया संचाशी सरळ जोडलेले नसते, तेव्हा त्याला ऑफ लाईन असे म्हणतात.

off-line equipment – **मार्गबाह्य उपरकण** – संगणकाच्या मध्यवर्ती प्रक्रियेशी प्रत्यक्ष संपर्क नसलेले उपकरण.

off-line system – **मार्गबाह्य पद्धत** – संयोजनाशिवाय माहिती मिळविण्याची पद्धती.

offprint – **सुटी मुद्रित प्रत** – उदा. नियतकालिकात प्रकाशित झालेला प्रत्येक लेख संबंधितास दिला जातो.

offset printing – **अक्षरप्रतिरूप मुद्रण.**

omissible – **वगळण्यायोग्य** – (१) मजकुरातून गाळण्याजोगे. (२) वगळण्यायोग्य मजकूर.

omission – **निष्कासन/वगळलेला.**

omission factor – **निष्कासन घटक/वगळलेला घटक.**

omission mark / ellipsis – **गाळलेल्या शब्दांसाठी चिन्हे.** (उदा. तीन पूर्णविराम...)

omnibus book – **समग्र वाङ्मय ग्रंथ** – छोट्या गोष्टींचा पुनर्मुद्रित एकत्र ग्रंथ.

omnibus edition / colleted edition – **सर्वसमावेशक आवृत्ती/समग्र आवृत्ती.**

online – **सहमार्गी/तारमार्गी** – संगणकावरील माहिती शोधण्यासाठी आदान-प्रदान क्रियांसाठी एका केंद्रावरून साधलेला परस्परसंबंध, यात केंद्र आणि संगणक हे तारांनी (Leased Lines) जाळ्यांनी (Networks) किंवा दळणवळणाच्या इतर साधनांनी (जसे टेलिफोन, उपग्रह) जोडलेले असू शकतात.

online catalogue – संगणकीय तालिका.

on a probation / on approval – पसंतीसाठी ग्रंथालयात आलेले ग्रंथ.

on sale – विक्रीसाठीचा (मोफत नसलेला) ग्रंथ.

on demand publishing – मागणीनुसार प्रकाशन – वाचकाला हवे असेल तेव्हाच प्रकाशन उपलब्ध केले जाते. संगणकावर माहिती उपलब्ध असते. आवश्यकतेनुसार छापील प्रत दिली जाते.

onlay – ग्रंथवेष्टनाचे अलंकरण.

online access – सहमार्गी/तारमार्गी प्रवेश – संगणकाद्वारे सरळ प्रवेश, माहितीशोध.

online database – सहमार्गी/तारमार्गी आधार सामग्री – संगणकावरील माहितीसंचय.

online infromation retrieval / online searching –सहमार्गी/तारमार्गी माहिती पुनर्प्राप्ती – दूर अंतरावरची माहिती मिळविण्यासाठी संगणकाचा उपयोग करून हवी असलेली माहिती शोधणे.

online search service – सहमार्गी/तारमार्गी सेवा – संगणकाद्वारे माहिती जाळ्यापर्यंत शोध सेवा.

online searching – सहमार्गी/तारमार्गी शोधन – १) संगणकाद्वारे माहितीचा शोध घेणे. २) आपल्याजवळील संगणक पद्धतीच्या साहाय्याने परस्परांच्या डेटाबेसमधून माहितीचा शोध घेणे. वाचक व्हिडिओ डिस्प्ले यूनिटच्या आणि दूरसंचारणाच्या माध्यमातून संपर्क साधतो आणि संगणकावर प्रतिसाद मिळवतो.

online system – संगणकाची पद्धती.

online thesaurus – संगणकावरील शब्दकोश.

Online Puclic Access Catalogue / Open Public Access Catalogue (OPAC) – उपयोजकांसाठी संगणकीय तालिका – ग्रंथालय उपयोजक स्वत: वापरू शकतील अशी संगणकीय तालिका.

online center of library of congress / Ohio College Library Catalogue (OCLC)

op. bit. (Abbr. for opere citaro) – तळटीप देताना अन्य तळटीपांनंतर लेखाचा संदर्भ आल्यास पुनरावृत्ती टाळण्यासाठी वापरण्यात येणारा शब्दसमूह.

on loan – उसनवार – उसने देणे–घेणे.

open – मुक्त.

open access – मुक्त प्रवेश/मुक्तद्वार प्रवेश – यामध्ये वाचकांना ग्रंथाच्या कपाटाजवळ जाऊन ग्रंथ हाताळण्याची मुभा असते. विविध ग्रंथ पाहून वाचक आपल्या आवडीचे ग्रंथ निवडू शकतो.

open array – मुक्त पंक्ती.

open entry – खुली नोंद – अधिक माहिती लिहिणे शक्य होईल अशी नोंद. मालेमध्ये नंतर प्रकाशित होणाऱ्या खंडाविषयी माहिती लिहिण्यासाठी सोय.

open joint / french joint – बांधणीसाठी फ्रेंच पद्धतीचा जोड.

open notation – खुले चिन्हांकन.

open order – **खुली मागणी** – ग्रंथविक्रेत्याकडे पुरविलेल्या ग्रंथाशिवाय इतर ग्रंथांची केलेली मागणी.

open purchase – **खुली खरेदी** – अनेक ग्रंथविक्रेत्यांना ग्रंथपुरवठा करता येईल अशी पद्धती.

operating system (O.S.) – (१) संगणक व उपयोजक यांच्यात समन्वय घडवून आणणारी यंत्रणा. (२) संगणकास वीजप्रवाह पुरवठा गेल्यावर विशिष्ट आय.सी. मधील काही आज्ञावलींमध्ये संगणकाचे कार्य मानवाच्या सहभागाशिवाय सुरू करण्याचे सामर्थ्य असते. हा ओ.एस.चा मूलभूत उपयोग आहे.

operating time – **परिचालन काळ** – संगणक संयोजना तयार करणे, विकसित करणे व इतर कामांसाठी लागणारा कालावधी.

operation manual – **कार्यवाही पुस्तिका** – ज्या पुस्तिकेत विशिष्ट कार्याची सूचना व मानके दिलेली असतात.

operations research – **क्रिया संशोधन तंत्र** – एखादे कार्य पार पाडण्यासाठी किंवा एखादा निर्णय सुनिश्चित करण्यासाठी किंवा विशिष्ट प्रश्नांचा अभ्यास करून त्यावर उपाय शोधण्यासाठी या तंत्राचा उपयोग केला जातो. हे तंत्र प्रमुख्याने गणितशास्त्र व संख्याशास्त्र यावर आधारित असून त्याद्वारे वेगळ्या चाचण्या, प्रतिकृती तयार केल्या जातात. यात नियोजित कार्यासंबंधीचा भविष्यवेध घेण्याच्या तंत्राचाही उपयोग केला जातो.

operator – **कार्यवाहक/तंत्रज्ञ** – जी व्यक्ती यंत्रावर अनेक कामे करते.

operators (boolean) – **कार्यवाहक (बुलियन)** – उदा. AND, OR & NOT

opinion – **मत** – एखाद्या व्यक्ती किंवा गोष्टीबाबतचे मत खास करून वस्तुस्थिती किंवा ज्ञान यावर न आधारलेले.

optical disk – **माहिती साठविण्याचे साधन** – ही माहिती संगणकाद्वारे वाचली जाऊ शकते.

optical fibre cable – **प्रकाशकीय तंतू तार** – याचा वापर संदेशवहनाकरिता केला जातो.

oral communication – **मौखिक संप्रेषण** – तोंडी संपर्क.

order – **क्रम/आदेश** – वस्तूंची मागणी करण्याची सूचना, मांडणी.

order of an array – पंक्तीचा क्रम.

order-card – **तालिकापत्राचा क्रम** – प्रत्येक मागणी केलेल्या ग्रंथाची संपूर्ण नोंद ठेवलेले पत्र.

decreasing extension order – व्याप्ती अवरोह असलेला क्रम.

order department – ग्रंथमागणी विभाग.

order of a class – वर्गांचा क्रम.

order of chain - शृंखलेचा क्रम.

order form - आदेशपत्राचा नमुना.

order list - आदेशाची यादी.

order of a link - कडीनिहाय क्रम.

ordinal - क्रमवाचक - क्रममूल्य असणारे अंक.

ordinal name - क्रमवाचक नाव.

ordinal number - क्रमवाचक अंक - अनुक्रम लक्षात येईल असे चिन्ह.

ordinal notation - क्रमवाचक चिन्हांकन - श्रेणीयुक्त रचना टाळून क्रमवाचक पद्धतीने केलेले चिन्हांकन.

ordinal symbols - क्रमवाचक संकेत चिन्ह - अशी चिन्हे जी केवळ अनुक्रम दर्शवितात व मूल्यविरहित असतात.

ordinal value - क्रमदर्शक मूल्य - गणितीय मूल्य नसणारी संख्या.

ordinary - सामान्य/सर्वसाधारण.

ordinary composite book - सामान्य संयुक्त ग्रंथ.

ordinary letter - साध्या पोस्टाने पाठविलेले पत्र.

ordinary publication - सामान्य प्रकाशन.

organisation - संघटन/संघटना - विशिष्ट हेतूने एकत्र आलेला व्यावसायिकांचा किंवा मंडळींचा गट.

oriental book - प्राच्यविद्या ग्रंथ.

orientation course - परिचयात्मक/उद्बोधन अभ्यासक्रम.

orientation class - उद्बोधन वर्ग - माहितीपर व्याख्यानांद्वारे व्यावसायाचा परिचय करून देणारे प्रशिक्षण.

orientation lecture - उद्बोधन/परिचयात्मक व्याख्यान.

original - मूळ/मूलभूत/प्राथमिक.

original catalogue - मूळ तालिका/ग्रंथविक्रेत्याचे मूळ सूचीपत्र.

original edition - मूळ आवृत्ती/पहिली आवृत्ती.

original sources / primary sources - माहितीची मूलभूत प्राप्तीस्थाने/प्राथमिक प्राप्तीस्थाने.

original work - मूळ रचना.

out of date - कालबाह्य - जुना, उपयोगात नसलेला.

out of print / exchausted edition – प्रकाशनबाह्य ग्रंथ – प्रकाशकाकडील सर्व प्रती संपलेल्या असून पुनर्मुद्रणाचा विचार नाही असा ग्रंथ.

out of stock – साठा संपलेले/संग्रही नसलेला ग्रंथ.

outlier library – बाह्यस्थित/सहकारबाह्य ग्रंथालय – राष्ट्रीय ग्रंथालयातर्फे देवघेव करणारे ग्रंथालय.

output – उत्सर्जन – संगणकातील संस्कारित माहिती, कर्मचाऱ्याने केलेले काम.

output device – उत्सर्जन युक्ती/यंत्र – संगणकातील माहितीचे परिणाम दर्शविणारी उपकरणे. उदा. छपाईयंत्र.

output record – कार्योत्पादन अभिलेख – संगणकाद्वारे छापील स्वरूपातील नोंद.

outside source – ग्रंथालयबाह्य प्राप्तिस्थान – विशेष ग्रंथालयाच्या ग्रंथपालांद्वारे ग्रंथालयाबाहेरील प्राप्तीस्थानाचा संदर्भ वाचकाला काहीवेळा दिला जातो.

outside user – बहि:स्थ वाचक/सदस्येतर वाचक.

over due – मुदतीबाहेर/प्रलंबित – (१) दिलेल्या कालावधीपेक्षा अधिक काळ बाहेर असलेले. (२) वाचकाने देयदिनांकापेक्षा अधिक काळ वापरलेले पुस्तक.

over book – मुदतबाह्य ग्रंथ.

over charges – अतिरिक्त शुल्क – अतिरिक्त शुल्क, मूळ किमतीवर आकारली जाणारी जास्तीची रक्कम.

over notice – विलंबाबाबत सूचना.

overflow – भरून वाहणे – क्षमतेपेक्षा जास्त होणे.

overhead projector – प्रक्षेपक – प्रक्षेपण करण्यासाठी वापरले जाणारे उपकरण.

overlapping – परस्परव्यापक.

overlapping subjects – परस्परव्यापक विषय.

oversized book – असाधारण ग्रंथ – (१) मोठ्या आकाराचा ग्रंथ (२) नेहमीपेक्षा वेगळ्या आकाराचे आणि ग्रंथमांडणीसाठी अयोग्य असे मोठे पुस्तक.

overstrike – अधिरेखाटन – एकाच स्थानावर दोन अक्षरे वा चिन्हे मुद्रित करणे. (उदा. S आणि I यांचा वापर करून $ चिन्ह छापणे.)

overwrite – अधिलेखन करणे – संगणकामध्ये आधीच्या माहितीच्या जागेवर नवीन माहितीसंचय करणे.

ownership mark – स्वामित्व/मालकीहक्काचे चिन्ह– (१) शिक्क्याच्या किंवा चिठ्ठीच्या साहाय्याने स्वामित्व दर्शविणारी खूण. (२) ग्रंथाच्या मालकीचा ठसा.

P

package – *संगणकीय तयार सूचनासंच (समावेष्टन)* – अनेक उपयोजकांच्या गरजा पूर्ण करण्यासाठी तयार केलेला संगणकीय सूचनासंच.

package library – *पुस्तिकासंग्रह ग्रंथालय* – कात्रणसंग्रह ग्रंथालय.

packet notation – *वेष्टित चिन्हांकन* – सहसंबंधित चिन्हांचा वर्गांक तयार करण्यासाठी केलेला उपयोग. उदा. दशांश वर्गीकरणामध्ये कंस ( ) या चिन्हाचा वापर करून अंक जोडला जातो.

packet switching network – *समूहजोडणी करणारे संगणकजाळे.* संगणक समूहामध्ये परस्पर माहितीची अदलाबदल नियंत्रित करणारे संगणक जाळे.

packing – *आवेष्टन* – मूळ वस्तूच्या संरक्षणासाठी असलेले वेष्टण.

packing slip – *आवेष्टन चिठ्ठी.*

page – *पृष्ठ/पान* –(१) ग्रंथाच्या पानाची एक बाजू. (२) पुस्तकाचे पान किंवा संगणक पडद्यावरील एक पान.

page break – *पृष्ठ खंड* – संगणककार्यामध्ये पान उलटून पुढे जाण्याची प्रक्रिया.

page catalogue – *पृष्ठतालिका* – एका पानावर थोड्या नोंदी अंतर राखून केल्या जातात. नवीन नोंद समाविष्ट करण्यासाठी, क्रम राखण्यासाठी अंतर सोडून नोंदी केल्या जातात.

page headline – *पृष्ठशीर्षक* – ग्रंथातील प्रत्येक पृष्ठावर लिहिलेले शीर्षक.

page layout – *पृष्ठ आराखडा* – पृष्ठावरील मजकुराची मांडणी.

page make up – **पृष्ठ प्रतीपूर्ती** – पृष्ठावर मजकूर, आकृती, चित्रे यांची सुयोग्य रचना.

page printer – **पृष्ठ मुद्रक** – एकावेळी संपूर्ण पानाची छपाई करणारे छपाईयंत्र.

page reference – **पृष्ठसंदर्भ** – ग्रंथसूचीमध्ये एखाद्या विषयाच्या उल्लेखाविषयी दिलेला पृष्ठक्रमांकाचा संदर्भ.

pages per minute (ppm) – **छपाईवेग मोजण्याचे एकक**.

pagination – **पृष्ठगणन/पानांकन/पृष्ठांकन** – (१) ग्रंथातील प्रत्येक पृष्ठाला दिलेले क्रमांक.
    (२) तालिकानोंदीमधील ग्रंथाची पृष्ठसंख्या दिलेला उल्लेख.
    (३) ग्रंथाच्या पानांना क्रमांक देण्याची पद्धती.

paging – **पृष्ठन** – संगणकाच्या पृष्ठावरील माहिती मुख्य संचामध्ये समाविष्ट करून वेळ वाचविण्याचे तंत्र.

paleography – **लिपीशास्त्र/लिपीविज्ञान** – पुरातन हस्तलिखितांचे अभ्यासशास्त्र. यामध्ये लेखनाच्या प्रकारावरून हस्तलिखिताचा दिनांक ठरविण्याचे शास्त्र अंतर्भूत आहे.

palmset – हस्तलिखितावर केलेले पुनर्हस्तलेखन.

palm leaf book – **तालपत्र ग्रंथ** – तालपत्रावर हस्तलेखन केलेला ग्रंथ.

palm top computer – **करतल संगणक** – तळव्यात मावेल एवढा संगणक.

pamphlet – **पत्रक** – दोन किंवा चार पृष्ठांचा छापील मजकूर.

pamphlet file – **पत्रक पंजी/संचिका**.

pamphlet volume – **पुस्तिका खंड** – अनेक पुस्तिकांची एकत्र बांधणी केलेला खंड.

paper – **कागद** – वनस्पती तंतूपासून बनविलेले मजकूर लिहिण्यायोग्य पातळ साहित्य.

paper back / paper bound – **कागदी बांधणी असलेले पुस्तक**.

paper bound / paper backed – **कागदी बांधणी केलेले पुस्तक**.

paperback edition – **स्वस्त आवृत्ती** – याची बांधणी कागदी असते. छपाईसाठी वापरलेला कागद कमी प्रतीचा असतो.

paperless office / electronic office – **कागद विरहित कार्यालय** – लँकास्टर यांनी १९८० मध्ये मांडलेली संकल्पना. एक संकल्पना.

paperless society – **कागदविरहित समाज** – अशा समाजात सर्व संप्रेषण संगणकाद्वारे केले जाते.

paper size – ग्रंथाच्या कागदाचा आकार.

papers – वैयक्तिक व कौटुंबिक कागदपत्रे.

papyrus – **पपायरस** – प्राचीन काळात काही झाडांच्या खोडापासून बनविलेले साहित्य ज्याचा उपयोग लिहिण्यासाठी केला जात असे.

paragraph – **परिच्छेद.**

parallel arrangement – **समांतर ग्रंथरचना** – नेहमीपेक्षा वेगळ्या आकाराचे ग्रंथ, मांडणीतील असमानता टाळण्यासाठी जवळच पण वेगळे मांडण्याची पद्धती.

parallel classification – **समांतर वर्गीकरण** – विशिष्ट वर्गीकरण केल्यानंतर ग्रंथाचा आकार, वैशिष्ट्ये याप्रमाणे पुन्हा वर्गीकरण करण्याची पद्धती. उदा. एकाच विषयाची पुस्तिका, चित्रे, पुस्तके वेगळी मांडणे.

parallel computer – **समांतर संगणक** – एकापेक्षा अधिक गणितीय व तात्त्विक एककांचा समावेश करून समांतर प्रक्रिया करण्याची सुविधा असलेला संगणक.

parallel data transmission – **समांतर माहिती प्रक्षेपण** – संगणकाद्वारे केलेले समांतर माहितीप्रक्षेपण.

parallel edition – **समांतर आवृत्ती** – एकाच मजकुराची विविध प्रकारे छपाई एका ग्रंथात केलेली आवृत्ती. उदा. भगवद्गीता व दुसऱ्या भाषेत भाषांतर, एकत्रितरीत्या छापलेली आवृत्ती.

parallel index – **समांतर निर्देश** – ग्रंथपृष्ठावर कडेला छोट्या अक्षरात निर्देशन संज्ञेचा केलेला उल्लेख.

parallel mark / paragraph mark – **समांतर चिन्ह** – उदा. तळटीप चिन्ह (।)

parallel processing – **समांतर संस्करण** – संगणकामध्ये एकावेळी दोन वा अधिक समांतरप्रक्रिया संस्कारित करणे.

parallel publishing – **समांतर प्रकाशन** – ग्रंथस्वरूपात व इलेक्ट्रॉनिक स्वरूपात एकाचवेळी केलेले प्रकाशन.

parallel storage – **समांतर संग्रह** – संगणकामध्ये अंक, अक्षरे, शब्द यांची समांतर साठवण.

parallel title – **समांतर ग्रंथनाम** – (१) ग्रंथाला दिलेले अन्य भाषेतील ग्रंथनाम. (२) मजकुरापेक्षा वेगळ्या भाषेत किंवा वेगळ्या लिपीमध्ये लिहिलेले ग्रंथनाम.

parallel translation – **समांतर भाषांतर** – मजकूर व भाषांतर समांतररीत्या उभ्या स्तंभामध्ये छापलेले प्रकाशन.

parameter – **प्रमाणक** – संगणक आज्ञावलीतील कार्यक्षेत्र सीमा.

paraphrase – **सविस्तर अर्थकथन** – एखादे भाषिक किंवा लेखन दुसऱ्या शब्दांत पुन्हा सांगणे, अर्थानुवाद करणे, एकभाषिक अनुवाद करणे.

parchment – **चर्मपत्र** – प्रक्रिया केलेली कातडी ज्याचा उपयोग लिहिण्यासाठी केला जातो.

parenthesis – **गोल कंस** ( ) – वाक्यामध्ये गोल कंसात दिलेले स्पष्टीकरण.

parenthetical references – **गोल कंसात दिलेले संदर्भ.**

parent organisation – **मातृसंस्था** – विशेष ग्रंथालय, ज्या संस्थेला घटक म्हणून स्थापन केले जाते ती पालक संस्था.

part – **भाग** – विभाग, कप्पा.

part publication – **प्रकाशनाचा एक छोटा भाग** – अनेक छोट्या भागांमध्ये केलेले प्रकाशन.

partial bibliography – **आंशिक ग्रंथसूची** – समाविष्ट करण्याच्या ग्रंथसाहित्यावर मर्यादा. केवळ नियतकालिके. ठरावीक काळात प्रकाशित झालेली नियतकालिके याप्रमाणे निवड करून तयार केलेली ग्रंथसूची.

partical contents note – अनुक्रमणिकेतील काही महत्त्वाच्या नोंदी समाविष्ट केलेले टिपण.

partial title – **आंशिक ग्रंथनाम/ग्रंथनामाचा उत्तरार्ध.**

partition – **विभाजन** – संगणक स्मरणिकेतील माहितीचे विभाजन.

passive documentation – **मागणीनुसार प्रलेखन** – वाचकाने माहितीची मागणी केल्यानंतर केलेले प्रलेखन.

password – **प्रवेश संकेतशब्द** – संगणकाला कामासाठी सुरुवात करताना उपयोजकाने प्रवेश मिळविण्यासाठी लिहिण्याचा सांकेतिक शब्द.

patent – **एकस्व/व्यक्त/प्रकट सनद/विशेषाधिकार** – पेटंट कार्यालयाद्वारे नोंदणी आणि प्रसिद्ध केलेले प्रकाशन ज्यामध्ये संशोधकांनी केलेल्या संशोधनासंबंधीची पूर्ण माहिती लेटर्स–पेटंटद्वारे शोध लावणाऱ्याचे संपूर्ण हित विशिष्ट काळाकरिता सुरक्षित ठेवण्यात आले आहे.

patent Act – **एकस्व अधिनियम/नियम** – मूळ शोधकास स्वामित्व प्रदान करणारा कायदा.

patent office – **एकस्व कार्यालय.**

patent Law – **एकस्व कायदा.**

patent literature – **एकस्व साहित्य** – संशोधनाच्या हक्काबद्दल सनद मिळविणे. अशी सनद उल्लेखिलेले साहित्य हे नवीन माहिती देणारे असते.

patent right – **एकस्व हक्क** – विशिष्ट शोधाबाबत स्वामित्वाचा अधिकार.

path – **मार्ग/दुवा** – संगणक जाळ्यातील कोणत्याही दोन संगणकाचे कार्य साधणारा दुवा.

patron / user / reader / clientele / member – **विशेष सभासद/आश्रयदाते** – ग्रंथालयाचे नोंदविलेले मुख्य सभासद.

patron record – **वाचक अभिलेख/दस्तऐवज.**

patronymic – **पूर्वपरंपरागत.**

pattern – **नमुना/साचा/पद्धती.**

pause instruction – **विराम सूचना** – स्थगिती सूचना चालू असलेले संगणककार्य तात्पुरते स्थगित करण्यासाठी संगणक आज्ञावलीला दिलेली सूचना.

pause entry – **विराम नोंद** – संगणक जाळ्यामध्ये माहितीचे प्रसारण करताना प्रसारण त्रुटी निर्माण झाल्यावर कितीवेळा परत प्रयत्न करावा, तसेच यशस्वी प्रसारणामध्ये कितीवेळ काम करावे याविषयी पर्यायी सूचना उपयोजकाने देण्यासाठी तयार केलेली संगणकजाळे नियंत्रण आज्ञावली.

payment – **पगार/शोधन** – कामाचा मोबदला/वेतन.

penname / pseudonym / nick name – **टोपणनाव** – व्यक्तीने लेखक म्हणून घेतलेले दुसरे नाव उदा. वि. वा. शिरवाडकर (कुसुमाग्रज)

pending (books) – **प्रलंबित (पुस्तके)** – वाचकाने वेळेवर परत न केलेली पुस्तके.

penumbral – **उपछाया/पडछाया.**

penumbral region – **पडछाया क्षेत्र.**

penultimate – **उपान्त्य** – अंत्यच्या मागचा.

penultimate class – **उपान्त्य वर्ग.**

peer review – **काळजीपूर्वक परीक्षण.**

peer reviewed journal – प्रकाशनास स्वीकारण्यापूर्वी लेख तज्ज्ञांकडून तपासून घेणारे नियतकालिक.

perfecting / perfect printing – **दुपाठी मुद्रण** – एकावेळी कागदाच्या दोन्ही बाजूस केलेली छपाई.

perfect binding – **दुपाठी बांधणी.**

perforation stamp – **छिद्रण शिक्का** – कागदावर छिद्र पाडून उमटविण्यात येणारा शिक्का.

performance evaluation – **कार्यमूल्यमापन** – सेवक कामे कशी करतात याविषयीचे मूल्यमापन, मूल्यांकन.

peripheral – **बाह्यपरिघीय** – एखाद्या विषयाच्या जवळील/परिचीय विषय, उपविषय.

period bibliography – **कालसंबद्ध ग्रंथसूची** – विशिष्ट कालमर्यादिसाठी केलेली ग्रंथसूची.

period division – **कालविभाजन**– (१) वर्गीकरण पद्धतीमध्ये केलेले विशिष्ट काळातील ग्रंथांच्या वर्गीकरणासाठीचे विभाजन. (२) तालिकेतील विषयशीर्षकाचे काळानुसार विभाजन. उदा. भारतीय स्वातंत्र्य लढ्याचा इतिहास इ.स. १७५७–१९४७

periodical – **नियतकालिक** – (१) जे प्रकाशन सहसा एकाच नावाने ठरावीक कालावधीने प्रकाशित होते व ज्यास सलग अंक व खंड क्रमांक असतात. (२) विशिष्ट कालावधीनुसार प्रसिद्ध होणारे प्रकाशन.

periodical article – **नियतकालिकातील लेख.**

periodical bibliography – नियतकालिकांची सूची – बरेचदा अनेक भागांमध्ये प्रसिद्ध केली जाते. विस्तारित पुरवणी प्रकाशित केली जाते.

periodical database – नियतकालिकांचा माहितीसंग्रह.

periodical holding list – नियतकालिकांची उपलब्ध यादी.

periodical index – नियतकालिकांचा निर्देश – (१) नियतकालिकाच्या एक वा अधिक खंडांसाठी दिलेला निर्देश. (२) नियतकालिकांच्या गटातून तयार केलेला विषयनिर्देश. हा बहुधा थोड्या थोड्या कालावधीने प्रकाशित करून संग्रहित केला जातो.

periodical collection – नियतकालिकांचा संग्रह – ग्रंथालयात असलेल्या नियतकालिके, वृत्तपत्रे, मालाप्रकाशन यांचा सुट्या स्वरूपात, बांधणी केलेला वा सूक्ष्मस्वरूपात असलेला ग्रंथ.

periodical display rack – नियतकालिके प्रदर्शनी – नियतकालिक प्रदर्शित करण्यासाठी बनविलेले कपाट.

periodical indexing – नियतकालिकांचे निर्देशन.

periodical list – नियतकालिकांची यादी.

periodical room – नियतकालिक कक्ष/खोली.

periodical section/division – नियतकालिक विभाग.

periodicity – नियतकाल – (१) नियतकालिकाचा प्रसिद्धी काळ. (२) दोन अंकांच्या प्रकाशनामधील कालावधी ज्यावरून प्रकाशनाची वर्गवारी होते. उदा. दैनिक, साप्ताहिक, पाक्षिक, मासिक इत्यादी.

peripheral units – संगणकाला जोडलेली इतर यंत्रसामग्री.

permission – अधिकृत परवानगी – लेखातील परिच्छेद, चित्रे यांचा उल्लेख करण्यासाठी मालकीहक्कानुसार घेतली गेलेली अधिकृत परवानगी.

permuted – क्रमसंचयित अदलाबदल.

permuted subject index – क्रमसंचयित विषय निर्देश – गुंतागुंतीच्या ग्रंथविषयातील प्रत्येक महत्त्वाच्या विषयाचा केलेला निर्देश.

permutation indexing – अदलाबदल निर्देशन – ग्रंथाच्या शीर्षकामध्ये परिचयात्मक टिपण, विभागाचे शीर्षक, अनुमान यामध्ये लेखकाने महत्त्वाच्या उल्लेखिलेल्या शब्दांची, वाक्यांची निवड निर्देशनातील नोंदीसाठी करणे.

permuted title index – अदलाबदल/क्रमसंचयित ग्रंथनाम निर्देश – ग्रंथनामातील प्रत्येक महत्त्वाच्या शब्दानुसार नोंद निर्देशामध्ये केली जाते.

personal – वैयक्तिक/व्यक्तिगत/व्यक्तिनिष्ठ/स्वत:चा.

personal author – व्यक्ती ग्रंथकार – व्यक्तिगत दायित्व असणारा ग्रंथकार.

personal authorship – **वैयक्तिक लेखकत्व** – संस्थेच्या कोणत्याही मदतीशिवाय स्वत:च्या जबाबदारीने स्वीकारलेले लेखनाचे लेखकत्व.

personal bibliography – **व्यक्तिनिष्ठ ग्रंथसूची** – व्यक्तिविषयी किंवा व्यक्तीने लिहिण्याच्या ग्रंथाची सूची.

personal catalogue – **व्यक्तिविषयक तालिका** – विशिष्ट व्यक्तीने लिहिलेल्या आणि त्या व्यक्तीविषयी लिहिलेल्या ग्रंथांची नोंद केलेली तालिका.

personal collection – **व्यक्तिगत संग्रह** – एखाद्या व्यक्तीने केलेला खासगी स्वरूपाचा ग्रंथसंग्रह.

personal communication – **व्यक्तिगत संप्रेषण** – दोन व्यक्तींमधील संप्रेषण.

personal computer / microcomputer – **वैयक्तिक संगणक.**

personal library – **व्यक्तिगत ग्रंथालय/खासगी ग्रंथालय** – एका व्यक्तीचा स्वत:चा ग्रंथसंग्रह.

personal name / forename – **व्यक्तीचे स्वत:चे नाव.**

personal papers – **खासगी कागदपत्रे** – विशिष्ट व्यक्तीचे, व्यक्तीविषयक खासगी कागदपत्रे.

personal service – **व्यक्तिगत सेवा.**

personal secretary – **खासगी सचिव/स्वीय सचिव** – अधिकाऱ्यास मदत करणारा साहाय्यक.

personal staff – **स्वीय कर्मचारी.**

personal facet – **व्यक्तिपैलू/मुख** – वर्गीकरण करताना ग्रंथाविषयीच्या अंगभूत अक्षरांचा सर्वात महत्त्वाच्या घटकांचा विचार करून विषयांची अविभाज्यता, अन्यसाधारणत: हे वैशिष्ट्य व्यक्त केले जाते असा डॉ. रंगनाथन् यांनी विशद केलेला विषयाचा विभेदक गुण.

personality isolate – **व्यक्तित्व उपांग.**

personnel – **कर्मचारी वर्ग.**

personnel management – **सेवकवर्ग/कर्मचारी वर्ग व्यवस्थापन** – एखाद्या संस्थेतील सर्व सेवकवर्गाचे व्यवस्थापन. त्याद्वारे जास्तीत जास्त काम व्हावे या दृष्टीने प्रयत्न करणे.

phase – **प्रावस्था/विषयांग/अंग** – वर्गीकरणामध्ये गुंतागुंतीच्या विषयांचा एक भाग. साधारणत: वेगळ्या विषयांची आंतरक्रिया म्हणजे 'प्रावस्था नातेसंबंध' याचे साधारणत: पाच प्रकार. (Form, Bias, Influencing, Comparision & Tool phase) प्रारूप, कल, प्रभावी, तुलना, साधन प्रावस्था.

phase analysis – **प्रावस्था/विषय विश्लेषण.**

phase relation – **प्रावस्था संबंध** – दोन बाजूंतील (विषयांमधील) संबंध.

philosophical classification – **तत्त्वज्ञानात्मक/ज्ञान वर्गीकरण** – अनेकविध माहितीचे विषयानुसार केलेले वर्गीकरण.

phoenetic writing – **ध्वनिलेखन** – चिन्हांचा अर्थ, वस्तू वा कल्पनेपेक्षा विशिष्ट ध्वनी दर्शवितो.

phoenix schedules – **फिनिक्स अनुसूची** – एका ठिकाणी अगोदर असलेली अनुसूची नाहीशी करून त्या जागी नव्याने तयार केलेली अनुसूची घालणे. जळाल्यानंतर स्वतःच्या राखेतून परत उत्पन्न होणारा एक पक्षी, 'फिनिक्स पक्षी' म्हणून 'फिनिक्स' या नावावरून या अनुसूचीस 'फिनिक्स' असे म्हटले आहे.

phonogram – **ध्वनिचिन्ह** – विशिष्ट ध्वनीसाठी वापरलेले चिन्ह.

phonograph – **ध्वनिमुद्रणाचे साधन** – ध्वनीची नोंद करण्यासाठी वापरण्याचे साधन.

phonograph record / gramophone record – **ध्वनिमुद्रिका** – ध्वनीचे मुद्रण करण्यासाठी वापरण्याची तबकडी.

phonoroll – **ध्वनिपट.**

photo copier / xerox machine – **छायाचित्रपत्र यंत्र** – छायाचित्रपत्र, छायाप्रत काढण्याचे यंत्र, झेरॉक्स यंत्र.

photocopy / xerox copy – **छायाचित्रपत्र** – झेरॉक्सच्या साहाय्याने प्रत तयार करणे.

photography – **छायाचित्रमुद्रण** – छायाचित्र काढण्याची कला.

photolithography – **छायाशीलामुद्रण.**

photomicrography – **सूक्ष्मछायाचित्रण.**

photostat – **लेख छायाचित्र.**

photozincography – **फोटो झिंको मुद्रण** – चित्रे, रेखाचित्रे यांचे पुनर्मुद्रण करण्याचे तंत्र. जस्ताच्या तबकडीवरील नक्षी, चित्र यांचे छायाचित्रण तंत्राने केलेले मुद्रण.

phrase searching – **पदबंध शोध** – पदबंध, शब्दसमूह देऊन घेतलेला शोध.

physical bibliography / descriptive bibliography – **वर्णनात्मक ग्रंथसूची** – ग्रंथाचे संपूर्णतः प्रत्यक्ष वर्णनाची नोंद केलेली ग्रंथसूची.

physical description – **खंडपृष्ठादिवृत्त.**

physical area – **ग्रंथरूप निर्देश क्षेत्र** – तालिका नोंदीमधील प्रत्यक्ष वर्णनाचे क्षेत्र.

physical form of catalogue – **तालिकेचे प्राकृतिक प्रकार.**

pica – **पाइका** – मुद्रणातील ठशाचा एक प्रकार. बारा पॉईंट = एक पायका

pictography – **चित्रलेखकला** – चित्रमय साहित्य.

pictorial map – **चित्रमय नकाशा.**

picture book – **चित्रमय पुस्तक.**

picture collection / picture file – चित्रांचा संग्रह.

pin pointed – लक्ष्यभेदी/विशिष्ट.

piracy – अनधिकृत ग्रंथप्रकाशन – स्वामित्व, हक्क धारण करणाऱ्याच्या परवानगीशिवाय केलेले प्रकाशन.

pirated edition – अपहृत आवृत्ती/ अनधिकृत आवृत्ती – लेखकाच्या/प्रकाशकाच्या परवानगीशिवाय प्रकाशित केलेली आवृत्ती. लेखन हक्काचे अधिकार डावलून काढलेली आवृत्ती.

placard catalogue – फलकतालिका – ग्रंथालयात मोठ्या फलकावर प्रदर्शित केलेल्या ग्रंथांची सूची.

place bibliography – स्थानीय ग्रंथसूची – विशिष्ट स्थानाविषयी लिहिलेल्या ग्रंथांची सूची.

place of publication – प्रकाशनस्थळ – तालिका किंवा ग्रंथसूचीमध्ये नोंद करताना ग्रंथ कोठे प्रकाशित झाला याचा केलेला स्थान उल्लेख.

place names – ठिकाणांची/स्थळांची नावे.

plain paper copier – साध्या/कोऱ्या कागदावरील छायालेखनयंत्र – साध्या, कोऱ्या कागदावर लेखांच्या प्रती काढण्यासाठी वापरण्यात येणारी साधनसामग्री वा यंत्र, झेरॉक्स यंत्र.

plagiarism – वाङ्मयचौर्य – दुसऱ्या व्यक्तीच्या लेखनातील मजकूर स्वतःचे लेखन म्हणून वापरणे.

plan – योजना/कट – विशिष्ट कामाचे केलेले नियोजन.

plan grants – योजना अनुदान – योजनांतर्गत खर्च, पंचवार्षिक योजना, वार्षिक विकास योजना अथवा प्रकल्पासाठी मंजूर केलेल्या व टप्प्याटप्प्याने प्राप्त होणाऱ्या रकमा.

planning – नियोजन – नियोजनाची कृती.

plane – स्तर/पातळी/क्षेत्र अवस्था – (१) विचारांचा, अस्तित्वाचा स्तर (२) द्विबिंदू वर्गीकरणामध्ये डॉ. रंगनाथन् यांनी वापरलेली संकल्पना. तीन प्रकार– विचार, चिन्हांकन, शाब्दिक अवस्था.

plate – चित्रपृष्ठ – ग्रंथामध्ये समाविष्ट केलेल्या छायाचित्रांचे पृष्ठ.

plates volume – खंड प्रकाशनामध्ये मजकुराशी संबंधित केवळ चित्रपृष्ठ असणारा खंड.

plotter – आलेखित – संगणकातील चित्रे, तक्ते, रेखाचित्रे यांच्या छपाईसाठी वापरले जाणारे विशिष्ट साधन.

pocket book – क्षेत्रफळाने/आकाराने छोटे पुस्तक – हातात मावेल एवढे पुस्तक.

pocket card charging / Browne charging system – नीना इ ब्राऊन यांची ग्रंथपत्र नोंदींद्वारे ग्रंथ देवघेव करण्याची पद्धती.

pocket edition – लघु आवृत्ती/छोटी आवृत्ती – संपूर्ण आवृत्ती छोट्या आकारात उपलब्ध ग्रंथाची लहान आकारातील आवृत्ती.

point – बिंदू/दशांशचिन्ह.

point measurement of type – मुद्राक्षर बिंदूमापन.

pointer – दर्शक – संगणकातील माहितीचे अचूक स्थान दर्शविण्यासाठी असलेला दर्शक.

policy – नीती/धोरण.

polygot – **बहुभाषिक ग्रंथ** – एकाच मजकुराचे अनेक भाषांमध्ये साधारणपणे समांतर स्तंभांमध्ये केलेले लेखन.

polygraphic book– अनेक ग्रंथकारांनी लिहिलेले पुस्तक.

polygraphy – अनेक प्रकारचे एक किंवा अधिक ग्रंथकांचे एकत्र लेखन असलेले पुस्तक.

pool of libraries – ग्रंथायतन – ग्रंथालयांचा समूह.

popular book – **लोकप्रिय ग्रंथ** – जास्त प्रमाणात वाचकांची मागणी असणारा ग्रंथ.

popular edition – **लोकप्रिय आवृत्ती** – हलका कागद, कमी चित्रे वापरून लोकप्रिय ठरावी अशी कमी किमतीत उपलब्ध केलेली आवृत्ती.

popular journal – लोकप्रिय नियतकालिक.

popular name – **लोकप्रिय नाव** – (व्यक्तीचे/संस्थेचे) रूढ नाव.

pornography – **अश्लील वाङ्मय** – अश्लील मजकूर असलेले साहित्य.

portable computer / laptop – **सुवहनी संगणक** – लहान आकाराचा, सहज जवळ बाळगता येणारा संगणक.

portable document format (PDF) – **सुवहनी प्रलेख प्रारूप** – ॲक्रोबॅट रिडरच्या साहाय्याने वाचनीय प्रारूप.

portolan chart / portulation chart – १३ ते १६व्या शतकादरम्यान खलाशांसाठी तयार केलेला मार्गदर्शक तक्ता.

portrait – **व्यक्तिचित्र** – एखाद्या व्यक्तीचे काढलेले चित्र किंवा त्याच्या प्रत्यक्ष रूपानुसार तयार केलेले छायाचित्र किंवा चेहऱ्याचे छायाचित्र.

postal circulation – **डाक परिचलन** – डाक सेवेद्वारे ग्रंथांचा पुरवठा करणे.

poster – भिंतीचित्र/भित्तीचित्र.

post co-ordinate indexing system – **पश्चात-समन्वय निर्देशन पद्धती/उत्तरान्वयी सूचीकरण**– (१) ज्यामध्ये शब्द सोप्या क्रमाने असतात. ज्यामुळे वाचकांना संयुक्त विषय शोधणे सोपे जाते अशी सूचीकरण पद्धती. (२) निर्देशकाने शीर्षक म्हणून साध्या संकल्पनांची निवड करून त्याखाली अनेक नोंदी केलेल्या असतात. उपयोजकाने त्यातील नोंदी एकत्रित विचारात घेऊन विषय लक्षात घेणे आवश्यक ठरते.

post dated - प्रत्यक्ष तारखेनंतरचा प्रकाशन दिनांक.

posteriorising - **परावर्ती** - नंतरच्या क्रमाने येणारा.

posteriorising common isolates - **उत्तरावर्ती/परावर्ती सामान्य उपविभाग** - (१) द्विबिंदू वर्गीकरण पद्धतीमधील सामान्य उपविभागाचा प्रकार. (२) द्विबिंदू वर्गीकरणामध्ये सखोल माहिती दर्शविण्यासाठी जोडचिन्हाचा वापर करून दर्शविलेला उपविभाग. उदा. अहवाल, चर्चा इ. दर्शविण्यासाठी उपयुक्त. उदा. चं-टीका तसेच द - चं वाङ्मयीन टीका.

posteriorising sub-division - **उत्तरावर्ती सामान्य उपविभाग.**

posthumous work - **मरणोत्तर प्रकाशन** - लेखकाच्या मृत्यूनंतर झालेले प्रकाशन.

postulate - **आधारतत्त्व गृहीते** - स्वीकृत कल्पना जिची सत्यता पडताळली जात नाही. याचा उपयोग ग्रंथ वर्गीकरण व तालिकीकरणात केला जातो.

postulate of concreteness - **निश्चितपणाचे आधारतत्त्व.**

postulate of fundamental - **मूलभूततेचे आधारतत्त्व.**

postulate isolate facet - **उपांग पैलूचे आधारतत्त्व.**

postulate of level - **स्तराचे आधारतत्त्व.**

postulate of round for energy - **ऊर्जेच्या चक्राचे आधारतत्त्व.**

postulate of rounds for personality & matter - **व्यक्तित्व आणि पदार्थांच्या चक्राचे आधारतत्त्व.**

postulate of sequence - **क्रमाचे आधारतत्त्व.**

postulate sequence in a round - **क्रमचक्राचे आधारतत्त्व.**

postulate space & time facet - **स्थान/काळ पैलूंचे आधारतत्त्व.**

postulate - **Based permuted Subject Indexing (POPSI)** - प्रलेखन संशोधन आणि प्रशिक्षण केंद्र, बंगलोर यांनी विकसित केलेली एक निर्देशन पद्धती.

practical - **प्रात्यक्षिक** - केवळ सिद्धान्तापेक्षा प्रत्यक्षपणे करता येणारा प्रयोग.

practically - **व्यावहारिकता** - उपयोगिता, तर्कशुद्धतेऐवजी उपयुक्तता.

preamcle - **हेतू/प्रस्ताव** - हेतू, कारणे, उद्देश इ.चा उल्लेख असणारा प्रस्ताव.

pre-co-ordinate indexing system - **पूर्वसमन्वय/पूर्वन्वयी निर्देशन पद्धती** - (१) प्रलेखाचे निर्देशन करताना संज्ञांचा समन्वय केला जातो. नोंदीमध्ये संज्ञा-समन्वय दर्शविला जातो. (२) मागणीचा अंदाज घेऊन अशी पद्धती तयार केली जाते. जी संज्ञा समन्वय साधते किंवा एकत्रित करून एक विषय बनविला जातो. सर्व वर्गीकरण पद्धती म्हणूनच पूर्वसमन्वय पद्धती होत.

preface – **प्रस्तावना** – (१) ग्रंथातील लेखकाचे उत्तरदायित्व ज्यात उद्देश/पद्धती, उपयोगिता ह्यांची माहिती व विचार यांचे दिलेले प्रास्ताविक.

prefered term – **प्राधान्य संज्ञा** – थिसॉरसमध्ये प्राधान्य संज्ञा देऊन समानार्थी संज्ञा या त्याखाली क्रमाने दिल्या जातात.

preliminaries / preliminary part – **विषयपूर्व भाग** – मुख्य मजकुरापूर्वी येणारा (ग्रंथशीर्षक पृष्ठ, प्रस्तावना, अनुक्रमणिका) ग्रंथाचा भाग.

preliminary cataloguing – **प्राथमिक तालिकीकरण** – ग्रंथालयशास्त्र पारंगत व्यक्तिव्यतिरिक्त कर्मचाऱ्याने केलेले तालिकीकरण. या तालिकीकरणाची नंतर तालिकाकार ग्रंथानुरूप तपासणी करतो.

preliminary edition / provisional edition – **प्राथमिक आवृत्ती** – मुख्य आवृत्तीपूर्वी तयार केलेली आवृत्ती.

preliminary leaf / pages – **प्राथमिक पृष्ठे** – ग्रंथातील सुरुवातीची क्रमांक न दिलेली पृष्ठे.

prenatal – **प्रकाशनपूर्व** – ग्रंथावर प्रकाशनपूर्व तांत्रिक सोपस्कार करणे.

prenatal cataloguing / cataloguing in publication – **प्रकाशनपूर्व तालिकीकरण** – ग्रंथाचे प्रकाशन करताना ग्रंथामध्ये तालिकानोंद उपलब्ध करणे.

prenatal classification – **प्रकाशनपूर्व वर्गीकरण** – ग्रंथाचे प्रकाशन करताना ग्रंथामध्ये वर्गांकाचा उल्लेख करणे.

pre-paid – **पूर्व प्राप्त** – पूर्वीच रक्कम मिळाली असल्याचे प्रमाणित करणे.

pre-print – **पूर्वमुद्रिते/मुद्रितपूर्व साहित्य** – (१) संपूर्ण पुस्तकाचे प्रकाशन होण्यापूर्वी काही भागांची मुद्रिते. (२) परिषदवृत्ते प्रकाशित होण्यापूर्वी प्रकाशित झालेला लेख.

pre-processed book – **पूर्व संस्कारित ग्रंथ** – ग्रंथविक्रेत्याने दिलेला पूर्व-संस्कारित ग्रंथ.

pre publication – **प्रकाशनपूर्व वितरण** – वैज्ञानिक किंवा तांत्रिक लेखांची प्रकाशनापूर्वी काही प्रतींमध्ये वितरण करण्याची व्यवस्था.

pre publication cataloguing – **प्रकाशनपूर्व तालिकीकरण** – राष्ट्रीय ग्रंथालयामध्ये प्रकाशनाचे ग्रंथ-परीक्षणासाठी दिलेल्या ग्रंथाचे तालिकीकरण.

pre publication price – **प्रकाशनपूर्व किंमत** – प्रकाशन दिनांकापूर्वी मागणी नोंदविल्यास द्यावी लागणारी ग्रंथाची किंमत. ही बहुधा सवलतमूल्य असते.

prescribed – **निर्धारित/विहित/क्रमिक** – नेमून दिलेला, विहित.

prescribed book – **क्रमिक पुस्तके** – वाचनासाठी, अभ्यासक्रमासाठी नेमलेली पुस्तके.

prescribed curriculum / syllabus – **विहित पाठ्यक्रम** – एखाद्या अभ्यासक्रमासाठी नेमलेला अभ्यासक्रम.

presentation copy – भेटप्रत – भेट देण्यासाठी विशेष ग्रंथप्रत.

preservation – जतन/संरक्षण – (१) महत्त्वाच्या ग्रंथांचे सुरक्षितरीत्या जतन करणे. (२) खराब होण्यापासून वस्तूंची काळजी घेणे.

Perserved Context Indexing System (PRECIS) – प्रेसिस – डेरेक ऑस्टिन यांनी ब्रिटिश राष्ट्रीय ग्रंथसूचीसाठी विकसित केलेली निर्देशन पद्धती.

press – छापखाना – वाचनसाहित्य छापण्याचे ठिकाण.

press and registration of books Act. – मुद्रण आणि ग्रंथनोंदणीचा १९५२ साली मंजूर केलेला कायदा.

press clippings / press cuttings – वृत्तपत्रातील कात्रणे – वृत्तपत्रातील उपयुक्त माहितीचे कात्रण काढून जतन करण्याचे काम.

press errors – मुद्रणातील त्रुटी – ग्रंथछपाईतील चुका.

press marks – मुद्रणचिन्ह.

press release – विमोचन/प्रकाशन – वृत्तपत्रांना पुरविलेली अधिकृत माहिती.

presumed author / attributed author / supposed author – संदिग्ध ग्रंथकार –लेखकत्वाविषयी संशय असल्यामुळे ज्याला ग्रंथलेखनाचे श्रेय मिळते तो संदिग्ध ग्रंथकार.

primary – प्राथमिक/मूलगामी/मूळ.

primary access – संगणकप्रक्रियेमध्ये माहितीसंचासाठी मिळणारा प्राथमिक प्रवेश.

primary bibliography – प्राथमिक ग्रंथसूची – ग्रंथालयात उपलब्ध असलेल्या ग्रंथांची सर्वसाधारण सूची.

primary literature material – प्राथमिक साहित्य.

primary periodicals / primary journal – प्राथमिक/मूलगामी नियतकालिके – अशा नियतकालिकांमध्ये आजपर्यंत प्रकाशित न झालेली अशी नवीन संशोधनात्मक माहिती असते. संशोधनात्मक लेख प्रकाशित करणारे नियतकालिक.

primary publication – प्राथमिक प्रकाशन – मूलभूत मजकूर (उदा. संशोधनाचे निष्कर्ष) असलेले प्रकाशन.

primary source – प्राथमिक स्तोत्र/साधन – मूळ साहित्य.

primary sources of information / original sources – प्राथमिक माहिती साधने/प्राथमिक प्राप्तीस्थाने – (१) मूळ हस्तलिखिते समकालीन अभिलेख किंवा लेखकांचे ग्रंथ किंवा अन्य वाङ्मयीन संकलन करताना उपयोगात आणलेले मूळ साहित्य. (२) माहिती पहिल्यांदा प्रकाशित करणारी प्रकाशने. उदा. मूळ हस्तलिखित प्रत, नियतकालिके, पेटंट्स, परिषदवृत्ते इ.

primary school library - प्राथमिक शालेय ग्रंथालय.

primary education - प्राथमिक शिक्षण - माध्यमिक शिक्षणापूर्वीचे शिक्षण.

principal author - प्रमुख लेखक - मुख्य लेखक.

principle - सिद्धान्त/तत्त्व - व्यक्तिगत वर्तनाचा नियम, नीतीनियम.

principle of alphabetical sequence - अनुवर्णक्रमाचे तत्त्व.

principle of away from position - स्थितीपासून दूरतेचे तत्त्व.

principle of bottom upward - तळ ऊर्ध्वमुखाचे तत्त्व.

principle of classification - वर्गीकरणाची तत्त्वे - वर्गीकरणकाराने वर्गीकरण पद्धती तयार करताना वापरायची तत्त्वे.

principle of clockwise - घड्याळाच्या गतीच्या दिशेने प्रवासाचे तत्त्व.

principle of commercial sequence - व्यापारी क्रमाचे तत्त्व.

principle of increasing concreteness - वाढत्या मूर्ततेचे तत्त्व.

principle of increasing complexity - जटिलता वृद्धीचे तत्त्व.

principle of inversion - स्थानबदलाचे/पर्यसनाचे/व्युत्क्रम तत्त्व.

principle of later-in - evolution - उत्क्रांतीनुसार रचनेचे तत्त्व.

principle of later-in-time - कालगणनेनुसार रचनेचे तत्त्व.

principle of left to right - डावीकडून उजवीकडे क्रम असणारे तत्त्व.

principle of literary warrant - साहित्य-निर्मिती प्रमाणाचे तत्त्व.

principle of special contiguity - विशेष सान्निध्यानुसारचे तत्त्व.

printed - मुद्रित/छापील.

printed catalogue - मुद्रित तालिका - पुस्तक स्वरूपात छापलेली ग्रंथांची यादी.

printer - छपाईयंत्र.

printout - संगणकावरून काढलेला मुद्रित संदेश.

prison library / jail library - तुरुंग ग्रंथालय/कारागृह ग्रंथालय - कैद्यांसाठी असलेले ग्रंथालय.

private library - खासगी ग्रंथालय - संस्थेचे वा व्यक्तीचे खासगी वापरासाठी असलेले ग्रंथालय.

probation - उमेदवारी - उमेदवारी अगर उमेदवारीचा काळ.

proclem - प्रश्न/विवक्षा - समजायला किंवा सोडवायला अवघड अशी गोष्ट.

procedure – **रीती/कार्यपद्धती** – एखादी गोष्ट करण्याचा नेहमीचा किंवा योग्य मार्ग.

procedure manual / work manual – **कार्यपद्धती निर्देशपुस्तिका.**

process – **प्रक्रिया/उपस्कार** – एखादी गोष्ट साध्य करण्यासाठी केलेल्या क्रिया.

proforma invoice / bill – **देयपत्रक.**

proceedings – **इतिवृत्ते** – सभा, परिषदा, कार्यशाळा इ.ची वृत्ते.

processing of books – **ग्रंथोपस्कार** – ग्रंथावर करण्यात येणाऱ्या ग्रंथालयीन प्रक्रिया.

proctustean bed – ग्रीक पौराणिक कथेतून एकरूपता निर्माण करणारी प्रवृत्ती.

profession – **व्यवसाय** – विषयाचे खास ज्ञान आणि कौशल्य लागणारा व्यवसाय.

professional assistant – **व्यावसायिक साहाय्यक.**

professional staff – **व्यावसायिक/प्रशिक्षित कर्मचारी** – व्यावसायिक कौशल्य अवगत असलेला कर्मचारी.

professional tax – **व्यवसाय कर** – व्यावसायिक/नोकरदार यांचेवर शासनाने आकारलेला विशिष्ट कर.

profile – **रूपरेषा** – विषयाची रूपरेषा (संचयी) माहितीपत्रक.

program – **आज्ञावली** – (१) संगणकाची आज्ञावली (२) विशिष्ट काम संगणकाकडून करवून घेण्यासाठी त्याच्या भाषेत लिहिलेल्या आदेशांना 'आज्ञावली' असे म्हणतात. सर्वसाधारणपणे कुठलीही एक क्रिया करण्यासाठी ज्या आज्ञा संगणकास दिल्या जातात त्यास 'आज्ञावली' असे म्हणतात.

programme – **कार्यक्रम** – कार्य पार पाडण्याकरिता विचार समूहाशी समन्वय साधणे.

programmer – **सूचनापटकार/आज्ञावलीकार** – संगणकाची आज्ञावली तयार करणारी व्यक्ती.

Programme Evaluation Review Technique/Critical Path Method (PERT/CPM) – **कार्यमूल्यमापन आणि अवलोकन तंत्र** – संगणकावर आधारित अशी नियोजन आणि नियंत्रण पद्धती. यांचा उपयोग हा वरिष्ठ स्तरावरील व्यवस्थापनास आवश्यक असतो.

project oriented – **प्रकल्पाभिमुख/प्रयोगाभिमुख.**

projected book – **प्रक्षेपित ग्रंथ** – सूक्ष्मचित्रफितीवरील ग्रंथांचे शारीरिक अपंग व्यक्तींच्या सोयीसाठी केलेले प्रक्षेपण.

projection – **प्रक्षेपण करणे** – पृथ्वीच्या पृष्ठभागाचा संपूर्ण किंवा काही भाग सपाट भागावर दाखविण्यासाठी नकाशाकाराने वापरलेली पद्धत.

proliferation – **अनियंत्रित वाढ** – प्रमाणाबाहेर आणि वेगाने वाढ.

promotion – पदोन्नती/प्रगती/उत्कर्ष – उत्तेजन देणे किंवा प्रोत्साहन देणे, उत्पादन सेवा, संस्था इत्यादी.

promotion of reading habits – *वाचन सवयीची वाढ.*

proof – *खरडा* – ग्रंथाची अंतिम छपाई करण्यापूर्वी काढलेली प्रत.

proof reader – *मुद्रित वाचक/मुद्रित शोधक* – ग्रंथ/मजकूर छापण्यास जाण्यापूर्वी कच्चे मुद्रण तपासणारी व्यक्ती.

prompt copy – *मार्गदर्शक प्रत* – वाचकासाठी पडद्यामागे त्वरित मार्गदर्शन करणाऱ्या व्यक्तीसाठी तयार केलेली नाटकाची प्रत. यात वेशभूषा, अभिनय, स्थान, पात्रांचे वैशिष्ट्य यांच्या उल्लेखांसह संवाद छापले जातात.

proper names – *योग्य/उचित/बरोबर नावे.*

pronounceable notation / syllabic notation – *सहज उच्चारता येण्याजोगे चिन्हांकन.*

property counter – *मालमत्ता कट्टा* – ग्रंथालयाच्या प्रवेशद्वाराजवळ असलेला काउंटर. जेथे वाचक आपल्या जवळील वस्तू, जसे पिशवी, ग्रंथ, छत्री ठेवतात. त्याबद्दल वाचकाला बिल्ला अथवा टोकन देण्यात येते. या वस्तू ग्रंथालयात नेण्याची परवानगी नसते.

property phase relation – *गुणधर्म वस्तुमुख संबंध.*

property tax – *जिंदगी/मिळकतकर/मालमत्ताकर.*

proprietary information – *संस्थेतील गोपनीय माहिती.*

prospectus – *माहितीपत्रक* – संस्थेचे/ग्रंथालयाचे माहितीपत्रक.

protocols – *नियमावली/संदेशाचार* – संप्रेषण पद्धतीतील दोन वा अधिक संगणकदुव्यांमध्ये माहितीची अदलाबदल करण्यासाठी साहाय्यक असा नियमांचा संच.

provisional edition / preliminary edition – *प्राथमिक/तत्पुरती आवृत्ती* – मुख्य प्रकाशनापूर्वी काढलेली आवृत्ती, टीका, टिप्पणी, निरीक्षणे, सूचना यांचा विचार करून अंतिम आवृत्ती काढली जाते.

proximity – *जवळीक/सान्निध्य.*

pseudandry – *टोपणनावाने लिखाण करणे.*

pseudo – *छद्म/आभासी* – सत्य नसलेले, काल्पनिक, असत्य.

pseudo abstract – *सारांश प्रतिकृतीलेख* – पुढे लिहिल्या जाणाऱ्या लेखाचा सारांश. परंतु हा लेख नंतर प्रकाशित होऊ शकला नाही असा सारांश.

pseudo classic book – *आभासी अभिजात ग्रंथ* – अभिजात म्हणून मानण्यास पात्र नसलेले परंतु, समीक्षा किंवा विडंबन करण्यास उपयुक्त ठरणारे ग्रंथ अथवा वाचनसाहित्य.

pseudo entity – काल्पनिक अस्तित्व.

pseudo series – आभासी माला.

pseudonym / pen name / allonym – टोपण नाव – (१) ग्रंथकाराने धारण केलेले अवास्तव वा खोटे नाव. (२) व्यक्तीने लेखक म्हणून घेतलेले दुसरे नाव.

public library – सार्वजनिक ग्रंथालय –
(१) जनतेच्या पैशातून उभे केलेले, सर्वांसाठी सेवा देणारे ग्रंथालय.
(२) जनतेच्या पैशातून जनतेसाठी चालविले जाणारे ग्रंथालय जेथे जात, वंश, धर्म, असा प्रवेशासाठी भेदभाव केला जात नाही.

public library Act / Law – सार्वजनिक ग्रंथालय अधिनियम.

public library manifesto – सार्वजनिक ग्रंथालय घोषणापत्र/जाहीरनामा.

public library services – सार्वजनिक सेवा.

public library system – सार्वजनिक ग्रंथालय व्यवस्था.

publication – प्रकाशन – (१) प्रकाशित साहित्य. (२) विशिष्ट लेखन वाचकांना उपलब्ध करण्यासाठी संस्करण करून प्रसिद्ध केलेले साहित्य.

publicaton date / date of publication – प्रकाशन दिनांक – प्रकाशन केल्याचा दिनांक.

publication division – प्रकाशन विभाग.

publication year / year of publication – प्रकाशन वर्ष.

publisher – प्रकाशक – ग्रंथ प्रकाशित करण्यास जबाबदार असलेली व्यक्ती/संस्था.

publisher bibliography – प्रकाशन ग्रंथसूची – प्रकाशनांची नावे व इतर माहिती देणारी सूची.

publisher catalogue – प्रकाशकांची ग्रंथसूची/तालिका – प्रकाशकांनी विक्रीसाठी प्रकाशित केलेल्या ग्रंथांची यादी.

publisher's binding / edition binding – मूळ/प्रकाशक बांधणी.

publisher's series – प्रकाशनमाला – एकाच शीर्षकाखाली प्रकाशित होणाऱ्या ग्रंथांची मालिका.

punched cards – छिद्रितपत्र/अक्षपत्रे – प्रत्येक छिद्र विशिष्ट माहिती दर्शविते. या पत्राचा उपयोग माहितीची प्रतिप्रासी करण्यासाठी होतो.

puff title – प्रचारी ग्रंथनाम – १७व्या शतकात वापरलेली संज्ञा. लेखक किंवा प्रकाशकाने ग्रंथाची जाहिरात करण्यासाठी माहितीपत्रकामध्ये किंवा मुखपृष्ठावर द्यावयाचे 'गौरवपर शीर्षक'.

punctuation – विरामचिन्ह.

punctuation marks – विरामचिन्हे – वर्गीकरणासाठी व लेखनासाठी वापरायची चिन्हे.

purchase of books – ग्रंथखरेदी – ग्रंथोपार्जनाचा प्रकार, ज्यामध्ये साहित्य विकत घेतले जाते.

pure bibliography – शुद्ध ग्रंथसूची – ग्रंथातील मजकुराचे मूल्य ठरविणारी ग्रंथसूची. ग्रंथसमीक्षेचा अंतर्भाव यात केला जातो.

pure notation – शुद्ध चिन्हांकन – (१) ज्यात फक्त एकाच प्रकारची/एकाच संचाची चिन्हे वापरली जातात असे चिन्हांकन. (२) एकाच प्रकारचे चिन्हांकन वर्गीकरण चिन्हांमध्ये केले जाते. उदा. ड्युई यांच्या दशांश वर्गीकरण पद्धतीत फक्त अरबी अंकांचा वापर चिन्हांकनासाठी केला आहे.

purely enumerative scheme – शुद्ध परिगणनात्मक पद्धती.

putting knowledge work – ज्ञानाचे कार्यान्वयन.

pyramid – कोनस्तूप/स्तूप/शंक्वाकृती.

qualification – पात्रता/योग्यता/अर्हता.

qualify – पात्र ठरणे/पात्र असणे/पात्रता फेरी गाठणे.

qualifying examination – विशिष्ट पदाकरिता निर्धारित परीक्षा.

qualifications educational – शैक्षणिक पात्रता.

qualifications desirable – इष्ट/वांछित अर्हता.

qualifications essential – आवश्यक अर्हता.

quantitative order – संख्यात्मक क्रम – संख्येनुसार रचना.

qualitative order – मूल्यात्मक क्रम – गुणानुसार रचना.

quantity – परिमाण/मात्रा/राशी/संचय/साठा.

quarterly – त्रैमासिक – दर तीन महिन्यांनी किंवा वर्षातून चार अंक प्रकाशित होणारे नियतकालिक.

quarto edition – चतकोर आवृत्ती – छोट्या आकाराची आवृत्ती.

quasi – class – सदृश वर्ग – वर्गीकरण पद्धतीमध्ये जो ग्रंथ वर्ग म्हणून मानला जातो किंवा तालिकीकरणामध्ये ज्याचे ग्रंथनाम 'विषयशीर्षक' म्हणून वापरले जाते असा ग्रंथ. हा सहसा पवित्र ग्रंथ किंवा उच्च साहित्यिक दर्जाचा अगर अभिजात ग्रंथ असतो.

quasi classic – सदृश चिरसाहित्य/अभिजात साहित्य.

quasi digit – सदृश्य चिन्ह.

quasi subject –सदृश्य विषय – स्वतंत्र विषय नाही परंतु ज्यास स्वतंत्र दर्जा दिला आहे असा विषय.

quasi isolate idea – सदृश उपांग विचार.

queing theory – अनुक्रमतत्त्व – ही एक संख्याशास्त्रावर आधारित तत्त्वप्रणाली आहे. याचा व्यवस्थापनामध्ये उपयोग पुढील बाबींसाठी केला जातो; संस्थेतील वेगवेगळ्या घटकांचे परस्पर संबंध प्रस्थापित व निश्चित करणे, वेगवेगळ्या विभागांची स्थाने निश्चित करणे, संस्थेतील विभागास आवश्यक अशा सुविधा आणि रसद पुरविण्याची व्यवस्था करणे. ग्रंथालय व्यवस्थापनात याचा उपयोग प्रचंड मागणी असणाऱ्या ग्रंथांच्या उपयोगामध्ये सुसूत्रता आणणे अथवा येणाऱ्या ग्रंथाचे ग्रंथसंस्करण करणे, इत्यादींकरिता केला जातो.

query – पृच्छा/शंका/प्रश्न विचारणे.

question – प्रश्न – चर्चा करण्यासाठी गोष्ट, समस्या.

question mark / interrogation mark / mark of interrogation – प्रश्नचिन्ह.

questionnaire – प्रश्नावली – (१) माहिती मिळविण्यासाठी विचारावयाच्या प्रश्नांची यादी. (२) सर्वेक्षण करताना प्रश्नावली तंत्राचा वापर केला जातो.

questionnaire – **closed** – बद्धप्रश्न असणारी प्रश्नावली.

questionnaire – **open ended** – मुक्त प्रश्न असणारी प्रश्नावली.

quick reference collection – तत्काळ संदर्भ संग्रह.

quick reference service – शीघ्रसंदर्भ सेवा – कमी वेळात दिली जाणारी संदर्भ सेवा.

quick reference book – तत्काळ संदर्भग्रंथ – विविध विषयांवरील तयार माहिती दिलेला ग्रंथ.

उदा. Book of Fact

quick time – तत्काळ वेळ.

quinquennial – पंचवार्षिक (प्रकाशन) – पाच वर्षांनी प्रकाशित होणारे प्रकाशन.

quotation – दरपत्रक/निविदा/अवतरण – उद्धृत केलेले शब्द/वाक्य/परिच्छेद इ.

quotation mark – अवतरण चिन्ह, (''........'') – वाक्यातील शब्दाचे महत्त्व दर्शविण्यासाठी वापरलेले चिन्ह.

quotes – उद्धरण देणे – पूर्वीच्या लेखनाचा दाखला देणे.

rack – दरवाजा नसलेले उंच कपाट, ग्रंथसंग्रह ठेवण्याचे साधन.

radial – **अरीय** – केंद्रासंबंधी, किरणासंबंधी.

rag paper – चिंध्यांपासून तयार केलेला कागद.

Raja Ram Mohan Roy Library Foundation (RRMRLF) – राजाराम मोहन रॉय ग्रंथालय **प्रतिष्ठान** – सार्वजनिक ग्रंथालयांचा विकास करण्यासाठी राष्ट्रीय स्तरावर स्थापन झालेली संस्था (स्थापना– १९७६) कोलकाता.

range – **व्याप्ती असणे** – समावेशन करणे.

rare book – **दुर्मिळ ग्रंथ** – बाजारात सहजपणे उपलब्ध नसलेली पुस्तके.

rairities bibliography – **दुर्मिळ ग्रंथांची सूची.**

ramification – **विषय विभागणी** – विषयाचे विभाग व उपविभाग.

ramifying classification / branching classification – **शाखात्मक वर्गीकरण** – दोन वा अधिक उपवर्गांचे विभाजन करून पुन: पुन्हा केलेले उपवर्ग रूपांतर काही वेळा तक्तारूपात वर्गमांडणी.

random – **ऐच्छिक/स्वैर/विनाधोरण** – कसेही केलेले किंवा निवडलेले, अहेतुपूर्वक निवडलेले.

random sample – **स्वैर नमुना** – कोणत्याही विशेष गुणधर्मांचा विचार न करता केलेली निवड. उदा. यादीतील सम/विषम जागेवरील घटक.

random sampling – **स्वैरनमुना चाचणी.**

Random Access Memory (RAM) – **स्वैर निवेश स्मृती** – तात्पुरत्या स्वरूपात आवश्यक आज्ञावली आणि माहिती साठविण्याची संगणकाच्या प्राथमिक संकलन विभागातील वापरलेली जागा. विशिष्ट काम झाल्यावर अथवा वीजप्रवाह खंडित झाल्यावर ही रिकामी होते अथवा त्यावरील साठवलेली माहिती पुसली जाते.

Ranganathan, S. R. (Dr.) – **रंगनाथन् एस. आर. (डॉ.)** – भारतीय ग्रंथालय शास्त्राचे पितामह ज्यांनी या विषयाच्या विकासासाठी स्वत:चे जीवन वाहून घेतले. (जन्म १८९२; मृत्यू १९७२)

ranked isolate – **दर्जात्मक उपांग** – विश्वाच्या उपांग व्यवस्थेत अशी प्रतवारी निश्चित केलेले व दर्जा असलेले उपांग.

rapid selector – **जलद चयनक.**

raw data – **संस्करणपूर्व कच्ची माहिती.**

reader / user / borrower / member / clientele / patron – **वाचक/उपयोजक** – ग्रंथालयाचा वापर करणारी व्यक्ती.

reader area – **वाचन क्षेत्र** – वाचकांसाठी राखून ठेवलेले ग्रंथालयातील विशिष्ट क्षेत्र.

reader service – **वाचक सेवा** – वाचकांसाठी उपलब्ध सेवा.

reader ticket – **वाचक पत्र**- ग्रंथालयाने वाचकाला दिलेले सभासद पत्र.

reader's advisory sevice – **वाचक सल्लागार सेवा.**

reader's card – **वाचकांचे वाचकपत्र** – वाचकांना ग्रंथालयाचा वापर करण्यासाठी दिलेले पत्र.

reader's record – **वाचकांची नोंद.**

reader's ticket – **सभासदपत्र/वाचकपत्र.**

readily available – **चटकन् उपलब्ध असणारे वाचनसाहित्य.**

reading – **वाचन** – वाचन म्हणजे लिखित संकेतांचा अर्थपूर्ण अवबोध; यात शब्दांची प्रत्यभिज्ञा, प्रवाह, आकलन इत्यादींचा समावेश होतो.

reading circle / reading club – **वाचनमंडळ/वाचकमंडळ.**

reading list – **वाचनसाहित्याची यादी** – वाचनासाठी सुचविलेल्या ग्रंथांची यादी.

reading material – **वाचनसाहित्य.**

reading room – **वाचन कक्ष**- वाचकांना ग्रंथ वाचण्याकरिता ग्रंथालयातील जागा.

read about translation – **जुजबी भाषांतर.**

Read Only Memory (ROM) – **न पठनमात्र स्मृती** – संगणकास वीजपुरवठा मिळाल्यावर त्यास सुरू करणाऱ्या आज्ञावलीची जागा वीजपुरवठा खंडित झाला तरी ती पुसली जात नाही किंवा त्यात बदलही करता येत नाही.

ready reference – तत्काळ/तयार संदर्भ – वाचकाला शंकानिरसन करण्यासाठी ताबडतोब पुरविलेली माहिती.

ready reference service – तत्काळ/तयार संदर्भ सेवा.

reallocation of grants – अनुदानाची पुनर्वाटणी – अर्थसंकल्पातील तरतूद शिल्लक राहिल्यास वर्ष अखेरीपूर्वी अन्य शीर्षकाकडे वर्ग करणे.

real name – वास्तविक/खरे नाव.

real time – सद्य: अनुक्रिया – संगणकाला पुरविलेल्या माहितीवर संगणकाने ताबडतोब केलेले संस्करण.

re-back – ग्रंथाच्या कण्याची दुरुस्ती/पुन: पृष्ठनियोजन.

re-bound – ग्रंथाची पुनर्बांधणी – खराब झाल्यामुळे किंवा नवीन पाने समाविष्ट करण्यासाठी पुन्हा बांधणी.

recall – पुनर्प्राप्ती – विचारलेल्या प्रश्नांसंबंधी जे उपलब्ध असेल, त्याची माहितीच्या संचयातून प्रतिप्राप्ती करणे.

recall factor – पुनर्प्राप्ती घटक.

recall notice – ग्रंथपुनर्मागणी सूचना – वाचकाला ग्रंथ त्वरित परत करण्याबाबत दिलेली सूचना.

reacall value – मागणी/पुनर्प्राप्ती मूल्य – मागणी संभवणारे मूल्य.

recall & precision – पुनर्मागणी आणि अचूकता – निर्देशन पद्धतीने मूल्यमापन करण्याकरिता या तंत्राचा उपयोग केला जातो. वाचकास हवे असलेले संदर्भ अचूकपणे व चटकन् मिळवून देणारी निर्देशन पद्धती, हीच योग्य पद्धती आहे.

recent – नवा/नवीनतम.

recent additions – नव्याने प्राप्त झालेले – एखाद्या ग्रंथालयात दाखल झालेला अलीकडील उपयुक्त संग्रह.

recent edition – अद्ययावत आवृत्ती – नजीकच्या काळात प्रसिद्ध झालेली अद्ययावत माहिती दिलेली आवृत्ती.

recension/redaction/revision – नूतनीकरण – साहित्याचे नूतनीकरण करून प्रकाशनयोग्य स्वरूप करणे.

recognition – मान्यता/ओळख.

recommendation – शिफारस – ग्रंथाच्या खरेदीसाठी दाखविलेली अनुकूलता.

recommendation slip / call slip / requisition slip – ग्रंथखरेदीसाठी शिफारसपत्र.

recommended curricula – शिफारस केलेला पाठ्यक्रम (अभ्यासक्रम).

reconditioning – दुरुस्त केलेले.

record – अभिलेख/नोंद – संगणकातील फाईलमध्ये एक नोंद घेण्याची जागा. एका फाईलमध्ये अशी अनेक रेकॉर्ईस (उदा. प्रत्येक पुस्तकासाठी एक) असतात. या नोंदी माहिती घटकांमध्ये विभागलेल्या असतात किंवा आधारसामग्रीशी संबंधित बाबींचा संग्रह. तो संगणकीय माहिती प्रक्रियेसाठी माहितीचा एक घटक म्हणून समजण्यात येतो.

record office – अभिलेख कार्यालय.

record – ध्वनिमुद्रिका.

recorded information – ध्वनिमुद्रित माहिती.

record of rights – हक्कनोंद/हक्कदारपत्र.

recording of data – आधारसामग्रीचे अभिलेखन.

records management – नोंदविषयक कागदपत्रांचे व्यवस्थापन.

rectification – पुनर्शोधन– सूचनेची पाहणी व दुरुस्ती करण्याचे काम.

recto – विषम क्रमांकाचे पृष्ठ/उजव्या बाजूचे पान.

recurring expenditure – आवर्ती/नित्य खर्च – दरवर्षी होणारा खर्च जसे, ग्रंथ व नियतकालिके, टपाल, छपाई वा स्टेशनरी, आकस्मिक खर्च, बांधणी इत्यादी.

redaction / recension – नवीन आवृत्ती – साहित्याचे नूतनीकरण करून प्रकाशकांसाठी योग्य स्वरूप देणे.

reduction – संक्षिप्त करणे/लघुकरण –(१) मूळ दस्तऐवज आहे त्यापेक्षा लहान आकारात तयार करणे. (२) छायाचित्रप्रत मूळ मजकुरापेक्षा लघुस्वरूपात काढणे.

reduction of numbers – अंकांचे लघुकरण – वर्गांकातील शेवटचे अंक गाळून सुटसुटीतपणे केलेला वर्गांक.

reduction of schedules – सारण्यांचे लघुकरण – वर्गीकरणासाठी सारणी देताना नवीन आवृत्तीमध्ये व्यापक वर्गाची नोंद करणे. विशिष्ट वर्गांक कमी करणे.

redundancy – आधिक्य/अतिरिक्तता – माहितीची प्रतिप्राप्ती करताना एका संज्ञेसाठी अधिक शब्दांचा केलेला वापर.

redundant indexing – अनावश्यक निर्देशन – दोन वा अधिक संज्ञांचा अर्थ पूर्णपणे वेगळा सांगता येत नाही. अशा संज्ञांचे निर्देशन. प्रलेखातील समान माहिती दर्शविण्यासाठी केलेले निर्देशन.

refer from reference – 'च्या वरून' संदर्भ – 'पाहा' आणि 'आणखी पाहा'च्या उलट संदर्भ.

reference – संदर्भ –(१) वाचकांना माहिती साधनांकडे निर्देशित करणे. (२) एका विषयशीर्षकाकडून दुसरीकडे दिलेला संदर्भ.

reference assistant – संदर्भ साहाय्यक – ग्रंथालयात संदर्भसेवा देणारा साहाय्यक.

reference bibliography – संदर्भग्रंथांची सूची.

reference book – संदर्भ ग्रंथ – संपूर्ण मजकूर वाचण्याचा हेतू नसून फक्त शंका निरसन करण्यासाठी संक्षिप्त माहिती दिलेली असते.

reference card – संदर्भ पत्र – अधिक संदर्भ (cross reference) असलेले तालिकापत्र.

reference collection – संदर्भग्रंथांचा संग्रह.

reference department – संदर्भग्रंथ विभाग.

reference desk – संदर्भसेवा दिली जाणारा मेज.

reference entry – संदर्भदर्शी नोंद.

reference librarian – संदर्भ ग्रंथपाल – ग्रंथालयामध्ये वाचकांना हवी ती माहिती शोधण्यासाठी मदत करणारी प्रशिक्षित व्यक्ती.

reference library – संदर्भ ग्रंथालय – संदर्भ ग्रंथांचा संग्रह अधिक प्रमाणात करणारे ग्रंथालय.

reference list – संदर्भ यादी – संशोधकाने वापरलेल्या आधारग्रंथांची यादी.

reference marks – तळटीप चिन्हे – आधारग्रंथांचे ग्रंथवर्णन देताना वापरलेली चिन्हे.

reference material – संदर्भ साहित्य – संदर्भ म्हणून वापरण्यासाठी ग्रंथ, ध्वनीफीत यासारखे साहित्य.

reference question – संदर्भ प्रश्न.

reference room / section – संदर्भ कक्ष.

reference service – संदर्भ सेवा – वाचकाला संदर्भ मिळविण्यासाठी दिलेली सेवा.

reference source – संदर्भसाधन.

reference tools – संदर्भसाधने – संदर्भ मिळविण्यासाठी उपयुक्त वाचनसाहित्य.

reference work – संदर्भकार्य – लेखाच्या पूरकसंदर्भासाठी दिलेले इतर संदर्भ.

referral centre – संदर्भासाठी उपलब्ध केंद्र.

reflex copying method – प्रतिवर्तित प्रत पद्धत.

refund – परतावा – रक्कम परत करणे.

regional – प्रादेशिक/विभागीय.

regional bibliography – प्रादेशिक ग्रंथसूची – विशिष्ट प्रदेशातील माहितीविषयी ग्रंथांची सूची.

regional catalogue – प्रादेशिक तालिका – विशिष्ट प्रदेशातील ग्रंथालयांच्या ग्रंथसंग्रहाची तालिका.

regional classification – भौगोलिक स्थानानुसार केलेले वर्गीकरण.

regional computer network – प्रादेशिक संगणक जाळे – विशिष्ट प्रदेशापुरते मर्यादित संगणक जाळे.

regional library – प्रादेशिक ग्रंथालय – क्षेत्रीय गरजा भागविणारे ग्रंथालय.

register – नोंदवही – विशिष्ट माहिती लिहिण्यासाठी तयार केलेली वही.

register issue system – वहीरूप देवघेव पद्धती.

registration – पंजीयन/पंजीकरण – नाव नोंदणी करणे.

registration card – नोंदपत्र.

registration form – नोंदप्रपत्र – नोंदणी करताना भरावयाचा अर्ज.

registration record – पंजीकरण नोंद.

registration period – नोंदणीकाळ – सभासद कोणत्या तारखेपर्यंत ग्रंथालयसेवेचा लाभ घेऊ शकतो याची नोंदणी.

regulations – नियमन.

reinforced binding – मजबूत बांधणी.

re-issue – (ग्रंथाची) पुनर्देवाण – वाचकाला तोच ग्रंथ पुन्हा वाचनासाठी देणे.

rejection slip – नकारपत्र – प्रकाशकाने लेखकाला लेख अस्वीकृतीबाबत दिलेले पत्र.

related – संबंधित – एकाच प्रकारचा.

Related Term (RT) – सापेक्ष संज्ञा – माहितीची प्रतिप्राप्ती करताना एका संज्ञेशी संबंधित असणारी दुसरी संज्ञा.

related title – संबंधित ग्रंथनाम – माला प्रकाशनातील ग्रंथ किंवा आधीच्या ग्रंथाला लिहिलेले पूरक ग्रंथ सापेक्ष ग्रंथनामाचे आढळतात. उदा. कणेकर शिरीष – यादों की बारात, पुन्हा यादों की बारात.

related work – संबंधिक ग्रंथकार्य – तालिकीकरण करताना एखादा दुसऱ्या ग्रंथाला पूरक ग्रंथ असल्याचा उल्लेख. उदा. पुरवणी, निर्देश, नियमपुस्तिका इत्यादी.

relational database – सापेक्ष आधारसामग्री – उदा. ग्रंथालयातील सभासदांचे नाव, पत्ता आणि त्यांच्याकडे असलेली पुस्तके हे दोन वेगळे डेटाबेस असून ते सापेक्ष आहेत.

relational indexing – सापेक्ष निर्देशन – जटिल विषयांमध्ये समाविष्ट असलेल्या संज्ञांचे निर्देशन.

relative – सापेक्ष/विनिर्दिष्ट – दुसऱ्या एखाद्या गोष्टीशी तुलना करणारा.

relative index – सापेक्ष निर्देश – वर्गीकरण पद्धतीसाठी तयार केलेला निर्देश. यात प्रत्येक निर्देश नोंदीखाली सापेक्ष विषय व बाजूंचा उल्लेख केला जातो.

relative location – सापेक्ष स्थान.

relative order – विनिर्दिष्ट क्रम/सापेक्ष क्रम.

releif map – **उठावाचा नकाशा** – उंचवटे, सखलता असणारा पण भिंतीवर लावता येणारा नकाशा.

relevance – **संबंधता** – विचारलेल्या प्रश्नविषयी नेमलेल्या व संबंधित अशा बाबींची माहितीच्या संचयातून प्राप्तीसाठी उपयोग करणे.

relocation – पुनर्रचना, पुनर्मांडणी.

remainders – **अवशेष ग्रंथ/शिलकी ग्रंथ** – ग्रंथ प्रकाशनाची विक्री झाल्यानंतर काही काळाने विक्रिचे प्रमाण कमी होते अथवा नवी आवृत्ती प्रकाशित केली जाते. तेव्हा प्रकाशक उरलेल्या प्रती लिलावाद्वारे किंवा अतिशय कमी किमतीला दुकानदारांना विकतो. अशा प्रतींना 'शिलकी ग्रंथ' म्हणतात. ही संज्ञा विशेषत: अमेरिकेत वापरली जाते.

rename – पुनर्नामकरण (फाईल किंवा निर्देशाचे).

renew – नवीकरण/नूतनीकरण करणे.

renewal – नूतनीकरण/नवीकरण/नवीनीकरण.

renewal of book – ग्रंथाचे नूतनीकरण.

renewal of subscription – **वर्गणीचे नूतनीकरण** – नियतकालिकाच्या सभासदत्वाचे नूतनीकरण.

rental library – **सशुल्क ग्रंथालय** – विशिष्ट शुल्क भरूनच वापरता येते असे ग्रंथालय.

repeatable fields – **पुनरावर्ती घटक** – माहिती घटकामध्ये सतत त्याच प्रकारची माहिती येत असल्यास ती सामावून घेण्यासाठी केलेली सोय. उदा. एका लेखाचे एकापेक्षा जास्त लेखक असू शकतात. त्याची नावे संगणकात लेखकाच्या एकाच घटकामध्ये लिहायची असतात; अशा वेळी यासाठी चिन्ह देऊन एकानंतर एक ती लिहिता येतात.

repeating key – **पुनरुक्ती कळ** – संगणकाच्या कळपटावरील पुनरुक्ती कळ.

replacement copy – **बदली ग्रंथ** – वाचकाने हरविलेल्या ग्रंथाऐवजी ग्रंथाची दुसरी प्रत स्वीकारली जाते.

replica – **हुबेहूब प्रतिकृती** (एखादे चित्र किंवा शिल्प).

report – **अहवाल/वृत्तान्त** – (१) एखाद्या संस्थेच्या कार्याचा प्राथमिक अहवाल/वृत्तान्त.
(२) परिषदा, सभा यांच्या कामकाजाचे वृत्त/संस्थेच्या कार्याविषयी दिलेला वार्षिक आढावा.

report – **annual** – वार्षिक अहवाल.

report numbers – अहवाल/वृत्तान्त अंक.

repository – **संग्रहालय** – संघयोजनेतील मध्यवर्ती ग्रंथालय.

reprint – **पुनर्मुद्रण** – (१) एखाद्या ग्रंथात कोणताही बदल न करता पुन्हा मुद्रण करून प्रती काढल्या जातात. अशा पुनर्मुद्रणाचा क्रमांक ग्रंथनामवृत्ताच्या मागे लिहिला जातो.

(२) एखादा लेख नियतकालिकातून पुनर्मुद्रित करून किंवा छायाचित्रपत्र घेऊन तो स्वतंत्ररीत्या ग्रंथालयात ठेवणे.

reprint series – **पुनर्मुद्रितांची माला** – पूर्वी एखाद्या वा अनेक प्रकाशनांतर्फे प्रकाशित झालेले ग्रंथ. एकाच प्रकाशकाने एकाच मालाशीर्षकाखाली प्रकाशित करणे.

reprinted article – **पुनर्मुद्रित केलेला लेख.**

reprography / photocopy / xerox / photostat – **प्रतिरूपलेखन/छायाचित्रपत्र काढणे** – छायाचित्र घेऊन ते पुनरुत्पादन करण्याची प्रक्रिया किंवा छायाचित्रीकरण प्रक्रियेद्वारे प्रलेखांचे पुनरुत्पादन.

reprography service – **छायाचित्रप्रती सेवा.**

republication – **पुनर्प्रकाशन** – प्रकाशकाने बदल करून किंवा बदल न करता केलेले पुनर्प्रकाशन.

request – **विनंती.**

requester – **विनंतीकार.**

requisition slip / recommendation slip / call slip – **ग्रंथमागणी शिफारसपत्र** – (१) ग्रंथालयात विशिष्ट ग्रंथांची खरेदी करण्यासाठी दिलेले शिफारसपत्र. (२) ग्रंथमागणी करण्यासाठी भरून द्यावयाची पत्रिका/पत्र.

research – **संशोधन.**

research cubicle / carrel / study / alcove – **अभ्यासकक्ष.**

research institute – **संशोधन संस्था.**

research library – **संशोधन ग्रंथालय** – संशोधनासाठी उपयुक्त संग्रह असणारे ग्रंथालय.

research librarian – **संशोधनासाठी सेवा देणारा ग्रंथपाल.**

research monograph – **संशोधन हस्तपुस्तिका.**

research reports – **संशोधनाचा अहवाल** – संशोधनाच्या प्रगतीची प्रथम माहिती देणारा अहवाल.

research service – **संशोधन सेवा** – संशोधनासाठी विशेष ग्रंथालयाकडून दिलेली ग्रंथालयसेवा.

reservation – **आरक्षण** – हवा असलेला ग्रंथ ग्रंथालयात आरक्षित करण्याची प्रक्रिया.

reserved – **राखीव/आरक्षित** – खास वापरासाठी किंवा खास प्रसंगासाठी राखून ठेवलेला.

reserved book – **आरक्षित ग्रंथ** – हवा असलेला ग्रंथ, दुसऱ्या वाचकाकडून परत आल्यावर मिळण्यासाठी आरक्षण केलेला ग्रंथ.

reserved collection – **राखीव/आरक्षित ग्रंथसंग्रह.**

reserved card – **ग्रंथ आरक्षण पत्र** – ग्रंथालयातून बाहेर दिलेल्या ग्रंथाकरिता मागणी नोंदविणारे पत्र.

resources – साधने/सामग्री/साधनसंपत्ती.

resource centre – **वाचनसाहित्य संग्रह केंद्र** – शाळा व महाविद्यालयांना उपयुक्त अशा सर्व प्रकारच्या ग्रंथ व ग्रंथेतर साहित्याने युक्त अशी संग्रह ग्रंथालये.

resource sharing – **ज्ञानसाधनांची आंतर ग्रंथालयीन देवघेव** – (१) वाचन साहित्याचा सामुदायिक वापर. (२) अनेक ग्रंथालयांनी एकत्र येऊन ज्ञानसाधनांची देवघेव करणे.

responsive service – **प्रतिसादात्मक सेवा** – वाचकांना त्यांच्या विनंतीनुसार दिल्या जाणाऱ्या संदर्भसेवा आणि माहिती सेवा.

restricted access – **मर्यादित प्रवेश** – ग्रंथालयात प्रवेशासाठी विशिष्ट व्यक्तींना दिलेली परवानगी.

restricted loan – **मर्यादित उधार** – वाचकांना विशिष्ट संख्येने विशिष्ट मर्यादित कालावधीसाठी दिलेला ग्रंथ.

retiring room – आरामकक्ष/विश्रामकक्ष.

retrieval – **प्रतिप्राप्ती** – परत मिळविणे. हवी ती माहिती प्रत्यक्ष ग्रंथालयात संगणकावर शोधणे व ती मिळविण्याची प्रक्रिया.

retrieval device – **प्रतिप्राप्तीचे एक साधन** – हवी ती माहिती मिळविण्यासाठी उपयुक्त अशी क्रमिक पुस्तके, नियतकालिके, ग्रंथालयतालिका किंवा संगणकावरील माहितीसंचय.

retrieval system – **माहितीची प्रतिप्राप्ती पद्धती** – माहिती मिळविण्यासाठीच्या प्रक्रियांचा पद्धतशीरपणे लावलेला क्रम.

retroactive notation – **पूर्वलक्षी चिन्हांकन** – वर्गीकरण करताना गुंतागुंतीचा विषय असेल तेव्हा साहित्यप्रकाराच्या आधी दिलेले चिन्हांकन.

retroconversion – **पूर्वलक्षी परिवर्तन** – (१) एखाद्या कृती पद्धतीमध्ये बदल करण्यासाठी पूर्वींच्या साठ्यावर करावी लागणारी प्रक्रिया. (२) संगणकीय रूपांतरण.

retrospective bibliography / closed bibliography – **पूर्वलक्षी ग्रंथसूची** – आधीच्या वर्षांमध्ये प्रकाशित झालेल्या ग्रंथांची सूची.

retrospective search – **(साहित्याचा) पूर्वलक्षी शोध** – विशिष्ट साहित्य ग्रंथसंग्रहात उपलब्ध आहे वा नाही याचा शोध.

return – परत.

return counter – ग्रंथपरतीचा कट्टा.

return date – **ग्रंथपरतीचा दिनांक** – ग्रंथालयातून ग्रंथ विशिष्ट कालावधीकरिता दिला जातो. असा ग्रंथ परत करण्याचा दिनांक.

return key / enter key - **प्रवेश कळ** - संगणकाला द्यावयाच्या सूचनांपैकी अंमलबजावणीसाठीची कळ. ही कळ कार्यरत केल्यामुळे दिलेल्या सूचनांची उपयोजना केली जाऊन प्रतिसाद मिळतो.

returns - **परतीचे ग्रंथ** - विक्री न झाल्यामुळे ग्रंथविक्रेत्याने प्रकाशकाला परत दिलेला ग्रंथ. (१) ग्रंथखरेदीमध्ये प्रत्यक्ष पाहण्यासाठी दिलेल्या ग्रंथांपैकी न निवडलेले साहित्य.

revenue - **महसूल** - उत्पन्न, विशेषत: शासनाचा महसूल, प्राप्त मिळकत.

revenue district - **महसुली जिल्हा.**

revenue stamp - **महसुली तिकीट.**

reverse cover / back cover - **मलपृष्ठ** - ग्रंथाच्या मजकुराच्या शेवटच्या पानानंतरचे बाह्य पृष्ठ.

reversible relation - **उलटा करता येणारा संबंध** - असा संबंध जो उलटा करता येतो. यात वर्गीकरणातील दोन संमिश्र अंक फिरते असू शकतात किंवा त्यांची अदलाबदल होऊ शकते.

review - **ग्रंथपरीक्षण/ग्रंथ आढावा** - नवीन ग्रंथांचे परिचयात्मक टीपा देणारे लिखाण.

review copy - **परीक्षण प्रत** - ग्रंथ परीक्षणासाठी प्रकाशकाने वृत्तपत्राकडे दिलेली प्रत.

review periodical - **परीक्षण नियतकालिक** - सर्वसाधारणपणे विज्ञान व तंत्रज्ञान या क्षेत्रातील प्रगतीचा आढावा किंवा परीक्षण, समीक्षण प्रकाशित करणारे नियतकालिक.

reviewing periodical - **परीक्षणात्मक नियतकालिक.**

review of progress - **प्रगतीचा आढावा घेणारे प्रकाशन.**

revised edition - **सुधारित आवृत्ती** - चुका काढून टाकून, नवीन माहितीची भर घातलेली आवृत्ती.

reviser - **आढावाकार/संशोधक** - ग्रंथात सुधारणा करणारी व्यक्ती.

rexin binding - **रेक्झिन बांधणी** - ग्रंथ वेष्टणाकरिता रेक्झिन वापरून केलेली ग्रंथ बांधणी.

ribbon arrangement - **कप्पेवार रचना/मांडणी** - ग्रंथांची विशिष्ट कप्पेवार रचना. सार्वजनिक ग्रंथालयांमध्ये गरजेनुसार कथा-कादंब-या व इतर ग्रंथांची केलेली विशिष्ट रचना.

Rider's international classification - **राइडरची आंतरराष्ट्रीय वर्गीकरण पद्धती** - १९६१ मध्ये प्रेग्मॉन्ट राइडरने प्रकाशित केलेली वर्गीकरण पद्धती.

rigid classification - **स्थूल वर्गीकरण** - (१) आधुनिक वर्गीकरण पद्धती अस्तित्वात नव्हत्या तेव्हा ग्रंथाच्या विषयानुसार वर्गीकरण करण्यापेक्षा स्थानानुसार वर्गीकरण करण्याकडे ग्रंथालयांचा कल होता. (२) एकच ग्रंथवैशिष्ट्य लक्षात घेऊन केलेले वर्गीकरण.

ring network - **वर्तुळाकार संगणक जाळे** - प्रत्येक दुवा जवळच्या दोन संगणकांना जोडलेले वर्तुळाकार संगणक जाळे.

robot - **यंत्रमानव** - संगणकाद्वारे नियंत्रित.

robotics - **यंत्रमानव निर्मिती तंत्रज्ञान.**

rolled map – वेष्टित नकाशा – गुंडाळी नकाशा, गोलाकृती गुंडाळले जाणारे नकाशे.

roman numerals – रोमन अंक.

root directory – मुख्य निर्देशिका (निर्देशिकांची निर्देशिका).

rotated catalogue – परिभ्रमित तालिका – वर्गांकातील प्रत्येक वर्गाच्या क्रमांकामध्ये नोंद केलेली वर्गीकृत तालिका.

rotated entry – परिभ्रमित नोंद – निर्देशातील प्रत्येक शीर्षकाखाली केलेली संपूर्ण माहिती देणारी नोंद.

rotated indexing – परिभ्रमित निर्देशन – वर्गीकरण चिन्हातील प्रत्येक वर्गानुसार शीर्षकाखाली संपूर्ण नोंद असलेले निर्देशन.

rotational indexing – निर्देशनातील प्रत्येक संज्ञा – फाईलमध्ये प्रथम क्रमांकावर घेणे शक्य होईल असा सहसंबंधित निर्देश तयार करणे.

round – आवर्तन.

round back – ग्रंथाचा गोलाकार कणा.

routing – आवर्ती देवघेव – संस्थेतील कर्मचाऱ्यांकडे पद्धतशीरपणे केली जाणारी मासिकाची वा पुस्तिकेची देवघेव.

routine – नित्यक्रम – (१) नेहमीचा कार्यक्रम, शिरस्ता, परिपाठ. (२) संगणकाला दिलेल्या सूचनांचा गट/संगणक आज्ञावलीचे उपविभाजन.

royal society – रॉयल सोसायटी – १९६२ साली ब्रिटिश सरकारने लंडनमध्ये विज्ञानाच्या संशोधनासाठी स्थापलेली संस्था.

royalty – स्वामित्वधन – ग्रंथकाराला लेखनाबद्दल प्रकाशकाने दिलेला मोबदला.

rules & regulations – नियमविनियम.

rules & regulations of classification – वर्गीकरणाचे नियम.

runners – संदर्भासाठी दिलेले अंक किंवा अक्षरे.

running title – आवर्ती ग्रंथशीर्षक – ग्रंथातील पृष्ठाच्या सुरुवातीला छापलेले ग्रंथनाम किंवा विभागाचे शीर्षक.

run on – सुरू ठेवा.

rural library – ग्रामीण भागातील ग्रंथालय.

rush books – प्रासंगिक मागणीचे ग्रंथ – तात्कालिक मागणी असलेले ग्रंथ. विशिष्ट चर्चेतील विषयावर आधारित ग्रंथ. उदा. युवराज्ञी डायना यांच्या चरित्राला त्यांच्या मृत्यूनंतर आलेली अधिकाधिक तात्कालिक मागणी.

S

sacramentary – संस्कार ग्रंथ – धर्म विधींचे विवरण असलेला ग्रंथ.

sacred book – पवित्र/धार्मिक ग्रंथ – भगवद्गीता, कुराण, बायबल, गुरुग्रंथसाहेब यासारखे ग्रंथ.

sacred work – पवित्र/धार्मिक कार्य.

salient features – प्रमुख वैशिष्ट्ये/गुणविशेष.

sales tax – विक्री कर – वस्तूंच्या विक्रीवरील शासकीय कर.

sample copy – नमुना प्रत – ग्रंथालयात, नियतकालिकाची वर्गणी भरण्यापूर्वी नमुन्यादाखल मागविलेली प्रत.

sample pages – नमुना पृष्ठे – संकल्पित ग्रंथांची निवडक पाने. ही पाने छपाईसाठी नमुना म्हणून संपूर्ण ग्रंथाची प्रतिकृती सादृश पृष्ठे म्हणून ठेवली जातात.

sample survey – नमुना सर्वेक्षण/नमुना चाचणी – मुख्य माहिती संकलनापूर्वी मिळविलेली अल्प प्रतिसादकांची माहिती.

sampleback – ग्रंथकणा नमुनापट्टी – ग्रंथाचा कणा बांधणी करताना, कोणता रंग, साहित्य वापरायचे यासाठी तयार केलेली नमुनापट्टी. रंगाची, साहित्याची जुळणी करण्यासाठी ही पट्टी वापरली जाते.

sampling – नमुना चाचणी – मोठ्या संख्येने उपलब्ध प्रतिसादकांपैकी थोड्या प्रतिसादकांची प्रतिनिधित्व असणारी निवड करणारे तंत्र.

satellite broadcasting – उपग्रहाद्वारा प्रसारण – माहितीची अदलाबदल. प्रसारण उपग्रहाद्वारा करण्याची प्रक्रिया.

satellite communication – उपग्रहाद्वारे संदेशवहन.

satellite network – **उपग्रहाद्वारा संगणकजाळे** – उपग्रहाद्वारा नियंत्रित केलेली माहितीची अदलाबदल करणारी संगणकांची जाळीदार रचना.

save – **जतन करणे** – संगणकाच्या स्मरणिकेत माहितीचा साठा करणे.

save the time of the reader – **वाचकांचा वेळ वाचवा** – डॉ. रंगनाथन् यांनी दिलेले ग्रंथालयशास्त्राचे चौथे सूत्र.

scale (maps) – **मापन** – वास्तुशास्त्रीय चित्र, नकाशा, पृथ्वीगोल किंवा उभा भाग यात दाखवलेले अंतर आणि ते प्रतिरूपीत करणारे पृथ्वीच्या पृष्ठभागावरील प्रत्यक्ष अंतर यांचे प्रमाण.

scanner – **प्रतिकृती यंत्र** – संगणकाला जोडलेल्या या यंत्राद्वारे कागदावरील प्रतिकृती संगणकीय स्वरूपात साठविली जाते.

scanning – **क्रमविक्षण/अवलोकन** – नोंदी शोधण्याचे कार्य.

scatter – **विखुरणी/निर्देशातील नोंदी विखुरणे** – एकाच विषयातील नोंदी या एकवचन/अनेकवचन किंवा इतर कारणांमुळे अनेक ठिकाणी विखरून कराव्या लागतात.

scatter reference – **विखुरलेले संदर्भ** – निर्देशामधील एक उलट संदर्भ. ज्याचा बोध विशिष्ट विषयाच्या शीर्षकाद्वारे होत नाही परंतु पर्याय सुचविले जातात.

scattered – **विखुरलेले** – जवळ नसलेले, पांगलेले.

scenario – **चलचित्रवत् योजना/पटकथा** – (१) घटनांची काल्पनिक साखळी. (२) चित्रपट, नाटक वा इतर रंगमंच सादरीकरणाची संक्षिप्त आवृत्ती. त्यांचे तालिकीकरण करताना नाट्यप्रकारानुसार नोंद केली जाते.

schedule – **अनुसूची/तक्ता/जोडपत्र सारणी** – (१) वर्गीकरण पद्धतीतील उपवर्गांची वर्गानुक्रमे दिलेली सूची. अनेक अंक असलेली कोष्टके ज्यात सर्व विषय त्यांच्या शाखा, उपशाखा, अनुक्रमे ००० ते ९९९ या क्रमांकाने दशांश वर्गीकरण पद्धतीच्या दुसऱ्या खंडामध्ये ही अनुसूची आहे.

schedule of classification – **ग्रंथवर्गीकरणाच्या अनुसूची/तक्ते** – पायाभूत किंवा मूळ विषय, त्यांचे विविध पैलू, उपांगे इत्यादींची संज्ञा वापरून बनविलेली पद्धतशीर/क्रमबद्ध अशी यादी.

scheduled mnemonics – **सारणीतील स्मृतीसुलभता/स्मृतिसुलभ अनुसूची** – डॉ. रंगनाथन् यांची संकल्पना – वर्गीकरणासाठी चिन्हांकन तयार करताना वर्गवारी, तक्ते, सारण्या यातून निवड करून तयार केलेली अनुसूची.

scheme – **पद्धती** – योजनांचे पूर्ण वर्णन.

scheme assortment – **निवडीची पद्धत** – ग्रंथवर्गीकरणातील नियमांची मांडणी.

scheme of classes – **वर्गरचना पद्धती.**

scheme of classification – वर्गीकरणाची पद्धती – एखाद्या वर्गीकरण पद्धतीची सारणी, निर्देश व वर्गीकरण नियमावली असा संपूर्ण संच.

scholarly journals – विद्वत्ताप्रचुर नियतकालिके – अशा नियतकालिकांत एखाद्या विषयातील नवे प्रवाह/संशोधन यावर आधारित लेख असतात.

scholarly source – विद्वत्ताप्रचुर साधन.

school – प्रणाली/संप्रदाय/मत/शाळा/संकुल.

school edition – शालेय आवृत्ती – शालेय वापराचे उद्दिष्ट समोर ठेवून तयार केलेली आवृत्ती.

school librarian / teacher librarian – शालेय ग्रंथपाल – शालेय ग्रंथालयाची व्यवस्था पाहणारी व्यक्ती.

school library – शालेय ग्रंथालय – शालेय विद्यार्थी, शिक्षक, कर्मचारी यांच्यासाठीचे ग्रंथालय.

school of thought – विचार प्रणाली/मतप्रणाली.

science – विज्ञान.

science fiction – विज्ञानाधिष्ठित कथा/कादंबरी – शास्त्र, प्रात्यक्षिक, उपयोजन असणारे विषय. काल्पनिक कथांमध्ये वैज्ञानिक सत्य, प्रगती यांचा भरपूर वापर केलेला असतो. उदा. प्रेषित – डॉ. जयंत नारळीकर

scientific – शास्त्रीय/शास्त्रशुद्ध.

scientific management – शास्त्रीय/शास्त्रशुद्ध व्यवस्थापन – वैज्ञानिक आधार असलेले, शास्त्रीय.

scientific expeditions – वैज्ञानिक शोधयात्रा.

scientific terms – शास्त्रीय संज्ञा – विशिष्ट वस्तूचे शास्त्रीय नाव.

scope – व्याप्ती/मर्यादा – विषयाची/संशोधनाची व्याप्ती.

scope note – विषयव्याप्ती टिपण – (१) माहितीची प्रतिप्राप्ती करताना विशिष्ट विषयाचा अर्थ व व्याप्ती स्पष्ट करणारे टिपण दिले जाते. यामुळे एकसारख्या दुसऱ्या, संबंधित अथवा समानार्थी शब्दांमुळे निर्माण होणारी अडचण टाळता येते. अचूक माहिती मिळविणे शक्य होते.
(२) एखाद्या नोंदीचा विषय, नाव, उपविषयनामाची व्याप्ती स्पष्ट करणारी वा वर्णन करणारी टीप.

scramble – संगणकामध्ये माहितीची सांकेतिक स्वरूपात केलेली साठवण.

screen – पडदा/पटल (संगणकाचा पडदा).

script – लिपी – (१) छपाईप्रमाणे लिहिलेली हस्ताक्षरीत प्रत.
(२) कोणत्याही भाषेची लिखित स्वरूपातील अभिव्यक्ती.

SDI (Selective Dissemination of Information) - **माहितीचे निवडक प्रसारण** - उपलब्ध माहिती आणि उपयोजकाची गरज यांचा मेळ घालून विशिष्ट उपयोजकाला विशिष्ट माहिती पुरविण्याची ग्रंथालयाची सेवा.

search - **(माहितीचा) शोध घेणे** - प्रत्यक्ष ग्रंथ वा इतर साहित्यामध्ये किंवा संगणकाच्या मदतीने माहितीचा शोध घेणे.

search aid - शोधतंत्र सहायता.

search engine - शोधयंत्र.

search record - **शोध नोंद** - माहिती मिळविण्यासाठी उपलब्ध साहित्य, प्रकाशने, व्यक्ती यांची नोंद.

search method - शोध पद्धती.

search point - शोध बिंदू.

search room - **शोध कक्ष** - साहित्य शोध घेण्यासाठी ग्रंथालयामध्ये नियतकालिकांचे निर्देश, सारांश, खंड, ग्रंथसूची ठेवलेले दालन.

search service - शोधतंत्र सेवा.

search statement - शोध निवेदन.

search strategy - **शोधतंत्र/पद्धती** - (१) विशिष्ट चौकशीची पूर्तता करण्यासाठी वापरलेली शोध पद्धती. (२) हवी असलेली माहिती संगणकातील माहिती संग्रहातून मिळविण्यासाठी तर्कसंगत संकल्पना वापरून शोधबद्ध एकमेकांस जोडून शोध समीकरण (Search Expression) तयार करण्याचे तंत्र.

search term - **शोधशब्द संज्ञा** - (१) विशिष्ट माहिती मिळविण्यासाठी साधन म्हणून उपयोजकाने वापरलेला शब्द, वाक्यरचना इ. (२) संगणकावरील माहितीसंग्रहात शोध घेण्यासाठी तयार केलेला शब्द. हा अंक/अक्षरे/एकापेक्षा अधिक शब्दांनी बनलेला असू शकतो. अशा वेळी आशय दर्शविणारे शब्द.

searching - **शोधन** - ग्रंथालयात आलेला ग्रंथ ही दुबार प्रत आहे, नवीन आवृत्ती आहे की ग्रंथालयात समाविष्ट झालेला ग्रंथ आहे हे ठरविण्यासाठी ग्रंथालय तालिकेतील नोंदी तपासण्याची प्रक्रिया.

second half-title - ग्रंथाच्या आतील भागात पुन्हा लिहिलेले ग्रंथशीर्षक.

second indention - **द्वितीय समासांतर** - तालिकेतील नोंद करताना वापरावयाची संज्ञा.

second section - **दुसरा अनुच्छेद** - तालिकेच्या नोंदीत संबंधित ग्रंथाचा उल्लेख करणाऱ्या अनुच्छेदाला 'दुसरा अनुच्छेद' असे म्हणतात.

second vertical - **तालिकापत्रातील दुसरी उभी रेषा.**

secondary access - **दुय्यम प्रवेश** - माहितीची प्रतिप्रासी करताना एका नोंदीशी संबंधित दुसऱ्या नोंदीची पाहणी करणे.

secondary bibliography – **दुय्यम ग्रंथसूची** – प्राथमिक ग्रंथसूचींचा वापर करून संपादित केलेली विशिष्ट विषयाच्या ग्रंथांची सूची.

secondary documents – **द्वितीयक प्रलेख** – प्राथमिक प्रलेखांची अधिक माहिती देणारे प्रलेख. उदा. सारलेख.

secondary document sources – **दुय्यम माहिती साधने** – मूळ प्राथमिक प्रलेखातील मजकूर/ आशय संक्षिप्त स्वरूपात सादर केलेले सार. सारांश वा संक्षेप देणारी सूची/यादी. यामुळे मूळ प्रलेखाचे स्थान समजते आणि तो प्राप्त करणे सुलभ जाते.

secondary element – **नोंद प्रथमेतर संज्ञा** – नोंद प्रथमेतर संज्ञा म्हणून न निवडलेल्या आणि म्हणून त्यांच्या नंतर लिहावयाच्या पदाला अथवा पदसमुच्चयाला नोंद प्रथमेतर संज्ञा असे म्हणतात.

secondary entry – **दुय्यम नोंद** – तालिकेमध्ये प्रमुख नोंदीव्यतिरिक्त केलेल्या इतर नोंदी.

secondary literature – **दुय्यम साहित्य** – पूर्वीच्या संशोधनाची पुनरुक्ती देणारे लिखाण.

secondary periodicals – **द्वितीयक/दुय्यम नियतकालिके** – मूलगामी/प्राथमिक नियतकालिकांमध्ये प्रकाशित होऊन गेलेल्या लेखनसाहित्यामधून पुन्हा तीच माहिती सारांशरूपाने वा लेखसूचीस्वरूपात देणाऱ्या नियतकालिकाला 'दुय्यम नियतकालिक' असे म्हणतात. यामध्ये निर्देशात्मक, सारकारी, समीक्षात्मक नियतकालिकांचा समावेश होतो.

secondary publication / secondary sources – **द्वितीयक प्रकाशन/द्वितीयक प्राप्तिस्थाने** – प्राथमिक प्राप्तिसाधनांचा वापर करून तयार केलेली प्रकाशने उदा. लेखांचे सार, निर्देश, यांचा उद्देश उपलब्ध माहितीचे विशिष्ट उपयोजकांसाठी पद्धतशीरपणे प्रसारण करण्याचा असतो.

secondary service / abstracting service – **दुय्यम सेवा/सारलेखन सेवा** – एखादी व्यक्ती वा संस्था यांनी उपयोगितेनुसार तयार केलेले सारलेख.

secondary source – **दुय्यम साधन**.

secondary title – **दुय्यम शीर्षक** – मुख्य शीर्षकाबरोबर स्वतंत्र विभाग दर्शविणारे शीर्षक. उदा. महाराष्ट्राचा भूगोल–मराठवाडा विभाग.

second-hand book – **दुसऱ्यांदा किंवा त्यानंतर विकले गेलेले पुस्तक**.

secret literature / clandestine literature / under ground literature – **गोपनीय साहित्य** – सुरक्षा विभागाचे अहवाल किंवा युद्धप्रसंगी वापरले जाणारे साहित्य.

secret press / clandestine press / underground press – **गोपनीय छापखाना** – गोपनीय साहित्य छापखान्याचे ठिकाण.

section – **विभाग**.

section headling – **विभागीय शीर्षक** – ग्रंथातील विशिष्ट विभागाचे शीर्षक.

section mark – **विभाग चिन्ह** – (१) विभाग अंकापूर्वी द्यायचे चिन्ह उदा. चौथे संदर्भचिन्ह म्हणून तळटीप देताना वापरण्याचे चिन्ह (✲✲)

sectionalized index – **उपविषयानुसार निर्देश** – विविध विभागानुसार तयार केलेल्या नियतकालिकाचा निर्देश. यात विभाग विशिष्ट प्रकारे केले जातात. – (१) महत्त्वाचे मोठे लेख, (२) छोटे परिच्छेद व वृत्तविषयक स्फुटलेखन, (३) विविध लेखनसाहित्याचे सारांश इ.

sector– **क्षेत्र** – उच्च शब्दाने सुरू होणारी अंकांची मालिका किंवा एक रिकामा अंक किंवा दोन्ही रिकामे अंक असणारी रांग.

sector device – **क्षेत्र/विभागीय युक्ती/क्लृप्ती** – वर्गीकरणासाठी वापरायचे तत्त्व.

sector notation – **क्षेत्राधिष्ठित चिन्हांकन.**

sectoral centre – **विभागीय केंद्र** – विषय/शाखा कार्यशील असलेली माहिती केंद्रे.

see – **पाहा** – तालिकीकरण करताना केलेली विशिष्ट नोंद. ज्या शीर्षकाखाली नोंद नाही त्या शीर्षकाला पर्यायी शीर्षकाकडे 'पाहा' म्हणून केलेली नोंद. उदा. ILA 'पाहा' Indian Library Associaton.

see also – **आणखी पाहा** – (१) तालिका अथवा वर्गीकरण सारणीमधील 'आणखी पाहा' या टिपेसाठीची संक्षेपाक्षरे. यामुळे निरनिराळ्या संज्ञा असलेला एकच विषय शोधण्याकरिता वाचकास मार्गदर्शन केले जाते. उदा. विशेष ग्रंथालये 'आणखी पाहा' औद्योगिक ग्रंथालये.

see also entry – **'आणखी पहा' नोंद** – तालिकेसाठी तयार करावयाची 'आणखी पाहा' मजकुराची नोंद.

see also reference – **'आणखी पाहा' संदर्भ.**

see reference – **पाहा संदर्भ** – या नोंदीचा वापर केला जात नाही मात्र नोंदीकडून ज्या नोंदीचा वापर होतो असे मार्गदर्शन केले जाते.

see safe – **प्रकाशन व ग्रंथविक्रेते यांच्यातील एक करार** – ग्रंथविक्रेत्याकडील प्रती विकल्या गेल्या नाहीत तर दुसऱ्या ग्रंथाच्या प्रती घेऊन न विकलेल्या प्रती प्रकाशकाला परत केल्या जातात.

segregate – **दूर ठेवणे/निराळा ठेवणे/बाजूला काढणे/वेगवेगळे करणे.**

selected bibliography – **निवडक ग्रंथांची सूची** – विशिष्ट विषयावरील निवडक ग्रंथांची सूची/ यादी. निवडक अशा दृष्टीने केलेली असते की अनावश्यक साहित्य त्यातून वगळलेले असते किंवा विशिष्ट लोकांच्या गरजा भागविण्यासाठी अशी ग्रंथसूची बनविली जाते.

selective dissemination of information – **निवडक माहितीचे प्रसारण.** पाहा 'SDI'

select list of references – **संदर्भसाहित्याची निवडक सूची** – उपलब्ध संदर्भसाहित्यातून निवड करून तयार केलेली सूची.

selected term co-ordination – निर्देशन करताना शीर्षकामधील महत्त्वाच्या संज्ञांबरोबर सह–संघटन करणे.

selective cataloguing – **निवडक तालिकीकरण** – तालिका नोंदीतील अनावश्यक वाटणारा भाग वगळणे, जास्त वापरल्या जाणाऱ्या पुस्तकांचीच फक्त पूर्ण नोंद करणे. याद्वारे तालिकीकरणाचा वेळ व खर्च वाचविला जातो.

selective classification – **निवडक वर्गीकरण** – कमी वापरल्या जाणाऱ्या ग्रंथांचा मोठा गट वेगळा करून वर्गानुक्रमानुसार अथवा दाखलअंकानुसार मांडणी केली जाते. या ग्रंथाबाबत वर्गीकरण व तालिकीकरण यांचा खर्च वाचविता येतो.

selective record service – **निवडक नोंद सेवा** – यजमान ग्रंथालयाच्या डाटाबेसमधून वेगवेगळ्या ग्रंथालयांना उपयुक्त ठरणाऱ्या तालिकानोंदींची निवड करण्याची पुरविलेली सेवा.

self–charging system / self issue system – **स्वयं-देवघेव पद्धती** – वाचक स्वतःच अंशतः अथवा संपूर्ण नोंद करून ग्रंथ वाचनासाठी घेतो.

self–checkout machine – **स्वयंचलित यंत्राद्वारे साहित्य बाहेर नेणे.**

semi – annual / half yearly / bi–annual – **अर्धवार्षिक/षण्मासिक** – सहा महिन्यांनी प्रकाशित होणारे नियतकालिक.

semicolon – **अर्धविराम** (;)

semi–monthly / fortnightly / bi–weekly / half–monthly – **पाक्षिक** – दर पंधरा दिवसांनी प्रकाशित होणारे नियतकालिक.

semi–professional – **कनिष्ठ कार्यकुशल कर्मचारी/अर्धकुशल कर्मचारी** – ग्रंथालयातील कनिष्ठ स्तरावरील प्रशिक्षित कर्मचारी.

semi – weekly / twice weekly – **अर्धसाप्ताहिक** – आठवड्यातून दोन वेळा प्रकाशित होणारे नियतकालिक.

seminal mnemonics / unscheduled mnemonics – **बीजसुलभ/स्मृतिसुलभता/अनुसूचिबाह्य स्मृतिसाधके.**

seminar – **चर्चासत्र/परिसंवाद/सभा** – विशिष्ट विषयावर तज्ज्ञ व्यक्तींनी केलेली चर्चा/युक्तिवाद यांचे सत्र.

seminar room – **परिसंवाद / चर्चासत्र/चर्चा कक्ष** – चर्चा, वादविवाद आयोजित करण्याकरिता निर्माण केलेले कक्ष.

sequel – **उत्तरभाग** – **साहित्यातील एखादी कृती** – बरेचदा कादंबरी परिपूर्ण असते. परंतु, आधीच्या साहित्यकृतीचा तो उत्तरावर्ती भाग असतो. उदा. झोंबी-नांगरणी-घरभिंती-काचवेल (आनंद यादव)

sequence – **अनुक्रम** – घटना, कृती वगैरेंचा क्रम.

serial – **क्रमकालिक** – (१) विविध भागांमध्ये केले जाणारे प्रकाशन. नियतकालिक, वृत्तपत्र, वार्षिक यांचे विशिष्ट काळाने पण नियमित होणारे प्रकाशन. (२) भागांमध्ये प्रकाशित होणारे पुस्तक. शीर्षक समान असते. (३) हप्त्याने प्रकाशित होणारी प्रदीर्घ कथा.

serial catalogue – **कालिकांची तालिका** – ग्रंथालयातील क्रमकालिकांची तालिका.

serial control – **कालिकांचे नियंत्रण**.

serial number – **अनुक्रमांक** – माला प्रकाशनातील विशिष्ट ग्रंथाचा प्रकाशनक्रमांक.

serial publication – **कालबद्ध प्रकाशन** – नियमितपणे प्रकाशित होणारे प्रकाशन.

serials – **कालिके** – नियमित कालावधीनंतर प्रसिद्ध किंवा प्रक्षेपित होणारी मालिका, प्रकाशन.

serials librarian – **कालिक ग्रंथपाल** –कालिकांची व्यवस्था पाहणारी व्यक्ती.

series – **माला** – (१) एकामागून एक घडणाऱ्या घटनांचा, गोष्टींचा गट. (२) एका विशिष्ट विषयासंबंधित समान मालाशीर्षकाखाली प्रकाशित होणारे खंड.

series area – **मालानोंद क्षेत्र** – तालिकेतील नोंदीमध्ये मालाविषयक उल्लेख करण्याचे स्थान.

series (name of) entry – **मालानाम नोंद** – ग्रंथसूची वा तालिकेमध्ये केलेली मालाशीर्षकाखाली प्रकाशनाची नोंद.

series note – **माला/टीप/टिपण** – ग्रंथसूची वा तालिकेमध्ये प्रकाशनाची नोंद करताना मालाशीर्षकाचे केलेले टिपण/मार्गदर्शक टीप.

series number – **मालाक्रमांक** – (१) मालिकेतील प्रकाशन क्रमांक. (२) प्रकाशकाने मालेतील प्रत्येक ग्रंथाला दिलेला क्रमांक.

series statement – **माला उत्तरदायित्व** – उत्तरदायित्वाची तालिकेतील माहिती.

series title – **मालाशीर्षक** – प्रकाशकाने ज्या मालेअंतर्गत ग्रंथांचे प्रकाशन केले आहे त्या मालेचे शीर्षक.

server – संगणकाच्या नेटवर्किंगसाठी सेवा देणारा मुख्य संगणक.

service – **सेवा** – ग्रंथालयातून वाचकांसाठी दिल्या जाणाऱ्या सुविधा.

set – **संच** – एकाच प्रकारच्या वस्तूंचा गट किंवा संघ.

shared – **सहभागी** – संयुक्त, सहकारी.

shared authorship – **सहकारी ग्रंथकारिता** – दोन व्यक्तींच्या सहकार्याने एकत्र केलेले संकलन, संपादन, भाषांतरे, रूपांतरण या स्वरूपाचे लेखन.

shared cataloguing – **सहकारी तत्त्वावरील तालिकीकरण** – (१) अनेक ग्रंथालयांनी एकत्र येऊन सहकारी तत्त्वावर ग्रंथखरेदी करणे–नवनवीन प्रकाशकांनी खरेदी करणे यामुळे शक्य होते. (२) खरेदी केलेल्या ग्रंथांचे लवकरात लवकर तालिकीकरण करून ते सभासद ग्रंथालयांना उपलब्ध करून देणे.

shared responsibility – संयुक्त जबाबदारी – ग्रंथाच्या निर्मितीसाठी दोन वा अधिक संख्या किंवा व्यक्ती जबाबदार असतील तर त्यास 'संयुक्त जबाबदारी' असे म्हणतात.

shareholders – भागधारक – संस्थेच्या भांडवलात हिस्सा असणारे.

sharemarket – समभाग बाजार.

sharpening – सूक्ष्म करणे – धार आणणे, टोक करणे, विषय स्पष्ट करणे.

sheaf – चिठ्ठी – कागदाची पट्टी(साधारण आकार).

sheaf catalogue – चिठ्ठीरूप तालिका – कागदाच्या चिठ्ठीवर तयार केलेली तालिका. ही तालिका विशिष्ट बांधणीमध्ये लावली जाते. यात नवीन चिठ्ठीरूप तालिका योग्य क्रमाने समाविष्ट करण्याची सोय असते.

sheet – ताव/कागदाचा मोठा तुकडा – (१) एखाद्या पदार्थाचा पातळ सपाट ताव किंवा तुकडा. (२) कागदाचा मोठा ताव.

sheet index – (नकाशांसाठी) पाननिर्देश – नकाशातील उठाव, क्रमांक पद्धती याविषयी निर्देश.

sheet map – कागदाच्या एका बाजूस काढलेला नकाशा.

sheets – (ग्रंथबांधणीपूर्वी) छापलेल्या कागदांचा संच.

shelf – कपाट/मांडणी.

shelf arrangement – कपाटावरील ग्रंथरचना.

shelf capacity – कपाटाची क्षमता – ग्रंथ सामावण्याची कपाटाची क्षमता.

shelf guide / shelf label – ग्रंथमांडणी केलेल्या कपाटावर कोणते ग्रंथ मांडले आहेत याची मार्गदर्शक चिठ्ठी.

shelf list – स्थान यादी – ग्रंथालयातील कपाटांमध्ये मांडलेल्या ग्रंथांची यादी.

shelf number – ग्रंथालयातील कपाटाला दिलेला क्रमांक – या क्रमांकाचा उल्लेख ग्रंथांकामध्ये काहीवेळा केला जातो. यामुळे ग्रंथाचे निश्चित स्थान समजण्यास मदत होते.

shelf mark – कपाटावरील खूण/चिन्ह – ग्रंथावर केलेली चिन्ह/खूण, ज्यावरून त्याचे कपाटातील स्थान दर्शविले जाते.

scheduled mnemonics – अनुसूचीबद्ध स्मृतिसुलभता – वर्गीकरणाच्या अनुसूचीमध्ये वापरलेली एक नियमावली, एकच संज्ञा.

shelve – फळीवर ठेवणे.

shelving – ग्रंथालयातील कपाटांमध्ये ग्रंथ जागेवर ठेवण्याची कृती.

shelving of book – कपाटामध्ये ग्रंथ जागेवर लावण्याची क्रिया.

shift key – संगणकाच्या कळपटावरील एक कळ – याच्या वापरामुळे मोठ्या (capital) लिपीतील अक्षरे उमटतात.

short cataloguing – लघु तालिकीकरण – तालिकेतील नोंदीमध्ये लेखक, प्रमुख शीर्षक व प्रकाशन दिनांकाचा उल्लेख केला जातो.

short discount title – कमी सूट देऊन मिळणारा ग्रंथ.

short range reference service – शीघ्रसंदर्भसेवा – कमी वेळात संदर्भ उपलब्ध करून देणारी सेवा.

short story – लघुकथा – साधारणत: १०,००० पेक्षा कमी शब्दांचा वापर केलेली कथा.

short term loan – कमी कालावधीसाठीचे कर्ज.

short title – लघुशीर्षक/संक्षिप्त ग्रंथनाम – तालिकेतील नोंदीवरून ग्रंथ ओळखता येईल असे ग्रंथशीर्षक.

short title system – लघुशीर्षक पद्धती – प्रकाशनांमध्ये ग्रंथसूचीचा संदर्भ देताना एकदा संपूर्ण उल्लेख केला असेल तर नंतर लघुस्वरूपात ग्रंथशीर्षक देण्याची पद्धती.

showcase – प्रदर्शन पेटी.

signature – स्वाक्षरी/सही.

signed article – स्वाक्षरित लेख.

signed edition / autographed edition – स्वाक्षरित आवृत्ती – (१) लेखकाची स्वाक्षरी असलेली आवृत्ती. (२) लेखकाने स्वाक्षरी केलेली मर्यादित स्वरूपातील आवृत्ती.

significant title – अर्थपूर्ण ग्रंथनाम – अशा ग्रंथनामामुळे ग्रंथाचा विषय लक्षात येतो.

simple book – साधे/साधा ग्रंथ.

simple heading – साधे शीर्षक.

simple notation – साधे (सुलभ/सोपे) चिन्हांकन.

simplified cataloguing – सुलभ तालिकीकरण – तालिकीकरणाच्या पद्धतीप्रमाणे करावयाच्या नोंदीतील काही भाग वगळणे, यामुळे तालिकीकरणामध्ये सुलभता येते.

simultation technique – प्रतिआभास तंत्र – संगणकावर आधारित असे हे तंत्र असून त्यावर एखाद्या कार्यप्रणालीचा प्रतिभास निर्माण करून तो अत्यंत कार्यक्षम पद्धतीने अंमलात आणण्यासाठी योग्य असा पर्याय निवडण्यास मदत केली जाते.

signed page – स्वाक्षरीत पृष्ठ.

single entry system – एक नोंद पद्धती – ज्यामध्ये फक्त खर्चाची नोंद केली जाते अशी नोंद पद्धती.

single volumed book – एकखंडीय ग्रंथ.

site – स्थळ/जागा.

size – आकार – कोणत्याही वस्तूचे बाह्यस्वरूप.

size of book – (ग्रंथाचा) आकार – ग्रंथाच्या उंचीवरून आकार ठरविला जातो.

size notation – ग्रंथाचा आकार दर्शविण्याची पद्धती – सेंमी किंवा इंचानुसार आकार दर्शविला जातो.

slanted abstract – कलदर्शक सारलेख – लेखातील विशिष्ट मजकुराचा दृष्टिकोन लक्षात घेऊन सारलेखन केले जाते. याद्वारे विशिष्ट वाचकसमूहाचे लक्ष वेधून घेतले जाते.

slide – दृश्यपट्टिका – पडद्यावर दाखवायचे छायाचित्रणाच्या फितीवरील छायाचित्र, पारदर्शिका, सरकचित्र.

sliding shelves – सरकती मांडणी – कपाटे पुढे ओढण्याची सोय केलेली मांडणी.

slip – चिट्ठी – कागदाचा चिठोरा.

society – समूह – धार्मिक परोपकारी, सांस्कृतिक, सहकारी, राजकीय, देशप्रेमाच्या किंवा इतर कारणांकरिता एकत्र आलेल्या व्यक्तींचा समूह.

society publication – संस्थेचे प्रकाशन.

soft currency – सुलभ मुद्रा – सुलभ म्हणजेच रोख चलन.

soft key – मृदुकळ – संगणकाच्या कळपटावरील एक कळ (उदा. F1).

software – आज्ञावली – विशिष्ट बाबींशी संबंधित लिहिलेल्या वेगवेगळ्या आज्ञावलींचा एकत्रित वापर करताना वापरलेले संबोधन. सॉफ्टवेअर आणि प्रोग्रॅम ही नावे अनेक वेळा परस्परपूरक वापरली जातात.

sort key – क्रम कळ – संगणकाच्या कळपटावरील एक कळ. समान गुणधर्मानुसार निरनिराळे गट करताना माहिती गटातील क्रम ठरविण्यासाठी वापरायची कळ.

sorting – वर्गवारी विभागणी – समान गुणधर्मानुसार केलेली वाटणी. माहितीची समान विषयानुसार विभागणी.

sought heading – इष्ट शीर्षक/वांछित शीर्षक.

sought link – इष्ट दुवा/वांछित दुवा.

sound library – ध्वनिमुद्रितांचे ग्रंथालय.

source – प्राप्तिस्थान/उद्गम – ग्रंथालयात माहिती ज्या ग्रंथातून मिळते त्या माहितीचे प्राप्तिस्थान.

source book – साधन ग्रंथ.

source document – साधन प्रलेख/माहितीचे मूलस्थान – माहिती उपलब्ध असलेले वाचनसाहित्य.

source index – साधन निर्देश/प्राप्तिस्थानांची माहिती दिलेला निर्देश – विविध शंकांचे निरसन करताना प्राप्तिस्थाने म्हणून वापरलेल्या साहित्याचा तयार केलेला निर्देश.

source language – साधन भाषा – माहिती उपलब्ध असलेल्या साहित्याची मूळ भाषा.

source list – साधनयादी – लेखकाने वापरलेल्या माहिती प्राप्तिस्थानांची यादी.

source material – **साधन सामग्री** – माहितीचे प्राप्तीस्थान असलेले साहित्य.

souvenir – **स्मरणिका** – एखाद्या माहितीचे समारंभानिमित्त तयार केलेले प्रकाशन.

space bar – **अंतरदंड** – यामुळे अक्षरछपाईमध्ये अंतर राखले जाते.

space facet – **स्थलमुख/स्थलपैलू** – वर्गीकरणासाठी एक लक्षण गुण. ग्रंथविषय हा विशिष्ट भूभागाशी माहिती देणारा असेल त्यावेळी वर्गांकामध्ये त्याचा निर्देश करण्यासाठी स्थल पैलू उपयुक्त ठरतो.

space isolate – **स्थल विभक्तक/उपांग.**

spacing – **अंतर संयोजन** – मजकुराची मांडणी करताना शब्द व वाक्य यामध्ये केलेले समायोजन.

spam – **अनपेक्षित इ-मेल किंवा जंक मेल.**

spatial contiguity – **स्थलसंलग्नता.**

special – **विशेष/खास/वैशिष्ट्यपूर्ण.**

special bibliography – **विशेष ग्रंथसूची** – एकाच विशिष्ट गुणाचा विचार करून तयार केलेली ग्रंथसूची.

special classification – **विशेष वर्गीकरण** –(१) ज्ञानाच्या एकाच विभागासाठी उपयुक्त असलेले वर्गीकरण. (२) एखाद्या विषयापुरते मर्यादित वर्गीकरण.

special edition – **विशेषावृत्ती** – इतर आवृत्तीपेक्षा काही विशिष्ट कारणाने विशेषत्व प्राप्त झालेली आवृत्ती. उदा. कागद, चित्रे यांची विशिष्ट रचना.

special librarian – **विशेष ग्रंथालयाचे ग्रंथपाल.**

special librarianship – **विशेष ग्रंथालयाचे ग्रंथपालन.**

special library – **विशेष ग्रंथालय** – प्रमुख विषयावरील ग्रंथांचे उद्दिष्ट ठेवून संग्रह केलेले ग्रंथालय.

special number / special issue – **विशेषांक** – नियतकालिकाचा विशेष प्रसंगी प्रसिद्ध होणारा किंवा विशेष विषयावर प्रसिद्ध होणारा अंक. उदा– दिवाळी अंक.

special isolate idea – **विशेष उपांग विचार.**

specialist – **विशेषज्ञ** – एखाद्या विषयातील तज्ज्ञ व्यक्ती.

specials – **विशिष्ट ज्ञानशाखा** – (एखाद्या विषयाच्या).

species – **उपवर्ग/उपजाती** –(१) ग्रंथांचे वर्गीकरण सखोलरीत्या करताना वर्गांचे पाडलेले विभाग. (२) विशिष्ट गुणधर्म असलेला आणि परस्परांत प्रजोत्पादन करू शकणारा प्राण्यांचा गट.

specific – **विनिर्दिष्ट/विवक्षित** – विशिष्ट गोष्टीबाबतचा.

specific cross reference – **विशिष्ट वक्र संदर्भ** – तालिकेमध्ये दिलेला विशिष्ट शीर्षकाचा संदर्भ.

specific entry – **विशिष्ट नोंद** – प्रत्यक्ष विषयाच्या शीर्षकाखाली केलेली नोंद.

specific index – विशिष्ट निर्देश – एका विषयाखाली एकच नोंद केलेला निर्देश.

specific information – विशिष्ट माहिती.

specific reference – विशिष्ट संदर्भ – तालिकेमध्ये पहा नोंदीखाली अचूक विषय शीर्षक दिले जाते तो संदर्भ.

specific subject – विशिष्ट विषय – (१) वर्गीकरण करताना विशिष्ट प्रलेखाला अचूक दर्शविणारा विषय. (२) ज्ञानशाखेचा असा विभाग त्याची वृद्धी/व्याप्ती आणि सखोलता ग्रंथातील प्रतिपाद्य विषयाशी मिळतीजुळती असावी.

subject entry – विशिष्ट विषय नोंद – ज्या ग्रंथात संबंधित विषयावर माहिती दिलेली असते तो ग्रंथ दाखविणारी जी नोंद असते तिला 'विशिष्ट विषय नोंद' असे म्हणतात.

specification / specificity – निश्चितपणा/विशिष्टीकरण/विशेष निर्देशन – (१) ग्रंथात प्रतिपाद्य केलेल्या विषयाचे मुख्य विषय आणि घटक विषय अथवा पैलू वर्गांकामध्ये दाखविण्याची सोय.

specifications – विवरणे/मानक – प्रमाणित आकार, रचना, मांडणी.

specificity – विशेषत्व – बारकाव्यासारख्या, जर प्रगणनाद्वारे बारकावा प्राप्त करता आला तर विशेषत्वही संश्लेषणातून प्राप्त होते. विशिष्ट विषयांतील सर्व घटकांचे प्रतिनिधित्व करण्याची वर्गीकरणाची क्षमता.

speech recognition – उच्चार ओळख – बोलीभाषेचे रूपांतर संगणकभाषेत करण्याची प्रक्रिया.

speech synthesis – उच्चार विश्लेषण – संगणकावरील ध्वनिवर्धक सूचना.

spell checker – शुद्धलेखन तपासनीस – संगणकामध्ये इंग्रजी शब्दरचना तपासणारी यंत्रणा. चूक आढळल्यास पर्यायी शब्द पुरविणारी यंत्रणा.

spine of the book – ग्रंथाचा कणा.

spine title – ग्रंथाच्या कण्यावर छापलेले शीर्षक – ग्रंथशीर्षक पृष्ठावर लिहिलेल्या शीर्षकापेक्षा हे शीर्षक छोटे असते.

Sponsor Classification – स्पेन्सर वर्गीकरण – विज्ञान वर्गीकरणामध्ये दिलेल्या वर्गपद्धती ज्या १८६४ मध्ये हर्बट स्पेन्सर यांनी तयार केल्या.

spiral binding – सर्पिल बांधणी.

split catalogue – विभाजित तालिका – (१) विविध शीर्षकांखाली विखुरलेली तालिका. (२) विस्कळितरीत्या ठेवलेली तालिका. (३) विभाजित तालिका.

spooling – रांगेत लावणे – संगणकामध्ये मूलभूत माहितीचा तात्पुरता संचय करणे.

sports library – क्रीडाविषयक ग्रंथालय.

square book – आयताकृती ग्रंथ.

square brackets – **चौकटी कंस** – [ ] तालिकीकरण व ग्रंथसूचीमध्ये नोंद करताना मूळ ग्रंथामध्ये न दिलेली माहिती तालिकाकार देतो.

stabbing – **सळी बांधणी.**

stack room / book stack – **ग्रंथसंग्रह दालन** – (१) जेथे ग्रंथसंग्रह ठेवलेला असतो. (२) एकाहून अधिक मजल्यांवर ग्रंथ साठविण्याची कपाटे मांडण्याची सुविधा.

stack guide – **ग्रंथसंग्रहातील फलक.**

staff – **कर्मचारी/सेवक/कर्मचारी वर्ग.**

staff manual – **कर्मचारी संहिता/निर्देशपुस्तक/कार्य मार्गदर्शन संहिता** – कर्मचारी वर्गाच्या दैनंदिन उपयोगासाठी तसेच कार्य मार्गदर्शनार्थ पुस्तिका.

staff room – **कर्मचारी कक्ष/खोली.**

stalwarts – **जाणकार/तज्ज्ञ** – अत्यंत नावाजलेली व्यक्ती.

stamp – **ठसा/शिक्का.**

stamping – **मुद्रांकन/शिक्के मारणे.**

stand – **घोडा** – फळा अथवा छायाचित्र प्रदर्शित करण्यासाठीचे कटघर.

standard – **मानक** – अधिकृत, प्रमाणित, दर्जेदार नमुना, मार्गदर्शिका किंवा मार्गदर्शनासाठी नमुना, दर्जेदार, प्रमाणित, अधिकृत.

standard author – **प्रतिष्ठित लेखक** – साहित्यक्षेत्रातील मोठा सहभाग असलेली व्यक्ती.

standard book – **दर्जेदार ग्रंथ.**

standard book number – **अधिकृत ग्रंथांक** – प्रत्येक ग्रंथाला दिला जाणारा नऊ अंकी क्रमांक.

standard card – **विहित आकाराचे पत्र.**

standard copy – **दर्जेदार/मान्यताप्राप्त गुण असलेली प्रत.**

standard edition – **प्रमाणित आवृत्ती** – एखाद्या स्वस्त आवृत्तीपेक्षा अधिक चांगली आवृत्ती. यात परिचय व टिपांचा समावेश केला जातो.

standard format – **विहित/मान्यताप्राप्त/प्रमाणित स्वरूप** – एखाद्या पुस्तकाच्या ग्रंथवर्णनाचा सर्वसाधारणपणे स्वीकृत नमुना, साचा, आराखडा.

standard number – **विहित क्रमांक.**

standard subdivision – **सामान्य उपविभाग/स्वरूपविभाग** – वर्गीकरण पद्धतीतील चिन्हांकन दर्शविणारा आणि कोणत्याही विषयाला किंवा ज्ञानशाखेला जोडता येतात तसेच तक्त्यातील वर्गांकालाही आवश्यकतेनुसार जोडता येतात असे उपविभाग.

standard title – **अधिकृत शीर्षक** – तालिकेमध्ये ज्या शीर्षकाखाली नोंद केली जाते असे शीर्षक.

standard work – **दर्जेदार काम/लिखाण** – कायमस्वरूपी बहुमूल्य असणारा ग्रंथ.

standard for library service – **ग्रंथालय सेवेसाठी प्रमाणके** – ग्रंथालय सेवेचे मूल्यमापन करता येईल अशी प्रमाणके.

standardization – **प्रमाणीकरण** – प्रमाणित रचना सुचविण्याची क्रिया.

standing – **स्थायी**.

standing committee – **स्थायी समिती**.

standing order – **स्थायी आदेश** – नेहमीसाठी कार्यान्वित राहू शकेल असा आदेश.

standing vendor – **स्थायी विक्रेता** – नेहमी ग्रंथपुरवठा करणारा विक्रेता.

star map / astronomical map – तारकांच्या साहाय्याने काढलेला नकाशा.

star network – **तारकाकृती संगणकजाळे** – संगणक जाळ्यातील प्रत्येक संगणक मध्यवर्ती संगणकाला जोडलेला असतो.

starter – **आरंभचिन्ह** – [C] दशांश वर्गीकरण पद्धतीमध्ये वर्गांच्या सुरुवातीला दिला जाणारा पहिला अर्धा गोल कंस.

state library – **राज्य ग्रंथालय** – राज्य शासनाने दर्जा दिलेले राज्य ग्रंथालय.

statement – **उत्तरदायित्व/विवरण**.

statement of responsibility – **उत्तरदायित्व विधान** – ग्रंथातील विचारांना जबाबदार असलेल्या व्यक्तींची वा संस्थांची माहिती म्हणजेच उत्तरदायित्व विषयक विधान.

state - of - art - report – **सद्य:स्थितीदर्शक अहवाल** – एखाद्या विषयातील ताज्या लेखांचे संदर्भ पुरवणे, नियतकालिकातील लेखांची प्रत अथवा भाषांतर पुरवणे.

state central library – **राज्य मध्यवर्ती ग्रंथालय** – राज्याचे प्रमुख ग्रंथालय.

state central librarian – **राज्य मध्यवर्ती ग्रंथालयाचा ग्रंथपाल**.

state central library services – **राज्य मध्यवर्ती ग्रंथालय सेवा**.

state library council – **राज्य ग्रंथालय परिषद** – राज्यातील सार्वजनिक ग्रंथालयांच्या विकासाचे मार्ग शासनाला सुचविणारी समिती.

stationary – **लेखनसामग्री**.

statistical bibliography – **ग्रंथसंख्यात्मक ग्रंथसूची** – ग्रंथालयातील ग्रंथ व नियतकालिकांची संख्यादर्शक सूची.

statistical data – **सांख्यिकीय माहिती** – अंकीय प्रारूप माहिती.

statistical source - सांख्यिकीय साधन.

statistics - संख्यात्मक माहिती - वस्तुस्थिती संख्याशास्त्र.

statistics (library) - (ग्रंथालयाची) आकडेवारी.

status - स्थान/प्रतिष्ठा.

statute - नियम/अधिनियम - वैधानिक संस्थेने अंतर्गत कारभारासाठी तयार केलेले मान्यताप्राप्त नियम.

statutory - सांविधितक/संविधीमान्य/कायदेशीर.

stereotyping - साचेबंद मुद्रण.

stock - साठा/संग्रह.

stock book - ग्रंथसंग्रहाची नोंदवही.

stock checking - ग्रंथसंग्रह तपासणी.

stock in - उपलब्ध आहे.

stock register - ग्रंथसंग्रहाची नोंदवही.

stock taking - ग्रंथसंग्रह पडताळणी - ग्रंथालयातील सर्व वाचनसाहित्य आहे की नाही याची तपासणी.

stock taking register - ग्रंथसंग्रह पडताळणीची नोंदवही.

stock verification - परिगणन/ग्रंथपडताळणी.

stopword - विरामक शब्द - साठवण, थांबवून ठेवणारे शब्दमुद्रा. उदा - ए, ॲन, द

storage - संचयीकरण - (१) भविष्यकाळात उपयोगी पडण्यासाठी जमा करणे. (२) संगणकामध्ये केलेला माहितीचा साठा.

storage capacity - संचय क्षमता/साठवण क्षमता.

storage devices - संचयन साधन - संगणकामध्ये माहिती समाविष्ट करणे, साठवण करणे, जतन करणे व काढून घेण्याचे साधन.

stray issue of periodical - नियतकालिकाचा फुटकळ अंक - नियतकालिकाच्या सर्व अंकाऐवजी एखादा अंक.

striking title - ठळक ग्रंथनाम.

string - साखळी - निर्देशन करताना तयार केलेली शब्दसमूह साखळी.

strip index - पट्ट्यांवरील निर्देश - कागदाच्या पट्ट्यांवर नोंदी करून निर्देशन केले जाते.

structural – संरचनात्मक/रचनाधिकृत/रचनात्मक.

structural indexing language – रचनाधिकृत निर्देशनभाषा.

structural notation – रचनात्मक चिन्हांकन – वर्गीकरण पद्धतीची संरचना दर्शविणारे चिन्हांकन.

structure – आराखडा/योजना करणे.

student's card – विद्यार्थी पत्र.

study / carrel / cubicle / alcove – अभ्यासिका.

study circle – अभ्यास मंडळ – एखाद्या विषयाशी संबंधित घटकावर सखोल चर्चा घडवून आणणारे मंडळ.

study group – अभ्यासगट – विशिष्ट विषयाचा सखोल अभ्यास करणारा गट.

style guide – शैली मार्गदर्शक – संशोधन अहवाल लिखाणाचे तंत्र स्पष्ट करणारे नियम.

style manual – शैली नियमपुस्तिका – लेख लिहिताना आवश्यक मांडणी सुचविणारे नियम.

sub – उप/कनिष्ठ.

sub class – उपवर्ग – मुख्य वर्गाखालचा दर्जा असणारा विषय.

sub committee – उपसमिती – मुख्य समितीतील काही सदस्यांची विशिष्ट कामाकरिता नेमलेली समिती.

sub division – उपविभाग – उपविभागणी वर्गीकरण करताना केलेली विभागणी.

sub device – उपप्रयुक्ती.

sub editor – उपसंपादक – संपादकापेक्षा लगेच खालच्या दर्जाची व्यक्ती.

sub entry – उपनोंद – निर्देशन करताना संपूर्ण नोंदीतून नोंद करण्याचा शब्द वगळता उरलेल्या मजकुराची केलेली नोंद.

sub heading – उपशीर्षक.

sub index – उपनिर्देश – निर्देशामध्ये असलेला निर्देश.

sub title – उपग्रंथनाम – मुख्य ग्रंथनामानंतरचा ग्रंथनामातील भाग.

subfields – उपघटक – एकाच घटकामध्ये लिहिल्या जाणाऱ्या माहितीचे वेगवेगळे भाग सामावून घेण्यासाठी करावी लागणारी सोय. उदा. लेखकाच्या दोन उपघटक (subfields) असू शकतात. एकात लेखकाचे नाव तर दुसऱ्यात त्याची भूमिका (संपादक, भाषांतर वगैरे) लिहिता येते. याचा उपयोग घटकामधील संपूर्ण माहिती प्रत्येकवेळी प्रदान करण्याऐवजी विशिष्ट घटकामधील माहिती प्रदान करण्यासाठी किंवा विशिष्ट उपघटकातील संगणकात निर्देश तयार करण्याकरिता होतो.

subject – विषय – ग्रंथातील मजकुराविषयी ठळक वर्णन.

subject analysis – विषयनिहाय विश्लेषण.

subject analytical entry – **विषय विश्लेषणात्मक नोंद** – (१) ग्रंथाच्या विषयाचे विश्लेषण अंतर्भूत असलेली नोंद. (२) विशिष्ट विषयाची माहिती ग्रंथाच्या ज्या भागात दिलेली असते तो भाग दाखविणारी नोंद.

subject arrangement – **विषयनिहाय ग्रंथरचना** – विषयानुसार केलेली ग्रंथरचना.

subject authority file – **विषयाची अधिकृत नोंद** – विशिष्ट तालिकेमधील विषयशीर्षक व त्यांचे संदर्भ यांची संगणकीय सूची.

subject bibliography – **विषय ग्रंथसूची** – समान विषयावर लिहिलेल्या ग्रंथांची सूची.

subject catalogue – **विषयदर्शक तालिका / विषय तालिका** – विषयानुसार नोंदीची रचना केलेली तालिका.

subject classification – **विषय वर्गीकरण** – ज्याची रचना ब्लिस यांनी केली.

subject department / subject libraries – **विशिष्ट विषयानुरूप ग्रंथालय विभाग.**

subject device – **विषय क्लृप्ती / युक्ती** – डॉ. रंगनाथन् यांची संज्ञा. वर्गीकरणासाठी वापरण्याचे तत्त्व. विषयाला प्राधान्य देऊन वर्गांक तयार करण्याची क्लृप्ती / युक्ती.

subject directroy – **विषय निर्देशिका.**

subject entry – **विषयानुसार / विषयदर्शक नोंद** – (१) ग्रंथाचा विषय दर्शविणाऱ्या शीर्षकाखाली केलेली नोंद. (२) ग्रंथातील विषयाबद्दल माहिती देणारी नोंद.

subject focus – ग्रंथालयात प्राधान्य दिलेला विषय.

subject gateways – **विषय मार्गपथ** – विषयातील मुख्य घटक.

subject guide / topic guide – **(ग्रंथालयातील) विषयानुरूप मांडणीचे मार्गदर्शक.**

subject heading – **विषय शीर्षक** – तालिकेतील नोंद करण्यासाठी वापरला जाणारा ग्रंथातील मजकुराला विषय दर्शविणारा शब्दसमूह.

subject librarian – **विषय ग्रंथपाल** – विशिष्ट विषयाबाबत मार्गदर्शन करणारी ग्रंथालयातील व्यक्ती.

subject reference – **विषयाचा संदर्भ** – एका विषयाकडून दुसऱ्या विषयाचा नोंदीमध्ये दिलेला संदर्भ.

subject search – विषय शोध.

subject series – **विषय माला** – प्रकाशकाने एका विषयावर छापलेली पुस्तके, एका मालाशीर्षकाखाली छापली जातात. अनेक लेखकांनी लिहिलेली पुस्तके.

subject specialist – विषयतज्ज्ञ / विशेषज्ञ.

subject specialization – **विषय विशिष्टीकरण** – एका भौगोलिक क्षेत्रातील ग्रंथालयांनी एकत्र येऊन विशिष्ट विषयांची पुस्तके सहकारी तत्त्वावर खरेदी करणे. काहीवेळा काही ग्रंथालयांमध्ये विशिष्ट विषयाच्या बाबतीत 'संग्रही ग्रंथालय' ही भूमिका घेतली जाते. काढून टाकले जातील असे ग्रंथ केवळ संग्रही ठेवले जातात.

subject specific – **विशिष्ट विषय** – ग्रंथात प्रतिपादन केलेला प्रमुख विषय.

subject work entry – **विषयदर्शक शब्दनोंद** – ग्रंथाचा विषय दर्शविणारा ग्रंथशीर्षकातील शब्द निवडून त्या विषयशीर्षकाखाली केलेली नोंद.

subjective – **वैयक्तिक/आत्मनिष्ठ/व्यक्तिनिष्ठ.**

subordinate – **गौण/आश्रयी/दुय्यम** – विषयाचे सूक्ष्म अगर लहान विभाग.

subordinate class – **दुय्यम वर्ग.**

subordination – **वर्गीकरण सारणीमध्ये विषयसंज्ञेला मिळालेले अचूक स्थान.**

subscriber – **नियतकालिकाचा वर्गणीदार/सभासद.**

subscriber's edition – **वर्गणीदारांसाठी आवृत्ती** – प्रकाशनपूर्व मागणी करण्यासाठीच फक्त प्रसिद्ध केलेली आवृत्ती.

subscription – **वर्गणी** – नियतकालिक भागविण्यासाठी लागणारे मूल्य/किंमत.

subscription books – **वर्गणी ग्रंथ** – संस्थांद्वारे प्रकाशित होणारी, विशिष्ट कालावधीने प्रकाशित होणारी व वर्गणीदारांना दिली जाणारी पुस्तके.

subscription library / circulating library – **वर्गणी ग्रंथालय** – वार्षिक वर्गणी घेऊन सेवा देणारे ग्रंथालय.

subscription price / pre publication price – **प्रकाशनपूर्व किंमत** – ग्रंथ प्रकाशनापूर्वी असलेली किंमत बहुधा ग्रंथ प्रकाशनानंतरच्या किमतीपेक्षा कमी असते. प्रकाशकाला प्रकाशन विक्रीबाबत मार्गदर्शन मिळविण्यासाठी अशी किंमत जाहीर केली जाते.

subseries – **उपमाला** – (१) दुसऱ्या मालिकेतील ग्रंथांशी सहसंबंधित मालेतील पुस्तके. (२) मालेमध्ये असलेली दुय्यम माला म्हणजे व्यापक मालेबरोबर त्याचा एक विभाग असणारी माला.

subsidiary – **गौण** – (१) ग्रंथातील मजकुराव्यतिरिक्त शेष भाग – यात ग्रंथसूची, निर्देश, मलपृष्ठ यांचा समावेश होतो. (२) कमी महत्त्वाचे.

subsidiary rights – **शेष हक्क** – ग्रंथाच्या लेखनाव्यतिरिक्त लेखकाला नाट्यरूपांतर, भाषांतर, चित्रपट, मालिका यासाठी असलेला मालकी हक्क.

sub-subsection – **उप-उपविभाग** – उपविभागाची पुढील विभागणी.

subsystem – **उपपद्धती.**

sub–title – उपशीर्षक – (१) मुख्य शीर्षकाचा आशय अधिक स्पष्ट करणारे शीर्षक मुख्य शीर्षकाचा उत्तरार्ध म्हणून येते. (२) द्वितीयक किंवा दुय्यम ग्रंथनाम. काहीवेळा ग्रंथनामाचे विश्लेषण करणारा हा भाग असतो. हा भाग एकतर ग्रंथनामाचा विस्तार करतो किंवा ग्रंथनाम मार्गदर्शित करतो.

suggestion card / recommendation slip / requisition slip – ग्रंथखरेदीसाठी दिलेले शिफारसपत्र.

summary – सारांश/संक्षिप्त – (१) एखाद्या लेखाचा आढावा घेणारा संक्षिप्त मजकूर. (२) डेसिमल वर्गीकरण पद्धतीत असलेली ज्ञान विभाजनाची प्रमुख रूपरेषा. अशा सारांशाच्या तीन रूपरेषा आहेत. त्यात वाढत्या श्रेणीने तपशील दिलेले आहेत.

summum genus / basic class – मूळ वर्ग/आधारभूत वर्ग – वर्गीकरणाचा गाभा.

superannuation – सेवानिवृत्ती/निवृत्ती – नियत बयोमानानंतर कार्यालय सोडणे.

super computer – उत्कृष्ट संगणक – अतिशय कार्यक्षम, जास्त माहिती साठविणारा, उच्च गती असलेला संगणक.

super imposition device – अधिसमावेशन क्लृप्ती/युक्ती – द्विबिंदू वर्गीकरणामध्ये एकाच पैलूदर्शक दोन केंद्रे असतात. तेव्हा प्रभावी व गौर केंद्र दर्शविण्यासाठी (–) या संयोगचिन्हाचा वापर करण्याची क्लृप्ती/युक्ती.

superoridinate class – प्रमुख वर्ग – उदा. ३०० सामाजिक शास्त्रे.

supervisor – निरीक्षक – अशी व्यक्ती कर्मचाऱ्यांच्या कामामध्ये समन्वय साधते व कार्य करून घेते.

supplement – पुरवणी – एखाद्या प्रकाशनाला पूरक माहिती दिलेले वेगळे प्रकाशन.

supplement number – पुरवणी अंक – मूळ ग्रंथात भर घालणारा ग्रंथ क्रमांक.

supplement facet – पुरवणी पैलू.

supplement to author statement – लेखकाचे उत्तरदायित्व सांगणारी पुरवणी माहिती.

supplement to a periodical – नियतकालिकाची पुरवणी.

supplementary classification – पुरवणी वर्गीकरण – एक दृष्टिकोन वर्गीकरण (जसे यु.डी.सी. ड्युई डेसिमल वर्गीकरण/जे विषयाचे त्यातील दृष्टिकोनानुसार विभाजन करते. त्यातील वर्गानुक्रमे निर्देश मात्र एका विषय संज्ञेखाली हे सर्व दृष्टिकोन एकत्र आणणे, याला 'पुरवणी वर्गीकरण' म्हणतात.)

supplied title – पूरक शीर्षक – संशोधन व अभ्यास चालू असलेल्या एखाद्या ग्रंथाला तालिकाकाराने दिलेले पूरक शीर्षक.

supplier – पुरवठाकार/पुरवठा करणारा – जो वस्तूंचा मागणीनुसार पुरवठा करतो.

supposed author / attributed author / presumed author – संदिग्ध ग्रंथकार – ग्रंथाच्या लेखनाबाबत अधिकृतता साशंक असल्यामुळे ग्रंथाचे श्रेय ज्याला दिले जाते तो 'संदिग्ध ग्रंथकार.'

supporting staff – साहाय्यक कर्मचारी.

suppressed – निषिद्ध (वाङ्मय) – अविश्वसनीयता, अचूकतेचा अभाव किंवा अनैतिकता यामुळे लेखक, प्रकाशन व शासनाने निषिद्ध ठरवलेले साहित्य.

surname – आडनाव – (१) कुटुंबाचे नाव. (२) एखाद्याने आपल्या व्यक्तिनामासोबत जोडलेले कुलनाम अथवा आडनाव. तो हे नाव त्याच्या आप्तमंडळातील इतर सदस्यांबरोबर, सामाईकपणे धारण करतो. आडनाव पुष्कळ वेळा त्याच्या व्यक्तिनामाचा उल्लेख न करता वापरले जाते आणि कधी कधी वैयक्तिक ओळखीच्या बाहेर त्याचा उल्लेख, त्याची पदवी आणि पत्त्यासह वापरले जाते. तालिकेमध्ये अगर ग्रंथसूचीत नोंदीसाठी 'शीर्षक' म्हणून त्याचा वापर केला जातो.

surname indexing – आडनावानुसार निर्देशन.

suspended publication – स्थगित प्रकाशन – बंदी घातल्यामुळे अगर अडथळ्यामुळे स्थगित केलेले प्रकाशन.

syllabic notation / pronounciable notation – उच्चार चिन्हांकन – विशिष्ट क्रम असलेले उच्चारता येण्याजोगे चिन्हांकन.

symantics – भाषेतील चिन्हे – (शब्द, वाक्प्रचार, वक्तव्ये) आणि वस्तू, संकल्पना यांच्यातील संबंधाचा अभ्यास करण्याची पद्धती.

symbol – चिन्ह/संकेतचिन्ह – एखाद्या शब्दसमूहाऐवजी त्याची प्रतिनिधिक अशी खूण.

symposia – परिसंवादाचे वृत्त देणारे प्रकाशन.

symposium – परिसंवाद – नव्या विषयाचा परिचय करून देणारा परिसंवाद.

syndetic – संबंधक – उलट संदर्भ दिलेल्या नोंदी माहितीची प्रतिप्रासी करताना उपयुक्त असलेले रोम वा अधिक संबंधित प्रलेख.

syndetic catalogue – संबंध तालिका – उलट संदर्भ देणारी कोशतालिका–व्यापक विषयाकडून संकोची संज्ञेकडे जाणाऱ्या विषयांच्या उलट संदर्भ दिलेल्या नोंदी.

syndetic index – संबंधक निर्देश – विषयनिर्देशातील नातेसंबंध दिलेला निर्देश. निर्देशनामध्ये उपशीर्षकांचा व उलटसंदर्भाचा केलेला उपयोग.

syndetic structure – संबंधक आराखडा/संरचना.

synecdoche – उपलक्षण/लक्षणा (अलंकार) – एखाद्या व्यापक शाखेसाठी वापरला जाणारा बोलीभाषेतील रूढ शब्द. उदा. 'भाकरी' (अन्न या व्यापक संज्ञेसाठी.)

synonym – समानार्थी शब्द/समानार्थक.

synopsis – **आराखडा/सारांश/रूपरेषा/सार** – (१) ग्रंथाचा आढावा घेणारा परिच्छेद. (२) एखाद्या पुस्तकाचा, लेखाचा, प्रबंधाचा सारांश, रूपरेखा, रूपरेषा.

synoptic journal – **रूपरेखात्मक नियतकालिक** – नियतकालिकामधील लेखांची रूपरेषात्मक ओळख देणारे नियतकालिक.

syntax – **वाक्यरचना** – संरचनेतील शब्दांचा अचूक वापर करण्यासाठीची नियमावली.

synthesis – **संश्लेषण/एकत्र आणणे** – उपविषयांना वा घटक नियमांना एकत्र आणून त्यांचा एक पूर्ण वर्गांक तयार करणे.

synthesis of number – **अंकांचे संश्लेषण** – अंकबांधणी/वर्गांक तयार करणे यासाठी असलेली दुसरी संज्ञा.

synthetic classification – **संश्लेषणात्मक वर्गीकरण** – गुंतागुंतीच्या विषयांचे वर्गीकरण करण्याची पद्धती.

synthetic indexing – **संश्लेषणात्मक निर्देशन** – गुंतागुंतीच्या विषयांचे निर्देशन करताना विषयशीर्षक निवडण्याची पद्धती.

synthetic indexing language – **संश्लेषणात्मक निर्देशन भाषा** – गुंतागुंतीच्या विषयांसाठी विषयशीर्षक तयार करण्याचे नियम व विषयशीर्षके यांची सूची.

systematic – **क्रमबद्ध/व्यवस्थित** – विशिष्ट पद्धती वापरून तयार झालेले, पद्धतशीर.

systematic bibliography – **पद्धतशीर ग्रंथसूची** – ग्रंथसूचीतील नोंदीची अभ्यासपूर्ण संदर्भासाठी तर्कशुद्ध व उपयुक्त मांडणी करणे.

systematic catalogue – **पद्धतशीर तालिका** – वर्गीकरण पद्धतीनुसार तयार केलेली वर्गीकृत तालिका तर्कसिद्धरीत्या केलेली नोंदीची मांडणी.

systems – **विशिष्ट प्रणाली** – एखाद्या विषयाच्या कल्पना वगैरेंचा संच.

systems analyst – **प्रणाली विश्लेषक/संश्लेषक** – (१) संगणकपद्धती विषयक तज्ज्ञ व्यक्ती.

systems analysis – **पद्धती विश्लेषण** – एखाद्या संस्थेच्या कार्याचे विश्लेषण करणे, त्यातील प्रत्येक बाबीचे योग्य असे स्थान ठरवून एक कार्यप्रवण असा संच तयार करणे, ज्यायोगे सर्व साधनांचा योग्य असा उपयोग केला जाईल.

systems analysis & design – **प्रणाली विश्लेषण व संरचना.**

tab key – पृष्ठनाम कळ – संगणकाच्या कळपटावरील एक कळ – या कळीच्या साहाय्याने स्थानदर्शक ५ जागा सोडून पुढे जातो.

table – सारणी/तक्ता – रेघा व स्तंभाच्या रचनेमध्ये स्पष्ट करून लिहिलेली माहिती.

table of contents – अनुक्रमणिका – नियतकालिकातील वा ग्रंथातील लेखांची शीर्षकयादी.

table of precedence – प्राधान्यक्रम तक्ता – वर्गीकरणामध्ये सारणीतील उपविषयांसाठी अनेक लक्षणगुणांचा वापर करून अचूक वर्गांक तयार करण्यासाठी दिलेली सारणी.

tabulation card – कोष्टक पत्र.

tabulor classification – तक्तानुरूप वर्गीकरण.

tag – label – खूणचिठ्ठी/खूणदर्शक – माहितीची प्रतिप्राप्ती करताना खूणदर्शक उपयुक्त.

tailored – काटेकोर – निश्चित किंवा काही उद्देशाकरिता तंतोतंत विचार असणे.

talking book – बोलके पुस्तक – अंधांसाठी उपयुक्त असा ध्वनिमुद्रित ग्रंथ. उदा. कुहू–कविता महाजन.

talking newspapers – बोलकी वृत्तपत्रे – बातम्यांच्या समावेश असलेल्या ध्वनिमुद्रित फिती.

tape – फीत.

tape (audiotape) – ध्वनिफीत – केवळ आवाज नोंदविता येणे व ऐकणे यासाठी उपयुक्त फीत.

type (videotape) – ध्वनिचित्रफीत.

tape record – ध्वनिमुद्रण.

taperecorder – **ध्वनिमुद्रक यंत्र** – ध्वनि नोंद करून ते हवे तेव्हा ऐकविणारे साधन.

task-force – **अभ्यासगट अथवा समिती** – एखाद्या विशिष्ट प्रश्नाचे पृथक्करण वा मार्गदर्शन करण्यासाठी अथवा सोडवणूक करण्यासाठी अथवा उत्तर शोधण्यासाठी नेमलेला अभ्यासगट अथवा समिती.

tax – **कर** – सरकारला सार्वजनिक कामासाठी द्यावयाचा पैसा (आर्थिक) कर.

taxonomy – **वर्गीकरणाचे शास्त्र.**

teacher - librarian / school librarian – **शाळेतील ग्रंथालयाचे कामकाज सांभाळणारा शिक्षक.**

teacher's book – **शिक्षकांसाठी उपयुक्त पाठ्यपुस्तक** – काही वेळा यामध्ये प्रश्न-उत्तरे स्वरूपातील नोंदी असतात.

teacher's handbook – **शिक्षकांसाठी हस्तपुस्तिका.**

team librarianship – **सांघिक ग्रंथपालन** – ग्रंथालय संघटनेतील छोट्या विभागांचे कार्य, दोन वा अधिक ग्रंथालयांना वाटून दिले जाते.

technical – **तांत्रिक** – एखाद्या औद्योगिक किंवा वैज्ञानिक विषयाच्या तपशीलवार व्यावहारिक ज्ञानासंबंधीचा, तंत्रज्ञानविषयक.

technical acstract bulletin – **तंत्रलेखन सारांश नियतकालिक** – तांत्रिक लेखांचे प्रसिद्धीनंतर लवकरात लवकर त्यांचे सारलेख प्रसिद्ध करणारे नियतकालिक.

technical information centre – **तांत्रिक माहितीचे केंद्र** – तांत्रिक माहिती मिळविणे, त्यांचे संस्करण करणे व प्रसारण करणे यासाठीचे तंत्रज्ञान केंद्र.

technical information system – **तांत्रिक माहितीसेवा यंत्रणा** – माहितीचे संस्करण व प्रसारण करण्यासाठी सुविधा पुरविणाऱ्या माहितीसेवांचे संगणकजाळे.

technical journal / technical periodical – **तंत्रज्ञानविषयक पत्रिका/नियतकालिक** – तंत्रज्ञानाच्या विशिष्ट शाखेशी निगडित माहिती पुरविणारे नियतकालिक.

technical library – **तंत्रज्ञानविषयक/तांत्रिक ग्रंथालय** – तंत्रज्ञानविषयक ग्रंथसंग्रह असणारे ग्रंथालय.

technical report – **तांत्रिक अहवाल** – (१) विशिष्ट विज्ञानशाखेतील संशोधन व विकास यांची सद्य:स्थिती दर्शविणारा अहवाल. (२) वैज्ञानिक संशोधनाचे निष्कर्ष पुरवणारे अहवाल.

technical services – **तांत्रिक सेवा** – (१) ग्रंथालयातील तांत्रिक सेवा यामध्ये उपार्जन, वर्गीकरण आणि तालिकीकरणाचा समावेश होतो. (२) ग्रंथालयातील साहित्य प्रत्यक्ष वापरासाठी साहित्य मिळविणे, संघटन करणे व संस्करण करणे यांच्याशी संबंधित असलेल्या क्रिया.

technical qualification – **तांत्रिक ज्ञानविषयक पात्रता.**

technical terms – **तांत्रिक संज्ञा/शब्द.**

technician – तंत्रज्ञ – ग्रंथालयातील तांत्रिक साधनांचा वापर करण्याबाबत तज्ज्ञ असलेली व्यक्ती. उदा. दृक्-श्राव्य माध्यमे, संगणक यांचा वापर करणारी ग्रंथालय कर्मचाऱ्यांशिवाय असलेली व्यक्ती.

technique – तंत्र/पद्धत/प्रक्रिया/कौशल्य – एखादी संकल्पना यशस्वी करण्याचे तंत्र.

technological gatekeeper – तांत्रिक द्वाररक्षक.

technology – तंत्रज्ञान/तंत्रविज्ञान/तंत्रविद्या – व्यवहारोपयोगी गोष्टींसाठी केलेला विज्ञानाचा अभ्यास आणि वापर.

telefacsimile – दूरलेखन – एका ठिकाणाहून इतरत्र मजकूर मुद्रित स्वरूपात पाठविण्याचे तंत्र.

teleordering – संगणकीय ग्रंथमागणी – ग्रंथविक्रेते संगणकावर ISBN क्रमांकानुसार ग्रंथमागणीची नोंद करतात. ही माहिती मध्यवर्ती संगणकामार्फत प्रकाशकाकडे नोंदविली जाते. नोंदणीतील चुका व त्रुटी ग्रंथविक्रेत्यांच्या संगणकाकडे परत पाठविल्या जातात.

telescoped notation – संमिश्र चिन्हांकन – वर्गीकरण करताना एकापेक्षा अधिक पैलूंचा वापर करून केलेले चिन्हांकन.

tell us – आम्हास सांगा (सूचनापेटी किंवा इ-मेलद्वारे) – वाचकांचा प्रतिसाद मिळवण्याचे एक साधन.

ten main classes – दहा मुख्य वर्ग – दशांश वर्गीकरण पद्धतीतील प्रमुख वर्ग. यालाच सारांशाची प्रथम रूपरेषा म्हटले जाते. हे दहा प्रमुख वर्ग दहा प्रमुख ज्ञानशाखा दर्शवितात.

tender – निविदा – विशिष्ट कामाच्या दरासाठीचा प्रस्ताव. असे दर मोठ्या रकमेच्या खरेदीसाठी मागविले जातात.

term – संज्ञा/पारिभाषिक शब्द.

term indexing – संज्ञेद्वारे निर्देशन – मजकुरातील शब्दांचा विषयशीर्षक म्हणून घेतलेला शोध.

term truncation – संज्ञा छाटणी – मुख्य शब्दास योग्य जागी छाटून त्यापुढे छाटणी चिन्ह (Truncation Symbol) देण्याची क्रिया. संपूर्ण शब्द शोधशब्द म्हणून वापरला तर फक्त त्याने शब्दसंच शोधता येतो. परंतु छाटणी केल्यावर त्यापुढील भागात कितीही फरक असला तरी ते सर्व शब्द शोधता येतात.

terminal – अंतस्थायी – (१) संगणकातील माहितीवर प्रक्रिया करणाऱ्या यंत्रणेशी संवाद साधण्यासाठी उपयोगात येणारे व निविष्टी (input) आणि निष्पत्ती (output) घटक असलेले सयंत्र (device). (२) संगणकयंत्र व कळपट यांचा एकत्र संच.

terminology – परिभाषा/व्याख्या/संज्ञांचा संच.

terms & conditions – अटी आणि शर्ती.

tertiary – तृतीयक – तिसऱ्या क्रमांकातील, तिसऱ्या दर्जाचे.

tertiary bibliography - **तृतीयक साहित्याची ग्रंथसूची** – द्वितीयक साहित्याची सखोल माहिती देणाऱ्या साहित्याची ग्रंथसूची.

tertiary sources - **तृतीयक साहित्य साधने** – प्राथमिक व द्वितीय साधनांच्या आधाराने तयार केलेली साधने. उदा. निर्देशिका, ग्रंथसूची वार्षिके यासारखी द्वितीयक साहित्याची अधिक माहिती देणारी साधने.

text - **विषय/गाभा/मजकूर** – (१) ग्रंथाचा प्रमुख भाग. (२) शब्द व अंकस्वरूपातील माहिती/ मजकूर.

text book - **पाठ्यपुस्तक** – (१) निर्धारित अभ्यासक्रमानुसार अध्ययन अध्यापनासाठी तयार केलेले पुस्तक. (२) विशिष्ट अभ्यासक्रमासाठी/शिक्षणासाठी नेमलेले पुस्तक.

text editor - **मजकूर संपादक** – संगणकातील माहितीत बदल करू शकणारी आज्ञावली.

text library - **पाठ्यपुस्तकांचे ग्रंथालय.**

textual - **पाठभेददर्शक/चिकित्सक.**

textual bibliography - **पाठभेददर्शक/चिकित्सक ग्रंथसूची** – (१) चिकित्सात्मक ग्रंथाभ्यास, फलित ग्रंथपाठ, (२) मजकूर व त्याची मुद्रणे, आवृत्ती यांचा अभ्यास व तुलना.

theoretical - **सोपपत्तिक/तात्त्विक.**

theory - **सिद्धान्त/उपपत्ती/वाद/तत्त्व/मीमांसा/वाद/नियम.**

thesaurus - **शब्दकुल कोश/संज्ञाकोश** –
(१) सामान्यपणे लहान विषय विभागाच्या संबंधातील संरचनात्मक यादी. अंतर्गत संबंधाच्या व्यतिरिक्त अशी यादी अशी संज्ञांमधील पसंतीक्रम दर्शविते. संज्ञाकोश म्हणजे एखाद्या क्षेत्रातील, विषयातील संबंधित संज्ञांची सूची होय.
(२) अर्थानुसार शब्दरचना असलेला शब्दकोश. समानार्थी शब्दांची मोजणी असलेला शब्दकोश.

thesis - **प्रबंध/विधान/स्थितीविधान/प्रमेय/पूर्वपक्ष/साधकबाधक/प्रतिपादन** –
(१) विद्यापीठाच्या पदवीसाठी एखाद्या विषयावर लिहिलेला प्रबंध.
(२) उच्चपदवी मिळविण्यासाठी अभ्यासक्रमाचा एक भाग म्हणून तयार केलेला अहवाल. शैक्षणिक संस्थांमधून विशिष्ट क्षेत्रासाठी पूर्ण केलेल्या कामाचा अहवाल.

thought - **चिंतन/विचारप्रणाली/विमर्श/प्रज्ञा/शाखा** – विचारांची माला किंवा विषय.

thought content - **विमर्श.**

tie-bound periodicals – पुठ्ठ्याच्या साहाय्याने नियतकालिकाचा खंड तात्पुरता बांधून ठेवणे.

tier - **मजला/माळा** – मागे-पुढे किंवा वर-खाली असणाऱ्या रांगातील एक रांग.

time - **काळ** – द्विबिंदू वर्गीकरण पद्धतीतील एक मूलभूत पैलू जो कालावधीकरिता वापरतात.

time facet – कालपैलू/कालदर्शक पैलू – वर्गीकरण करताना लेखनाचा काळ (वर्ष) लक्षात घेऊन चिन्हांकन तयार करण्याचे तत्त्व.

time lag – कालव्यय.

time numbers – कालांक/कालदर्शक अंक – ग्रंथाची रचना लेखकानुसार वा अनुक्रमानुसार करण्यापेक्षा दाखलअंकानुसार करता यावी म्हणून तयार केलेले अंक वा अक्षरे.

time out – समयातीत – संगणकाला सूचना देण्यासाठी लागणारा अपेक्षित वेळ.

time table – वेळापत्रक (समयसारणी).

time sharing – वेळ सहभाजन – एकावेळी अनेक उपयोजकांना संगणक वापरण्याची सुविधा.

title – ग्रंथशीर्षक/ग्रंथनाम/शीर्षक – शब्द/शब्दांचा समूह ज्यामुळे ग्रंथाच्या नावाचा बोध होतो.

title analytical entry – ग्रंथनाम विश्लेषक नोंद.

titlecard – ग्रंथनामपत्र – तालिकेमधील ग्रंथशीर्षकानुसार केलेले नोंदपत्र.

title catalogue – शीर्षकांची तालिका – ग्रंथांच्या नावांची आद्याक्षरनिहाय तयार केलेली तालिका.

title entry – ग्रंथनाम नोंद – तालिकेमध्ये ग्रंथशीर्षकानुसार केलेली नोंद.

title index – ग्रंथनाम निर्देश – ग्रंथशीर्षकाच्या आधाराने तयार केलेला निर्देश. उदा. KWIC

title leaf – शीर्षकपृष्ठ – ग्रंथाच्या मुखपृष्ठानंतर आतील पहिल्या पानावर ग्रंथशीर्षक.

title page – ग्रंथनामदर्शक पृष्ठ – ग्रंथाच्या आतील ग्रंथशीर्षकासह लेखक, प्रकाशनविषयक पूर्ण माहिती, ISCN मुद्रक यांची माहिती देणारे ग्रंथशीर्षक, पृष्ठाच्या मागील पृष्ठ.

title search – शीर्षक शोध – शीर्षकाच्या नावानुसार घेतलेला ग्रंथशोध.

title section – शीर्षक विभाग – तालिकेतील नोंदीमधील ग्रंथनाम लिहिण्यासाठी असलेला विभाग.

title statement – ग्रंथनाम विवरण.

tool phase – साधन प्रावस्था – डॉ. रंगनाथन् यांची संज्ञा. ग्रंथामध्ये अंतर्भूत असलेल्या मजकुराच्या विषयांपैकी एका विषयाचे स्पष्टीकरणासाठी दुसरा विषय साधन म्हणून वापरण्याची प्रावस्था.

topical collection – प्रचलित विषयसंग्रह.

top margin – वरचा समास – ग्रंथपृष्ठाची वरची कडा व मजकुराची पहिली ओळ यातील रिकामी जागा.

topic – उपविषय – ग्रंथाची नोंद करताना मुख्य विषयानंतर नोंद करण्याचा उपविभाग.

topic guide / subject guide – उपविषय मार्गदर्शक – कपाटामधील ग्रंथमांडणीचे मार्गदर्शन करणारे उपविषय मार्गदर्शक.

toipcal bibliography – उपविषय साहित्याची सूची.

topographical catalogue – स्थानीय विषयाशी संबंधित ग्रंथांची तालिका.

topographical index – ग्रंथांचा स्थाननिर्देश.

topographical map – स्थलस्वरूप नकाशा.

tracing – नोंददर्शक टिपण/पूरक नोंद टिपण – ग्रंथालयीन तालिकीकरणामध्ये शीर्षकाखाली पूरक नोंदी केलेल्या असतील त्या नोंदशीर्षकांची यादी.

tracing section – शोध अनुच्छेद/अन्वेषण अनुच्छेद/नोंददर्शन विभाग – ग्रंथाच्या सर्व पूरक नोंदी दाखविणाऱ्या तालिकापत्रावरील अनुच्छेदाला 'शोध अनुच्छेदन' असे म्हणतात.

tract – प्रचार वाङ्मय.

trade – व्यापार.

trade bibliography – व्यापार ग्रंथसूची – ग्रंथव्यवसायाला पूरक अशी बनविलेली ग्रंथसूची.

trade catalogue – व्यापार तालिका – देशामध्ये प्रकाशनांतर्फे असणारे ग्रंथ व परदेशातील प्रकाशित ग्रंथासाठी दलाल म्हणून नेमलेल्या देशी ग्रंथविक्रेत्यांच्या उपयोगासाठीची सूची.

trade directory – व्यापारी निर्देशिका – एखाद्या व्यापारशाखेला उपयुक्त असणारी निर्देशिका.

trade discount – व्यापारी सूट/बट्टा – मुद्रित/छापील किमतीवर देण्यात येणारी वजावट.

trade edition – व्यापारी आवृत्ती – प्रकाशकाकडून ग्रंथविक्रेत्याला नियमितपणे काही प्रती घाऊक दराने दिल्या जातात.

trade journal – व्यापारी नियतकालिक/पत्रिका – विशिष्ट व्यापारशाखेशी निगडित नियतकालिक.

trade list – व्यापारी सूची – ग्रंथविक्री व्यापाऱ्यांना उपयुक्त अशी प्रकाशकाने तयार केलेली प्रकाशनांतर्गत ग्रंथांची सूची.

trade literature – व्यापारी वाङ्मय/साहित्य – (१) व्यापार वाढविण्यासाठी/लोकप्रिय करण्यासाठी प्रकाशित केलेले साहित्य. (२) उत्पादनांची माहिती देणारे साहित्य.

train of characteristics – लक्षणमालिका.

trainee – प्रशिक्षणार्थी – प्रशिक्षणात सहभागी असणारी व्यक्ती.

trainer – प्रशिक्षण देणारी व्यक्ती.

trained – प्रशिक्षित – प्रशिक्षण पूर्ण केलेली व्यक्ती.

training – प्रशिक्षण – प्रात्यक्षिक सेवा शिकविण्यासाठीचा कार्यक्रम.

training library – प्रशिक्षणार्थी ग्रंथालय.

transactions – संस्थांच्या सभांच्या लेखी नोंदी/अहवाल.

transformation – रूपांतरण.

translation – अनुवाद/भाषांतर – एका भाषेतील साहित्य मूळढाचा न बदलता दुसऱ्या भाषेत रूपांतरित करणे.

translation bank / translation pool – अनुवाद पेढी.

translation index – अनुवाद निर्देश – अनुवादित साहित्याची नोंद केलेला निर्देश.

translation pool / translation bank – भाषांतर पेढी – भाषांतराची उपलब्धी असण्याचे केंद्र.

translation rights – भाषांतराचे हक्क – मालकीहक्काचा एक भाग म्हणजे प्रकाशनाचे, दुसऱ्या भाषेतील भाषांतराचे हक्क.

translation service – भाषांतर सेवा – व्यक्ती वा संस्थेची मूळ लेखांचे अनुवाद करून देण्याची सेवा.

translator – अनुवादक/भाषांतरकार – एका भाषेतील साहित्य दुसऱ्या भाषेत मूळ विषयगाभा न वगळता रूपांतरित करणारी व्यक्ती.

translator entry – अनुवादक नोंद – तालिकेच्या नोंदीमध्ये अनुवादकाच्या नावे केलेली नोंद.

transliteration – लिप्यंतरण – (१) एका भाषेतील शब्द दुसऱ्या भाषेच्या लिपीमध्ये लिहिणे. विशेष नामांचे लिप्यंतर करतात, भाषांतर करीत नाहीत. भारतीय राष्ट्रीय ग्रंथसूचीमध्ये रोमन लिपीमध्ये इतर भारतीय भाषांतील शब्द लिप्यंतर वापरून लिहितात.
(२) एका भाषेतील माहिती जशीच्या तशी दुसऱ्या भाषेच्या लिपीमध्ये लिहिणे. उदा. (कोसला) Kosala by Bhalchandra Nemade

transmission – संचारण/प्रक्षेपण – एकीकडून दुसरीकडे माहिती स्थलांतरित करणे.

travel guidebook – प्रवासी मार्गदर्शक ग्रंथ – (१) प्रवास करणाऱ्या व्यक्तींना संबंधित प्रदेशाची, गावाची, इमारतींची, सोयी–सुविधांची माहिती देणारा ग्रंथ. (२) प्रवास करणाऱ्या व्यक्तींना उपयुक्त ठरेल अशी पर्यटन स्थळांची आनुषंगिक माहिती देणारे पुस्तक.

travelling library / mobile library / librarine – फिरते/चल ग्रंथालय – जे ग्रंथालय वाचकांना सेवा देण्यासाठी एका ठिकाणाहून दुसरीकडे जाऊ शकते.

tray – खण/तबक/कप्पा.

treastise – विवेचनात्मक निबंध – (१) विशिष्ट विषयाचे विशिष्ट पद्धतीने केलेले विवेचन. (२) एखाद्या विषयावरील निबंध/प्रबंध.

treatment – विवेचन/वर्णनपद्धती.

tree of porphery – पॉर्फिरी वर्गीकरण रचना.

trolley – ढकलगाडी – हातांनी ढकलावयाची दोन/चार चाकांची छोटी गाडी.

trolley / book trolley – ग्रंथासाठीची ढकलगाडी – ग्रंथ व इतर ग्रंथालय साहित्य एका ठिकाणाहून दुसरीकडे वाहून नेण्यासाठी वापरण्यात येणारे वाहन.

truncation – छेदून छोटे करणे.

trustees – विश्वस्त मंडळ.

tutor librarian – शिक्षक ग्रंथपाल.

tutorial – स्वाध्याय – विद्यार्थ्याने स्वयं अध्ययनाद्वारे करावयाचे लिखाण.

tutorial system – उपनिषद पद्धती – स्वाध्यायाद्वारे अध्ययन–अध्यापनाची पद्धती.

twigging – विद्याभ्यास या नियतकालिकाची विभागणी करून प्रकाशकाने विशिष्ट विषयाची दोन/तीन नियतकालिके प्रकाशित करणे.

typographer – मुद्राक्षरकलाकार/मुद्रक.

typograhical error – मुद्रण त्रुटी – मुद्रण दोष.

typography – मुद्रणकला – छपाई करण्याची कला.

ultimate class / unitary class – अंतिमवर्ग/एकशेष वर्ग – (१) वर्गीकरण स्वीकारलेला अत्यंत लहान विस्तार असलेला वर्ग. (२) ग्रंथाच्या विषयाला न्याय देणारा अचूक वर्ग.

ultimate commodity – अंतिम वस्तू.

ultimate service – अंतिम सेवा – परिणामकारक सेवा.

unaccessioned book – पंजीकृत नसलेले ग्रंथ – ग्रंथालयाच्या दाखल नोंदवहीत नोंदविलेला नाही असा ग्रंथ.

unauthorized edition – अनधिकृत आवृत्ती – (१) स्वामित्व हक्क धारण करणाऱ्या परवानगीशिवाय प्रकाशित केलेली (झालेली) आवृत्ती.

unambigue – निस्संदिग्ध.

unbound volume – नियतकालिकाचे सुटे अंक.

uderground literature / secret literature – गोपनीय साहित्य – युद्धप्रसंगी किंवा राजकारणी महत्त्वाचे साहित्य.

underground press / clandestine press – गोपनीय छापखाना – गोपनीय साहित्य मुद्रणासाठी उभारलेला छापखाना.

underline – अधोरेखन – मजकुराचा वेगळेपणा, उपशीर्षक दर्शविण्यासाठी वापरायचे चिन्ह.

uneven pages – विषम क्रमांकाची पाने – ग्रंथाचे उजव्या बाजूचे पान.

unexpurgated edition – विरोध असलेल्या मजकुरासहित प्रसिद्ध केलेली आवृत्ती. मजकूर कोणत्याही कारणाने न गाळता तयार केलेली आवृत्ती.

uniform edition – एकरूप आवृत्ती – एका लेखकाच्या सर्व कृतींची एकत्र बांधणी केलेली आवृत्ती.

uniform heading – सर्वसमान शीर्षक (तालिकेतील नोंदीसाठी).

uniform title – सर्वसमान/एकरूप ग्रंथनाम – (१) एकाच कृतीच्या विविध आवृत्त्यांच्या नोंदी तालिकेमध्ये एकत्र याव्यात म्हणून वापरलेले ग्रंथनाम. (२) एकच ग्रंथ अनेक स्वरूपांमध्ये, विविध ग्रंथनामाने प्रसिद्ध झाला असेल तेव्हा ते नाव सर्वरूढ झाले असेल व तालिकेतील नोंदीसाठी निवडले असेल ते ग्रंथनाम.

uniformity – एकरूपता/सारखेपणा/एकवाक्यता.

union – संघ/संयुक्त समूह.

union catalogue – संघतालिका/संयुक्त तालिका – (१) एकापेक्षा अनेक ग्रंथालयांच्या संग्रहाची तालिका ज्यामध्ये ग्रंथ कोणत्या ग्रंथालयात मिळेल याची माहिती असते.
(२) अनेक ग्रंथालयांची किंवा विभागीय ग्रंथालयांची एकत्र तालिका.

union list – संघयादी – विशिष्ट विषयाची किंवा विशिष्ट साहित्याची अनेक ग्रंथालयांची वा विभागीय ग्रंथालयांची मिळून तयार केलेली यादी.

union trade catalogue – संयुक्त व्यापारतालिका – विशिष्ट व्यापारासाठी उपयुक्त अशी सूची.

unit – गट/एकक – विशिष्ट काम करणाऱ्यांचा गट, पथक.

unit bibliography – घटक ग्रंथसूची – समान शीर्षकाच्या ग्रंथांच्या विविध आवृत्त्यांची सूची.

unit card / unit entry – एकक पत्र/घटक नोंदपत्र – (१) ग्रंथाचे एकक तालिकापत्र ज्याच्या प्रतीवरून त्या ग्रंथविषयक इतर नोंदी बनविता येतात व त्या तालिकेत आवश्यक तेथे वापरता येतात.

unit cost – कार्यघटकाचे मूल्य – एका कार्य घटकाचे मूल्य. उदा. एका ग्रंथाच्या तालिकीकरणासाठी येणारे खर्च.

unit operation – एकक संक्रिया.

unit record – सादृश्य/मूळ ग्रंथ.

unit system of catalogue – एकक तालिका पद्धती.

UNESCO (United Nations Educational, Scientific and Cultural Organisation) – युनेस्को – युनोच्या आंतरराष्ट्रीय विकास व सामंजस्य यासाठी कार्य करणारी संघटना.

UNISIST (United Nations Information System in Science and Technology) युनिसिस्ट – युनेस्कोच्या सहकार्याने वैज्ञानिक माहितीच्या देवाणघेवाण कार्यात काम करणारी संस्था.

uniterm index – एक संज्ञा निर्देश/एकक संज्ञानिर्देश – (१) प्रलेखातील मजकुराचा आढावा घेणाऱ्या संज्ञा निवडून तयार केलेला निर्देश. (२) एका संज्ञेसाठी एकच पर्यायी संज्ञा देणारा निर्देश.

universal – सार्वत्रिक/वैश्विक/विश्वव्यापी/सर्वव्यापी.

universal bibliography – जागतिक ग्रंथसूची – विश्वव्यापी ग्रंथसूची ज्यामध्ये सर्व देश, सर्व भाषा आणि सर्व प्रकारचे प्रलेख यांचा समावेश असतो.

universal bibliographic control – जागतिक ग्रंथसूचीय उपलब्धी नियंत्रण – जगातील प्रत्येक ग्रंथाची ग्रंथसूचीय माहिती उपलब्ध करून देण्यासाठीची यंत्रणा.

Universal Decimal Classification – जागतिक दशांश वर्गीकरण – १९०५ मध्ये पॉल ऑटलेट आणि डी.ला. फाऊन्टेन यांनी तयार केलेली ग्रंथ वर्गीकरण पद्धती. (यू.डी.सी.)

universe of subjects – ग्रंथबद्ध असे विषयविश्व.

universe of knowledge – ज्ञानविश्व – उपलब्ध सर्व ज्ञान दर्शविणारे विषयक्षेत्र.

university – विद्यापीठ/विश्वविद्यालय.

UGC (University Grants Commission) – विद्यापीठ अनुदान आयोग – भारत सरकारद्वारा, देशातील विद्यापीठे व त्यांच्या कक्षेमधील महाविद्यालये यांचा शैक्षणिक विकास घडवून आणण्यासाठी शासकीय अनुदान देणारी आणि दर्जेदार उच्च शिक्षण देण्यासाठी प्रयत्न करणारी संस्था.

university library – विद्यापीठाचे/विद्यापीठ ग्रंथालय – विद्यापीठातील यंत्रणेद्वारा शिक्षक,संशोधक व विद्यार्थ्यांसाठी चालविलेले ग्रंथालय.

university library committee – विद्यापीठातील ग्रंथालय समिती – विद्यापीठ तसेच संलग्नित महाविद्यालयातील ग्रंथालयाच्या कार्याबाबत विद्यापीठास सल्ला देणारी समिती.

unix – संगणकात वापरली जाणारी युनिक्स कार्यपद्धती – एकावेळी अनेक संगणकाबरोबर कार्यरत असणारी कार्यपद्धती.

unload – अवभार – माहितीसंग्रहातील माहिती ISO-2709 (फॉरमॅटमध्ये) रूपात प्रदान करण्याच्या (output) सोयीस, CDS/ISIS मध्ये वापरेला शब्द.

unknown document – अज्ञात प्रलेख – वाचकांना परिचित नसलेला प्रलेख.

unpaged book – पृष्ठसंख्यारहित ग्रंथ – ज्या ग्रंथातील पृष्ठांना पृष्ठक्रमांक दिलेले नाहीत असा ग्रंथ.

unprocessed book – प्रक्रियारहित ग्रंथ – ज्या ग्रंथाचे वर्गीकरण/तालिकीकरण इ. प्रक्रिया पूर्ण झाल्या नाहीत असा ग्रंथ.

unscheduled mnemonics / seminal mnemonics – शाब्दिक स्मरणसुलभता – अनुसूचीबाह्य स्मृतीसाधके – वर्गीकरणासाठी चिन्हांकन तयार करताना वापरली जाणारी अनुसूचीतून न निवडता सहसंबंधित असणारी स्मृतीसाधके.

unsought link – अवांछित/अलक्षणीय दुवा – (१) ज्या विषयशीर्षकाद्वारे वाचक ग्रंथाची मागणी करण्याची शक्यता नाही असे विषयशीर्षक.

(२) वर्गीकरण करताना शृंखला निर्देशनामध्ये चिन्हांकनाचा स्तरीकरणामधील अनावश्यक दुवा. काही वेळा वर्गीकरण पद्धतीमधील चुकीच्या स्तरीकरणामुळे आलेले चिन्हांकन.

unrecorded communication – न नोंदविलेले संप्रेषण.

update – माहिती अद्ययावत करणे – विशिष्ट पद्धतीने संगणकातील मुख्य फाईलमध्ये अद्ययावत माहिती समाविष्ट करून बदल करणे.

updated version – सुधारित आवृत्ती – जुन्या आवृत्तीमधील चुका सुधारून नवीन माहिती समाविष्ट केलेली आवृत्ती.

upload –प्रसृत करणे – ISO-2709 फॉरमॅटमधील माहिती एखाद्या माहितीसंग्रहात अंतर्भूत करण्यासाठी CDS/ISIS वापरलेल्या सोयीस दिलेले नाव.

up time – संगणक कार्यरत असतानाचा वेळ.

up-to-date – अद्ययावत– परिपूर्ण.

urban library – नागरी/नगर ग्रंथालय.

usage – परिपाठ/वापर.

user / reader / borrower / member / clientele / patron – वाचक/उपयोजक –
(१) संगणक सुविधा वापरणारी व्यक्ती वा संस्था.
(२) ग्रंथालय सेवा, सुविधा वापरणारी व्यक्ती वा संस्था.

user cost – वाचक खर्च – प्रत्यक्ष उपयोग करणाऱ्याला पडणारा खर्च/परिव्यय.

user education – उपभोक्त्यांसाठी शिक्षण – ग्रंथालयाचा वापर कसा करावा याविषयी उपयोजकांना दिलेले शिक्षण.

user friendly program – वाचक सहयोगी कार्यक्रम – सहज/सुलभतेने वाचकांना उपयोग करता येण्याजोगा कार्यक्रम.

user group – वाचकांचा गट – विशिष्ट संगणकप्रणाली वापरणाऱ्या उपयोजकांचा गट.

user interface – वाचक दुवा – निवडक माहितीच्या प्रसारण सेवेत अभ्यासक आणि संदर्भ (माहितीसंग्रह यांना साधणारा दुवा म्हणजेच ग्रंथपाल).

user need survey – वाचक गरजा पाहणी – वाचकांच्या गरजा माहिती करून घेण्यासाठी पद्धतशीरपणे केलेली पाहणी व सर्वेक्षण.

user port – उपभोक्ता मुखद्वार.

user profile – **उपभोक्ता पार्श्वरूप** – अभ्यासकाच्या वैशिष्ट्यांसंबंधीचे माहितीपत्रक. निवडक माहिती प्रसारण सेवेत अभ्यासकास स्वारस्य असलेल्या विषयांची माहिती देणारी प्रश्नावली. ही वापरून वाचकांसाठी शोधसमीकरण तयार करता येते.

user relevance – **उपभोक्त्यांसाठी माहितीची सापेक्षता** – वाचकाला अपेक्षित असलेल्या माहितीच्या प्रतिप्राप्तीमध्ये माहितीची असलेली सापेक्षता.

user satisfaction – **उपभोक्त्यांचे समाधान** – संस्थेच्या वाचकांना दिलेल्या सेवेबाबत वाचकाला मिळालेले समाधान.

users services – **उपभोक्त्यांसाठी सेवा** – ग्रंथालयाने वाचकांसाठी दिलेल्या सेवा.

user studies – **वाचकांचा अभ्यास** – वाचकांना अपेक्षित कोणत्या सेवा, सुविधा, चुका, त्रुटी आहेत याचा केलेला अभ्यास.

user survey – **वाचक सर्वेक्षण** – वाचकांच्या वाचनसाहित्य विषयक गरजा माहिती करून घेण्यासाठी वापरण्यात येणारी ही एक संशोधन पद्धती आहे. या पद्धतीमध्ये प्रश्नावली, मुलाखत इत्यादी तंत्रांचा वापर केला जातो.

username – **उपयोजकाचे नाव.**

utilitarian classification – **उपयुक्तेनुसार वर्गीकरण.**

utilitarian scheme – **उपयुक्तेनुसार पद्धती.**

utility – **उपयुक्तता/उपयोगिता** – ग्रंथालयसुविधा किती उपयुक्त आहे याची तपासणी/पडताळणी.

utility characteristic – **उपयोगिता लक्षण** – वर्गीकरणासाठी उपयुक्त वैशिष्ट्य.

utility programme – **उपयोगिता आज्ञावली** – संगणकातील माहिती प्रत्यक्ष उपयोगात आणण्यासाठी उपलब्ध असलेली सुविधा.

vade-mecum – संदर्भांसाठी सहज- ने-आण करण्याजोगे छोटे पुस्तक.

valid upto – विधिग्राह्य.

Value Added Network (VAN) – **संगणकजाळे** – अद्ययावत माहिती आधारित संगणकजाळे.

Value Payable Post (VPP) – **मूल्यदेय डाक** – (१) डाकेचा मोबदला दिल्यानंतर मिळणारी डाक (२) विशिष्ट रक्कम भरल्यानंतर प्राप्त करता येणारे टपाल.

variable field – परिवर्तनशील क्षेत्र.

varient edition – दुरुस्त आवृत्ती/पाठभेद.

variorum edition – **पाठचिकित्सात्मक आवृत्ती** – आधीच्या ग्रंथांचा तुलनात्मक अभ्यास करून तयार केलेली आवृत्ती.

vedic classification – **वैदिक वर्गीकरण** – उपनिषदांतील वर्गांची पद्धती जी नंतर पुराणे, भगवद्गीता आणि तंत्रांमध्ये स्वीकारली आहे.

velvet – **व्हेलवेट** – रेशमी कापडाचा प्रकार, जो ग्रंथ बांधणीसाठी वापरला जातो.

vendor – **विक्रेता** – वस्तू/माल विकणारी व्यक्ती.

Venn Diagram – **व्हेन आकृती** – जॉन व्हेन ह्या इंग्रजी तर्कशास्त्रज्ञाने दोन विषयांतील सुसंगती दाखविण्यासाठी तयार केलेली आकृती.

verbal – **शाब्दिक** – शब्दांनी किंवा पारिभाषिक शब्दांनी केलेला व्यवहार.

verbal plane – शब्दांकन स्तर/पातळी/क्षेत्र – शब्दाने व्यक्त केलेले क्षेत्र.

verbatim report – भाषण/परिसंवाद यांचा शब्दश: अहवाल.

verification – सत्यशोधन/पडताळणी/परिगणन.

vernacular – राष्ट्रीय (भाषा) – उदा. भारताची राष्ट्रीय भाषा हिंदी, स्थानिक भाषा.

versatile – अष्टपैलू – वैशिष्ट्यपूर्ण, ज्याचा सहजपणे वापर करता येतो असा.

version – सुधारित वा रूपांतरित आवृत्ती.

vertical filing – सम क्रमांकाचे पृष्ठ/डावे पृष्ठ.

video – दृश्यचित्रसाधन.

video cassette / tape – दृश्यमुद्रित फीत/चित्रफीत.

video library – दृश्यमुद्रित फितींचा संग्रह केलेले ग्रंथालय.

view point – दृष्टिकोन.

viewer – प्रेक्षक – पाहणारी व्यक्ती.

village library – ग्राम/खेडेगावचे ग्रंथालय.

virtual library – सर्वथैव ग्रंथालय.

virus – व्हायरस (विषाणू) – संगणकाच्या कार्यात व्यत्यय आणणारी आज्ञावली.

visible index – दृश्यनिर्देश – चौकटीत बसविलेला सहजपणे न्याहाळता येणारा निर्देश.

visitor's book / register – अभ्यंगत नोंदवही – भेट दिलेल्या व्यक्तींची नोंद ठेवणारे पुस्तक जे प्रवेशद्वारा जवळ ठेवतात.

visual – दृष्टिमूलक – शिकविताना/अभ्यास करताना वापरायचे चित्र, चित्रपट, व्हिडिओ यासारखे साधन.

visual aids – दृक् साधने. उदा. चित्रपट.

vocabulory – शब्दसंग्रह – निर्देशनासाठी उपयुक्त असणाऱ्या शब्दांचा संग्रह.

vocabulory control – शब्दसंग्रह नियंत्रण – निर्देशन पद्धतीतील सुसज्जता आणता येण्यासाठी निर्देशातील शब्दांची निवड व मांडणी करणे.

volume – खंड/ग्रंथ – सर्वसाधारणपणे एका वर्षामध्ये प्रसिद्ध होणाऱ्या एका नियतकालिकाच्या सर्व अंकांचा मिळून एक खंड तयार होतो. यानुसार वर्षामध्ये प्रसिद्ध होणाऱ्या किती अंकांचा मिळून खंड होईल ते प्रकाशक नमूद करतात. काही नियतकालिकांचे एका वर्षात दोन वा अधिक खंड प्रसिद्ध होतात.

volume capacity – खंड धारिता/क्षमता.

volume facet – खंडदर्शक पैलू.

volume number – खंडांक/खंड क्रमांक –अंक– खंडांच्या अनुक्रमानुसार ग्रंथाला दिलेला क्रमांक.

volumen – एखाद्या वस्तूस गोल पद्धतीने गुंडाळून ठेवणे.

voluminous author – **बहुग्रंथ लेखक** – खूप लिखाण केलेला लेखक.

voluminous book – **अनेक खंड ग्रंथ** – मोठ्या आकाराचा किंवा अनेक खंड असलेला ग्रंथ.

voluntary – **ऐच्छिक** – स्वखुशीने स्वीकारलेले काम.

volunteer – **स्वयंसेवक** – स्वखुशीने विनामूल्य सेवा करणारी व्यक्ती.

voucher – **पावती** – पैसे दिले आहेत याचा पुरावा असणारे प्रमाणपत्र किंवा पावती.

waiting list – **प्रतीक्षा यादी** – ग्रंथालयाच्या सभासदत्वासाठी वाचकांची प्रतीक्षायादी.

wall picture principle – **भित्तीचित्र सिद्धान्त/तत्त्व** – ग्रंथ वर्गीकरण करताना विषयातील महत्त्वाचा घटक आणि दुय्यम घटक ठरविण्याकरिता वापरलेले तत्त्व.

web page, web search, web site – **वेब स्थळ** – जाळे **www** साठी वापरतात.

weeding out / negative selection / withdrawl / discarding – **काढून टाकणे/रद्दबातल करणे. निष्कासित करणे/निर्लेखन** – (१) निरुपयोगी साहित्य ग्रंथालयातून रद्दबातल करणे. (२) ग्रंथालयाच्या संग्रहातील निरुपयोगी ग्रंथ काढून टाकणे.

weekly – **साप्ताहिक** – (१) जे प्रकाशन आठवड्यातून एकदा परंतु ठरावीक दिवशी प्रकाशित होते. (२) दर आठवड्याला प्रकाशित होणारे प्रकाशन.

whole organ principle – **पूर्ण भाग तत्त्व** – ग्रंथवर्गीकरण पद्धती तयार करताना प्रथम संपूर्ण शरीराशी संबंधित विषय व नंतर शरीराच्या अवयवाशी संबंधित विषय अशी रचना करावी हे स्पष्ट करणारे तत्त्व.

Who's Who/Who Was Who – **कोण आहे/कोण होता/व्यक्ती परिचय कोश** – (१) विशिष्ट क्षेत्रातील व देशातील व्यक्तींची परिचयात्मक माहिती. (२) कोण आहे/कोण होता याबाबत व्यक्तींचा चरित्रकोश.

whole number – **पूर्णांक** – नियतकालिकांच्या सुट्ट्या अंकाला वा मालाप्रकाशनातील प्रत्येक ग्रंथाला प्रकाशकाने दिलेला क्रमांक.

Wide Area Network (WAN) – बृहत्परिसर संगणकजाळे.

windows – विंडोज – विंडोज पॅकेजेसमधील माहितीची देवाण–घेवाण सुलभ करू शकणारी संगणक आज्ञावली.

wisdom – प्रज्ञा/बुद्धी/चातुर्य/विवेक – ज्ञान समजण्याची क्षमता.

withdrawal / weeding out / negative selection / discarding – रद्दबातल/निंदणी/काढून टाकणे/निष्कासित करणे – (१) एखादी नोंद दाखल नोंदवहीतून किंवा कपाटातून काढून टाकण्याची प्रक्रिया.

withdrawal processing – रद्दबातल सोपस्कार.

withdrawal register – रद्दबातल नोंदवही.

wood engrawing / xylography – काष्ठकोरण – लाकडी ठसा कोरून केलेले मुद्रण.

word – शब्द/अक्षरसंच – (१) वर्णांचा समूह ज्याला काही अर्थ वा उद्देश असतो. (२) माहितीची प्रतिप्राप्ती करताना माहितीचे चिन्ह म्हणून आलेला अक्षरसंच.

word by word arrangement – शब्दानुसार क्रमरचना.

word–by–word alphabetisation – शब्दानुसारी वर्णानुक्रम रचना – वर्णानुक्रम रचनेत ज्या अक्षरांनी (वर्णांनी) आरंभ होतात यानुसार नोंदीची रचना त्या नोंदीमध्ये असलेल्या पहिल्या शब्दानुसार केली जाते. येथे शब्द (वर्ण नव्हे) म्हणजे एक घटक कल्पिला जातो. या पद्धतीस (Nothing Cefore Something) पद्धती असे संबोधले जाते. इंटरनॅशनल स्टँडर्डस इन्स्टिट्यूशन या संस्थेने या पद्धतीस मान्यता दिली आहे.

word entry – शब्दमूलक नोंद.

word group – शब्दांचा समूह/गट.

word length – शब्द विस्तार.

word processing – शब्द प्रक्रिया – विवरणात्मक/परिच्छेदात्मक लिखाण संगणकाद्वारे विशिष्ट आज्ञावली (software) वापरून करायची पद्धत. संगणकावर सुरुवातीला या आज्ञावलींचा मोठ्या प्रमाणावर वापर होतो.

work – कार्य/काम/कृती/लेखकाचा ग्रंथ/लिखाण/साहित्यकृती – भाषेद्वारे अथवा संकेताद्वारे अथवा अन्य प्रकारे केलेले विचार संप्रेषित करण्याकरिता तयार केलेली कृती.

work assignment – काम नेमून देणे.

work load – कार्यभार – करावयाच्या कामाचे प्रमाणक.

work manual / procedure manual – कार्यनिर्देश ग्रंथ/कार्यपद्धती निर्देशपुस्तिका – कार्यालयातील पदनिहाय कामे व कामाचे प्रमाण स्पष्ट करणारी पुस्तिका.

work slip – मार्गदर्शक चिठ्ठी.

work space – कामाची जागा.

work sheet – कार्य विश्लेषण – CDS/ISIS मध्ये कळफलक वापरून माहिती इनपुट करताना संगणकाच्या पडद्यावर दिसावी या उद्देशाने जे फॉर्म्स् तयार केलेले असतात त्यांना दिलेले नाव, एक कार्यपत्र अनेक घटकांचे असते.

world wide web (www) – विश्वव्यापी महाजाळे.

wrap case – वेष्टन पेटी.

wrapper – आवरण/वेष्टन.

write – लेखन – संगणकाच्या तबकडीवर केलेली नोंद.

write off – निर्लेखित करणे/रद्दबातल करणे.

write protect – माहितीमुद्रणाची सुरक्षितता.

writer / author – लेखक/ग्रंथकर्ता – ग्रंथ, लेख लिहिणारी व्यक्ती.

xenix – झेनिक्स – एक प्रकारची कार्यप्रणाली पद्धती.

xerography – शुष्कछायामुद्रण.

xerox / photocopy / photostat – छायाचित्रमुद्रण/प्रतमुद्रण/झेरॉक्स/छायाप्रत – झेरॉक्स यंत्राद्वारे प्रत काढणे.

xerox copy – छायाप्रत/प्रतिलिपीकृत प्रत – झेरॉक्स तंत्राच्या साहाय्याने मूळ ग्रंथाची तयार केलेली सादृश्य प्रत.

xerox machine – छायाप्रत तयार करणारे यंत्र.

xylographic book – काष्ठकोरण ग्रंथ – लाकडावर कोरलेला ग्रंथ.

xylography / word engraving – काष्ठकोरण.

xylotype – काष्ठ उत्कीर्णपासून मुद्रांकन किंवा छपाई.

year – वर्ष.

year book – **वार्षिक/सांवत्सरिक ग्रंथ** – (१) गतवर्षातील घटनांची माहिती देणारे व दरवर्षी प्रकाशित होणारे प्रकाशन : साधारणपणे वार्षिक ही देशाप्रमाणे माहिती देतात. (२) दरवर्षी प्रसिद्ध होणारे प्रकाशन.

year facet – **वर्ष पैलू/कालपर्व पैलू** – वर्गीकरणासाठी वापरण्याचा लक्षणगुण.

year number – **वर्षांक/वर्षांक चिन्ह** – ग्रंथप्रकाशनाचे वर्ष दर्शविणारे चिन्ह.

year of publication / date of publication / imprint date – **प्रकाशन वर्ष** – (१) ग्रंथ ज्या वर्षात प्रकाशित झाला ते वर्ष. (२) ग्रंथ प्रकाशनाचे वर्ष.

yearly – **वार्षिक** – वर्षातून एकदा प्रकाशित होणारे प्रकाशन.

yellow press – **पीत प्रेस** – सनसनाटी आणि रोमांचकारी बातम्या प्रकाशित करणाऱ्या वर्तमानपत्रांसाठी वापरली जाणारी संज्ञा.

Z

zero - शून्य.

zerography - जस्तचित्रांकन/कोरडी/शुष्क छपाई - ग्रंथातील काळी-पांढरी चित्रे व आकृत्या यांच्या मुद्रणासाठी वापरण्याचे तंत्र.

zebra number - बारकोड लेबलवरील नंबर वितरणासाठी वापरणे.

zincography - जस्तचित्रांकन.

zonal - क्षेत्रीय - विभागीय.

zonal analysis - क्षेत्रीय विश्लेषण.

zonal isolate - क्षेत्रदर्शक उपांग.

zone - क्षेत्र/परिमंडल/विशिष्ट/विशेष विभाग.

zone analysis - क्षेत्र विश्लेषण.

zoom - **समीप दृश्य** - संगणक पडद्यावर माहिती वा चित्र मोठ्या स्वरूपात पाहणे.